W9-CPO-874

BLUESTONE RONDO

Walker Smith

SONATA BOOKS
2014

Bluestone Rondo
Copyright © 2012, 2014 by Walker Smith
Published by Sonata Books, LLC

All rights reserved. No part of this book may be reproduced (except for inclusion in reviews), disseminated or utilized in any form or by any means, electronic or mechanical, including photocopying, recording, or in any information storage and retrieval system, or the Internet/ World Wide Web without written permission from the author or publisher.

For further information, you may contact the author at:

walkersmithbooks.com

or by email:

walkersmithbooks@gmail.com

Cover concept/design
Walker Smith, David Williams, and Jerome Anthony Davis
Cover model - Kenneth Stepter

Printed in the United States of America

Bluestone Rondo
ISBN 978-0-9904996-1-9

ALSO BY WALKER SMITH:

The Color Line

Letters from Rome

The Incredible Story of Jack the Rapper

Acknowledgments

David—First in my heart and soul forever, you are my husband and the love of my life. Thank you for all the love, encouragement, patience, and laughter you give to me. I treasure the beautiful music we have made of our marriage.

Theresa—You keep me rooted. I am humbled by your vast capacity for love as you go about your daily mission of saving the animals. Your unforgettable Anthony inspired the character of Miles.

Daniel—You are the strongest person I know. It was an honor growing up with you in the last days of the Huck Finn era, playing barefooted and free before the onset of this daunting adventure called life.

Vincent—In your soul resided a beautiful dreamer in constant battle with a violent intruder. Now for all time the dreamer prevails, across the dangerous footbridge, safe at last.

Elizabeth Quinn—You push me intellectually and I am blessed that you take me along in your unique exploration of the deep spiritual places. May we be fellow Bobby-Soxers forever—SMNO!

Eddie Pugh—You believed in me as a musician and as a writer. You will always be my friend.

Lynnette Brandon and Rene Williamson—My lifelong sisters. Thank you for staying strong and REAL and for giving me the voices of Pearl and Stella.

Gary Askins—Your little-boy voice and wit will never leave my memory. You breathed life into the character of Nick.

Michael Rice—For your enduring soul, and for loving *The Color Purple* as much as I do.

Taryn Nash—You are my "friend in the fireworks." No matter where you roam, keep writing.

To Jerome Davis, Joe Donn Martin, Karen Sweet, Nadine Barrois, Dale Gray, Jack "The Rapper" Gibson, Carolyn Butts, Frank Wildhorn, and Keb Mo for all your help over the years.

To Dalton Trumbo, Ring Lardner Jr., Dashiell Hammett, Richard Wright, Howard Fast, Langston Hughes, Paul Robeson, Arthur Miller, and all those who suffered persecution as a result of the Blacklist; and to Edward R. Murrow, Kirk Douglas, and Otto Preminger for doing their part to end it.

To Dave Brubeck, Robert Johnson, Frank Sinatra, Bird, Trane, Dizzy, and Miles, Billy Strayhorn, Marvin Gaye, and Sam Cooke for laying down the score.

To the Mighty Mississippi River, the City of New York, and the City of New Orleans for their music and for the timeless stories they told my soul.

And last but not least, thanks to all the radios that gave my life its own unique soundtrack.

All were essential elements in the composition of this song.

—WS

Dedication

For the drummer and his lady
Two sleepy people who once lived and loved in a city of glass
1954-1973

"Sing, Antoninus, sing."

—Dalton Trumbo

rondo (*noun*) — a musical form with a recurring theme
that often repeats in the final movement

Chicago – 1952

What a difference a day made...

It was just a song on the radio. At least that's what Joe told himself. An unfeeling bit of musical electricity delivered by airwaves, like a million other songs on a million other radios.

But he didn't believe it. That song had hunted him down as surely as McCarthy hunted down Reds on the Black List.

The tall windows let in just enough light to illuminate half the room. Joe was sitting on the dark side of the bed smoking a cigarette and staring at the radio's eerie glowing dial.

What a difference a day made...

Twenty-four hours ago, success was only a ten-minute drive up North Fairbanks Avenue at the Chez Paree. Joe had been scheduled to appear there as the headliner for a sold-out weekend engagement. On his way from the airport to the hotel, his limousine had passed the nightclub and he had seen his name in lights on a marquee for the first time.

But just one day later, everything he had worked for, lied for, and sold his soul for was gone. So here he was—high above the city lights in a glamorous joint called The Palmer House—trapped in a room with his worst enemy, that radio, and his best friend, a .38-caliber revolver. If he wasn't so hungover and miserable, he might have laughed at the irony.

His gaze drifted over to a slanted rectangle of light near the window. Scattered there on the floor were several message slips and the Entertainment section of the *Tribune*, which was soaked and littered with jagged pieces of a broken glass. All night he had been trying to deaden the pain and quiet the voices on the radio with a mix of scotch and Benzedrine. But he had finished off the scotch, and the Bennies weren't working anymore. All he had left was his trusty .38. He had never actually shot anyone with it, but it did have a way of making a point in an argument.

Joe peered curiously at the gun as he loaded it. The smug little sonofabitch seemed to be gulping the bullets, eager to get to its big moment. "I only need one, ya know," he muttered.

In the distance, he heard a fuzzy, percussive sound. As it grew louder, he realized that it was someone knocking on his door. How long had it been going on? He shook his head. "No. That's not real. Nobody's there." Pointing at the radio, he yelled: "And you're not real either!"

As if on cue, the radio contradicted him in one of its many voices:

... Be sure to stay tuned for a full hour of romantic hits after this brief news break ... In an interview today, Roy

Cohn, counsel to Senator Joseph McCarthy, denied that U.N.
Assistant Secretary General Abe Feller's recent suicide was a
result of Blacklist-related harassment. "I can only repeat the
Senator's earlier statement," Cohn said. "If Feller's
conscience was clear, he had nothing to fear from us."
*   ... And now a word from our sponsor, pure, clean Ivory*
soap...

Joe squeezed his eyes shut as the words from the news and the advertisement jumbled together in his brain:

McCarthyBlacklistSuicideClearconsciencePurecleanIvorysoap...

He raised the gun to his head, but before he could position his finger on the trigger, a sound on the radio stopped him cold: Violins.

An orchestra was playing the intro to a familiar song. And in some hazy echo chamber of his mind, he could hear Magda, in her broken English, telling him her "great secret."

I let da tears flow out through fingertips into da bow. You see, Joe? I make da violin to cry.

The gun slipped harmlessly from his hand onto the bed as the song washed over him, drowning him in sorrow. The violin soloist played a short, plaintive interlude, conjuring up an image of Magda that was so real and so close—Joe could almost feel her heartbeat.

Then the last kick of his scotch/Benny high slurred the rest of the song into an incoherent mess, which struck him as funny—until the announcer slapped him back to reality:

*   That's one of the best torch songs ever put on wax, ladies*
and gentlemen—
*   "I'm a Fool to Want You"—nicely done by the one and*
only Frank Sinatra.

Joe's lips twitched into a feeble smile. "The one and only."

He watched his hand picking up the gun seemingly with a will of its own. The cold kiss of gunmetal on his temple caused him to flinch slightly. The phantom door knocking grew louder.

"You're not really here!" He shut his eyes again, trying desperately to conjure up Magda's face. But all he could see was the brother he had been running from all his life. He opened his eyes. "You're not really here, Calvin! Leave me alone! *Please* leave me alone!"

I'm here, Joe. And I ain't goin' noplace. I ain't goin' noplace. I ain't goin' noplace...

Joe curled his finger around the trigger. "It's okay," he whispered. "I'm dead already anyway."

PART I

OLD MAN RIVER

Chapter 1

Natchez, Mississippi - 1935

Calvin Bailey was singing again.

His wife Leah stared out at the River. It was flowing calmly today, almost distracting her from the pain in her head and ears. But as the old wagon creaked and rattled along the rutted levee road, her gaze drifted away from the River and back to Isabel's dusty gray rump. Isabel was more than a mule in the traditional working sense; she was also Calvin's pet and unlikely muse. There was something about Isabel's clopping rhythm that inspired him to sing every time he picked up the reins—and Calvin was a terrible singer. His pitch was so bad that no one on earth besides Leah could identify his badly wrecked version of "Crossroads Blues."

The levee road to Natchez was treacherously bumpy. And despite the shade from Leah's straw hat, the sun was making her headache more severe than usual. Her twin boys, Joe and Calvin Jr., were bickering in the back of the wagon, and she was already planning the stripes she would lay on their boney legs with the whipping belt once she got them home.

Suddenly, one of the wagon wheels hit a deep rut, raising a spray of road dirt. Then, in a head-splitting concert of racket, Isabel snorted loudly, Calvin hit an off-key note that sounded like the bleat of an injured sheep, and one of the boys let out a piercing scream.

As Leah reached back and snatched each boy by an arm, her straw hat flew off her head, setting her temper ablaze. "Y'all drivin' me crazy and now ya done made me lose my hat!"

"It was him, Mama!" Joe yelled, kicking at his brother. "Mud Boy hit me again!"

Calvin Jr. slapped Joe's hand away. "Shut-up, ya pansy! It was you!"

Leah only managed a few minor swats, but she had made her point. "Y'all stop screamin' and name-callin' now! When we get home, y'all gon' catch a *real* reason to holla!"

"Aww, Leah," Calvin Sr. said easily. "Calm down, now, honey."

"I can't calm down with them two fightin' and screamin'! And I'm coughin' up dust and then you go to caterwaulin'! Lawd, Calvin, you *know* you can't carry a tune in a bucket."

Calvin nudged her shoulder and grinned. "Ain't never stopped me befo'." Then he planted a noisy kiss on her cheek, and went back to singing "Crossroads," which set the twins to giggling.

Joe covered his ears. "Uh-oh, here he go! Calvin Bailey's singin' again!"

Leah finally gave up and laughed. "Isabel," she called to the mule, "you my only friend."

Calvin pointed out the group of buildings in the distance and patted Leah's hand. "We almost there, honey. Maybe Mr. Elderwood got one'a them headache powders or sump'm."

When they reached the edge of town, Leah turned to watch her sons as they saw Natchez for the first time. Until today, their whole world had been Mr. Manley's farm with its plows and mules, and those monotonous cotton fields. Leah chuckled. Just as she had expected, the boys were gaping wordlessly at the sights on Commerce Street: three- and four-story brick buildings, a huge Confederate flag rippling outside the Post Office, a barbershop pole with swirling red and white stripes, and an open mahogany coffin surrounded by huge floral arrangements that filled the display window of Kendall's Funeral Parlor. The wagon finally slowed to a stop between Elderwood's General Store and Hackett's Grain & Feed.

"Calvin, *please* talk to them two 'fo you go," Leah pleaded.

"Awright, I ain't forgot." He twisted around with a stern expression and shook his finger at the boys. "Now this is town, dammit! So ya can't be runnin' 'round actin' like triflin' skunks! I gotta go see 'bout some work, but I'm comin' back to load this wagon. So you best mind yo' Mama, or I'ma lay that strap 'cross *both* y'all narrow li'l behinds when we get home, hear me?"

"Yes, sir." Sincerity dripped in unison.

Leah rolled her eyes as she helped the boys down. She had just gotten their feet on the ground when an angry looking white man hurried out the door of Hackett's Grain & Feed.

"Move that wagon, black boy!" he shouted at Calvin. "Got me a delivery comin'!"

Leah knew the man on sight—Ben Hackett, a known member of the Klan. She jerked her gaze back to her husband, who was sitting frozen in his seat, breaking the longest-standing rule of the South. He was staring that white man directly in his eyes. Leah gathered her boys close.

"I *said* move it, ya worthless nigger!" Hackett said, stepping closer to the wagon.

Leah watched helplessly as Calvin dropped the reins and slowly climbed down. Her pulse began to race when Hackett strode around to the back of the wagon to meet her husband in the street. "Sweet Jesus, Calvin," she whispered, "don't give him no cause."

Without acknowledging Hackett, Calvin reached into the back of the wagon and retrieved some object she couldn't see. Then he handed Leah her hat. "You dropped this, honey." He climbed back up on the wagon, and gathered the reins. "Get on up, Isabel!"

Hackett's chest expanded with hard, angry breaths as he watched Calvin slowly ride away. He turned quickly in a long stride, but stopped short, seemingly unaware that Leah and the boys had been standing there. Then he leaned menacingly close to her. "You best tell him not to test me like that again, you hear me, gal? That's one stupid black boy there!"

Once Hackett had disappeared into the grain store, Leah gazed sadly down the road at the rigid figure of her husband riding away in silence. "G'on, Calvin," she whispered urgently. "Sing! G'on and sing yo' song." But all she heard was the lonely echo of Isabel's rhythmic clopping. Leah stared at the wagon until she felt a tug at her skirt, and finally looked down at her boys. The shock on their faces was almost as heartbreaking as her husband's silence.

"Daddy ain't no stupid black boy!" Joe cried. "How come he ain't *smack* that man?"

"We know yo' Daddy ain't no stupid black boy, but baby… you jus' can't go 'round smackin' no white man. Might as well learn that right now. It's jus' the way things is. So straighten up and act like you got some sense—and stop all that fightin'! Come on."

Firmly gripping their hands, she led her boys inside. A bell rang above the door, but the store appeared empty until a deep, angry voice spoke: "Who is this colored boy in my store?"

Calvin Jr. gasped and Joe clung to Leah's skirt. Peering down at them was a tall, spindly white man with shaggy gray hair and a forbidding frown.

"Mornin', Mr. Elderwood," Leah said.

Mr. Elderwood's name was a perfect fit for his craggy face. It was thin with deep crevices, like the bark on an ancient cedar tree, and his rheumy eyes peered out from under brows that looked like two gray tangles of Spanish moss. But then he smiled, and handed peppermint sticks to Calvin and Joe. "Mornin', Leah," he said amiably. "Wait a minute. These *both* your boys?"

"Yes, suh," Leah said softly. She watched Mr. Elderwood closely as he studied her sons. Their smiles were almost identical, with dimples on each boy's left cheek. But aside from the smile, they were a study in contrast. Calvin's silky infant ringlets had tightened into wooly, black hair, and his skin was the traditional sienna-brown of his father and generations of Baileys. Joe's hair was an unlikely tangle of soft, smoke-colored curls that framed a pale beige face. Mr. Elderwood glanced at Calvin's ink-black eyes, but gazed into Joe's for a long, suspended moment. Joe's eyes were neither brown nor black, but a pale mixture of both, with a liquid, transparent quality that created the illusion of a bottomless well.

Leah knew the reason for Joe's light features; it was a flesh-and-blood reason with a name she hated—Edwin Longchamp—a white plantation owner and the father of five babies born to Leah's great grandmother, who was a slave. Leah had escaped the pale reminder of Edwin's genes, inheriting her dark complexion and aquiline nose from her mother Helene, a half-blooded Natchez Indian. But her piercing black eyes that seemed to gaze into the souls of folks were a gift from her great grandmother. Jane Longchamp had run away from Edwin at the end of the war, taking her five mulatto children with her. With each telling of Jane's story, Leah's resentment of Longchamp's name weighed on her spirit like a heavy ancestral chain.

On the day Leah married Calvin, she knew that her words puzzled him: *Thank you for helpin' me break free.* With great joy, she joined her life with Calvin's, while breaking her last link to Edwin Longchamp. That is, until her unusual twins were born.

Leah touched her boys' shoulders. "They twins, but they ain't—'zackly the same."

"Huh? Oh, well, yes, I can see that," Mr. Elderwood said, still unable to break Joe's stare. "Mm-hm. I seem to recollect folks talkin' about some mismatched twins bein' born to some coloreds in Nede County a few years back. 'Round the time of the big flood in '27, wasn't it? Guess that'd make you fellers about eight years old then, wouldn't it?"

"Yes, suh," Joe said, stepping forward. "I be the lightest one in the family."

Mr. Elderwood laughed and handed Joe another peppermint stick. "You sure are! A high yella little booger, ain'tcha!"

Joe grinned bashfully. "High—*yella*?"

"That's what I said, boy. Yella. Like a little ball'a sunshine." The bell rang over the door, and Elderwood hurried over to assist two elderly white women who were walking in.

"That's good, ain't it, Mama?" Joe said. "If he call me a ball'a sunshine?"

"I s'pose so," she said absently as she reached for a box of baking powder on the shelf.

Calvin leaned close to Joe and whispered, "He called ya a *booger* too, stupid."

Joe turned away. "Mista Elderwood ain't mean like that white man outside, huh, Mama?"

"Well, he better'n most."

Calvin rolled his eyes and walked away, peeking into barrels filled with everything from peanuts to spools of thread. "Look!" he squealed, reaching for a comic book. "Detective Dan!"

Joe came over to look. "Yup, that's it. The Gangsters' Frame-Up!"

Leah slapped Calvin's hand. "No! We can't afford nothin' but necessities, you hear me?"

Calvin jerked away, and Joe tugged at Leah's skirt. "Hey, Mama! What's *that?*"

Resting on a shelf above a crate of red apples was a gleaming cathedral-style radio. Leah stared at it; then Calvin touched one of the knobs. "Yeah, Mama. What is it?"

She slapped his hand again. "It's sump'm you ain't supposed to touch, that's what it is!"

"But what is it, Mama?" Joe asked sweetly. "Guess *that* be some'a them—necessities, huh?"

"No, Mr. Smart-Aleck, it ain't." But her voice softened as she gazed at the radio. "Sho' would be a fine thing to have though. Jus' like all them rich white folks in the movies!" She reached for the dangling price tag and let out a soft whistle. "Twenty dollars!"

"But what *is* it, Mama?" Joe repeated impatiently.

"Is it a toy?" Calvin asked.

Mr. Elderwood appeared behind them again. "No, Sonny, that ain't no toy. It's a Philco—a real grand radio. I bet your Mama'd like to take *that* home."

"Oh, no, suh," Leah said, shaking her head. "We ain't got no twenty dollars!"

"That's a knocked-down price, Leah, on account'a it bein' second-hand. Here, listen to this—" He turned one of the knobs and the radio began to squeak and buzz. "Come on, now. Hard as you and Calvin been workin' this year, you ought'a be able to spare some'a that cotton money for— Oh, that's right. I plumb forgot Manley ain't got electricity out there yet."

Just then, a voice spoke from the speaker: And now a word from our sponsor, Burma Shave.

Calvin gasped and yanked Joe's arm. "It talked!"

"Ouch!" Joe yelped. "I know! I heard it."

"It sings too!" Calvin chortled. He pointed at the knobs. "Are these the eyes right here?"

Mr. Elderwood laughed and rubbed Calvin's head. "Tell you what. If you're good and don't make a ruckus, you can sit and listen to *The Shadow*. That's comin' on in a minute."

Calvin and Joe stared wide-eyed at the radio as it played the jingle for *Cracker Jack*.

"I'ma be on the other side'a the sto' shoppin'," Leah whispered to the boys. "But I'ma be checkin' on you two, so none'a that fightin'!" She pinched of them on the arm. "I *mean* it!"

"Oww! Yes, ma'am!"

All was quiet for a few minutes, but then Leah heard two loud crashes, followed by Mr. Elderwood shouting: "Get *out*, you li'l roughnecks! You can wait for your Mama outside!"

Leah dropped her things on the counter and hurried out the door after the boys, with Mr. Elderwood right behind her, shaking his fist.

"Little hooligans broke two of my jars of pickles throwin' 'em at each other! You're gonna have to pay for that, you hear me, gal?"

"I will, suh. I will," Leah said as she tried to untangle the boys. Calvin suddenly pulled free and smacked Joe's face, causing him to shriek. Leah slapped Calvin on the side of his head.

He grabbed his ear. "Oww, Mama! My other brother made me do it! He *hates* Joe!"

"What other brother?" She was staring at Calvin with a mix of rage and curiosity when Joe lunged forward and jabbed his fingers at Calvin's eyes.

"Oww!" Calvin yelled. "He poked me in the eye, Mama! *Kill* him!"

Joe dropped to his knees in the street. "Don't *kill* me, Mama," he wailed dramatically.

A group of white townspeople had gathered, amused by the brawl. One of the men snickered loudly, "Ain't gotta worry about them two endin' up like that Lindbergh baby. Nobody'd try to kidnap them little black devils!"

As the crowd laughed, Joe scrambled up, sobbing hysterically. "Not *me*! I ain't no black devil!" He pointed at his brother. "*He* is! Not me!"

As the crowd dispersed, Leah sat her boys on the sidewalk for a tongue-lashing. But before she could say a word, she saw a strange, distant expression in Calvin's eyes. And with his face still wet with tears, Joe began to smile. They were listening to something. Then Leah heard it too—a deep, spine-chilling voice coming from that twenty-dollar radio in Mr. Elderwood's store.

Who knows what evil lurks in the hearts of men?... The Shadow knows.

Chapter 2

Throughout the 1930s, the Great Depression cast its curse of deprivation over every large city and small rural town in America. At the bleakest point, unemployment rose to twenty-five percent, and former working-class citizens found themselves standing in bread lines that stretched for miles. Vacant eyes stared out from the faces of unclaimed children begging pennies, while the elderly died of hunger and illness in the cold, damp doorways of inner-city tenements. Veteran heroes of the Great War lived as worthless rejects in packing boxes on the outskirts of towns. Makeshift families gathered in makeshift shanty villages they called "Hoovervilles"—a swipe at President Hoover, who they blamed for the 1929 Crash and its miserable aftermath. Hobo camps sprang up near water tanks and whistle stops, and the trains themselves bore witness to the great equalizing effects of the Crash. Wall Street losers who hadn't taken the Black Tuesday Leap shared boxcars with lifelong "hoe-boys." Forgotten men in tattered overalls sat alongside forgotten men wearing worn-out suit jackets and expensive shoes that had long since lost their shine. Race and social status had no meaning here. They were all brothers now, whether they knew it or not, heading west on the rails. Always west.

Despite the widespread poverty, an elite handful of industrialists and financial wizards had managed to outsmart the Crash or were too wealthy to be touched by it. They resided with their families in big-city penthouses that towered high above the bread lines.

In the Midwest, severe drought conditions killed crops as well as hope and expelled farmers from the land their families had worked for generations. A newspaper reporter named Robert Geiger dubbed the region "the Dust Bowl" in one of his articles, and the name stuck.

And from coast to coast, radios were playing America's most popular song, "Brother, Can You Spare a Dime?"

In the South, King Cotton had been dethroned. The lush soil of the Mississippi Delta had fared better than the ravaged Midwest, but ripple effects, both financial and ecological, eventually struck. Cotton's pre-Crash value had topped out at twenty cents per pound. At the nadir of the Great Depression, the per-pound price had tumbled to less than six cents.

But in Nede County, where the Bailey family lived, hard times were nothing new.

Calvin Bailey had spent his life working the cotton fields alongside his friend Gerald Moore. As tenant farmers on Horace Manley's plantation, the two men lived with their families in houses that were little more than shacks—two rooms with no running water or electricity—no different from any other tenant farmer's dwelling in Nede County. The two families shared everything—a well, an outhouse, tools, food, joy, and misery. In the Great Flood of 1927, Calvin and Gerald had fought side by side to save the crumbling levees as Leah gave birth to the twins in a dripping canvas tent. After spending over a year in a Vicksburg colored refugee camp under state mandate, they learned that the water had finally receded. The return to Manley's farm meant another year of rebuilding, repairing, and cultivating before planting could even begin. They agreed to fractional profit splits, because splits were better than starvation.

Calvin could not remember the first time he had heard the word "Depression," but he remembered the grim-faced white man in the dark suit stepping out of his automobile in front of Mr. Manley's house. And he remembered Mr. Manley begging for more time to make his mortgage payments. Calvin walked out to the fields and stared toward the Midwest, thinking of the farmers there. He knew that Mr. Manley's trouble was somehow connected to that Wall Street Crash and those dust clouds that were killing crops and choking livestock in Texas and Oklahoma. And he knew that life's most dire decisions had to be made in the solitude of a man's own mind. He could not help Mr. Manley any more than Mr. Manley could help him. He had only one valuable asset left—Isabel. But he needed her to work his crops. Calvin stood stroking the mule's muscular neck as he worked the trouble around in his head.

"My kids hongry, Isabel. Runnin' around like two li'l skeletons, and ain't had no shoes since—" He stopped suddenly, and thought of his father, who had beaten him for crying when he was twelve years old. Calvin hadn't shed a tear since that day, but now he felt a great sob rising inside him. "So now what, Lawd? What the hell we s'posed to do now?"

Within weeks the answer came.

Ever since his election, President Roosevelt had been aggressively attacking the Depression on all fronts. His new plan to subsidize southern farmers in exchange for plowing up their cotton crops was praised by his admirers and condemned by his critics. The intended effect was to force cotton prices back up, but no one knew what the long-term effects would be. According to Mr. Manley, the short-term effect of a subsidy check would pay the mortgage—for the time being.

By 1938, Calvin and Gerald were planting full crops again and working harder than they had ever worked before. It was the year that bonded them forever as brothers—if not by blood, then certainly by sweat and hardship. The cotton was abundant and of the highest quality that year. It sold for top dollar, even if top dollar was still only a fraction of what it once had been. Many other tenant farmers had no choice but to abandon their land, but the Manley farmers hung on. The Great Depression was not over, but they found ways to survive, one harsh day at a time.

≈∞≈

To clear his head of worries, Calvin often slipped away to a place he had discovered as a boy. Shaded by the branches of the old oak trees lining the west bank of the Mississippi, he had cut his own trail to a secluded clearing with a panoramic view. Century by century and inch by inch, the River's current had reclaimed silt and stone to create a widening slope where the calm water gathered speed and roiled into white-capped rapids. This was the pinnacle of the magnificent Mississippi, where its most diverse and elemental aspects, tranquility and power, met.

Calvin would stand at land's edge listening to the whispering bulrushes as he waited for the magical animation of sunrise: white-tailed deer foraging for breakfast as they moved quietly among the trees; birds rustling branches and chirping the first songs of morning. As he observed nature's daily miracles, great and small, Calvin learned that stars not only existed in the sky, but also inside the globular dewdrops shimmering on the leaves. He discovered that the land along this River was patient land—a place to watch a transformed caterpillar wriggle out of a cocoon for its maiden flight on bright new wings. A place where tiny diaphanous rainbows flickered in the wet mist that rose from the shallows. These were the spectacles that made Calvin question something church folks always said: *Give glory to God!* How could a man even dream of *giving* glory to that Somebody who had made the glory of rainbows and sunsets and water that leaped up to touch the blue face of the sky? Glory needed only Acknowledgement.

He brought his sons to the River to teach them the things that boys should know—like how to throw rocks for distance and how to catch slippery green bullfrogs and then release them so they could observe their athletic escape leaps. When he told the boys one of his passed-down stories about the wise old Mississippi River, he saw the wonder in their eyes and felt a little taller on the walk home. Even a poor black man had treasures to pass on.

But most times, Calvin visited the place alone, to talk to the River about making a better life for his sons and building a bathroom for Leah, who always grumbled about bathing in a rusty washtub. And the River never laughed at Calvin's singing the way that Gerald did. Lately, all Gerald talked about was President Roosevelt and his "New Deal" programs. Calvin distrusted all politicians, and barely tolerated Gerald's nonstop Roosevelt sermons.

But early one morning Gerald knocked on his door with news that Calvin couldn't ignore. "Mawnin', Calvin. Sorry I woke ya up, but I got some big news. What'chu gotta do today?"

Calvin sighed and dropped into a chair. "Hell, man. Same thing as yesterday! Guess you ain't seent all that cotton out yonder we gotta bring in. Ain't nothin' changin' 'round here."

"Oh, yes it is too, Calvin. Sump'm *big* fixin' to change 'round here."

"What the hell's changin'?" Calvin snapped. "Damn sun comin' up over yonder, we' hongry, and white folks still in the lead. Same as yesterday."

"Man, you wrong jus' like you *always* wrong! Roosevelt got this new thing called 'Rural 'Lectrification Act' and Mista Manley gon' wire up the farm! And get plumbin' too!"

Calvin glared at him. "Gerald? Don't let that do'knob hit'cha in the ass on yo way out."

"Shut up and listen, fool!" Gerald said. "You seent all them poles they been puttin' up along the main road? Well, now they stringin' up the wire! We fixin' to get 'lectricity, man!"

"Oh, Lawd. Manley gettin' some 'lectricity ain't gon' mean nothin' to a mule like you."

"Manley ain't payin' for this. The gub'ment is! We jus' pay fa' the 'lectricity *in* the wire."

"Gerald, what the hell a mule like you need with 'lectricity comin' out a damn wire?... Oh, yeah. Plumb forgot all them fancy plug-in lights you got in yo' *mansion* over yonder."

Gerald took a playful swing at him. "Ya got one mo' damn time callin' me a mule fo' I hitch yo' ass up to my wagon and make you pull it."

Calvin laughed and held up his hands in surrender. "How we gon' pay for 'lectricity, man?"

"Little extra work is all."

"'Cause Lawd knows we ain't got enough to do. How much extra work you sign us up fo'?"

Gerald reached for Calvin's arm. "Let's go see Mista Manley and find out."

≈∞≈

It took three months, but the REA electrician and plumbing crews finally began work on every major structure on the Manley farm. Whenever they could, Calvin and Gerald followed the workers around to observe the installation of fuse panels, lighting circuits, and plumbing pipes.

On the day the work was completed, Leah and Rita prepared food for a sunset picnic and Gerald brought out two jars of his homemade whiskey. When it was finally dark, the eldest child from each family ran inside their respective houses to wait at the switch for the signal.

"Now!" Calvin shouted, and the windows of both houses glowed with electric lights for the first time. The children yelped and turned clumsy cartwheels in the grass, and Calvin and Gerald stayed up late, drinking and making impossible plans.

"Awriiight, Gerald," Calvin said, once he was thoroughly drunk. "I guess ol' man Roosevelt ain't sa'bad after all... Matter a'fack, I'm finna sing'um a song..."

When Calvin began his teeth-rattling rendition of "Happy Days Are Here Again," Gerald covered his ears and yelled, "Somebody call the law! Calvin Bailey's singin' again!"

≈∞≈

The two men spent the better part of a year hunting through salvage yards, and finally scraped together the materials for a bathroom, including an old clawfoot tub that was badly chipped, but still in working condition. As they hoisted the tub up onto his wagon, Calvin spotted a large chair, upholstered in faded green broadcloth, lying on its side in the rubble. A closer examination revealed a broken leg and a few tears on the arms, but the cushions were in passable condition. Calvin smiled. Cleaned up with a little stuffing and mending, it would make a fine king's throne.

Once the bathroom was finished, Leah took her first bath in the clawfoot tub. Calvin sat proudly in his mended green chair, listening to her joyful crying as he counted the days until Sunday. That was the day he would spring one last surprise that had taken six weeks of saving.

Calvin never attended church services with the family, despite Leah's weekly warnings about a "one-way ticket to hell for heathens." His answer was always the same. Preachers were pickpockets, and he could do his praying free of charge at the River. And playing dominoes with Gerald on Sunday afternoon was God's gift to him for a week of hard work.

But on the Sunday of the big surprise, Calvin skipped his gift-from-God dominoes game and waited for Leah and the boys to return from church. When he heard them coming up the path, he leaned out the window and began to sing a loud performance of "Crossroads Blues."

Leah laughed as she took off her hat. "Lawd, Calvin! The dogs is howlin' out here and runnin' 'round in circles! And you bed'not *never* run into Robert Johnson neither, 'cause he'd haf'ta shoot the fool that been singin' his song so wrong!" But she stopped talking when Calvin's prickly voice was replaced by the smooth sounds of Duke Ellington's orchestra.

Leah ran inside and saw Calvin standing next to the radio from Mr. Elderwood's store. She let out a squeal and then jumped into his arms. "How'd you know 'bout that radio, Calvin?"

"Them two li'l skunks a'yours told me," he said, smiling at her. "Lawd, Leah, look at'cha. Ya got runnin' water, 'lectricity, *and* a radio. You a fancy lady now!"

"But Calvin—twenty dollars? You ain't joined up with them bank robbers, is you?"

Calvin raised his hands. "Ya got me, G-Man! Ya done caught Purty Boy Calvin!" Then he hugged her to muffle her groan. "Aw, Leah! Mr. Elderwood been markin' that price down till it got to six-ninety-five. So I done me some extra haulin' and I went on and bought it. So, now— 'fo you rattle off any mo' questions, ya think I could get me a dance?"

Leah worked in the fields with the men to bring in the cotton at harvest time, but during the rest of the year, she helped Mrs. Manley with household chores, free of charge. Calvin disapproved, but Leah felt it was her Christian duty. Mrs. Manley had six unruly children, but her youngest boy was sickly. He was seven years old and had never spoken a word.

One afternoon as Leah was hanging laundry on the clothesline, Mrs. Manley called her inside to meet someone. "This is Miz Chapman, Leah," she said. "She's lookin' to hire a girl."

"Afternoon, ma'am," Leah said, trying not to stare at the fur piece around the woman's neck. She had seen Joan Crawford wear one in a movie at the Grand Marquee, and Joan Crawford was the last word in glamour, according to Mrs. Manley. But up close, in broad daylight, Leah found the fur piece anything but glamorous. It looked like two terrified squirrels sewn together, with tails and paws dangling from their dead, flattened bodies. To make it worse, the animals still had teeth and claws, and their eyes had been replaced with black gemstones that glittered eerily in the light. Leah shivered and took a step back.

After answering a few questions, she hurried back outside to finish the laundry.

When Mrs. Chapman's automobile drove away, Mrs. Manley rushed outside. "I knew she was gonna like you! See, Leah, some folks are gettin' through the Depression just fine. Miz Chapman's husband is some kind'a big muckety-muck over to the bank. He's the one that helped Horace with our loan trouble. But here's the best part, Leah. They're loaded!"

Leah couldn't hold back her laughter. "*Loaded*, ma'am?"

"Mercy! I sound just like one'a them gangster movies, don't I? What I mean is you'll get a fair wage, Leah! A good recommendation was the only way I could repay you for the help you been givin' me all these years. But my Missy's eleven now, and that's old enough to start helpin' out. And that means you can go work for the Chapmans and get paid for a change."

"I sho' do appreciate it, ma'am."

"The Chapmans live in Natchez. Can you get all the way out there every day, ya think?"

"I sho' can, ma'am," Leah said, smiling. "Even if I gotta walk all the way."

≈∞≈

Leah's daily journey to the Chapmans' home in Natchez began at 5:00 a.m. After nearly four years of employment, she had never once been late. So on her boys' twelfth birthday, she woke them at 4:30 to celebrate with a birthday-cake breakfast.

After Calvin returned from driving Leah to work, he unhitched Isabel and called the boys inside. "Y'all 'member last year when we couldn't give you no present and I said things gon' get better this year? Well, stick out'cha hands." Counting out eight quarters, he smiled. "That be fo' bits apiece. Ought'a set y'all up widda pitcha show and enough popcorn to choke a hoss."

"Naw, Daddy," Joe said as he counted the quarters. "It be a whole dollar apiece, don't it?"

"Not if you splittin' it up with them two little knuckleheads y'all be runnin' with all'a damn time. Butch and—what the hell that other skunk's name?"

"Zachary!" Calvin shouted. "Thanks, Daddy!"

"Y'all be sho' and ask they mamas' permission, and be careful crossin' them railroad tracks, now! You behave in that theater and git y'all narrow li'l behinds back home 'fo dark!"

A matinee at the Grand Marquee in Natchez was the next best thing to Christmas, as far as Joe and Calvin were concerned, and almost as rare. On the big silver screen of the Grand Marquee, Edward G. Robinson, James Cagney, Paul Muni, and Humphrey Bogart took turns killing each other in eye-popping, gangster-themed motion pictures.

Calvin and Joe picked up Zachary and Butch, hen hurried to town, hoping for a double feature like the one they had seen at the end of the summer—*Little Caesar* and *The Public Enemy*. The boys had stayed all day for that one, and memorized the best scenes.

As they ran up the street to the theater, Calvin was the first to spot the colorful posters over the entrance. "Look, y'all! *The Roaring Twenties*! Cagney *and* Bogart!"

Butch let out a delirious squeal. "Look! Joe Louis! A Joe Louis newsreel! Come on!"

But Joe remained on the other side of the street. "Y'all go ahead. I'll come in a minute."

Calvin took a slap at the air. "Who cares about Joe anyhow," he said. "Let's go on in."

After the boys went inside, Joe went to the ticket booth to pay his quarter. "One, please."

The white woman inside pushed her eyeglasses up on her nose and smiled. "Well, ain't you handsome? Where'd you get them pretty gray eyes, sugah? Your Mama or your Daddy?"

Joe stared at her a moment and then grinned. "My Daddy. Mama's eyes are… blue."

She slipped his ticket and change under the window. "Enjoy the show, honey."

Joe stepped inside and scowled at the Colored Section sign—the Mason-Dixon Line for Negro theatergoers. Then he pulled his cap low on his face and hurried past the usher.

"Hey, hold it, buster!" the usher said, grabbing his arm. "I ain't seen yer ticket!"

"Here it is," Joe mumbled as he produced the torn half of his ticket.

"Okay, follow me," the usher said. "There's still some seats down front."

Joe followed him to the white section and took a seat. No one had stopped him.

Then the usher was back. "Hey, could you move down? Got me a party of four here."

Joe moved over, and four white children hurried into the row—three boys and a girl who looked about ten. The girl smoothed her pink dress and sat down next to him. "Hi," she said.

Joe squirmed and smiled back at her. "Hi."

"My brother hates it when I tag along, but I don't care. I love the pitcher show."

"Me too," Joe said, as he watched the girl's fingers entwining her blonde pigtail. The lights dimmed as the newsreel started, but then the picture froze and the houselights blazed on.

The audience buzzed, but the usher's voice cut through the noise: "Hey, you!" He pointed at Joe and gave him a disdainful up-and-down look. "Yer—brother's lookin' for ya."

Joe's knees were shaking as he stood up and moved past the blonde girl. When he reached the aisle, the usher grabbed him by the collar. "One'a them high-yella ones, huh? You *know* the colored section's up in the balcony. Stay where you belong next time, hear me, boy?"

Everyone was laughing as Joe ran to the exit. But when he got to the balcony steps and saw his brother standing there with his elbow resting on the Colored Section sign, Joe stopped.

"I ought'a tell Mama you was tryin' to pass," Calvin said contemptuously.

Joe smirked and pushed past him to go up the stairs. "Not *tryin'* to pass. I *did* pass."

"Shit! Not for long! And it ain't *never* gon' work. Not long as I'm around."

≈∞≈

It was late afternoon when the boys passed the old train depot and took the turn onto Highway 61. Lining the highway was the evidence of an early Mississippi spring. Rows of oak trees stripped bare by winter were already sprouting tightly curled, green buds along their skeletal limbs, and the Acacia trees were beginning to bloom. The boys took their time walking home, throwing rocks, slapping at tree branches, and acting out favorite scenes from the movie.

Calvin ran ahead and fired at Joe with his imaginary Tommy-gun. "You seen that fool beggin' when Cagney was fixin' to plug him? Just like Joe—talkin' tough till Cagney whupped out his gat. Shee-it! Turned yella! I *told* y'all he was gon' turn out to be yella!"

"Shoot!" Butch laughed. "You ain't told nobody nothin'! Yo' mouth was too busy chompin' up all the daggone popcorn! But Cagney sho' did drill that mug, huh?"

"Yeah," Joe said, "but did you get a load of them sharp suits Bogart had on? And Cagney wearin' them hats with the high crowns? Them mugs is rollin' in dough! And all them fast cars!"

"Dillinger use'ta drive a flathead Ford V-8, man!" Zachary said. "That car was fast!"

"Cagney drives a V-8 too!" Joe said. Then he curled his top lip in disgust. "All we got is that old mule wagon. That's all cotton pickers get to drive... Shoot! One day I'ma hightail it out'a here and make me some dough. Get me one'a them V-8s and a couple'a dames too! Watch me!"

Zachary let out a skeptical snort. "How?"

"I'ma go to Hollywood and be a movie star, like Cagney—or get me a band and sing on the radio. Then I'ma buy me a whole closet-full of pinstripe suits—all in different colors too."

Calvin jerked up his chin. "So? I'ma be a boxer like Joe Louis... *and* a Hollywood gangsta! Kind'a like the colored Jimmy Cagney! Get me some guns and a big stack'a C-notes."

"Hollywood?" Zachary hooted. "Maaan, crazy must run in y'all family! They don't give no niggas no guns and suits in no Hollywood! And *sho'* not no C-notes!"

"You might could get a big stack'a shoe-shine rags!" Butch laughed.

"Or be the new Rochester," Joe said tartly. "But not me, 'cause I can pass. I did it today—till you squealed. I could go to New York and tell folks I'm I-talian—or maybe a Ay-rab sheik!"

Calvin glared at his brother. "Shut up, stupid!" Leaning down, he scooped up a handful of pebbles and sent them sailing in the direction of Joe's ankles. "Ay-rab sheik? Shee-it!"

Joe dodged the hail of pebbles. "You dead, Calvin! I done shot you twice, so lay down!"

"I ain't dead. I only got wounded in my leg, see?" Calvin said, developing a sudden limp.

"Shee-it!" Butch jeered. "Then how come you grabbed yo' chest and not yo' leg, nigga?"

"So what?" Calvin snarled. "How come y'all ain't say nothin' 'bout Joe takin' all them Tommy-gun bullets I done put in *his* chest? Shee-it! You the one dead, Ay-rab sheik!"

Joe rolled over and fired a round at Calvin. "Oh. A wise guy, huh? Hey, *I'm* Jimmy Cagney, fool. I *can't* die. 'Cause I'm the only one smart enough to run the bootleggin' operation."

"Naw, you ain't. And don't make me play Joe Louis on yo' monkey ass to prove it to ya neither. Ya ain't no I-talian; ya ain't no Ay-rab sheik; and ya *sho'* ain't no Jimmy Cagney."

Joe smirked. "Oh, so I guess *you* supposed to be Cagney, huh? *And* Joe Louis? No, I'll tell you who you are—you that yella Bogart. I'ma finish you off in the last reel, sucka."

Calvin jerked up his chin and narrowed his eyes at Joe. "I *said* I killed you. Why can't you really die, Joe? How many times I gotta kill you 'fo you *really* die?"

Zachary emitted a gasp. "Uh, let's go on to y'all house and get some'a that cake."

But his suggestion died in the evening breeze, and suddenly the only sound was the rustling of the branches above the boys' heads. Butch began to back away timidly.

Calvin landed the first blow in the center of Joe's chest, causing him to fall hard. Joe let out a pained groan, but scrambled up quickly and lunged at his brother with his shoulder. Butch bolted toward the Bailey house, but Zachary remained near the twins, just out of swinging range.

"There go Butch!" he choked through a nervous laugh. "Bet he headin' to y'all house to tell yo' Daddy." He flinched as Calvin knocked Joe down again, then tried reasoning with them, Cagney-style: "And ya know that punk Butch. So maybe y'all mugs ought'a lay off, 'cause soon as y'all Daddy come outside, Butch gonna saaang like a canary boid! And ya know what that means—" He made a throat-cutting gesture with his index finger. "Curtains! For both'a y'all!"

There was an audible smack as Calvin's knuckles connected with bone through the soft flesh of his brother's face, and the first blood of the afternoon trickled down Joe's chin.

His lips parted in a grin of bloody teeth. "Come on, Mud Boy. That the best you can do?"

Chapter 3

Christmas of 1941 was overshadowed by a nationwide panic sparked by two fateful words: Pearl Harbor. The terrible lessons of the Great War had kept many Americans neutral when it came to the conflict between the Allies and the Axis countries. But Japan's December 7th attack on Pearl incited a national outcry. For the second time in twenty-three years, the world was at war.

Leah Bailey's radio was no longer a source of entertainment; it was a vital source of information and the family's nerve center. Each night, Calvin and Joe listened to the news with heart-pounding anxiety. This was no radio show with sound effects and scripts; this was a real war correspondent, reporting from Europe, where real bombs were killing real people.

The war seemed to unite everyone in Nede County. Enlistment rolls swelled, and Calvin and Joe forgot their squabbles and worked together, collecting used newspapers, old rubber tires, and scrap metal for the weekly drives at their school.

But as weeks dragged on, their shared fear of the war took a natural psychological turn to a need for distraction. Calvin gravitated to athletics, both as participant and fan. He enjoyed spending time with his father and Gerald Moore as they listened to the Friday night fights on the radio. Gerald would bring a jar of his homemade whiskey and they would sit tensely on the edges of their chairs, staring at the radio until the bout was over. Calvin's favorite fighter was Joe Louis, who took on any and all challengers in his "Bum of the Month Club."

Hello, sports fans! This is Don Dunphy welcoming you to the Gillette Cavalcade of Sports, live from Madison Square

Garden. Tonight's bout is the last appearance for heavyweight champ Joe Louis before he reports for duty with the U.S. Army...

Inspired by the fight broadcasts and newsreels, Calvin would wait each evening for the setting sun to cast shadows on the wall so he could get in some shadowboxing before dark. He threw murderous combinations as he muttered the blow-by-blow commentary of his imaginary title fights, and he was always crowned Champ when the final bell sounded.

Meanwhile, Joe was developing an intense passion for music. After joining the church choir, he began to learn basic harmonies and spent long hours with Mrs. Mason, who played piano. She helped him with pitch and sharpened his knowledge of chord structures, but his tonality and range were instinctive, untaught gifts. Within weeks, he won a spot as one of the choir's soloists.

The resulting squabbles over the radio were inevitable. On fight nights, Calvin always won the battle the minute his father settled onto his chair with his whiskey jar. Everyone but Joe loved *King Biscuit Time*, which was the only show that featured Negro blues artists. Their mother sometimes listened to *The Jack Benny Show* and *Command Performance*, and she never missed President Roosevelt's fireside chats.

Joe sang along with musical programs and studied the polished voices of the actors on detective dramas and the announcers hawking soap, razor blades, and cigarettes. The radio lifted him into the dream world of Harry James, Glenn Miller, and Benny Goodman. But when Tommy Dorsey introduced a new singer named Frank Sinatra, Joe was stunned and envious, and his daydreaming turned into a burning ambition to croon. He practiced every night, singing along softly with the radio after his father went to bed. One night he was sitting on the floor lost in a fantasy—filling in for Sinatra with the Dorsey band—when a booming voice startled him.

"Boy, what the hell you doin'?"

Joe jumped and blinked up at his father, who was standing in the doorway looking at him with an expression of angry exhaustion. "Nothing. J-just listening to Tommy Dorsey."

His father shut off the light. "And squallin' ya fool head off too."

"Aww, Daddy. Tomorrow's Saturday. No school."

"My, my! A no-school day fa' Mista Radio Man. Well, it be a five-o'clock-in-the-mawnin' work day fa' me, boy! So you stop all that damn back-sass and git'cho ass in the bed—now!"

≈∞≈

After church services one Sunday, Joe's mother stomped into the house, removed her hat, and confronted her husband. He was listening to *The Lone Ranger* in his green easy chair as he waited for Gerald to bring the dominoes for their weekly game.

"Tell him, Joe," Leah said firmly. "You speak up for ya'self now, boy."

Joe cleared his throat. "Well—it sure would be nice if we had a piano, Daddy."

Leah nodded her head with a jerk and placed her arm around Joe's shoulders. "Amen."

"A *what?*" Calvin Sr. yelled. "I *know* I ain't jus' heard you say you want a *gotdamn* piano!" He straightened up in the chair and sighed. "Boy, when I was yo' age, I had to take my black ass out every damn mawnin' to work them cotton fields in the hot sun. Why the hell you think I can barely read? Ain't had no schoolin', that's why! And why the hell you think I work my ass off with every job I can dig up?… Shut-up! I'ma tell ya why! So you and yo' knucklehead brother can go to school instead'a bein' a field worker like me, that's why! Or diggin' ditches or shinin' white folks' gotdamn shoes! I ain't havin' that for my boys—you ought'a know that by now."

Joe was already turning to leave. "Yes, sir," he mumbled.

"I ain't through wit'chu, boy! Turn yo' ass around!… Now what the hell was I sayin'?"

"You were talkin' about how you work all those jobs so me and Calvin won't have to shine shoes and dig ditches. Oh, and you said Calvin was a knucklehead, too."

A pebble flew into the room from the direction of the back door, and Calvin Sr. yelled over his shoulder, "Dammit, boy! You stop throwin' shit while I'm talkin' to yo' brother 'fo I drag both y'all sorry asses out to that shed, hear me?" Then he shook his forefinger at Joe. "What I should'a did was drag y'all out to them cotton fields long time ago! I'ma do it this summer. See how ya like the kind'a work a man gotta do when he ain't got no book-learnin'."

Joe gulped and took a step back. "Never mind, Daddy. Really. I shouldn'ta asked."

"Damn right you shouldn'ta! Comin' in here like Mista High Horse… Take a good look at me, boy," he said, stretching out his arms. "Do I look like a rich white man to you? Huh?"

"No, sir."

"Damn right. I'm a black man doin' the best I can in a white man's world. Barely scrapin' by tryin' to keep clothes on ya back. Now you got this here fancy radio to sing along with, so you ain't need no damn piano! And ya bed'not *ever* ask me sump'm that gotdamn stupid again, hear me?" He finished with a warning glare at Leah to keep her from pushing the matter further.

"All that blasphemin'!" Leah said. "We jus' talkin' 'bout a second-hand piano, Calvin. The Chapmans done bought a new one for the parlor so they sellin' that old one. It don't cost much."

Calvin ended the argument by twisting the radio's volume knob to the right and turning his attention to Tonto's conversation with the Lone Ranger.

≈∞≈

The boys' first year at Douglass High School was uncommonly peaceful due to the polarity of their interests. But as the second year began, some intangible force blew in again, hurling them at each other like the conflicting gusts of a Wednesday-born hurricane.

September to May was one long, furious fight—predictably violent and unreasonable. Joe pulled off a sneak attack by joining the track team, which was Calvin's domain. Calvin responded with an ambush after school, which left Joe with a black eye. Calvin was annoyed when Joe showed up at track practice the next day, but didn't show it. He outweighed Joe by fifteen pounds of muscle and knew that his brother could never outrun him. But between piano and choir activities, Joe somehow had found the time to practice, and managed to beat Calvin at the next big track meet—not as a sprinter, but as a hurdler.

And then there was church. Every Sunday as Joe sang his solos and basked in the praises of the congregation, Calvin felt the razor-sharp teeth of jealousy chewing at his insides. He hated Joe for invading his territory on the track team, and he was sick of his brother's satisfied grin. So Calvin decided that it was time for some biblical retribution.

After the next Sunday's services he waited until the church was empty and hesitantly asked the choir director for a tryout. Brother Mason nodded toward the front of the church, and Calvin walked up the aisle to stand beside the pulpit. His knees shook all the way through the first verse of "Precious Lord" before Brother Mason stopped him.

"Boy, stop! Please!… Now, I don't know who was the fool tol' ya to try out for the choir—'cause boy, you couldn't sing a lick if yo' life depended on it."

The laughter of several boys erupted from outside under an open window, and Calvin immediately recognized Joe's mocking voice: "Save me, Lawd! Calvin Bailey's singin' again!"

Calvin shot out of the church like a freight train with no brakes, and caught Joe near the road. By the time they got home, he had cracked one of his brother's ribs, but not the smile.

≈∞≈

Joe's practiced indifference was his only weapon against his brother. No matter how severe the beating, he dusted himself off and infuriated Calvin with a cavalier grin. He had always heard that a light complexion was supposed to be the most valuable asset a colored person could possess, but Joe hated the term "light, bright, and damn near white." The hard truth about being light-skinned was that "damn near" was still damn far. He had seen too many damn-nears laboring their lives away, just like his father and all the other darker Negroes in the cotton fields.

As summer approached, he dreamed up excuses to avoid the threatened fieldwork, and settled on a mysterious, heat-induced illness. Once, for effect, he even forced himself to throw up, and the ploy worked. While Calvin worked in the fields alongside his father, Leah insisted that Joe remain indoors.

At the end of June he peered at his pale reflection in the mirror with a new certainty. He was no longer a damn-near. Joe Bailey was as white as most of the white folks in Nede County.

≈∞≈

The following Sunday it was Calvin who played sick to avoid church. He was stretched out on the floor listening to *Captain Midnight* when Leah and Joe returned.

"Boy, what'chu doin' out here when you supposed to be sick in the bed?" Leah yelled as she swatted his leg. "Lyin' to the Lawd on a Sunday! But'cha can't fool the Lawd, busta! He know you for a pitiful liar, and the Lawd don't like ugly! And you missed yo' brother's big solo too! He made eb'body cry!"

Calvin sighed loudly and then turned up the volume on the radio.

"Calvin!" Leah shouted. "Turn that thing down! And where yo' Daddy at?"

"Out back tryin' to fix them steps," he muttered.

Leah headed to the back door and winced as she peered out. Her husband was leaning over a sawhorse cutting a piece of wood. And he was singing again. "Crossroads Blues"—possibly. She laughed softly and then stepped outside. "Calvin?"

He wiped the perspiration from his forehead, then squinted up at her. "Yeah?"

"I wish you could'a heard Joe today," she said, smiling. "That boy sho' can sing."

"Hell, Leah, I know the boy can sing. Better'n his ol' man, that's fa' damn sho'! But you gon' haf'ta get on away from here and tell me 'bout it later 'cause I'm tryin' to finish up here."

She sighed impatiently. "Well, you sho' picked a awful hot day to do it, Calvin."

"Gotdamn, woman! You been on my back to fix the damn steps and now I'm fixin' 'em!"

"Blasphemin' on a Sunday! Sho' hope the Lawd don't run out'a mercy for you, Calvin!"

Just then, a loud crash erupted from inside the house, followed by the sound of Calvin and Joe yelling. Flinging his saw to the ground, Calvin pushed past Leah and stomped into the house. "That's it, gotdammit!" he shouted. "I'm 'bout to beat the hide off them boys…"

"Calm down, now, Calvin," Leah fretted as she followed him inside. "Please…"

Calvin bulled his way between his sons, wrestled them apart, and backhanded each of them. Then he shoved them to neutral corners and glared at them as he tried to catch his breath. "One gotdamn word'a back-sass out'a either one'a y'all—and I bet'cha I beat the taste out'cha mouths!… Y'all think you big enough—to take on the old man—ya best think twice— 'cause next time—" He gasped suddenly, and then seemed unable to breathe at all. His arms dropped to his sides and he stared at Leah with a look of utter shock as he crashed straight to the floor.

Chapter 4

Daddy's gone.

For the next few nights, that was the only thought in Calvin Jr.'s head. When he managed to sleep, he suffered disturbing dreams that his father was trapped somewhere, trying desperately to return home. Shortly after the funeral the dreams began to subside, only to be replaced by a cold feeling of emptiness.

He watched his mother grow old in a matter of days. The heavy weight of grief slowed her steps, slumped her shoulders, and extinguished the light in her eyes. She went back to work for the Chapmans, then began taking in washing at night, and barely spoke a word to her sons. She drifted quietly from day to day, like a ghost caught between this world and the next, and her silence was as jarring as a screamed accusation. Calvin took care to stay out of her way.

He took long aimless walks until he remembered that place by the River that his father had loved so much. The thought of it sent a surge of adrenaline into his legs and Calvin began to run.

When he reached the spot, his heart was beating like the wings of the startled birds flying up from the surrounding trees. He gazed into the distance at the expanse of rushing water. He had almost forgotten how magnificent it all was. It was one of earth's preordained points of natural convergence, where the rain returned from journeys over distant lands to dance with the rapids in a joyous reunion. Where Calvin stood, at land's edge, the shallows were calm and clear enough to see the darting minnows near his feet. He could hear the water trickling over small, clean rocks before gathering enough speed to merge with the rapids, and he remembered what his father had said about the River "singing songs."

The song it was singing now brought long forgotten memories welling up in Calvin's mind, clear and true—even visions of things that had happened before he was born. He saw his father's whole life—years of backbreaking work, daily humiliations, and hundreds of lost dreams. For the first time he understood his father's joy in the simple things—talking to the River, drinking Gerald's homemade whiskey, listening to the fights on the radio, or singing those juke joint songs when he thought no one was around to complain. He had worked hard, loved one woman, and raised two strong sons. These things had given him all the reason he needed to stand tall through the worst days of a black man's life. Calvin felt the burn of tears and shut his eyes tightly. His father felt as real and present as the cool River mist all around him. It smelled sweet and green, and it was alive with his father's voice. He was telling one of those old stories about how the River had no beginning and no end, and how the ancient Indians knew that it was the source and the lifeblood of the whole territory long before anybody called it "Mississippi."

That be a mighty River right there, boy. Can't nothin' stop it! Livin' right with the land, turnin' any way it want to. Ain't paid no mind to no county lines, no states neither. Folks always killin' each other over lines on some map. But them Indians knowed the truth. That's why they been sayin' the same thing for a hun'ud years. White man come, divide up the land, and think they own it. But in the end, the land gon' own 'em all. An' the River gon' swallow up they blood.

Calvin's eyes opened. He saw the images that still lived in the mist of that River. He saw it running red with blood as snapping dogs chased people dressed in rags—runaway slaves, trusting the River to guide them to safety along the Underground Railroad. The rushing rapids sounded like a mournful wail, and he saw soldiers on horseback—both Union and Confederate—whispering prayers as they rode through the water to face death. The images and sounds swirled in Calvin's brain—guns of the Civil War, explosions, and violent screams. Then—it stopped.

Out of the stillness, Calvin heard the River's exultant roar. *The war is over!* But from the height of joy, it fell abruptly to a shushing moan of sorrow. He blinked to be sure he was not dreaming, but his mind was clear. He continued to listen, and suddenly knew what the troubled sound meant. The River had witnessed it all, and it was grieving the cold, lingering divisions of Reconstruction—divisions that had widened over time as the people continued to distance themselves, one from the other, seeing only their differences, and not their common humanity. Generation after generation had closed their eyes so tightly to pray for miracles from above that they did not see the miracle of each other, or the gift of the earth that sustained them.

Daddy? Where' heaven at?

Heaven? Well, boy, some folks say heaven be up in the sky someplace. But me, I b'lieve heaven might jus' be smack in the middle a'that ol' River...

And Calvin felt the first light taps of a summer shower on his shoulders. And he looked out at the gentle splashes the rain made as it returned to the River that had given birth to each drop, no matter how small. And he knew that his father was there.

≈∞≈

For those precious few days at the River, Calvin's grief was gone. But when the voices began to fade and fall silent, the pain and loneliness returned, fresh and sharp, as if his father had died a second time. In his anger, Calvin walked away from the River, determined never to go back.

The rest of the summer passed in a slow burn, finally dying into lazy embers that August. Calvin passed the time by running, and the last thing he expected to find on the school's dirt track was good fortune. But there she was—Michele Littlejohn—his beautiful stroke of luck.

It was nearly dark, and Calvin was still running time sprints. When he stopped to stretch, he was surprised to see Yvonne Jackson, one of the stuck-up girls from last year's history class, cutting across the track with a girl he had never seen before. "'Evenin', ladies," he called.

"Oh, hi, Calvin," Yvonne said, barely glancing at him.

But the other girl walked over to talk. She was even prettier up close, with a smooth caramel-candy complexion. The cotton blouse she wore could not conceal the fact that the Lord had blessed her with more than her share of man-pleasing bosom. Calvin forced his eyes back to her smile and noticed that her teeth were slightly crooked. This small imperfection gave him the courage to start a conversation. "Ain'tcha gonna introduce me to your friend, Yvonne?"

Yvonne had already walked away, but turned around and sauntered back. "This here's my cousin from Virginia—Michele Littlejohn. She stayin' with us a spell till her family get here in October." She nudged Michele and gave her a slit-eyed look that made Calvin want to knock her down. "This here's Calvin Bailey," she said flatly.

Michele smiled and extended her hand. "Hi, Calvin. You on the track team or sump'm?"

He noticed her furtive glances at his body, so as he took her hand, he flexed his left pectoral muscle and watched her eyes widen. "Yeah. I'm anchor of the relay team and—"

Yvonne cut him off. "Yeah, yeah, but we gotta go now. See ya in two weeks, Calvin."

"Two weeks? What's in two weeks?"

"You so stupid, Calvin," Yvonne cackled. "*School* be startin' in two weeks, 'member?"

Calvin's face felt hot, but he ignored her. "So, Michele, you goin' to Douglass too?"

Michele smiled again. "Mm-hmm. And I'ma go to one of them track meets and watch you run sometime. I bet you gonna win all kinds'a ribbons this year!"

≈∞≈

Unlike Joe, Calvin had never been confident around girls, so when school started, it took him a full week to ask Michele for a date. He took her to a church picnic and they began seeing each other every weekend. In October, Joe's girlfriend Elizabeth threw a party and Calvin went, only to please Michele. But at the end of the night, when "Mood Indigo" played on the phonograph, Michele nestled closely to him and rewarded him with a long, passionate kiss. Calvin couldn't resist sneaking a peek at his brother. For once, Joe was not grinning. What was that look? When Calvin realized what it was, he smiled maliciously at Joe with his eyes. The look was envy.

Shortly after Elizabeth's birthday party, Calvin's relationship with Michele began to heat up. She breathlessly permitted necking and petting in the back seats of the Grand Marquee, and then told him to sneak around to her bedroom window after her parents were asleep. Although their whispered love talk at the window was steamy, he could never convince her to climb down and slip away somewhere with him. Calvin suffered weeks of almost unendurable teasing before Michele whispered to him that maybe, just maybe, Christmas would be the night.

Frederick Douglass High School sat on a plot of land that had once been a farm, and the old barn now served as a gymnasium. The students had decorated it for the big Christmas dance, and they chattered loudly among themselves, catching up with the latest gossip and dance steps. Since Michele had volunteered to serve punch, Calvin agreed to man the phonograph.

After Melvin Thomas and Carolyn Washington won first prize in the dance contest, the requests began to roll in for slower numbers. Calvin placed "Mood Indigo" on the phonograph and craned his neck to look for

Michele. He asked Raymond, a luckless boy with no date, to take over
the phonograph, then headed to the refreshment table. "Hey, Cynthia.
You seen Michele?"

"Huh? Oh, hi, Calvin. Umm, yeah. Michele—she went out to the
bathroom. She be back in a minute. Hey! Could you play 'Creole Love
Call' next?"

"Sure, yeah. Listen, when Michele gets back, tell her I'm lookin' for
her, okay?"

"Mmm-hmm. I'll tell her. 'Creole Love Call,' Calvin. Don't forget."

"Mood Indigo" was just fading out when Calvin returned to the
phonograph. As he searched for "Creole Love Call," he felt a sharp jab in
the ribs. Carolyn Washington was beside him, smacking her chewing
gum and bouncing on her heels in a rapid Lindy Hop rhythm.

"Where' yo' brother at tonight, Calvin? I wanted to Lindy wid' him."

"I don't know—off somewhere with Elizabeth. So you gonna have to
Lindy by yo'self."

Carolyn rolled her eyes. "Shoot! I been tryin'! But I can't Lindy to
nothin' with that square, belly-rubbin' music you been playin'. Throw on
sump'm that jumps, Calvin. Come on."

He sighed as he took "Creole Love Call" off the turntable and replaced
it with "Stompin' at the Savoy." "Hey, Carolyn! You seen Michele? I ain't
seen her for about twenty minutes."

"Oh, she ain't told you? Shoot, that girl's sick, Calvin. She went home."

Before Carolyn could say another word, Melvin Thomas whirled her
out to the dance floor for a high-flying Lindy. Calvin cursed loudly, then
spotted Raymond still standing awkwardly at the end of the table. "Hey,
Raymond. Take over these records, man. I'm goin' home."

"Uh, well, what do I play?"

"Shit, I don't know, Raymond. Take requests. And if it skips, just
nudge the needle."

Calvin headed home, cursing and kicking the dirt in the road. He
knew that his mother was serving a late party at the Chapmans', and that
meant that Joe and Elizabeth were at the house carrying on in Joe's bed.
And in the time it took him to walk home, Calvin had hatched a sinister
plot. As he quietly opened the front door, he heard the radio playing a
Frank Sinatra song—"I Fall in Love Too Easily"—accompanied by the
rhythmic creaking of springs from Joe's bed.

Calvin tiptoed to the bedroom door, flipped on the light, and saw his
brother's pale rear-end positioned between Elizabeth's clinging naked
thighs. He started to laugh, but then stopped when he saw Joe lean away
from her. The legs wrapped so shamelessly around his brother did not

belong to Elizabeth at all. They belonged to Calvin's one and only angel, Michele. And she didn't look the slightest bit sick.

In that painful moment, Calvin knew that his first impression of Michele Littlejohn had been correct. She truly had turned out to be a beautiful stroke of luck—bad luck.

Somehow he survived his humiliation. With the exception of silent passages at school, nearly three months passed before he had to face Michele again, on his eighteenth birthday.

Calvin came home with Butch and two other friends that his mother refused to allow in her house. After several minutes of arguing, Calvin kicked open the front door and walked out.

"Calvin!" Leah shouted. "You better turn around right now, boy! Don'tchu test me! And tell them hoodlums to get on out'a here! All they do is get you into fights and stir up trouble! Now I done told you we got company inside. So tell them roughnecks they gotta go and then you git'cho behind back in here and speak to Miss Michele like a gentleman!"

Calvin turned around slowly. "Who?"

"Michele Littlejohn's here, Calvin, in the kitchen. Ain't you heard a word I been sayin'?"

Calvin strode past his mother and saw Michele seated at the kitchen table, staring at him.

"Happy birthday, Calvin," she said softly.

Calvin stared at her in silence until Leah smacked him on the back of the head.

"Boy! You hear Miss Michele talkin' to you?"

Calvin's lips curled into a scornful smile. "Hello, *Miss* Michele. Nice to see you back here again. You *were* here before. I *saw* you, 'member? You were with Mista *Sunshine* and I—"

Joe came in and bumped Calvin from behind, and then leaned down to kiss Michele. "Hey, what's goin' on? I thought we were havin' a party. Where's the cake and stuff, Mama?"

Calvin turned to leave. "I'm leavin' anyway. I got some shit to do."

Leah yanked out a chair and pointed at it. "Boy! You git'cho nasty-talkin' behind back in here! You don't use that kind'a language in my house! Now you sit down. Right *now*!"

Calvin glared at her for a moment, but then slumped into the chair and closed his eyes.

"Now," she said, "I know all about you and yo' brother fightin' over Michele but—"

"Mama, I don't want to talk about that," he said with a pleading look.

Leah sighed. "Well, did you see the birthday present Michele done give to Joe?"

Joe grinned. "Gold cuff links, see? Sharp, huh? What'cha call these stones, baby?"

"Aquamarines or—or blue topaz—sump'm like that. But it ain't no real gold or nothin'."

Leah beamed. "Michele saved up her money from her library job. Ain't that sweet?"

"Yeah," Calvin sneered. "Sweet. So what'cha get *me*, Michele?"

She gave Joe a "help-me" look, and Calvin saw it. "Seem' like you always givin' things to Joe and you ain't give me *nothin'*. Like that Christmas present—'member that?"

Michele covered her face with her hands. "Oh, Joe, make him stop!"

Leah slapped the table. "Stop it! Y'all done killed yo' Daddy with all that fightin', and I ain't havin' it! You hear me, Calvin? Joe?"

Joe flashed a self-satisfied grin. "Yeah, Calvin," he said. "Let's have a party."

Leah turned to Calvin. "And what about you, busta?"

"I'll stay a few minutes," he snapped. "But then, like I said, I got some *shit* to do."

"You stop that cussin', boy!" Leah shouted, but then softened her tone. "Calvin," she said gently, "She Joe's girl now. You go on and find yourself somebody else."

Calvin glared at her. She was wearing the same patronizing smile he remembered from his childhood—when she had beaten him with a belt and then told him it was for his own good.

"Mama? Why ain't you just take my balls and stick 'em on top'a the damn birthday cake?"

Ignoring his mother's shouts, Calvin stood up, kicked his chair over, and walked out.

Chapter 5

In the six days following his birthday Joe saw his brother twice. He had no idea where Calvin was spending his time and didn't care. When he got home from school that Thursday, he heard the radio warming up, but no one was around. "Mama?" he called. "Where are you?"

"Out back," she answered. "Bringin' in this laundry so I can start ironin' yo' shirt, baby."

Joe met her at the back door as she came in. "Now, how'd you know I needed that shirt?"

"It's yo' favorite, ain't it?" she said, spreading out the shirt on the ironing board. "I figured you'd be wantin' it for choir practice tonight. What time you leavin' out?"

"'Bout an hour. I'm going in to wash up now."

A few minutes later Joe came out of the bathroom, but stopped when he saw his mother. She was standing at the ironing board, just as he had left her, but there were dark clouds of steam rising from his badly scorched shirt, and his mother's shoulders were slumped and shaking. He ran over to retrieve the iron, and saw that she was sobbing. "Mama! What's wrong?"

Leah just shook her head and stared at the radio. The announcer was in the middle of a news bulletin, and his voice cracked with emotion: ... *I repeat, President Roosevelt is dead.*

≈∞≈

It was dark when Joe heard the front door slam. He was sitting at the table eating soup and didn't look up. He recognized his brother's heavy steps.

"Where Mama at?" Calvin said in his usual belligerent tone.

"In her room," Joe said. "But don't go in there right now."

"Why not? I got sump'm to tell her and I wanna get the shit over with."

"Didn't you hear the news about the President dying today?"

Calvin looked at Joe with an expression of genuine shock. "Nah. Roosevelt's *dead?*"

"It's true, and Mama's been crying all day. So whatever you have to tell her can wait."

Calvin dropped into a chair and stared out the kitchen window. "Roosevelt was her hero."

"He sure was. I can't believe he's dead. He's the only President I can even remember."

"Well, what happened to him?" Calvin asked softly. "And why ain't the radio on?"

Joe shook his head. "I turned it off. It was breaking her heart."

Leah walked in just then, staring at Calvin with red eyes. "What'chu got to tell me, boy?"

Calvin squirmed in his chair. "Nothin', Mama. It can wait."

She sighed and leaned against the wall. "I'ma ask you again. What'chu got to tell me?"

He looked at the floor. "You ain't gonna like it."

"Boy! I ain't got no patience now!"

"It's just—I ain't gon' graduate, Mama. Joe is, but not me." He saw her quick tears and groaned. "Aww, come on, Mama. I'll graduate next year is all."

"No, you won't," Joe muttered.

"Shut up," Calvin hissed.

Leah started to say something, but then just shook her head and walked out without a word.

≈∞≈

Joe's graduation was bearing down on Calvin with an inescapable pressure. Letters from family members began to arrive, and Leah was planning a big meal. Each time the subject came up, Calvin fought her to a draw about not going, but her tears finally defeated him.

When the day came, Calvin reluctantly put on his best Sunday pants, shirt, and necktie. As he waited outside, all he could think about was *Angels With Dirty Faces* and Jimmy Cagney's long walk down that dark hallway to the electric chair.

The graduation ceremony bored Calvin to sleep until he felt his mother's elbow jabbing him awake. When it was over, visiting family members and Joe's friends headed back to the Bailey house. Uncle Cyrus had traveled from Baton Rouge with his own stash of liquor, a phonograph, and a stack of records. Judging from the number of times he played it, "Minnie the Moocher" was his favorite. With Cab Calloway's voice grating on everyone's nerves, Joe basked in the praises of the uncles, who called him "graduation man" and patted him on the back. Calvin was left to the sympathy of the bosomy aunts, with their smothering hugs and comments about trying harder next year. He finally ducked into a corner and watched the minutes drag on the clock. At 10:05, Uncle Cyrus drowned out a chorus of groans with a drunken roar. "*Got*damn! I done tol' y'all I seent Cab Calloway at the Renaissance Ballroom back in '33, ain't I? Up in Harlem, beautiful Harlem! Thash my lady!… Hey, Leah! Come on an' dance with ol' Cyrus one time!"

"No! And sit down, ya drunk fool!"

"Come on now, Leah! Bus' out another bottle and les' all us' chillun git *blind!*"

Calvin closed his eyes. *Time to go.*

The last thing he heard as he left was Uncle Cyrus's off-key chorus of hi-de-hi-de-hos.

He headed toward Highway 61, feeling the need to run. Clawing at his necktie, he ripped off his shirt and bunched it up in his fist. *Faster.* A moment before, the night breeze had felt cool, but now he was burning up and running faster than he had ever run before. In his head he could hear voices murmuring in a rapid, discordant cadence that grew to a steady roar. Then he saw a figure up ahead at the railroad crossing, and stopped so abruptly he nearly fell. As he regained his footing, he saw who it was.

Joe. Grinning, girlfriend-stealing Joe. Graduation man.

"Hey, Calvin. What are you doin' out here?"

Calvin stared at his brother's untroubled smile. He was surprised to see Joe strolling closer to him, like an unwitting bug into a spider's web. The voice in Calvin's head was laughing like a cold-blooded thrill killer: *Better back up, Joe.*

"I slipped out around nine," Joe was saying. "Couldn't take any more of Uncle Cyrus's singing. I was gonna go see Michele, but she's still not home from Cynthia's party, and I didn't feel like goin' over there. So, uh, you never said what you're doing out here."

Calvin felt the rapid rise and fall of his chest, and continued to stare silently at his brother. Then he saw what he had been waiting for—that flicker of fear in his eyes.

Joe backed up a step and sighed heavily. "Aww, shit, Calvin… Come on, not tonight."

Should'a ran, Joe. Should'a ran for your life.

Joe attempted to sidestep his brother. "Look, aren't you over that girl *yet?* I mean—"

Calvin was on him before he could finish his sentence. Anger and adrenaline had swirled together, eclipsing every thought but one: *Nobody's around this time.*

It took less than a minute for Joe to begin begging for his life. "Awww, God, pleeease—"

As Joe clawed at his forearms, Calvin could see the terror in his eyes. He swung harder, connected, and felt the skin on his knuckles split with the impact. When Joe fell, Calvin yanked him to his feet just for the pleasure of knocking him back down.

"Wait!" Joe screamed. "Calvin! You're killin' me! Stop—*please!*"

A solid right smacked a wheezing sound out of him, and Calvin became dizzy with an urge to finish him off. But suddenly, he was surrounded by a shock of bright headlights. Each blink of his eyes felt like thunder in his head as he peered over his shoulder at a dark-colored automobile prowling up behind him.

Joe let out a feeble sob and tried to get up. "Help me, pleazzsh! He's—killin' me!"

Calvin shoved him back down and strode over to the driver's door. Staring out at him with a horrified expression was the face of Miss Anson, his history teacher from Douglass. One of the F's responsible for his failure to graduate. Calvin leaned in menacingly and bared his teeth. "Get out'a here, bitch!" Then he lunged at her, thumping the car door with his knee.

Miss Anson gasped, jerked the car into reverse, and sped away with tires screeching.

"Wait!" Joe cried as he crawled toward the car. "Aww, God. Don't leave me here!"

The interruption momentarily jolted Calvin out of his rage. He blinked uncertainly at Joe, who was still struggling to crawl away. Then something glittered in the moonlight—the stone from one of the cuff links. Calvin felt his lips stretch tightly over his teeth, and he jerked Joe up by the collar.

"Look at me!" he yelled. "I said *look* at me! Who got the gotdamn grin now, huh?... Hey! Wake up! This ain'tcho regular ass whuppin', Sunshine! I ain't done yet!" Snatching the cuff links from Joe's sleeves, he shoved him back down and heard a dull clunk when his head hit the tracks.

"Come on!" Calvin screamed. "Call me Mud Boy now!" He kicked Joe's leg, but there was no reaction. He stared at him for a long, still moment, and then kicked him again. Nothing. Calvin backed away slowly, and then began to run as fast as he could toward town.

By the time he got home, Calvin had lost all sense of time. The house was dark, so he crept in quietly, squinting at the clock by the moonlight from the window. But before his eyes could adjust, the kitchen light blazed on.

Leah stood there glaring at him until her gaze lowered to his blood-stained undershirt. "Oh my Gawd, Calvin!" she gasped. "You all bloodied up! What'chu gone and did now?"

"Nothin'," he snapped. "Where eb'body go?"

"They gone. And where that blood come from? Lawd, please don't let my Joe be hurt!"

Calvin felt his back teeth grinding together. "How you know this ain't *my* blood, Mama?"

Leah narrowed her eyes and gathered the collar of her robe tightly around her neck. "It ain't *never* yo' blood, Calvin. Who you been beatin' on this time? Next thing you be tellin' me is that crazy story about yo' *other* brother makin' you beat on folks, huh?"

He smirked and reached for a hunk of bread. "Mama, you must'a dreamed that. What the hell I need with another damn brother? I wish I ain't had the one I got!"

"Don't you say things like that, Calvin! Now where my Joe at?"

Calvin stuffed the bread into his mouth. "Who? Oh, you mean Gradua-tion Man? Shoot! Ain't my job to be lookin' out for him. He grown."

≈∞≈

Calvin refused to worry about Joe until three days had passed. Waking earlier than usual, he glanced over at his brother's bed, still made up, just as he had left it on graduation day. Gazing around the room, he tried to ignore the gnawing feeling in his gut. Above Joe's bed were his tacked-up Frank Sinatra photos and articles, and the popular swimsuit pin-up of Betty Grable smiling seductively over her shoulder.

Calvin scowled. "Joe sho' do love hisself some damn white folks."

Leaning his head back, he looked up at the photos of Joe Louis and Sugar Ray Robinson that he had pinned on the wall over his own bed. He had considered hanging a pin-up of Lena Horne, but decided against it. Beauty queen or not, Lena Horne was a female, just like Michele Littlejohn, and not to be trusted. He cut his eyes at Betty Grable. "Shit. You ain't so purty."

His gaze drifted back to Joe's empty bed, and there was that digging feeling in his belly again. "Damn!" he snapped, getting up suddenly to dress. "He prob'ly jus' tryin' to worry Mama so she'll be fussin' over him when he finally brings his sorry ass back home… Shit. I'ma catch hell when Mama sees what I done to Pansy Boy's face."

He stopped buttoning his shirt when he heard his mother crying in the other room. She was usually at work at this hour. A cold shudder went through Calvin and he closed his eyes, only to see an image of Joe lying face-down on the railroad tracks. Completely still. Unconscious.

Naw. I ain't beat him that bad—did I? But what if he—wandered off someplace and—

A surge of panic propelled him out of his room. "Mama, how come you ain't at work?"

Leah sat down slowly. "Miz Chapman gimme the day off. She let me use her phone last night to call the police, and they comin' today. Sump'm terrible done happened to Joe."

"No, Mama, look—I was jus' leavin' out to go find him. I think I know where he is."

"You don't know where he is," she said, then gave him a cold stare. "Or maybe you do."

There was a sound outside—the crunch of automobile tires in the rocky dirt. Calvin touched his mother's hand. "Don't go out there, Mama… Please."

When she heard the knock, she didn't move for a moment. But finally, she placed both hands on the table and pushed herself out of the chair. "You tell 'em what you know, boy."

Calvin felt as if his feet were nailed to the floor as he watched her walk out. When she returned with two white men, he still hadn't moved. The man in front was tall and slender with slicked-back reddish hair and hooded blue eyes, and behind him was a shorter, more muscular man, who looked younger than his partner, despite his balding head.

"Mornin', Miz Bailey," the taller man said with a thick Mississippi drawl. "I'm Detective Jansen and this here's my partner Detective Masterson. This yer son?"

"Yessuh. This Calvin."

Calvin could feel the detective's eyes giving him a calculating once-over. He gripped the back of a chair and tried to respond, but his mouth had dried out, so he just nodded.

Jansen tapped out a Camel and stuck it in his mouth. When he struck a match to light it, Calvin flinched, drawing all eyes to him. Jansen smiled artfully. "Why don't we all sit down?"

"I—got some coffee on the stove," Leah said nervously. "Can I git'cha a cup?"

Detective Masterson shook his head. "None for me, but—mind if I look around a little?"

"No suh. That be fine."

Calvin sat down, but kept his eyes Masterson as he disappeared into the back room.

Jansen took out a notepad. "I'll take some'a that coffee, Miz Bailey—no cream or sugar. Now, on the phone you said yer boy ain't been home since graduation. That right?"

"Yessuh." Leah poured the coffee into a cup and handed it to him.

"And that'd be what? 'Bout three days ago, right?"

"Y-yessuh. And my Joe ain't never stayed away that long. He a good boy."

"Mm-hmm. I'm shore he is, Miz Bailey." He leveled a pinpoint stare at Calvin as he sipped the coffee. "So, tell me, Calvin. When's the last time *you* saw yer brother?"

"Same as Mama. Graduation." He glanced quickly in the direction of his room, wondering what Masterson was doing back there.

Jansen scribbled on his pad, then dropped it carelessly on the table and looked away, giving Calvin a chance to sneak a look at what he had written:

Son sweating on a cool morning. Scraped knuckles and arms.

Calvin quickly hid his hands under the table, angry at his slip-up.

Jansen turned back to Leah. "Miz Bailey, did anything odd happen on graduation night?"

"Well, Calvin come in— He come in real late." She looked at the clock, then at Calvin.

No, Mama, don't say it. Please.

Jansen leaned forward. "Was that strange—him comin' home so late? Was he alone?"

"Yessuh. He was alone, but he was— His shirt was—"

Calvin shifted slightly in his chair.

Leah's voice was a whisper. "Lawd, I pray you ain't did nothin', son. Please, Lawd—"

Calvin was about to pitch his hastily prepared alibi when Detective Masterson walked back into the room carrying a pair of scuffed shoes and a cigar box with the top flipped open.

Placing the shoes on the table, Masterson pointed at a bundled handkerchief in the cigar box. "Found this under a bed in that back room with these shoes. These yer shoes, Calvin?"

Calvin hesitated a moment, then tried to sound casual. "Yessuh."

"Where'd you get the scratches on your hands and arms, Calvin?" Jansen asked.

Calvin jerked up his chin defiantly. "Don't remember."

Jansen untied the handkerchief and a cuff link dropped out onto the table. "What's this?"

The sound of Leah's sharp gasp hit Calvin like a punch to the midsection. "That belongs to—to *Joe!*" she screamed. "Oh, Calvin, what'chu *do?* Oh, my Gawd!"

Jansen narrowed his eyes at Calvin and flashed a smug grin. "Well, well. Looks like you got sump'm sticky on your brother's cuff link, Calvin. Looks like blood to me."

Calvin lowered his head and stared at the floor as his mother sobbed for Joe.

Detective Jansen stood up. "Looks like you're comin' with us, Calvin."

Chapter 6

In the following weeks Calvin did not fight the nightmare that had become his life; he burrowed deep into the core of it, coiling his thoughts and emotions into a tight, self-protecting knot. Finding a strange comfort in the dictated order of the Natchez County Jail, he spoke to no one and regarded his cell as a cruel but reliable hiding place. It was the outside world that he feared now. Nothing there made sense anymore and any thoughts of life before his arrest tortured him with questions that had no answers. *Where is Joe at? If he dead, then where his body at?*

His court-appointed lawyer, Kenneth Green, advised Calvin that the prosecution's case likely would hinge on the theory that he had viciously murdered his brother and disposed of the body in some unspeakable manner. Green repeatedly bombarded him with questions about graduation night, but Calvin only shrugged. As long as Joe was missing, he knew his answers were pointless. *Where is Joe at?* The question filled his days, and after lights-out the nerves in his legs began to twitch. After a few sleepless nights, he knew the reason. In the sliver of space too small for pacing, his athlete's legs were rebelling, screaming at him their need to run.

≈∞≈

On the opening day of the trial, Calvin got his first glimpse of the prosecuting attorney. The white man whose mission was to convict him was a typical throwback to the vanguard of the old South—a theatrical character with the fitting name of Beauregard Davis, Esquire.

Davis swept into the courtroom, wearing a white seersucker suit that perfectly matched his unruly shock of snowy hair. In a room filled with spectators busily waving paper fans to fight the late summer heat, Davis appeared cool. When Calvin caught his eye, the white man's imperious gaze confirmed that this trial would be business as usual in the old southern tradition.

It took several minutes for Calvin to work up the courage to look back at the colored section. Seated beside Gerald Moore, his mother was staring down at him with wounded eyes. Calvin quickly looked to Gerald, hoping for a sign of understanding or forgiveness from his father's lifelong friend. But all he saw was accusation and disappointment from a man missing a much-needed day of work. Calvin turned around and never looked back.

The white citizens in Nede County had exhibited only mild curiosity about a colored boy killing his brother until the newspapers reported that Davis would prosecute the case personally. Soon the crowds outside the courtroom began to grow. Jury selection was completed with almost no objection from Calvin's lawyer, who seemed more than eager to bring the ordeal to an end.

Davis's opening statement exceeded anything Green had predicted, with its graphic imagery of severed limbs buried in holes or tossed into the Mississippi. As Davis strode back and forth gesturing and raising his voice for effect, Calvin stopped listening, and withdrew into his own thoughts. Some days he stared at witnesses as they testified, and never heard a word they said.

But then Davis called his star witness to the stand.

Gertrude Anson was the only eyewitness to the beating Calvin had repeatedly denied. After being sworn in, she sat rigidly in the witness box waiting for her big moment. For once in her mundane life, she was the center of attention, and she had dressed for the occasion: a rose-print dress made from her favorite Butterick pattern; a white pillbox hat covered with multi-colored posies, and a pink neck-scarf tied in a jaunty bow. She held her eyeglasses in her gloved hand.

Davis hung his jacket on the back of a chair, rolled up his shirt-sleeves, and strolled over to the witness stand. "That is quite a colorful ensemble, darlin'! Just like a garden in springtime."

Miss Anson smiled bashfully. "Thank you, sir."

"You're welcome. Now, please state your full name and occupation for the court."

"Gertrude Lee Anson, sir. I'm a history teacher at Douglass High, right here in Natchez."

"Thank you. Now, Miss Anson, was Joseph Bailey a student of yours?"

"Yes, sir, he was. I taught him and his brother Calvin in my senior history class last year. Joe passed the course, but Calvin failed.... And his conduct was no better."

"He was disruptive, wasn't he?"

"Objection, Your Honor," Kenneth Green interjected in a flat tone.

Judge Lockhart tapped his gavel lightly. "Now, Beau, let's not testify for the witness."

"My apologies. Miss Anson, did you attend the graduation at Douglass this past June?"

"Yes, sir, I certainly did. It was June the 10th."

"And did you see Joseph and Calvin Bailey at the graduation?"

"Yes, sir. I did."

"Did you happen to notice whether or not Joseph was wearin' cuff links?"

"Yes, sir. They were light blue. He told me his girlfriend gave 'em to him for his birthday."

Davis brought a tagged item over to Miss Anson and showed it to her. "Miss Anson, is this one of the cuff links you saw Joe Bailey wearin' that evenin'?"

"Why, yes, sir, I believe it is."

"Your Honah," Davis said, "the court should know that this bloody cuff link was found in the possession of the defendant Calvin Bailey three days after his brother was last seen."

After the spectator buzz over the cuff link died down, Davis continued. "Miss Anson, did you notice whether the Bailey brothers left the graduation together?"

"Yes, sir. They were with their mother."

"And do you remember seein' both boys together again that night?"

"Yes, sir. I did. It was about ten-thirty or eleven that same night—graduation night."

Calvin looked at the jurors and shook his head. Lyle Hart, Ben Hackett and his son Harlan, and nine other possible Klan members.

"Miss Anson, in your own words, please tell us where you were and what you saw between ten-thirty and eleven on the night of June 10th."

"Well, I was drivin' my Daddy's Plymouth that night, and I got lost out by the railroad tracks. That's when I saw Calvin beatin' Joe up—just like he always did in school."

"Just stick to what you saw that night," Davis said. "You're sure it was the Bailey boys?"

"I drove closer to see. It was them all right. Calvin was beatin' the daylights out of Joe."

"And for the court record, could you please point out the boy that was doin' the beatin'?"

After squinting over at Calvin, she put on her eyeglasses and took another look. Then she sat up straight, extended her arm, and pointed rigidly at Calvin, like a well-trained hunting dog.

"Let the record show that the witness has identified the defendant," the judge said. "Go on."

"Well, as soon as he saw the car, he stopped beatin' Joe and stared at me."

"He stared at you?" Davis asked. "Do you think he recognized you?"

"Well, not at first. Not till I crept up a little closer. I—I don't know why I did it, but it just seemed to me that somebody had to stop him. That's when Joe called out."

"And what did Joe say?"

"I heard him quite clearly. He said, 'Please help me. My brother's killin' me.'"

Calvin closed his eyes. He could still hear the terror in Joe's voice as he begged for his life.

Pandemonium erupted in the courtroom. Judge Lockhart pounded his gavel to no avail. When Calvin heard his mother wailing loudly from the colored section, his blood ran cold.

It took fifteen minutes for things to calm down enough for Davis to present his big finish. "And now, Your Honah, I have here a few photo exhibits I'd like to show to the jury."

Judge Lockhart looked at the photos, then directed the bailiff to pass them on to the jurors.

"Miss Anson," Davis said, "tell the jury how we found the stretch of road in these photos."

"Yes, sir." Miss Anson took off her glasses and faced the jury. "Well, sir, when those detectives came to my house askin' me questions about Joe's disappearance, I took 'em back over to Highway 61 right to the spot where I saw that Calvin killin' his brother."

Kenneth Green issued a barely audible objection. Calvin cut his eyes at him in disgust.

"If the jurors will direct their attention to Exhibit B-3," Davis said, "they'll see a smeared blood trail near the railroad crossing, as if the victim had been dragged off the road."

This time Green stood up. "Objection! That could've been a deer that was hit by a car."

Davis held up two small brown envelopes and then handed them to the judge. "If it please the court, I have two exhibits for the jury to look at. In that first envelope are teeth, Your Honah, and not from a deer. What you're holdin' there are human teeth—a molar, if I've got my dental jargon right, and an incisor that's broken off at the root, like it was knocked out of somebody's mouth. And in that other envelope is a hank of curly brownish-colored hair, that I also doubt belonged to a deer—not unless said deer just had himself a home permanent, Your Honah."

Laughter broke out in the courtroom, and Kenneth Green stood up again. "Objection."

"Sustained," the judge said, covering a laugh. "Good Lord, Beau! Control yourself!"

"I'm sorry, Your Honah. What we plan to do is call the boy's Mama to the stand to identify the hair. And in any case, we *will* be presenting corroborating expert testimony."

Calvin cringed at the now familiar sound of his mother's sobs from the colored section.

Davis continued: "Now, Miss Anson. After you came upon the murder scene—"

"Oh—objection!" Kenneth Green cried. "Murder scene? It hasn't even been established that a murder was committed! There's not even a body, for God's sake!"

Judge Lockhart tapped his gavel lightly. "Beau—"

"I'll rephrase it, Your Honah. Miss Anson, after you bumped into the Bailey boys, havin' their little *tussle* that night—" He waited for the snickers to die down. "What happened next?"

"Well, then he—well, he came over to the driver's side door."

"In a threatenin' manner, Miss Anson?"

"Yes, sir. In a *most* threatenin' manner. And then he said—"

"Objection," Kenneth Green groaned. "Leading the witness by her willing little nose."

Davis cast a surprised glance at Green. "Withdrawn, Your Honah. However, I have a serious objection to Mr. Green's insulting attack on my witness."

Judge Lockhart glared at Green. "Sustained."

"Now, Miss Anson," Davis continued, "what did the defendant say next?"

Miss Anson crimsoned. "Well, sir, I can't repeat such vulgar language, but he told me to get the—the blankety-blank on out'a there, and then he kicked my Daddy's Plymouth! It's still got the dent too. And then I went home and called the Sheriff's office. Deputy McGinnis told me he'd go check on Joe, but when he called me back, he said he didn't see anybody out there. I thought everything was all right till those detectives told me Joe was missin'."

"Well, thank you, Miss Anson. You've been very helpful. No further questions."

"Sir? I'd like to say one more thing if I may. I don't know what he did with the body, but that boy killed Joe as sure as I'm sittin' here. I saw him—with my own two eyes."

Kenneth Green's objection was lost in a sea of angry, shouting voices.

≈∞≈

Beauregard Davis, Esquire had a reputation for closing argument theatrics. When he held up an enlargement of Joe's school photo, its intended impact was clear. The picture had been taken in the dead of winter, when Joe's complexion was its palest. Calvin gazed at the shocked faces of the all-white jury. The boy in the photograph could have passed for one of their own.

Chapter 7

Adam Delavigné stood at the front door of the Redbird Club mumbling in a mixture of Cajun French and English, the traditional vernacular spoken by many New Orleans natives. He blew aside a strand of gray hair that fell over his left eye as he juggled his keys, a paper cup filled with hot coffee, and a stack of papers. Standing on one leg and balancing the papers on the other knee, he gripped the damp paper cup in his teeth and managed to unlock the front door. Dropping the keys and papers onto the floor, he hurried behind the bar and dumped what was left of the coffee into a mug, then crumpled the paper cup in his fist. "Rex and his cheap goddamn paper cups!"

He pulled the chairs off of one of the tables, then picked up his papers and spread them out. Everything from sheet music to bookkeeping records lay before him demanding attention. As he arranged the papers into stacks, he sipped his coffee and continued his grumbling.

Outwardly, Adam Delavigné seemed angry and unapproachable, but solitude was the only thing he trusted, and carping against life's annoyances was his only fun. He had lived a hard life; he had been divorced twice, and then lost his beloved third wife and their son in an automobile accident. After two years of drinking and mourning, he had finally managed to rejoin the living when he bought the Redbird and built it up from a broken-down juke joint into one of the more successful nightclubs in the French Quarter. In all the fifty years of his life, it was the only thing he had loved that had not let him down or left him.

He drained his cup and grunted happily at the coffee's mild energetic buzz before turning his attention to the sheet music. As he scowled at Pat Gibson's boring arrangements, he heard a tap on the door and saw someone peering at him through the tiny wrought-iron window. Adam shook his head and held up one hand. "Not open yet. Come back later."

Another more persistent tap sounded.

"*Mon dieu*! *Now* what the hell?" He stood up, headed to the door, and opened it a crack. "Look. This is a nightclub. No food. Come back at two when the bar opens."

"Wait, Mister. I'm not a customer. I'm lookin' for a job. I'm a singer."

Adam gave the hungry looking stranger the once-over. He was wearing a shabby plaid shirt and patched dungarees. "Here, kid—take this dollar and go up to that diner on the corner of Dauphine. Tell that good-for-nothin' sonofabitch Rex to give you some breakfast and coffee."

"But I—"

Adam waved him away and began pushing the door shut. "Go eat! Then you come back and see me, and I'll tell you whether or not you're a singer."

Forty-five minutes later, the stranger was back with two paper cups filled with coffee. "Compliments of Rex," he said, grinning. "That guy sure likes to talk!"

Adam scowled. "Goddamn Rex and his goddamn lousy paper cups." He took the cups and nodded in the direction of the bar. "Reach back there and get two real cups!" he barked.

Ducking behind the bar, the kid found the cups and placed them on the bar. "Got 'em."

Adam poured the coffee into the ceramic cups. "How'd you get that eye, kid?"

"Bumped into somebody's fist. You should'a seen me a month ago."

"Yeah. Bumped into a couple'a fists in my time, too."

"So can I ask you a question, Mr. uh—?"

"It's Delavigné. And what the hell's your question?"

"Uh, well, why'd you send me to Rex's Diner if you hate him so much?"

"Hate him? Shit! Rex is the best friend I got! It's his goddamn cheap paper cups I hate. So, kid. You come here to sing or ask me personal questions that ain't none'a your damn business?"

"Oh, I'm here to sing." He turned to scan the room. "Have you got a piano?"

"Of course we got a goddamn piano! What kind'a joint you think this is? Have we got a piano…! It's in the main room behind those curtains. This is the classiest club in the Quarter, kid. We been packin' 'em in ever since V-J Day. Or at least till I screwed up and booked that goddamn Pat Gibson. You wanna sing? So sing. But don't waste my time. You better be good."

The kid took a seat at the piano and played a few chords, then closed his eyes and began to play a unique, heavy-handed intro to "You Go to My Head." The sound of his voice was a shock in contrast to his blocky piano style; his tones were smooth and the lyrics glided along like a heady breeze. But somehow, it was a complementary combination— when the voice surged, the piano backed away, and vice versa, before swirling back together, like a couple dancing.

Adam walked to the back of the room. The kid was definitely a crooner. Each phrase was like velvet, as if he were whispering intimate secrets that somehow carried to the back row of tables. He was no matinee idol, but if that tooth could be fixed, his dimpled smile was disarming, and his smoky eyes were just the sort that made women surrender their hearts, as well as their clothing. Adam tried to picture him cleaned up in a new suit, and nodded approvingly. When the song ended, the last note hung in the air, reverberating, making the ears crave more.

The kid opened his eyes and stared at Adam. "Well?"

Adam grunted, and the kid looked dismayed. "Okay, look. I can do another song—"

"Relax, kid, you convinced me that adding a singer wouldn't be a bad idea. Been listenin' to Sinatra, ain'tcha? But hell, you got somethin' else too. Somethin' here in New Orleans we call 'lagniappe.' It means 'that little somethin' extra.' Somethin' that bum Pat Gibson never had. No talent, no personality, no lagniappe... So, kid, that arrangement—yours?"

"Yeah, just foolin' around. Look, it'll sound better with a band. And I can change it."

"Don't change it! Let's see what the band can do with it. They'll be draggin' their asses in here for rehearsal in a couple'a hours. Always late, the sonsabitches, but talented. All but Pat, and I'm getting' rid of him today. I can salvage the rest of the band. Shit, the drummer would probably volunteer to assassinate the no-talent bastard! So, kid. How many numbers you know?"

The kid grinned. "Enough to wing it till we replace that no-talent bastard Pat."

Adam's face contorted into an uncharacteristic smile. "How old are you?"

"Uh, twenty-one," the kid mumbled, fidgeting with something in his pocket.

Adam grunted. "Sure you are. Hey, what's that you keep foolin' with in your pocket?"

"Cuff link. Lost the other one. I just keep this one for—good luck, I guess."

"So, listen, you got a name? I can't keep callin' you kid."

"Yes, sir, Mr. Delavigné. My name's Joe."

"Joe," he said sourly. "Well, hell, that narrows it down. Come on! Ya got a last name?"

After a short pause, Joe flashed his best smile. "Oh. Yeah, it's Bluestone. Joe Bluestone."

≈∞≈

Within three months, the Redbird Club's new headliner was attracting an unprecedented following. Adam rewarded Joe by raising his pay, buying him a new wardrobe, and fixing his teeth. He claimed that it was an investment, but it was clear to every other employee of the club that Adam's new star had become like a son to him. Every night at the end of the last set, he meandered over to the stage, his customary frown betrayed by a proud pat on the back for Joe.

"Kid, hirin' you was the smartest thing I ever did."

"Thanks, Adam. You gave me a chance when nobody else would. I won't forget it."

Adam nudged him. "Hey, the two broads to your left are beggin' for some body heat."

Joe glanced at the two white girls and shrugged. "Nah, I've seen cuter."

Adam made a sound that was almost laugh-like. "Particular, huh? Did you see that Creole girl that was sittin' up front? Hot little bombshell, that one. Hey, kid, lemme take you to Tremé. They got some real cute colored broads down there. Great music too."

"Nah, not tonight. Maybe some other time, Adam."

Adam's face twisted into the grimace/smile now familiar to Joe. "Yeah, yeah. You'll change your mind one'a these nights. They *all* do! But at least let me get you a drink at the bar."

"You know I don't drink, Adam. All I need is a walk, some fresh air, and some shut-eye."

"No booze, no women—no *Tremé*? Hah! Ya don't know what you're missin', choirboy!"

Joe laughed. "G'night, Adam."

On the way out, Joe passed two band members, Eddie and Gil, who were drinking Hurricanes with a Negro couple. The easy interaction between the races in New Orleans still surprised Joe. Eddie and Gil were white, but seemed indifferent to any color line between themselves and the other band members, or any other Negroes in the club.

Joe nodded and smiled. "Man, Gil, you fellas were wailin' tonight."

"You too, jazz man! Hey, why you headin' back to the pad so early?"

"Gotta get unconscious so I won't feel this heat."

"Baby, we *like* it steamy! And besides, they ain't got Mardi Gras up north, y'eard me?"

"I know, I know— Gotta love the steam," Joe laughed. "I'm workin' on it, Gil."

He was halfway out the door when he overheard his own name in a half-whispered exchange. First Eddie's voice, then the voice of the Negro he had been talking to:

"When'd you guys pick up that Creole singer, man? He pretty good."

"Naw, man, he ain't Creole. He's from up north someplace."

Gil laughed. "Y'all always wanna claim the talent when it comes to the singers. But this one bats for the white boys' team, baby! Hundred percent Caucasian."

Joe smiled and stepped outside. It was nearly 2:00 a.m., and the after-hours musicians were just getting warmed up. He rolled up his shirtsleeves as he walked, pausing at each open door to peer into rowdy bars and nightclubs. He was still curious about New Orleans night life— why people seemed to anticipate each and every sundown like a grand holiday that would never come again. Maybe it was because at the last sign of daylight everything in the French Quarter changed. The old purple- and green-painted structures that appeared garish by day looked glamorous bathed in nighttime neon. And the damp streets were a beautiful impressionist blur of molten gold, red, and aqua after one of New Orleans' frequent rain showers. Jazz, in all its exotic incarnations, bounced crazy decibels from the gutters up to the wrought-iron balconies, which were always crowded with people finding excuses to celebrate. It was a manic mix of heat, sounds, sights, and smells—laughter and screech horns, whiskey and stale perfume. A glittering, haphazard arrangement of multicolored beads—remnants of long-ago Mardi Gras parades—still dangled from the branches of the trees lining Jackson Square. They were distinctly French Quarter trees that towered above the visiting revelers like a line of tall chorus girls dressed up in their costume jewelry, swaying with the breeze in whatever tempo King Jazz dictated.

A familiar gravelly voice belting "Won't You Come Home, Bill Bailey" was stirring up an exodus of tourists, all hurrying to Bourbon Street toward the music. Joe laughed as he watched them spilling their drinks and checking the film in their cameras. He knew that Louis Armstrong was not in town tonight; the voice belonged to Junior Thibodaux, an Armstrong imitator, who was performing with Alton Purnell all week at the Famous Door. Any other time, Joe might have followed the crowd, but tonight his senses were pulling him in the opposite direction, toward the River. As the sounds of Bourbon Street faded behind him, the humidity itself seemed to undulate with the sexual rhythms of a distant riverboat band, slowing Joe's pace to a lazy shuffle. He inhaled deeply. Someone was cooking gumbo in one of those all-night waterfront eateries. By the time he turned the next corner, he felt as if he had stepped back in time. The hulking Delta Queen was moving slowly on the dark water, creating a trail of glittering ripples from the reflected lights. The paddle wheel creaked as it swept the water high, then sent it cascading back into the River of its origin. The slow, hypnotic rhythm reminded Joe of a Paul Robeson song from a movie that had made his mother cry a lifetime ago at the Grand Marquee—"Old Man River."

The Riverboat sounded a doleful whistle, and for a long, indulgent moment Joe imagined swimming out to it, climbing aboard, and letting the River carry him home to his mother. He stood there thinking of her until the boat disappeared around the bend; then he began walking slowly toward Dauphine Street. At the corner of Royal and Bienville, he saw a couple necking in a doorway, and stopped to watch them. Shadows hid their faces, but their bodies were tightly entwined, and there was a heated desperation in the movement of their hands. Without knowing them, Joe knew their story—illicit lovers with no place to be together—a brief tryst that turned that doorway into a momentary heaven. He gazed at them until a green paper streamer fluttered down from a balcony and stuck to the perspiration on his forearm. He brushed it off and shot one last envious glance at the couple before heading to his boardinghouse.

As tired as he was, Joe barely slept that night. The small electric fan that sat on a chair at the foot of his bed blew nothing but hot air, and the sheets were sticky and uncomfortable. And when he did manage to doze off, he was troubled by heart-pounding dreams he couldn't remember upon waking. But as the sky began to lighten with the sunrise, he finally fell into a deep sleep and didn't wake until nearly two in the afternoon.

After taking a cold shower and dressing, he headed out in search of food. Stepping outside, he decided to go to Rex's Diner, which was just up the block.

As Adam had told him, Rex Belhomme was indeed his best friend, even though the two men were polar opposites. Adam was white—French on his father's side—and his personality was anything but outgoing. His penchant for grumbling concealed his generous spirit, and he was often misunderstood. He hated going to the barber, so his mop of unruly gray hair always fell into his eyes, adding to his list of constant gripes. Rex, on the other hand, was a dark-skinned Negro, energetic and gregarious, with a clean-shaven head. He ran his diner efficiently, regaling his customers with local news and New Orleans history, while cooking up some of the best food in the French Quarter. He nagged his regulars about their health and kept a stash of colorful umbrellas for tourists unprepared for Crescent City weather. Adam ate nearly all of his meals at Rex's, and Joe enjoyed listening to the comical bickering between the two men. They were like an old battling married couple who couldn't live without each other.

When Joe stepped inside the diner Rex had his back to him, but turned around at the sound of the squeaking door. "Well, now. How's my buddy, the singin' star?" he called.

Joe laughed and waved. "Fine, Rex."

There were only two other people in the diner, two middle-aged white men, huddled over their respective lunches and newspapers at opposite ends of the counter. Joe took a seat at a table near the window and Rex hurried over with a cup of hot coffee.

"Too bad you just missed Adam. He left with the last of the lunch crowd. So how ya doin', Joe? You sho' lookin' prosperous. New shirt?"

"Custom made," Joe said, grinning.

"Lawd, boy, you done come up in the world! First time I seen you, you was hungry and boney, and ain't had eye-water to cry with, y'eard? And now ya wearin' custom made shirts!"

"Yeah, but I'm still just as hungry," Joe laughed. "What's cookin'? It sure smells good."

Rex stepped back and smiled broadly. "Got me a *mean* pot of gumbo simmerin', but it won't be ready for a while. Ya know, for the supper crowd."

"Mm-mmm," Joe said, smacking his lips. "You know, I've tasted a lot of gumbo since I've been in New Orleans, but yours is the best by a mile, Rex. I'm not kiddin' either."

"It's all in the roux, boy. Just like everything else in Louisiana. All in the roux."

Joe grinned. "Another one of those New Orleans words. You guys have got a whole different language than the rest of the country, but okay. I gotta know. What's *roux* mean?"

"Well, cookin' folks'll tell you it's the base of the gumbo or whatever dish you be makin'. But when I talk about the roux, I'm talkin' 'bout New Orleans! The history and the people—Mardi Gras Krewes, Tremé, Storyville—or even the ol' Kingfish, Huey P. Long, y'eard me? Then you got gris-gris and all that goin's-on at Congo Square. That's some deep-down roux *there*, boy. But that's a lot to take in, so I'll explain it to you the way my Mama use'ta tell folks. Whatever it is you talkin' about, the roux is the *soul* of the thing."

Joe stared blankly at Rex for a moment, and then smiled. "Well, hell, Rex. Guess I gotta come back for supper now that I know all about your gumbo's *soul* and all. But right now, I'll be happy with some iced-tea and one of those fat, luscious ham sandwiches you make."

Rex grinned. "I'll throw ya in a slice a'pie, son, as a reward for not makin' me fire up that hot ol' grill again. That pot a'gumbo is steamin' up that kitchen as it is, so I don't need that ol' grill addin' to the heat. And that sandwich is comin' right up."

"Thanks, Rex." As Joe sipped his coffee, he stared across the street at a carriage pulled by a mule wearing a flowered hat. He thought of his father's old mule Isabel, then frowned, as he always did when childhood memories surfaced in his mind. In the distance he heard a mournful coronet, blending with a trombone, in an extremely slow call-and-response rhythm. It was a funeral dirge, played in that unique New Orleans style—spiritual, magnetic, and mystical.

Rex brought Joe's sandwich and pie, then peered out the window. "There go ol' Mista Moreaux," he murmured sadly. "Passed last Thursday, ya know."

"Friend of yours?" Joe asked, attempting politeness as he sneaked a bite of his sandwich.

"Mista Moreaux was a *good* friend. Hard workin' man and a Trail Chief with the Creole Wild West Tribe—a Mardi Gras Indian—till he come down with that pneumonia last year. Back in '23 he saved about thirty kids in a big fire at a school in the lower 9th. Got his picture in the newspaper and everything." Rex smiled. "Young folks 'round here don't remember all that, but old folks like me and Adam sho' do. And he gon' get that good send-off too. I heard they got him a spot smack in the middle of St. Vincent de Paul No. 2—and that's sayin' sump'm, boy."

Joe took a swallow of his tea. "Okay, wait. You're goin' too fast, Rex! What do you mean he was a 'Trail Chief' and what in the world is that St. Vincent No. 2 thing?"

"St. Vincent de Paul No. 2 Cemetery, just off Louisa over yonder! You ain't seen that?"

"No, not that I can remember."

Rex's eyebrows shot up. "Ain't you seen our cities, boy?"

Joe gave him a puzzled look. "Cities?"

Rex slid into a chair and scooted closer. "Go on and eat while I tell you about 'em. They call 'em Cities of the Dead—all them above-ground cemeteries we got all over New Orleans."

"Oh, yeah," Joe said. "I pass a lot of those when I walk places."

"You need to stop walkin' past 'em and walk *through* one sometime, boy. You can feel all the souls just like flesh-and-blood people standin' there. All the dates and names on the crypts—that's history, boy, starin' right at'cha. And that's what them Mardi Gras Indians are all about. They go back to the time when the slaves and Indians got together and started minglin' all that blood and culture. Tourists always snappin' pictures of 'em, thinkin' they just part'a the entertainment, but they wrong! It's New Orleans tradition, and it's about pride and respect." Rex smiled. "But you'll understand come Carnival time." The band's music grew louder, and again, Rex gazed outside. "They gon' be out there today."

"Who?"

"The Indians. They gon' be out there for Mista Moreaux, Gawd love him." Rex heaved a gloomy sigh. "Ya know, he use'ta be here every Monday mornin', waitin' for me to open. And we'd solve all the troubles of the world while the coffee perked. He loved my beignets better'n Du Monde! Always said if it wasn't for my coffee and beignets, he would'a never got through all them blue Mondays in his life. Then he'd pick up his old lunch pail and head on off to work. Yes, Lawd. Black with two spoons a'sugar… Monday mornin's ain't never gon' be the same."

Out of a long silence, he glanced over at the two men seated at the counter. One had just stood up to leave, and the other man was folding his newspaper. Rex hurried over to settle up with them. "Thank you, Mista Charles. You too, Mista Laramie. And I'll see y'all tomorrow." When they left, he locked the door behind them and pulled down the shade, then hurried back to the counter, wrapped up a beignet, and fixed a cup of black coffee with two spoons of sugar.

Joe laughed when he saw Rex carefully slip the paper cup into a second one for reinforcement. "How come you never taught Adam that trick?"

"And take away his favorite thing to gripe about? Not me! Come on, Joe. We gon' pay our respects to Mista Moreaux. And you fixin' to see what the *real* New Orleans is all about."

When they stepped outside the brass band was just passing the diner. There were nine instruments: a coronet, two trombones, two trumpets, a tuba, a bass drum and a snare, all played by Negro musicians perspiring heavily in black suits. Most of them wore black captain's hats with the word "Eureka" emblazoned in brass above the brims, but the coronet player wore a black derby with purple, green, and gold ribbons trailing down his back. He led the procession with a slow side-to-side step as he played "The Old Rugged Cross," and two women shielded him from the sun with bright green umbrellas. A tired looking gray mule pulled the wagon carrying a white casket covered with red carnations, and about forty mourners trailed behind. About half were Negroes dressed in church attire, followed by an unusual mix of white and black tourists and locals, some reverent, others apparently following out of simple curiosity. Joe watched Rex place the beignet atop the flowers on the casket, then wondered how and when he would serve his dead friend that final cup of coffee, prepared the way he had liked it—black with two spoons of sugar. The band turned under a wrought-iron archway that read "St. Vincent de Paul Cemetery

No. 2." There the pallbearers removed the casket from the wagon and carried it through a labyrinth of stone structures of different heights and shapes. It was exactly as Rex had described it—a city. It had a jagged skyline of ancient, miniature skyscrapers each with its denizen's name and history etched into the facade. The mourners trailed along until they reached the open tomb that awaited Mr. Moreaux. A frail looking black man in full priest's robes was there, peering at the mourners through a pair of thick eyeglasses. His prayer book was already open in his hands.

Inexplicably, when the music stopped, Joe felt his heart begin to pound.

The priest's voice rose and fell in a dramatic recitation of the Catholic prayer for the dead: "Ashes to ashes, dust to dust." A woman wailed loudly, and Joe flinched.

As the mourners began tossing flowers over the casket, Rex stepped over with his paper cup and poured a bit of coffee over the flowers, and the rest onto the ground. "This is for you, Mista Moreaux, and for all the folks who ain't here to see you off... We sho' gon' miss you."

Rex stepped back and the priest began to pray again, but a sound from the front gate of the cemetery suddenly seemed to electrify the crowd. A tambourine, accompanied by a primitive sounding drum beating out an unusual rhythm, then the low chanting of men's voices. Joe turned around and craned his neck. All he could see were three high, fluffy arcs of bouncing colors—green, yellow, and peacock blue. He nudged Rex. "What is *that*?"

Rex smiled proudly. "Mardi Gras Indians," he said. "I told you they was gon' be here."

The priest finished quickly, surrendering to the hypnotic power of the Indians' drums and chanting and tambourines. The band began to play "When the Saints Go Marching In," and the mourners moved back to the street in a pulsing parade of bouncing umbrellas and smiles. "Second-line!" Rex shouted, and then began a high-stepping, elbow-flapping dance.

Joe was startled, but he had to get a closer look at the Mardi Gras Indians. He inched through the crowd until he saw a black man covered in a mountain of feathers, with a glittering chestplate of blue and silver sequins in the image of a standing peacock. A huge headdress of turquoise ostrich plumes and peacock feathers fanned out above his face. His eyes never opened as he beat his tambourine and continued chanting. Joe stared at him until he danced away.

Then Rex's voice startled him from behind. "What's wrong, son?"

Joe turned and shook his head. "I guess—I just don't understand New Orleans funerals."

Rex placed his hands on Joe's shoulders and gazed at him with knowing eyes. "Ain't a time for understandin', son. It's a time for *feelin'*.

Now, I was feelin' sad a while ago, watchin' 'em carry ol' Mista Moreaux off to that crypt, but soon as our Indians showed up, I found my joy! They ain't just here to pay their respects, son. They come to remind us that we all belong to the same family. And it's time to stop cryin' about a death, and get to celebratin' our brother's life! Remember what I told you about the roux? Well, baby, that's what second-linin' is all about, y'eard? Dancin' down the streets, pickin' up all the sinners and the tourists and anybody feelin' the music. It's the act of *gatherin'*, boy! That's what turns a whole bunch'a strangers into one big family of saints! Don'tcha see? It's the gatherin'... The gatherin' is the *roux*."

≈∞≈

By the time Joe returned to his room that night, his mood had zigged and zagged as erratically as Mr. Moreaux's funeral. He tossed his *Times-Picayune* onto the bed and read the headlines:

100,000 MORE DEATHS FOR HIROSHIMA
IN A-BOMB AFTERMATH.

Joe shuddered. *Ashes to ashes.* He turned on the fan and the radio, then counted the savings in his coffee can and returned it to his suitcase. As he stretched out on the bed, he heard the beginning of "Sophisticated Lady," followed by the velvety phantom voice of an announcer:

Time once again for an evening of music, presented to you
by the American Tobacco Company, makers of Lucky Strikes
cigarettes. Tonight's broadcast comes to you from the exotic
Cotton Club in New York City. So let's take a ride on the A-
Train with the world-renowned Duke Ellington Orchestra...

Setting the newspaper aside, Joe turned to his new copy of *Radio Review*, which featured Frank Sinatra on the cover. After studying the photo, he found the corresponding article:

Frank Sinatra made his highly anticipated return to the
Paramount Theater in New York last week and once again
incited a riot. Since his first solo triumph at the Paramount in
1942, not much has changed for the singer—not as far as the
female population of planet earth is concerned. "Frankie
Frenzy" is alive and kicking with the undeniable force of a
million saddle shoes. From coast to coast, "The Voice" still
sends bobby-soxers into swooning spells, something the critics
call "Sinatrauma."

After lingering over a photo layout of Sinatra and his family at their Hoboken home, Joe spotted a piece that mentioned Benny Goodman and Lionel Hampton:

*In response to vibraphonist Lionel Hampton's recent
attempt to stay in a segregated hotel, bandleader Benny
Goodman spoke out against racial restrictions…*

Joe scowled. "So the great Benny Goodman gets mad, and somebody
prints an article," he muttered. "But Hampton probably ended up staying
in some shack on the dark side of town anyway. Shit. Nothin' ever
changes in good old damn Dixie." He glanced over at the newspaper.
Ever since spotting the first article on his brother's trial, he had tried not
to think about it, but now that it was winding down he had to know the
outcome. He found it on page four:

*A controversial fratricide trial in Natchez, Mississippi
ended today. Calvin Bailey received a life sentence for the
murder of his brother Joseph Bailey, whose body was never
found. The jury based their verdict on eye-witness testimony,
blood evidence, and scraps of teeth and hair identified to be
that of the victim.*

*The defendant refused to reveal the location of the body,
and it was the testimony of his own mother that finally sealed
his fate. Leah Bailey stated that her son Calvin came home
covered in blood on the night Joseph was last seen alive.
Judge Lockhart stated at trial's end: "Calvin Bailey should be
facing a date with the electric chair."*

As Joe stared at the words "electric chair," his heart began to thump
rapidly. His only intention had been to escape Natchez and start a new
life. He had never given Calvin's fate a second thought until he had
begun reading the trial coverage a week earlier.

"Poor Mama. Maybe I ought'a let her know I'm okay… No… *Shit*,
no! If I go back now, I'll never get to New York. Calvin deserves to be
locked up anyway." He leaned back on his pillow, and fought the guilt by
focusing, detail by detail, on the night he had paid his passage with blood.

He had awakened that night at the edge of Highway 61 coughing up
blood, but relieved to be alive. In his ringing ears, the night creatures
seemed louder, as if amplified. An owl swooped low, and Joe cringed into a
fetal position. After a minute, he blinked up at the sky. Each blurry star had
a double, and there were two full blue moons, connected like a glowing
figure-eight. With great effort, he dragged himself off the road, but then
slipped in the gravel and scraped his hands. He brushed something off his
left palm, and saw a fuzzy metallic glint as it hit the ground. It was one of
his cuff links. He felt the rips in his sleeves and knew that Calvin must have
taken the links and then dropped one. Picking it up, he stumbled into the
woods and collapsed under a tree. As the branches blurred above him, he
drifted into a half-dream; he was a casualty, killed on the same battleground

of his childhood war games. The little-boy voices of Calvin, Butch, and Zachary swirled in his head, and then disappeared into a dark silence.

When Joe woke for the second time, the sky had lightened; it was nearly dawn. When he moved, a searing pain screamed through every fiber of his body, telling him to remain still. He touched his face and gasped at the feel of his misshapen skull and swollen lips. A lump over his left eye was the size of an egg, and his midsection registered hot, stabbing pains with each breath he took. In his dazed condition, all he could think of was getting away before Calvin returned to look for the cuff link he had dropped. He finally got to his feet and stumbled in a circle trying to regain his sense of balance. Then he walked slowly back to the highway and headed in the opposite direction of his home. After stopping twice to rest and once to throw up, he saw a pair of high headlights—a truck. He staggered out and waved feebly.

The truck stopped, and a white man wearing a straw cowboy hat leaned out his window. "What happened to you, boy? You hurt bad?"

"Uh, yes, sir. I—I need to get away—to the next town—or wherever you can take me."

"Son, yer in bad shape! Lemme take you to a doctor. We ain't far from town."

"No, sir. See, my Daddy—he beats me. I gotta get away. You ain't headed east, are you?"

"Lord, boy! Yer *Daddy* beat'cha like that?" He sighed. "Well, I'm takin' this produce to New Orleans. Guess I could take ya that far."

Joe nodded. "New Orleans? I got an aunt livin' there. That'd be fine."

The driver shook his head slowly. "I sure do wish you'd let me take you to a doctor."

Joe glanced anxiously down the road. "Please, Mister. My aunt—she'll fix me up good."

"Well—okay." The man hopped out and hurried around to help Joe up. "You okay?"

"Yes, sir. I'm fine now, sir."

"You ain't got to call me sir. Just call me Billy, like my friends do."

"Thanks, Billy. Thanks a lot."

Within minutes, Natchez was only a blurry image in the truck's side mirror. Along the way, Billy stopped to buy bandages, and then shared a sandwich with Joe. When they reached New Orleans, he handed him a dollar for food and a nickel for the payphone, and wished him luck.

≈∞≈

Joe smiled as he thought about Billy, even though it had all happened months ago. But his smile faded as his thoughts returned to his mother.

The Cotton Club program was over and he turned off the radio. He found a pen and paper and began to write: *Dear Mama—*

"And then what? I'm fine and by the way, I'm still alive?" Again, he pressed pen to paper:

> *I know you must be shocked to get this letter, but try to understand. I never meant to hurt you. I can't tell you where I am, but I'm okay. Please don't try to find me.*

He stopped and threw the pen down. "Stupid! She'll take the letter to the prison and get Calvin out. First thing he'll do is track me down and finish me off."

Before he could change his mind, he crumpled the letter into the ashtray and burned it.

≈∞≈

The first set at the Redbird Club always started at 9:00, but on the night of Joe's anniversary party, he was late. The band covered for him by playing an instrumental set, but at 10:15 Adam finally lumbered up to the bandstand and motioned for Gil to cut the number short.

"Where the hell is he, Adam?" Gil whispered.

Adam scowled at him. "Gone!"

"Gone? Where?"

"Just gone!" Adam barked. "I sent Jaymo to get him, and—hell, you know the routine! Empty closet and no forwarding address. So make the goddamn announcement."

As Gil spoke to the audience, the room quieted and Adam heard the front door creak open. Someone walked in—not Joe—but from outside Adam could hear a train whistle—the 10:18. Something about that sound reached in and touched a lonely spot in his soul, waking him from a happy but unrealistic dream.

As the patrons scattered, Adam felt a comforting hand on his shoulder. Rex Belhomme guided him back to the office and shut the door. "He took off, didn't he? And quit all that pretendin' and mean-muggin', Adam. I know what that boy meant to you."

Adam dropped into his office chair. "How could he leave like that, Rex? Guys like him don't just *leave* New Orleans. Not like *that.*"

Rex opened the desk drawer and pulled out the scotch and two glasses that Adam always kept there. "What'cha mean guys like him?" he asked as he sat down and poured the scotch.

"Hell, I don't know. Guys who show up lookin' like—like—"

Rex nodded. "Like they don't belong noplace. See, Adam, you can't understand it 'cause you got'cha roots in New Orleans. And that boy ain't got no roots *noplace.*"

"Bullshit. And it still don't explain why he left without sayin' a goddamn word to me. After all I did for that ungrateful little bastard. I even paid that thievin' dentist to fix his goddamn teeth, Rex! And what does he do? He takes his shiny new Hollywood smile and blows town!"

"Man, it wasn't nothin' you could'a did to make that boy stay. And before you go to askin' me why, I'ma tell you, so shut it on up!" Rex pulled his chair closer. "We all get lonesome, Adam. And when somebody comes along at one'a them lonesome times, we try to make 'em out to be sump'm they ain't. Like women! Men can be ten different kinds a'gotdamn fool over a good-lookin' woman sometimes, can't we? Treat the nice ones like dirt, and the dirty ones like angels—till ya wake up and find out your angel done *rolled* ya for all the cash in your wallet! And women make us out to be they dream man, till they catch us wrong—lyin' and skunkin' around with some she-devil from Airline Highway." He chuckled. "Must be human nature."

Adam screwed his face into a sour-milk expression. "What kind'a drunk shit are you—"

"I ain't drunk and I ain't finished! So suck down that damn scotch and listen to me! It ain't no shame in it. We all do it!" Rex softened his tone. "Adam—you tried to make that boy into your son. But all he could be was who he really was—a drifter—runnin' away from trouble. Fellas like that ain't nothin' but shadows on the wall. Disappear soon as the light changes."

Adam stared across the desk at Rex, but said nothing until he heard the band beginning their next set. "Well, I'm gonna miss him just the same. Guess that makes me crazy."

"Naw, Adam, it don't. It makes ya a human fool, just like the rest of us. And ya ain't gotta worry. I ain't gonna tell nobody 'bout your soft spot for that boy."

The band's music echoed in the hallway, and Adam's face twisted into a smiling grimace. "Ya *better* not. Might spoil my reputation as the meanest sonofabitch in New Orleans."

Rex held up his glass. "And here's to ya, ya mean sonofabitch!"

Adam touched his glass to Rex's. "So I guess the goddamn show must go on, huh?"

"That's all life is, Adam. A big ol' messy show that must go on."

Adam finished his drink and looked up. "What the hell is that? What's he playin' out there?"

Rex listened for a moment, then sighed. That's that new one they added to the show just last week, special for Joe. It's called, 'Do You Know What it Means to Miss New Orleans.'"

Adam grunted as he refilled his glass. "Goddamn that Gil."

PART II

EAST

We interrupt this program for a salute to all the side-men...

So long, Kingfish!
Uptown to down—
Salt Peanuts with a rebop sound
Skin-popping jitterbugs and Juilliard squares
on Bird's Thoroughfare—
The Voice is on the air

Strung out harmonics—
Needles bless and bobby-socks swoon
Damn! Just how high IS the moon?
Dancing in the dark 'round midnight
but 5:00 a.m. comes fast—no sleep
Crash course class in Ornithology

Scattin' the rebop
scat the repeat—
Grooves real sweet on 52nd Street!
Birth of the Cool—
Still not enough?
Hit me with a hot note, Daddy! Count it off...

Chapter 8

"Penn Station!" the bus driver called over the shushing sound of the brakes.

After an exhausting three-day trip, Joe was the first passenger to step off the Greyhound. As he was stashing his bags in a locker he spotted a poster on the wall. He read it and grinned.

Don't miss Frank Sinatra at the Capitol Theater!
November 13th — 8 Great Shows!

When Joe stepped outside, 7th Avenue greeted him with the ugly, beautiful sounds of a New York street symphony—honking horns, echoes of bebop, distant police sirens, pedestrians speaking in foreign languages, and the squealing brakes and grinding gears of taxicabs darting through traffic in a never-ending game of chicken. He walked for blocks, gawking at the towering buildings and animated signs. Then he turned a corner that brought him to a dead stop.

He was standing at the edge of Times Square, and it was grander than he had ever imagined. The Strand, the Selwyn, a huge blinking Automat sign, and two statues—a man and a woman—like 50-foot bookends to a waterfall framed in blinding neon above the Bond Apparel Store. The centerpiece of Times Square was so imposing it seemed to have forced the division of the street through sheer intimidation—a stack of gargantuan signs for Pepsi Cola, Ruppert Beer, Kinsey Whiskey, and Chevrolet—one on top of the other, climbing skyward like a Tower of Babel dreamed up by the Madison Avenue boys. Joe laughed at the huge Camel cigarette billboard, with actual smoke rings drifting out of the pictured man's open mouth.

A passing stranger grinned at Joe without breaking stride. "Yeah, I seen that sign a million times and it still makes me laugh!"

"Hey," Joe called, "you happen to know where the Capitol Theater is?"

The man pointed down the street. "Sure, pal. 51st and Broadway."

≈∞≈

On the day of Sinatra's opening, the bobby-soxers were waiting in legion numbers, snaked around the Capitol Theater four deep, chanting "Frankie, Frankie, Frankie…" When a shiny black limousine prowled past, the chant sharpened into a feral shriek. "It's *Frankeeee!*"

Joe crossed the street and stared at them in dumbstruck awe. The bobby-soxers themselves were a phenomenon, so how would he react when he finally saw Sinatra in person? But as he watched the girls push past security guards to swarm the limo, he got an idea and hurried over to the guard at the entrance door. "Excuse me," he said. "You think I could—"

The guard cupped his hand to his ear. "Can't hear you over the screaming!" he yelled.

Joe leaned closer and shouted, "Do you think I could go inside to use the bathroom?"

The guard smirked. "Nice try. These nutty girls have been tryin' that one all morning."

Joe grinned. "Come on. I'm no bobby-soxer! Look, I really need to use the bathroom."

"Sorry, pal. Try the automat down the street."

"But I'll lose my place in line and it's general admission," Joe pleaded. "I'll never get a good seat after this herd stampedes the joint! Come on. I was hopin' to pick up a date today!"

"No chance'a that happening. These girls won't give you the time of day." But when he saw Joe's disappointed expression, he sighed. "Okay, kid. Just so your day ain't a complete loss, I'll let you use the can. Lemme see your ticket." After examining the ticket, he opened the door. "But if you're thinkin' about sneaking somebody in the side door, they're under heavy guard."

Joe slipped inside just as the girls began running up behind him. "Thanks, Mister!"

The guard gestured at the usher, who was standing inside. "He's okay. He's got a ticket."

The door slammed shut just as the bobby-soxers reached it and began pounding.

"Sinatra's causin' another Columbus Day Riot, huh?" the usher said. "I don't get it."

Joe grinned. "But those girls sure get it. Hey, which way to the bathroom?"

"Around the side and down that corridor. And if I was you, I wouldn't try going back outside into that angry mob. Just hang around the lobby till I open the doors."

"Hey! Thanks, pal. I'll get a great seat now!" Joe headed toward the corridor and opened the bathroom door, letting it shut loudly without going inside. After peering around to make sure he was alone, he walked toward a door marked "No Entry" and tried the knob. It was unlocked. When he opened it, he found himself in a long, dark hallway that sloped downward. Noticing light on the floor at the end of the hallway, he continued in that direction until he heard the loud slam of a heavy door, followed by the echo of male voices and distant screams of "Frankie" from outside. By the time Joe reached the end of the hallway, the men's murmuring was clearer.

"Okay, door's locked," a voice said. "Once again, we save your ass, ya sonofabitch."

A laugh. "Thanks, Tony."

"Hey. You okay, Frank?" a gravelly, New York tough-guy voice asked.

Joe peeked through the half-closed door and spotted Sinatra surrounded by four men in suits. He was brushing off his jacket and straightening his collar as he grinned at a hefty, leather-faced man. "Come on, Sol!" he cackled. "Ya gotta love 'em!"

Sol groaned. "Oh, no, I ain't! *You* love 'em! I'm sick'a bein' beat up by them—them socks-broads! Them little hellions scratch like alley cats! And it ain't like I can belt 'em if one of 'em rips my ear off for a souvenir thinkin' it's yours... Say, you *sure* you're okay, Frank?"

"Shit! They got my watch and tie again! But lemme check. Yeah, I still got all my vital body parts," he cracked. "I think."

Sol began fanning himself with his hat. "I can't take this pressure," he groused. "Gettin' your ass from the limo into the theater is worse than stormin' the goddamn beach at Normandy on D-Day. And I was there, ya know."

Frank rolled his eyes and waved his hand. "We know, we know."

Sol scowled. "A picnic compared to them savages outside!"

Frank shrugged. "Look, Sollie. So they're a little pushy! They're here, aren't they? The loyal little darlings! And look! You still got both ears! So whadaya beefin' about?"

"They ought'a be locked up in Bellevue," Sol muttered. "The psych floor."

"Aww, come on!" Frank said. "Can I help it if they love me to pieces? Literally?"

Sol finally cracked a small grin and began nudging Frank toward the stairs. "Very funny. So what's say we shovel all ya pieces onstage and see if yuz can still croon—*Frankie*."

Frank glared at him playfully as he sang a line from "I Get a Kick Out of You," then stopped and nudged Sol. "Hey, Sollie—"

"I know, I know. So the Voice is in poifect voice. So what am I? Surprised?"

Joe knew that once Sinatra disappeared up those steps, any chance of meeting him would be lost. Impulsively, he stepped into the room. "Uh—Mr. Sinatra?"

Sol spun around. "What the hell are you doin' in here?" he said in a growling monotone.

"I'm sorry. I didn't mean any harm. I was just hoping to—I don't know. I never *actually* thought I'd meet you, Mr. Sinatra!"

Sol glared at him. "Ya ain't *met* Mr. Sinatra. Ya met Mr. *Sol*. And if you don't wanna get *intimately* acquainted with Mr. Sol's fist, I recommend that you toin around and *blow*."

Frank snorted a loud laugh. "Aww, come on, Sollie! Leave us not *kill* the boy!"

"I'm sorry, sir," Joe said, "I really am. It's just that—I knew I didn't stand a chance of meeting him if I stood around with those—those rabid *wolves* out there."

"Hey!" Frank said. "Watch how you talk about my she-wolves! I'd be nothin' without those little howlers! Relax, Sollie," he deadpanned. "I bet the kid's not even packin' heat."

"Cute," Sol said. "It's a good thing he ain't packin' a camera. Okay, kid, make it quick."

Sinatra shook Joe's hand as if he had known him for years. "How ya doin', kid?"

Joe tried to answer, but his mouth had gone dry. None of the photographs he had seen of Sinatra did justice to the man shaking his hand. The disarming grin, the pointed chin and prominent cheekbones framed by tousled, longish dark hair. And the famous blue eyes—like two neon lights, twinkling with devilish amusement.

"It's okay, kid. I felt the same way when I first met Harry James. So where ya from?"

"Huh? Oh! New Orleans. I was a singer, like you, in the French Quarter. I mean, not like you. Nobody's like *you*, but I—I came to New York to try to—" He stopped when he heard Sol's impatient sigh. "Oh, I'm sorry, Mr. Sinatra. You've got a show to do and I'm holding you up."

"Not at all, kid, not at all. Sol's a pussycat! Hey! One'a you mugs got a pen? And somebody find Sol's squeaky-mouse so he stops his yowling."

Sol scowled as he handed him a pen. "You're a riot today, Frank, ya know that?"

The gray-haired man fumbled in his briefcase until he found an 8-by-10 photo, and Frank began scrawling a message on it. "So what's your name, kid?"

"Joe. Joe Bluestone."

"Bluestone?" Frank looked up at him curiously. "Americanized?"

"Huh?"

"Never mind. It's just an unusual name for an Italian."

Joe laughed. "Italian?"

"Not Italian? Boy, you sure *look* Italian." He grinned and hit Joe's shoulder playfully. "Probably on your mother's side. So where did you sing in the French Quarter, Joe Bluestone?"

Joe shrugged. "Aw, just your typical dive."

Frank chuckled as he handed the signed picture to Joe. "Then I'm sure I must've played the joint. But, hey, don't knock the dives, kid. I got my start singing in a dive. Sheesh, what a dive! Look, everybody's gotta start somewhere, right? Listen, you got a ticket to the show today?"

Joe held up his ticket. "Right here! And thanks. You don't know what this means to me."

Frank grinned as he backed toward the stairs. "Enjoy the show, paisan!"

Joe waved and then eagerly read the message on the photo:

To my pal Joe Bluestone—Keep singing and always leave them begging for more. —All the best, Frank Sinatra.

Tucking the picture safely inside his jacket, Joe sprinted back out to the lobby just as the usher was opening the doors. Well ahead of the bobby-soxers, he found a good seat near the front before they began swarming in. Two blonde girls in full skirts and petticoats bounced in beside him just as the newsreel started. The audience chatter stayed at din level.

By the end of the first feature, Joe had struck up a conversation with the girl next to him. She was the All-American cheerleader type, an energetic blue-eyed blonde. Her name was Elsie.

"Gosh, you're an odd duck," she said. "Most guys *hate* Frankie 'cause they're jealous."

"That's crazy. He's the best entertainer to study when you're a singer like me."

"Oooh!" she squealed. "You're not *really?* Do you record and stuff, like Frankie?"

"Naw, nothin' like that. But I headlined at a club in New Orleans."

"But that's just how Frankie got started, Joe—as a club singer." Elsie tapped her friend's arm. "Cora, this is Joe. He's a singer—and guess what? He's crazy about Frankie too!"

"Well, good," Cora said. "Most guys show up just to heckle him."

Elsie nodded. "One guy even threw an egg at him! We took care'a that creep, but good."

"Yeah, well, if some wise guy pitches an egg today, I'll make the bum eat it."

Elsie giggled. "So, are you, uh, singing anywhere in Manhattan?"

"Still auditioning. But hey, tell me your story, Elsie. You in college or sump'm?"

"Nursing school. And I do volunteer work at night sometimes too. I stay pretty busy."

"Too busy to give me your number?"

As Elsie wrote her number on a scrap of paper, the curtain began to rise to the opening strains of "Begin the Beguine." Joe craned his neck and spotted a bass drum with the initials "SH" on a high riser at center stage.

The bandleader stepped to the microphone. "Hello, ladies and gentlemen. I'm Skitch Henderson and we have got one great show for you today. Lovely Lorraine Rognan, the talented Will Mastin Trio, and of course, the dashing young man you've all been waiting for."

Screams erupted in the theater, and Henderson laughed. "Not yet, ladies. He'll be out in a few minutes, but first—" On his cue, the tempo of the music picked up, and the drummer broke into a wild solo. The girls in the audience poured into the aisles to dance.

Joe continued his shouted conversation with Elsie until the tap-dance trio took the stage. When he saw that it was a Negro act, he fell silent. The youngest performer, introduced as Sammy Davis Jr., stole the show with his celebrity impressions, dancing, and singing.

Joe was so envious of his voice, he couldn't wait for Davis to finish. After the trio left the stage, the band played the intro to "Saturday Night is the Loneliest Night of the Week," and the noise of stomping feet filled the theater. He looked at Elsie, who was sobbing. "What's wrong?"

"That's Frankie's big song. He's coming out now," she sniffled. "I always cry."

Just then, there was a break in the song, followed by a dramatic drum roll. The lights dimmed, and Skitch Henderson shouted, "Okay, ladeeees! Hang onto your bobby-socks! Here he comes! The one and only Frrrrrank Sinatra!"

An earsplitting blast of screams rose to the rafters, and Joe's heart began to thump. He stared in slack-jawed wonder at the man walking to center stage with a follow-spot glowing blue against his black jacket. Sinatra was as sleek as a panther stalking his prey through a shaft of moonlight. Confident, elegant, and radiating sex from every pore. He reached for the microphone, smiled at his screaming devotees, and shook his head when a few of them sank to the floor—the first casualties of the afternoon.

Joe barely heard the rest of "Saturday Night," but then Sinatra motioned for quiet and the clamor diminished. The soft swell of violins was followed by the first line of "I Fall in Love Too Easily." And Joe realized that this was not "Frank," the wisecracking regular guy he had just met. This was "The Voice"—the national phenomenon. And he sounded like a one-man choir of angels compared to the inferior version Joe had heard on his mother's radio. By the time Sinatra ended the song, Joe's spine was tingling with the physical vibrations of the double-basses. He had never dreamed that a live orchestra could sound so clear and powerful.

Next came "All of Me," swinging like Joe had never heard it swing before. He marveled at Sinatra's phrasing, gestures, and facial expressions. The way he closed his eyes, as if lost in a never-ending climax. The pauses and sighs that milked every nuance from the lyrics. "I Get a Kick Out of

You" prompted the traditional tossing of one of Nancy Sinatra's handmade bow-ties into the crowd, and a brawl ensued.

Sinatra finished with a torchy show-stopper, "One For My Baby," that sent the weeping females into delirium. As he left the stage, the wails rolled into a cacophony of screams, and the thunder of stomping feet demanded an encore, but The Voice was gone. Joe grinned and patted the photo inside his jacket, remembering its message: *Always leave them begging for more.*

≈∞≈

As the nighttime sparkle of Broadway wore off, Joe discovered the broad-daylight reality that was New York City. The thrill of meeting Sinatra faded quickly in the face of a cold Manhattan winter, and Joe began to think of the whole experience as one of those high-speed silent movies in grainy black and white. The faces of strangers rushed past him in varying shades of gray, their movement the only thing distinguishing them from the lifeless skyscrapers towering overhead.

Each day he perused local musicians' magazines for audition notices, then trudged blocks of sidewalk, from 28th Street and the area once known as Tin Pan Alley, all the way to 52nd Street, with its legendary jazz club lineup—the Onyx, the 3 Deuces, and the Royal Roost, among others.

The first snowfall was early that year. Intersections became rivers of slush that looked as dreary as the leaden sky, and each night Joe returned to his cold rooming house, discouraged and tired. Even his pale blue cuff link looked too gray to be a good-luck charm anymore.

With his savings nearly gone, Joe found work as an elevator operator in the Chrysler Building, which required him to wear an ill-fitting uniform with huge gold epaulets. When he put it on and looked in the mirror he did not see a singing star; he saw a hungry-looking toy soldier.

As spring approached, he felt himself fading into utter insignificance. Day after day, businessmen in tailor-made suits breezed past him as if he were invisible. Only at night did he feel human as he haunted nightclubs in pursuit of "the big break."

By summer he was desperate. Each audition chipped away at the confidence he had built up in New Orleans. His style was all wrong. Not enough experience. He couldn't sight-read. He couldn't scat. When he got word of three auditions on one Saturday, he summoned his last bit of hope, figuring he had nothing left to lose.

The first two went as expected: "Don't call us, we'll call you." And now he was standing in front of a building more run-down than the last. "So this is the Metronome." Sighing, he squinted at an address on a matchbook cover. "Rehearsal room B—or is it a G? Shit." Opening the door, he peered into a dimly lit hallway and stepped inside. On the wall he spotted a crooked arrow scrawled on a ripped piece of notepaper with the message: *Auditions: Bass, vibes(?), any kind of damn horns (sight-readers only), vocalist.* Joe groaned. "Oh, yeah. Now *this* is class."

He followed the arrow to a half-open door and looked in. He saw two white men who looked to be in their early thirties. One was the bookish type—thin, with sparse brown hair and sallow skin. Slumped at an old upright piano with his neck angled forward, he resembled an undernourished turkey marking his sheet music. Hanging from the corner of his mouth was a half-smoked cigarette, and his horn-rimmed glasses were precariously close to sliding off his nose. The other man was facing the open window with muscular outstretched arms, as if begging for a breeze. He looked Italian, with an olive complexion and bushy black hair badly in need of a barber's attention. He too had a cigarette affixed to the corner of his bottom lip. Neither man wore a shirt, but both sported suspenders holding up oversized pleated slacks that tapered snugly at the ankles. New Orleans musicians had called them "drapes"—the bottom half of a Zoot-suit. The only sound in the sweltering room was the low hum of an ineffectual oscillating fan.

Joe stepped inside. "Is this Room B?"

The window man gave him a skeptical look. "Only if you can sing—or play a horn."

"I'm a singer," Joe said. "So then—the gig's still open?"

The window man finished his cigarette, dropped it on the floor, and stepped on it. "Zig, ya think the young lad's got the chops? Whadayou, kid? Fourteen?"

"Lay off him, man," the piano man said. "After the parade a'squares we had to listen to today, if he's twelve and knows half the notes in Happy Birthday, I'll be tickled pink." He peered over the top of his glasses at Joe, then stood up and extended his hand. "What's jumpin', Jack? Name's Ziegler, but call me Zig if you want to live. The shifty bum with all the lip we refer to as King or Mr. Long Weekend, *sometimes* even 'the drummer'—but that's a stretch. We gave up tryin' to find out his real name months ago." Zig gestured to the side of his head in a circular "crazy" motion. "Psychotic. Cat goes around naming people—claims it's his duty as a *royal*."

"I'm incognito," King deadpanned. "The hobo threads are a cover. I'm actually filthy rich."

Zig shook his head. "Just filthy."

King laughed. "Ignore us, Jack. We're cooked and stir crazy from so many hours in this oven. Insanity's our only entertainment." He pulled a cigarette from behind his ear. "Nail?"

Joe stared at the two men, and then heaved a tired sigh. "Okay, look. First of all, my name's not Jack—it's Joe. And you can actually *call* me Joe. I'm not fourteen or twelve; I'm twenty-one. I don't smoke 'nails' and I don't scat. I'm tired and I'm hungry. The last audition I was at, they waited till I sang my head off and then told me they were looking for somebody who could scat. So if that's what you're looking for, I might as well tell you now it's not what I do. Me, I'm more of a crooner." He plopped down onto a stool and stared at the floor, prepared for rejection.

King shot Zig an amused look, and then lit the cigarette for himself. "So croon already."

Joe looked up. "Oh, okay. Let's see—do you know, uh, 'I've Got You Under My Skin'?"

Zig snorted. "Don't be forever a nebbish. Ask me if I know 'Chopsticks,' why don'tcha?" He sat back down and began playing a series of intros that modulated up and down, skillfully transposing "Under My Skin" all over the keyboard. Then he shot Joe an impatient glance. "You can jump in here anywhere, Mr. Crosby. Lemme know when I hit that diggable key."

"Oh! Yeah, okay," Joe laughed. "Right there's good."

When Joe got halfway through the first verse, King picked up his sticks and began playing on a snare drum. By the time the last piano chord faded, the three men were dripping with perspiration, but grinning.

King nodded at Joe. "Welcome to the lava pit, baby. You're in."

≈∞≈

Zig and King continued to hold auditions for their rhythm section, but couldn't find a bass man to fit their style. Day after day, they sweated through the auditions of mediocre players until a dour-faced character with dark, unruly hair ambled in. When he played, his slumping shoulders and long arms embraced the neck of his upright bass in such a natural line that it appeared to be a part of his body. Standing at a gangly six feet four, he was long in height and short on conversation. During a rapid-fire session of improvisation, he not only kept up, but seemed to anticipate King's every rhythmic rise and fall, surprising him with the unexpected placement of his fills and spaces and his mastery of inverted chords. His name was Richard Ritenour, but King christened him "Reet" and loudly proclaimed him an innovative, bottom-dwelling genius.

Two days after the discovery of Reet, a brown-skinned stranger arrived at the Metronome and ingratiated himself to the band without speaking a word or playing a note. With a quick glance at King and Zig who were shirtless, the short, muscular Latin placed his saxophone case and battered valise on the floor, then calmly peeled off his dress shirt, then his undershirt. A long, gold watch-chain dangled well below the knee of his baggy, pleated trousers. After pulling his suspenders back up over his bare shoulders, he lifted his alto sax out of the case and hooked it to his neck strap. Placing a palm at the top of his forehead, he spread his fingers and ran them straight back like a comb through his thick black hair. He nodded, and then began warming up with a fluid confection of sound. Reet and Zig began to play along and their blend evolved into a lush rendition of "Passion Flower." Then the sax man picked up the tempo and improvised a wild solo that was shades of Charlie Parker with a heavy dose of Latin rhythm.

"Get me a hypo!" King yelped. "Strayhorn and uncut Cubop, straight from Havana, baby!"

The man stopped playing. "Lounge, gringo! I never been to Cuba in my life—and before you ask—no, I ain't a Puerto Rican either." Leaning back in a Zoot pose, he reached for his dangling watch chain and swung it like a pendulum. "Mendoza's the name—Oliver Mendoza, Mexican sax master. But hey, look, if you got your heart set on a Cuban..."

"Shit, no!" King said. "You send me, baby! I don't care if you're a one-eyed albino from—"

Zig groaned. "Ignore the drummer. His deck's about ten cards short. But since we're on the subject, where *are* you from? You ain't local, 'cause I would've gotten the wire about you."

"Just got into town—from L.A.," Oliver said. "East L.A., to be *exactly* exact."

King's smile faded. "East L.A.? Oh, man, we heard about that trouble the Zoot-suiters had out there in '43. You see any of that?"

"See it? Hijolé, man, I was *in* it! L.A. went loco after that Sleepy Lagoon shit hit the newspapers! Me and my cousin Tino got beat up, and then he got *locked* up for a few days. But me?" He smiled a sly smile. "I gave 'em the slip."

King glanced at Zig. "Heard they tried to play the whole thing as a Commie conspiracy."

"Yeah. Me and Tino never could figure out how wearing Zoot-suits was supposed to make us *Commies*! All we wanted to do was play jazz and pick up chicks."

"Wait," Joe said. "They thought you were a *Commie* just 'cause you wore a Zoot-suit?"

"Red Scare, baby," Zig said. "Ya know—America's resident fascists? Joe McCarthy and the HUAC boys? Come on, you must've heard about it on the radio. The Blacklist?"

Joe shrugged. "I guess I heard some of that on the news, but I don't really get it."

"Me and King'll hip you to it later. Even the part about the Zoot-suits."

"Hey," Oliver interjected, "maybe you can hip *me* to it while you're at it, 'cause I *still* don't get that shit. A lot'a my *carnals* stopped wearin' their drapes after a few night-sticks to their skulls." He paused and grinned. "But when Bird and Dizzy finally made it out to Billy Berg's on the West Coast, *nobody* was gonna keep me from wearin' my killer-diller-reet-pleat reds! Man, I *promise* you vatos—you ain't *never* heard "Night in Tunisia" the way I heard it live in '45, baby."

Zig and King chimed in with the essential question: "Did you sit in?"

"For an *hour*, baby! A whole hour! And I been tryin' to get to New York ever since."

Zig grinned and tossed him a cigarette. "52nd Street, to be *exactly* exact."

"This cat digs me," Oliver laughed. "So what are my chances with you all-stars?"

Zig grabbed his pencil. "Already writin' your solo, baby. Hope you can sight-read."

"Shit! Like a champ."

"Okay, hold it, champ," King said. "Hip me to sump'm here… *How* in the hell did a sight-reading, sax-blowin' Zoot-suit Commie cat like you get stuck with a shitty name like Oliver?"

"Chalé!" Oliver chuckled as Zig lit his cigarette.

King's eyes widened. "Nah, man. That's worse than Oliver."

Oliver coughed up a puff of smoke and laughed. "Not *Charlie*, gringo, *chalé*!"

"Yeah, gringo!" Zig said. "Hit the pedal! He's talkin' about your mother in Spanish."

"Hijolé! How 'bout everybody just call me Señor. And *maybe* I'll spare you vatos from the wrath of my blade." He flashed a sarcastic grin. "We *all* carry switchblades, ya know."

King hit his crash cymbal. "Translation—we're supposed to line up and kiss his Mexican ass! Hey, what's that mean anyway—vatos? That's Spanish for cats, right?"

"A *gato* is a cat," Oliver said dryly. "Not *vato*. And stick to drums, *please*, not Spanish."

Zig howled. "Oh, this gato I *dig*, baby! Death to the rest'a yuz."

King grinned and extended his upturned palm. "Okay, Señor Gato, skin me. You are officially *in*. Life sentence, no chance for parole."

≈∞≈

With the band assembled, full rehearsals began. As everyone became musically acquainted, Joe tried to pick up the crazy slang they called "bop talk." Everyone griped about early rehearsals and whose turn it was to buy cigarettes, and the chore of devising a song list sparked a war of sarcastic one-upsmanship. But things changed when King rushed in one night to tell them about a new trumpet player he had hired.

"For any a'you squares who ain't hip to Doc Calhoun, man, this cat is *class*, baby! Real cool and sophisticated. Middle register—hot as a bonfire, but quiet, dig? Like a low, *intense* simmer."

Reet interrupted in his unrushed monotone. "Intense? Okay, so—is he a good kisser?"

"You *do* sound like you're talkin' about a woman," Oliver said. "Is 'Doc' really a nurse?"

King grimaced. "Hilarious. Hey, Zig. Edify these music lesson drop-outs, would'ja?"

Zig nodded. "Doc Calhoun has just what we need to thicken up our sound. And he'll *definitely* add some class to you third-rate bums. Man, this cat is the most!"

"And his high register's a *muthafucker!*" King gushed. "With his voicing against Oliver's alto style, it'll be like—like a horny couple in the throes of passionate musical intercourse, man!"

"Throes?" Zig yelled. "And horny musical… *intercourse*? No! A thousand times, hell no!"

Oliver crossed his arms and glared at King. "You can include me *out*, baby. 'Cause I ain't throwin' *no* kind'a horny intercourse with nobody named Doc."

Reet tapped out his last cigarette, and threw the empty pack at King. "Go get laid, man."

≈∞≈

The highly anticipated arrival of Doc Calhoun came as a shock to Joe. When the tall, serious-looking man walked into the Metronome, Joe's insides went cold. King had never mentioned that his trumpet-playing idol was a Negro. He appeared to be in his late forties, with a sprinkle of gray at his temples. He wore a conservative blue suit that clashed with the rag-tag Zoot wardrobe of the other musicians, and his complexion was the color of dark, bittersweet chocolate.

After a few weeks, it was clear that "bittersweet" summed up his personality, as well. Doc Calhoun had a bone-dry sense of humor, delivering observations of life with a deadpan wit. He could find a way to critique King on a subpar paradiddle with comedic insults against his mother until she ended up with the reputation of a red-light-district pro. The band would take five, and Doc would light a cigarette and ease into a chair, his frown betrayed by his twinkling black eyes.

Joe had seen it before—this game that dazzled the band members. It was called "the dozens" and his Uncle Cyrus had been an expert at it, drunk or sober. Joe remembered sneaking out of bed with his brother to witness the outlandish "signifying" duels between their father and uncle, and then laughing themselves silly in their room. It was his only pleasant memory of Calvin.

But Joe was deeply disturbed at the way Doc made him think of his childhood and home. Maybe it was the way his brother suddenly walked through his mind uninvited. Or maybe it was the way Doc looked at him when playing his solo version of the dozens, as if he expected Joe to know the game when the others didn't.

Chapter 9

As the summer's triple-digit temperatures finally began to drop, it was Doc who came up with the perfect name for the band: "Beat the Heat." From the minute he first saw Joe, he referred to him as "Junior." And to Joe's annoyance, the name stuck.

After several auditions, the owner of the Café Nocturne signed the band to a limited engagement. During rehearsals, the band members tried to coax Joe into scatting, and each time he refused. As his performances improved, Zig began pushing the issue again.

"It's just improvisation, man, like when we trade fours and eights," Zig explained. "You'll be trading fours with us. Just make sounds like an instrument, that's all. It'll be hip, baby!"

"I can't even figure out how *you* guys do it. How do you know when it's your turn?"

Doc blew a smoke ring and smiled. "It's dialogue, Junior. Spontaneous musical dialogue."

"Yeah—a friendly conversation," Zig said. "I ask Doc a question on the piano—"

"And I repeat it or answer it—on my trumpet," Doc explained.

Oliver nodded. "Or make your own statement—like me. But it's gotta fit the chord."

"*And* be in rhythm," Doc said. "Chords are the language, but rhythm makes it poetry."

"Dig it," Zig said. "Don't mean a thing if it ain't got that swing, baby!"

Reet was working out a figure on his bass, and shook his head without opening his eyes. "No, man, no. Stop confusing the kid. It's not swing *or* language… It's sex, man."

"Sex?" Joe repeated incredulously.

"Yeah, baby," Reet said. "Remember? Musical intercourse. Music is *loaded* with sex."

A lewd grin lit up King's face. "Triple tonguing and ticklin' the ivory, baby."

Doc caressed his trumpet. "Lips on her mouthpiece, and she opens riiight up to Papa."

"Ooh, and drums," King gushed, "with *skin*. If it's nice and tight, I can vamp all night!"

"Oh, yeah, baby," Zig said breathlessly. "The harder the bop, the sweeter the pop!"

"That's after you pluck the G-string," King panted. "Ya *gotta* pluck the G-string."

"And finger the screech horn," Doc deadpanned. "Hot licks and layin' in the cut."

"Oralé!" Oliver groaned. "Just roll the stag film already! Ignore these stupid vatos, Joe. 'Cause when we're trading fours and everybody's really smokin'—man, it's *better* than sex!"

Everyone began nodding and murmuring in unanimous agreement, and Joe laughed. "Trading fours is better than *sex*? Okay, okay, I guess I gotta try that. So when do we start?"

Doc cackled dryly. "Hit the pedal, Junior. What do you think we've just been doin'?"

≈∞≈

After the first two weeks, the band began to generate a buzz that filled the club to near-capacity every night, and Joe slowly relaxed into his new life. Even his uneasiness around Doc diminished, as long as the other band members were around. Everyone seemed to adore the black man and everything he did—from his grumbling one-liners to the methodical way he chain-smoked. He was the only person Joe had ever seen who lit a fresh cigarette from the end of the one he was finishing. But it was not just personality traits that set him apart; it was his innate ability to adapt to any person or situation, as if he'd seen it all before. And then there was his talent—that goosebump-inducing musical style that came without the usual dose of screaming ego. Somehow, Doc Calhoun was both chameleon and nonconformist, quietly defying categorization, whether cultural, musical, or racial. Trapped by uncertainty, Joe fretted over his future with the band and his inability to grasp the complexities of jazz. But his deepest fear was that his Caucasian masquerade would be exposed. The one thing he knew for sure was that he had never met anyone, black or white, with the commanding presence of Doc Calhoun.

In short order, the other members of the band split into two comfortable factions: Reet would join Zig at his apartment in Brooklyn to listen to his avant-garde jazz collection. The two of them could sit for hours listening to Django Reinhardt or Thelonious Monk, with only an occasional nod or a grunt as a sign of approval for a particularly impressive segment.

Oliver and King embraced jazz with a noisy passion and shared a manic take on life. Once, while standing with them outside a record shop on 42nd Street, Joe was struggling to comprehend Charlie Parker's newest release when some feat of saxophonic brilliance elicited a yelp from King. When Oliver collapsed in a pratfall in apparent delirium, New York pedestrians stepped over him with barely a glance. There was nothing for Joe to do but laugh. Oliver and King were too much fun for him to worry about being a self-conscious jazz outsider.

Of course, Doc shifted easily from one group to the other, and Joe was left to try and follow conversations about composition, theory, and stylization. Some guy named Clark Terry had a technique nobody had ever seen before, and hard bop was going to change the world. Doc, King, and Zig stayed up late writing complex charts of epic lengths, then fought wars over them, tore them up, and started over again. And sprinkled in like seasoning were stories about the jazz all-stars, which sounded to Joe like bald-faced fiction told in a foreign language.

Rehearsals at Zig's apartment were usually long, weird nights, with little actual rehearsing. Lining one wall were floor-to-ceiling shelves containing a haphazard arrangement of records, interspersed with an eclectic collection of books. Without fail, Zig would find an excuse to stop rehearsing, play a new jazz cut on the hi-fi, yank out one of his dog-eared books, and begin reading progressive poetry aloud. He informed Joe that music and poetry created a symbiosis that was irresistible to the soul of an artist. Joe had no idea what symbiosis meant, but he took note of the amused expression on Doc's face whenever Zig performed his hammy recitations.

Despite the chaos, the show had shaped up nicely, and rehearsals were cut to once a week.

≈∞≈

Reet ambled in for the regular Tuesday rehearsal, wearing dark glasses and a scowl.

"The late Reet Ritenour," Doc intoned. "A moment of silence."

Oliver blew the first few notes of "Taps," and Reet threw a cigarette at him, which he caught. "What's jumpin', dead man? Hey, light me up so we can start this *pinché* rehearsal."

Ignoring Oliver, Reet lifted his glasses to squint at the chart. "What is this, Ziegler?"

"What's what?" Zig muttered without looking up.

"Here in letter B— Oh, okay! A Diz dominant seventh with a Bird flatted ninth." He yawned theatrically. "How original."

Oliver took his first look at the chart and whistled. "You think I got the chops for this? Oralé! Man, I'm flattered! That's what I call genius, baby."

"No, man," Doc said as he lit the cigarette clenched in his teeth. "It's called larceny."

Zig was at the piano, scribbling on a chart. "We're all influenced, Doctor Calhoun," he murmured. "Even you. And don't commit it to memory; I'm making another change here."

Doc sighed. "Just finish the damn chart so we can rehearse, man."

"Aw, come on, baby," King said, "Give him a tick or two to make it so complicated nobody can play the shit. The audience'll dig that the most."

Doc finished cleaning his trumpet and was checking the valves. He peered at Joe, who was in a corner reading an article in *Down Beat.* "Junior, is that a Mr. B collar you have on?"

Joe smiled. "Yeah. Probably goin' out later. Does it look okay?"

"It *looks* hip, but Mr. B's more than a singer in a hip shirt. He's a musician and a composer. Now that's *really* hip. But you? You can't even sight read. We'll give you till next week."

Oliver blew a note that sounded like a hysterical goose-honk, and shoved Doc with his shoulder. "Hijolé, hombre! Lay off the kid, man!"

"I'm just suggesting to our resident freshman, by way of extreme sarcasm, that he should get his nose out of that *Down Beat* and start payin' attention. He checks out every time we get to the sheet music 'cause he can't read it. But there's other ways to learn. Some of the most innovative musicians in the world play by ear—Errol Garner, for one—without knowin' the difference between a treble clef and a coffee stain on a goddamn chart. Junior needs to dig that jazz begins with the soul, not the sheet music."

"Sez you," Zig snarled. "Errol Garner ain't here and I personally ain't got a soul, so right now, this shit begins *and* ends with the sheet music. As a matter of fact, everybody give me back your charts so I can make this one last brilliant change."

After a group groan, the change was made, and the rehearsal began. But less than a minute in, Doc grimaced and waved his hand. "Goddamn, girls! We sound like a train wreck!"

"What's wrong?" Joe asked.

"We just compromised the shit out of the chordal integrity of my arrangement, that's what's wrong," Zig whined. "And somebody's axe is way the hell out of tune."

"My mistake, man," Oliver muttered, staring at his chart. "I got it now."

"Sight-reading champ, my ass," Doc grumbled. "And everybody tune up, for chrissakes!"

After the brief interruption, they ran through the complete show, only stopping twice to argue creative points. At rehearsal's end, they were packing their instruments when King grabbed Joe's shoulders, startling him. "Hey, Junior. Where the hell's the good doctor?"

"Out in the hall—went to the can or sump'm. But you know Doc. He might'a left."

"Go see if you can catch him while I pack up my shit."

Joe stepped out and saw Doc at the end of the hallway with his back turned. He was clutching the pay phone receiver and arguing loudly with someone. His burning cigarette hung limply between the fingers of his free hand, its ashes falling onto the floor.

"I *said* where the hell are they?" he shouted. "Where?... Well, congratulations! That makes *one* goddamn thing you got right today." Then he slammed down the receiver, threw the cigarette to the floor, and crushed it with an angry grind of his shoe.

Joe quietly ducked back into the rehearsal room before Doc could see him.

"Don't tell me that was Doc blowin his cool like that." King said.

Before Joe could answer, Doc walked back in. "Those other bums headed to Minton's?"

Joe shrugged. "They told me they were 'making the scene at a— laboratory'?"

"That's Minton's. And I ain't in the mood for a crowd tonight. What about you, King?"

King grinned. "Let's blow, baby! Come on, Junior. Tonight you roll with me and Doc."

"Well, okay, but where are we rolling to?" Joe asked.

Doc blew a smoke ring toward the ceiling. "It's a surprise."

After a short subway ride to a midtown walkup on 3rd Avenue, Joe trudged up the dimly lit flight of stairs behind King and Doc.

"Goddamn, King!" Doc snapped. "How many flights? I'm gettin' a nosebleed, man!"

"Come on," Joe grumbled. "Somebody tell me where we're going. Let me in on it."

"Church," Doc called back over his shoulder. "If I don't have a heart attack on the way."

"Come on! This is no church!"

"It's the church of bebop, Junior!" King called down. "My pad. You got the undeserved honor of loungin' with the good doctor and me while we fly high on Bird's most latest."

Joe groaned. "I wish you guys would speak English once in a while."

Doc peered back at Joe with a wry smile. "All he's sayin' is that we're gonna light the fuses on a couple'a twists and realize some new wax. That's all."

"Huh?"

"Don't worry, Junior. The band's chippin' in to hire you a translator from the U.N."

"Oh, that's real hilarious."

"Goddamn, King!" Doc yelled. "I ain't climbin' my old ass but one or two more flights!"

A door flew open and an angry, middle-aged white man stepped out. "Pipe down, will ya?"

Doc paused and smiled at him calmly. "Good evening," he said, with a courtly bow.

The man blinked at him in apparent confusion, went back in, and slammed the door.

King laughed from above. "Stop scarin' the squares with that black Count Dracula routine! Come on. One more landing! Deep breaths, Daddy-O. All them nails put the wheeze on you!"

"Okay, that I got," Joe said. "Cigarettes, wheeze. And by the way, Dracula fits you to a tee."

Doc ignored him and kept climbing. When he reached the top, he suddenly clutched the handrail with one hand and grabbed his chest with the other.

King's face registered panic as he grabbed Doc's shoulder. "You okay, man?"

After a short pause, Doc cackled and then reached into his pocket for his cigarettes. "I'm just messin' with you, man. I live in the nosebleed section of a walkup my damn self."

King sighed. "See that, Junior? Cat's always springin' surprises. I shouldn't let his wise ass inside my luxurious hacienda." He leaned against the wall, mugging the seductive pose of a prostitute, and batted his eyes at Doc. "*But*—I'm easy, sailor. I can be *had* for chocolate."

Doc lit a cigarette and blew the smoke into King's face. "Don't take this wrong, Mam'zelle. But there ain't enough reefer, paper bags, or liquor in the state of New York."

King laughed as he stumbled inside. "Okay, okay, so this is the pad. Entre vous and cop a squat. Services, libation, and sleeves comin' up!"

Joe stepped in behind Doc and looked around as King disappeared into the kitchen. The room was neat and stylish; even the gray, deep-pile rug looked new. Hanging over a black leather sofa with royal blue throw pillows was a framed pen-and-ink rendering of Charlie Parker in mid-solo. The coffee table was covered with jazz records, and a phonograph in an oak cabinet stood against the opposite wall between two black Art Deco-style club chairs. Above that was a small framed certificate. Joe peeked over Doc's shoulder at it. "What's it say?"

Doc let out a low whistle. "Juilliard. I'll be damned."

"That's that music school you guys are always talking about, right?"

"That is *the* music school, Junior. For classically trained musicians, not bums and sidemen."

"Oh… You surprised?"

"Well, yeah. I figured he was a straight Moeller-method, Chapin-book type'a cat."

Joe rolled his eyes. "Whatever that is. But look at this place! I expected it to be more like—"

"Nagasaki after the bomb?" King said, walking in from the kitchen. "You bums shouldn't talk so loud when you're judging a book by its cover. Johnnie Walker and Coke comin' up."

"No!" Joe called. "Just a Coke for me."

Doc peered at Joe with an amused expression. "The Johnnie Walker's for me, Junior."

"Oh, I thought he meant, you know, mixed and—"

"Hit the pedal, baby," King called.

"Huh?"

"Accelerate," Doc said, shaking with soft laughter. "Keep up, man!"

Joe sighed. "I thought hit the pedal meant to shut-up or sump'm."

"That's hit the brake. Come on, you gotta be semantically hip by now. At least mildly."

"*What?*" Joe held up his hand. "Never mind… but can I ask you sump'm, Doc?"

"You can ask. Doesn't mean I'll answer."

"Well, I was wondering… You talk like—like an educated guy. Did you go to college or sump'm? I mean, maybe not that Juilliard, but some colored college or university, right?"

Doc narrowed his eyes. "Yeah. That'd be the university of none'a your goddamn business."

"Okay, okay. Guess I walked into that one."

"Yeah, you did," Doc chuckled. "I read, that's all—and not just music charts. *Books*, Junior. Maybe I'll take you to a library one day. But tonight, we're workin' on your *musical* edification." He flipped through a stack of records and held one up. "Hey, King! What's this Robert Johnson wax doin' here? I never figured you for one'a those raw blues cats."

"Roots, Daddy-O!" King shouted. "Gotta dig the evolution in the revolution, baby!"

"'Crossroads Blues,'" Doc murmured. "This one *really* told a story."

Joe sat down to peruse the records. "Yeah, my Daddy loved that song," he said absently.

Doc gave him a pointed look. "*Your* Daddy was hip to Robert Johnson?"

An icy chill danced down Joe's spine. "He liked—all kinds'a music," he stammered.

King set the drinks on the coffee table, and then reached for the record. "Lay it on me."

Doc was still staring at Joe with a vague smile. "Naw. Not this one. Here—Ellington."

King sighed as he slipped the record from its sleeve. "Guess Bird's new cut can simmer while we lock lobes to some chamber music for a tick or two."

Doc grimaced. "Chamber music? Hey, man, Ellington's always been in the groove. And when the groove changes, he riffs over."

Joe was thankful that King had changed the subject. "Do you guys ever speak English?"

"Junior," Doc said sternly, "you need to pay attention to this."

"English at last. Okay, you got my attention."

"I want you to dig sump'm. You're always beefin' that you don't get jazz, so this is a nice, easy piece to start with. Close your eyes and listen to this."

"Okay." Joe closed his eyes and smiled as he listened to the record's intro of exotic drumbeats and unusual horn melodies. "Oh, I know that one. That's 'Caravan.'"

"Right. What do you see?" Doc asked.

Joe opened his eyes. "Huh?"

King pulled up a chair and leaned forward. "How's the gravy, Dad? What's it taste like?"

"Okay, first you tell me it's conversation. Then you tell me it's sex. And now it's *gravy*?"

"It's all those things," Doc said. "If you want to learn, then you've gotta listen. Technically, it would take you years to understand jazz, but you can dig the philosophy. It's all about stories, Junior. Jazz tells *stories*, and it's got a soul that you can dig without knowin' an E-flat from a—"

"I know, I know—a coffee stain. But maybe I can't, Doc. I mean, I know I'll be sorry for admitting this, but I really need lyrics to know what a song's about."

Doc groaned. "No, you don't! Hey, King. Start it from the top."

As King started the record over, Doc settled onto the edge of a chair. "Close your eyes again, Junior," he said. "This piece has a specific *flavor* from a specific region. It's like Bauza and Chano's influence on Dizzy's music. You know, man—that Afro-Cuban meets bop sound."

"Cubop, baby!" King said. "Remember 'Manteca'? That piece Oliver's always playing?"

Doc nodded. "A *very* tasty morsel. But this one's different. So what does it sound like?"

Joe closed his eyes. "Oh, okay! It sounds like one of those Ali Baba movies, right? Like the Arabian Nights. So it's about—Arabia or sump'm?"

"Right. Sand dunes and sheiks. And camels dancin' along in a line. See it?"

Joe opened his eyes. "Hey, I really *can* see that! No wonder they called it 'Caravan.'"

Doc lit a joint and held Joe with a penetrating stare. "Right."

"You ain't just a hairhead after all!" King said. "Now lemme spin Bird's new wax and see what kind'a scene *that* puts in everybody's cranium."

Doc clenched the joint in his teeth at a rakish upward angle a 'la FDR. "I'm a colored man, King. Don't send me out tryin' to beg up a taxi to the Deuces with a goddamn cuttin' jones!"

King chortled as he brushed the dust off the phonograph needle, "It's cuttin' time, baby!"

Joe let out a frustrated sigh. "I'd do better with Chinese."

"Nighty-night, Junior," Doc laughed. "Those pillows look real comfortable."

≈∞≈

After a long, inadvertent nap, Joe woke up. For a moment, he forgot where he was and his heart began to pound. He slowly became aware of Doc's voice. He was in the middle of a story.

"Maaan, he's got the wickedest left hand in the hemisphere," he was saying. "And speaking of the hemisphere, there was that story about Birks when he flew *all* the way out there."

King nodded. "Oh, man, I got the wire! That was where? The Onyx?"

"Minton's. And I was *there*, baby! Diz held that note for at least five minutes without takin' a breath." Doc took a pull from the joint he was relighting, then passed it to King.

King grunted as he hit the joint. "Circular breathing, man."

Joe began fanning the air with his hands. "Your dope smoke burned up all the air in here!"

Both men ignored him.

"Not circular breathing, man!" Doc said. "I'm tellin' you—the cat left earth, went beyond, *orbited*, and then… landed again! It changed him! And *that's* why he plays like he does now."

"Which is?"

Doc glared at King. "Which is? What I just said, man! Like a cat who went beyond and orbited and then landed again! Hit the pedal, dope fiend!"

Joe groaned. "You guys sound so stupid."

"That's—that's 'cause we're—ossified, Junior," King stammered solemnly.

"Whatever that means."

Doc chuckled. "Guess I better go load Junior's ass onto a train. The squares'll be reporting to their plantations any damn minute, and I *don't* want to realize that midtown stampede, man."

Joe was shuffling toward the door with his eyes half-shut, but then stopped. "What?"

King laughed, then relit the joint. "Wait, Doc, don't split yet! Hip me to that part about Bud Powell. That was you yankin' my chain, right? He didn't really get *bounced*?"

Stepping into the hallway, Joe leaned his forehead against the wall and waited for Doc to finish what he hoped would be the last story of the night.

"Yup," Doc said, "bounced from Minton's. For pretending to play the eighty-eights without touchin' the keys." He pantomimed and shook his head. "Weird, baby, weird."

"Daaamn!" King gasped. "The great Bud Powell—deported!… From the lab yet!"

"Don't nail him up for it, man. Word is the cat was fucked up on sump'm that wasn't stepped on right."

Joe groaned. "Look, I got ten dollars. It's all yours if you'll start speaking English."

Doc patted Joe on the back. "That's mighty *white* of you, Junior, but you don't have ten dollars. We picked your pocket for a liquor run a couple'a hours ago."

Chapter 10

After two months, Joe began to appreciate the ability of the band to switch from hardcore bebop to the slow, sexy love songs Zig had carefully chosen for him: "Autumn in New York," "Where or When," "I Only Have Eyes For You," and the newest addition, "Lush Life."

He still felt like an outsider, but continued to observe the other musicians. They were like five fingers on one artistic hand, united by their reverence of a music that was impossibly mathematical, carnal, and spiritual, all at the same time. An enigma not unlike Doc, himself.

Over time, Joe had acquired an intense craving for that ethereal late-night world of time that King called "the witching hour." The last set was instrumental improvisation, which freed Joe to sit and listen, and learn. The other band members shook off the alcoholic cobwebs of too many scotch-rocks, then followed Doc like apostles into uncharted musical territory. Complex riffs and unexpected chord progressions floated on cigarette smoke and soft sighs of *Holy Jesus!* And Joe realized that he was like all the others. Like it or not, he was moth to Doc Calhoun's flame.

Each night after the last set, he bombarded Doc with questions. "How the hell do you do that, man? You never play it the same way twice. What can I do to catch up? I gotta get *better*."

Doc chuckled as he put his horn in its case. "Slow down! You're jumpin' to the coda, baby!"

"But if I could understand the music better, maybe my vocals would be better," he said, frowning. "King says it might help if I learned to read music. He said my pitch is okay, but my dynamics would be better if I started thinking like an instrument. Like technique, right?"

"Wrong. Not technique, Junior. *Feeling*. Break their hearts, man. Make 'em cry."

"Oh. I thought that was the *one* thing I had right. I thought I *was* feeling it."

"Junior, I'm gonna tell you this one more time: Jazz tells stories, man. Let yourself get lost in one of 'em. And some night one'a those antiseptic songs you croon is gonna grow a soul."

Joe heaved a heavy, frustrated sigh as he walked toward the door behind Doc.

Doc looked back at him with an amused expression. "You followin' me, Junior?"

"Not really. But now that you mention it, where are you headed?"

"Remember that university I told you about?"

Joe grinned and shoved his hands into his pockets. "G'night, Dracula." As he watched Doc walk away, he felt a sudden pang—a jarring rush of color, sound, and memory. But it came and went so fast, he was unable to tell if it was joy or sorrow.

≈∞≈

Joe always tried to catch a nap before the show, but lately sleep had been a stranger. He turned on the radio and stretched out in bed. *Johnny Dollar* was in mid-episode, and the droning voices quickly lulled him to sleep. But after dozing awhile, he woke to the beginning of a news report:

> *This just in on the recent suicide of Secretary of Defense Vincent Forrestal. Authorities have now released this unfinished note found in Forrestal's room at the Bethesda Medical Hospital: "No quiet murmur like the tremulous wail of the lone bird, the querulous nightingale." When asked to comment on the meaning of the note, Senator Joseph McCarthy stated his belief that it was the Communists who hounded Forrestal to his death… And now a word from our sponsor, Alka Seltzer…*

Joe sighed. Lately, there was just no escaping the Red Scare. McCarthy and his gavel-pounding HUAC Committee seemed to hound those pathetic witnesses around the clock. The radio and the front page of every newspaper screamed indictments on the creeping evil of Communism, with an occasional dissenter arguing the case for the First Amendment. Zig and King had tried to explain it to Joe by telling him about the people they called "the hunted ones." Writers and fellow musicians who had fled to Europe or Mexico—overnight expatriates whose refusal to "name names" had ended their careers, divided their families, and driven more than a few to suicide. Some had faced McCarthy's Un-American Activities Committee to answer un-American questions about their private thoughts and beliefs, the people they knew, where they had come from. *Are you now or have you ever been a member of the Communist Party?* Each time Joe heard the question, it was a mental pinprick that bled into a messy, vivid picture of what would happen to him if someone dug into his past. *Are you now or have you ever been a Negro?* And Joe realized that he knew those people—the hunted ones—those people whose names appeared on an ominous document, real or mythical, simply called "The Blacklist."

He stared at the radio and wondered which side had hunted Forrestal into that corner where there was nothing left for him but an unfinished poem and a sixteen-story leap. Had he been one of the hunters? Or one of the hunted? Perhaps he had been both.

≈∞≈

When Joe walked into the club that night, Zig was loudly responding to the band members' complaints over the new chart he had just handed them.

"Too complex? Whadayou? A bunch'a B-flat sidemen playin' your first Bar Mitzvah? Why don't we go ahead and play "Melancholy Baby," for chrissakes!"

Joe grinned. Surrounded by the noisy, wisecracking denizens of the Nocturne, he felt safe.

Four hours later, the club was nearly deserted. The crowd usually thinned out early on Sundays and Mondays, but the show always went on for the loyal handful of bleary-eyed die-hards who waited patiently in the fog of stale cigarette smoke for Doc's last number.

Joe yawned and sat on a stool near the drums as the waitresses cleared the empty tables.

King handed him his half-empty highball glass. "Hold this for me, Junior."

"What the hell are we playin'?" Oliver asked.

"Ask Doc. If he ever finishes that drink and drags his ass up here," King said loudly.

Doc glared at him from the bar, then headed to the bandstand. "Deafening professionalism, man. I don't know *why* you're not playin' Carnegie Hall. Where's Zig?"

King nodded in the direction of the bathroom door. Zig was already heading their way.

Leaning close to the microphone, King murmured, "Good evening to all the lovers left in the joint, old and young. We've got a request from the muses—don't know what it is yet, but the venerable Doctor Calhoun will make you realize it as soon as he dreams it up."

Joe's gaze was already fixed on Doc. It was the witching hour. Even on a dreary Monday night with a near-empty house, he prepared as if he were about to play a command performance for royalty. As always, Joe was fascinated by Doc's ritual. His palms pressing their moisture into the folds of his handkerchief before picking up the horn. The repetitive licking and pursing of his lips in preparation. The deliberate adjustment to settle the mouthpiece into the perfect position. The expansion of his chest as he filled his lungs with the rarefied kind of air that seemed to know it was fated to be music. Spotlight. His left shoulder dropped slightly; then he turned and stared at Joe with eyes full of conversation. *Jazz tells stories, Junior. Listen…*

Joe closed his eyes and the images rushed in. The first notes were fragile and plaintive, drawn out like the fearful cries of something barely alive. He saw a sapling, surrounded by stronger, larger trees, and he heard its desperation to survive. Then a melodic surge of full-bodied, confident notes, climbing higher and higher. Youthful virility, flashy in its full-blown foliage. A sudden scream of angry, red notes. Stark and defiantly discordant. The sounds of struggle and defeat, followed by a barren winter. Hopeless dry branches reaching desperately for life, like the arms of a dying man. Then the soothing, fluid tones of a waterfall. Sounds of love, gentle and verdant, like the rebirth of spring. New leaves and new vitality. A second chance.

More images appeared in Joe's mind, scattered among fragments of stories, but somehow Doc's trumpet made sense of them all. And in that moment, a door opened in Joe's mind. He suddenly understood why jazz made philosophers of musicians—why they all wore that familiar glazed expression when rhapsodizing over Bird or Billie Holiday or Mingus. It was his first peek into a world of jazz infinity that existed somewhere behind the eyes—that secret place he longed to visit, where the jam sessions were nonstop. Where living musicians sidestepped the notion of mortality by smoking joints and trading fours with masters long thought dead by reasonable folks. It was the kind of nonsensical world only junkies and dreamers could understand. An addictive personality paid the dealer in full, and music was the drug of choice.

Joe kept his eyes closed and floated on an atmospheric high.

When he finally opened his eyes, he blinked at Doc. They were the only two people left on the bandstand, and the manager was waiting for them at the door. "Where'd everybody go?"

Doc was buckling his horn case. He looked over at Joe with an amused smile. "Scattered to the winds. Set's *been* over, Junior. So I guess the question is—where'd *you* go?"

Joe stood up and grinned. "On a caravan, man."

Lighting a cigarette, Doc slowly headed to the door. "So you realized me on that love song."

"I did."

Doc exhaled upward and the cloud of smoke drifted back down slowly, encircling his head. "A classic story about all the hate in the world."

Joe's smile faded. "You just said it was a love song."

"It was both. Remember when we told you about improvisation being like conversation?"

Joe grinned. "And sex. Yeah, I remember that."

"Sex *is* conversation, of a sort. And so is jazz. But, hell, it's more than that and I wish I could—" Suddenly, he stopped. "Hah! How 'bout that? It just hit me. Standin' here in this empty club, tryin' to find a way to explain this one who-gives-a-damn-Monday-night-song to your youngster ass… Junior, you dug that last song because it was about love *and* hate. It was birth and death and all the conversations in between. The sweet talk and the arguments and the heaven and the hell. 'Cause every now and then—maaaan, it's perfect." He put his hand on Joe's shoulder. "Junior," he said softly, "jazz is just—life."

≈∞≈

Two weeks later the band's engagement at Café Nocturne came to an end. As they packed their instruments and griped about their uncertain prospects, Mr. Ramsay, the proprietor of the club, opened his office door and motioned to King.

King followed him in and returned ten minutes later with a stunned expression. "You're never gonna believe this!" He peered back over his shoulder and whispered, "Cat wants us to be the house band! And when I realized how bad he wanted us, I hit him for double the bread!"

Doc lit a cigarette and smiled. "Oh, that's my *favorite* kind'a bread. So?"

"So— It seems we gave the cat's business a nice jump last month."

"And?"

Reet groaned. "Whadayou? Alfred Hitchcock with all this goddamn suspense? And *what*?"

King pantomimed a fisherman reeling in a whopper. "And, I tossed out a line about another offer, and the cat hopped right on my hook. So we're back here Monday with fat pockets, baby."

Joe stood there grinning until he heard Elsie shriek, "Ooh, Joe! That's swell!"

He groaned softly. The band members had welcomed Elsie in the beginning. She had distributed flyers at the hospital and brought large groups of friends, which increased the band's initial popularity. Joe had enjoyed her attention at first, but now it was just embarrassing. To hear Elsie tell it, Joe was the star and the other band members were mere sidemen.

"Okay, look," Doc said. "I was plannin' to surprise you criminals by feedin' you so you wouldn't go commit suicide, but since we all want to live now, let's change the wake to a party. Food's still included, but we take up a collection for the liquor. Deal?"

"Deal!" King shouted. "We finally get invited to the hallowed digs of the good Doctor!"

"Joe," Elsie called, "could I talk to you a second?"

"Shit. Now what?" he muttered.

King let out a derisive cackle. "Got them ball an' chain blues, Junior?"

"Oralé," Oliver said. "You gotta run along with Mommy?"

"Just give me a minute," Joe said. He hopped off the stage and grabbed Elsie's arm.

"Hey!" she said. "What are you doing?"

"I'm puttin' you in a cab."

"Oh, no you're not. You're not *putting* me anywhere. Why don't you just tell 'em that your girlfriend goes wherever you go. Unless you don't *want* me at your party."

Steering her outside, he waved frantically at an approaching cab. "It's not that. It's just— Look. This is a band celebration. Nobody's bringin' girls." He glanced at her and groaned. Her lower lip was trembling and her face had that pinched-up redness that always meant tears.

"You're tired of me, aren't you?" she said. "Y-you want to break up, don't you?"

Joe stared at her, glad that she could not read his mind: *I wish you'd just put your ass in this cab and get out'a my life.* Instead, he gave her his most engaging smile. "Look, baby. It's just a jam session. All those hams do is trade solos and I hardly get to sing at all. They'll be drunk and cursing and I don't want you around all that. I'll call you tomorrow, okay?"

"No. I want to go with you, Joe."

Joe narrowed his eyes at her. "Have you ever been to Harlem, Elsie?"

"Harlem? Well—no, but—"

"Well, that's where Doc lives."

"Oh." Elsie swallowed hard, then jerked up her chin. "Well, have *you* ever been there?"

"Not yet, but the other guys go up there all the time—to nightclubs and places like that. Besides, I don't have a problem with Harlem like you do."

"Who said I have a problem with Harlem?"

"That sick expression on your face, that's who."

"I don't care," she said, crossing her arms. "I'll be with you so I don't care… Okay?"

He stared at her and then sighed. "Come on."

≈∞≈

An hour later Joe emerged from the subway steps on 125th Street and took his first look at Harlem—the colorful shops and the locals going about their business. He realized that his fear of coming uptown alone had been unwarranted. Still, he felt more at ease in the company of the other band members. As he thought of all the stories Uncle Cyrus had told him about Harlem, he smiled. Then he felt the heat of Doc's penetrating gaze. "What?"

Doc grinned and blew a mist of smoke into the air. "Nothin', Junior."

Joe felt Elsie's fingernails digging into his arm as she clung to him. He endured it for as long as he could, but finally shook his arm free.

"Nobody's gonna hurt you, okay?" He glanced over at Doc and when their eyes met, he got the feeling that he was reading his mind.

He shook off the feeling and continued to take in the sights of Harlem. It was no longer the cultural Mecca it had been during the Renaissance years, but its old soul was still intact, and the rhythm of its heartbeat still vibrated right up through the sidewalks. A wide spectrum of local characters made it beautiful in a crazy-quilt sort of way. Prostitutes painted up for an evening of brisk business peacefully coexisted with well-dressed couples peering into shop windows on their way to the movies. A tall, honey-colored man in a blue sharkskin suit and a matching pork-pie hat scribbled on a small notepad as people clustered around him murmuring numbers. A fight nearly broke out when one of the players shouted "Pickpocket!" and a small, wiry man stumbled from inside the group. A hefty woman swatted him a few times with her pocketbook but that didn't stop her from shouting her numbers to the policy man. Joe laughed so hard he nearly bumped into a boy selling newspapers under the Apollo Theater marquee. "Sorry, kid." He tugged Elsie's arm. "Come on! We're a block behind everybody!"

The atmosphere was almost spoiled when he spotted a junkie nodding on the steps of a run-down building on the corner of Lenox Avenue. The man lifted his head and stared vacantly at Joe, then muttered something unintelligible and leaned back into the shadows. Joe turned away quickly and focused on a young couple at the bus stop holding hands and talking. They were locked in an intimate gaze, and their faces were bathed in the unique glow of new love.

In the distance, he heard a bouncy arrangement of "Perdido" and Joe began snapping his fingers. Apparently, sundown was the cue for a pickup in the rhythm on 125th Street. The energy reminded him of New Orleans, but there was a distinct difference. In New Orleans, it was overt—flashy, joyful, and loud. Harlem's nighttime energy was subtle, but as overpowering as the unspoken attraction between the two lovers he had seen at the bus stop. He gazed at a golden sunset reflected in the windows of the Hotel Theresa, and felt a gentle breeze against his face. *No wonder Uncle Cyrus always called Harlem a lady.*

They followed Doc into his building on the corner of 126th Street and 7th Avenue, then trudged up the dark, narrow staircase to his apartment.

When Doc opened the front door, they were greeted by a tall, striking woman the color of bronze. Stretching up, she kissed Doc's neck quickly. "Hi, baby," she said softly.

Joe's knees almost buckled at the sound of her voice—a deep, velvety contralto that resonated with equal parts of elegance and sex.

Doc wrapped his arm around her waist. "This is my wife Pearl."

King stepped into the room and nudged Joe. "Did he say *wife*?"

"That's what the man said."

King walked in a small circle, shaking his head. "Told'ja, Junior. He's full of surprises!"

When Pearl smiled, Joe had to check to make sure that his tongue was still inside his mouth. Doc's wife was the most stunning woman, black or white, he had ever seen. She was slender and tall—about 5'9, with black, slightly straightened shoulder-length hair. He noticed that she wasn't particularly large-breasted—just exquisitely shaped, from head to toe. She wore a black sweater and matching toreador pants that clung just enough to reveal a pair of long, shapely legs and a rear-end with the provocative curves of a pear. Joe forced his eyes away from her body and back to her face. The only thing not quite perfect there was the tiredness in her eyes. They were dark, expressionless eyes, rimmed by faint circles, but even this flaw only added to her mystery and made her sexier. She dropped to her knees and stretched out her arms to a little boy of about five and a baby girl just old enough to toddle around on wobbly legs.

"Mama!" the baby cooed.

Joe blinked at Pearl. He had never seen anyone who looked less like a "Mama" in his life.

"This is Shay," Doc said, "and Edward. Tell 'em who you're named after, Edward."

The boy looked at the floor shyly. "Edward Kennedy Ellington. Ya know, the Duke."

King extended his hand. "Greetings, Duke. I'm King. Slip me some'a that royal skin!"

Edward giggled as he slid his palm over King's and tried to snap his fingers.

"Dig it, gate! I bet you can even work the eighty-eights like the Duke. Come on over here and we'll serenade the peons with our royal talent!"

Hand in hand, King and Edward headed across a faded blue battlefield of carpet-scars—the evidence of a well broken-in jam session area—to an old upright Steinway in the far corner of the room. The clunky strains of "Chopsticks" rang through the apartment, followed by King's shouts of encouragement: "Swing it, Duke! Make me realize it, baby!"

As more people arrived, the noise swelled with introductions and conversation. It took several minutes before Joe remembered to check on Elsie, who had found a place on the small sofa near the door. There was only one lamp in the room, but it illuminated her angry expression like a spotlight. Joe sighed and sauntered over to her. Although everyone else seemed to be having a good time, Elsie resembled a ceramic statue of some martyred saint. Shoving his hands into his pockets, he remained standing as he stared down at her. "You asked to come, Elsie."

"I know," she said stiffly. "I'm fine."

Joe suddenly felt the hair on the back of his neck dance on end and knew that Pearl was standing behind him. He turned to look at her and his lips automatically curled into a smile.

Even holding a baby, Pearl was effortlessly sexy. Smiling down at Elsie, she said, "Anything I can get'cha, sugah?"

That deep, sexy voice again. Joe shivered and felt his pulse pound.

"No, thank you," Elsie replied.

As Pearl tried to coax Elsie, the baby began to squirm restlessly. "Oh, Lord, this child's gettin' fussy—no nap today." Shay continued to whimper and then jerked her body to one side, causing Pearl to lunge forward to prevent a full-blown fall right into Elsie's lap. She leaned on her shoulder briefly before righting herself. "Oh, sugah! I'm sorry. You okay?"

Elsie's eyes widened as she stared at Pearl's left arm. "I'm fine," she murmured.

Pearl quickly pulled down the sleeves on her sweater, which had bunched up on her arms from the near-accident. With one more glance at Elsie, she turned to Joe. "I got some enchiladas in the oven and there's a pie on the kitchen table, uh, Joe—? Wasn't that your name?"

"Yeah, Joe. And thanks, Pearl. I'm as hungry as a bear! Hey, Elsie? I'll be in the kitchen."

As he followed her down the hall, he gazed at the photos hanging on the wall—Doc and Pearl cuddling in a smoky nightclub, then smiling with the children at an amusement park. He squeezed into the kitchen and Pearl served him a plate of hot food. It was a tiny kitchen, painted bright yellow, with a black and white tile floor and a few houseplants fighting for sunlight on the windowsill. Joe ate slowly, watching Pearl as she chatted with Doc and fixed his plate.

"Thanks, baby," Doc said, leaning close to her for a kiss.

As Joe's eyes zeroed in on the kiss, all other activity and sound in the room ceased. Or it seemed that way to him. A silent, slow-motion movie close-up: Doc's lips seeking the sweetest spot to touch. Pearl's head tilting in an offering of that luscious neck. Lips lingering just below her left ear, and then—contact. Her eyes closed, and Joe's heart pounded like a conga drum.

But then Oliver's voice broke the spell and the room was noisy again. "Hey, Pearl! You sure you ain't from Guadalajara, baby? These enchiladas are the most!"

"Thanks, sugah." She reached down to pull Shay out of harm's way as the kitchen became overcrowded. "Hey, look out for the little folks!

One'a you big oxes knocks my baby down—I will take you apart with my own boney little hands."

Doc grinned broadly, and Joe stared at him. He was sure he had never seen him smile that way before. He glanced down the hall at Elsie and felt hollow inside, but when he looked back at Doc and Pearl, his heart resumed its lascivious thumping. They seemed incapable of passing one another without a touch or a confidential look. And that kiss was *not* a "married" kiss. Joe suddenly thought of the couple he had seen in the shadows of that French Quarter doorway over a year before. He remembered feeling an odd blend of jealousy and sympathy for the lovers; they seemed to be squeezing a lifetime of lovemaking into the brief time they had together.

When Pearl left the kitchen, Joe snapped out of his reverie and walked over to Doc. "How come you never mentioned you were married?"

"A, you never asked, and B, it ain't none'a your goddamn business, Junior," he said with an amused grin. "You still ain't tired of hearin' me say that, huh?"

Joe laughed. "But she's a knockout! If she was mine, I'd shout it from the rooftops."

Doc's smile faded suddenly, and he answered in a somber voice that sounded like someone else's. "That woman doesn't belong to me, Junior."

Something told Joe to keep his mouth shut.

After a pause, Doc was himself again. "Hey, don't get any ideas now. We *are* married."

"I get it, man. Loud and clear. Guess I better go check on my *own* girl."

He had only taken a few steps from the kitchen when he spotted Elsie. She was now sharing the sofa with two black men—both drunk and very attentive. When he saw her terrified expression, he hurried back to the kitchen, pulled Doc into the doorway, and pointed down the hall at Elsie. Then he ducked back into the kitchen with Doc right behind him.

"Doris Day comes to Harlem," Doc laughed. "You better go rescue her, man."

"Do you know those guys?" Joe sputtered.

"Sure. The one layin' all the dialogue is Roy. Married with four kids. He's harmless."

Joe sat down and grinned as he offered Doc a chair. "Then let's not spoil Roy's fun."

A few minutes later a loud cheer went up from the front room for somebody named Manfred, and Joe stepped out to investigate. Apparently, Manfred was the guy taking bows for bringing his drum kit, which King was loudly helping him set up next to the piano. Joe laughed and then glanced over at Elsie. She had gotten rid of Roy and his friend, and was sitting alone. He could tell by her expression that she was steaming, so he sighed and headed her way.

"Get me out of here," she hissed as he approached her.

"Nothin' doin', baby. You wanted to come, so sit tight. It's gonna be a long night."

"But—I thought it would just be the band," she said. "I didn't know there'd be so many—"

"So many *what*?"

Elsie's lips pressed together in a tight line and she glared at him. "Of *them*! And I don't care if that makes you mad. That woman—Pearl—she has needle marks on her arm, Joe!"

"What? Stop lying! You didn't see anything like that."

"I *know* what I saw. I work in a hospital, Joe. I know needle marks when I see 'em."

Joe shot her a dirty look, then looked back at Pearl, who was kneeling on the floor, finishing the last snap on her little girl's pajama top and kissing her goodnight. He smiled at her and she smiled back—a maternal smile, but still sexy. *She can't be a junkie*, he thought. *Impossible.*

Once the children were in bed, Manfred kicked things off with an inventive piece played with his brushes. Pearl walked back in and laughed. "Brushes? On account'a *my* kids? Man, those two could sleep even if you were usin' jackhammers for sticks. Go on and swing, fellas."

Doc's smile seemed to draw her to his side, and she pressed herself neatly into his arms like an interlocking piece of a jigsaw puzzle. As the musicians played, Joe continued to steal glances at Doc and Pearl. They spoke in low whispers, laughing and touching, and seemed to generate a heat that Joe could feel from across the room. It was a subtle dance of sexual foreplay hidden in plain sight—her hand moving over Doc's chest as he nuzzled her hair and snapped his fingers to the music. Joe was lost— a helpless voyeur, unable to stop staring until he heard King call him.

"Hey, Junior! Come on and croon sump'm, man. Sing the kids a lullaby."

Joe laughed nervously. "Naw, man. I'm takin' the night off."

Doc nudged Pearl toward the piano. "Why don't you sing tonight, baby? Just this once."

She gave him a strange, sad look and shook her head. "I ain't sang in years, baby."

He stared into her eyes, and the room fell silent. "Come on. Sing for me. Like you used to."

Out of a long, still moment, she nodded and walked slowly to the piano. The piano player smiled at her and began to play a few chords. "How you doin', Pearl? Been a long time, huh?"

"Yeah, Larry. A long *rusty* time," she murmured. "Matter of fact, you gonna have to take it down a half-step, sugah. I don't think I can hit *any* of them notes you playin' anymore."

After a moment of searching, Larry found a comfortable niche for Pearl, and his freestyle playing began to take on the personality of "God Bless the Child."

Pearl took a seat on the piano bench, facing Doc. She closed her eyes and began to sing in a sultry, resonant voice. It was clear that she was no amateur.

What had Doc said about singing with feeling? *Break their hearts, man. Make 'em cry.*

When Pearl opened her eyes, her gaze was already on Doc, who was staring back at her. Joe tried to read the look, but couldn't. It was in their own private code.

Chapter 11

Joe's female following at the club was growing, which meant a sharp slip in the ranks for Elsie. Notes with phone numbers and suggestive postscripts found their way to the bandstand, and Joe made a game of matching the note to the girl. The first note had come from a blonde who sat at a corner table all night staring at him with dark bedroom eyes. Without even knowing her name, he took her home for a sexual marathon. Then there was that tall brunette—an artist of seduction—who always sat at the front table. No note needed. Slowly and repeatedly, she would cross and uncross those long, shapely legs that promised—and delivered—hours of delightful debauchery.

But tonight was Elsie's night off from the hospital, which meant that she would sit front and center, ruining all of Joe's better prospects. He managed to limit contact with her until the last set ended, but as he was about to slip out the side door with Oliver, he heard her calling him.

"Shit!" he whispered. "Where are you guys headed, man?"

"Oralé!" Oliver said, rolling his eyes. "Where do us broke, starving vatos always go at two in the morning? The cheap, all-night automat."

"Okay, look," Joe said. "Here she comes. Run interference for me, would you?"

Oliver groaned. "Aww, man! How?"

"Shit, I don't know. Introduce her to one of your friends or sump'm, man!"

"I ain't got no friends, man! I hate all you vatos!"

"Come on, man! I'll lam out the back door and hang out in the alley until she gives up and leaves. Then I'll meet you guys at the automat in a few minutes."

"Okay, okay," Oliver muttered. "I'll introduce her to the bartender. He looks lonely."

≈∞≈

By the time Joe finally walked into the automat and headed to the band's usual corner, Zig and Reet had left, and the table was littered with leftovers on small white plates. He sat down and helped himself to a partial slice of pumpkin pie. "You're through with this, ain'tcha, Doc?"

Doc shrugged and lit a cigarette. "Shit, I guess I am *now*. What took you so long, man?"

"Elsie," Joe said, with a pointed glare at Oliver. "*Somehow*, she caught me in the alley."

"What's jumpin', Junior?" Oliver laughed. "Hey, sorry, man, but to be *exactly* exact—the bartender didn't send her."

Joe groaned. "Great. You're a poet now?"

"The bartender didn't send her!" King laughed. "Sounds like a Sinatra groove to me."

"So how'd you shake her anyway?" Oliver asked.

Joe grabbed his stomach and let out a theatrical moan, then grinned. "Acting skill."

"Man, I'll never understand gringos. I could dig it if you ditched Elsie for that fine contraption in the tight red skirt who was sitting at that front corner table."

King let out a wolf whistle. "Chick had some dangerous equipment squeezed into that skirt! I had plans for her myself, but some cat in Wall Street threads got away with the goods."

Ignoring King, Oliver continued to press Joe. "But *you* pass up a sure lay with Elsie to hang out at the gotdamn automat with a bunch of ugly, drunk vatos like us? Hijolé!"

Joe grinned. "So, King, what's on for after-hours? It's only three."

"Chinatown!" King roared, slamming his empty coffee mug onto the table.

"Goddamn, man!" Doc snapped. "Think you can turn up your broadcast? I don't think the Chief of Police heard you. And we are *not* takin' Junior to no goddamn Chinatown."

"What's in Chinatown?" Joe asked.

Doc blew a smoke ring. "Nothin' to worry your pretty little head about, Junior."

"Well, I tell you vatos what I'm gonna do," Oliver announced through a yawn. "I'm takin' *my* pretty little head home and dropping it on my pillow. On nights like this it sure feels good to climb into bed with a warm woman, even if she *is* my wife."

"Aw, shit," King grumbled. "Nothin' as boring as one'a those upright, downright, forthright squares rushin' home to the warden."

"Cabron!" Oliver laughed, scooting his chair back. "You're just jealous 'cause you struck out again and I got my warm, suavé female who rolls over into my arms the minute I touch her."

"Shit!" Doc hooted. "Beatriz probably doesn't act any different than any wife would when her husband comes crawlin' home at three in the mornin'—E-V-I-L. In fact, you'll be lucky if your suavé female doesn't hit your pretty little head with a not-so-suavé skillet!"

"So I die a quick death and get some sleep. And anyway, ain't *your* warden got a skillet?"

"Pearl's—different."

"Aw, come on, Oliver," King complained. "You're not really gonna split?"

Oliver saluted them as he backed away from the table. "So long, you rotten vatos."

"Damn!" King said. "Cat gets married, all his cool evaporates."

Joe rolled his eyes. "Come on. How do you know he was any cooler when he was single?"

"Shit! A cat's always hipper before they clamp on the leg irons, man."

Without lighting a fresh one, Doc crushed his cigarette butt in the ashtray. A sure sign the night was over. "Come on, King. Let's put Junior on his train."

"Not me," King said. "I'm goin' to Chinatown! Kick that gong and keep my high, Sly."

"Would somebody tell me what the hell's in Chinatown?" Joe demanded.

Doc shrugged. "It's like Cab says, man. It's a place to kick the gong around, that's all."

Joe squinted at him. "Thanks. That really cleared it up for me."

"*Narcotics*, Junior," King said. "Illegal D-O-P-E! That clear enough for you?"

"Lay off the kid and blow," Doc said crossly. "I'll put his ass on the train."

King took a nip from his flask and headed for the door, grinning stupidly and singing an altered version of "Minnie the Moocher."

The instant Joe heard that familiar melody, he was smothered by thoughts of his brother and graduation night—Uncle Cyrus's drunken rendition of "Minnie the Moocher." He blinked, and the memory flashed in his mind like lightning—the isolated dirt road, that eerie full blue moon, and his blood-soaked shirt, wet and heavy against his cracked ribs. He let out a short, inadvertent gasp, and looked up, half-expecting to see his brother. But it was only Doc who was staring at him, and they were alone.

"You all right, Junior? You look sick or sump'm."

"Huh? No, man. It's just— Look, I know how to put my own ass on a train." He knew he sounded jittery, so he stopped talking.

Doc lit a fresh cigarette, calmly and deliberately. "Cool. But I want to talk to you first."

Joe looked away, but he could feel Doc's probing eyes on him. "About what?"

"Two things, actually. First, don't worry about King. He can handle himself. Just walk the other way when he gets into one of his Chinatown moods." Doc reached into his pocket and dropped some change onto the table. "Go get yourself a sandwich and a coffee for me, Junior."

Joe fished out the nickels from the change. "Look. What kind'a stuff is King doin'?" he whispered. "I mean, he can get reefer at the club—and besides, I thought he liked bourbon."

"All true. But see, Chinatown's got sump'm King most *particularly* likes."

"What?" Joe asked, his eyes widening.

"Lounge, man. He ain't skin poppin' or anything like that—" Doc stopped abruptly.

Elsie's words about Pearl's needle marks were bubbling up in Joe's mind, but he kept his mouth shut. He walked over to the rows of tiny glass doors and found the one marked "turkey on rye." Slipping the nickels into the slot, he reached in for the sandwich. Then he filled two cups with coffee from the urn and returned to the table. Doc was still staring into space.

"So, Doc… what the hell's Chinatown got that King most particularly likes?"

"Huh? Oh. He just goes to the opium dens sometimes. That's one of his highs—opium."

"Opium… Okay, I know you're gonna laugh at me, but—what's opium?"

"There's no reason you should know about opium. It's one of those narcotics King was talking about. You *smoke* it, Junior. In a gong. It's like a pipe, but they call it a gong. Kick the gong, pass the pipe. Dig? Anyway, he rarely goes to the dens anymore."

"Oh, okay. And I guess you're right. Chinatown ain't my kind'a place." He studied Doc's face as he stirred his coffee. "So, what about you? You been to those—dens with him? Or—"

"What're you drivin' at, Junior?"

The question was left hanging in the air, and Joe felt moisture beading on his forehead.

"I *said* what are you askin' me? You a goddamn G-man or sump'm?"

"Aww, never mind. Just forget it."

Doc narrowed his eyes at him. "I saw the way you were lookin' at my wife."

"What?"

"Look, I'm only gonna tell you this one more time." Leaning closer, Doc blew a mist of smoke directly into Joe's face and enunciated each word: "Don't get any ideas, boy."

"Aw, wait a minute, Doc. You got me all wrong. I was just—"

"Look, I know she's still a beautiful woman."

"What do you mean she's *still* a beautiful woman?"

"What do I *mean*? She's still beautiful. I meant what I said."

"But—but why *still*? She's not old or anything. And why did she quit singing?"

Joe wondered why he couldn't make himself shut-up.

"Man, who the hell are you all of a sudden? One'a Joe McCarthy's goons? Look, Junior. My *wife* is none'a your business. I do *not* hang out in Chinatown. And no, I am not now nor have I ever been a member of the goddamn Communist Party! That about cover it for you?"

"Aw, come on, Doc! I would *never* make a pass at your wife. I was watching both'a y'all—and bein' kind'a jealous of—you know, your—the way you are *together*."

Doc groaned and leaned back in his chair. "Damn. I forgot how naïve you are, Junior. You think everything's a goddamn Frank Sinatra musical in glorious Technicolor."

"Man, stop talkin' to me like I'm some dumb kid!"

"Okay, then answer my original question. What—are—you—drivin'—at, man?"

"All right, look… I wasn't gonna say anything but—" He saw Doc glaring at him. "Okay! Elsie told me—she saw marks on Pearl's arms. Needle marks."

Doc's expression took a slow turn from anger to surprise to pain. "Look," he finally said, "Pearl's a real good woman." As he silently scrutinized Joe, he slowly rubbed off the burning end of his cigarette with his bare fingertip, then dropped the dead butt in the ashtray. "Okay, boy.

What I'm gonna tell you now is strictly between us. And goddammit, I mean *strictly*."

Joe gazed at Doc's scorched fingertip and felt a strong urge to run away. The curiosity had been rattled out of him, but he didn't dare leave his seat.

Lighting a cigarette, Doc exhaled and stared into the smoke as if it were a vision of his past.

"Pearl..." He said her name in a low, sustained E-flat and then stopped, as if it hurt.

Finally: "See, Pearl was married to another cat before me—a musician I worked with name'a Melvin Fulsome. Her and Melvin were in this band together, and he hired me for the gig when their regular horn man quit. Damn. Ain't thought about Melvin in a long time. Cat blew a hot sax, man, but he was a mainlinin' dope fiend. And he's the one that got Pearl hooked."

Joe felt a shiver run down his back. *Stories, Junior. Jazz tells stories.* He could almost hear the melody that went with this one. It was slow and blue, and Doc was about to solo...

"She was a real classy blues singer," he said. "She couldn't read music or play any instruments, but she had instinct, man. Her phrasing reminded me of a horn, but the best part was the way all that feeling came risin' up out of her. Even before I got to know her I knew she'd been through some shit in her life just by the way she sang." He smiled. "That's what I was tellin' you before, Junior. About the difference between technique and feeling."

Joe nodded quietly.

"Anyway, she already had my attention with her singing, and she was pretty easy on the eyes too. Maaan, you should'a seen her on that stage. She looked like one'a those magazine cover models, you know? I mean, she didn't have much money or anything. Shit, none of us did. But she had this one black dress and a pair of silk stockings that she took good care of, and a pair of black high heels that looked so good on those long legs. She had to wash out her dress and stockings every night 'cause that's all she had to wear onstage." He took a pull from the cigarette and chuckled as he exhaled the smoke. "You know, Junior, it's funny how you're attracted to a woman for sump'm like legs and a pretty face. That might be the thing that pulls you to her in the beginning, but it's a completely different thing that makes you want to spend your whole life with her. But anyway... After a while, I couldn't help noticin' how bad Melvin was treatin' her. He was a real jealous hot-head, and that was usually the problem, but sometimes I use'ta wonder if it was more than cats makin' passes at her. I think he was jealous of how good she was comin' along as a singer. And man, she was so young. Only about eighteen—and already usin'."

"But—well, how'd you end up—I mean, how'd they split up?"

Doc took one last pull from his cigarette, then used it to light a fresh one. "*That* was a real bad scene, Junior. She missed a few gigs, and I got worried. Hell, I was prob'ly already in love with her by that time—just hadn't admitted it yet, I guess. Anyway, I stopped by the apartment one night to drop off some charts, but I was really checkin' on her. So here comes Pearl openin' the door with a shiner 'bout the size'a Melvin's fist, and I had a hard time keepin' my cool. But I did. I didn't even act like I noticed her eye, just asked where was Melvin. So she told me, I said goodnight, and then I went to kill him."

"So wait—is *that* what you meant by a real bad scene? You *killed* him?"

"Naw, Junior. Fucked him up pretty good, though. And of course, he had to retaliate, so there were some main events in the alley behind the club—even a little blade-play one time. And this shit went on for a few weeks—you know, durin' breaks and after the set—that kind'a thing."

"You mean you still played in the band together?"

"Hell, man, business is business. We both needed the bread even if the music had to suffer. Clearly, we weren't swingin' any kind of groove while all this was goin' on."

"So what happened? They finally get divorced or what?"

"No. Melvin didn't show up at the club one night. So now it's no singer, no sax. Then at the end of the last set, we got word that Melvin had O.D.'d—overdosed and deceased."

"Wow. So—how'd Pearl take it?"

"Well, by this time, she was gettin' tired'a bein' Melvin's punchin' bag. But she's the one who found him, and that scared the hell out of her. She'd run away from him after a fight and went home to her Mama for a few days. Then, I don't know whether she went back to him 'cause she was missin' his sorry ass or 'cause she needed to fix up, but she went back. And there he was layin' on the floor—needle hangin' out his arm and rigor mortis—the typical ugly, sordid scene, man. But one good thing came out of it. It scared her off the needle and straight to me."

"Just like that?"

"No, man! Gettin' off junk is *never* just like that!"

Joe shifted in his chair. "Listen, can I ask you sump'm?"

Doc grimaced. "Shit. Can I stop you?"

"Did you ever try it? The—the needle?"

"Rude question, but I'll answer it. Yeah, I tried it. Long time before I met Pearl."

"What was it like?"

"Another rude question, but it's the same thing I wanted to know when I was young, so I'll tell you what was told to me. I asked an expert—and I am *not* givin' you his name, in case that was your *next* rude question. All he told me was how it liberated his playing and how heavenly it felt. And then he told me he'd beat my ass if he ever caught me tryin' it—talkin' out'a both sides of his mouth. So, naturally, that only made me want to try it more. So I did. But not for long."

Joe scooted his chair closer to the table. "And was it heavenly, like he said?"

Doc's smile was tinged with sarcasm. "Let's see... Okay, imagine some woman comes walkin' into the club one night. She's drop-dead gorgeous and stacked—in an illicit kind'a way. And for some misguided reason, she sizes up the band and decides you're her dream man. So she drives you to a moonlit beach, strips off all her clothes, drops to her knees, and goes to work on you, beggin' for all the sex you can give her. Then, next thing you know, the waves are crashin' all around you, she's screamin' your name, and just when you hit that explosive climax—" Doc pounded the table for emphasis. "Pow! She pulls you into the water and drowns your silly ass."

"Come on, man," Joe groaned. "That's not heavenly—and it sure the hell ain't funny."

"Oh, it's heavenly, all right. The drowning part doesn't happen till you try to quit. So now you can see why so many folks ride that needle all the way to the graveyard."

"Well, then how'd *you* quit, wise guy?"

"I *had* to, man. All I'd ever heard was how junk was supposed to give you some magic jolt—take your playing to some new heights. So I'd hit that needle right before I went onstage, and then go to revolutionizing the whole art form. At least I thought I was. Then one night I was playing 'Body and Soul'—I'll never forget it. I was cool with the melody, but when I went for my solo it felt like—like I'd just fallen into some dark vacuum. Nothin' I was doin' satisfied me. Like I'd already played everything and there was nothin' new to reach for. Hell, for all I know, I was playin' some brilliant shit that night, but I just couldn't *feel* it. It was like—death, man. I know that sounds crazy, but it's the only way I can explain it. So I stopped—cold kicked—and that's the worst kind'a sick you ever want to be, Junior. I never touched junk again."

"But what about Pearl?"

"After Melvin died, I talked her into stayin' with me so I could take care of her."

"And she quit?"

"It was hell for a long time, but she finally kicked. For nine whole years, man."

"Well, shit! Why in the world would she start up again?"

"My fault," Doc said softly. "My fault…"

"You?"

"Yeah, me. Things were real cool after we got married. We got a gig with this band—lot'a one-nighters, but at least we were together. Bouncin' around on that bus—too hot in the summer, too cold in the winter, eatin' lousy food at crummy roadside joints. But she never complained. She'd fall asleep with her head on my shoulder and a smile on her face every night. We finally lucked up and settled down with a local house band, and she sang till she got pregnant with Edward. Man, that made her happy. She told me she was ready to quit singing and have babies."

Joe gazed at him, waiting for the rest of the story. And for the first time he saw a crack in the armor—a searing pain that rarely showed in those enigmatic black eyes.

Doc murmured a seemingly incongruous word—Hartford—followed by a heavy sigh.

"After we had Shay, I hooked up with a real swingin' band. We were just gettin' hip to bebop, and I just lost my mind—it was so limitless. Then the demand skyrocketed so we hit the road for a couple'a months of one-nighters. Just before headin' back to New York, we were stayin' in this little dump outside Hartford, Connecticut. It happened to be my birthday, and I took this local hot-tail back to my room. Not something I normally did, but I was just drunk enough to think it was a good idea. So just as things start heatin' up, somebody knocks on my door. I figured it was one of the fellas, but they just kept knocking. So I went to the door to run 'em off, and there's Pearl, smilin' at me and holdin' a goddamn birthday cake all wrapped up in wax paper. Tellin' me she'd left the kids with our neighbor and caught a bus to Hartford to surprise me. She—wanted to ride back with me on the bus with the band… like the old days."

"Shit, man! What did you do?"

"What the hell *could* I do, man? I'm standin' there in my damn draw's, guilty as shit! So I'm tryin' to clear the liquor out'a my head and think up a story, but before I can put two words together, Pearl's in the room staring at this chick stretched out in the bed—all stripped down, just waitin' for the birthday boy. Next thing I know, Pearl pitches that birthday cake across the room like she's goddamn Satchell Paige! And I ain't gotta tell you who she was aimin' at. Man, I never saw a woman go from naked to fully clothed so fast in my natural life!"

"So—how was Pearl's aim?" Joe said, trying not to laugh.

Doc chuckled softly. "Bull's-eye. Smack upside the head. So now I'm playin' referee, tryin' to keep Pearl from committin' outright murder, and the chick's over there cussin' and tryin' to get dressed with frosting all on the side of her face and in her hair and— That part *was* funny, but believe me, it sure wasn't funny when Pearl slammed the door behind that girl and it was just me and her left in the room. Man, Junior, I never sobered up so fast in my life. Pearl crumpled down on that goddamn floor and cried like somebody'd just cut her heart out."

"Aww, damn… So that's what made her go back to the needle."

"Well, that was a big part of it, yeah. But after we got back home and we were tryin' to work things out—with me beggin' an' shit—her Mama died. Unexpected. Just dropped dead one day hangin' up a line'a laundry."

Joe shook his head silently.

"Oh, but that was just the beginning, Junior. Pearl had a brother— Ronnie, and they were real close." He gave Joe a long probing look. "He was a nice cat—and he was a homosexual."

Joe showed his teeth in a grimace.

"I see you have a problem with homosexuals, Junior."

"Hell, yeah! I got no use for 'em, if you know what I mean."

"Junior, you have no idea how many homosexuals you get along just *fine* with. You talk to 'em every day, man. Musicians, friends, relatives of the band members— As a matter of fact, a lot of your favorite records were cut by those cats who you claim to have no use for."

"Come on, man. That's a lie. You make it sound like there's millions of 'em."

The corners of Doc's mouth twitched with amusement. "Never mind. Guess Ronnie was the only one. Anyway, unlike *you*, Junior, I wasn't scared shitless of the big, bad boogie-man who happened to be my wife's baby brother. I actually got along great with him. Real quiet cat—but once I got him talkin' he turned out to be pretty cool, in a philosophical sort of way. But he fell apart when their Mama died. He kept callin' the house all hours of the night, pretty hysterical, and Pearl was barely holdin' herself together as it was. Guess he was too, but all I was thinkin' about was Pearl and how those calls upset her. I was pretty rough on him about that—told him to stop callin' and we'd see him at the funeral… So, of course, that was the night—" Doc fell silent again and rubbed the bridge of his nose.

"That was the night that—what? What happened?"

"He checked out, man… Razor blades with a whiskey chaser."

Joe leaned back hard in his chair. "What?"

"He hit his limit, man. His Mama was gone and—if only I would've let him talk to Pearl that night … Look, it's obvious that you don't know much about that kind'a life—Ronnie's, I mean. A Negro *and* a homosexual? Shit, that meant two strikes against him. He was probably the loneliest person I ever met. I didn't know him very long, but I have some real clear memories of him, for some reason..."

Doc smiled. "I remember this one time—it was when Edward was born and I'd just brought him and Pearl home from the hospital. Ronnie and Alva came by—that was Pearl's mother's name—Alva. Anyway, they came by to see the baby, so I threw some supper together for everybody. After we ate, Pearl and the baby fell asleep and Alva went home, but me and Ronnie still wanted to celebrate. And Ronnie liked wine. We were both broke as the ten commandments, which wasn't unusual, but we managed to put enough chump change together to actually have a choice. We could buy one bottle of some passable table wine, or three bottles of the cheap stuff. So naturally, quantity beat the hell out'a quality, and we stayed up all night, talkin' and gettin' blasted on Thunderbird." He sighed deeply. "I guess that night stands out in my memory 'cause of sump'm he said that really hit a nerve—especially a couple'a years later when he died like he did. And I won't forget it as long as I live." Doc's pensive expression hardened into a penetrating stare. "He asked me—if I ever felt like a shadow."

"A shadow? What the hell's that supposed to mean?"

"He told me that his whole life he felt like he was nothin' but a shadow. Maybe that's why I never forgot it. It's the kind'a thing that can keep you up at night, Junior. Thinking and thinking. About folks you never gave much thought to before. All those folks who live like shadows."

Doc stopped talking again, and Joe sighed. He had an annoying way of saying something mysterious, and then shutting down into a sudden rude silence. Like blowing a single hard note on a screech horn and then packing up and walking off the stage.

Finally: "You ever been to a double funeral, Junior?"

"No."

"Lucky you," Doc said, mildly sarcastic. "Anyway, Pearl got through it somehow. Or it seemed like she did at the time. But the next night, I knew she needed rest so I took the kids to our neighbor Rose's, and then I had a gig to get to across town. When I got back, she was gone."

"Aww, shit. So that's when—"

"She was gone three days. And the minute she got back, I knew. I could see it all over her face. I'd just broke her heart layin' up with some tramp, she loses her Mama, and then her baby brother eats up a pack of goddamn razor blades? Shit, man. Too many nails in the cross."

"Well, why can't she quit again, like the first time?"

"Goddamn, Junior, hit the pedal. It damn near killed her *that* time."

"But there must be some kind'a way. I mean, *you* quit. Can't she try that—cold kick thing?"

"It's a different grade, Junior. Real addictive, so when she tries to quit she just gets—so sick… off a few days, then back on. Once I went and got the shit for her myself 'cause I thought she was gonna die. But then—she needs more. Always more." He frowned at Joe. "Look, she *does* take care of the kids. And when she can't, she makes sure I'm with 'em, or Rose."

Doc's eyes glazed over again. Then out of long silence, he looked up suddenly. "I know what you're thinkin', Junior. But we're *all* livin' on borrowed time, not just her. Ask not for whom the bell tolls, man. 'Cause it tolls for all of us. Even you."

Joe stared at him quietly, and finally murmured, "Sorry I asked about—Pearl."

"It's okay. Made me think a little. Made me wonder what possessed me to risk losin' everything over some B-girl whose name I can't even remember. Thank God I didn't lose Pearl."

"Yeah, okay."

"And Junior? I don't have to tell you I don't like bein' in Winchell's column, right?"

"Winchell? You mean you've been in Walter Winchell's column?"

Doc winced. "Come on, boy! Winchell wouldn't know my ass from a pothole! Just don't broadcast my business, that's all I'm saying."

"Oh, right. I won't say anything."

"So, I guess you're wonderin' why I told you all that, huh? And that brings me back to my original subject, which would be *you*, Junior."

Joe blinked, and then shifted his gaze to the clean-up woman's dustpan.

"And there it is again. You *cannot* look me in the eyes whenever we start talkin' about *you*. I knew what it was till you got me all off-track, eyeballin' my wife."

Joe felt his heart thumping—panic. Something was off, out of place. Then it hit him. Doc had told that long story without smoking. He hadn't touched that last cigarette since lighting it. Joe glanced quickly at the ashtray, and saw the unsmoked remains, collapsed in a long, burnt ash.

Doc leaned forward and smiled, ever so slightly. "You aren't white. Are you."

It was a statement, not a question. They stared at each other in a long, silent showdown that had been a long time coming. Doc's story was a labyrinth that ended in a trap, and Joe had walked right into it.

"You suck me in with that story and then ask me sump'm like *that*?"

"Aww, lounge, Junior," Doc said calmly as he lit a fresh cigarette. "First of all, every word of that story was true. I just wanted to point out that confession is good for the soul."

Doc's amused expression made Joe want to belt him. "I got nothin' to confess," he hissed. "And that was a shitty thing to say."

"Boy, would you calm down? Look. I ain't the type'a cat to blow the whistle on anybody's groove. We all do what we gotta do to survive."

"Survive *what?*"

"I am *not* a threat to you, Junior, so lounge. No white cat in the world is gonna spot you. You look Caucasian, except a little shade in your facial features—the eyes and nose—"

"What the hell are you talkin' about? What's wrong with my eyes and nose?"

"*Wrong?* I didn't say anything was *wrong* with your eyes or your nose, Junior. But see, that's exactly the kind'a remark that colored folks pick up on and white folks don't. Of course, there's always the remote possibility that I could be wrong."

"You *are* wrong."

Doc taunted him with a laugh. "Come on, Junior. Tell the truth and shame the devil."

"I don't even know what you're talking about."

Then Doc's smile disappeared. "Stop it, boy," he said sharply. "I could tell by the look on your face when you got off the train in Harlem, man. All us wall-to-wall niggas made you sweat. Now Elsie—she had that regular ol' scared-shitless-please-God-don't-let-'em-kill-me look that every Caucasian with the exception of King gets whenever they're surrounded by Negroes. But you didn't look scared—just a little nervous. And you were *so* fascinated by it all. Like some part'a you was comin' home. Oh, and then that Robert Johnson slip was a dead giveaway, man."

"What the hell are you talkin' about now?"

"'Crossroads.' You told me your Daddy loved that song that night when we were at King's."

"You don't know what I said. You and King were high as two kites on all that reefer."

"I wasn't as high as you thought I was, Junior. I remember *exactly* what you said."

"So *what* if my Daddy liked that song? He—he used to go to this place—"

"What place? A juke joint?"

"If you'd let me finish—I'm *tryin'* to tell you—"

"You're *tryin'* to tell me that your *white* Daddy dug some gutbucket nigga blues and hung out in juke joints. And I'm tellin' *you* there's sump'm *real* crooked about that line."

"No! There's sump'm real crooked about *this*. You got a lotta goddamn nerve—"

Doc remained cool. "But you wrong me, Junior! I'm just an observer. You got the talk right and you croon just like Crosby." He grinned impishly. "Oops. Better make that Sinatra."

"*Why* are you telling me all this? You planning on telling everybody this shit?"

"As usual, you're missin' the point. Look, I've lived a lot longer than you, and I've only known about three, four cats in my life. Oh, they might have different names and come from different towns. Sometimes they're white and sometimes they're colored. *Sometimes*, they're even shadows. But they're all the same cats… Oh, yeah, I've seen you before, Junior. Peolas just like you, with bright faces and curly, pretty-boy hair, who just can't wait to jump across that color line. And don't act like you don't know what a peola is, man. Don't insult me like that."

"I *don't* know! I don't know about *any* of this shit you're talking about!"

"Passing, Junior. I'm talkin' about *you* passing."

Joe stood up, but Doc caught his arm. "Sit down, boy," he hissed. "This is for your own good, and nobody's gonna pull your coat to this but me. You're tryin' the oldest trick in the goddamn book and you ain't even good at it! I bet you don't even know *why* it's called passing."

Joe sat back down. "Passing under the radar. Passing for white! Which I'm *not* doing!"

"Wrong!" Doc shouted, then lowered his voice when the night manager looked over with an alarmed expression. "You *can't* be that simple, boy. It *ain't* just passin' for white under some goddamn imaginary radar! It's passing *away*. Junior… You're *dying*, man."

When Joe made a move to stand up again, Doc sprang to his feet and pushed him back into the chair. "Sit'cho ass down! 'Cause you ain't goin' nowhere till I finish schoolin' you. Now—all that passin' under the radar shit you heard? That's true, for folks who don't look any deeper. But I've seen it, Junior, and I look *real* deep. I know what it does to a mother who can't face the ugly truth—that her child could just leave her to worry herself to the grave. *That's* why it's passing in the sense of dying. They let their families give 'em up for dead; some even had funerals. They had to *die* just so they could be white. At least to their families they were dead. And there they were—livin' it up in white man's heaven. But they were dead, all right."

Joe let out a harsh, frustrated sigh. "Doc, man, you got this all wrong!"

"No, Junior. I got this all *right*. 'Cause I know a shadow when I see one. You told me you had no family." Doc's eyes narrowed into a skeptical leer. "Mama and Daddy both dead, right?"

"That's right. That's what I told you because it's true."

Doc shook his head slowly. "Wrong again. It ain't *them* that's dead, Junior. It's *you*."

Doc's words echoed in the quiet of the empty automat, and Joe felt suffocated. He made a desperate grab for his cup and took a gulp of cold coffee. "Sermon over?"

Doc stared at him for a long time, then chuckled softly. "Okay, man. Sermon's over."

"You're wrong about me, Doc. I don't know how to convince you—"

"Lounge, man. It's not my story to tell, just like my story isn't yours to tell. So it looks like we've got each other in check." He smiled. "Besides, you got this all wrong, man. All I was doin' was tellin' you a story about these three, four cats I knew, that's all. So… we cool?"

When Joe didn't answer, Doc extended his hand. "Name's Doc Calhoun, Junior—not *God*. I'm not judgin' you." He settled back and flashed that go-to-hell grin Joe had seen so many times, then mugged an Amos 'n' Andy affectation: "'Cause eb'body know Gawd's some *white* folks. Now ain't that right?"

Chapter 12

Joe didn't fall asleep until nearly noon the next day, and woke about six hours later to the sound of loud knocking on his door. "Yeah? Who'zat?" he called.

"Hope your drapes are pressed, Junior," King's voice shouted. "'Cause we got a 24-hour pass from the plantation, in case you forgot, and we're blastin' off to Dempsey's for some hots. Get threaded, man! Me and Doc'll be downstairs."

≈∞≈

Jack Dempsey's Restaurant wasn't very crowded when they got there, so they were immediately seated at a booth near the front window. As a waitress took their order, Joe stared out the window at the traffic on Broadway, then at the interior of the restaurant. On the other side of the polished brass rails was a long oval-shaped bar, and behind it was a huge mural of the Dempsey-Willard championship fight. King and Doc were discussing a medley that Zig was working on, and Joe was only halfway listening. Suddenly, he felt a foot nudging his leg under the table.

"Hey, Junior," King whispered. "He ain't here, man."

"Who?"

"Dempsey."

"But they said—" Joe grimaced, knowing that he'd fallen into a trap.

"I knew it!" King shouted, slapping the table. "Goddamn, Doc, the farmboy's starstruck! He's on the lay for Dempsey so he can tell the folks back home he met the champ!"

The waitress arrived to serve the food, and King snickered under his breath until she walked away. Doc thanked her and rolled his eyes at King. "Whadayou? Twelve?"

King continued to razz Joe. "G-golly, Mr. Dempsey! Could I g-get your autograph, sir?"

Doc smiled at Joe. "He usually gets here around eight for the supper crowd, Junior. Hey! Maybe he'll bring Sinatra, and you can go hob-nob with the royalty. We'll wait."

Joe cut his eyes at Doc. "Ha-ha. You two ought'a be on the radio with that comedy act."

"Hey, King," Doc said as he reached for the pepper shaker, "that combination you been workin' on really went over cool the other night, man. Good dynamics and high hat work."

"Here we go," King said. "I feel a *but* coming on."

Doc's sly grin made him look like a cat about to pounce on an unsuspecting mouse. "*But*—if you could *ever* learn to keep time, it'd be a definite plus."

King threw a few french fries at Doc, making sure that Joe got caught in the crossfire.

"Man, why don't you two murder each other and leave me out of it!" Joe snapped.

"Shut-up, Junior," Doc said. "Nobody's talkin' to you, so just lounge. Hey, King."

"What?"

"Somebody was askin' 'bout'cha Mama yesterday, man."

"Aww, shit. Lemme guess. Willie-the-pimp from up in your neck'a the jungle, right, Doc?"

"Now is that any way to talk about'cha sweet little ol' Mama?"

King wouldn't bite. "I hope you told Willie that Mama's got some new representation. Cat lets her keep a bigger percentage and everything, man."

Doc shook his head solemnly. "Nope. It wasn't Willie, man. I'm tellin' you."

"Okay, man. I give. Who the hell was it?"

"The Atlantic Fleet."

"Oh, them," King said with a yawn. "Sure they weren't lookin' for *your* mother, Doc? 'Cause my mother is strictly U.S. Marine Corp. all the way, man."

"Nah. The Marines have *standards*, man. And your Mama's so damn ugly—"

"*My* Mama? Hey, let's see a picture of *your* Mama, wise guy!"

"Come on, man!" Joe groaned. "I didn't come here to listen to y'all's *Mama* dozens."

"Y'all?" King chortled. "Did you just hear Junior say *y'all*, Doc?"

"Yeah. And I heard him say *dozens* too. What'chu know about the dozens, *y'all*?"

Joe sighed, but didn't look at Doc.

"Oh, well," King said. "What did we expect? Junior's from down south, where the Ku's and the Kluxes and the antelope play. Down home, all the Confederates say *y'all*. Right, Junior?"

"Yeah, Shakespeare," Joe said sarcastically. "Y'all. I believe you Yankee New Yawkahs have a woid for it too. Yuz."

King sat up straight, feigning outrage. "Ya mean *yous*? So what's wrong with yous? You, singular, plus you, another singular, equals the plural. So ya add an 's' and ya got 'yous.' Or, as they say da Bronx— *yuz*." He slapped his hand on the table. "And that, my friends, is the King's English, taught in every grammar school in every borough in the great state of Nooo Yawk!"

Doc grunted in playful contempt. "Vaudeville is now officially dead. Let's go hit the lab."

"Minton's again?" Joe complained. "We always go to Minton's."

King laughed. "Always? You've been there twice, Junior, to be *exactly* exact, so quit bellyaching. But okay. So it's no to Minton's. How 'bout the Deuces?"

"Nope."

"Okay, Junior," Doc said. "The evening is young. You pick the joint. Where to?"

Joe held up Doc's horn case, which had been resting next to him in the booth. "You had it planned all the time! That's why you brought your horn! Y'all know you've been dying for the place to open. Excuse me. Make that *yuz* know. And yuz foither know that the grand opening is tonight. So what are we waiting for?"

King grinned at Doc. "To Boidland, then, Doctor Calhoun?"

Doc groaned as he stood up. "Only if both'a yuz walk ten paces behind me—'cause I don't want yuz bums sperlin' my goddamn entrance."

≈∞≈

The entire region surrounding the new club was chaotic. The bottleneck of cars and taxis began at The Onyx Club, then stretched around the corner to Broadway and continued past the front entrance of Birdland. It was instantly apparent that the nightclub dedicated to Charlie Parker was the new bebop capital of the world, and legendary 52nd Street now stood in its shadow.

Joe stepped out of the cab into the street, which was still wet from a light rain. He smiled down at the blurred reflection of multicolored neon lights, and listened to the crazy mix of music and automobile horns echoing up and down the block. Looking up, he spotted the black awning with the word "Birdland" written in white block letters. Someone inside was blowing a melodic saxophone solo, which was being accented nicely by a clean, innovative drummer.

"Philly Joe, man," King said, bouncing on his heels. "I bet'cha a fin."

"Naw, man," Doc said. "That's not Philly Joe. It's Max. And pay the driver, man."

King dug into his pocket for the fare and yelled, "Max? What're you smokin' anyway? Who do you say it is, Junior? Philly Joe, right?"

"Eleanor Roosevelt, for all I care. Let's just get in there before there's no room left."

"Ugh," King yelped, "corn-belt humor! No more Jack Benny for you, Baby Snooks."

When they stepped inside, a uniformed doorman directed them to a narrow stairway leading down to the first of two lower levels. Joe spotted a sign hanging above his head, which he read aloud: "Welcome to the jazz corner of the world. Through these doors pass the most!"

King peered into the room and let out a whistle. "Low lights, wavy broads, and musical Nirvana!" He grabbed Joe by the shoulders. "Give it to me straight, man! They dropped the A-bomb on our cab and we're dead, right? 'Cause this has *got* to be heaven, baby!"

"Shit," Doc said. "Third-rate bum like you in *heaven*? Man, find me the door marked *hell*."

As they threaded their way slowly through the press of bodies, Joe could feel the floor pulsating with rhythm. He stretched up to catch a glimpse of the stage. Through the thick haze of cigarette smoke, he saw Lester Young soloing on his tenor sax.

King pointed at the stage. "Who's that on drums behind Prez? Philly Joe! So cross my palm with that fin, wise guy... Hey, anybody seen Bird? This is all for him, right?"

Doc snorted as he handed King the five. "Bird? Man, he'll be late for his own funeral. He'll probably roll in here around midnight—*after* he makes that stop. Come on, man. This way."

"Hey," King said, "you don't think they snatched his cabaret card, do you? I heard—"

Doc stopped him with a pointed look. "Pretty loud broadcast, Mr. Murrow."

King shrugged apologetically, then reached into his pocket for his flask.

"But why?" Joe whispered. "Why would they take his cabaret card?"

Doc lit a cigarette. "They've been watchin' him," he said softly. "Bird's got that jones."

"What jones?"

"That jones you and I were talkin' about last night." Doc exhaled a smoke-filled sigh, and stared through the crowd of patrons as if they weren't there. "Bird's like all them others," he finally said. "Tryin' to find God in that needle." Then he flashed that enigmatic smile—like a man who knew too much. "Come on, man. Let's find us a piece'a wall to lean on."

He led the way through the packed room to a good vantage point near the stage, then they pressed themselves close to the wall as a steady stream of patrons moved past.

"Ray Brown," King said, nodding in the direction of the entrance. "Right there."

Doc nodded and began pointing out to Joe several other known musicians, who all appeared anxious for a turn to sit in. Billy Strayhorn was with his regular Minton's group, staring intently at every move of Bud Powell's hands over the piano, and some unidentified vibes player was setting up on a precarious corner of the stage. Joe coughed and cleared his throat, irritated by the cigarette smoke. Then he picked up the scent of flowers hovering around the head of a girl trying to pass him. A waitress nearly dropped a tray of drinks on the girl, and she twisted her body to avoid a collision. Joe grabbed her waist to steady her and for a moment her body pressed tightly against him. When he got a good look at her face, he nearly lost his breath. She was stunning, with the most unusual eyes he had ever seen. They were blue, but not the penetrating cobalt blue of Sinatra's eyes; this girl's eyes were a pale ice-blue, like the clear water of a pristine lake, and framed by thick, black eyelashes. All her features were dark, even though her skin was alabaster white. Her thick, shoulder-length hair was so black it gleamed blue in the dim light, and her lips were the deep red of roses. Two black eyebrows arched in surprise and she blinked at him, apparently nervous. As she pulled away, Joe tried to disarm her with a smile. "Are you okay?"

She nodded, then smiled and disappeared into the crowd. Joe craned his neck and spotted her clinging to the arm of a white-haired man who looked at least seventy. He felt a nudge, and saw Doc grinning at him. "Okay, okay," Joe laughed. "So maybe he's her grandfather."

"Sure, Junior," Doc laughed. "Her sugar-daddy grandfather. Man, she's out'a your league."

"Yeah, who am I kidding?" Joe laughed. "She looks like Liz Taylor, for chrissakes!"

Just then, a roar went up from the entrance and Joe looked over to investigate. In an attempt to see over the other curious patrons, he climbed up onto a recently vacated chair.

King laughed. "Like a kid at Yankee Stadium. So who the hell is it, Junior? Jack Dempsey?"

"Very funny. Anyway, I'm tryin' to see—there's somebody with a big crowd around him and—Holy shit!" Joe squealed. "It's Dizzy Gillespie, man! And he's with Charlie Parker!"

Doc stretched up to peer at the entrance. "Bird's *early*?"

"Hey!" Joe yelled. "There's Red Rodney too!"

"Who else?" King asked.

"Oh, God," Joe murmured.

Doc groaned. "Never mind, man. My chances of sittin' in are already a million to one."

Joe stared dumbly at the group coming in behind Dizzy and Bird. "It—it's him! Sinatra!"

King laughed. "Aww, shit! Don't swoon yourself off that chair, man."

"Yeah, yeah," Joe muttered, still staring at Sinatra's entourage. "Hey, wait a minute! Man, you'll never believe who he's with! I think it's—"

"His son Jesus?" Doc said.

King held his drink high in the air. "Hot diggity dog! Jack Dempsey at last!"

Joe shot him a dirty look. "Ya know what? I'm saving up all my money 'cause if I ever *do* meet Dempsey, I'm gonna pay him to black both your eyes, ya wise sonofabitch."

"Yeah, yeah. I'm trembling all over. So who the hell is it, Junior?"

"Ava Gardner." Joe smiled triumphantly and placed his hand to his ear. "Oh, so what is that? Silence? I finally shut up that big mouth?"

Shoving Joe off the chair, King climbed up and gawked unashamedly at Ava Gardner. She had just tilted her head back to laugh at something Sinatra was saying, and King's jaw dropped as he stared at every detail: the curve of her long neck; that sassy smile of red lips and perfect white teeth; the defiant dimpled chin. She was wearing a strapless, form-fitting cocktail dress the color of emeralds, which set off her green eyes, and her long hair was dancing like black bohemian silk on her bare shoulders.

King carefully stepped off the chair, stunned into near-sobriety. "Okay," he said quietly. "When the hell did Frank graduate from children in bobby-socks to sex goddesses?" After a pause, he was himself again and punched Joe's shoulder. "Singers! You goddamn singers *always* get the prime-cut women!"

Doc winced. "Prime-cut? Man, no wonder you always strike out with women. No romance skills... Hey, wait. Look over there. That's the Mastin trio! Wait'll you see this kid, Junior—"

"I did see him! That's Sammy Davis. He opened for Sinatra at the Capitol. He was great!"

Sinatra led his entourage slowly through the room, smiling and chatting with several people as two waiters carried another table over near the stage for them. Joe cleared a path with his arms as Sinatra passed, then impulsively stuck out his hand.

Frank reached around Ava's waist to shake Joe's hand. "Hey, pal. Good to see you."

Joe's smile faded. It was obvious that Sinatra didn't remember him. But suddenly, the polite smile changed to a grin of recognition. "Doc! You sonofabitch! How the hell are you?"

Doc shook Sinatra's hand. "Can't complain." Jerking his chin in Ava's direction, he added, "I see life's treating you nicely."

Sinatra laughed and shrugged as his group began nudging him away. "Take it easy, Doc!"

Joe stared dumbly at Doc as Sinatra disappeared into the crowd. "You *know* Sinatra?"

"Aw, hell, I filled in for his horn player a couple'a times on some local gigs, that's all."

"Well, how come you never mentioned it?"

"I was afraid you'd want me to ask him for a lock of his hair to put under your pillow, man."

Joe scowled. "He didn't even remember me. I told you I met him that time."

"Junior. He meets millions of people. I'm amazed he remembered *me*, and I played some brilliant shit makin' him sound good. And pipe down, would'ja? Bird and Diz are goin' on."

The next two hours surpassed anything Joe had imagined as a dreamy-eyed teenager in Mississippi. The Birdland stage pulsed with musical brilliance as the all-stars of modern jazz made it look easy: Charlie Parker, Bud Powell, Dizzy Gillespie, Philly Joe Jones, Ray Brown, and dozens more with the good fortune to sit in with them. When the great Gillespie stepped aside to allow Bird's protégé to sit in, a hush fell over the room. The reed-thin black man in the gray Brooks Brothers suit wore his hair in a wavy conk, and his expression was an odd mix of nervousness and arrogance. He stood there quietly, his horn at his side, glowering at the audience until Charlie Parker finished his simple introduction: "Ladies and gentlemen—Miles Davis."

The smattering of applause stopped when a raw, sustained note emanated from Davis's muted horn. After an unusual improvised intro, he blew a steamy rendition of "Summertime" and ended it on the same sustained note. The standing ovation and Doc's nod of approval told Joe to keep his eye on the newcomer. Miles Davis had the makings of a future all-star.

It was nearly dawn when Joe, King, and Doc shuffled out with the other first-nighters. Doc chuckled as the door shut behind him. "Well, damn! Here's your hat, what's your hurry?"

Although King was thoroughly drunk, he pulled out his flask and tapped the last few drops of bourbon into his mouth. "Bum's rush, Doc. Story of my life." He draped his arm around Joe's neck as they staggered down the sidewalk. "So, Junior. How the hell wuzzat gravy, baby?"

Joe grinned and smacked his lips. "Just like Mama used to make."

Doc shot Joe a surprised look, and then laughed all the way to the subway entrance.

≈∞≈

The music of Birdland was still playing in his head when Joe got back to his room. He slipped off his clothes and fell into bed for a few hours of sleep before afternoon rehearsal. But for some reason, he was unable to forget the girl he had seen at Birdland. The thought of her pale blue eyes aroused him and transformed his need for sleep into a physical need for a woman he knew he'd probably never see again. And even if he did, there was that rich sugar-daddy. . .

After nearly an hour of tossing and turning, Joe sat back up and stared at the alarm clock. There was only one possible candidate at 6:55 a.m.—Elsie.

When he knocked on Elsie's door, it took several minutes for her to open it. She peered out at him, looking sleepy and disheveled. Joe gulped. He had never seen her without makeup.

"Joe? What—what happened to you the other night? You said you'd call."

"Can I come in, Elsie?"

She gave him a long, icy stare, but finally let him in.

Joe tried to loosen up her rigid mood by wrapping his arms around her waist and nuzzling her neck. It didn't work. She crossed her arms and began her speech, but Joe barely heard her. He couldn't help comparing her to the exotic girl from Birdland. Elsie's eyes were dark blue—steely and flat—and what in God's name had happened to her eyelashes?

"Well, Joe?"

"Huh? Oh, I'm sorry, baby. What were you saying?"

Elsie shrugged one shoulder and looked at the floor. "I said—do you love me or not?"

"Aw, baby, why do you think I'm here? Let's go in your room and I'll show you."

Elsie looked up with teary eyes. "That's all you want, huh? I *knew* it was a mistake—"

"A mistake? Oh, baby, how can you say that? I thought you liked it." Without touching her, he leaned close enough to breathe a soft sigh into her ear. "Don't you?"

"Well—yes, Joe, but—"

He felt her weakening and kissed her neck. "But what, baby?"

"You know you were the first. I wouldn't have let you if I didn't think you were serious."

"I *am* serious. Let me show you." He began easing her toward her bedroom door.

"Stop it, Joe!" she hissed. "You're talking about sex and I'm talking about—marriage."

Joe fought to keep a straight face. "Marriage? What— I mean— *marriage?*"

"I thought that's what love is all about, Joe. That's why I—let you."

As Joe was plotting his next move, Elsie's roommate Cora walked in and shot him a dirty look. "Shouldn't you be getting ready for work, Elsie?" she said. "You'll be late."

Joe leaned closer to Elsie and whispered, "Call in sick. I want to talk about our *plans*."

Bull's-eye. Elsie's frown turned into a matrimonial smile. All she needed was the white veil.

"Just go on without me, Cora," she said. "I'm calling in sick."

Cora grabbed her purse and rolled her eyes. "Yeah, you're sick, all right."

After the door slammed shut, Joe grinned and lifted Elsie into his arms. "Alone at last!"

"Oh, Joe," she giggled. "Where are you taking me? As if I didn't know."

He was impatient as he eased her onto her small bed. *All this song and dance just to knock off a barely average piece of ass.* He hurried through his standard routine—the hungry gaze up and down her body, which took a bit of acting skill. In her bulky white robe, Elsie resembled a dishwater blonde Michelin Man. After a couple of passable kisses, he went for his best move. Grabbing her hands, he forced her arms above her head onto the pillow, while smoothly rolling his body on top of hers. Domination played as sincerity—a passion song of empty promises. He made a mental note to ask Zig to explain "counterpoint" to him again.

"Joe? I—I thought we were gonna talk about our plans," Elsie whispered breathlessly.

Joe was busy trying to get her robe off. "Sure, baby, but let's talk about the wedding *after*."

Elsie moaned and kissed him, ready to cooperate.

Damn, I'm a bastard, he thought as he pulled off his shirt.

≈∞≈

The second Joe walked into the club that night he was struck with an eerie feeling that something was wrong. The instruments were all set up on the bandstand, but the band members were missing. Then he heard the drone of a news reporter's voice and spotted the band crowded around the radio at the end of the bar. He walked over to find out what was going on.

"Hey, what happened? How come—"

Doc shot him an annoyed glance and jerked his chin in the direction of the radio.

A spokesman for the Peekskill American Legion stated that their aim, to prevent the concert appearance of leftist agitator Paul Robeson, had been reached, but had no comment on the violence that followed. According to eyewitnesses, fourteen cars were overturned and scores of people required medical attention. State police were called in to escort concert organizers to their vehicles... Now, I've just been handed a transcript of Mr. Robeson's recent speech at the World Peace Conference in Paris. This is a direct quote: "We in America do not forget that it was on the backs of white workers from Europe and on the backs of millions of blacks that the wealth of America was built. And we are resolved to share it equally."

Well, there you have it, ladies and gentlemen. The subversive sentiments of one Paul Robeson... And now we must break for a word from our sponsor, DeSoto—the car designed with you in mind.

"Turn it off," Doc said. Then he finished his drink, stood up, and headed for the bandstand. Without a word, the others followed. Several minutes later the patrons began drifting in.

The mood remained uncharacteristically solemn, even after King kicked off the first set. Something about the night gave Joe the feeling that he should be looking over his shoulder. The Blacklist had always bothered him, but now it had taken up permanent residence in his mind, along with the blue-eyed girl from Birdland—the girl he was certain he would never see again. He couldn't stop thinking about Doc and Pearl and their hell-and-back kind of love, and he knew it was time to stop stringing Elsie along. On his first break, he called her and told her the truth—that he had never intended to marry her. Then he apologized and advised her to wise up before a worse scoundrel than himself came along.

After an instrumental rendition of "A-Train," King introduced Joe, who stepped to center stage. Zig played a sensitive piano intro, which Reet punctuated with a melancholy creeping up and down the strings of his bass, and King switched from drumsticks to the whisper of his brushes. Joe closed his eyes and saw her again. The girl from Birdland. It occurred to him that he had never even heard the sound of her voice. Zig had to play the intro to "Stardust" twice before Joe snapped out of his fantasy. It was time to sing.

When he finished the song, he was so distracted he barely heard the applause. Then he felt a sharp nudge and heard Oliver's voice: "Hey, vato! What're you, deaf? Number four, man!"

Joe had to think for a moment. Number four was "Nature Boy." This time he came in on cue, but it was suddenly becoming clear to him that all the singing he had ever done was just as insincere as his lovemaking to Elsie that morning. A forgery. And he realized that Doc was right. He hadn't learned to feel the story—not yet. He closed his eyes and as he sang the lyrics, he wondered for the first time what "Nature Boy" was really all about.

Calvin. Joe's voice caught, and his eyes fluttered open. Why did this song remind him of his brother? A rush of thoughts that he had buried deep in his mind began pushing to the forefront. How far he had traveled, in every sense of the word, to escape his black brother. Joe gazed into the darkness beyond the spotlight, and felt like a stranger in some isolated town who had just missed the last train home.

When he finished the song, Doc nudged him. "Nice story, Junior. You almost made me realize it." He grinned and held up his thumb and forefinger as a measure. "You were *this* close."

Joe wasn't in the mood. Without responding, he headed for the bar and ordered scotch. He rarely drank, but he hoped it would soften the sharp edges of his thinking. He choked down a few sips and stared into his glass. It made no sense, but his brother, who he hadn't seen in years, and a girl he didn't even know were inextricably joined in his mind, thoughts of one setting off thoughts of the other. He jumped when he heard a voice beside him, and saw a tall white man in an expensive looking suit.

"That was a great set, Joe," the stranger said as he took a seat beside him.

Joe obligingly shook his hand and smiled. "Thanks. I'm glad you enjoyed it."

"My name's Albert Crandall. I'm developing a jazz label here on the East Coast along the lines of Blue Note, and I'm looking for talent. As a matter of fact, I'd like to record you, Joe."

Joe finally looked up into the man's eyes. "Are you—on the level?"

Crandall handed him a card. "On the level. You are *some* singer. Call me."

"Wait—uh, Mr. Crandall. You're talking about recording the whole band, right?"

Crandall laughed. "Sure! What did you think? We'd record you with a kazoo?"

Chapter 13

It took less than two weeks for Albert Crandall to set up the first recording date. He booked a weekend at a studio called The Black Orchid, operated by Sid and Margo Friedland.

The Friedlands had left America in 1929 in search of a more colorful life in Paris. When the Nazi invasion forced them back to the States a decade later, they missed the music and cosmopolitan attitudes of the French, and in 1942 opened their own recording studio and made it a haven for jazz musicians and other free spirits. The Friedlands were in their mid-sixties, had no children, and were unashamedly devoted to each other. They were intellectually sophisticated, earthy, and offbeat, preferring the world of jazz and all its eccentric trappings to the conventional existence of other couples their age. Sid's usual attire was a turtleneck sweater, dark glasses, and a red beret, which was occasionally replaced by the gold-trimmed, royal blue yarmulke he wore for Jewish holidays and other personal reasons. He functioned mainly as engineer, but he also filled in for musicians if the tune wasn't too difficult. He played just about every instrument, but never pushed the issue when paying artists came in to record.

When the band came to check out the studio and meet the Friedlands, King took an instant liking to Sid. He smiled at the energy of the elderly beatnik with the gray goatee and the flashy yarmulke, and promptly christened him "Jazz Rabbi."

Like Sid, Margo was a bundle of contrasts. With her girlish figure, she still looked good in her comfortable pedal-pushers and loose sweaters. She defiantly refused to dye her gray hair, and wore it in a high ponytail. She was proud of the roadmap of lines on her face—each one earned by the smiles and tears of her life. Her passions ranged from jazz, modern art, and ballet to literature and global politics. Hurrying around the studio in her black flats, she was a blur of efficiency, handling bookings and making sure the coffee was always fresh. But she and Sid were equals when it came to whipping up a world-class breakfast after an all-night session.

The Black Orchid was a cramped, run-down studio, cluttered but functional, and its bohemian ambience was magnetic to musicians. Debates—philosophical, political, and artistic—blended with nonstop jazz, courtesy of the revered hi-fi or live in session, to flood the senses. Scrambled eggs and Irish coffee for breakfast; espresso and blackjack at midnight. A wild collage of conversations covering everything from Bird to politics to Nietzsche—religion, Salinger, the Blacklist, Coltrane, Einstein, and back to Bird again. That was the Black Orchid.

On the day of the first session, the band members trailed in early to get a feel for the place. By the time Doc showed up, everyone was having coffee and chatting amiably with Margo.

"Hello, girls," Doc said in a flat, hungover baritone. "I don't suppose you'd consider silence while I die over here in a corner. It won't take long."

"Oh, no ya don't," Margo said, shoving a cup of coffee into his hand. "Drink this, you'll live forever. Hell, it's the only thing keepin' Sid and me on this side of the dirt. Cream and sugar?"

Doc's eyebrows shot up, but he accepted the coffee. "Black's fine. Uh, thank you."

Just then, Sid rushed into the room, clapping his hands for attention. "Good morning, fellas! Everything's set up in the main room and I'm ready when you are. Follow me."

Doc cringed and stuck a finger in his ear, but quietly followed the band into a room equipped with microphones, a baby grand, and a setup of five music stands and stools.

King had already set up his kit and was tuning his floor tom. "Hey, Rabbi! Ya got a nail?"

Sid laughed and shook his head. "Margo found my stash and got rid of it. Let me run to the corner and pick you up some smokes. What's your brand, drummer man?"

"No, Sid, that's cool. Thanks, really, but one'a these criminals can spare a nail. Come on, somebody. I'm in dire need of tobacco and alcohol *now*! Before I get the D.T.s, man!"

Doc sat gingerly on the piano bench and rested his head on the keyboard at middle C. "I'll give you a whole pack of nails if you promise to play every tune with your brushes, man."

Enter Albert Crandall. "Good morning, everybody."

Joe hurried over to him, hoping that somehow he hadn't noticed Doc sprawled over the piano. "Good morning, Mr. Crandall."

Crandall peered over Joe's shoulder at Doc, who hadn't moved. "Rough night?"

Doc's eyes didn't open. "Not to worry. I've got my magic life-giving coffee here…"

Crandall smiled. "And I thought I heard somebody say he had the D.T.s?"

King stood up and stretched his arm high in the air like a third-grade genius who couldn't wait to shout out the right answer. "Right here, man! My flask is dry as a Sahara bone. You got a bottle of sump'm, Pops? Or maybe a smoke? The legal kind, of course. It *is* still daylight."

Crandall held up a pack of Chesterfields. "The cigarettes are on me, fellas, but let's stick to coffee until we hear how we sound. Now, let's get things organized. And Joe—relax."

After working out song structures and the order of solos, they devised a few inventive endings. By noon, they were ready to record. First was Zig's sultry arrangement of the Gershwin classic "Our Love is Here to Stay," which was always a hit at Café Nocturne. After two run-throughs and a false start due to technical problems, the song was put on wax.

Next was an odd but interesting choice, an old Marlene Dietrich song called "Falling in Love Again." Zig had restructured it with a 5/4 time signature, and the result was a fresh, jazzy setting for Joe's voice. Crandall raved from the booth when the last chord faded.

The final song was Zig's original composition, "Lady Blue." As the band worked on tempo and musical attitude, Joe stared distractedly at the lyrics. He jumped when he heard Doc's voice.

"Come on, girls! Just play it. Close your eyes and use your last hangover as inspiration. Hell, it always works for me. And Junior, here's your chance to tell that story."

When the recording light flashed on, King nodded a silent count, and the intro swelled with a perfect blend of tension and sensitivity, meeting Joe's voice like a kiss. As he sang the first few words, he felt that stab of loneliness again.

> *I once knew a lady / dying of the blues*
> *Sad and lonely / pretty lady / Why do you seem so blue?*
> *Had herself a secret / wouldn't tell me who*
> *Said he lied when she was true / nothin' really new*
> *Just another broken heart / nothin' more to lose*
> *Nothin' really new / nothin' special / just the blues*

As he sang, the music was a sharp, beautiful pain that splintered his emotions into flying shards of sound. He tried to gather himself for Zig's planned ending, and in that moment he felt an intense longing to love somebody—anybody—but then wondered if he were capable of it. His voice caught and he leaned close to the microphone, turning the word "blues" into a drawn-out, mournful lament. Zig did a quick rearrangement and followed him into the depths, playing a series of descending chords against Joe's single-note fadeout. The result was stone silence.

After a moment, Joe looked up. "Sorry, Mr. Crandall. Can I try it again?"

"Are you crazy? Joe, that was the best thing we cut all day! Wait till you hear the playback."

≈∞≈

Joe's spirits climbed over the next couple of months. After Crandall persuaded two local radio stations to place "Lady Blue" on heavy rotation, Café Nocturne began to do turn-away business. But to increase national record sales, Crandall recommended a road trip. King gave Mr. Ramsay notice to temporarily end the band's commitment to Café Nocturne, and they began rehearsing a new show. Joe was relieved when he checked the itinerary and saw no dates scheduled in the deep South. As far as he was concerned, stepping across the Mason-Dixon line would be like stepping off the end of the earth. With the excitement of his new life, his past had grown steadily dimmer until he had almost completely blotted it out. He was thrilled at the prospect of being on the road and couldn't understand the others' grumbling.

"We've *been* on the road, Junior," Doc informed him. "You haven't."

"I *love* the road," King said. "But I'll lay odds Junior cries eight to the bar for the duration."

≈∞≈

It didn't take long for King's prediction to come true. What had started out as a two-month road trip stretched into four months of cheap motels and roadside greasy-spoons. The clubs were no better, and the one-nighters were causing short tempers. When they received word from Al that the record had bottomed out, Joe was ready to head back to New York.

"What a joint!" he griped as they began setting up in one of the seediest places on the trip. He dropped into a chair and sighed. "Look at this clip joint!"

Doc sat on a wobbly chair and took a look around as he lit a cigarette. "Paint peeling off the walls, bandstand the size of a goddamn postage stamp... nice low ceiling for some shitty acoustics—and *what* is that smell? Damn! This is worse than the chitlin' circuit."

"Where the hell are we anyway?" Joe asked.

"Outhouse, West Virginia," King muttered. "Goddamn! Somebody open a window."

Zig opened a window and called back, "Hey, Junior, fire up the radio, man."

"Hey, who's got my *Down Beat*?" Joe called as he turned on the radio.

"Read a newspaper, Junior," Doc said. "Man cannot live by *Down Beat* alone."

The radio crackled and buzzed as it warmed up; then a newscaster's voice came through:

> *... And after pressure from Robeson's lawyers, a HUAC spokesman stated the reason for their actions: "Mr. Robeson's frequent criticism of the treatment of Negroes in America should not be aired in foreign countries. It is a family affair. Therefore, Mr. Robeson's passport has been revoked until further notice."*

"Zig," King said in a grave tone, "they actually pulled Robeson's passport, man."

Zig gazed at him blankly for a moment, and then began playing a slow, moody song on the low register of the piano. "So what're you? Surprised? At the HUAC boys? They shut down Café Society, for chrissakes! Nothing they do surprises me anymore."

Reet rumbled a groan. "Are you kidding me? Rachmaninoff, for cryin' out loud?"

"'Piano Concerto No. 2,' wise ass. Funereal mood music for the lousy news."

Oliver rolled his eyes. "Hijolé, man, they pulled his passport, they didn't execute him."

"Hey, what's that place they closed down?" Joe asked. "That—Society place?"

"Café Society. It use'ta be one of the best joints in the Village. Barney Josephson's place. It was integrated even before the Cotton Club, wasn't it, Doc?"

"Yeah. That's where Billie first sang 'Strange Fruit.' Great place. Robeson appeared there, Ella, Prez, Sarah—all of 'em. Come on, King. After Peekskill, you should've expected this."

King shrugged. "But to pull his passport? For tellin' the truth? This is gettin' scary, kids."

The gloomy Rachmaninoff music was beginning to fray Joe's nerves. He wanted to change the subject, but he was curious. "So you never said why they shut down that Café Society place."

"Same reason they went after Robeson," Zig said. "The Blacklist... Hey Doc, you're one'a those subversive Negroes with a passport, ain'cha? I bet they haul your ass in next." His sarcastic humor seemed strained as he peered at Doc over the top of his glasses. "Are you now or have you ever been a *Red*, Doctor Calhoun?"

Doc aimed a cynical grin directly at Joe. "Better red than dead."

"I believe you've got it ass-backwards, ya communist," Reet said dryly. "The *official* slogan, rubber-stamped by the *official* committee, is 'better dead than red.'"

"Hence my ass-backwards interpretation."

Zig stopped playing abruptly, and the room fell into a long, uneasy silence. Joe broke the lock on Doc's stare and forced his eyes back to his magazine until Zig suddenly began pounding a sour key on the piano. Joe jumped, and his eyes went straight back to Doc, who was still watching him through that ever-present haze of cigarette smoke. "I wonder when the local piano tuner died?" Zig muttered. "How many more bookings we got anyhow?"

"Four," King said, taking a quick swallow from his flask. "A one-nighter in Baltimore; then it's off to the jumpin' metropolis of Wilmington, Delaware, kids, for two glamorous nights at a joint called—get this—The Rusty Bucket. Then when *that* thrill wears off—"

"Hey, dig," Zig said, pointing at a man who was walking over. "Kilroy's here, man!"

"Huh?" King turned and blinked at the bald white man who was staring at him. As he scanned the man's beady, close-set eyes and long, bulbous nose, he grinned. "Hah! And we all thought Kilroy bit the dust on V-E Day with Laughing Boy and his Nazi sidemen!"

The man gave King a confused look that quickly changed to anger. "Oh, a wise guy," he snapped. "The name's Roger, pal. You the bandleader?"

"That's the nasty rumor, Roger. Listen, your cleaning lady let us in. And speaking of cleaning, we couldn't help but notice the uh, *odor* problem in here."

"Yeah, yeah, I know. Plumber's on the way. But I need to talk to you a minute. Over here."

King followed him to a far corner of the room as the others watched from the bandstand. It was clear from the way he leaned his head that the discussion was highly confidential.

"Wonder if King got the dates screwed up or sump'm?" Oliver said. "Wouldn't it be *ghastly* if we didn't get to play this glamorous joint?"

Suddenly, King's voice resounded through the empty club, rattling the coils on his snare drum. "*What?*... No, man! He's the standout!"

"Calm down a minute, pal," the manager said, glancing nervously at the bandstand.

"I ain't your *pal*, muthafucka! And just to prove it—get yourself another goddamn band."

Roger didn't bother keeping his voice down when he answered. "You better think twice, wise ass. We got a contract, and you're not hangin' *my* ass out to dry—not with all the business I'm expecting from these college kids in for the holidays. So you better check with Al."

King stood glaring at him for a moment, then turned and strode back to the bandstand.

Doc lit a fresh cigarette and smiled. "Let me guess. They're pullin' my passport?"

"Wait a minute," Joe said. "You mean he won't let Doc play?"

King stared at Doc. "He wants you to come in through the back door, play your set, and then go outside for breaks. Can you believe that shit? We're not even in dear old *Dixie* and these cats are scared you might sit next to one'a their women at the bar or sump'm."

Doc blew a lazy smoke ring. "I *am* irresistible to white women. Word must'a leaked out."

"It's not funny, man!" King seethed.

"Sure it is," Doc chuckled. "Preposterous shit is always funny."

"Wait a minute," Zig said. "Don't tell me any other Negro musicians put up with this?"

"No, man," Reet said, as he replaced a broken string on his bass. "Kilroy's sore 'cause this kind'a slip-up doesn't usually happen. Al probably didn't pull his coat about Doc's paint job."

"But I thought this was a *jazz* club, man," Oliver said. "Who the hell do they book in this joint? There ain't but ten or twelve *white* jazz musicians in the whole world! Shit! I ought'a scare him with my Commie Zoot-suit." He glared at the manager. "*Tu madre*, Kilroy!"

"Yeah!" Zig called. "Ditto! 'Cause if that meshuggenah cat's got a problem with Doc, he's definitely got a problem with me... Hey, Kilroy! What're your feelings on *kikes*, baby?"

"Christ, man," Reet deadpanned. "I forgot you were one'a those full-blooded *Hee-brews*! Me, I'm only half. My mother's an Irish Catholic *mick*, so that ought'a qualify me for the country club, right? I just renounce my Jewish daddy and I'm *in*, baby!"

The club manager began muttering, then walked out and slammed the door.

King made a snapping gesture with his thumb and top teeth. "*Baciagaloop!*" he yelled.

Joe groaned. "Aw, shit! English translation?"

"Chalé! What's your beef with that anyway, Junior?" Oliver snapped. "Since when does *anybody* in America speak English?... Now repeat after me, slowly: Kilroy is a *pen-de-jo*."

Doc stared at Joe as he exhaled a rush of smoke through his nose. "What's the verdict?"

"Time to split," King said. "That's my vote. How 'bout you, Zig?"

"Shit," Zig said. "Tell 'em to kiss my Hebrew ass and let my people go, man! What're they gonna do? Sue us? I dare you, Kilroy!" he yelled. "I got forty-seven lawyers in my family!"

Reet sighed. "Look, all I know is it took me hours to find bass strings today. Even a virtuoso like me can't keep Mr. Long Weekend in any kind'a pocket with a one-string bass. Let's jump."

King pointed at Oliver, who crossed his arms and nodded. "*Vámonos*, baby."

"So what's your vote, Junior?" King asked. "Not that it matters."

"Let's *depart*. That's English for jump, split, and *vámonos*, I think, in case anybody was—"

"We weren't," King said as he pulled a pen from his pocket. "And now, kids, it's time to leave a fond farewell for the management. Someplace good, so he won't find it till we're gone."

Doc groaned and headed for the door. "Shit, I'll be in the car."

"The rest a'yuz keep on the lookout for the enemy," King said as he hopped over the bar. On a lower cupboard door, he drew a quick indelible-ink sketch of the ubiquitous Kilroy—bald head and long nose peeking over a wall—but with the notable addition of a Hitler mustache. King cackled as he scrawled the caption: "*Sieg heil*, Kilroy! Your days are numbered, man!"

≈∞≈

A week after the band returned to New York, Al called for a meeting at the Black Orchid. Before he could begin, King said, "Some of these clubs were real toilets, Al. And we can't risk Doc's neck stumblin' into another one of those 'Strange Fruit' type'a joints either."

"Yeah, man," Oliver said, jerking at his collar. "I was gettin' nervous about my own neck. I think it was a little too brown for Kilroy. Uh, I mean Roger."

Al raised his hands. "I heard all about what happened. And that won't—"

King cut him off. "And four months is too long. "We couldn't take it another minute. Then the thing with Doc? Man, we just lammed. Sorry, Junior. Make that—we *departed*—post-haste."

"That club is off my list, but what I wanted to talk to you about was more recording."

"Frantic, baby!" Zig shouted. "Now you're talkin' bop!"

"Wait," Al said. "It'll be a little different this time. I know I told you we'd do some instrumental jazz, but from all the buzz about the last record, Joe's still our best bet for success."

King groaned. "Aw, man. We keep doin' that slow-drag crooner shit and the next thing you know we'll be playin' chamber music and opening for a dog act. Nothin' personal, Joe. It's just that we got some material that really jumps! Come on, Al, why can't we record that?"

"Because we need backing. And the backing I've found is for Joe. The backers want to record him as a solo, but you guys'll still be the rhythm section, and the pay is great. You'll be working with an orchestra, and we'll try to squeeze in a few solos for you, but it'll be Joe's name on the record... Look, I know you're disappointed, but I've gotta get back to these guys with an answer. So—are you in or out?"

Everyone stared at Al in silence until King finally spoke up. "Come on, kids," he said. "This shit was inevitable. Joe's always been a crooner, and we bent as far as we could to swing with it. So we go back to the Nocturne. I don't know about the rest a'yuz, but I dig the joint, and Ramsay gave us an open invitation. And Junior, anytime you want to sit in, it's cool."

"Wait," Joe said. "You mean you won't be my rhythm section for the record?"

"Relax, Joe," Al said. "I'll get you a great rhythm section and another singer for these guys. What about that guy filling in for the regular singer over at the Midnight Sun this week?"

"No! Not that vato!" Oliver yelped. "Hijolé! Just go ahead and set me on fire, man! That's gotta be less painful than playing behind that deadpan cigar-store Indian."

Reet patted Oliver's shoulder. "Okay, okay. We dig your drift, man."

"No, you don't! I think he skin-pops embalming fluid or something! I stopped in last Friday and caught a set. And you should'a *heard* that pathetic vato tryin' to sing 'Caldonia.'"

Everyone stared at Oliver until King let out a loud laugh. "No!"

"Yup. 'Caldonia.' The band made him sing it. Chalé! They must hate him."

Even Al began to laugh. "A disaster, I take it?"

Oliver made a mock sign of the cross. "No survivors, man. The audience ran for the exit."

"Okay, Oliver," Zig chuckled. "How 'bout no singer at all?"

"But you've gotta have a singer," Al said.

"Al," Zig said with a motherly smile. "Al, Al—my pal, Al." Wrapping his arm around Al's shoulder, he walked him to the other side of the room. "You gotta jump off the beaten path, baby! Bird and Diz rarely use singers—and the stores can't keep their wax on the pine!"

King grinned at Oliver. "Give Zig a minute with Al, and we'll be layin' some frantic instrumental wax and chasin' the all-stars' asses up the charts."

"So—you're sure you guys are okay with this?" Joe asked.

"Sure, Junior," King said. "Ya got our blessing. Go knock Sinatra's crown off."

Chapter 14

After meeting with Al's attorney to discuss legalities, Joe signed his first solo contract.

Within a week he was standing in the plush lobby of the Weingarten Recording Studio gawking at the dove-gray carpeting, a massive Art Deco-style desk, a long blue sofa, and a lavender wall covered with framed records and awards. He wondered if he should sit down and wait for Al or ask the chesty blonde receptionist to show him around. Then she looked up.

"Good morning," she said. "Are you here for the Joe Bluestone date?"

"Yes, I am. Actually, I'm Joe Bluestone."

"Oh! Well, it's a pleasure to meet you, Mr. Bluestone. I'm Jill."

Joe smiled at the curves of Jill's snug pink sweater. "The pleasure's *all* mine."

"Follow me," she said. "You're in Room 2, and the orchestra's just about ready for you."

When he stepped into Room 2, Joe was overwhelmed by all the instruments—woodwinds, brass, percussion, and strings. The musicians were tuning up and studying their charts, and Joe noticed that three of them were women. Then one of them—the violinist sitting in the front—turned his way. It was her. The girl from Birdland.

The receptionist was introducing him to a distinguished looking man in a brown suit, but Joe barely heard his name. He couldn't stop staring back at the girl every few seconds to make sure it was really her. As the receptionist walked away, Joe realized the man was talking to him.

"Uh, I'm sorry, sir. I didn't quite hear your name."

"No need to apologize. I'm Paul Ballantine, the conductor. Please call me Paul."

"Nice to meet you, Paul. Wow. Strings and the whole shot, huh? Just like Sinatra."

"Actually, we worked on Frank's last album. And he's *very* particular about strings."

"Well, I'm really impressed."

"Al wanted you to have the first-class treatment. Listen, what would you like to start with?"

Joe grinned. "You mean it's up to me?"

"You're the artist, Joe. Whatever makes you comfortable. What about the song your friend wrote. I understand he'll be here to help us with that one. Mr. Siegler?"

"That's Ziegler. Jerry Ziegler. He'll be here any minute, I'm sure."

"Good. Well, we've got the basic charts, so we'll run through it while we wait for him."

Joe glanced back at the girl from Birdland, and then spotted Zig wandering into the room. "Ziegler!" he called. "Over here."

"Hey!" Zig shouted. "Nice joint, Dad. Makes the Orchid look like a real shit-hole!"

Joe grimaced and gave Zig a hard nudge. "Paul, I want you to meet Jerry Ziegler."

Zig cut his eyes at Joe as he shook Paul's hand. "*Jerry*? Man, call me Zig. Everybody does. When they're acting *normal*, that is. Damn, Junior! All those cat scratchers here for you?"

Paul laughed. "Cat scratchers?"

"He's talking about the violins. Sorry, Paul. My friend only speaks English *occasionally*."

"No English required, as long as you're fluent in music. Listen, you two are familiar with this tune. Why don't you work on vocals while I warm up the orchestra?"

Zig nodded distractedly as he eyed the copper timpanis. "Hey, dig the crazy skins, baby!"

Joe nudged him toward the piano. "Just play, man, and try to fake some class."

"Just screwin' around with you, man. Truth is, I'm impressed. This is big-time, baby!" He threw his arm around Joe's shoulder and grinned. "Dig us, man! Just loungin' around waitin' for our Philharmonic side-cats to warm up for my tune!"

"Just play the song, Zig."

Within a half-hour, Joe took his place on a raised pedestal directly in front of the girl from Birdland, and she smiled politely. When he began to sing, he saw her watching him.

As the final chorus began, Paul suddenly waved his arms. "First violin!" he said impatiently. "That's the third mistake you've made. Are you having trouble, Magda?"

The girl closed her eyes and the color rose in her cheeks. "I—I'm sorry. No. I—I mark wrong da music, I'm afraid, Paul. I—I fix it. It don't happen no more."

Joe stared at her. So her name was Magda, but where was she from? What was that accent?

By the end of the second run-through, Ballantine was smiling. "Magda, I liked that embellishment going into the bridge. Why don't you repeat it at the end? Okay with you, Joe?"

Joe beamed at Magda. "Best idea I've heard all day."

≈∞≈

The minute the recording session ended that evening, Joe approached Paul on his way to the control room. "Hey, Paul, I'd like to tell your first violin how much I liked her work today."

"Sure, Joe. She'd love to hear that. She's right over there, packing up her things."

Just as he reached her, Joe saw her drop her sheet music. When he bent down to help her, she twisted away and swept her long skirt over her legs. Then he saw what she was trying to hide—a thick metal brace running down her left calf and the heavy boot that anchored it.

He smiled at her. "I just wanted to tell you how much I liked your playing today, Miss—"

"Skouros. Magdalena Skouros I am."

He stared into the startling blue world of her eyes. "You were my inspiration all day."

She dropped her pencil. "Oh, my Gott! I am such da clumsy girl, I'm afraid."

Joe picked up her pencil and smiled. "No, you're not. A clumsy girl couldn't play the violin the way you do. Here, let me help you carry your stuff. Do you have a ride home?"

"No—I mean, yes. I wait on da front door of my ride. But I carry by my—myself."

"Nonsense. I'll carry your stuff and we can talk while you wait for your ride."

"Please to forgive me. Is not so good, my English, I'm afraid. What dat means—dat *stuff*?"

"Oh, stuff just means your things—your violin, your pocketbook. And in your case, that pretty face is some *very* nice stuff. And your English is okay. I understand you just fine." He reached for her violin case. "Besides, I generally do most of the talking."

She hesitated and cast an uncertain glance at Paul, who nodded his approval.

"Go ahead, Magda. But don't forget, we're back in here at nine tomorrow morning. Don't be late. Oh, and Joe, we'll be ready for you around ten. That all right?"

"Just fine, Paul. So long. And thanks again for everything."

Joe and Magda walked along in silence until they reached the entrance. "Well, I sank you again, Mr. Bluestone," she said stiffly. "Goodnight."

Joe frowned. "Look, I don't mean to be pushy, but—are you waiting for your boyfriend or something? I don't want to get you in trouble. I just—"

"No!" She paused, obviously struggling with her words. "Professor Tosca—he pick me."

Joe blinked at her. "He pick you? Oh! He *picked* you—for what?"

"No, is wrong. He pick me *up*. In car. I must learn new words. I am such da stupid girl."

"You are *not* stupid. Stop saying that! And tell me more about the Professor."

She shrugged. "Well, in da house of Professor and wife I live. And very kind too, but all da time Professor tells to me—practice, practice, practice. No time for talking with boys."

"I see. But where are your parents? I mean, why do you live with the Professor?"

"In Greece are my parents. I am very more lonely for dem."

"Oh, I see. How long have you been here?"

"Almost one year. Is bad, my English, I know," she mumbled apologetically. "Like—to be here one day only, I'm afraid. To not talk very more. I must practice, practice, practice."

Joe took her arm gently and led her outside. "Well, if it won't make you too nervous, I'd like to meet Professor Tosca. Maybe he won't mind since I'm working with you."

"Oh, no! Da Professor tells to me, 'don't get cotch—' Wait. Is wrong word again. Cotched?"

Joe smiled. "Let's see—catch? No, you mean caught!"

"Yes, yes! Caught. He tells to me, 'Magda. Please to don't g-get *caught* by da New York musician.' Oh, how he tells to me? Oh, yes! 'Dey all are liars wanting for one thing only.' What is da one thing only, Mr. Bluestone? He don't tell to me dis one thing only."

Joe was trying to think up an answer when a black Lincoln pulled up and Magda hobbled over to it. As soon as Joe opened the door for her, the driver's door swung open and a white-haired man got out—the same man who had been with Magda at Birdland.

"Hello, sir," Joe said, walking around the car. "Good to meet you."

Professor Tosca narrowed his eyes at Joe. "You are with the orchestra, young man?"

"No, sir. Actually, this is my project. I'm Joe Bluestone."

"Ah, yes," the professor said stiffly as he shook Joe's hand. "Paul told me about this project. You are what they are calling one of these *crooners*—no?"

"Well, yes, but I'm also a serious musician who appreciates talent. And your student is very talented. You'd have been proud of her today." He detected a slight raise of the professor's right eyebrow, and Joe knew that he wasn't fooling him for one minute. So he shifted gears. "Excuse me, sir, but—you look so familiar. Didn't I see you at Birdland once?"

Finally, the Professor smiled. "Why yes, my boy. I am most interested in this modern jazz. Especially Charlie Parker and Dizzy Gillespie."

"But you teach classical music, isn't that right?"

"My boy, music is music! You must know the close relationship between classical music and jazz! The complicated arrangements and chord structures—"

Joe shot a quick glance at Magda, who was sitting in the car looking nervous. "Listen, Professor," he said, "I wish I had more time. See, I'm late for an appointment, but I'd love to get together again to talk this over. I know! Why don't you drop by for tomorrow's session and help us with some ideas?"

Professor Tosca smiled. "Wonderful! What time shall we be here?"

Joe walked over and tapped on the passenger window until Magda rolled it down about an inch. "What time did Paul say to be here, Magda?"

"Nine o'clock."

"Okay. And Magda, don't forget to bring your *stuff.*"

Her grin was a captivating mix of surprise and amusement. "Goodnight, Mr. Bluestone."

It took two weeks before Joe won Professor Tosca's trust. On the night he arrived to pick up Magda for their first real date, the professor greeted him warmly. "Come in, my boy!"

Joe followed him past a winding staircase and into an enormous wood-paneled room with a wet bar. A concert grand piano graced the far end of the room near a bay window with a view of a lighted garden, and at the entrance was a long coffee-colored sofa and three matching wing chairs. The finishing touch was a huge stone fireplace surrounded by redwood shelves containing hundreds of books. As the professor poured himself a glass of wine, Joe took a seat at the bar. "Wow! This is some beautiful room!"

"Thank you, Joe. It's my study and also my music room. I spend most of my time here."

"Is this where Magda does all her 'practice, practice, practice'?"

"Yes, it is. As much as she grumbles about it, you probably imagined it to be a dungeon."

"Well, this is sure no dungeon."

"Thank you, my boy. And will you have a glass of wine with me while you wait?"

"No, thanks. I really don't drink. Only on rare occasions."

"I see you have a rose for little Magda. You have the soul of an Italian, my boy."

"Well, thank you, Professor."

The professor gazed at Joe quietly for a moment. "I wanted to speak to you before you leave—about Magda—" A sound on the staircase stopped him. "Oh, but there she is now."

Joe stood up and saw Magda slowly descending the stairs in a burgundy-colored dress that flattered her slender waist. He walked over to meet her and handed her the rose.

"Oh, sank you! Please to wait. I will find for water dat—um—vase."

When she was gone, the Professor said, "I will be quick, Joe. She has had a hard life. Not only the Polio, but the poor child survived the Nazi invasion during the war. She saw things that no girl should see. So when my wife and I brought her here to study, we were very protective of her. But I'm afraid we made a mistake with a young man in the orchestra who played at romance and then broke her heart. You see, he could never truly see our little Magda—only her handicap. And with each tear she cried, I vowed that it will never happen again. Do you understand me?"

"Yes, sir. I understand completely."

When Magda returned, the professor smiled. "Our little princess deserves a night out after all her practice, practice, practice in the dungeon. Don't you think so, Joe?"

Joe laughed. "Yes, she does. And your royal taxi awaits, little princess."

≈∞≈

The Toscas' home was located on the outer edge of Morristown, New Jersey, and the long taxi drive back to Manhattan gave Joe a chance to draw Magda out in conversation.

"So how did you meet the Toscas? He told me they came here from Italy and you're from Greece. I remember reading in the newspapers that Italy *invaded* Greece during the war."

Magda began her halting story. "Well, you see—Professor Tosca—he help da partisans of Italy. Very more danger for him, but Mussolini don't cotch him for to kill him. Den he travel to Athens for to visit my teacher, Professor Polodouris—after da war, of course. My teacher tells to him I am very good student—good for symphony. So Professor Tosca travel to look and he tells to me—he take me to America. In America he will make a school for his very own, and so Mama—I'm afraid she cry and cry, but—" Magda smiled. "At last Mama let me to go traveling to here. I am afraid, of course, but I make my courage and I go on dat boat, Joe. And so here am I, da Greek girl, in America with Italian Professor and wife. I send Mama den one record of Bing Crosby dat my violin I make to cry, and so now Mama—she don't cry no more."

Joe grinned broadly. "I love the way you talk."

A deep blush crept up Magda's face. "Oh, Joe. You make me to talk more—and my words are so bad, I'm afraid."

"No they're not. But there *was* one thing you said before that I didn't understand."

Magda sniffed. "One thing only?"

"One thing only. I got the part about you playing on a Crosby record and sending it home to Mama, but what did you mean when you said you made your violin—cry?"

"Yes! Professor Tosca tells to me, 'Da violin is much *poignant*—'" She smiled. "Poignant—to mean touch da heart—to make happy or sad. He teach to me dis English word."

"Well, then that's a perfect word to describe how you play the violin."

"But you know why is dat, Joe?"

Joe shook his head and smiled. "No. Tell me."

"Da violin is much poignant of all instruments, because da violin alone cries on da music. Professor tells to me, 'Stop to be worrying all da time to play da perfect notes. In your *soul* feel da music, Magda. Let da tears flow through fingers into da bow and violin. Make da strings to cry.' Dis is great secret what Professor teach to me, Joe. More practice it takes me, but I learn dis secret. I make da strings to cry." She fell quiet and looked down. "But never before do I hear da poignant crying on singer. Until you. Dat is why I look at you when da first day I hear you sing. And Paul cotch—no, *caught* me to play dat mistake. I feel da crying, Joe, and so I miss my cue."

Joe felt a lump in his throat. "That's the nicest thing anybody's ever said to me," he whispered, "in my whole life. I only hope I can live up to what you think you heard."

"Oh, yes, Joe. I know dat sound of crying on da music. I hear it on your mouth."

Joe leaned his head back and laughed.

Magda slapped his arm softly. "Again you are laughing at Magda's English?"

"No! I *love* your English. You're the coolest frail on the coast. Classy chassis and real reet."

Magda's eyes widened. "What *dat* means?"

"I'm just trying to show you that there are lots of ways of talking. That's just bop talk. You were at Birdland, you heard how the musicians talked, didn't you?"

"Ah, yes! Solid, Jackson," she mugged playfully. "I tell to Professor 'solid, Jackson' all da way home, for to make him laugh!" Suddenly, her mouth dropped open. "Birdland! I bump next to you at dat Birdland, Joe! I am thinking dis face I see one time before."

"*Finally* you remembered! You know, I thought about you a lot since then. But the last place I thought I'd see you again was at a recording session for my own record."

"Professor Tosca tells to me, da world is small, no?"

"Yes it is. So, did you like Birdland? Do you like jazz as much as the professor does?"

"Oh, yes, Joe. First he tells to me about da man name of 'Bird' and how great is he. Da records he play but I don't understand. Not like music in Athens. So he take me for to hear dat Bird. But I like more dat other man, Joe, with name of—umm—Crazy? Or—Silly?"

"I don't remember anybody named Crazy or Silly."

She shook her head. "No, no. Da man making dat fat face when he play dat horn."

"Oh! Dizzy! You're talkin' about Dizzy Gillespie."

"Yes! Dizzy! Dat is name! I like dat way Dizzy play his horn, Joe… You know, in America I only first time to see many Negro people."

Joe stiffened. "What do you—what do you think about 'em?"

She smiled thoughtfully. "I like. Professor Tosca tells to me da white American people close da ears to musicians of jazz because of da black skin. But not you, Joe?"

"No," he murmured. "No, I like jazz no matter who's playin' it."

Magda gazed at him softly. "Yes, you are nice dat way. I like. And I like dat rose you give for me tonight. It is da more—uh, much? Da *much* beautiful one—ever I have see."

"No… you are the much beautiful one ever *I* have see." He leaned closer, surprised at the pounding of his heart over something as routine as a kiss. She held his gaze until he touched her face and took his first taste of her mouth. "God, your eyes are gorgeous," he whispered. "I could get lost in your eyes."

When the taxi pulled up to Café Nocturne, the driver turned around and grinned. "I ain't seen kissin' like that since V-J Day! Hate to break it up, kids, but the meter's still runnin'."

Joe looked at the meter and whistled. "Wow! What would you do if we stiffed you?"

"Drive back to Daddy Warbucks in Jersey and collect from him."

Joe paid him and grinned at Magda. "Okay, prepare to meet the weirdest cats on the planet."

They walked into the club and made their way to a table. The band members were at the bar on a break, but when they saw Joe, they headed over to the table.

"Skirt alert!" Zig shouted. "Hey, King! Our old crooner's makin' the scene! And dig the talent he brought with him."

"This is Magdalena Skouros—" Joe began.

Before he could say another word, Zig peered over his glasses at Magda. "Wait a minute—weren't you lead cat scratcher at the session a few weeks ago? Yeah! You kept our boy Junior distracted all day, droolin' over the premium upper and lower parts of your chassis, baby."

"Hey!" Reet said. "Nix the nomenclature, Nunzio. The skirt's got a lady in it."

Oliver elbowed Zig. "And he said her name's Magdalena, not *baby*. A little respect?"

King chimed in with a crazy mix of Shakespeare and Brooklynese. "Cease and desist thy panting, ya glassy knave! Thou cawn't call the fair frail 'baby' or bellow references to her private, albeit curvaceous, chassis! Thy head must roll! Somebody sober up the executioner!"

Magda laughed. "My hero! And what your name is, young man?"

King's eyebrows shot up. "And from what far yon village dost the fair frail hail?"

"Hail?" Magda played along in a haughty tone. "I before hail in Athens, my young man, but I for almost two years hail in village of New Jersey, and I am da Queen. Please to kiss my hand."

King barely controlled his laughter as he kissed her hand. "Ah, there's the rub, fair Queen. You see, I outrank thee. For I am King of the Land of Ludwig." He pointed at his drum kit on the bandstand. "Canst thou not see my throne upon yon stage? And alas, I must now bid you adieu and return to my kingdom." He turned and flounced away toward the bandstand.

Joe rolled his eyes. "He belongs in the kingdom of Alcoholics Anonymous. Oh, wait a minute! Here comes Doc. I really want you to meet Doc."

As Doc approached the table, he was already giving Joe one of those penetrating looks that made him squirm. "My, my. Looks like you finally found your Ava, huh, Junior?"

Joe's smile faded. "This is Magda. She plays violin with Paul Ballantine's studio orchestra."

"It's very nice to meet you, Magda," Doc said.

King's voice boomed from the speaker: "Your majesty. Please send forth my musical peons." As the musicians trudged to the bandstand, he began playing a hammy march cadence.

"Oralé!" Oliver groaned.

After a few bars, the band eased into an improvised version of "Caravan." Doc stepped up last, and played a sparkling solo that reflected the mood of the evening.

Joe cuddled close to Magda at their table. "Hey, you really give out with the personality! And here I was thinking you were shy."

Magda smiled. "You make me to feel happy, so—I give da personality."

"Well, you sure made a hit with my buddies."

When "Caravan" ended, the band began playing a slow number that caught Magda's attention. The notes floating out of Oliver's soprano sax were perfect creations of music as form—wet tropical flowers and birds in flight—enticing lovers to the dance floor for a bit of sultry upright necking. Magda watched them with wistful eyes. "What dis song is called, Joe? Is so pretty."

"It's called 'Passion Flower.' Perfect song for a dance," he said, rising from his chair.

Her eyes widened. "Oh, my Gott! You are crazy or something? I— How I can dance?"

"What do you mean? Sure you can dance. I'll lead. Come on." But when he saw her eyes fill with tears, he sat back down. "Hey, I didn't mean to upset you. I just thought—"

"My shoes, Joe! Dey are boots—like for army soldiers. Dey make me to look clumsy."

"No, they don't. I've known you for weeks and I have *never* seen you look clumsy." He lifted her chin with his fingertips. "You're the one with the classy chassis, baby. Remember?"

"But Joe, my shoes—and I never learn—dancing."

"Just try. Hang on to me and walk in a circle, that's all. Come on, before the song's over."

She gazed at him and let out a shaky laugh. "Okay, Joe. I make my courage—and I try."

He led her to the dance floor and pulled her tightly to his chest. Swaying to the creeping rhythm of Reet's bass, he led her with slight shifts and gentle nudges of his thighs. After a minute or two, he felt her relax in his arms. He nuzzled her hair and laughed lightly. "See?"

She sighed deeply. "Oh, Joe, to dance is so wonderful!"

Just as "Passion Flower" faded out, King's voice broke the spell. "Okay, break it up, Junior. You ain't gettin' out'a here without a song. So get up here and name your poison."

Joe took Magda back to the table. "Looks like I'm being drafted. Be right back. Hey! Don't get picked up while I'm gone." Adjusting the knot in his tie, he headed to the bandstand.

"You guys still remember 'Tenderly'?" he called.

King rolled his eyes, mugged a big yawn, and started a slow count. "One, two, three—"

As Zig played the intro, the house lights dimmed, and memories of all those nights came racing back into Joe's mind—all those empty love songs he had sung to girls he would take to bed but never love. He focused on Magda's face and knew she was different. "This is for you."

He didn't take his eyes off her until he finished the song to enthusiastic applause. Before he could turn to say goodbye to the band, King jabbed him in the back with a drumstick.

"Damn, Junior! Your chick's a knockout, man! She got any promiscuous sisters?"

Zig shook his head. "No, baby, no. You know what they say. Heavenly creatures like that never come in twos. If there *is* a sister, you can lay odds she's a real schnauzer, man."

King hit a rim-shot. "So what? I'm in dire need, man! If the mutt's got a pulse, I got eyes."

Joe laughed. "You bums'll never change. Thanks for the song."

"Singers," King grumbled. "You singers get all the prime-cut women."

$$\approx\!\infty\!\approx$$

After a few weeks of dating, Joe caught himself tumbling headlong into the idea of marriage. The gentleman routine was different, but he had never met a woman like Magda. And each time she looked at him with those pale blue eyes, he felt himself falling deeper in love with her.

On the two-month anniversary of their first date, they left their favorite restaurant, and Joe hailed a taxi. "Morristown," he told the driver. "104 Janina, just off West Park."

As the cab pulled into traffic, Magda said, "Joe? Please to answer for me one question."

"What is it, baby?"

After a short pause she said, "Well, why you don't—never take me to your bed?"

Joe was momentarily stunned. "Uh, well— Okay, first, the professor would skin me alive, and second—" He grinned and held up two fingers. "He'd probably skin me two times."

"Please to be serious, Joe. I am thinking dat—maybe—" Her gaze traveled to her leg brace. "Maybe you love me only like—like da love for—crippled child?"

"Wait," Joe laughed. "That's what you think? That I feel sorry for you? Oh, baby, relax! 'Cause if you could read my mind, believe me, you'd slap my face. I forgot all about your leg brace weeks ago!… Magda—don't you know how beautiful you are?"

Again, she looked at her brace. "But my ugly leg, Joe— You are sure it don't bother you?"

He stared at her for a long quiet moment, then tapped the cabbie's shoulder. "Sorry, but we changed our minds. Drop us at MacDougal and Sixth." He looked back at Magda. "Okay?"

She smiled. "Yes, Joe. Is okay for me."

"The professor's gonna kill me when you don't show up on time. You know that, right."

She smiled. "Yes. He will skin you two times. But I want to go with you, if you are sure."

Joe leaned back and kissed her. "I am sure. You'll see."

When the taxi pulled up to Joe's apartment, he paid the driver and helped Magda out. As they walked up the stairs, he whispered, "Last chance. You can still change your mind."

"No, thank you very much, Mr. Bluestone. Please to take me to your bed."

"Shhh!" he laughed softly. "Neighbors! Turn down your broadcast!"

He opened the front room and they walked inside. "Here, give me your coat. It's not a very big place, but I don't spend that much time here. Hey, you want some ginger ale?"

"Oh, yes, please, Joe."

Magda was still standing when he brought in the drinks. He turned on the radio and then stretched out on the sofa. "See? It folds out into a bed. Come wees me to za casbah, my dahling," he said, trying to loosen her up with his barely-passable Charles Boyer impression.

When she didn't respond, he got up and gently nudged her to a sitting position on the sofa. Then he knelt on the floor in front of her, slid the hem of her dress up over her left knee and gently began unfastening the buckles on her brace. The radio was playing "Two Sleepy People."

When Joe finished the last buckle, he untied the shoelaces and looked up. Magda's eyes were shut. With one last gentle pull to the heel of the boot, he slipped it off. Resting her small, atrophied calf in his left hand, he eased the brace off with his right. When she finally opened her eyes, he smiled at her and folded his arms. "So, is this what you were so scared for me to see? Magda. Your leg is not ugly. It's just a little smaller than your other leg, that's all." He quickly removed her other shoe and reached for her hands. "Now, stretch out here and relax with me."

She heaved a sigh and settled into his arms. "You are sure it don't bother you—my leg?"

"Not in the least." As he was about to kiss her, the radio played the intro to "Sing, Sing, Sing." Joe got up and turned it off. "I don't know about you, but Krupa pounding his drums is not my idea of romance. I got a better idea anyway. I'm gonna give you a music lesson."

Magda sighed. "All da time, practice, practice, practice."

"Yeah, but this is a different kind of music lesson." He gazed into her eyes as he slipped off his undershirt, and then he placed her palm on his bare chest. "Feel that?" he whispered. "My heartbeat. That's the rhythm of life. The first thing that shows we're alive when we're babies and the last thing to stop when we die. So you see, this is my drum."

Magda snuggled closer. "More, please."

He rested his lips against her neck. As he began to unzip her dress, he heard her sigh. "So, you're the expert on notes, Miss First Violin. What was that sigh? B-flat?"

"I am not thinking of notes now. Please to tell da story of your drum."

"All right. But first I want to show you how your drum sounds against mine." Without taking his eyes off her face, he eased Magda's dress over her hips.

"I think dat you undress many girls in your days of time, Mr. Bluestone."

"Hey," he laughed, "don't change the subject. Back to the drum. In the National Geographic magazine it says the drum is the oldest instrument. Villages used it to send news back and forth, and to prepare warriors for battle. But mostly, to stir everybody up for sex."

"Sex? Oh, dat you learn from da magazine, too?"

"Nah. The sex-drum theory I got from an oversexed conga player in the French Quarter. But forget about all that. Back to this rhythm our drums are making. Now listen… closely." Brushing his lips over her ear, he eased his body over hers and parted her legs with his knee.

After a lingering kiss, she smiled. "I see. Now we must practice… practice… practice…"

Chapter 15

As weeks melted into months, Joe's life had surpassed any of the fantasies he had dreamed up as a sharecropper's son back in Mississippi. On the day his record broke into the top forty, he decided to surprise Magda with a special six-month anniversary of their first date. It started with a movie at Radio City Music Hall.

They sat down just as the newsreel began. Joe stared at the screen and sighed. A shouting, gavel-pounding HUAC hearing. It was like a bad off-Broadway play that wouldn't die.

> *—You will be responsive to the question or I will have you removed. Now I will ask you once again. Are you now or have you ever been a member of the Communist Party?*
>
> *—And once again I will invoke my rights under the First Amendment, Mr. Chairman.*
>
> *—Leave the witness chair... Sergeant, take this witness out of my sight...*

The questions and gavels continued pounding in Joe's head until the title *On the Town* splashed across the screen and a bouncy overture filled the theater. Unable to keep his mind on the movie, Joe patted the velvet box in his pocket and smiled. But suddenly, the house lights came on, the screen went white, and he was in the grip of a sickening childhood memory:

One'a them high-yella ones, huh? You know the colored section's up in the balcony. Stay where you belong next time, hear me, boy?

"Joe?"

Joe jerked up in his seat. "Huh?"

Magda was staring at him curiously. "You are all right?"

"Yeah, sure. But why—" Before he could finish his question, a loud musical interlude sounded from the speakers, and the audience cheered. Joe turned around in his seat, bewildered. "What the hell's goin' on? What happened to the movie?"

A voice from the seat behind him said, "Say, don't you know the music from *Amos 'n' Andy*? They always interrupt the movie for *Amos 'n' Andy*. If they didn't, everybody'd stay home and not come to the theater on Saturdays. Relax. The movie'll be back on in a few minutes."

Joe turned back around, and cringed at the cartoonish dialogue:

> *—Holy mackerel, Andy! You gon' haf'ta run dat by me agin.*
>
> *—Lawd a'mussy, Kingfish! I done tol' ya twice awready! Now here's da plan...*

Magda touched Joe's arm. "Joe? You don't like da *Amos 'n' Andy* program?"

"No, I don't," he snapped. "I can't believe they interrupt the movie for this bullshit."

Magda frowned. "No bad words, please, Joe."

He sighed and patted her hand. "I'm sorry, baby. I guess I can stand this till the movie starts again. That's what we came to see. But then I'm taking you someplace very, very special."

Three hours later, Joe had forgotten the night's unpleasant start. As he and Magda gazed at the view from the 65th floor of the RCA Building, he knew that he had chosen the perfect spot. Surrounded by the Art Deco elegance of The Rainbow Room, Joe proposed marriage to the girl of his dreams, and she said yes.

≈∞≈

When Professor Tosca and his wife Lavinia learned about the marriage, they insisted on handling all the arrangements. Each time Joe visited Magda, Mrs. Tosca rushed then into the den to select flowers, invitations, bridal gown, groom's tuxedo, bridesmaid dresses. It was all a blur to Joe.

An occasional problem arose, but Joe improvised neatly. He explained the absence of a family with a sad story about his parents dying in a long-ago fire that had also destroyed family documents, including his birth records. It was a simple matter to talk Zig into arranging for affidavits in lieu of a birth certificate through his uncle, who was a lawyer. Marriage license problem solved. His final hurdle was meeting Magda's parents. Professor Tosca flew them in from Athens a week before the wedding, and they responded easily to Joe's charms.

But the wedding day started badly for Joe. He woke in a cold sweat after a nightmare filled with terrifying chaos: Magda in her wedding gown standing next to a preacher who looked like Joseph McCarthy. A screech horn playing a piercing rendition of the Wedding March as Calvin walked up the aisle swinging chains attached to his wrists and pounding a gavel on the back of each pew. *Are you now or have you ever been—a nigga like me?* Over and over… The only thing that finally woke Joe was the feeling of Calvin's chains striking him on the chest.

He stumbled into the bathroom and stood under a cold shower for several minutes.

When King and Doc finally arrived to pick him up, he greeted them with emotional hugs.

The two men exchanged an amused look, and then burst into unsympathetic laughter. Doc stepped back and looked him up and down. "Blues walkin' like a man," he said.

Joe stared at him, sullen and mute.

Doc chuckled. "Your daddy would'a laughed at that."

"Look at him, man!" King laughed. "Sweatin' like he's goin' to the electric chair!"

"I'm just nervous, okay?" Joe snapped.

"Don't come cryin' to me," King said. "I still don't know what she sees in you, ya bum."

"Let's get him to the church before he passes out or sump'm," Doc recommended.

"No," Joe said. "Remember? We're meeting up at the Toscas' house and then everybody's following us to the church. Wait a minute—Where's Pearl? Isn't she with you?"

Doc took his time lighting a cigarette before answering. "Pearl couldn't make it today."

≈∞≈

Upon their arrival at the Toscas' house, the first person Joe saw was Magda's father, Stavros Skouros. Forty hard years as a fisherman were evident in his short, powerful build and his brown, weatherburned face. His thick hair was steely gray and his eyes were the same cold color. He was standing on the front porch staring at Doc with a stupefied expression.

"Good morning, sir," Joe said, as he nervously studied his future father-in-law's eyes.

Doc removed his hat and aimed a blank, silent gaze at Mr. Skouros.

Professor Tosca hurried over. "Good morning. Are, uh, introductions in order?"

When no one answered, he began to speak quietly in Greek to Mr. Skouros.

As Joe searched for something diplomatic to say, Doc took the direct approach. "Looks like your in-laws have a restricted guest list," he said loudly. "White-only."

King nodded gravely. "Pretty accurate diagnosis, Doctor Calhoun."

"No, man," Joe murmured. "It can't be that."

But there was no need for translation as Mr. Skouros began ranting in heated Greek.

Doc turned around and put his hat back on. "Maybe I ought'a just blow."

"No, wait," Joe whispered, grabbing Doc's sleeve.

Mr. Skouros looked at Joe as if he were a traitor, and then strode into the house.

"I am *so* sorry, Doc," Professor Tosca said. "He is just—unfamiliar with you people and—"

King threw up his hands. "Gotdamn! Not the 'you people' speech again!"

"No, please," Professor Tosca pleaded. "It's just that Mr. Skouros is not very cosmopolitan. He is from a very small village and... No. There is no excuse for it. And please forgive me for handling this badly. But he said he will not attend the wedding. My God, I am so sorry."

"So what are you saying, Professor?" Joe shouted. "That Doc's gotta leave? Because that's out of the question. I invited him and he stays." After an awkward silence, he lowered his voice. "Look, Professor, just explain to Mr. Skouros that these are two of the guys in the band playing at the reception, and the other guys just won't play without Doc."

Before Tosca could answer, King flung his half-smoked cigarette to the ground and crushed it with his shoe. "Which won't be a lie, 'cause I'm blowin' this plantation right now."

"Wait," Joe pleaded. "You're my best man! You can't leave! What about the reception?"

"I told you, Junior. I don't go for this shit, man. If Doc's not good enough for your wedding, then I'm not either. So excuse me while I split, *vámonos*, and *definitely* depart."

"But what about the music?" Joe called as King climbed into his station wagon.

King gunned the engine, then leaned out the car window and glared at him. "Hell, I don't know, Junior. Why don't you get up and serenade 'em with a swingin' arrangement of "Look Away, Dixieland." That ought'a go over big with this crowd. A real Confederate toe-tapper."

"Oh, come on! The guy's a Greek, not a Klan member, for chrissakes."

"It all translates to the same bullshit." He leaned over and pushed open the front passenger door. "Come on, Doc. Let's jump. You ain't gotta ride in the back of *this* bus."

"I'm comin', man. I just need a few last words with the groom here."

"I am so sorry, Doc," Professor Tosca said. "You are always welcome in my home."

"I understand your position," Doc said, offering a patient smile.

When the professor was gone, Doc gripped Joe's hand, and drilled a hard stare into his eyes. "You remember that song you told me your Daddy dug so much? 'Crossroads Blues'?"

Joe jerked his hand away. "Aw, come on, man. Not that shit again. Not now."

Doc jabbed his index finger into Joe's chest. "*Right* now, Junior. Guess he never explained that song to you, huh?"

Joe sighed. "Look, I'm sorry about all this, but—"

"It was a song about a broke nigga with nothin' but lint in his damn pockets. He meets Satan at a crossroads and sells him his soul...Well? Don't you wanna know what he sold it for?"

Joe didn't answer. From inside the house he could hear Magda's mother sobbing a tragic Greek opera, and King's idling car engine was rumbling its ominous underscore.

"Don't wanna know, huh?" Doc whispered. "Well, I'ma tell you any goddamn way. Legend is that Robert Johnson sold his soul so he could play that guitar better than any man on earth. So what I wanna know is— what was *your* deal, Junior? Sure hope you didn't sell it cheap."

Joe reached for Doc's arm. "Wait a minute—"

"Look, son," Doc said, shaking off Joe's grip, "it's time for you to face facts. This is *not* some glamorous movie that comes out all happy in the end. This is your real life, man! You are *not* Frank Sinatra and Magda is *not* Ava Gardner." He sighed and shook his head. "Hell, Frank and Ava aren't even Frank Sinatra and Ava Gardner."

"What the hell does that mean?"

"It means they're real people, man! Not those characters the fan magazines invented! They have real problems just like everybody else."

"So *what* has all this got to do with my wedding?"

"You know why you're marrying this girl? Because she's pretty and she's *white*. Come on, man. You *saw* the way her daddy looked at me. So things are gonna get real gritty when the truth about you comes out. And there won't be some director there to save your ass by yellin' 'cut'!"

Joe glared at him, but said nothing.

"Junior. It's time for you to wise up. If you can't be honest with this girl about who you are, then it'll just be one lie on top of another, and then—"

Joe held up his hands. "You know what? You're right. You ought'a just go now, Doc."

"Okay, I'm going. But you might want to think about this: When they threw *me* out, they were also throwin' out your family—whoever they are and *wherever* they are." Doc gazed at him blankly as he backed away. "The world is full of people duckin' and hidin' and running away from the truth, Junior. So what about you?… Are you now or have you ever been—a shadow?"

≈∞≈

The rest of the day was a blur. When it was over, Joe was almost surprised to find himself on the church steps with his bride, smiling at the happy white faces of the guests throwing rice. But each time he closed his eyes, all he saw were the dark, angry faces of the disinvited.

Chapter 16

Moonlight Point was a romantic lodge that catered to honeymooners, with a private veranda and a panoramic view of Vermont's blazing autumn colors. But when Joe and Magda were finally alone in the suite, they forgot the scenery. They ordered champagne from room service and turned on the Sparton Bluebird on the nightstand. The radio became a compatible friend, serenading the honeymooners as they made love into the late hours of each night.

At about 2:00 a.m. on their last night in Vermont, Joe woke from a dream he couldn't remember. He sat up and quickly shook off the vague disturbance, then gazed down at Magda, who was sleeping soundly. Suddenly, in the absolute stillness of the room, he felt someone watching him. He turned away from Magda to look over his shoulder and was startled by his own reflection in the blue-mirror finish of the radio. As he stared at his blue face, an old Fats Waller song ran through his mind. *What did I do to be so black and blue?*

He was still awake when the sun came up.

≈∞≈

"New York City, Grand Central Terminal!"

The second Joe heard the train conductor's announcement, the relief washed over him like a cleansing rain. Honeymoon sex had been bliss for his body, but his nerves had been jumping ever since the wedding. He smiled. New York was like a faithful mistress, always there to welcome him, no matter how long he had been gone or how many other women he had loved.

The first challenge for Joe and his new bride was to combine their belongings in his small apartment. They both had musical session commitments, and when they had time, they returned duplicate wedding gifts. Once they had settled in for their first free weekend together, Magda suggested inviting the band over for supper.

"Dey are always hungry cats, no?" she asked, smiling.

"They are always hungry cats, *yes*. And how 'bout after supper we go see the show?"

"Solid, Jackson. You call da hungry cats and I go for to shop da food." She extended her hand and smiled. "So please to cross my palm with da bread, Daddy-O. No, da... fin?"

Joe laughed and handed her a five dollar bill. "You're gettin' pretty hip. Okay, here's a fin." He reached into his pocket. "Wait. Better make it a sawbuck the way those bums eat."

≈∞≈

The get-together was on a Saturday evening, and for the first time, the apartment was noisy. King, Zig, Joe, and Oliver were crowded around a small card table, playing a rowdy hand of poker. Reet was sitting on the sofa with his eyes shut, listening to a new Charlie Parker record on a radio-record-player combo that Joe and Magda had received as a wedding gift.

Doc was the last one to arrive. Peering in, he surveyed the cramped room. A sewing machine was wedged between Joe's bookcase and the sofa, and an enormous armoire was blocking the cutout between the kitchenette and the front room. Stacked neatly against any available wallspace were unpacked boxes and rows of phonograph records.

"Don't mind me, Junior," he cracked. "I'll just cop a squat out here on the fire escape."

Joe smiled, relieved that Doc seemed to have forgotten the unpleasant scene at the wedding. "Okay, Doc, so get over here and quit'cher bitchin'. You're just in time for this hand."

Zig stood up and threw his cards on the table. "Cool. Take my seat. I'm tired of losing anyway. Hey, Reet. Start that cut from the top, man."

Doc took Zig's chair and lit a cigarette as Joe shuffled and dealt the cards. "Hey, Junior. What have you done with the Missuz? Don't tell me you stashed her in the can?"

"No, she's in the kitchen. Beatriz is trying to teach her how to cook," he whispered.

"Uh-oh," Doc chuckled. "And we're the Guinea pigs." He scowled as he looked at his cards. "Goddamn, man, deal me some decent cards! I can't do shit with this hand."

"Lounge!" King bellowed as he tossed a quarter into the center of the table. "You in or out? 'Cause nobody's goin' for that dusty old bluff strategy of yours. And gimme a nail."

Doc cut his eyes at King and tossed him a Camel. "I'm in, and just for wisin' off, I'ma have to lay an old fashioned ass whuppin' on you, you goddamn amateur."

King clenched the cigarette in his teeth. "Kiss my ass and light me up."

Doc scowled as he reached into his pocket for his lighter. "How come you ain't in Korea anyway? Have you registered with the Selective Service, young man?"

"Section eight!" Oliver laughed. "And stop changin' the damn subject."

"What subject? There *is* no subject, man," Doc mumbled.

"The subject is how come King's suckin' down that Camel and I ain't! What is this? The Alamo all over again? And I might remind you vatos that we beat your pale asses there too."

Doc shook his head as he arranged the cards in his hand. "Whose pale ass? If *I'm* pale, then you gotta be the goddamn invisible man, Oliver."

Joe looked up. "*What* in the hell does the Alamo have to do with anything, Oliver?"

"I'm talkin' about a siege, man! If I don't get a nail soon! This vato's passin' out Camels like it's Christmas—to everybody but the Mexican."

"Hey!" Zig shouted. "*Us* vatos are tryin' to listen to some actual musicians over here! Shoot it out if you wanna kill each other, but shut *up!*"

"No shooting," Reet murmured. "Blades are quieter. Somebody get 'em blades."

Doc grinned and tossed Oliver a cigarette. "See all this shit you started? Why the hell don't you fold and take a goddamn siesta or sump'm, man, 'cause that's my last nail."

"*Tu madre*," Oliver muttered. "Hey, lay some matches on me, Joe. Ain't I a guest?"

Doc groaned when a female voice erupted in rapid, angry Spanish. It was a well-known fact that Oliver's wife could not abide foul language.

"You dirty-mouth dogs! And you, Doc! You are the worst one!"

"Help, man!" Doc muttered, sinking lower in his chair. "Smooth it out, Oliver!"

"Forget it," Oliver chortled. "You're blowin' a solo, baby."

Beatriz gave each man the evil eye as she walked in carrying two steaming plates piled high with fried chicken, gravy-covered mashed potatoes, and asparagus. Magda followed behind her with a basket of hot French bread and a pitcher of beer.

Cheers of approval went up from the men, who began reaching for plates.

"Oh, baby!" Joe said. "This really looks good! You learned how to fry chicken!"

"Beatriz teach me how is da way, Joe. Southern fried chickens, of course."

Oliver grinned as he bit off the end off of a jalepeño and squeezed the juice over his chicken. "And *this* is south-of-the-border fried chicken."

Beatriz tapped Magda's shoulder. "They don't deserve this, you know."

Magda smiled at Joe. "You like da chickens, Joe?"

He grinned and crooked his finger at her. "It's chicken, not chickens. And c'mere." When she leaned close, he wiped a smudge of flour off the tip of her nose. "Thanks for doing all this."

After everyone ate their fill, Beatriz sat down at the poker table and cracked her knuckles.

"Uh-oh!" Oliver hooted. "*You* vatos better prepare for humiliation. In case I never mentioned it, Beatriz comes from a family of cardsharps. The East L.A. Galindo Gang."

"Oh, come on, man," King laughed. "We're supposed to be scared of little Beatriz?"

Beatriz smiled and raised one eyebrow. "Excellent. A sucker. Deal the cards, por favor."

Doc grinned. "Oliver! A challenge from the little lady? Maaan, I'm *in*."

"Well, I been beat by her and her brothers too many times. So while you vatos get wised up, I'm gonna help Magda with the dishes. We'll see who's still smiling after my wife cleans you out." He patted Beatriz's shoulder and kissed her head. "Bring home the bacon, baby."

The front door suddenly squeaked open and Pearl Calhoun walked in. "Anybody home?"

King stood up and pulled out his chair. "Doc, you didn't tell us Pearl was coming!"

"Hello, everybody," Pearl said as she made her way over to the chair.

"So you're suddenly feelin' better?" Doc said in a caustic tone.

Pearl smiled languidly. "Yeah. I'm feelin' *much* better now, baby."

"Uh, Pearl, you met Beatriz before, didn't you?" Joe asked.

"Mm-hmm. At the club." She leaned over to hug Beatriz. "How you been, sugah?"

Before Beatriz could respond, Doc cut in: "Who's watchin' the kids, Pearl?"

Pearl gave him a pointed look. "The kids are okay. They been with Rose all afternoon."

"*All* afternoon?"

Pearl tapped out a cigarette and Joe lit it for her. She stared at Doc through a mist of smoke. "All afternoon, sugah."

After a long, awkward silence, Joe said, "Listen, Pearl, I want you to meet my wife. Hey, baby! Come in here and meet Pearl."

Magda walked in, wiping her hands on a dish towel. "I am so happy to meet you, Pearl."

Pearl smiled. "Me too, sugah."

"Joe tells to me how wonderful you sing."

"Well, I don't sing anymore, but thank you."

Magda glanced uncertainly at Doc and then back at Pearl. "So you are hungry to eat? Or you are playing da throat-cut cards with dese bums too?"

Pearl's deep laugh broke the tension in the room. "Sugah, let me help you clean up."

"No, no! You are guest! And Oliver helps me."

"Nonsense! We'll throw him back to these—what was that you called 'em? Throat-cut card bums? Lord, sugah, I sho' do love the way you talk."

≈∞≈

Four nights later, Magda was startled from a deep sleep by the sound of the front door slamming. She fumbled for the lamp in the darkness and turned it on. "Joe?"

"Sorry I woke you up," he said in a flat tone.

"Something is wrong, Joe?"

When he didn't answer, Magda sat up and watched him as he roughly yanked off his undershirt. She softly repeated her question. "Joe? Something is wrong?"

He strode into the bathroom without saying a word. Magda heard the squeak of the shower faucet, and leaned back against the pillows to wait.

A few minutes later, Joe returned to the bedroom, set the alarm clock, and turned off the lamp. Then he settled into bed, facing away from her.

Tentatively, she touched his back. "Joe?"

"I don't want to talk about it. We'll talk tomorrow. Just let me get some sleep, okay?"

"Okay, Joe. You sleep... I love you."

He sighed. "I love you too. Now go to sleep. I gotta get up early."

The next morning Magda eased out of bed quietly and blinked at the clock in the semi-darkness. Without putting on her brace, she hobbled out and closed the bedroom door softly. After plugging in the percolator, she began fixing breakfast.

A few minutes later, Joe walked in and put his arms around her.

"I—I don't hear dat clock ringing, Joe."

"I turned it off," he murmured, nuzzling her neck. "I heard you get up. And I didn't sleep very good last night. Guilty conscience, I guess."

"Why?"

"You know why. I came home mad and took it out on you. I'm sorry, baby."

Magda poured him a cup of coffee and turned the eggs over in the skillet. "So you tell to me now what is wrong?"

Joe sat down and sighed. "Music, what else? It was a lot more fun when we got to work together. I sure miss the Weingarten Studio. This place Al's got me in now is a real cut-rate joint. And the songs! Sheesh! What garbage! I guess until a guy's a star, they never let him call the shots. And now... Now they're even messing with my style."

Magda hobbled to the table. "Your style? What dat means, Joe? No more crooner songs?"

"No, it's not that exactly. It's just that— Hey! Where's your brace? Magda, you know what the doctor said about walking around without your brace." He stood up, scooped her into his arms, and carried her back to the bedroom.

"But Joe," she protested. "I—I make too much da noise when I want for you to sleep."

"And you were scared I'd wake up acting like I did last night. Damn!" Putting her down on the bed, he reached for the brace and shoes. "Here. Put 'em on right now."

"But Joe," she said as she pulled on a sock, "Da eggs will burn!"

"Forget the eggs. Next time I come home acting like that, just hit me with a lamp, okay?"

"Joe, please!" she laughed. "Please to let me make eggs again before I go."

Joe sprinted to the kitchen, turned off the burner, and wolfed down the eggs. "Just the way I like 'em, baby—crunchy." He poured a cup of coffee and walked back to the bedroom. "Hey, did you say you were going out? You got a session today? Wait, don't tell me—at the Weingarten?"

"Yes. I'm sorry, Joe…"

"It's okay. I'm a *little* jealous, but I'm glad you get to play at a class joint, even if I don't. So who's the date for?"

She finished the last buckle on her brace and smiled. "You are ready to be impressed?"

"I am ready to be impressed," he said, raising the coffee cup to his lips.

"Only Nat King Cole, of course."

Joe's cup froze in mid-air and a strange expression flickered in his eyes. He took a sip of coffee and smiled. "That's great, baby. Nat King Cole. That's—big time."

≈∞≈

After a long, difficult day in the cramped studio, Joe shifted on the stool in front of the orchestra. His shoulders were slumped and he was unable to concentrate. He had been staring at the lyric sheet for so long that the neat lettering was beginning to look like nonsensical black spiders.

Skip Steiner tapped the music stand with a pen. "Come on, Joe, just sing it, for chrissakes."

"I can't, Skip."

The musicians began muttering, and Joe shot them a defiant glare. "And I don't care what any of you bums think. This song is strictly from hunger, if you want my opinion."

Jay Stringfield, the songwriter, shouted at him, "We don't!"

Skip stepped between the two men. "Look, Joe, we went over all this yesterday and we all know how you feel. But you gotta trust me on this. Novelty songs are selling like crazy, man."

"Well, let 'em sell without me."

"Fine. Guess I'll just call Al and tell him to find another singer."

Joe threw the lyric sheet to the floor. "Wait a minute, goddammit! Whose date is this anyway? When you call Crandall, you can tell him I'm picking my own songs from now on."

Jay Stringfield smirked and walked away.

Skip stepped closer to Joe. "You're making enemies with the wrong guy, Joe. Al's got a long history with Stringfield. Payoffs for favors and that kind of thing. You know how the industry works. If I were you, I'd just grit my teeth and sing the song."

Joe felt concession creeping up and hated himself for it. "It's not my style," he mumbled.

Skip rested a persuasive hand on Joe's shoulder. "I know it, man. That's why I'm trying to walk you through it. Come on and let's just get it over with. Believe me, the next one'll be like cake and icing with your voice, Joe. Right up your alley."

Joe sighed and slumped back down on the stool. "All right, Skip. I'll give it a try."

Once Joe began to cooperate, they finished the first song quickly. Then, after they ran through the second song, it became clear that Skip had been right. It sounded like a hit to everyone, including Joe. But by the time he settled into a cab for the ride home, all he could think about was that first song. He grimaced as he envisioned the title in the center of the label:

"My Salt 'n' Pepper Baby (She Sure Can Cook)"
by Joe Bluestone

"Oh, well, shit. If Sinatra had to own up to the goddamn "Hucklebuck," then I guess…" He stopped muttering when he saw the cab driver's amused expression in the rear-view mirror. "Hey," he snapped, "I changed my mind. Drop me at 47th and Lex."

≈∞≈

When Joe stepped inside the Weingarten Studio, he could hear the faint sounds of the recording session in progress. When someone opened the door to step out of the control room, Nat King Cole's velvety voice floated out into the corridor. Joe immediately took note of the lyrics, which were far superior to "My Salt 'n' Pepper Baby."

He saw Jill, the blonde receptionist, leaning against the desk scribbling notes in a scheduling book. "Hi, Jill," he said. "Remember me? Joe Bluestone. Okay to go in?"

Jill looked up. "Closed session, Joe," she said. "That's Nat Cole."

"I know. My wife's with the orchestra. So—do you think I could watch—if I'm real quiet?"

She looked up again and shrugged. "Well—I don't know, but let me check."

Joe followed Jill to the control room door and watched as she whispered something to the man seated at the console. He glanced back at Joe and impatiently pointed at a seat. After this brief acknowledgment, Joe spent the next hour feeling invisible and irrelevant.

The session abruptly ended when Nat announced that he was tired and exited by a side door. As the musicians began packing their instruments, Joe went in to get Magda. But as he headed over to her, he could tell that she hadn't seen him. The piano player seemed to be flirting with her by trying to get her to take a puff of his cigarette. At first, she just giggled and shook her head. But then, to Joe's surprise, she allowed him to place the cigarette between her lips. After inhaling, she coughed and laughed, and then handed the cigarette back to him.

By the time Joe reached her, he was in a rage. "Having fun, sweetheart?" he hissed.

The piano player turned away. "G'night, Magda." His tone was casual, dismissive.

Joe grabbed his shoulder and spun him back around. "Wrong! That's *Mrs.* Bluestone. And *if* Mrs. Bluestone smoked—which she *doesn't*—she wouldn't be smokin' your brand." He finished by swatting the cigarette neatly out of the piano player's mouth.

Magda glanced around the room nervously. "Joe, please! My work is here."

The piano player smacked Joe's hand away. "You're screwin' with the wrong guy, Mac."

Joe grinned and his eyes glittered dangerously. "How would you like a couple'a broken fingers, ya sonofabitch? Couldn't hurt your lousy playin'—that's for goddamn sure."

Magda looked around. Everyone was staring at them. "Please to take me home now, Joe," she pleaded. "You make me to lose my job—and we need da money."

Joe glared at her. "*What?* Look—you better get this straight, baby. Any goddamn money we need *I'll* make! You understand that?"

Paul Ballentine hurried over. "Hey!" he said sharply. "What's the problem here?"

Ignoring Paul, Joe grabbed the violin case and then pulled Magda by the hand as he strode to the door. She was stumbling to keep up, and by the time he managed to hail a taxi, she was sobbing. He opened the door, pushed her into the seat, and climbed in after her.

"Let me tell you sump'm, *baby*," he snapped. "You are *not* supporting me—get that? And let me tell you sump'm *else*. The next time you embarrass me like that I'll—" Suddenly aware that the taxi was not moving, he glared at the driver. "What the hell are you waitin' for?"

The driver, a burly roughneck type, turned completely around in his seat to address Joe. "Okay, now let me tell *you* sump'm, *baby*. Here's what I'm waitin' for. I'm waitin' for this goddamn wise guy who's stinkin' up my cab to apologize to the pretty lady and then do sump'm *genius*, like givin' me an address. Then maybe I'll *think* about not kickin' your ass out and stompin' it under the sidewalk. Get that, baby?"

Joe got out and slammed the door. "Give him the address and go home, Magda."

≈∞≈

When Magda woke the next morning, she was surprised to see Joe asleep beside her. Without putting on her brace, she stole quietly into the living room and dialed Paul Ballantine's number.

"Paul?" she whispered. "I—I am sorry—to call so early—"

"Perfectly all right, Magda. I was already up working on these charts and I was going to call you this morning anyway. I was worried about you after what happened last night."

"Oh, I am fine, Paul. Everything is—fine."

"Why are you whispering and stammering if everything's fine? Magda, I know your personal life's not my business, but when Joe brings it to the studio, that *makes* it my business."

"I am so sorry, Paul. Joe don't mean to be dat way… I'm sorry. I am now fired?"

"Of course not. How could I fire my first violin? Besides, it was Joe's fault, not yours. But look—I can't have that kind of nonsense going on at my sessions. And Nat—he's too busy to put up with it. If he'd still been there, we could've all been fired. So I don't want Joe at any more sessions. If he gets mad, tell him to talk to me. As far as I'm concerned, he's banned."

"Banned? What dis mean—dis 'banned'?"

"Sorry, Magda. It means he's not allowed—he can't come in."

"But Paul—how I tell to him dis—he is banned?"

"Tell him to call me if you want to, Magda. It's his own fault. Now, are you still coming today? Nat loved what we did yesterday."

"Yes, I come. I tell to Joe. He will understand and—yes, I come today."

"Good. See you at ten."

As she placed the receiver back in the cradle, Joe's voice startled her from behind.

"Tell to Joe *what*?"

"Oh! Joe—I—I wake you up."

"Tell me what? Who the hell was that?"

Magda stared at him, but said nothing. She attempted to walk past him, but he gripped her arm and spun her around to face him. "You hurt my arm, Joe! Stop, please!"

"I asked you a question. Answer me and I'll let you go."

Magda bit her lip to keep from crying out. "Paul tells to me—you are banned! No more you come to da studio, Joe. You make trouble for me and for Paul too!" She jerked her arm free and swept her hair off her face. "Now—I get dressed and go to work. Is okay for you?"

Joe's angry expression slowly transformed into a grin that lay somewhere between amusement and lunacy. It was a look Magda had never seen before, and it instantly chilled her anger into fear. She felt herself stumbling backwards.

"Go ahead," Joe said smoothly. "And tell Paul he'll be beggin' to work for me someday."

≈∞≈

Joe hated unfamiliar stages and this one had particularly bright, hot lights. He couldn't see the audience and recoiled at the impenetrable darkness of the rows of seats. Suddenly, the house lights came on. "Carnegie Hall," he whispered. Then he heard the bandleader begin to sing the opening to "Minnie the Moocher."

Joe gazed at the white audience. Middle-aged matrons dressed in mink and diamonds and gentlemen in tuxedos were buzzing disapprovingly. He hurried over to the bandleader to suggest a different song. Cab Calloway spun around in his white tuxedo and shook his long, tousled hair.

"What'sa matter, Joe?" he shouted. "Forget the words?"

A man who looked like Lionel Barrymore stood up in the audience, squinted through his monocle, and pointed at the stage. "They're niggers!" he shouted. "Niggers in Carnegie Hall!"

As Joe stared at the man, he spotted one black face in the audience, dead center in a sea of white: Calvin. And he was headed straight for the stage.

"Somebody call the police!" Joe yelled. "He's a killer!"

As Cab Calloway continued his insane dancing, Calvin got closer. Now he was less than a foot away, eagerly clenching his fists. "Look me in the eye, Joe… I *said* look at me!"

"I—I can't."

"Then I'ma haf'ta beat'cha, Joe. You know that."

Then came the rain of fists. A stinging right, followed by that destructive left hook Joe had always tried to avoid. As he fell, he heard echoes of applause and bravos from the audience.

He woke to the sound of his own cry and felt wet all over; the sheets on the bed were soaked with perspiration. For a confused moment, he felt a terrifying presence in the dark room and fumbled with the lamp. Blinking at the sudden brightness, he took a frantic look around the room. Nothing. No Calvin. Nothing but a thick, smothering silence. Instinctively, he picked up the telephone, but then quickly hung up. He couldn't call Magda—not in this condition—whimpering like a scared baby. And not after the way he had treated her when he left town.

A long stretch of lonely night lay ahead, so he turned on the radio, hoping to find a late program. After it warmed up, he found surprising comfort in the smooth voice of a radio announcer extolling the heavenly flavor of Chase & Sanborn coffee.

≈∞≈

The next evening, Magda heard Joe's key in the lock and went to meet him at the door. He stepped inside and dropped his suitcase. When she saw his angry expression, her heart sank.

Finally he said, "Well, that's it. I'm finished. So much for a goddamn hit record."

"I am so sorry, Joe. It—it don't go so good?"

He scowled. "No, it don't go so good. So now I guess I've gotta stand here and tell you every detail about my failure so you won't feel like I'm 'shutting on you the door,' huh?"

"Please to don't mock my English, Joe. And—it was maybe not so bad like you think."

"Oh, yeah," he sneered. "I guess playing to empty chairs isn't so bad, huh? Just leave me alone, Magda. You don't know what you're talking about. You weren't there."

"But I *want* to be there," she said. "And you will make dat hit record someday, Joe."

"You don't understand," he moaned. "I can't stand being a—a nobody! You don't know what I had to do to just— Look, it's not just a hit record, Magda. I wish I could make you understand." He squeezed his eyes shut and dropped into a chair. "I *need* this."

"But—I want to understand, Joe. I try—but you don't talk to me no more."

"Just—leave me alone. I'm depressed. You know what that word means, Magda? You expect me to come home and just turn it off. But this is my whole life!... Look. Just leave me alone." He stood up and strode into the bedroom, shutting the door.

Magda sank onto the sofa, paralyzed by the silence for several minutes. Finally, she walked into the bedroom, where she found Joe stretched across the bed, sound asleep. She gently eased off his shoes and loosened his tie. His forehead was moist with perspiration, causing the edges of his hair to curl into tight, sticky ringlets. She gazed at his face for a moment, remembering the happy times before their marriage, and wondered what had gone wrong. As usual, she had no answers, so she headed into the bathroom for a long soak. After removing her brace and turning on the faucets, she rubbed the deep red indentations on her leg for a moment, then climbed into the tub. As the bathroom filled with steam, she stared at the white porcelain "hot" and "cold" knobs until she felt tears streaking down her face. She laughed bitterly at the blurred knobs. "Hot and cold," she whispered, "like marriage. No warm. Only to burn or freeze."

The cooling of the water was the only clue as to how much time had passed, and Magda got out and dried off. Pulling on her robe, she opened the door slightly to let out the steam, and then sat on the edge of the tub. She stared at her brace, hating it more than usual. As she sat rubbing the fading marks on her leg, the bathroom door opened, and she looked up. Joe walked over and knelt in front of her. He didn't say a word as he gently massaged her leg. Any other time, she would have been touched by such a tender, wordless apology, but this time she only stared down at him, preparing herself for the next cold spell.

Chapter 17

After an initial mediocre climb, Joe's record had dropped to the bottom of the charts. The only thing worse than his sagging career was his marriage, which seemed to have fallen off a cliff.

But then something happened to boost his spirits. After a guest appearance on a radio program in Los Angeles, the show's producer introduced him to an agent named David Smythe, who was the most energetic human being Joe had ever met. As they discussed career ideas, Smythe put him in mind of a fizzy fountain drink about to bubble over the top of a glass. The most attractive idea he suggested was pitching Joe to both Clef and Capitol. Smythe had connections with both labels and told Joe he would be a good fit at either one. Capitol Records was more prestigious, but jazz impresario Norman Granz was generating innovative sounds and big sales over at Clef. Without giving his first mentor Al Crandall a passing thought, Joe impulsively signed a representation contract with David Smythe.

Smythe seemed to have all the answers—even a solution for Joe's recent difficulty sleeping. He whipped out a business card and wrote the name of a doctor on the back. "He's in New York, Joe. He's got an office on the upper east side. Go see him when you get back."

"Wait a minute, David. I'm not crazy about the idea of sleeping pills. I heard they have a sort of hangover effect and we're gonna be busy. I can't be draggin' around all day."

Smythe snapped his fingers in front of Joe's face. "Hey, baby! Where the hell have you been? Show business runs on Bennies, man! The trick is not to get hooked. An occasional dose just gives you a boost for a couple'a days. Same thing with the sleeping pills. Temporary. Only when you really need it, man. That's all."

Over the next few days, Smythe met with executives from Capitol and Clef to talk over possible deals, and called Joe every morning with progress reports. After booking studio time to record a demo, he dropped by the apartment to check Joe's schedule for the day.

"Oh, hi, David," Joe said as he let him in. "You're just in time for coffee."

"Thanks. Don't mind if I do. So are you ready to take a look at some musicians today?"

Joe grinned as he poured the coffee. "You mean—I get final word on the musicians?"

"Sure. We can even use your wife's orchestra if you want to. Ballantine, right?"

"Uh, well—" Joe shrugged. "I'm open to other suggestions, if you know what I mean."

"Loud and clear, baby. But meanwhile, I'm about an inch away from booking you into an elite jazz club in Connecticut. I represent the house band and the owner's dying to add a singer to the act. I figure you could appear there on weekends between recording sessions. If you like their sound, you could use them as studio back-up too. And strings we can get. I know a guy—"

Joe laughed. "Hey, slow down, David! Give me a chance to catch up."

David raised his hand and snapped his fingers several times in rapid succession. "I move fast, kid. It's the only way to keep my acts working. And I really think you'll like this band."

"But I'm still solo, David. I record as a *solo*. They'll understand that, right?"

"Sure, baby, sure. And you'll be the featured attraction at the Sundown until we get you signed and cut that hit record. Look—let's drive up to Hartford later and I'll introduce you to the owner. We'll catch a show and tie up all the loose ends."

"Sounds great, David."

"Leave it to me, kid. I'll make some calls and get back to you in a couple of hours."

≈∞≈

Joe was convinced that signing with David Smythe was the smartest thing he had ever done. Within a week, Smythe had booked him into the Club Sundown in Hartford, Connecticut and hired the band for the recording date. The band members were so glad to get the studio work they treated Joe like a king. The only bad news was that Capitol had passed on signing him.

"I'm sorry, Joe, but they make a good point," David explained. "They've got Nat King Cole *and* Dean Martin. I hear the project Dean's working on now is a definite chart topper, and lately, every song Nat cuts turns into instant gold."

Joe bristled at the mention of Nat King Cole. "Yeah, they must be *delirious* with him."

"Yeah, but don't forget—I've still got that meeting with Norman Granz later tonight."

"Wait, David. Are you sure Granz hasn't got a full stable of singers? What label's that new guy on? Every station on the dial is playing 'Because of You' seven days a week. What's that guy's name?" He snapped his fingers. "Bennett. Tony Bennett. What label's *he* on?"

David laughed. "Don't worry, Bennett's with Columbia. Now, as it stands, Clef Records leans more towards instrumental jazz, but that's how I plan to pitch you. You said it yourself. Radio's playing Tony Bennett constantly and Frank and Nat are selling like ice cream in July. Granz'd be crazy not to grab a piece of that action! All I gotta do is convince him that Joe Bluestone is the boy to deliver. I'll call you the minute I find out something."

≈∞≈

The next morning David called early. His voice was hoarse but upbeat, as always. "Well, kid. It took a lot of talking, but Granz just called me back. He wants to sign you."

"What? Holy shit, David! When?"

"We'll probably meet with everybody to sign early next week."

Magda walked into the room and Joe grinned at her. "You're the greatest, David!"

"Working with that bebop band influenced your style. Granz is excited about your future."

"Yeah?"

"Yeah. Okay, look, kid. I gotta hit the streets. I'll call you later."

"Sure thing, David. And thanks again!"

After hanging up, Joe grabbed Magda and kissed her. Then he hurried into the bathroom and reached into the medicine chest. After swallowing his morning pill, he went to the closet and pulled out a shirt. Magda stood in the doorway, staring at him curiously.

"I know, I know," Joe laughed. "I'm acting like a nut. But baby, I'm with Clef!"

≈∞≈

Pearl Calhoun had given Magda her phone number the first time they met, pointedly telling her to use it if she ever needed a friend. When Magda finally called, they talked for nearly two hours. Pearl told her about her children, and they exchanged stories about Harlem and Greece. Magda felt so comfortable talking to her that she began telling her about her troubled marriage, and found wisdom in her new friend's thoughtful advice. On an impulse, she asked Pearl if she would like to come to the apartment for coffee.

Pearl arrived early the next morning with a smile and a curious question: "Sugah, do you have any trouble climbin' stairs?"

After coffee, the two women headed to Penn Station, where they picked up a handful of schedules. They boarded the A-Train for a short ride. Then Pearl said, "Here's our stop, sugah."

Magda gamely made her way up the subway stairs. When she reached the top and looked around, the thrill of accomplishment eclipsed her exhaustion. "We travel to Harlem, Pearl!"

Pearl smiled. "We sho' did! And once you catch your breath, you fixin' to travel to my building. Then next time, you'll know how to get there by yourself. You gotta do things by yourself sometimes, sugah. That's the only way to learn independence. And then it'll be my turn to make the coffee."

≈∞≈

Every Friday, Joe would blow through the apartment like a maniacal whirlwind, packing and racing for the train. And upon his return from Hartford each Sunday, it was a mad rush into midtown to spend hours in the studio. Although he allowed Magda to join him for the first few weekends in Connecticut, her invitation was angrily withdrawn the first time her schedule conflicted with his. The minute he was gone, she dialed Pearl's number.

"Hello, Pearl?"

"How you doin', sista?" Even over the phone, Pearl's deep voice was comforting.

Magda sighed. "Oh, I am okay, I suppose. But Joe is mad with me again."

"Oh, Lord, that Joe… What was it this time, sugah?"

"Well, I tell to him I have dat recording session tomorrow. I tell to him I will take da train later to meet him in Connecticut after da session, but he tells to me I am—banned...Why Joe is always mad with me when I must work, Pearl? And we need da money for dat house he buys."

"Oh, so you made up your mind about that house? He finally took you to see it?"

"Yes. Is little house in New Jersey near to da Holland Tunnel. But I tell to Joe why we don't look for a house in Harlem to be near to you—and den he is mad with me again, of course."

Pearl chuckled. "Harlem? Yeah, I bet that *did* make him mad."

"But why, Pearl? I will like to live near to you."

"Well, sounds like he's set on that house in Jersey. Where'd you say it was? Hoboken?"

"No—Hackensack. But dat house will cost much money and we save only little bit. But Joe tells to me don't worry. He will make money from selling—um, da hotcakes?"

Pearl rumbled a deep laugh. "Not sellin' hotcakes, sugah. It's sellin' records—*like* hotcakes, and good luck to him, 'cause that ain't easy. But how do *you* like the house?"

"Is nice with big grass and two doors on da front. And many windows and flowers on da wallpaper." She sighed. "But I don't know, Pearl. Is more far from Harlem on da train, I think."

"Sugah, once you get moved in, I'll come over and show you how to get to the Essex Street Station. And it's a breeze from there, so don't you worry. Long as there's buses and trains, ain't nothin' gonna keep us from havin' our coffee together."

≈∞≈

Preparations for moving into the new house kept Magda's mind occupied for a while, and once they were settled in, there seemed to be no end of things to do. When she wasn't working, she shopped with Pearl and lost herself in decorating her new house. She still practiced her violin every evening, but on her anniversary, she stopped early to fix Joe a special dinner. As she placed a pot of potatoes on the burner, the phone rang. She hurried out to answer it. "Hello?"

"Oh. Uh, hello, Magda. It's Al Crandall."

"Al! You don't call for such da long time. Everything is okay for you?"

"No! Everything is *not* okay. In fact, your husband is giving me the dirtiest screw of my life! Sorry for the language, but after all the money I laid out for that bum—I'm pretty angry."

"Oh, my Gott, Al! What Joe do to you?"

"Oh. It figures he wouldn't tell you about it. Look, I'm just calling to find out his reaction to the papers he was served with yesterday. Is he there?"

"No, Al. What papers?"

"I'm sorry, Magda, but I'm suing your husband—and Smythe too, if I can. I had to do it. I'm a businessman and your husband did me wrong. So just give him the message. No, better yet, just tell him to call my lawyer. The number's on the papers he was served with."

After he hung up, Magda walked slowly back to the stove and stared into the pot of potatoes until the sound of the front door bell startled her. "Please to wait," she called.

When she opened the door, a delivery boy smiled at her from behind a huge bouquet of red roses in a large red and white mosaic vase. "Delivery for Mrs. Bluestone."

She pointed at the entry table and the boy placed the roses on it. Then Magda reached into a candy bowl for some change and handed it to him. "Thank you."

She closed the door and read the note:

"Magda—Please forgive me for not being home to spend our anniversary together. I had to work, but I promise, tomorrow is all yours. I love you—Joe."

She read the note again, and then dropped it into the trash can.

"Always tomorrow with you, Joe."

≈∞≈

With Joe gone more than he was at home, Magda felt a constant loneliness beginning to overwhelm her. She told herself that Joe loved her and that things would work out, but it wasn't helping. She visited Pearl more frequently, and tried to fill the lonely nighttime hours with marathon practice sessions on her violin.

One night, she stopped in the middle of a song, suddenly realizing that her marriage to Joe had been a mistake. In a moment of panic, she called Professor Tosca, hoping that he would squeeze her in for more intense study.

"We were going to call you this week, my dear," the Professor said gently. "My daughter has just presented us with a grandson, and Lavinia and I will be leaving next week for Italy."

"Oh, that is so wonderful, Professor!" Magda said. "But when you get back—"

"I'm afraid there is more," he said. "For some time now, Lavinia has been worrying about my health. And now, with my new grandson, we have decided to move back to Italy for good."

As he continued to tell her about his plans, Magda's mind drifted back to her first terrifying months in America when Professor Tosca and his wife had been both parents and teachers to her. They had helped her learn English and encouraged her to reach new musical heights. And now they were leaving. She was barely able to say her goodbyes before the tears overwhelmed her.

She dialed Pearl's number, but then quickly hung up, remembering her first words of advice: *You gotta do things by yourself sometimes, sugah. That's the only way to learn independence.*

≈∞≈

In the following weeks, Magda made up her mind to save her marriage. Thanksgiving was fast approaching, and she decided to cook a big dinner for Joe. She was sitting on the sofa reading some recipes Pearl had given her when Paul Ballantine called.

"Hello, Paul! How are you today?"

"Hi, Magda. I'm fine. I was calling to find out your plans for next week. I hope you're not cooking a big turkey dinner, because I really need you in the studio this weekend and the first half of next week. I'm not sure we'll be finished by Thursday."

"Oh," Magda murmured. "I *was* planning to cook, I'm afraid. And Joe will be coming home dat Wednesday night, just because I cook dat turkey."

"Well, I hate to tempt you but it's for Dean Martin—double scale."

"Oh, Paul! For how many songs?"

"Six. And I can't do it without you. Come on, Joe's in the business. He'll understand."

"Well, okay, Paul. I call Joe and ask him."

"No, Magda. Call Joe and *tell* him. This is important. How would he feel if he couldn't count on his musicians when he needed them?"

"You are right, of course, Paul. I call him now."

Magda hung up, but kept her hand on the receiver. Then she quickly dialed the number for the Park Ridge Hotel in Hartford. A pleasant sounding male voice answered.

"Good evening. Park Ridge Hotel."

"Good evening to you, sir. Will you please ring da room of Joseph Bluestone?"

"Hold a minute, please. I'll connect you."

Joe picked up after four rings. "Yeah?"

"Joe?"

"Oh, hi."

Magda winced at the annoyed edge in his voice. "Something is wrong, Joe? You sound—"

"Nothing's wrong. Look, I'm just having a bad day is all. Now tell me what you called for."

Magda took a breath. "Well, I have good news for you and I have bad news too."

"Well, I'm already in a bad news mood, so you might as well hit me with that first."

"Okay. I—I'm afraid I will not be cooking dat turkey Thanksgiving dinner, Joe."

"Oh, is that all? So we'll find a restaurant. No catastrophe. So, what's the good news?"

"I have work with Paul in da studio. Four days—maybe more. And for da double scale too."

"Double scale? Who for?"

"Dean Martin."

After a long silence, Joe muttered, "Perfect."

"You are now mad again, Joe?"

"No. It's just a lousy ending to a lousy day, that's all."

"Joe, why you are mad with me when I have work?"

"It's not that. Look—Dean Martin's with Capitol, remember? And Capitol turned me down for a recording deal. They said they already have enough crooners—good ol' Dino boy, for one. Then you call to tell me you're doin' a session with him. How do you think that makes me feel?"

"But you don't tell me about Capitol, Joe—only dat you sign to dat Clef label."

"Never mind. You know what happened to me today? David tried to book me at the Paramount as an opening act, and they turned me down. Said I got no marquee value. And my radio play is slipping. All they want is Dean and Nat and Frank."

"I'm sorry, Joe."

"Why should you be sorry? Stop throwin' me bones, for chrissakes."

"I—I call only for to tell you dat news, Joe."

"Of *course* you did. I bet you couldn't wait to tell me."

"Stop it, Joe!" she shouted. "I don't know how to please you! Always you are mad!"

"Aww, shit," he muttered. "And now you're crying."

Magda slammed down the receiver. For a moment, it felt good. But only for a moment.

She cried until 2:30 that morning, and finally dialed the Hartford number.

"Good evening. Park Ridge Hotel."

"Hello. Will you please ring da room of Joseph Bluestone?"

"Certainly. Hold the line a moment, please."

After three rings, a female voice answered. "Hello?"

Magda froze.

"Hello? Is anybody there?" the strange woman snapped.

Magda hung up and stared at the telephone for a long time before redialing.

"Good evening. Park Ridge Hotel."

"Joseph Bluestone, please. I think before—I get maybe da wrong room."

"My apologies. Please hold the line."

Only one ring this time. The same woman's voice answered. "Hello?"

Clutching her forehead, Magda croaked, "Please. I call for Joe Bluestone."

"He's in the shower and who are *you*? How do you know Joe?"

Instead of answering, Magda quietly placed the receiver back on the hook.

≈∞≈

When Joe returned home the next night, Magda was seated comfortably on the sofa, listening to the radio. She saw him open his mouth to say hello, but her cold, silent stare stopped him. After an awkward moment, he strode into the bedroom and shut the door.

Magda heard the suitcase drop to the floor, followed by Joe's angry muttering, and drawers opening and slamming shut.

"You are now mad with me, Joe?" she whispered. "Good. I make my courage already, so you come back. I wait." Doris Day was singing "Sentimental Journey" on the radio, and Magda began singing along.

Suddenly, Joe flung open the bedroom door, strode back into the living room, and turned off the radio. Then he turned and glared at her. "What the hell's wrong with you *now*?"

Magda stood up and reached around Joe to turn the radio back on, louder this time. She returned to the sofa and stared at him flatly as Doris continued to croon.

Joe reached down and yanked the plug out of the wall. The radio emitted a squeaky, electronic yelp, and Doris Day fell silent.

"I said what the *hell* is wrong with you, Magda?" he shouted.

Magda shrugged one shoulder. "Nothing the hell is wrong with me," she said calmly. "You are da one with something wrong. You want for me to go away, Joe? Tell to me. I go."

"What the hell are you talking about?" he countered.

"Always you are angry, Joe. Going away all da time and shouting at me. It is easier if I just go away, no? Den you can go away all da time and not worry about me. Tell to me now, Joe, and I go. Simple." She narrowed her eyes in a chilly, pinpoint stare. "You think I am not serious?"

After a long silence, he lowered his voice. "What brought this on? Would you tell me that?"

"Sure. I tell. We fight yesterday and I call you to make up, but your girlfriend—she answer da telephone, Joe. She tells to me she waits in your bed while you take a shower."

Joe's reaction didn't surprise her. She watched as he began shouting and gesturing angrily. "You know what? You're crazy! Don't tell me you're gonna be one of those insecure, suspicious wives always accusing me of things I'm not even doing. Did it ever *occur* to you that they might've just rung the wrong number? Huh?"

"Yes. Dat is why I call back again, and—"

"And what?" His tone was icy.

"And I don't believe you, Joe."

A sad expression crossed his face; then he sat down slowly. "You know," he whispered, "that's the first time you ever stood up to me like that. Maybe you should've done it sooner."

Magda stared coldly at him, disappointed in his artless tactic. He was actually trying to shift her attention with this fake act of contrition. "Who was dat woman in your room, Joe?"

"All right," he said softly, there *was* a girl. But not like you think. When you hung up on me after our fight, I got mad. I had to get to the club for rehearsal and I tried to put it out of my mind, but I was—I was just a lot more upset than I thought. I wasn't thinking straight, baby. Look, I never would'a given that girl a second look any other time but—"

Magda stood up, but Joe reached for her hand. "Wait! Please. . ."

She sat down quietly and gave him an expectant look.

He took a deep breath. "Okay. I—I guess she was just at the right place at the wrong time and interested in picking up one of the musicians. She came on to me and I was still mad so I thought, why not? But when we got to the room, I got cold feet. I went to take a shower so I could think up a way to get rid of her. When the phone rang I thought it might be you, but she told me it was a wrong number and—"

"And?"

"And I told her to get out. Look, *nothing* happened, baby. That's the truth. And I hurried right home because I wanted to make up with you so bad."

Magda was still studying Joe's eyes. They reminded her of the time she had fallen into deep water when she was twelve. She had nearly drowned and then contracted Polio.

"So why you don't call me after dat girl leaves?"

Joe looked down at her hand and touched it gently. "I wanted to make up in person, baby. Do you know—" He stopped, and was quiet for a long time. When he looked up, there were tears standing in his eyes. "Do you know how much I need you? I'm sorry for hurting you, I really am. Look—I'll be leaving for California next week, and I want to spend all my time here with you before I go… Please don't ever talk about leaving me again, baby. I really *need* you. If you ever left me—I don't know what I'd do."

Magda tried to resist when he reached for her, but his tears were a shock, and her anger changed to confusion. When he kissed her, she was overwhelmed by a new feeling for Joe—pity.

Chapter 18

Magda's most precious memories were measured in seconds. Her first few steps after months of childhood paralysis. The first time she coaxed the sound of tears from the strings of a violin. Her first kiss. And now there was a new one.

Each time she reached the top of the subway steps of the 125th Street Station, she felt a thrill. She wasn't sure whether it was because of her new-found independence or her friendship with Pearl, but Magda had fallen in love with Harlem. She breathed in the chilly air and looked around. With Christmas just around the corner, the shops along St. Nicholas Avenue glittered with red and green decorations.

She walked into the flower shop, where she always bought a small bouquet for Pearl's table. The bell over the door jingled and Maybelle's voice rang out: "How ya doin', Miss Magda?"

"I am fine, Mrs. Maybelle. How you are feeling today?"

"Jus' fine, baby. Got some new arrangements in this mornin'. Be hard to choose."

"Oh, yes!" Magda said as she looked over the flowers. She finally chose a small bundle of red and white roses, nestled among a sprig of holly and two silver Christmas ornaments.

After chatting with Maybelle, she walked to Pearl's building and began the climb to the sixth floor. She heard the children and saw the open door, so she went in. "Hello?" she called.

Pearl walked out of the kitchen. "Hey, sista! What's that you got there—? Oh, flowers!" She hugged Magda and set the flowers on the table. "Thanks, sista. You doin' okay on them stairs?"

"Yes, Pearl, but my brace—still I bump each step. I make noise."

"Oh, don't worry about that, sugah! I'm just checkin' on you. Those stairs wear me out—" She stopped and caught Edward by the arm as he tried to sneak past her. "Okay, dammit! Where you think you goin'? You *know* you still on punishment for rough-housin' with that baby! So you *ain't* goin' out."

"Come on, Mama," Edward pleaded. "She ain't hurt."

"Not this time, but she's little and you gotta learn to be more careful."

Doc was sitting on the piano bench with his horn at his side. He was marking his sheet music, but looked up sternly. "Boy, don't make me take off my belt! Mind your Mama and go play in your room."

"Yes, sir," Edward mumbled as he slunk down the hallway to his room.

"Have a seat, sugah," Pearl said. "I just made coffee. Doc, you want some coffee, baby?"

"None for me, thanks," he said. "Hello, Magda. How are you doin'?"

Magda shrugged. "I guess I am fine."

Doc stood up and stretched. "That didn't sound very convincing to me."

"I do okay, I guess, Doc."

Doc kissed Magda's cheek. "Hey, you been practicin' that two-step we taught you?"

"No one to practice with, I'm afraid. Joe is all da time gone so I come here to practice."

"Well, that's cool, but remember we were gonna teach you to jitterbug today." Placing his horn on the bench, he sat back down at the piano and began playing a loud boogie-woogie.

"Oh, my Gott, Doc! To jitterbug? I don't know—"

"Sure, sista!" Pearl said, handing her a cup of coffee. "Little Lindy Hoppin', beboppin'. . ."

Magda took a sip, then laughed. "Well, maybe I make my courage after we shop."

"Oh, yeah, sista! We gotta get to Macy's. Lemme see if I can talk this man into babysittin' his little pride and his little joy."

Doc grimaced as he stood up slowly and loudly jingled the change in his pocket. "Who wants a sodapop?" he called. "Edward, you got a twenty-minute parole, boy."

Edward hurried back into the living room grinning, and Shay ran in behind him, shrieking as she jumped into her father's arms.

Pearl quickly kissed all three faces. "We probably won't be here when you get back. But we'll only be gone a couple'a hours or so. You kids be good for Daddy."

Doc helped the children put on their coats, and finally the front door slammed shut.

Pearl sighed. "Okay, let me just finish foldin' these clothes and we can catch our train."

"Of course, Pearl," Magda said. "What I can do to help you?"

"Well, I guess you could put these away," Pearl said, handing her a small stack of folded undershirts, "in the bottom drawer of that big chest in my room."

Magda carried the stack into Pearl's room and opened the drawer. As she pushed aside the other clothes to make room, she gasped. A scene of death stared back at her from the bottom of the drawer—a postcard depicting a Negro man hanging from a tree. His shirt was gone, and his trousers were ripped and bloody. Some bulky object was stuffed into his mouth, and his neck was twisted in a macabre angle. But more horrifying than the broken man were the white people, smiling and pointing at him as if he were a trophy. Magda stared at the caption: *"The only good nigger is a dead nigger."* Her hand shook as she turned the card over to read the handwritten message: *"Cleaning up the South—one sassy nigger at a time. —Ed and the Dixie Brigade"*

In the distance, she heard Pearl's voice calling to her. "Sugah? What'cha doin' in there? I'm 'bout finished now so we can get goin'."

A moment later Pearl appeared in the doorway. Unable to speak, Magda stared at her, then held out the postcard as tears spilled from her eyes.

"What's that you got there, sugah?" Pearl asked as she reached for the postcard. "Oh, Lord," she moaned softly. "So that's where he put it." Sinking slowly onto the edge of the bed, she patted the space next to her. "Sit down, sista, so I can explain this to you."

"How you can explain, Pearl? Dat horrible picture! Why—why dey kill dat man?"

"Could'a been anything. Talkin' too proud to a white man. Havin' sump'm they ain't got… Lookin' at a white woman."

Magda shook her head. "I never see *nothing* so horrible before. Why dat can happen—?"

"I can't explain *why*, sugah. Okay, look. Do you ever notice how white folks stare at you and me when we go shoppin'? Don't you know they're thinkin' I'm your maid or sump'm?"

"My maid? But—why?"

"Because they could never accept the fact that we're such close friends." Pearl sighed. "Oh, maybe if you were raised here, it might be easier for you to understand. It's a little different from that trouble my husband had at your wedding."

Magda lowered her head. "Papa was very bad to hurt Doc dat way."

"That's okay, sugah. Joe told us all about how you fought your Daddy on that."

"Papa never is seeing much Negroes in Athens, Pearl. But still he is wrong."

"Yes, he is. But see, it goes deeper than that. Now, I know you heard about slavery, right?"

"Yes," Magda sniffled. "In school I learn. And da Civil War—and Abraham Lincoln."

"Well, the Civil War was nearly a hundred years ago, but deep down inside, white folks ain't changed a lick. Oh, we get *paid* now, but they'd still rather keep us workin' the same ol' slave jobs—cleanin' and cookin' and shinin' shoes— Lord, it's a wonder we got ourselves as many colored doctors and teachers as we do. And honey, believe me, even here in the North, they had to work twice as hard to get those jobs, and they still make pitiful money. But as bad as that is, there's sump'm much worse in the South. It's called segregation, sugah."

"Seger—seger-gation? What dis word means, Pearl?"

"It means—to divide folks up—by their color. They do it with signs and laws, and worse things sometimes. See, there's places Negroes ain't allowed to go. White-only places."

"But dat picture, Pearl! Why Doc keeps dat horrible picture?"

"Okay, sista. I'm gettin' to it. It was back when I was pregnant with Shay. See, Doc was with this white band and they were headin' out on a road trip. He didn't tell me they were dippin' down south, 'cause we'd been hearin' all about the race trouble they had down there that summer, and he knew I'd worry." She paused, and then continued in a deeper, troubled tone. "When he got back, he was real quiet for a few days. Drinkin' more than usual and smokin' too many cigarettes. But I finally got it out of him, and then he pulled that postcard out of his pocket. He told me somebody sent it up to the bandstand with a drink. A message to get out'a town. He said he threw it on the floor, but the next morning, it turned up again—under the windshield wiper of the band's station wagon. So they left town, and quick."

"Oh, Pearl! You worry for Doc to be killed—like dat poor man in da picture?"

Pearl's eyes went flat. "A Negro woman lives with that fear every single day of her life."

Magda gasped. "Oh! Please to forgive me for my questions, but *why* he keeps dat picture?"

"For Edward, sugah," Pearl said patiently.

"No! A little boy don't need to see dat horrible picture! He will have bad dreams!"

"He won't show it to him until he's older. But he needs to see it."

"But why, Pearl? *Why* he needs to see?"

"Same reason you needed to see it. Look, sista. Sometimes we gotta look evil right in the face. That's all there is to it. Edward needs to protect himself. But how's he gonna protect himself if he don't know what's out there?" She touched Magda's arm. "Stop worryin' about it, sugah," she whispered. "It's just one'a them things you can't change."

≈∞≈

Magda knew that Pearl was trying to cheer her up as they rode the subway to Macy's. By the time they arrived, she made up her mind to stop thinking about the postcard and enjoy the day.

The elevator operator was in good voice as he finally called out the floor she had been waiting for. "Housewares! Appliances, linens, crystal, and fine china."

Magda smiled as she stepped off the elevator. She loved everything about Macy's, but her favorite department was housewares, with its gleaming copper pots, and showcases filled with crystal that dazzled like diamonds under the bright lights. All dressed up for the holidays, Macy's could put the crabbiest pessimist in the world in the Christmas spirit.

"Got most of your Christmas shoppin' done, sista?" Pearl asked.

"Oh, no. Better to shop many days. I like to ride my subway and come to da stores."

"So what'cha shoppin' for today?"

"I shop for Joe a gift, but towels we need, too. And I am seeing so much more things!"

"I know," Pearl said. "About a hundred more things, huh? Me too, sista."

Magda smiled. "Sister—always you call me. No one before ever calls me *sister*, Pearl."

"That's right, huh? You don't have any brothers or sisters, do you?"

"No. But I think maybe now—I find one."

Pearl hugged Magda. "That's right, sista. You and me. We gotta stick together, 'cause these men can be a mess sometimes. And speakin' of men—how's Joe doin' these days?"

"Oh, Joe is like—like elevator we ride, Pearl. He is up—den he is down."

"Well, that ain't so bad. There's worse things, I suppose."

Magda stared at the floor. "Pearl?"

"Yes?"

"Well, for you and Doc—things are still very wonderful? To be in love?"

"Why would you ask that, sugah? Things gettin' that bad with Joe?"

"Oh, not so bad, I suppose. But Doc—he talks to you, Pearl?"

"Just try stoppin' him! Oh! Look at this little moo-cow cream pitcher, would you?"

"But—Doc—he tells to you things—about his business?"

"Well, we ain't got any secrets from each other if that's what'cha mean—not anymore. But we had some rough times in the beginning." Pearl put the cream pitcher back down. "Why? What did Joe do?"

"I think he is not so happy with me no more, Pearl. If I cook, he is not hungry. If I don't cook, he is mad. He is only happy when he is going away."

Pearl shook her head. "Takes men longer to grow up, seems like."

"But Pearl, I make him happy before—"

"Oh." Pearl softened her tone. "And you think you don't make him happy anymore?"

"Oh! Sometimes he is happy like hopping over da moon! And he will talk and talk like before. But when I think everything is okay, he is all da time screaming again. Will you believe it, Pearl? Da other night, Joe wakes me up at four o'clock in da morning to dance."

"Lord," Pearl laughed. "Four in the mornin'?"

"Yes! 'Dance with me, baby,' he tells me. But I am too sleepy, so he is mad with me again. And den when I find out what he do to Al Crandall—"

"Al Crandall? I thought they parted amicably."

"Amic—? Amica— What dat word means, Pearl?"

"Sorry, sugah. Amicably means—oh, friendly, I guess."

"Friendly? No, Pearl. Al Crandall is mad with Joe to sign to dat Clef Records. He sues him."

"A lawsuit, huh? Well, the way Joe switched labels on him *did* seem a little dirty to me."

"Yes! Dirty! Dat is how Al tells me. Dirty screw."

Pearl showed her teeth in a grimace. "Whoo! That *does* sound unfriendly. So that's what's botherin' you, huh? The way he treated an old friend. Mm-mm-mm."

"Joe tell me David has many lawyers who will make dat lawsuit to go away, but—" Her voice softened. "I don't know dis man I married no more. I think he is hating me sometimes."

"Oh, sugah. Nobody could hate you."

"Pearl… I know about da other girls."

Pearl fell silent for a long moment. Then she tugged at a loose strand of Magda's hair. "You know what? Too much talk about Joe. Let's get your mind off him. I can't afford to buy nothin' today anyway, but I do have a couple'a quarters for one of those fattening banana splits down at the automat. Let's go cheer ourselves up and then come shop for your towels after."

Magda opened her mouth to answer, but something caught her eye— a young couple holding hands while looking at dishware. The man was a Negro and the woman, Caucasian.

"What's wrong?" Pearl asked, turning to follow Magda's gaze.

"Look, Pearl," Magda whispered urgently. "Da white man at da counter is staring at dem."

"Oh, sugah, I'm sure they're used to it. They know what they're up against. That white woman probably lost her whole family 'cause of that colored man. And as for him—"

Magda's eyes widened. "Dey will *kill* him?"

"This ain't the South, sugah, and you need to stop thinkin' about that postcard."

"Dey must *never* go to dat South."

"They won't even entertain the notion. And here, they'll just get stared at a little."

"But not me," Magda said firmly.

Pearl smiled. "Well, thank the Lord for white folks like you, sugah. But to be honest, colored folks can be pretty narrow-minded about it too, you know."

"But not you, Pearl?"

"Well, not *those* two, I guess. But now, if that was my man standin' over there hugged up with some woman, *whatever* color she was, we wouldn't even be havin' this conversation. 'Cause I would'a made a stop at the cutlery department and copped me a meat cleaver. Then I'da done a job on both of 'em till they was both the same color—red!"

Magda giggled. "*Murder*, Pearl?"

"Don't laugh, sista! It's true! Long as that woman didn't steal *my* man, I got no problem with her. Just lookin' at 'em as a couple'a strangers—what the hell. They ain't hurtin' nobody."

Magda gazed at the couple again and smiled. "You are right, Pearl. Dey make courage, yes? She is woman—he is man. Nothing wrong with dat."

Pearl's smile faded and her eyes went vacant. "Well—since you brought that up, there's other kinds of folks in the world—like my brother—" She fell silent and stared at the floor.

"Please to forgive me, Pearl. I make you sad with too much questions today."

"Sugah, did you ever know anybody who didn't have any hate inside? None at all? Well, my brother was like that. But—they finally taught him how to hate. They taught him to hate *himself*."

Pearl swallowed hard, and finally managed a smile. "Oh, sugah, I'm sorry. I gotta shake off these damn blues. Let's go get those banana splits. Come on, there's our elevator!"

They managed to squeeze into the elevator just as the doors were closing, and made space among the crush of chattering shoppers, who were all loaded down with bags and packages.

"Express elevator to floor one!" the elevator operator sang out. "Perfume, jewelry, and today we're presenting six new designer evening gowns worn by our strolling Macy's models."

As the elevator began to descend, Magda noticed two middle-aged white women who were staring at Pearl. "Merry Christmas," Magda said sharply. The chattering in the elevator stopped and everyone looked at her. "I say Merry Christmas to you," she said, her voice edgier this time.

Pearl linked arms with her. "Yes. Merry Christmas."

The two women ignored them, so Magda leaned closer and spoke loudly. "I am Christmas shopping, you see, with my friend and sister Pearl—who is *not* my maid, of course."

The women remained mute, suddenly intent on staring at the lighted numbers above the doors. The only sound in the elevator was the soft whir of the motor until Pearl snorted an inadvertent giggle. She clapped her hand over her mouth, but her shoulders continued to shake with silent laughter. When the doors finally opened, the white women hurried out, with Magda in hot pursuit, forcing her heavy brace into a surprisingly fast gait.

"What is wrong?" she shouted as Pearl tugged at her coat. "Is sega—*seguration* elevator or something? You never before see two friends walking together in da Macy's? You must be all da time frowning and whispering?"

As Magda continued to pursue the two women, she collided with one of the Macy's models, who was strolling through the store reciting an advertisement for her full-skirted evening gown. The model stumbled, and would have fallen if Pearl had not caught her by the arm.

"We are *so* sorry, Miss," Pearl sputtered, trying to hide her laughter.

"Shit!" the model muttered as she leaned down to disentangle the heel of her evening slipper from the hem of the gown. When she straightened up, she gave Pearl and Magda a confused look; then, after an awkward pause, she smiled professionally and continued her routine as if nothing had happened. "I'm wearing Moonlight Magenta, from Macy's own Winter Evening Collection. Influenced by Christian Dior, the narrow boned bodice is strapless and slopes in a graceful line to a full-length skirt featuring five yards of Moonlight Magenta *peau de soie*. Only one hundred and twenty dollars in ladies formal fashions on the fifth floor."

Pearl was doubled over with laughter, but Magda just stood there, gaping wide-eyed at the evening gown. The model executed a graceful runway turn, and then disappeared down the main perfume aisle, repeating her Moonlight Magenta speech.

"Oh, Pearl," Magda sighed. "Did you see dat beautiful dress?"

"Yeah, sugah, I got a real good close-up look at it when you tackled that model."

Magda gasped, then laughed. "I *tackle* da model, Pearl? To knock her down dat means?"

Pearl hugged Magda as they both shushed each other and tried to get their laughing under control. "Sista, you sure are good for my soul! All day I been studyin' some sad ol' memories, but you sure brought me back!"

"Shh!" Magda laughed. "I must have dat dress, Pearl, for New Year's Eve."

"Well, amen to that, sista, 'cause you deserve that pretty dress, and Joe deserves to pay for it." She straightened her blouse and smoothed her hair. "The lady said fifth floor, didn't she?"

Magda linked arms with her and smiled. "Yes, Pearl. Fifth floor."

"Okay, sista, I'm game. Let's go see what kind'a damage we can do up there."

≈∞≈

Magda cooked and decorated for the holidays and hoped for the best. But Christmas turned sour shortly after she and Joe exchanged gifts. He loved the camel hair coat she had given him, but as he fastened the clasp on her new diamond bracelet, the telephone rang. Joe spent the rest of the day talking to David, and then over dinner he broke the news that he would be working in California on New Year's Eve.

The week passed in a chilly silence until Joe left on New Year's Eve morning. That night Magda dressed up in her new evening gown and took a taxi to Café Nocturne to meet Pearl and Beatriz. The night began on a high note, but ended in disappointment. Pearl never showed up.

Chapter 19

After two weeks in California, Joe was exhausted and agitated. He had called home several times and got no answer. Then he called Doc's number only to hear from Pearl that Magda was there, but didn't want to speak to him. Racing around for radio interviews and club dates distracted him, but the flight home gave him plenty of time to think. By the time he landed at LaGuardia, he was steaming. He stashed his suitcase in a locker, then stepped outside into a brisk New York wind and hailed a taxi. "Stork Club," he said.

When the cab pulled up to the club, the door man welcomed Joe with a broad smile. "Mr. Bluestone! Good to have you back!"

"Thanks, Mike," Joe said, reaching into his pocket for a tip. "Good crowd tonight?"

"Oh, yeah. All the regulars and a few people from the coast—you know, out here to make a movie with some'a those new kids over at the Actor's Studio."

Joe chuckled. "Oh. The artsy crowd, huh?"

"Yeah. Kazan's in there with Kim Hunter, and he said Brando might be stopping by later, but I'm not looking for *that* kook. The more they beg him to hob-nob, the harder he resists. Oh, yeah! Martin and Lewis are here tonight too—with some suit yelling about how everything's on him. You know the type—studio executive showing off his expense account. How much you wanna bet those two are holding up Paramount for a better deal?"

Joe shrugged. "Well, that rubber-faced kid's sure worth it."

The door man gestured at the maître d'. "Get Mr. Bluestone a good table, would you?"

"Thanks, Mike," Joe said. He adjusted his necktie and smiled as he stepped inside. After checking his hat and coat, he passed the Cub Room and heard the unmistakable voice of Jerry Lewis, clowning for everyone free of charge, followed by one of Walter Winchell's salty quips. The result was uproarious laughter, and Joe peeked in until he heard a female voice calling to him from the direction of the bar.

"Hello, Joe."

He turned and saw blonde, blue-eyed Shirley, his favorite cigarette girl, standing at the bar with her long, shapely legs on full display. He leaned against the doorframe to the Cub Room and gave her a seductive grin.

"Thought you forgot about us," she said, pouting.

"*Heavens*, no, baby," he said, letting his gaze roam down the length of her body. "How could I *ever* forget the way you girls pack those red-hot costumes you wear?"

"Oh," Shirley said as she walked slowly over to him, "so it's *girls* and not *girl*."

As he watched the undulation of her hips, Joe let out a low moan. "Here they come, ladies and gentlemen. The sexiest legs in the joint. Shirley, *please* tell me you got those legs insured."

"Just like Betty Grable, baby," she said.

Joe laughed and eased his arm around her waist. "So tell me, do you still get off at two-thirty? 'Cause I sure am in the mood to spend some time with you. I got some ideas—" Before he could finish, someone bumped him from behind.

"Hey! Watch who you're pushin'!" he shouted.

The man shot Joe a surprised look that quickly changed to a smug grin. "Well, if it isn't Joe Bluestone—the Sinatra impersonator. How's the comedy circuit these days, Joe?"

Joe glanced back at the empty space where Shirley had been standing, and her sudden disappearance enraged him. "Kiss my ass, ya wise sonofabitch," he hissed.

The man's cool, irritating smile widened. "Hank," he called to a man standing behind him. "Get a shot of small-time here. I might just run a little piece on him tomorrow."

Before Joe could respond, the flash of a camera blinded him, and he was lunging at the man who had given the order. After managing just one lukewarm punch, Joe grabbed him by the lapels. "Who the hell do you think you are, you sonofabitch?"

The man shoved Joe away and brushed off his jacket as his companions intervened. "Read the *Times* tomorrow, you no-talent bum. I'm Tony Byrdyn and you might just as well bend over and kiss your ass goodbye as far as your career goes. And I use the term 'career' laughingly."

Joe's second attempt at a punch failed because several Stork employees had now arrived on the scene. "Time to go, buster," said a hefty man Joe recognized as the bouncer.

"Wait a minute," Joe protested. "This guy started the whole thing!"

"Yeah, yeah, sure, sure," the bouncer sing-songed. "You're innocent as a newborn babe."

As Joe was half-carried to the front door, he heard Byrdyn's scornful sendoff: "Might have to print a little of that pickup scene you were doing with Shirley too. Bad boy. Seems I heard somewhere you're a married man, Joe. It'd be just *dreadful* if your wife reads about it."

≈∞≈

The next morning Joe tried to steer his thoughts away from Byrdyn's threat, but couldn't. He wandered around, still uncomfortable in the new house, and avoided Magda. After downing two Bennies with his lunch, he lost the battle against his own curiosity and called David Smythe.

"Hey, listen, David. Have you seen the *Times* today?"

"No, Joe, I haven't. Why?"

"Can you pick one up for me and bring it to the house? I need to go over a few things with you anyway, so plan on staying for supper. How 'bout it?"

"Sure, Joe. I'll be there around four."

Joe was watching out the front window when David's car finally pulled up. He hurried to the door and opened it before David had a chance to knock. "Come on in."

"Hiya, Joe. Where's Magda?"

"In the kitchen—fixing supper or something. Can I get'cha anything? A drink?"

"Nah. I had a late lunch. Too much food and coffee, and too early for booze. I'm just making my afternoon paper delivery, and then I'm gonna relax right here and have a smoke." David tossed the newspaper to Joe and flopped down on the sofa. "Mind if I turn on the radio?"

"Go ahead," Joe said as he anxiously scanned the entertainment section. His jaw tightened when he saw the unflattering photograph of himself. "Shit."

"Uh-oh," David said. "Guess you found what you were lookin' for."

Joe sprang to his feet. "You ever heard of this guy Tony Byrdyn? Well, listen to this…"

There are artists and there are singers. Only last year this reporter was guilty of mistaking new vocalist Joe Bluestone for an exciting new artist on the jazz scene, but as it turns out, he was just another lounge act. With the release of his newest effort "Late at Night"—well, my kind nature won't allow me to go further than to say that the word "late" is the most appropriate part of the title. Too late. Wake up, Joe. It's been done—by a guy named Sinatra.

And since we're on the subject, just how many Sinatra impressions must we endure? Especially when even the original is beginning to fray around the edges. The best thing about "Late at Night" is the arrangement, tastefully played by a few local stars of the studio circuit. Too bad an instrumental version isn't available. And too bad the few sparks of artistic fire evident in Bluestone's debut effort "Lady Blue" are nowhere to be found on "Late at Night."

Oh, I nearly forgot. I've been asked by the management of the Stork Club to pass along a little message to Joe: Married men are off-limits to Stork Club cigarette girls.

Apparently, our boy Bluestone is a leg man.

"Shit!" Joe said, flinging the paper to the floor. "What am I gonna do if my wife sees this?"

From the radio, Walter Winchell was barking out his familiar machine-gun rhythm:

Good evening, Mr. and Mrs. America and all the ships at sea. This is Walter Winchell, your roving reporter. Let's go to press… Here's the latest on that Hollywood slacker whose ego has gone completely out of control. No need to mention his name; suffice it to say that he's a has-been crooner whose latest pictures haven't exactly been boffo at the box office.

While his wife waits at home with the kiddies, this Casanova is
out romancing none other than Ava Gardner, and slugging it
out with any reporter who dares to photograph them together.
Like the song says, and I'm being perfectly <u>frank</u>, it's time to
straighten up and fly right before the public abandons you
altogether…

"Shut-up," Joe muttered as he turned it off. "So now Winchell's crucifying Sinatra, and I got this goddamn Junior G-man Byrdyn measuring me for my own cross." Falling back onto the sofa, Joe shut his eyes and sighed. "Shit. At least I'll be in good company when they nail me up."

"Relax, Joe," David said. "Byrdyn's just a hound with a new bone. He'll drop it as soon as he finds another one. Besides, you know what they say—there's no such thing as bad publicity—as long as they spell your name right."

≈∞≈

For two weeks, Byrdyn's column was proof that Joe had acquired a formidable enemy. At first he laughed it off when he discovered that David had been right; the column was having the opposite of its intended effect. Joe's record sales were up—only slightly, but still up.

But when Byrdyn took to writing about him in the form of an open letter, Joe began to panic under the scrutiny. One particular question opened a door that he thought he had safely locked:

… And what about that name—Bluestone? That can't
possibly be your real name, Joe. And where did you come
from? I asked around and it strikes this reporter as odd that
nobody seems to know from whence Joe Bluestone came. This
calls for a little journalistic research.

≈∞≈

There were no mentions in Byrdyn's column for a while and Joe's mood soared. He also found it easy to function on very little sleep. Empowered with nonstop energy, he had no idea that his flashes of temper and paranoia were the flipside of his beloved Bennies. He was spending more time in hotel rooms than at home, and becoming an expert at packing for trips. He never traveled without an extra shoe bag, which contained his three most essential possessions: sleeping pills, Benzedrine, and a new .38-caliber handgun.

On his longest road trip to date, Joe spent nearly a full month in California for a series of appearances designed to boost his record sales. During his stay, he managed to involve himself in two fistfights, and was tempted to break in the new .38 on more than one occasion. He knew that

David and the musicians were alarmed by his short fuse, but he laughed off each episode as "just one of those things" and always managed to be ready by showtime. But then something happened that sent him into a quiet terror for several days.

It happened on a Friday night when he returned to the Chateau Dumont hotel after a radio appearance. As he waited for the desk clerk to check for phone messages, he overheard a heated argument between the hotel manager and a group of people huddled at the other end of the front desk. He glanced over and recognized the woman in the group as Billie Holiday. She was staring grimly at the desk clerk as the white musicians with her argued her case. Then suddenly, all the talking stopped in an apparent standoff. After a chilly moment, the manager recited a stiff apology: "I'm sorry, Miss Holiday, but it's hotel policy and there's nothing I can do."

Billie took a deep pull on her cigarette and blew the smoke into his face. "Fuck it. Let's go."

Joe stood watching for a moment, then turned to walk to the elevator. As he looked back over his shoulder to see if Holiday's group had left, he collided with a stranger hurrying past.

"What the hell's wrong with you, ya sonofabitch?" Joe yelled. He pushed the man away angrily, and then gasped when he saw his brother's dark face staring uncut hatred at him. Stumbling backwards, he looked away for a split-second to keep from falling. When he looked up again, he saw that it wasn't Calvin at all. It was a hotel kitchen employee dressed in a white uniform. His only resemblance to Calvin was his coloring and the bitterness in his eyes. Joe straightened his tie and jerked up his chin. "You always go around knocking down guests?"

The hotel manager suddenly appeared at Joe's side and began brushing off his jacket. "I'm *so* sorry, Mr. Bluestone." Then he glared at the employee. "Listen, boy," he hissed, "you've been told to stay out of the lobby. Use the kitchen entrance, you understand?"

"But Mr. Blake—there's a stalled delivery truck blockin' the door and—"

"Don't stand there talking about trucks! Apologize to Mr. Bluestone at once!"

After a tense pause, the man apologized through clenched teeth. "I'm sorry, sir."

"Now, get back into the kitchen. We'll discuss it in there." Mr. Blake took a deep breath and smiled at Joe. "Once again, Mr. Bluestone, on behalf of Chateau Dumont, I *do* apologize."

≈∞≈

For the duration of the trip, disquieting thoughts chased each other through Joe's brain. He couldn't stop thinking about that angry kitchen employee, and thoughts of Calvin returned. There was an uptick of news about the HUAC hearings on the radio, and the Billie Holiday incident sent a clear message to Joe that he was only a guest in this hotel on a pigmentation technicality.

Radio appearances kept him busy by day, but nights were difficult. He needed company and he no longer cared who it was—a cocktail waitress, a B-girl looking for a good time—anyone who would keep away the darkness. Even the drugs began to scare him. At first, he could fly for days on one or two Bennies, but as his system adjusted to the effects, it demanded more.

More. He remembered something Magda had asked him just before his trip to California: *Why I can't be enough for you, Joe?* He winced as he recalled his cold answer: *Because I need more.* Then he thought of something Doc had told him about Pearl's heroin addiction, and it suddenly rang with relevance. *But then she needs more. Always more.*

On the night before his flight home, Joe made a decision: "No more women," he muttered as he packed. "And I gotta get off these pills too, or I'll end up like Pearl, with a goddamn monkey on my back. I must be crazy. I've got the most beautiful girl in the world, so what more could I want? Maybe I'll take her away someplace—someplace romantic where we can start all over."

Pleased with his decision, he called home. After six rings, he hung up, knowing that she wouldn't answer. "It's okay, baby," he whispered. "I'm gonna make it right this time."

≈∞≈

Joe went straight home from the airport the next evening. As he opened the front door, he heard Magda playing a line on her violin, then stopping and repeating it. She was studying a new chart and trying to perfect her attack. When he walked into the bedroom, she didn't look up.

"Hi, baby," he said softly.

Magda stopped again to look at the chart. "Hi."

Joe stepped closer. "You all right? You seem—mad."

"I am fine, Joe. I must practice."

"Well, you don't seem fine. But I've got an idea that's gonna cheer you right up. You ever heard that song 'April in Paris'?"

"Yes, Joe. I hear dat song before." Her voice was tight and she still hadn't looked at him.

"Well it'll be April in two days and we're flying there."

She finally looked up with a surprised expression—minus the smile. "We fly—to Paris?"

"Can you think of a better place for a second honeymoon?"

"I don't know."

He touched her face and gazed into her eyes. "You still—love me, don't you, baby?"

She looked away.

Joe knelt on one knee beside her chair. "Look. I know I've been an ass. But I promise I'll make it all up to you. I want everything to be good between us again—the way it used to be."

Magda stared at him for a long time, then finally smiled. "Okay, Joe. We go to Paris."

≈∞≈

Everything about Paris whispered romance, but Magda seemed remote. They didn't fight, but the lovemaking was tepid and conversation never rose beyond small talk. He bought a pack of French cigarettes, hoping they would help ease him away from the Benzedrine. As he walked with Magda along the Champs-Élysées in an uncomfortable silence, he felt like a miscast actor on a painted movie set. There was nothing to do but stare blindly at the scenery and chainsmoke.

When they returned to New York, it was only a matter of days before they settled back into their previous cycle of squabbles and icy silences. Joe regarded David Smythe as a savior when he called to rattle off the dates of his upcoming schedule. With no time to worry about his marriage, Joe went back to work and hoped that somehow things would work themselves out.

In mid-May, Magda announced that she was pregnant, and Joe was overjoyed. He was sure that a new baby would change everything. Three days later, David called to tell him that he had booked him at New York's Paramount Theater as a guest vocalist with Count Basie's orchestra.

Joe breezed through the next week, rushing to rehearsals with Basie and keeping a close watch on *Billboard's* best-selling retail charts. His new record was climbing the charts, and he was sleeping better at night since he'd cut back on the Benzedrine. Each time he went home, he brought Magda a gift, and lavished attention on her. But she was having a difficult pregnancy, and her bouts of sickness prevented her from joining him at the Paramount for his appearance.

Joe was happily surprised when David showed up in a limousine to pick him up on the night of the show, and laughed when he ceremoniously opened the door for him.

"Get used to it, kid," David said, popping the cork on a bottle of Dom Perignon. "After tonight, you're on a straight track to the stars."

Joe grinned. "Wow, the good stuff! But only a little, David. Really."

"Okay, okay, just a sip or two. But I feel the irresistible urge to make a toast."

Joe raised his glass to meet David's. "Fire away."

"To Joe Bluestone. The new king to legions of bobby-soxers around the world. Salute!"

"Aw, let's not be greedy, David. Legions? Nah. Just enough to fill the Paramount."

David chuckled. "I got news for you—you'll have to drive off the chicks with a stick after tonight. You're a good-lookin' kid. Like you didn't know that! Hey, I bet that kid you and Magda are having is gonna be a real looker. Who do you think he'll take after?"

Joe stared mutely at David for a long moment, then grinned and drained his glass. "Me, of course... Listen, you got a cigarette?"

"When did you start smoking?"

"Recently. Trying to cut back on the Bennies."

David gave him a cigarette and lit it. "Make it temporary, man. Bad for the pipes, ya know."

When they arrived at the Paramount, Joe stepped out of the limousine and grinned up at the building. "Wow! It just hit me, David! I'm actually playing the Paramount! Just like Sinatra!"

"You sure are, kid. But it ain't gonna happen here on the sidewalk. Come on!"

Everything after that moment was a blur until Joe found himself standing in the wings waiting for his introduction. He glanced down nervously to make sure that he was dressed properly; he couldn't quite remember putting on his suit. He dabbed his forehead and wished that Magda could have been in the audience. Then he heard Count Basie introduce him.

As he strode out to the dream world of center stage, he felt pinpricks of excitement all over his body. Basie's deferential nod; the sudden shift from full stage lighting to the prestige of the spotlight; the glorious music; and a sudden blast of female screams. Joe flashed the grin that had always worked for him, and a louder wave of sighs and squeals filled the air. He recognized the sound. It was the same adoration he had heard and felt at the Capitol Theater when he had seen Sinatra. He leaned close to the microphone and began singing "How High the Moon."

He stopped singing abruptly when he spotted a face in the audience. Calvin. He wondered if this was another nightmare, but a very real feeling in the pit of his stomach told him it wasn't. As he looked for a security guard, Basie shot him a questioning look and covered for him with a piano solo. Joe looked back to find his brother, but saw only a heavyset Negro woman wearing a black dress and hat. She smiled at him and Joe's knees nearly buckled with relief. But as he picked up the song, he struggled with the frightening prospect that he was losing his mind.

≈∞≈

The newspaper reviews of Basie's show lavished praise on Joe's performance, and a steady stream of work followed. By the time David called with the news that he had booked him into the popular Chez Paree in Chicago, Joe was almost expecting it.

"You'll be staying at The Palmer House, Joe. Class joint. But the best part is that you won't be an opening act or a guest singer at Chez Paree. This time, my friend, *you're* the headliner."

"Hey! A headliner? They finally think I can fill a joint, huh?"

"Well, why not? Radio's in love with you, and your record sales are better than ever. This is that straight track to the stars I told you about, Joe. Remember?"

"It's about time, too. Hey, thanks, David. I could've never done it without you."

David laughed. "I'm a blood-sucking agent, Joe. No work for you, no blood for Papa. Oh, but I was meaning to ask you—when's your wife due? I felt bad booking something this close to the baby's birth, but I couldn't pass up this opportunity. This appearance is a career-changer."

"Oh, she's not due for another four weeks or so. I'll be back in plenty of time."

≈∞≈

The lobby of The Palmer House glittered with European opulence— crystal chandeliers, a double staircase with marble steps and gleaming brass rails, towering arches and a massive expanse of Venetian frescoes overhead, statues and gilt wall sconces, plush, deep green chairs, and bellboys in gold-braided uniforms. When Joe stopped staring and approached the registration desk, the VIP treatment began.

"Mr. Bluestone! We have the Imperial Suite all ready for you, sir," the desk clerk said.

Joe smiled. "Thank you. I've gotta change and then get to the Chez Paree for rehearsal."

The hotel manager took over. "We'll have a boy take your bags up to your room so you can change, and I'll have the driver standing by. Will that be satisfactory?"

"Thank you. That'll be perfect."

A gangly, red-haired bellboy smiled at Joe, picked up the bags, and led him to the elevator.

When they reached the 22nd floor, he led Joe down the corridor to the Imperial Suite and opened the door. Joe walked in and smiled approvingly. "Nice room."

"Yes, siree, Mr. Bluestone. Best in the hotel. And get a load of this radio!"

Joe gazed at the large console radio facing the bed. "Wow! That's some contraption!"

"It's a Zenith," the bellboy said, turning on the radio. "Genuine maple cabinet. I asked the manager once. High-fidelity too. Get a load'a the sound when it warms up."

"I will. Hey, could you run down and get me some Camels? Just leave 'em on the nightstand for when I get back later. And keep the change."

The bellboy reached for the five dollar bill Joe held out. "Sure, Mr. Bluestone! And thanks!"

Joe closed the door behind the happy bellboy and fell into a garnet club chair. He gazed at the Oriental emblem in the center of the gold bedspread and noticed that it matched the color of the plush carpet. Removing his shoes, he took a foot-pleasing walk to the bathroom and flipped on the light. He grinned at the gleaming white sink, polished brass faucets, and a large golden bowl filled with soap in the shape of small white baseballs. But his smile faded as he gazed at the bowl of soap. A disturbing memory flashed in his mind—the gold filigree handrails along the stairs leading to the Colored Section in the Grand Marquee back in Natchez. When he walked back into the front room, the radio had warmed up and a news report was beginning:

> *More on the latest Blacklist-related suicide. Just days after being questioned by Roy Cohn, counsel to Senator Joseph McCarthy, U.N. Assistant Secretary General Abe Feller leaped to his death from the 12th floor of his apartment building...*

Joe turned off the radio, but it took nearly a minute to force his eyes away from it. He finally grabbed his coat and turned to leave. When he reached for the doorknob, his hand was shaking.

≈∞≈

The club manager greeted Joe at the door of the Chez Paree. "Sorry about the chaos, Mr. Bluestone. It's Tony Martin's last night, and he just ran through a new song with the band. But now they're all yours, ready to rehearse tomorrow's show with you. I'm George. I'm the guy to see if you need anything at all."

George's smile was like water from Lourdes, healing Joe's jitters immediately. His mood continued to rise as he looked around the large room buzzing with activity: musicians going over chart notations, an army of waiters rushing around smoothing tablecloths and fussing with floral arrangements. *Class joint.* He straightened his tie and headed up the center aisle to the stage.

The rehearsal went smoothly and he stayed around to talk to the band until Tony Martin's first set began. George seated him at a front table equipped with three beautiful blondes and complimentary drinks. During the show, Tony Martin introduced Joe as the next night's headliner and asked him to take a bow. Joe stood up and gave him a friendly wave.

By the time the night limousine driver arrived to pick him up, Joe was feeling good about himself. No more shakes. He had turned down a tempting offer from one of the blondes and he was headed straight back to the hotel, like a good husband. As he settled into the quiet comfort of the limousine, he glanced up at the marquee. Tony Martin's name was already gone, and a worker on a ladder had just finished placing the last neon "E" in "BLUESTONE." Joe grinned. "Officially a headliner. Finally."

"I beg your pardon, sir?" the driver asked in a clipped British accent.

"Oh, nothing," Joe said.

"Veddy good, sir. So will that be straight to the hotel then?"

"Yes, straight to the hotel, " Joe said, chuckling. This "Ronald Colman" limousine driver was a far cry from the "dese-dem-and-doze" types that drove New York taxicabs.

"As you wish, sir."

When he got back to the hotel, Joe went to the front desk and asked for messages. Different desk clerk—same respectful smile.

"Here are your messages, Mr. Bluestone. And just call if you need anything else, sir."

As Joe rode up in the elevator, he read the messages—one from Magda and one from Pearl Calhoun, both marked "urgent" and three from David. "Urgent" again.

He hurried into his room and dialed the operator. "Yes, could you get me David Smythe in Manhattan, please? CIrcle 7-4800."

When the call connected, David picked up on the first ring. "Joe?"

"Yeah, it's Joe. And what're you still doin' in New York? I thought you were—"

"Joe, look, things are crazy here so I'll get right to the point. Get yourself to Midway in the morning. Your ticket's paid for. United, flight number 410—the 7:15 to La Guardia."

"Wait a minute, David. Is this some kind'a joke? I'm not catching a flight to anywhere! Did it somehow slip your mind that I've got a show tomorrow night?... David?"

David finally answered in a grave tone. "Joe, Magda had the baby this morning."

"Wait—this morning? Why didn't you call me earlier at the club?"

"I did—about an hour ago, but they said you'd left."

"But if she had it this morning, then why didn't you call me then?"

"I didn't want to bother you at the club. I was trying to handle things myself, but—"

"Wait a minute, David. Magda's okay, isn't she? Nothing went wrong, did it?"

"She's fine. The—the baby's—healthy too. It was a—boy."

Joe sensed a long feared red flag waving wildly between the lines of this odd conversation. *It can't be that.* "So I'm a Daddy," he said stiffly. "So congratulate me."

"Look, Joe—"

Joe began pacing. "You said Magda and the baby were all right."

"They are."

"Well, then why the hell are you makin' like the goddamn grim reaper? I'll just do the show and fly home right after, man. Just call Magda and tell her— Never mind. I'll call her myself."

"No! Joe, listen to me. There are some—special circumstances. I tried to handle it myself, but—trust me. You've gotta fly back first thing in the morning. It'll look worse if you don't."

"*What'll* look worse?" he shouted. "*Nothing* could be worse than me not showing up for the show tomorrow night! Look, I'll call Magda and she'll understand. Now stop talking crazy!"

"Joe! Listen to me. You don't get it. There's something—wrong."

No! It can't be that. The unthinkable thought screamed through his brain. Joe gripped the receiver. "What's so wrong that I gotta run out on the most important show of my life?"

David sighed. "Not on the phone. Hotel operators listen in. Trust me. You gotta come back."

Joe could no longer ignore the clammy feeling in the pit of his belly. *No, please. Not that.*

"Look, just get to New York before the reporters get hold of this. Flight 410. United."

"*What* reporters... ? Wait a minute, David?... Hello?"

Joe sat in stunned silence for a moment listening to the dial tone before finally hanging up. Almost instantly, it rang again, causing him to jump. He snatched the receiver. "David?"

Then he heard a vaguely familiar voice: "No, not David. Hey, I just saw your kid, Joe."

"Who the hell is this?"

The only response was derisive laughter.

"Who the hell is this?" Joe repeated. "Byrdyn?"

"Aw, Joe. What you *should* be worrying about is the nigger who's screwing your wife."

Joe felt the blood drain from his face. "What... What the hell are you talking about?"

"Or maybe she was screwing a nigger all along. *Maybe*—she married one."

Joe scoured his brain for a response. "Who is this?" he murmured weakly.

"Just be sure to pick up a morning paper tomorrow, Joe, on your way out'a town."

"Fuck you, Byrdyn—I *know* it's you. I'm not buying any goddamn paper and I'm not leaving town! I'm sold out! I'm headlining at Chez Paree—tomorrow night."

Another laugh. "No, you're not... Daddy."

≈∞≈

At dawn, Joe was standing like a lone sentry in front of The Palmer House. He stared vacantly at a lamppost on the opposite side of the street until the rumbling of a truck broke the early morning quiet. As the driver tossed the bundles of newspapers onto the sidewalk, Joe heard the squeaking of a bicycle behind him. A lanky, light-skinned Negro boy jumped from the rickety bicycle, yanked off his gloves and dropped to his knees near the bundles.

The truck driver shouted, "Better start gettin' here on time if you wanna keep the job!"

The boy began muttering as the truck rumbled away, then ripped through the strings on the bundles with his pocketknife. He held up a paper and squinted at Joe. "*Tribune*, Mista?"

Joe answered with a silent nod and stared at the front page headline:

FORMER PRESIDENT TRUMAN
ATTACKS MCCARTHY'S HUAC COMMITTEE

"That'll be a nickel," the boy said.

Without taking his eyes off the headline, Joe handed the boy a five-dollar bill.

"Ain't got no change yet, Mista."

"Keep it." Joe finally looked at the boy, who grinned and thanked him, then pocketed the five and went back to his work. Joe tucked the newspaper under his arm, and stood there watching the boy a moment before finally walking back into the hotel.

When he got back to his room, he stared at the newspaper for nearly a minute, trying to work up the courage to read Tony Byrdyn's syndicated column. Finally, he turned the pages and tried to blink away the sting in his eyes that had come from a long night of replacing sleep with scotch and Bennies. When he found the column, the first three words screamed off the page at him. They might as well have been written in neon letters three feet high.

Holy Mackerel, Kingfish!

This columnist is unsure as to what sort of floral arrangement to send to new Papa Joe Bluestone today. Maybe you'll remember crooner Bluestone from his lukewarm records and his off-stage shenanigans with the ladies. I have official confirmation that at 5:55 Friday morning Joe's lovely wife gave birth to a bouncing baby boy, weighing in at six pounds, six ounces.

The baby had the proper number of fingers and toes. The birth certificate listed the mother as Magdalena Skouros Bluestone and the father as Joseph Bluestone. This would all be perfectly normal, if not for the fact that both parents are Caucasians, and the baby is only a shade or two paler than a Hershey bar.

One possibility is that skirt-chasing Joe finally drove his wife into the arms of another man—a man of the Negro persuasion. But who? I'm not saying he is and I'm not saying he isn't, BUT dear readers, this reporter has, on several occasions, observed Mrs. Bluestone in the company of a trumpet player by the name of Doc Calhoun, a member of Bluestone's former band "Beat the Heat" and a friend of the family. A very close friend... Perhaps.

But perhaps I'm wrong. Perhaps Mrs. Bluestone is innocent of committing adultery with a Negro. Perhaps she married one. Either way, rest assured that I'll be bringing you more details on this story as they surface, since it seems to be much more entertaining than anything Joe Bluestone has put on wax.

Now, back to my dilemma about what to send to Joe. Somehow, a bunch of yellow roses with the standard congratulatory card doesn't seem quite right. Perhaps a bereavement wreath would be more appropriate.

Joe shut his eyes tightly before reading the article again, trying to convince himself that somehow the words would change. *This isn't happening. This can't be happening. Not now.* He flung the paper to the floor, picked up the telephone, but couldn't think of a number or a name.

He slammed down the receiver and grabbed his coat. Propelled by a compulsion he could not comprehend, it wasn't until the elevator reached the lobby that he was able to identify it.

Escape. From his room, from Tony Byrdyn, and from his rapidly disintegrating life.

The instant the elevator doors opened, he was blinded by a camera flash. He finally made out the silhouettes of two reporters, and tried to yell at them, but his brain and vocal cords seemed disconnected.

"We're from *Hollywood Confidential*, Joe. That was *some* story in today's paper. Come on and give us a statement, 'cause we're gonna run our story with or without your side of it."

"Yeah, Joe. We already got pictures of the kid and—"

Joe lunged at the reporter and heard an inhuman noise come from his own throat. Before he knew what was happening, he felt several arms pulling him off the man.

"Shumbody call'a poleesh!" the reporter yelled. "Thish crazhy shummbish broke my jaw!"

Joe stared at his bloody face and began to tremble. He couldn't remember hitting him.

≈∞≈

Joe was too numbed by the day's events to know how long he had been locked up. When David arrived, the officer unlocked the cell door and Joe hurried out. "I thought you'd never get here!"

"I caught the first flight I could get on, Joe."

"What time is it?"

David checked his watch. "Five-thirty."

"Good. I got just enough time to shower and shave before the first show."

"Joe. Look—I don't know how to tell you this, but—the show's been cancelled."

"Very funny. Come on, David. It was a sell-out."

"Joe. *Listen.* There's no show tonight. I got things straightened out with the reporter, but—"

Joe jerked away from him. "Don't tell me you paid that sonofabitch off?"

"Joe! You broke the guy's jaw! I had to get him to drop the charges. Then the club manager cancelled the show. Too much bad publicity. First that story Byrdyn ran, and then you went and smacked that reporter. The local radio guys had a field day with that. Look, Joe, I really tried."

Pressing an envelope into Joe's hand, David softened his tone. "Here's your plane ticket. We'll go to the hotel and I'll help you pack. We'll talk things over."

Joe pocketed the envelope. "No, thanks. I'm okay. I'll just meet you at the airport. But I could use a smoke, if you got any. I left mine in the room."

David gave him a cigarette and flipped open his lighter. "Better watch it with these things, Joe. They're bad for your voice, and—" He stopped, and his thumb froze on the lighter wheel.

Joe stared at him, then lit the cigarette himself. The awkward moment took its time passing.

"I, uh, changed your flight to tonight—8:15... Hey, Joe? You sure you're okay?"

"Yeah. Sure... I'll be there at eight."

David shook his head. "You know," he said softly, "I never figured Magda for the type."

As he met David's gaze, Joe felt what was left of his world drop from under him. In that split-second, he saw a look of sympathy harden into a probing look of cold suspicion. The most lethal line of Byrdyn's column was written clearly in David's eyes: *Maybe she married one.*

≈∞≈

The lobby was crawling with reporters when Joe got back. Someone had tipped them off about his release. He pushed past them to get to the elevator, but the desk clerk caught up to him.

"Mr. Bluestone? I have quite a few telephone messages here for you."

Joe snatched the messages without looking at him, then ran to the elevator and pressed the button for the 22nd floor. He had only one thought in his head: *Escape.* When he shut the door to his room, it seemed to be nothing but four tight corners, and he was panting like a trapped animal. Wiping his forehead with his sleeve, he blinked at the phone messages and threw them to the floor. Then he hurried into the bathroom and stared at the haggard face in the mirror. An old song drifted through his mind like a ghost: *What did I do to be so black and blue...*

"But my skin is *white!*" he screamed.

He washed down two Bennies with what was left of the scotch, then turned on the radio, desperate for a friendly voice. He heard static, then a newscaster—with the latest on the Red Scare, of all things. Joe pressed the heels of his hands against his eyes to keep from crying.

> *... And in his continued attack on Senator McCarthy's*
> *Blacklist tactics, Former President Truman added: "It is the*

use of the big lie and the unfounded accusation against any citizen in the name of Americanism or security. It is the rise to power of the demagogue who lives on untruth; it is the spreading of fear."

In a related comment, newsman Edward R. Murrow confirmed his long-held belief that McCarthy would eventually overplay his deceptive hand, adding: "The obscure we see eventually; the completely apparent takes longer."

Stay tuned for Your Hit Parade, right after this message from our sponsor...

You'll wonder where the yellow went when you brush your teeth with Pepsodent!

Joe stared at the bed. A diligent maid—possibly someone like his mother—had arranged the bedspread with perfect fanned pleats at the corners. And now he had rumpled it. He smoothed it and carefully repositioned the pillows. Cugat's boys were kicking off a Rumba inside the radio.

But then the rhythm swirled away, replaced by eerie voices. Recent voices and voices from Joe's past—male and female, whispering and screaming their fatal words.

This ain'tcho regular ass whuppin', Sunshine! I ain't done yet!... Joe?... Joe? Why we are all da time screaming at each other?... So who is it, Joe? Who's the nigger screwing your wife? Did she marry one? Perhaps she married one...

Joe stared at the radio in terrified disbelief. The voices were coming directly from its speakers. He prayed for them to stop until a loud cheer went up for Robert Johnson, who began singing "Crossroads Blues."

Doc's familiar voice called over the music: *Hey, Junior! What was your deal, man? 'Cause I sure hope you didn't sell it cheap.*

And the priest from the New Orleans funeral: *Ashes to ashes, dust to dust...*

Then Robert Johnson's voice began to bend and roll out of pitch until he sounded like Joe's father singing. Joe grabbed a glass from the nightstand and threw it at the radio, but missed and hit the drapes. "Shut up!" he screamed. "This is all *your* fault! I bet that baby's as black as you!"

Joe's father laughed, but it was Doc who was doing the talking:

You really think it was Calvin that night at the Paramount, don't you, Joe?

Joe stared at the radio, too stunned to speak for a moment. "It *was* him," he finally whispered. "Or no... I—I guess it couldn't have been him. He's locked up—or dead."

I told you—it ain't them that's dead, Junior. It's you.

Then Doc's voice relaxed into the familiar cool of *The* Voice. It was the sound of twinkling blue eyes and it was nursing its third martini. *Relax, paisan! Take it from me, you gotta know when to get off the stage, capisce? Remember—always leave 'em begging for more.*

A chill prickled down Joe's spine; then he pointed at the radio. "None of you are really here!" he yelled. "I know that! You came out of a goddamn bottle!" He grabbed his head. "So stop it! I know it's just the booze—and too many goddamn Bennies. That's all it is."

He looked down at one of the message slips on the floor. *Please call Magda. Urgent.*

"Oh, God, baby, everybody's calling you a whore. You didn't do anything wrong, but nobody knows it." He wiped his nose on his sleeve and laughed. "Except maybe Byrdyn. Shit, who the hell knows?"

The Shadow knows, paisan. Are you now or have you ever been—a shadow?

Joe lit a cigarette, but his mind kept tilting. He tried to think of the name of that magazine. "*Hollywood Confidential*," he murmured. "Yeah. Same rag that ran that dirty story on you."

What was that, Joe?

He hurled another glass at the radio—a bulls-eye this time—and watched it shatter against the maple finish. "That rag that talked about you and Ava. And you tryin' to commit suicide—"

Did you say—suicide, Joe? the radio asked.

Joe held his breath and waited for the next voice.

Come on, paisan! One last bow and off! Trust me. They'll be begging for more!

Then, inexplicably, the voices stopped. Without knowing why, Joe hurried to the dresser for his gun. When he returned to the bed, the radio was playing music again.

What a difference a day made...

He dropped the cigarette in the ashtray and began to load the gun, but it began mocking him, just like the voices in the radio. Pushing it aside, he muttered, "I only need one, ya know."

A rapid, persistent thumping sound echoed from the door. "No. That's not real. Nobody's there. And you're not real either!" he yelled at the radio. "So shut up!"

The song finally ended, and some announcer was reporting on another HUAC-related suicide. It slurred into a soap jingle, and left a cacophony of sharp words crashing around in Joe's mind: *McCarthyBlacklistSuicideClearconsciencePurecleanIvorysoap...*

He raised the gun to his head, but then slowly lowered it when he heard the sound of violins playing the intro to a familiar song. Inside that music was a sweet, painful memory of Magda. A lone violin played a spine-tingling interlude that led the singer into a soft, sad finale. But then the song began to slur until the radio announcer woke Joe, once and for all, from his foolish damn-near dream: *That's one of the best torch songs ever put on wax, ladies and gentlemen—"I'm a Fool to Want You"— nicely done by the one and only Frank Sinatra.*

Joe's lips twitched, unable to form a fittingly sarcastic smile. "The one and only."

The knocking on the door grew louder, and again he raised the gun. When the cold muzzle touched his temple he flinched, then closed his eyes and tried to conjure up Magda's face. She was hazy, but she was smiling. A brief serenity washed over him until suddenly, her white skin began to darken, and her blue eyes hardened into Calvin's hateful, black stare.

"You're not really here, Calvin!" he cried. "Leave me alone! *Please* leave me alone!"

Then all the voices were back, blending together until they sounded like a demonic choir of Calvins: *I'm here, Joe. And I ain't goin' noplace. I ain't goin' noplace. I ain't goin' noplace...*

Joe felt a vein in his temple pulsing his heartbeat. Another memory: *The last thing to stop...*

He stared at Calvin, knowing that he was only a cruel figment of his own imagination, but it didn't matter anymore. "It's okay," he whispered to the apparition. "I'm dead already anyway."

There was an abbreviated fusion of sound and feeling—the first syllable of a tinny reverberation and a hard jerk to his body. And then—nothing.

Chapter 20

It was nearly midnight when Pearl returned home from the hospital. The apartment was dark, except for the small night-light she always kept burning just outside her bedroom door. She was just beginning to feel the full emotional weight of the day's events. As she reached for the light switch, she saw the orange glow of Doc's cigarette floating around in the darkness. He was sitting on the edge of the bed.

"Don't turn on the light," he said softly.

Pearl took off her shoes and slipped out of her dress, and then eased in next to him. "You home early, baby," she said. "When did you get here?"

"Hour ago. I figured the kids were with Rose."

"Mm-hmm. I called her earlier and she said she'd keep 'em till morning."

"How's Magda?"

"She's—in pretty bad shape."

Doc heaved a tired sigh. "Well, I guess that's to be expected."

Pearl kissed his shoulder. "I wasn't sure if you knew or not—about Joe, I mean. I'm glad you do, though, 'cause that ain't the kind'a news I feel like breakin' twice in one day."

"You mean *you* had to tell her?"

"Mm-hmm. The doctor asked me to. She was gettin' hysterical on account'a Joe hadn't called since the baby was born."

Pearl leaned against her pillow and studied her husband's profile, which was illuminated by the cigarette's glow each time he inhaled. There was more in his expression than just the pain of losing a friend. "Don't take it so hard, baby," she said softly.

"Yeah. I'm okay. So then, the doctor told you, but how'd he find out? Who told him?"

"David—Joe's agent. He called the hospital early this mornin'. Must'a been about nine."

Doc's shoulders slumped with another sigh. "Pearl... Have you been hearin' any of this radio talk? Or read that article in the newspaper?"

"No, baby. What article?"

Doc crushed his cigarette butt in the ashtray and looked directly at Pearl for the first time since she had stepped into the room. "They're hintin' around... They're sayin' I'm the father of that baby, Pearl. Couple'a the bastards even printed my name."

She recoiled slightly and Doc grabbed her hand. "It's *not* true, Pearl! It's only because the baby's dark, and I was the only colored man connected to Joe and Magda. But I'm not the Daddy, for God's sake! Aw, come on, baby—you gotta believe *that*."

"Oh, I do, baby. It was just a shock hearin' you say it, I guess. To tell the truth, that thought never even crossed my mind. I just figured Magda must'a had herself a colored man on the side."

Doc shook his head. "You're wrong, Pearl."

"No I'm not. There's *got* to be a colored man mixed up in this mess. How the hell else you gon' explain that baby's color? And she don't seem the slightest bit bothered by it either. Only time she smiles is when she's holdin' him. She calls him her 'healthy brown boy.' Don't *you* think that's a little strange?"

Doc shrugged, but said nothing.

"Well," Pearl continued, "my guess is that she met somebody on the uptown train. And you know she had me coverin' for her whenever Joe called here lookin' for her."

"She probably just didn't want to talk to him," Doc said. "She told me she didn't even answer the phone at home sometimes."

"Well, I can't blame her for that. Joe wasn't treatin' her right, baby, and I'm not just talkin' 'bout his foolin' with women. He was just plain cruel to her sometimes."

"You're wrong, Pearl."

"No, I'm not. You should'a heard some'a the things that child told me!"

"Not that. You're wrong about her havin' another man. In Harlem or anywhere else."

"Then how you gonna explain that brown baby? And it seems like he's gettin' browner every time I look at him, too."

"Joe Bluestone isn't white," Doc said quietly. "I mean, he *wasn't* white. He was passing."

"What?"

"I said—he was *passing*."

Pearl shook her head skeptically. "What makes you think that? He tell you that?"

"No. He denied it."

"Well, then—"

"They all deny it, baby. And when I confronted him with it, he looked at me like a—a goddamn rat with one paw caught in the trap and the other one in the cookie jar. He was passin', believe me. Hell, in every sense of the word, too. I'm tellin' you what I know."

"Well, I still think she had a man on the side. Wish he'd come claim that baby."

"She tell you that?" Doc asked.

"No, but—"

"Joe was passin', Pearl," he snapped.

Pearl was silent for a long moment, and then sighed pensively. "Oh, Ronnie, Ronnie…"

Doc looked at her. "What brought Ronnie into your mind?"

"Just—sump'm he use'ta say about truth and lies. He always said there's a whole lot'a truth hidin' in the lies folks choose to tell."

Doc nodded as he lit a fresh cigarette. "That sounds like Ronnie, all right. But Joe took all his lies with him. Anyway, the only lies I'm worryin' about are the ones in the newspapers. Damn! I need to wring somebody's goddamn neck for puttin' you through this shit."

Pearl slipped her hand inside his undershirt and began making rhythmic, restful circles on his back with her palm. "I ain't worryin' 'bout no talk, baby. We awright—you and me. And it's a good thing too, 'cause Magda's gonna need us now. 'Least till her folks get here from Greece."

"Aww, shit," Doc groaned loudly. "I forgot all about *them*."

"That's right. I forgot you met 'em. Were they that bad?"

"Well, I only met the father, and yeah, he was that bad. Ooh, man! When he gets a look at the color of that baby—the shit's gonna hit the fan."

"Oh, hell. That *is* bad."

"Yeah. But what the hell else would you expect from white folks?"

"But Magda's not like that. Neither is King—or the other fellas in the band for that matter."

Doc sighed impatiently. "I know. I didn't mean *them*. So, did she call her folks already?"

"No, and when I asked her about it, she said not to call 'em. Guess she knew how they'd act. Po' baby. Guess they both all alone now—her and that little boy."

"Yeah," Doc murmured. "Damn! What a mess."

Pearl rested her cheek against Doc's shoulder. "What the hell made Joe do sump'm so damn crazy? I never would'a figured him for the type."

Doc took a deep pull on the cigarette. His eyes were fixed and staring, as if searching for some answer hidden in the dark. "I tried to warn him," he murmured.

"What'cha say, baby?"

"Nothin'. Guess he must'a felt like everything was closin' in on him or sump'm. But I still don't know how he could'a done that to her."

Pearl felt the muscles in his back growing tense. "Baby," she whispered. "Ain't nothin' you can do about it. Now, why don'tcha just lay down so I can tend to you awhile."

Doc smiled at her over his shoulder, then crushed his cigarette in the ashtray on the bedside table. "And what makes you think I need tendin' to, woman?"

"Hell, I know what you need better than you do, Doc Calhoun. You too tired, too worried, and smokin' too damn many cigarettes. Now, lay down, fool, 'fore I fall asleep and you find out you done passed up some'a this good tendin'."

Chuckling softly, Doc eased off his undershirt and slipped off his trousers. Once under the covers, he raised up on one elbow and studied Pearl's face. "You straight?" he whispered.

She sighed and closed her eyes. "Yes, baby. I'm straight."

"I worry about you, you know—when you go off to that place."

"I know. But you said you don't want it in the house. I'm tryin', baby. Been spacin' 'em out pretty good. And I ain't been doin' so much. Just enough to get me straight so I don't get sick."

"I know. And I don't want you gettin' sick, so I guess—whatever it takes. I need you to be cool, 'specially now. So, whatever it takes, Pearl."

She touched his face gently. "I can handle it, baby. I can be straight when I need to."

Doc gazed into her eyes for a moment; then he buried his face in her neck. There was a catch in his breathing, and he began whispering her name over and over like a desperate prayer: "Pearl... Pearl..."

She held him as tightly as she could, unable to remember the last time she had seen him this way. The tears rushed up, but she kept her voice steady. "I'm right here, baby. I'm right here."

≈∞≈

Early the following afternoon, Doc and Pearl stepped into Magda's room at Mount Sinai. She was sitting in a chair near the bed, neatly dressed in a brown suit, pillbox hat, and white gloves, but her pale blue eyes were vacant and red-rimmed.

Doc walked over to her and smiled as he squeezed her hands in an unspoken promise of protection. "So I hear we're gonna have company at our house for a while."

No answer.

He gave her hands another light squeeze. "Magda. Did you hear me?"

"Sugah?" Pearl said gently. "Where's that pretty baby this mornin'? You nurse him yet?"

Magda blinked and nodded. "Yes. I—I nurse him. When I wake up, I nurse him."

At that moment, a Caucasian nurse with a hefty build breezed into the room pushing an empty wheelchair. Her loud, singsong voice bounced around the tension-packed room like a crazy rubber ball. "Good morning, Mrs. Bluestone!" she called. "Are you ready to go home?"

Magda lowered her head, and her shoulders shook with quiet sobs. Doc straightened up to glare at the nurse, but kept a gentle grip on Magda's hands.

Unruffled by the silence, the nurse positioned the wheelchair next to Magda's chair and continued her monologue. "First stop, Mommy, and next stop, Baby Bluestone!" With an uncertain glance at Doc, she directed her question at Magda. "These folks work for you, dear?"

"No disrespect intended," Doc snapped, "but apparently you didn't hear the news. Mommy and Baby Bluestone just lost *Daddy* Bluestone night before last. We're friends of the family and we'd appreciate it if you'd just do whatever you have to do here without all the *yak*."

Pearl placed a cautionary hand on his arm. "What my husband's tryin' to say is that we're Mrs. Bluestone's closest friends and we're here to take her home."

Doc turned his back on the nurse and continued grumbling. "I *said* exactly what I meant. I can do without all the goddamn *yak*."

Pearl frowned. "Like I said, we're here to take her home. Are we gonna have a *problem*?"

The nurse hesitated. "Well—"

"I was the one who brought her in to deliver, nurse. And I was with her all day yesterday too," Pearl said pointedly. "You weren't here yesterday, were you? Or the day before."

"I'm just back from vacation. Look, if you'll wait here I'll go check with the head nurse."

As Doc helped Magda into the wheelchair, the telephone rang. He nodded back at Pearl. "Get the phone, baby. Like a good little maid."

Pearl picked up the receiver. "Hello? Oh, hi, King... Yeah, we're takin' care'a things... No, she's—well, she's okay. We're takin' her home with us for a few days... Yeah... She just needs some peace and quiet... Yeah... We'll tell her... Bye."

Just as Pearl was hanging up, the nurse walked back in. "Well, everything's straightened out now. Sorry about the confusion. Poor little thing," she murmured, gazing at Magda.

Sidestepping the nurse, Doc wheeled Magda to the door. "Which way to the nursery?"

"To your right," the nurse said. "Oh, one more thing, folks. Dr. Aemel prescribed sleeping pills for her and they're quite strong. So no more nursing for that baby, you understand? Even if she wants to, don't let her. They gave her a pill last night and the nurse going off duty told me they had a real hard time waking her up this morning. So it's formula for this baby. We'll give you a list for the pharmacist."

Pearl stared at the nurse. "But—but then why'd they let her nurse him this morning?"

"Excuse me, but I'm *sure* they didn't."

Pearl frowned. "Excuse *me*, but she just told me she nursed that baby this morning."

"She isn't thinking clearly. There is no way they let her nurse that baby this morning."

"But she said—"

Doc stopped in front of the nursery window and cut his eyes at Pearl. "Hey, Magda!" he said loudly. "Would you look at all these babies! What'cha name yours?"

Out of a long silence, she murmured, "Charles. I name him Charles Nicholas Bluestone."

≈∞≈

After stopping at the drug store for the formula and the prescription, Doc helped Magda out of the taxi and up the steps to the apartment. Pearl followed behind them, carrying the baby.

"I'll run across the hall to Rose's and check on the kids," Pearl said as they stepped into the living room. "Here's Nicky. You get him and Magda settled, and I'll be right back."

Pearl returned a few minutes later and heated up a can of soup. She placed the bowl on the kitchen table for Magda, who sat staring out the window, her hands folded in her lap.

Doc stood in the kitchen doorway, watching quietly. "Kids okay?" he whispered.

"Mm-hmm," Pearl answered. "Where's Nicky?"

Doc grinned. "That makes twice you called him that. Thought his name was Charles."

"Well, his middle name's Nicholas and Nicky's cuter than Charles, don'tcha think?"

"Maaaan. The kid's only two days old and you already got his *cute* name picked out."

"Well, he is cute. And sweet as he wanna be, don'tcha think?"

"Wait till 4:00 a.m. when he starts that baby-howlin' shit and ask me that question again. Anyway, I dragged out Shay's old crib for him and put him in it. He's in our room."

"Good." Pearl picked up a spoon and offered it to Magda. "Come on now, sista. I know you got the blues real bad, but you gotta eat to keep up your strength."

Magda refused the spoon and her eyes filled with tears.

Pearl sat in a chair and scooted close to her. "Look, sugah," she whispered, "I know what misery feels like and sometimes the only escape is sleep. Now I got some sleeping pills for you, but you can't take 'em till you eat this soup. Don'tcha wanna take one and go to sleep? You'll feel better when you wake up. And don't worry. I'll take real good care'a the baby, okay?"

After a long pause, Magda nodded and reached for the spoon.

Doc sighed. "That'a girl."

≈∞≈

Magda slept through the night and most of the following day in Edward's bed. When she finally wandered into the kitchen, she was holding her head and stumbling. "Joe!" she croaked.

Doc sprang from his chair and grabbed her. "Calm down, baby. You're safe."

"Joe!" she shouted. She lunged forward, bumping into Pearl. Shay let out a frightened screech and buried her face in her mother's skirt.

"Oh, Lord!" Pearl moaned. "I shouldn't have brought these kids home so soon."

Magda stood there looking disoriented and sobbing, "Joe! Where he is?"

Doc lifted her in his arms and carried her back to the children's room, but she began fighting him. By the time he put her back in the bed, she was screaming hysterically. "I now remember! Don't lie to me! I make him to die!"

"Shhh, hush, Magda," Doc said, trying to calm her. "Pearl," he called over his shoulder. "You run the kids back over to Rose and—" Before he could finish, Magda caught him with a wild swing and scratched the side of his face with the stone of her ring.

Doc yelled, which startled the baby, who began to scream loudly.

"You take 'em!" Pearl said. "She'll listen to me. I'll calm her down."

"You can't handle her!" Doc shouted as he dodged Magda's slapping hands.

The wailing children and another one of Magda's wild swings sent Doc over the edge. "Goddamn, Pearl! Get these kids out'a here! They don't need to see this shit!"

After Pearl had herded the children out of the apartment, Doc grabbed Magda's shoulders and shook her. "Hey! HEY! It's time to settle down, you hear me? I don't mean to get rough with you, but I'm not having this in my house with these kids around, Magda."

She stopped struggling and he eased his grip. "Okay. Now Pearl's comin' right back and—"

She interrupted him abruptly. "I go to da bathroom."

"Uh, well, just wait a minute, and Pearl can take you."

"I am now in da house-jail?" she snapped.

"House-jail?" Doc rolled his eyes and allowed her to sit up. "No, Magda, this is not *any* kind'a jail. But you need to calm down. This won't do you any good—you or your baby."

Suddenly, her eyes changed from angry to tragic. "Where—is da baby?"

"He's across the hall at Rose's—with our kids, Magda. You scared him with all that yellin'. See, that's why you need to straighten up. That baby needs you."

The front door opened, and then Pearl walked into the room. "You doin' better, sugah?"

Magda wiped her nose with the sleeve of her nightgown. "I go to da bathroom, please."

Pearl and Doc exchanged an uncertain look, and she snarled, "I am now in da house-jail?"

"Of course not, sugah," Pearl said, reaching for her hand. "Here, let me help you."

Magda slapped Pearl's hand away and managed to get to her feet. "I want no help. I want only to be alone." She slowly made her way into the bathroom and shut the door.

Pearl leaned against the door and shut her eyes tightly as she listened to Magda sobbing.

"You think she's okay?" Doc whispered, handing Pearl his handkerchief.

Pearl blew her nose and composed herself. "Yeah, baby. She's just in there tryin' to—how's she say it? Tryin' to make her courage." She tapped on the door lightly. "Magda?"

Doc moved Pearl away from the door and knocked sharply. "Hey. Time's up, Magda. Now, open this door or I'ma have to open it for you. I know you're upset but—"

Muffled sounds emerged from the bathroom: loud scraping and an anguished half-scream. Doc tried the doorknob; it was locked. Stepping back, he threw his shoulder into the door, forcing it open. All he saw were Magda's legs thrashing; the rest of her body was halfway out the window. Only Doc's quickness prevented her from taking a six-story leap. Grabbing an ankle with his right hand, he clawed at her nightgown with his left until he managed to grip her waist. She struggled with surprising strength, kicking his head into the medicine chest mirror, shattering it. Finally, Doc braced his foot against the toilet tank for leverage and yanked her back in, which sent them both toppling backwards to the floor.

"Magda!" Pearl shouted as she tried to help them up. "What'chu tryin' to do, sugah?"

Scrambling to his knees, Doc pushed Pearl toward the door. "Get *out* before you get hurt!"

"Please to let me die!" Magda wailed. Twisting free, she crawled away from Doc. Again, he caught her ankle, and again, she kicked him with the other leg and wriggled out of his grasp.

"Block the door!" he yelled at Pearl.

Before Magda could escape, Doc found his opening. Twisting her around until she was facing him, he let fly a hard, fully extended backhand, which caught her on the side of the face. After a couple of unfocused blinks, her eyes rolled back and she slumped into his arms.

Pearl gasped. "You—you hit her!"

Breathing heavily, Doc struggled to his feet. As he hoisted Magda over his shoulder, he shot Pearl a look that was a mix of anger and bewilderment. "You goddamn right I hit her! And don't look at me like that. If she'd got past you, she would'a jumped right out that front window! Shit! My only regret is this main event wasn't in the Garden for some goddamn money! Now get me those sleeping pills." He paused at the door, closed his eyes, and sighed. "Please."

By the time he had settled Magda in Edward's bed, Pearl was back. She quickly eased a pill into her mouth and held a glass of milk to her lips. "Can you swallow this, sista?"

Magda's eyes fluttered open and she managed to swallow the pill.

"What's the milk for?" Doc whispered.

"So she don't get sick."

"Oh, yeah. We don't want the little hellcat gettin' sick, now, do we?" he said, pointing at his bleeding forehead. "Let's keep her healthy and strong for round two."

"Doc Calhoun! You know this ain't Magda's real nature. She's all out'a her head from this."

"I know," he said. "But damn! That little woman kicks like a mule. A big, *strong* mule."

"It's a strong feeling—wantin' to die," Pearl said softly. "Look what it did to Ronnie."

Magda's eyes opened again. "Yes. I die," she whispered. "Please to let me die."

"No," Doc said firmly. "And make that *hell*, no. That's what that fight was all about. We are not about to let you die, so stop that talk right now."

Magda closed her eyes and her head rolled slightly.

"I hope she goes to sleep for a while," Doc whispered as he closed the door.

Pearl went into the bathroom for antiseptic and bandages. "Oh, Lord, I gotta clean up all this glass before the kids can come back."

Doc was in the kitchen washing his cuts. "Shit. Wonder what a new medicine chest costs?"

Pearl walked into the kitchen and pressed a cotton ball to his forehead. "Here, let me do it."

"Look out now! That shit burns!"

"Hush. You're worse than Edward. She did get her licks in, though, I'll give her that."

Doc grinned. "I must be gettin' old. That skinny little woman took me the distance!"

"Oh, no," Pearl said suddenly. "I just thought of sump'm. What about the funeral?"

"Hell, I don't know. King said he'd go claim Joe's body at the airport and get it to the funeral home. But damn. I don't know if she can take a funeral. We might have to call that doctor and see if he can give her sump'm to calm her down."

After a long silence, Pearl nodded. "I guess so."

≈∞≈

At Dr. Aemel's instructions, Pearl and Doc woke Magda early the next morning just long enough to slip her another sleeping pill and get her into a taxi for the ride back to the hospital. Once she was admitted, they joined the doctor for a conference in his office.

Dr. Aemel sat down behind his desk and began to explain. "A husband's suicide is traumatic enough, but she's suffering from severe post-partum depression—a hormonal imbalance. And from all you've told me, I don't feel comfortable letting her near that infant." Removing his glasses, he rubbed the bridge of his nose. "I've weighed the options and my recommendation is electroshock therapy."

"You mean those shock treatments?" Pearl looked at Doc. "I read about that mess, baby."

"Now, Mrs. Calhoun," the doctor said, "When prudently administered in communion with a series of one-on-one sessions with a qualified psychiatrist, they've proven quite effective."

"Some standard sales-pitch bullshit if I ever heard it," Doc muttered.

Dr. Aemel's eyebrows shot up. "I beg your pardon!"

Doc's jaw tightened. "She's not a science experiment, man. She's our friend."

Pearl's response was horrified silence.

"I'm trying to help," Dr. Aemel said. "These methods are gaining widespread acceptance."

Doc shrugged uncomfortably. "Well, she *is* in pretty bad shape, baby. I mean, that scene in the bathroom and all. If I hadn't caught her when I did—"

"Exactly," Dr. Aemel said. "In my experience, electroshock therapy has worked wonders on extreme behavior such as this. We'll try it on a short-term basis and see how she does. And I'll give you my home phone number so you can call me if any problems arise with regard to the baby." He smiled. "I'm confident Mrs. Bluestone will respond positively. Trust me, please."

"Well—if it's the only way," Pearl murmured hesitantly. "But what's it gonna cost?"

"The same insurance policy that covered the baby's birth will cover this. But we will need your signature as the responsible party, Mrs. Calhoun. I'll get the authorization forms."

Pearl looked at Doc, who nodded resignedly. "Thank you, Doctor," she said.

≈∞≈

Eight days passed before Dr. Aemel approved visitors for Magda, which included a special exception for the baby. Doc entered the room first, and Pearl followed with Nicky in her arms. Forcing a smile, Doc tried to erase the image that leaped into his mind. Magda's face resembled the face of an emaciated Holocaust survivor he had seen once in a photograph—with dark hollows under vacant, haunted eyes. He looked back at Pearl and saw her reaction. But the cheerful note in her voice covered it well.

"Hey, sista! Look who came to see his Mama! Little Nicky!"

Magda's face contorted into a faded version of her old smile. "Nicky you call him?"

"Oh, I'm sorry, sugah. It's just a little nick-name."

Doc chuckled. "Ooh. That calls for a rim-shot. Where's King when we need him?"

"We can call him Charles if you like that better, sugah," Pearl said.

"No, I like," Magda said softly. "Little Nicky. Mama is so sorry." She gazed at Pearl, then at Doc, and her eyes filled with tears. "No good, I'm afraid. I am such da bad Mama."

"Aw, stop that now," Doc said. "You've just got the blues is all. Happens to everybody."

Magda pointed at Doc's scratches. "I'm sorry I act so crazy dat way. Please to forgive me."

"No, I want a rematch! I admit you caught me a few times with that left, but see, I've been training!" He shook his fist at her playfully. "And I will be ready for you next time."

Magda laughed as the tears streamed down her face. She wrapped both her hands around Doc's fist and kissed it. "You protect me when I act so crazy. And you make me to laugh again."

Pearl placed the baby into her arms. "Now don't you worry about the baby. I'm takin' real good care of him till you come home. You're gonna be a real good Mama, hear?"

"No, Pearl, please! I shake. I—I drop him or something. Please to take him."

"Nonsense," Doc said. "Just relax against the pillows while you hold him. He won't fall."

Magda nodded and held the baby closer. "He eats okay, Pearl?" she asked softly.

"Just like a little baby pig, sista!" Pearl laughed. "He's gonna be a bruiser, all right."

Magda seemed unable to take her eyes off the bundle in her arms. "He is a healthy boy—a good boy, yes? He don't cry, Pearl! See how quiet is my little Nicky—my healthy brown boy."

Doc grinned. "Yeah, he's definitely *brown*, all right."

"It's good to see you doin' better, sugah. Now, move over so I can sit with you."

As Pearl settled in, Magda rested her head on her shoulder. "My sister," she murmured.

"Damn right. Sista's right here, and I always will be. So—you feelin' better now?"

"Well, I feel all da time like crying, but not to—not to die no more. I think of da baby when—" She stopped and a frightened expression crossed her face. "Da treatments, Pearl."

"Oh, that must be scary, huh? But, sugah, it seems to be helping."

"Yes, but da needles and to be strapped down—and to hurt so bad." She sighed and smiled. "I'm sorry, Pearl. Is okay. I make my courage, and I dream of music after."

"I know you make your courage, sugah," Pearl said softly. "And dreamin' about music sounds real nice... Now, would you look at Nicky smilin'? He's so happy to see his Mama!"

"Baby smiles ain't nothin' but gas," Doc laughed.

"No. Is pretty smile on my little Nicholas. That is middle name of my Papa—Nicholas."

Doc grunted, and Pearl cut her eyes at him. "That's real nice, sugah," she said.

"First name is—" She clutched at Pearl's hand. "Pearl! I forget my Papa's first name!"

"It's the medicine makin' you forget," Doc said. "Don't worry. It'll come back to you."

Magda smiled at the baby. "Do people think my Nicky is da brother of Edward and Shay?"

Pearl laughed. "You know, one'a Rose's friends did, now that you mention it."

"Because he is a healthy brown boy! See how good is my little brown boy, Pearl."

A gray-haired nurse appeared at the door. "Time for your treatment, Mrs. Bluestone."

"No!" Magda wailed, holding Nicky tighter. "More time, please? So long I don't see him!"

"Sorry, but the treatment schedule is strict." The nurse glanced over her shoulder. "But I have some good news," she whispered. "Doctor said you might get to go home next week."

Magda's old smile made an amazing reappearance. "Next week?" She snuggled the baby happily. "You hear dat, Nicky? Mama comes home next week. Den I fix everything."

≈∞≈

A half-hour later Magda was staring at the ceiling in the electroshock therapy room, her fists clenched at her sides. *Next week—home to my boy.* As the attendant buckled the straps on her wrists, she said, "Please, sir. How many more treatments I must have?"

"Well, let me look at your chart… Two more after this. Then you can probably go home."

"Oh," she breathed. "Dat will be so wonderful. Thank you."

"Okay, now. It's important for you to relax, and it'll all be over soon. Here we go…"

≈∞≈

Magda had discovered an unusual way to tolerate her treatments. During the gradual waking phase, she experienced an oddly pleasant sensation on the other side of the convulsive ache. It was as if she had moved through a portal into a timeless, bodiless divinity where there was no pain or anxiety. It was a memory place, where favorite symphonies blended with rhythmic earthsounds and treasured moments of extreme joy. She knew it was a dream, but she felt safe there until the music finally guided her back to consciousness. In the first hazy seconds, all she could hear was her own heartbeat—a loud, fuzzy thumping in her ears—mallets on timpanis—that vibrated down her spine and into her extremities. A pulsing rhythm in her fingers—a violin tremolo. Then the happy pinging sound of rain dripping into a metal pot. Counting two measures more, the squawking slide-trombones transformed into the human voices of doctors and nurses. Magda would wiggle her fingers and toes, until the light appeared under her eyelids. She would blink to test her vision, whisper her name, and sigh with relief when everything still worked. The lingering pain in her head was a small price to pay for such a beautiful journey.

But this journey would be different.

She was still a few measures away from wiggling her fingers or opening her eyes, but she could hear the distant trombone voices beginning to form words:

> *"Where's Murphy?"*
> *"Out sick."*
> *"This patient coming in for treatment or finishing one?"*

"I don't know. My shift just started. Check the chart."

"Shows her coming in. Get her strapped down before she wakes up."

Chapter 21

The faint, faraway sound of a ringing telephone echoed in Pearl's ears. It was her old nightmare. She knew who it was and she knew that once she answered his call, he would keep talking, no matter how many times she begged him to stop. *Don't answer it. Just don't answer it.* But in the dream she always answered, just as she had on the night Ronnie had taken his own life. It was that same cold, disembodied voice that had called itself "Sergeant Gallo from the 28th Precinct."

Mrs. Calhoun?... We found your name and number in an address book belonging to a Ronald Sayles. You were listed as the party to contact in case of emergency, so I'm calling to inform you that Mr. Sayles' neighbor found him lying in his doorway, deceased, about an hour ago. It appears to be a suicide. There was a note, but it was unreadable...

Another ring ended the dream. Pearl's eyes flew open and she grabbed the phone. "Hello?"

"May I speak to Mrs. Calhoun?"

"Yes—" She paused to clear her throat and catch her breath. "This is Mrs. Calhoun."

"Mrs. Calhoun, this is Dr. Driscoll from Mount Sinai Hospital. I, uh—I'm afraid I have some bad news about Mrs. Bluestone. It seems she—"

Pearl's interruption was loud and edgy. "What happened to her?"

"I'm terribly sorry, Mrs. Calhoun, but it's against policy to give details over the phone."

"Is—is she dead?" Pearl shouted in a half-sob.

"No! I'm sorry, Mrs. Calhoun. She's alive, but there have been some—complications. Please just come to the hospital tomorrow at nine. Dr. Aemel will meet us here."

Pearl hung up and dialed Dr. Aemel's number. After four rings, she heard the doctor's tired hello. "Dr. Aemel? I just got a call from—"

"I know," he said. "I just spoke to Dr. Driscoll. I'll still need you to come in tomorrow, but I can tell you this much. It seems that Mrs. Bluestone has lapsed into a state of catatonia—"

"What the hell does that mean?"

"It means that she's—unresponsive. She can't speak or understand what's said to her."

"But she was fine just this morning! Maybe she just doesn't feel like talkin' to anybody."

"It's more than that, Mrs. Calhoun. There is simply no response."

"Well, maybe she just—maybe—passed out or sump'm. Just—just wake her up!"

He sighed. "Mrs. Calhoun, have you ever heard of people being in a coma?"

Pearl felt the tears welling up again. "You *can't* wake her up. That's what you mean."

"We're doing all we can and running more tests. The best way I can explain it is that she's in a sort of an awake coma. Her eyes are open but her mind is asleep."

"It was those goddamn shock treatments! I should'a never let you do that to her!"

"Mrs. Calhoun, please! I assure you, her condition is not a result of those treatments. Trust me, please. We'll talk it over tomorrow. You'll be at the hospital at nine?"

After a long silence, Pearl answered. "Damn right I'll be there."

≈∞≈

It was almost 3:00 a.m. when Doc returned home from the club. As he unlocked the front door, he heard a child's piercing scream—Shay. Dropping his keys and horn case on the chair, he ran to the children's room and flipped on the light. Shay was kneeling rigidly in her bed, wailing.

He scooped her into his arms and felt her tiny fingernails digging into his neck. "Calm down, baby. Daddy's here." He glanced over at Edward, who was still asleep.

"Daddy! My Daddy!" Shay sobbed.

"Yeah, yeah, baby. Your Daddy's here. What happened? You have a bad dream?"

"It was a monster, Daddy," she sniffled.

"Oh. That monster again, huh? He's not real, Shay. I told you that."

"He *was* a real monster! He made me bump my head! And he was growlin' at me too!"

"You bumped your head and he was growlin' at you? But I don't see any lumps."

She pointed at her head. "Right here. It hurts like a lump. It *really* hurts. Jus' like a lump."

"Aw, you're a tough girl. You can take a little lump. And you can go back to sleep now that I'm home. 'Cause monsters are scared'a me, you know. Especially those imaginary monsters."

"Good! I called Mama but she didn't come. How come Mama didn't come?"

"It's Daddy's job to get rid of imaginary monsters. Now, you need to go to the bathroom?"

"No, sir," she said in a sleepy voice. "Um, will it be morning soon, Daddy?"

He squinted at his watch. "It'll be morning about—one minute after you go to sleep."

"One minute? Are you *sure*?"

"One minute. So go to sleep and it'll be morning before you know it. Good night, baby."

After tucking her in, Doc strode down the hallway toward the ribbon of light under his bedroom door. His pulse was pounding a manic rhythm in his temples as he jerked the door open. "Pearl! Why you got the goddamn door shut when—" The angry words died in his throat. Pearl was sitting calmly on the edge of the bed with her right foot on the floor and her left leg stretched out over the twisted sheets. Doc's eyes took in everything at once: The red hot-water-bottle hose tied high on her bare leg. The needle shaking just before piercing the bulging vein that ran down the inside of her thigh. The series of purple to black bruises that marked her new favorite spot. The hypo drawing up that small, swirling tinge of pink—blood mixing with narcotic for a split-second before rushing back into her leg. He looked at her face. As she waited for the effect, her gaze was dispassionate—perhaps aimed at the bedside lamp, perhaps not—as if shooting heroin were an everyday task. She might as well have been washing dishes.

He didn't want to see the next phase—the wild-eyed ecstasy, the rolling of her head—so he sat down on the end of the bed and stared at the floor until she finished. He heard the shuddering gasp, the orgasmic moan, and finally, the long exhalation. "It just hit, huh?" he said bitterly.

The bedsprings squeaked as she fell back against her pillow. "Hit gooood, baby."

He got up to check on the baby, who was sleeping soundly. "What happened, Pearl?"

"What makes you think sump'm happened, sugah?" she cackled dryly. "Hell, it ain't like you didn't know I was a goddamn junkie."

"Keep your voice down! I *told* you never to fix up in the house! And here you are with your goddamn works all over the bed—" He hurled a scorched teaspoon at the venetian blinds in a loud metallic clatter. The baby stirred, but didn't wake up.

He grabbed Pearl's arm. "Listen to me! Shay's out there screamin' her head off, and you're in here fuckin' that goddamn stick! *Why* Pearl?... Hey! Are you hearin' me? *What* happened?"

Pearl smiled and began singing softly. "Them that's got shall have—"

"Answer me, goddammit!" he hissed. "*What* happened?"

She scowled and pulled her arm free. "You messin' up my high, man... Lemme alone, dammit! I'll tell you what happened... S'my fault. That hospital—messed up Magda's brain with those—goddamn treatments I signed for. *That's* what happened. Now she can't talk or— even go to the damn bathroom by herself no more. They tried to tell me it was sump'm else, but I know... I *know* it was those damn shock treatments. Those treatments I signed for. *Me.*"

Doc lifted one of the blinds and stared out. "So you bring that shit into the house and you get high. But guess what? Magda still can't talk or go to the bathroom by herself, now can she?"

Pearl laughed softly. "Hey, baby... you *said* whatever it takes."

Chapter 22

Three days later, Pearl was at Idlewild Airport with Dr. Aemel, who had agreed to act as liaison when Magda's parents arrived from Athens. She shared an uneasy alliance with the doctor, forged from distrust and a mutual need for assistance.

"So you'll do all the talkin', right, Doctor? 'Cause even if they spoke English, they probably wouldn't talk to me anyway. They don't have much use for colored folks."

"Well, my Greek is limited, but I'll make them understand the situation. Don't worry."

"Doctor, I really appreciate what you been doin' for Magda. Lord knows we can't afford it."

"And you've taken great care of the baby, Mrs. Calhoun. Magda's parents can take over now." He pointed at a TWA plane taxiing to a stop. "This looks like their flight."

They watched the passengers disembark and file into the terminal building. Each one hurried past or was met by a happy relation. Pearl was about to give up when she spotted a short, gray-haired woman, who was crying softly into a handkerchief. "Mrs. Skouros?" she called.

The woman nodded at her and approached them uncertainly.

Dr. Aemel began speaking to Mrs. Skouros in Greek, mixing in a few English phrases, and Pearl found her rigid opinion softening under the older woman's gentle gaze.

Suddenly, Mrs. Skouros pointed at her. "You are—Pearl?"

"Yes—yes, ma'am," Pearl stammered.

Mrs. Skouros retrieved what looked like a letter on blue stationery from her pocketbook and held it out. "Pearl—you friend for my Magdalena—she tell to me." Her eyes filled with new tears. "My husband—he no come. He no—*talk* my Magdalena—no more."

≈∞≈

Pearl was pacing in the hospital corridor, fidgeting with her wedding band and trying to ignore the familiar crawling-worms feeling in her belly. Her throat was tight and dry, and it seemed as if Mrs. Skouros and the doctor had been in Magda's room for hours. I'll *never get through this day without a fix—or at least a damn drink of water. But if I walk down to that water fountain and that nurse gives me the evil eye, I'm liable to belt her... And then run straight to the quarter house. Dance with that goddamn Hydra and never come back.* Her thoughts were cut short by the sound of Mrs. Skouros's sobbing as Dr. Aemel led her out of Magda's room and into his office. When the door closed, Pearl shivered and prayed for strength.

Another thirsty eternity passed before Dr. Aemel stepped out and asked Pearl to join them. She hesitated, then walked in. "Could I have a glass of water, Doctor?" she croaked.

"Of course, Mrs. Calhoun. Please have a seat." He poured a glass of ice water from a pitcher and handed it to her. "Mrs. Skouros has something she would like to ask you."

Pearl nodded absently and reached for the water. The ice cubes clinked musically and the glass was cold and damp on her fingertips. Pressing her dry lips to the rim, she sipped the water and felt the God-blessed coolness of it wetting her throat. After draining the glass, she felt better.

Mrs. Skouros was still crying. "Please, Doctor—my English... Please—you tell."

"Of course." Dr. Aemel refilled Pearl's glass. "It seems you were right about Magdalena's father, Mrs. Calhoun. Mrs. Skouros told me that when he learned about the child's color, he disowned his daughter. That's why he refused to come with his wife to see her. He said that when Magdalena took a Negro lover, she murdered her husband by breaking his heart."

Lord Jesus, I need that fix. Pearl took another sip and murmured, "It's a damn mean world."

"Yes, it is," the doctor agreed. "Mrs. Skouros is heartbroken that she can't take the baby."

Mrs. Skouros gestured with a shaky hand. "Da baby—yes—"

Dr. Aemel patted her hand. "I suppose you know what she wants, Mrs. Calhoun. She wants you to raise the baby. I told her that you'd want to discuss it with your husband."

"I already did," Pearl snapped. "We figured this was how it'd go. So you tell her that Magda is *family* to us. And colored families don't put their babies out—no matter *what* color they turn out. Damn right we'll take care of Nicky. He belongs with us anyway." Noticing Dr. Aemel's surprised expression, she added, "Well, I guess you don't have to tell her all that. Guess I'm a little on edge is all. Just tell her—we love Nicky and we'll be happy to take him."

Mrs. Skouros gave the doctor a quizzical look. "Nicky?"

"Yes," Pearl said. "Nicholas. In honor of Magda's missing-person Daddy."

Mrs. Skouros dabbed at her eyes. "Sank you," she said. "May Gott to bless you."

The doctor helped her to her feet. "I'm having a nurse drive Mrs. Skouros to a hotel for the night, but I'll be right back. Please wait. I'd like to discuss a few more details with you."

Pearl was pacing like a caged cat when the doctor returned. "Well, what did she say?"

The doctor sat back down at his desk. "Well, she was shocked to see her daughter in such a state and I begged her to take her time about deciding, but the poor woman has no choice. She can't go against her husband. I know it's wrong, Mrs. Calhoun, but I couldn't exactly force her."

"You mean they're just gonna *leave* her—laid up all alone in this hospital?"

"Well, I'll see to it that she can remain here until we make other arrangements. There are some excellent charity institutions that care for people like Magdalena."

"*Charity* institutions!" Pearl yelled. "You talkin' about a state hospital? Oh, hell, no! I've seen those places, and you are gonna have to come up with sump'm better for my friend."

"Please have a seat and calm down, Mrs. Calhoun. When you signed the papers for—"

Pearl interrupted him in a chilling baritone. "*You* need to cut the shit right now, 'cause I already know what you're tryin' to pull here. Yes, I signed the papers for those treatments, but whatever happened to Magda happened in *this* hospital under *your* watch. I know some lawyers that are *real* good at diggin' out details, and the papers are always lookin' for stories like this."

"Mrs. Calhoun, please—"

Pearl's palms hit the center of his desk with an audible smack, and she leaned so close to him that he jerked back in his chair. "And *then* there was that slip-up in the maternity ward when *somebody* let her nurse that baby when she was drugged up on those sleeping pills. Don't think for one minute I'm forgettin' about *that*! So, like I said, Doctor, y*ou* and this hospital are gonna have to come up with sump'm better than a goddamn rat-infested *charity* hospital for my friend!" She swallowed back the sob she felt rising in her throat and glared at him with dry eyes.

Out of a long silence, Dr. Aemel said, "I assure you this hospital is not responsible—"

Pearl grabbed her pocketbook and headed for the door.

"Wait, please! Perhaps—we can work out—better arrangements."

Pearl turned around and narrowed her eyes at him. "Perhaps?"

"Since you and your husband are willing to take the child, I'm sure I can convince the board to find a facility for Mrs. Bluestone that meets with your approval. Now, about the child—"

Pearl yanked out a chair and sat down stiffly. "I'm listening."

"There are two choices—you can take the child on a temporary basis as foster—"

Pearl slammed her pocketbook onto his desk. "His name is Nicky, dammit! Not *the child*. He's not some leftover problem for some goddamn board of directors to get rid of!"

"I'm sorry if I sounded insensitive, Mrs. Calhoun," the doctor said carefully.

"And we don't want nothin' temporary, Doctor. We'll adopt Nicky permanent."

Dr. Aemel smiled at her. "Mrs. Calhoun, you're an angel. A temperamental angel—but your temper is understandable. This is a unique case and I'm sure I can pull some strings."

≈∞≈

Two weeks later, Doc and Pearl were back at the hospital to sign the adoption papers.

"You know why that doctor's bein' so nice, don'tcha, baby?" Doc said.

"I'm the one who threatened him, remember? But if we really *had* tried to sue—"

"I know," Doc grumbled. "Lawyers cost money. Better to just leave it alone. But every time Smilin' Jack, M.D. walks in here, I wanna belt him. And when's that notary cat comin' back?"

"In a minute," she said, gazing distractedly out the window. "You know, now that we're makin' it official, I'm gettin' real nervous. What if— What if I can't raise that baby right?"

"Stop it. You're doin' fine with our kids. Nobody's a perfect parent, and we're already doin' the kid one big favor by changin' his name to Calhoun. 'Cause lately, it seems like anybody named Bluestone is a walking disaster. That is one bad-luck name. And besides—"

"Wait, baby," Pearl said. "I need to make sump'm right. I wanna promise you sump'm before that man comes back..." She sat down next to Doc and stared into his eyes. "I'm gonna kick, baby," she whispered. "I'm gonna really try hard this time. 'Cause I can't stand that I disappointed you—bringin' that mess into the house. And I—I want you to trust me again."

Doc smiled. "Pearl... We don't keep score, you and me. Remember?"

Chapter 23

1958

Nick clung tightly to Pearl's hand as they rode the elevator to the fourth floor of the Genesco Medical Center. The instant the door opened, he pulled his hand free and dashed down the hall.

"Nicky!" Pearl called softly. Casting a glance toward the nurses' station, she smiled and sighed. "Sorry, Hattie. It's his birthday today and he's just so excited to tell her."

Hattie was a lanky, dark-skinned woman with an energetic personality and a warm laugh. "It's okay, Pearl, and we all know it's that boy's birthday. He ran around last time you were here announcin' it to the whole hospital. So we got a little surprise for him."

"Hattie! That's so sweet, but you didn't have to do that."

"Oh, yes, we did! Girl, every nurse in the hospital loves that boy."

"Yeah, he's sweet—when he's here. But you ought'a see the little monster at home."

Just as Pearl and Hattie approached the door to Magda's room, Nick ran out, grinning broadly. "Look, Aunt Pearl! Mama got me a party in here! And a big ol' chocolate cake!"

Pearl stepped into the room and gasped. Hanging from the ceiling was a rainbow-arc of multi-colored balloons and streamers. Nick tugged her hand and she leaned down.

He placed his hand close to her ear and whispered, "You think Mama got me a kitten, Aunt Pearl? For a present—maybe? I *really* want a kitten. I told Mama last Sunday."

Pearl rubbed his head. "Baby, you know they don't allow dogs or cats in this place. So I'm sorry, but you won't be gettin' a kitten—not this year anyway."

Nick's expression turned tragic and his bottom lip quivered until he spotted Hattie lighting the candles on his birthday cake. The nurses and orderlies began singing *Happy Birthday*, and Nick giggled bashfully as he crawled into bed with his mother.

"How many candles you got on that cake, Nick?" one of the orderlies asked.

Nick snuggled closer to Magda and grinned. "Six."

"Six, huh? You're an old man, now. You ready to gobble up that cake?"

"Yes, sir, Mr. Jeff!" Nick shouted. "I'm ready! Hey! You want some too?"

"Nicky," Pearl said, "the cake's for everybody, and don't be hollerin' in here, baby."

As Pearl began cutting and serving the cake, Nick climbed down from the bed and tugged at her skirt. "I'll take Mama's cake to her, Aunt Pearl."

"Okay, sugah. Here's a piece for her right here."

"She likes chocolate cake a whole bunch, like me."

"I remember you tellin' me that, baby."

"And I could feed her too. She likes it when I feed her."

"Okay, climb up and use both hands." She helped him up and handed him the cake.

"It's chocolate, Mama," Nick whispered. "Open up."

Pearl was only half-listening to something Hattie was saying as she watched Nick with his mother. As always, Magda's face was an inanimate mask, expressing neither happiness nor sadness, but Nick was oblivious to the difference between her and the other people in the room.

"Open up, Mama," he repeated. "It's real good!"

When Magda finally opened her mouth, Nick grinned triumphantly. "I told'ja it's good!"

Pearl smiled. As she watched him feeding his mother and chattering his childhood news to her, she remembered the doctor's explanation, almost word for word: *The sense of smell triggers an innate survival instinct, which is why Mrs. Bluestone continues to accept food when it's fed to her. It requires no thought. But she will never be able to feed herself.*

Magda's body jerked suddenly and a grunting sound escaped her mouth. "Puh."

"That's good, Mama!" Nick said happily. "You talkin'!"

"Hattie," Pearl said suddenly, "could we have a little time alone with her?"

"Sure, honey. Just stop by the nurses' station on your way out. We got a gift for him."

"A gift too? Oh, thank you, Hattie. And thanks for all this."

When everyone was gone, Nick stared at Pearl. "Ain'tcha gonna come talk to Mama?"

"Sure, baby!" Slipping off her shoes, Pearl climbed into the bed and hugged Magda. "Sista, can you believe this boy is six years old today? Just growin' like a weed, ain't he?"

Nick grinned. "I'm a six-years-old healthy brown boy, right, Aunt Pearl?"

"That's right, Nicky. That's what she always called you—her big healthy brown boy."

"Mama's learnin' how to talk," he said matter-of-factly. "I'ma teach her some words."

Magda lurched forward again and made the same grunting sound: "P-puh."

"See, Aunt Pearl?" Nick yelped. "She's talkin' again! She's sayin' *Pearl*."

"No, baby," Pearl said gently, "that's the same sound she always makes."

"No, ma'am. She's sayin' *Pearl*." Then he pointed at Magda's hand. "See?"

Magda was clutching at the air with her fingers in the manner of a blind woman reaching for a familiar object to guide her. Pearl grasped her hand carefully and then held it gently against her face. "I'm right here, sista," she said softly. "And I been takin' good care'a your baby."

Nick scowled. "I ain't no baby, Aunt Pearl. I'm six now, 'member?"

"That's right, sugah. You sure are."

At that moment the door opened. A tall Negro man walked in and removed his hat. He wore a neatly-trimmed beard, but his head was shaved clean. "Uh, beg your pardon—"

Nick scrambled down off the bed. "Hi, Mista. You comin' to my birthday party too?"

"Listen, I'm sorry to interrupt," the man said, gazing at Nick and then at Magda.

Pearl stood up. "This is a private room. Who were you lookin' for?"

The man opened his mouth as if to speak, but no words came out.

"What are you doin' in this room?" Pearl asked sharply. "Come over here, Nick."

The man's eyes widened. "Nick? Uh, I thought your name was—Charles."

"Yes, sir," Nick said. "Charles Nicholas Calhoun. Nick for short, see?"

Pearl pulled Nick close. "How do you know this boy's name? Just who the hell *are* you?"

"I'm sorry. I should'a said that right off. I'm the boy's uncle, ma'am. I'm Calvin Bailey."

PART III EQUINOX

Silent shadows slip unseen
one for one
in lost, forgotten cold-sweat dreams
A misbegotten love supreme...
Brother—are you really there?
Or is it only hate that waits just east of fate
and fratricidal warfare?
Out of the shadows
and out of the night
Now run...
into the light and the bright
and the damn near white
OH! What did I do
to be so black and blue?
Outrun the shadows
outrun the night
Run, boy, run...
from get-back-black to broad daylight
hiding... in plain sight
What was my crime and
what did I do—to be so black and blue?
blue... blue... as a Blue Moon tune; a Trane refrain
Forgotten man—time to get in the game
Out of tune and off the beat but
cool... no rules
Where all the squares play musical chairs
So grab a seat and don't be scared
Nobody's ever really there... only shadows
Silent shadows—quick, unseen
air a shared unholy scream
One brother gone—a shadow fades
Let us pray...
Day is done, gone the sun...
Time has run, shadows come...
to leave their footsteps on your grave
Vernal eternal—Equinox!
One for one and son for son
Light eats dark, but dark in Autumn
drinks the light—
So what remains and WHO remains
when bright is pushed aside by night?
... That's right...

Chapter 24

Thanksgiving was colder than usual that year and the streets of Harlem were quiet. A light powder from the predicted storm had just begun to fall on Calvin Bailey's shoulders as he approached the Calhouns' apartment building. He stood there for a long time gazing at the chipped green paint on the cornice, then at the cracked lamp hanging in the portico until a scraping sound startled him—a window opening. Then he heard a child's voice shouting from above: "Up here, Mista Bailey! Hey! Up here! Apartment 602!"

Calvin looked up and saw Nick waving. He waved back, then stepped into the foyer and brushed off his coat. Secret-recipe smells were heavy on each floor as he made his way up to the sixth. Turkey, stuffing, sweets, and spices he couldn't name. He took off his hat when he reached Apartment 602, but the door swung open before he could knock. Hands reached for his hat and coat, and laughing voices competed with a jazz saxophone solo screaming from an old cabinet-style radio near the living room window. The smells from the kitchen were so strong he could almost taste them. "Hello, Mrs. Calhoun."

Pearl smiled. "Hello back at'cha, Mr. Bailey. Hope you're hungry. Okay, this big boy snatchin' off your coat is my son Edward... Dammit, boy! You're pullin' the man's arm off!"

Edward grinned. "Sorry, Mr. Bailey. Nice to meet'cha."

Before Calvin could respond, Pearl continued with the introductions. "And that's my little girl, Shay," she said, pointing at a girl who looked about nine, with the energy and rangy legs of a spirited filly. "Shay! Come back over here and say hello to Nick's uncle!"

"Hi," Shay called as she skipped down the hall to answer the ringing telephone.

"How you doin', young lady," Calvin called after her.

"You were raised better than that, dammit!" Pearl shouted. "And don't get on that phone! We're sittin' down to eat in a minute. Edward, take Mr. Bailey's hat and coat and put 'em in my closet. Now where's that little devil Nick? Lord, he was just here a second ago. Doc Calhoun! Could you turn down that radio long enough to come over and say hello to Nick's uncle?"

Doc walked over and stared at Calvin for a long, silent moment before speaking. "Sorry for starin' at you, man, but you are the answer to all Joe's riddles, standin' right in my living room."

From the kitchen came the crash of a glass dish hitting the floor. "Hey!" Doc yelled. "You kids are supposed to be helpin', not tearin' shit up!"

Nick appeared in the doorway, holding a wooden spoon. "Don't worry, Daddy. I got all the frosting on the cake 'fore I dropped the bowl. Hey! Hi, Mista Bailey! You found us, huh!"

Doc held up his hands in a praying gesture. "Pearl, these kids are killin' my groove!"

Pearl cut her eyes at him. "Join the club, you ol' grouch. And who the hell said you supposed to be the only one groovin'? These kids killed my groove years ago! And at least the boy *did* get the cake frosted before he broke the bowl. Now see, if you weren't so busy worshipping at the altar of god-almighty Charlie Parker—"

Doc's eyes widened. "Pearl! How are you gonna tell me you don't know Trane from Bird?"

Pearl glanced at Calvin's expression and laughed. "Lord, you must think we're all loony! Come on in the kitchen, Mr. Bailey. Let's see what kind'a mess your nephew's in there makin'."

"Please call me Calvin."

"Okay, Calvin. And you call me Pearl."

He started to follow her into the kitchen, but Doc stopped him. "Look, we'll talk later after all these kids fall asleep." Pointing at the radio, he backed away and grinned. "I don't mean to be rude, but they're playin' a tribute to Dizzy Gillespie! Tell Pearl I'll be in directly, would you?"

"I heard you, man," Pearl called from the kitchen. "Some host you are! Well, when you get hungry enough you'll come sniffin' around in here. And when you do, bring that extra folding chair with you. Nick can sit on that and a couple'a telephone books."

"Errol Garner sits on a telephone book to play his piano, huh?" Edward shouted.

Doc chuckled as he lit a cigarette. "I knew *somebody* was payin' attention to my stories."

"Come in the kitchen, Calvin," Pearl said, "and talk to me while I clean up Nick's mess."

The kitchen was cramped but cozy. After cleaning up the broken bowl, Pearl somehow managed to squeeze in enough chairs for everyone. In the center of the table was a small turkey, ready for carving, and several dishes containing all the traditional fare of Thanksgiving. After grace, Calvin sat quietly watching Doc carve the turkey as Pearl talked and served the food.

"Hey, baby," Pearl said, pointing at Doc's horn. "We might have a little more room on the table if you could part with your girlfriend there for an hour or so."

Doc placed a protective hand on his trumpet. "She ain't takin' up much room," he grumbled. Picking up the horn, he carefully rubbed the flare with his napkin, and then bared his teeth at Pearl, which caused the children to giggle. "But I'll move her," he said. "One a'your clumsy children might sling some gravy on her and gum up her valves."

"See that?" Pearl said dryly. "When they're slingin' gravy and killin' folks' grooves, they're *my* children. But just let one of 'em mess around and accidentally do sump'm *good*, and watch that man break his back takin' a damn bow! More gravy, Calvin?"

"Thank you. This sure looks good. This is the first Thanksgiving I been to in years."

"Aww," Pearl said, frowning. "No family? I mean, besides Joe?"

Calvin gazed at Nick. "Well, I guess I got some distant relatives left somewhere, but I done lost track of 'em all years ago. That's why I was tryin' to find Nick. He's about the closest blood relation I got. So I sure would appreciate it if you'd stop callin' me Mista Bailey, Nick. You can call me... Well, I guess you can call me Uncle Calvin—if you want to."

Perched atop his telephone books, Nick peered intently at him with a creased brow and a studious frown. Suddenly, he broke into a grin. "Okay, Uncle Calvin."

Calvin winked at him and Nick tried to wink back. Unable to close just one eye, he wrinkled his nose and squeezed both eyes shut tightly. Calvin suppressed a laugh.

Pearl finally sat down to eat. "Baby, did Calvin tell you he's in the music business?"

"No, he didn't," Doc said, reaching for more stuffing. "Are you a musician?"

"Me? I ain't got a musical bone in my body. And trust me—you do *not* wanna hear me try to sing. I just do promotion—for a company called Little Black Book Records."

"They have any jazz artists?" Doc asked.

"Naw. Nothin' you could call jazz. Rhythm and blues, rock and roll—that kind'a thing."

Doc groaned. "Rock and roll? Nothin' personal, man, but I'd rather listen to fingernails scratchin' on a chalkboard."

Pearl poked his shoulder and scowled at him. "That ain't nice, Daddy! Anyway, some of it's good. Matter of fact, I been hummin' 'Under the Boardwalk' all week."

Doc shrugged noncommittally.

"Little Black Book, huh?" Pearl said. "Well, they must not be *that* small. That girl that sings 'Starlight Love' is signed to that label. What's that girl's name, baby?"

"Oh, yeah. That one *is* nice," Doc said, nodding. "But I don't know her name."

"Mariette Winninger," Calvin said.

"That's her," Pearl said. "Mariette Winninger. She can sing! You promote her record?"

"Well, not Mariette. Right now I'm helpin' with promotion for Sam and the Alakazams—plus a few more acts."

"The Alakazams?" Edward grinned and began singing: "*I might not be a star, baby—*"

Doc interrupted him. "Aw, not that silly song you're always singin' around the house?"

"It ain't silly!" Edward grinned and snapped his fingers, then Shay began singing along with him as she bounced in her chair.

"My kids are painfully shy, as you can see, Calvin," Doc said, shaking his head.

Nick quickly scrambled off his chair. "No! Look at me, Mista Bailey!"

He squeezed his eyes shut, extended his arms, and began to sing loudly until Doc grabbed him and tickled him to a complete collapse on the floor. "You ever see such a ham in your life?"

"Naw, I never did," Calvin laughed. "Man, Nick, you remind me of a buddy I used to have back in—uh, back in the day. Little Man loved to sing, but he ain't had nothin' on you! You got *some* lungs there, boy! Where'd you learn to sing like that?"

Nick scrambled up from the floor and his expression suddenly turned serious. "I'll show you, Mista Bailey. Oh! I mean, Uncle Calvin. But it's a *secret*."

"You sit back down and finish your meal," Doc said. "You can show him after dinner."

"Yes, sir."

When dinner was over, Pearl excused Nick from the table, and he grabbed Calvin's hand.

"'Scuse us a minute, folks," Calvin said. "We'll be right back."

He followed Nick into a small room and took a seat on the edge of a narrow bed covered with a worn, green army blanket. He watched the boy scramble down on his hands and knees and reach for something hidden under the bed. When Nick pulled out a peeling, overstuffed Dutch Masters cigar box, Calvin stared at it and swallowed hard. That cigar box reminded him of something—something unpleasant—but he couldn't place it for a minute.

Then, suddenly, it all came rushing back in his memory: a white man's hands holding a pair of scuffed black shoes and a cigar box with the top flipped open. That detective. What was that detective's name? One was Masterson, but what was the other man's name?

Found this under a bed in that back room with these shoes. These your shoes, Calvin?

What was his name? He could still see the man's cold blue eyes penetrating all his defenses and smearing him with guilt for a murder he had never committed.

Looks like you got sump'm sticky on this cuff link, Calvin. Looks like blood to me.

"Jansen," Calvin said absently.

Nick had just placed the cigar box on the bed, and he looked up curiously. "Huh?"

"Oh, nothin'. Just sump'm I was thinkin' about. So what'cha got there, Nick?" He touched the corner of an old issue of *Down Beat* magazine that was sticking out of the box.

"Okay, Uncle Calvin, I'ma show you my treasure box," Nick said, his voice solemn.

Calvin leaned forward with interest. "Awright."

Nick opened the box slowly. Under the *Down Beat* was a 45-rpm record with a Clef label, a lumpy, black, velvet drawstring bag, and two publicity photos—one of Joe and one of Frank Sinatra, which he held up. "See, my Daddy use'ta be friends with Frank Sinatra. Not my Daddy in there," he said, pointing toward the kitchen. "My *blood* Daddy. He died."

Calvin smiled. "I know. He was my brother, remember?"

"Oh, that's right," Nick laughed. "When you was a lidda boy. I forgot."

Calvin read Sinatra's message on the photo and shrugged. "I guess that's pretty friendly."

Nick placed the picture back in the box and handed him Joe's photo. "And this is my blood-Daddy's famous pitcha right here," he said proudly.

Calvin stared at his brother's picture, and then at Nick. The boy had Joe's light, smoky eyes, but they looked warmer somehow. "So you wanna be a singer like your Daddy, huh?"

Nick sighed. "I'ma prob'ly be on the radio. Like my Daddy and Frank Sinatra. Hey! Did you sing too, like my Daddy?"

"Noooo!" Calvin laughed. "My singin' scared everybody to death. Can't sing a lick."

"That's too bad, Uncle Calvin," Nick said, giving him a sympathetic pat on the shoulder. "I bet you could do other stuff good though."

Calvin smiled and touched the velvet bag. "So what's in here?"

Nick glanced at the door. "My Daddy's blue diamonds he done lef' me. Wanna see?"

Calvin nodded, and Nick dumped out the contents of the bag: gold jewelry decorated with aquamarine stones, and one diamond ring. When he saw the cuff links, his heart pounded.

"Hey! You wanna hear my Daddy's record?"

Before Calvin could object, Nick was pulling the record out of its paper sleeve. "Aunt Pearl won't let us play the big hi-fi, but me and Shay got us a record player right here." Peering back at Calvin, he grimaced bashfully. "It got Donald Duck on it, but it works real good."

Calvin smiled. "Okay, buddy. Let's hear it."

≈∞≈

The mainstream music industry was beginning to acknowledge the demand for Negro recording artists, and Calvin had never been so busy. Creative promotion campaigns took him out of town regularly, but when he was in New York, his top priority was to spend time with Nick, despite having to win back his affections every time. Each time he told Nick he was leaving town, the same question arose: "You ain't never comin' back, are you? Like my blood Daddy."

After Calvin returned from a California trip that was extended by two additional weeks, Nick threw a tantrum and hid in the back of Pearl's closet for hours. He was still sulking the next day, but Calvin finally coaxed him into a visit to the Bronx Zoo, where they spent the day walking and staring at the animals. By the time the zoo closed, Nick was smiling again.

"I sure like them big skinny pink birds, Uncle Calvin," he said, yawning. "They was taller than me! What'cha call them skinny birds again?"

Calvin started the car and chuckled as he drove toward the exit. "Flamingoes, Nick. Yeah. The flamingoes were my favorite too."

≈∞≈

A few weeks later Doc and Pearl invited Calvin to join them at the Village Vanguard, a popular jazz club in Greenwich Village. King and a few new musicians were tinkering with a different sound, and Doc was appearing as a guest soloist.

The club was already crowded and hot when Calvin arrived, but he spotted Pearl waving at him from a front table. By the time he sat down, she was lighting two cigarettes. She handed him one and then nudged her copy of the *New York Times* in his direction. "Did you see this?" she asked, pointing at a front page article. "About Billie?"

Calvin squinted at the subhead above the photo: *Billie Holiday Dead at 44*. "Yeah, I heard it on the radio last night," he said. "And then they played all her songs for the whole program." He spotted Doc on the bandstand and waved at him. "But you know, Pearl, it ain't like everybody ain't seen that comin'."

Pearl stared into space for a moment. "I'm glad you're here, Calvin. Gives me somebody to talk to durin' the sets, 'cause I can't seem to shake these blues. I mean, we just lost Lester Young a few weeks ago—and now Billie. Mm-mm-mm."

Calvin studied Pearl's distant expression and said nothing.

"Feels like when Bird passed back in '55," Pearl continued. "That was like losin' family."

"Oh, yeah. I know Doc must'a took that hard. They were close, weren't they?"

"They were friends. But Bird wasn't *really* close to anybody. But you're right. Doc took it hard." Pearl shivered and crossed her arms. "Didn't talk to nobody but that bottle for days."

"Okay, look," Calvin said, "maybe it's time to change the subject and cheer you up."

Pearl blew a mist of smoke through here teeth. "Okay. I can use some cheerin' up."

"Well, I stopped by Rose's on the way over here—"

Pearl laughed softly. "Had to see that little devil Nicky, didn't you?"

Calvin grinned. "Yeah. I was hopin' he wouldn't be mad at me for this last trip, but he was. Wouldn't hardly talk to me. Makes me wonder… Look, don't get me wrong. I ain't tryin' to say nothin' about the way you bringin' him up or nothin'. It's just—I got so many questions—"

A soft, sustained note from Doc's muted horn brought a gentle halt to their conversation. When the melody of "Autumn Leaves" unfolded, the entire room hushed. Every eye and every ear turned expectantly to Doc Calhoun, and he did not disappoint. He played them a story of ill-fated lovers meeting under the falling red and yellow leaves of October in Central Park. Or Hyde Park. Or on the street where they lived. Any place and any autumn that lived in human memory.

Calvin hung on every intimate detail of the story—notes painted in star-crossed colors that transcended the complexities of race, sex, time, distance, impossible circumstances… He closed his eyes and saw a man and a woman in a small room, slowly swaying together in their uncomplicated dance.

As the song ended, he opened his eyes and looked around. Every face in the club was softened by a contemplative afterglow. Through the magic of his horn, Doc had told each of them their own personal story.

When the applause died down, Calvin took a deep breath and nudged the ashtray over to Pearl. "I don't know nothin' 'bout no jazz, but he sure can make you feel that music, huh?"

Pearl was still gazing up at her husband. "Yes, he can." She crushed her cigarette butt in the ashtray. "Now what in the world were we talkin' about?"

"Nick."

"Oh, Lord, that's right. Nicky. So what was it you wanted to know, Calvin?"

He shrugged. "Well, the tantrums worry me, I guess."

"Well, he's the sweetest little fella you ever want to know. He's always tryin' to help me with things, and always fusses over his Mama when we visit. But sometimes he just gets—upset. Sometimes angry. Saddest thing I ever saw was—" She paused and sighed. "One time we went to visit Magda, just me and Nicky. When I went out to talk to Hattie, he was in there with her talkin' his usual little happy talk, but when I walked back in, he was holdin' her face with his little hands, starin' at her and cryin' his eyes out. He kept sayin' 'Why won't you talk to me, Mama?' Took me twenty minutes to get him calmed down, then he acted like nothin' happened, all happy again. That really worried me, Calvin."

"But he seems okay most'a the time—"

Pearl reached across the table and patted Calvin's hand. "Oh, he is. Don't worry. But sometimes I think he saw too much when he was a baby—his Mama's breakdown and all that."

"But he was just a tiny baby, Pearl," Calvin said, shaking his head.

"Well, some folks believe things affect babies more than we think. But even if you don't believe that—there was sump'm else. Now I ain't no scientist, but I don't think Magda should'a been nursin' that baby after they gave her that medicine in the hospital. A little baby drinkin' in all those strong chemicals? Could'a messed up his nervous system or his brain. I don't really think it did, but what if it would have?… Listen, you got a cigarette? Those were my last two."

Calvin gave her a cigarette and then lit it for her. "So you were sayin'—"

"I was tellin' you about that damn hospital. Givin' her sleepin' pills and then lettin' her nurse that baby! And I guess we'll *never* know what went wrong with those shock treatments. Ruined her whole life. With all that talent she had, and she was so young…"

Calvin didn't respond. The band was playing a sultry rendition of "Summertime," and he let his thoughts drift away with the music. But then Pearl said something that brought him back.

"I guess takin' Nicky to see her in that sad state probably wasn't a good idea. I thought it was at the time, but maybe I was wrong. I just thought—"

"What?"

"Well, I know it sounds like wishful thinking, but I always had the feeling that Magda was—*there*, you know? I remember this one time we all heard a car backfire outside in the parking lot, and she jerked her head, like she heard it and it scared her. Doc said it was probably just involuntary or some mess, but I don't care. It was a *reaction*, and it made me believe that some part of her could hear us—or at least she had some kind'a sense that we were there... I just wanted her to see her baby now and then so she'd know I was takin' good care of him. Well—I guess 'see' is the wrong word, but—" Her voice trailed off.

"Anyway, the doctors just kept telling me it was hopeless, but I'd *still* take Nicky to see her. I wanted him to know there's all kinds of people in the world. And I wanted him to accept folks for whoever and *how*ever they are. And he does. He's not like most kids, Calvin. I think somehow deep inside he realizes that she's been—damaged, and he's just got this fierce protective streak when it comes to his Mama." She shrugged. "I want all my kids to be strong, Calvin, but I don't want 'em lookin' down on *nobody*. It's a hell of a balancing act, but they *need* to learn how to survive and still be good people. This is a damn mean world and I ain't gonna be around forever to protect 'em from it."

"Yeah," Calvin said. "That's the most important thing to teach kids, I guess—bein' strong."

Pearl leaned forward. "Yeah, but Calvin," she said urgently, "what if—what if I'm responsible for liftin' that boy's hopes so high like that?"

"Don't be so hard on yourself, Pearl. I probably would'a done the same thing—hell, if I ever thought that deep. But listen, tell me sump'm—if it ain't too personal... Don't you think it's a little confusing for him to call you 'Aunt Pearl' and then he calls Doc 'Daddy'?"

Pearl smiled up at her husband. He was waiting for his solo, eyes closed, fingers snapping. "My husband is the only father-figure that boy ever had. I know he goes around talkin' about Joe and callin' him his blood-Daddy, but Doc raised him, and those two love each other, Calvin. He's the real Daddy. Joe's more like some bedtime-story Daddy. He ain't real. I think Nick just loves the *idea* of Joe—his singin' and all that. But when it comes to Magda, that's different. He's been around her since he was a baby. I mean, he can see her and touch her. She's real and she's *Mama* to that boy." She stopped suddenly, and stared into the curling smoke of her cigarette. "Po' baby. I sure miss her sometimes."

"You too were—real close, weren't you? How'd you get so close?"

Pearl smiled sadly. "At first I just took her under my wing 'cause she seemed like a little kid—you know, naïve and all. But when I got to know her, I found out there was a lot more to her. She was a hell of a musician, and she—she reminded me of my brother Ronnie—just didn't have any hate in her at all. So there I was thinkin' she needed me, but it turned out I needed her. Ain't that somethin'? And maybe that's why I keep bringin' Nicky to see her. He needs to be around her, even if she can't talk to him. 'Cause asleep or awake, she got a good soul. You know she blamed herself for what that damn Joe did?"

King suddenly tripled the tempo of "Summertime" with a loud combination, and Calvin had to pull his chair closer to hear Pearl. "What was that you said?"

"I was talkin' 'bout Magda. I know she was drugged up and everything, but all she kept talkin' about the day we brought her home was how it was all her fault. Kept sayin' 'I kill Joe! I make him to die!' Oh, I can still hear her sayin' it—with all that guilt. Can you believe that, Calvin? Like that angel could hurt somebody as cold-blooded as Joe." She looked at him with an alarmed expression. "Oh, I'm sorry, sugah. I keep forgettin' he was your brother."

Calvin smiled. "Just 'cause he was my brother don't mean he wasn't a cold-blooded snake."

"Well, I still shouldn't speak ill of the dead. But whenever I think about Magda—I just wish we could'a done sump'm better for her."

"I know," Calvin said softly. "We all got regrets, Pearl."

She smiled vaguely, but her eyes were vacant. "Maybe that's what finally kills us, huh? Pile one regret on top of another… Oh, hell, I done got us all off the subject. What was it?"

"I was just wonderin' if it bothered you that he calls you Aunt Pearl and not—Mama."

"Oh, no. That don't bother me at all, sugah. I understand. That boy really believes Magda's gonna make some kind'a miraculous recovery. I know he must'a mentioned it to you."

"At least a hundred times." Calvin sighed. "It really is sad, ain't it? For the boy, I mean."

"Well, don't let Nicky hear you say that. He loves his Mama and believes with his whole little heart that she's comin' home someday. And that's why he calls me Aunt Pearl. So there won't be any confusion when his *real* Mama comes home."

Chapter 25

Saturday mornings were always the same for Nick when his uncle was in town. Although the arrival time never varied, he fretted nervously before each visit. It had been months since his last tantrum, and he was trying his best to be calm. He had just pulled a kitchen chair over to the front window to watch for Calvin's car when Pearl emerged from the bathroom.

"What'cha doin', sugah?" she asked as she stretched out on the sofa.

"Waitin' for Uncle Calvin. You feelin' better, Aunt Pearl? Did your toof fall out yet?"

"Juuus' came out, sugah," she said in a languid drawl.

Nick grimaced. "Did it hurt? I almosh shtarted cryin' when my toof came out. *Almosh.*"

Pearl laughed lightly. "Didn't hurt a bit, baby. It was so loose it slipped riiight on out."

Nick began bumping the heel of his shoe against the leg of the chair. "I hope my toof growzh fash, Aunt Pearl. Makin' me talk funny."

"Just a little lisp, sugah. Happens sometimes—when you lose both your front teeth. That first one's startin' to come in already, and the second one'll grow back before you know it. And then you'll be talkin' juuuus' fine again."

Nick touched his tongue to the space where his teeth used to be. "Sho where izh it?"

"Where's what, sugah?"

"Your toof! Ain'tcha gonna put it under your pilla tonight? You could get a dime! I shtill got minezh right here." Digging in his pocket, he pulled out the dime and held it up. "Shee?"

Pearl's soft humming ended with a lazy laugh. "It's *mine*, sugah, not *mines*—'member? But ya know, I forgot all about that ol' tooth fairy. Thanks for remindin' me. I'ma put that tooth under my pillow tonight so I can get my dime too."

"Good. Hey, you look like you feelin' better, Aunt Pearl. Did you take your medishin?"

"Mmm-hmm," she murmured. "Took my medicine and had me a niiice long bath, too. So now I'm feelin' juuuus' fine, sugah. Fine and mellow." She opened her eyes and gave him a serious look. "But remember, Nicky. That medicine—that's our little secret, okay?"

"Yesh, ma'am." Nick patted his hair. "Hey, Aunt Pearl? Do my hair look awright?"

"It's *does* my hair look all right.' And yeah, you look jus' like Chuck Berry, sugah."

Nick grinned as he looked out the window, then yelped. "Hot damn! He finally here!"

"Boy!" Pearl scolded softly. "I told you I don't want you sayin' that!"

Nick sighed and rolled his eyes. "Daddy shay it."

"Daddy says a whole lot'a things I don't *ever* wanna hear comin' out'a your mouth. And he *doesn't* go around sayin' 'do my hair look awright' either. That's those ignorant friends a'yours."

Nick wasn't listening. The only thing he heard was Calvin coming up the stairs.

Sighing, Pearl slowly stood up and opened the front door just as Calvin reached the landing. "Come on in, sugah. Maybe you can do sump'm with this boy."

Calvin loomed in the doorway, looking like a cross between Willie Mays and Superman. Nick ran over and leaped into his arms.

"Hey!" Calvin laughed. "You gettin' strong, little man! You squeezed the breath out'a me!"

"Nuh-uh!" Nick giggled.

"Aw, come on. Show me your muscle."

Nick pulled the short sleeve of his shirt over his shoulder and flexed his arm.

"Look at that, Pearl! For a little fella, he gettin' some sho-nuff man muscles, huh?"

"Oh, yeah," she said dryly. "He's a regular Charles Atlas."

"Look, Uncle Calvin!" Nick grinned with what should have been his front teeth. "Shee?"

"What? Oh! That other front tooth finally came out, huh?"

"Aunt Pearl'zh toof came out too, but herzh inna back where you can't shee it."

Calvin laughed. "But yours is in the front so you can show everybody, huh?"

"Yesh, shir! And I talk funny too. My tongue keepsh pokin' out where my teef ushta be!"

"Yeah, I noticed that."

Calvin reached over to rub Nick's head, but Nick frowned and leaned away. "My hair!"

"Oh! Sorry, pahtnah!" Calvin laughed.

"Oh, Lord, that child and his hair," Pearl said. "You want a cup'a coffee, Calvin?"

"No thanks, Pearl. Me and my pahtnah here got places to go and folks to see."

≈∞≈

As he rode along the parkway in Calvin's big tan Oldsmobile 98, Nick watched the billowing white sails on the boats gliding along the Hudson. A cool spring breeze was blowing in through the open windows and he opened his mouth to see if he could taste its sweetness.

Calvin laughed. "You tryin' to catch some bugs for lunch, boy?"

Nick made a sour face and shut his mouth with a quick clack of his back teeth. "Yuck! No!"

"Hey, Nick, guess where we goin' today."

"Where?"

"Okay, I'll give you a hint." Turning on the car radio, he twisted the tuner knob until the voice of Chubby Checker filled the car. Snapping his fingers, Calvin bobbed his head and began to sing along.

Nick clapped his hands over his ears and grimaced. "Aww, no, Uncle Calvin!" he shouted. "You a terrible shinger! Better let me do da shingin' around here."

Calvin took a playful jab at Nick. "Okay, wise guy. You do the singin'."

Nick grinned as he sang, then suddenly stopped. "Hey! Izh'at da hint, Uncle Calvin? We gonna meet Tubby Tecker?"

Calvin let out a loud laugh. "You tryin' to say Chubby Checker, ain'tcha?"

"I better try again, huh!"

"Sorry, pahtnah, I ain't mean to laugh at you."

Nick grinned. "Ish okay, Uncle Calvin. I'm laughin' at me too! I shound funny!"

"Yeah, you do, but to answer your question, no, we ain't gonna meet Chubby Checker."

"Oh, okay. Dat ain't da hint. Hmmm... Oh! Da twisht? We goin' to a party or shump'm?"

"No, man! I'm workin' today. The hint was the radio. I'm takin' you to a radio station."

Nick's eyes widened and he gripped the door handle tightly.

Within five minutes, they pulled up to the WLIB radio station and got out of the car. "See that, Nick?" Calvin said, pointing up at the giant transmitter.

"Uh-huh. Ish a big ladder, huh?"

"Not a ladder, man. It's a transmitter. That's how they send the music out to the radios."

Nick cut his eyes at Calvin. "Nuh-uh."

"Yeah, man. Through the airwaves."

"Wait a minute. You ain't tellin' me muzhic fliezh inna shky like— like Shuperman?"

"Yup. Just like Superman. Come on in and I'll prove it to you."

Nick shot Calvin another look that was pure skepticism, but followed him inside.

Standing near the coffee pot was a dark-skinned man with a stout, muscular build. He glanced over his shoulder and smiled. "Hey, Calvin! How you been, brutha?"

"Fine as wine, Lead. Nick, say hello to Mr. Leadbelly."

Nick extended his hand as he stared at the man's mid-section. "Hi, Mishter Leadbelly."

"Hi, Nick. What'cha lookin' at? You tryin' to figure out why they call me Leadbelly?"

Nick blinked and backed up a couple of steps. "Naw."

Calvin tapped Nick's forehead hard with his finger. "What did I tell you, boy?" he hissed.

Nick winced and rubbed the sore spot on his forehead. "Oh, uh, I mean—no, shir."

Leadbelly handed Nick a cookie. "That's okay. See, the original Leadbelly was a great blues man. Me, I just got a hard belly, so folks call me that too. Go on and try punchin' me."

"Oh, no, shir! Uncle Calvin might *kill* me!"

"No, he won't," Leadbelly laughed. "It's okay. Go ahead."

Nick grinned and punched Leadbelly. "Ow! Dey should call you... *Rock*belly!"

Leadbelly laughed. "How old are you, Nick?"

"Sheben."

"Seven? Well, that's a good age to be."

Nick pointed at the empty space in his mouth. "I jush losh my toof, shee? Now I talk funny."

"I noticed that! But don't worry, son, it'll grow back. Hey, Calvin. That's a good lookin' kid, man. I can really see the family resemblance."

"Yeah, I prob'ly looked about that goofy when my teeth were missin' too. But not quite."

As Nick bit into his cookie with his side teeth, he tugged Leadbelly's sleeve. "Shcuzh me, Mishter Leadbelly? Do muzhic really fly 'crosh'a shky? Dash what Uncle Calvin told me but—"

"He ain't tellin' stories this time, Nick. You *could* say music flies in the sky."

"I told him he could see how you send music out over the airwaves," Calvin explained.

"Okay, then. Come on in the back so you can see where it starts. Ray just started his show and you know how wild he is, Calvin. Grab your coffee. I think the kid's gonna love this."

As they walked down a narrow hallway, Calvin pulled a piece of paper out of his pocket and nudged Leadbelly. "Hey, man. You been playin' those sides we talked about last week?"

"Oh, yeah, man! 'Specially that new girl group. We got that one on heavy rotation."

Calvin pointed at his list. "But what about number 5? It ain't been gettin' much play."

"Hey, I been playin' it, Calvin. You know you're my man. Look, tell you what I'll do. I'll post up a note to remind the rest'a the fellas. But remember what I told you about Al—"

Calvin nodded. "Al with the extra pockets. Yeah, I'm workin' on that. Thanks, Lead."

As the two men continued to talk, Nick stretched up on his tiptoes trying to peer through the large window that was just above his head. Then Calvin lifted him up and Nick saw a small room, with floor-to-ceiling shelves packed with records. Perched between two spinning turntables was a young olive-skinned man with long, conked hair combed into a stylish D.A. He was wearing red-framed sunglasses and a loud pink jacket, and had a cigarette clenched tightly in his teeth. Nick watched, fascinated, as the man simultaneously pulled one record from the first turntable while placing another one on the second.

Suddenly, he leaned close to the mike and his high-speed voice screeched from the overhead speakers. "Saaaay, babeees! This is the one and only Ravishin' Ray, bringin' the newest beats right to the street, and that was The Platters, hot off the presses with 'Smoke Gets In Your Eyes.' And Ravishin' Ray digs it too, no jive. Now, I want you to hang on to ya wigs, all you luscious ladies and dapper Daddy-ohs, 'cause I got mah cool man Chuck Berry up next to blast ya brains out with 'Johnny B. Goode'!"

As the music started, he motioned for everyone to come in. When he saw Nick, he leaned back in his chair and grinned. "Well, cut off my legs and call me Shorty! It's Sammy Davis Jr.!"

Nick laughed. "Naw, shir. I ain't Shammy Davish Jr.! I'm Nick Calhoun!"

Ravishing Ray lowered his sunglasses and peered at Nick over the top of the frames. "What're you, man—about twenty-five? You here tryin' to steal Ravishin' Ray's job?"

"Naw, shir! I'm only sheben! Look at me! I'm jush a lidda kid, man!"

The three men laughed. "Man, I don't believe it," Ray said. "You got'cha hair fried and laid to the side like Billy Eckstine! You sure you ain't a midget out prowlin' for women?"

After teasing Nick for a minute more, Ravishing Ray held a finger to his lips. "Shh. Song's almost over. Look' like Johnny got about as good as the nigga was gon' get, so it's time for me to announce the next record, ya dig? So everybody be *real* quiet."

He faded out Chuck Berry and timed his intro perfectly, finishing just as Fats Domino hit the first syllable of "Blueberry Hill." "Okay, we can talk now—till Fats gets through."

"Hey, boy," Calvin said. "Ain't this your favorite song? You always singin' it."

Ravishing Ray crossed his arms. "Don't tell me Nick Calhoun's a singer?"

"Yesh, shir! Wait, okay—" Extending one arm, Nick began to sing his impression of Fats Domino's deep voice. His attempt at a bass growl combined with that lisp resulted in laughter from the men in the room, but Nick flashed a good-natured grin and plowed ahead with his song.

Sneaking the microphone to the "on" position, Ravishing Ray waited just long enough for Nick to hit his big finish, swallowed back a laugh, then launched into his lightning-fast ad libbing: "Maann, babies, Ravishin' Ray's just gotta be the hippest of the hip. Bringin' it to you live—no jive—the thrillin' sounds of that seven-year-old singin' sensation Nick Calhoun—wailin' with phenomenal Fats, ya dig? And you heard it here first on WLIB—home of the hits."

Calvin whispered into Nick's ear, "You were just on the radio, boy. How's it feel?"

"Nuh-uh!" Nick whispered, suddenly self-conscious.

"It's okay, you can talk out loud now," Ravishing Ray said. "The mike's off."

"Wuzh I really shingin' on da radio, Ravishin' Ray?" Nick asked.

"You sure were. The whole city of New York just heard Nick Calhoun on the radio."

Nick's mouth fell open and Calvin pushed him toward the door. "We better go, Ray, so you can do the news. Thanks a lot, and, uh, be sure and give my product some spins, man."

"Next hour, top of the lineup. Nick, you come back to sing for me again sometime, ya dig?"

"Yesh, shir!"

Calvin looked down at Nick and smiled. "You really like to sing, don'tcha, boy?"

"Yesh, shir! I wish I could shing all'a time!"

"Kid might have a future," Leadbelly said. "He sang the hell out that song! Lisp and all!"

Calvin nodded distractedly. "Yeah, Lead. You gave me sump'm to think about. Okay, Nick, say good-bye to Mr. Leadbelly, you little conk-head ham."

"I had me a good time, Mishter Leadbelly! It wuzh a lot more fun den da bread factory!"

"What bread factory?" Calvin said.

"Ya know, at shkool. Dey called it a field trip, but it wuzhn't really no fieldzh—only bread."

"Oh! Okay," Calvin said.

"Can I vizhit you again shumtime, Mishter Leadbelly?"

"Anytime, Nick," Leadbelly said as he shook the boy's hand.

"Take it easy, Lead," Calvin said, trying to cover his laughter. "And thanks for everything."

"You take care, now, Calvin. Bye, Nick!"

As they walked out, Nick tugged Calvin's sleeve. "I know why you laughin', Uncle Calvin."

Calvin stopped and looked down at Nick's toothless grin. "Why?"

Nick giggled. "'Cause dat time I whishowed, huh?"

Calvin leaned against the door and laughed until tears streamed from his eyes. "You tryin' to say—you *whistled*? You know what, boy? I'ma be kind'a sorry when them teeth grow back in."

Chapter 26

1963

Every June when the schools closed for summer, the children flooded Nick's block in something Doc called "the annual enemy occupation." Traffic slowed to a crawl as rubber balls bounced into the street, followed by little boys with faithful dogs in hot pursuit. On the sidewalks, neighborhood girls drew hopscotch squares, played jacks, and jumped double-dutch, while their brothers shot marbles in the small patches of dried-out dirt that had grown Harlem's Victory Gardens during World War II. The big kids played their radios and danced on the stoops. And on particularly hot days, someone would open a fireplug and cool off the neighborhood. But the most popular game on the block was stickball.

With Nick's eleventh birthday still five months away, he was surprised when one of the older boys named Ernie called him to play shortstop on his team.

The other boys jeered, but Ernie waved them off. "Aww, shut up! He got good hands and he's quick," he snapped, pulling Nick over to his position. "And he can catch too!" He handed Nick a beat-up glove and whispered, "You can catch, can'tcha?"

"I don't know."

Ernie grinned. "Better learn quick, man!"

Nick stood up as tall as he could and punched his glove. "Don't worry!"

Once the game began and he had fielded his first ball, the realization hit him. Nick Calhoun was finally playing stickball with the big boys—a rite of passage on 126th Street.

After ten days of playing, he had hit his first double. Now it was the bottom of the ninth, with the game tied at three-all, and he was at bat again, anxious to try for a home run. "Hurry up, William!" he called. "It's gettin' dark!"

Just as William wound up for his pitch, the street lights came on. "Hurry!" Nick yelled.

But a voice from above ended the game. "Ernie! Come on in now! Supper's ready!"

Nick groaned as he watched Ernie desert the chalk-drawn square that was third base. Then another mother's voice rang out, and all the players began to disperse. Nick dropped his mighty Louisville Slugger and watched it transform back into a broken broom handle.

Ernie grinned. "Hey, I was waitin' for you to hit another double and bring me in!"

"Shoot! William pitches too slow. I was 'bout to hit me a home run!"

"You got all summer to hit your first home run, Nick. See ya tomorrow!"

Nick was heading for the steps when he heard his Aunt Pearl's voice calling.

"Nicky! Go find Shay and get up here to Miss Rose's apartment right now!"

Nick couldn't find Shay among the children in the stairwell, but he went straight to Rose's apartment, as he was told. Pearl and Rose were sitting tensely on the sofa, Edward was standing with four adult neighbors, and everyone was staring at the television set. Something was wrong.

"I couldn't find Shay," Nick said. "What happened?"

Edward scowled at him. "Shh! The President's on TV. Sit down and pay attention."

Just then, Shay walked in looking confused, and Nick grabbed her hand. "Sit down," he whispered. "The President's talkin'. I hope it ain't them bombs again."

Shay sat down, staring fearfully at President Kennedy's serious expression as he spoke:

And when Americans are sent to Vietnam or West Berlin,
we do not ask for whites only. It ought to be possible,
therefore, for American students of any color to attend any
public institution they select.

Nick looked back when he heard Mr. Sanders muttering. "'Bout damn time! Took what King did in Birmin'ham to get Kennedy to open up his mouth. Now he need to do sump'm 'bout that goddamn Bull Connor and them fire hoses! And them goddamn dogs too!"

"Mr. Sanders," Rose said stiffly, "*please* watch your language around these children."

Nick had suffered nightmares after seeing Bull Connor and those attack dogs on the news. He looked back at the television and listened hard, trying to understand the connection.

If an American, because his skin is dark, cannot eat lunch in a restaurant open to the public, if he cannot send his children to the best public school available, if he cannot vote for the public officials who will represent him... then who among us would be content to have the color of his skin changed and stand in his place?

Nick looked back at Edward. His fists were clenched tightly, but he was smiling.

I shall ask the Congress of the United States to act, to make a commitment it has not fully made in this century to the proposition that race has no place in American life or law.

When the speech was over, Rose turned off the set and let out a shaky sigh. "Lord, Jesus, Pearl. I never thought I'd live to see this day."

Edward was exuberant. "You know that march on Washington everybody's talkin' about? I didn't give 'em a chance in hell of pullin' it off, but now—they might just do it."

"Boy, stop that cussin'," Pearl said. "And when's that supposed to happen anyway?"

"August," he said. "Wish I could go!"

Mr. Sanders was still frowning. "Took Birmin'ham to get the white man to speak up."

"Yes, sir," Pearl said as she walked him out. "But he finally did. Hey, Rose, why don't you come over later for some coffee and we'll talk. 'Night, Mr. Sanders. Come on, kids."

"Aunt Pearl?" Nick asked as they walked across the hall. "What's gonna happen now?"

"Yeah, Mama," Shay said softly. "What did all that mean?"

Pearl smiled. "Sugah... it means that Dr. King's gonna finally get some *real* help."

≈∞≈

Nick and Shay began to take a deeper interest in the news. Each evening, they went with Pearl to Rose's apartment to watch Walter Cronkite, and then bombarded any adults present with questions. They didn't quite grasp President Kennedy's speech in Germany, but they clearly understood the footage of southern governors blocking public school doorways to prevent the enrollment of Negro students. When Dr. King's March on Washington was televised that August, all the neighbors from Nick's floor crowded into Rose's apartment for a watch party. But less than three weeks after that happy day, there was more trouble in Birmingham. Four little Negro girls were murdered in a bomb blast at the 16th Street Baptist Church, and it was Shay's turn to have nightmares.

And nearly every day Walter Cronkite had something to say about a violent power struggle brewing on the other side of the world in a place called Vietnam.

But the approaching Thanksgiving holidays took the children's minds off the troubles of the world. Nick and Shay were trying to learn to dance the Mashed Potato to their favorite new song—"Fingertips" by Little Stevie Wonder. Winter was shaping up to be particularly cold that year, and Nick had already broken his record for slips on the sidewalk.

One day in mid-November, Calvin picked him up to take him to the arcade. The minute he reached the icy street, Nick's feet flew out from under him, and Calvin barely managed to catch him. "Careful, boy!" he laughed. "Anything happens to you, Doc gon' kill me dead!"

"Nuh-uh!" Nick said, grinning as he regained his footing.

"Oh, yeah! And then I bet'cha Pearl wakes me up just so she can kill me again!"

Nick laughed. "Too much ice, Uncle Calvin. Sure got cold fast, huh?"

"It ain't that bad," Calvin said. "Not like Detroit. Up there they got that blue hawk."

"What's that?" Nick asked.

"Come on, boy. You heard folks call cold weather the hawk, ain'tcha?"

"I guess so," Nick said, shivering. "So is today a blue hawk day?"

"Blue hawk won't make it out here for at least a month. This is just the regular hawk. He swoops down all that cold air and spits it in your face." Calvin grinned and pinched Nick's nose, making him giggle. "Then he bites on your nose with his beak. Regular hawk. He ain't so bad."

"Well, then what that ol' blue hawk do, huh?"

"Blue hawk—" Calvin paused and cupped a protective hand around his lighter, fighting the wind to get his cigarette lit. "Blue hawk carries a blade."

Nick grinned and stomped his feet to keep warm. "And he cuts you with it, right?"

Calvin pulled Nick's wool cap over his ears. "Nope. That ol' blue hawk's a *mean* one, Nick. He takes that blade and cuts all your buttons off your coat, and then he cuts so many holes in your pants and your shirt, they finally just fall off. Then he cuts off your shoelaces to loosen up your shoes till they just slip off in the snow. And *then*... there you are! Just standin' there freezin' your naked behind off, with your clothes behind you, all wet and raggedy in the snow."

Nick laughed. "Nuh-uh! Man, Uncle Calvin, you must think I'm Boo Boo the fool!"

"Well, you sho' do *feel* naked. And then that ol' blue hawk just flies off, squawkin' and laughin' at you while you freeze. Oh, yeah. That blue hawk's a mean one, Nick, I'm tellin' you."

$\approx\infty\approx$

November 22nd began like any other morning in the grip of winter. Nick and Shay were walking the fifteen blocks to PS 123 together, bundled from head to toe, complaining about the icy wind.

"Ooh! Uncle Calvin must'a been wrong about it bein' too early for the blue hawk, huh?"

Shay groaned. "You and that blue hawk! It's just cold, that's all I know. And we got ten more blocks to walk. So let's talk about sump'm *warmer*. What can we talk about that's warm?"

"I know!" Nick shouted. "Let's talk about fire!"

"You are *so* stupid," Shay said, smacking him on the shoulder.

Nick grinned. "You know, like fire on candles. Like the candles on my birthday cake tomorrow! I'm eleven!" he yelled. "I'm finally eleven!"

"You're not eleven yet, little squirt."

"Okay. I'm ten and ninety-nine tenths!"

"Ninety-nine tenths? Oh, Lord! I'll tell you what you are. You're somebody who needs to be workin' on your fractions, that's what you are. And stop all that hollerin', boy! So what'cha think you're gonna get for your birthday anyway?"

"Aunt Pearl's makin' me my chocolate cake, I know that."

"I'm not talkin' about a cake, fool! What presents?"

"Uncle Calvin said he got sump'm real important for me."

"Well, that's good, 'cause Mama and Daddy are broke as a joke this year."

"I don't care… Hey, Shay. Guess what!"

"What?"

Nick pulled his cap down around his ears. "You know Lenny from across the street who be bringin' that big dumb yellow lunch pail to school all the time?"

"Yeah, so what?"

"You know how come his sandwich is always all squishy and flat?"

Shay sighed impatiently. "Okay, why?"

"Because—" Nick giggled. "He got a can of spinach in there!"

"In his lunch pail?"

"Yup. A can of spinach and a can opener too! That's how come his sandwich is always squished. That can of spinach rolls around in there and squishes it!"

"That is *so* stupid, Nick. I never saw him eating any spinach at lunch."

Nick held out his mittened hands. "'Cause he don't ever eat it. He just keeps it 'cause—"

"Stop laughing and tell me, Nick. And this *better* be funny."

"Them junior high school boys took away his milk money twice awready. So he keeps the spinach 'cause next time he thinks he can eat it and get strong real fast—like Popeye!"

"Stop laughing at him. He's Ernie's brother and I thought Ernie was your friend!"

"Hey, lounge, baby! He *is* my friend! That's how come I only laughed at him a *little*."

"Stop tryin' to talk like Daddy. And what if those boys took *your* milk money and then I laughed at *you*? Maybe *you* ought to be eatin' some spinach, ya little squirt."

"It only works if you eat it every day! And I'd *kill* myself if I had to eat spinach every day!"

"Mm-hmm. Then what would you do if they caught *you*?"

Nick broke into a grin. "I'll do what Lenny did! I'll call Ernie the Sailor Man!"

Shay groaned. "Ooh. Your jokes are worse than your fractions. Come on, you corny little squirt. Let's run so we can warm up. But we cross streets together, hear me?"

≈∞≈

It was nearly three in the afternoon when Nick saw Shay again among the students pouring out the double doors of PS 123. "Come on!" she cried as she ran down the steps.

Nick stuffed his mittens and cap into his coat pockets and ran to keep up with her. The cold air stabbed his chest, but fear told him to keep running. As he watched the puffs of Shay's breath blowing along the sides of her head, Nick wondered if the blue hawk ever killed people.

By the time they reached their apartment building, Shay was gasping and sobbing loudly. Nick followed her up the steps to the sixth floor, where they found their apartment door open with the radio blaring. They pulled off their coats and ran into the kitchen.

"Mama!" Shay cried. "Where are you? Somebody shot President Kennedy!"

Nick ran back into the living room. "Aunt Pearl!" he screamed.

"I'm out here, sugah," Pearl called from across the hall. "Now come on over to Miss Rose's and be quiet. We're watchin' it all on her TV."

Nick and Shay hurried into Rose's apartment and sat on the floor directly in front of the television set. The shades were drawn, leaving the room in semi-darkness. The only light came from the glow of the television screen—gray images of people crying and pointing at a row of trees at the top of a low, sloping hill. Nick peeked over his shoulder and saw that Rose and Pearl were both sniffling into crinkled wads of tissue. "Is he okay now, Aunt Pearl? Miss Dawson said the doctor might could get the bullet out—"

Pearl reached out for Nick and he climbed up onto the sofa next to her. "No, sugah. They tried, but—the President passed away a little while ago."

As Pearl continued to talk, Nick leaned into her arms and pressed his face against her neck. He was no longer hearing her words; it was the low, soothing tone of her voice that he craved.

Shay hadn't said a word since they had gotten there, but her emotions finally broke in a soft sob. "Mama?… How come they killed him?… Was it 'cause he was—helpin' Dr. King?"

"Come here, baby," Pearl whispered. "Now, here's what we're gonna do. You and me and Nick and Miss Rose—we're gonna sit together and pray real hard, okay?"

≈∞≈

Despite the gloomy mood, Doc and Pearl managed to pull together a small birthday party for Nick the next afternoon. Mr. Goldstein, who owned the corner grocery store where Edward worked, brought an assortment of baseball cards wrapped up with green ribbon.

"So you like the baseball cards, do you?" Mr. Goldstein said.

"Yes, *sir!*" Nick gushed as he spread out a few of the cards on the table. "Roger Maris, Roy Campanella, Mickey Mantle… and Say-Hey-Willie-Mays! Thanks, Mr. Goldstein!"

"Well, the baseball cards are only part of your gift, Nicky. I've been thinking about your idea—about working for me after school and on Saturdays."

Nick's eyes widened. "Yes, *sir!*"

"Well, if it's okay with your folks, I think I could pay you to sweep up and help your brother unload the smaller boxes at the store. How does fifty cents an hour sound?"

Nick's mouth dropped open. "Fifty cents an hour?" he yelled. "I'm rich!"

Doc scowled at him. "Hey, not so loud, boy! Now what do you say to Mr. Goldstein?"

"Thank you, Mr. Goldstein! Do I go to work tomorrow?"

"No, I'm closed on Sunday. Just come in with Edward after school on Monday. Okay?"

"Yes, sir!"

Pearl cleared her throat and glanced at Doc. "Wanna give him our present now, sugah?"

Doc groaned, but he was smiling. "Yeah, let's go ahead and walk that plank."

"Go get it, Shay," Pearl said.

Shay walked over to the front door. "Be right back."

"Okay, sit down in that chair and close your eyes, boy," Doc said.

Nick sat down and shut his eyes. When he heard the slap of Shay's flip-flops approaching, he stretched out his arms and made grabbing motions with his fingers.

"Okay, stop that, little squirt," Shay said. "And keep your eyes shut. It's a box, and I'm putting it on your lap… Okay, *now* you can reach inside the box, but *gently*."

His fingers fumbled around the bottom of the box until he felt a soft ball of fur. Peering down, he saw two round copper-colored eyes staring up at him. Nick let out a short, muffled squeal, but aside from that, he was speechless.

"You been talkin' 'bout wantin' a kitten for a long time, sugah," Pearl said.

"Can I—can I pick him up?" Nick whispered.

"Sure, sugah. But be gentle with him. Edward, put that box out on the fire escape."

Nick carefully cuddled the kitten against his chest, then walked slowly over to Pearl. "But—how'd you remember, Aunt Pearl?" he asked in a choked-up whisper.

Pearl kissed his forehead and smiled. "Aunt Pearl remembers everything, sugah."

"But—where'd he come from?"

"Remember Miss Rose's sister? Well, her cat had some kittens."

Doc walked over and eyed the kitten. "Huh! Best thing about him was the price."

"Told you they were broke as a joke this year," Shay whispered.

"I don't care!" Nick said, snuggling the kitten. "He's better than a million dollars!"

Doc grinned at Pearl. "Okay, Nick. Thank your Aunt Pearl for being a financial genius."

"Thanks, Aunt Pearl!" Nick said. "Hey, hold him, Daddy."

Doc picked up the kitten and petted him with his index finger. "Puny little thing, huh? But he's a big responsibility, Nick. You have to feed him every day—get some muscles on him."

"Oh, I will, Daddy," Nick said, grinning. "Just like Charles Atlas!"

"I hope he likes discount cat food and table scraps. And you have to clean his sand box or dirt box or whatever a cat uses for a toilet. And that box stays on the fire escape, deal?"

"Deal!" Nick said.

Doc smiled. "I'll rig up some chicken wire or sump'm out there so he won't fall."

"What'cha gonna name him, Nick?" Edward asked.

Nick rubbed his cheek against the kitten's soft fur. "Umm... I know! Sylvester!"

Shay grimaced. "No! Sylvester on the cartoon is a black and white cat. This kitten's orange! You can't name him Sylvester!"

"Yes, I can, 'cause he's *mine*. And he's Sylvester."

Doc sighed. "Silly Sylvester. We can call him Silly, for short."

"Nuh-uh!" Nick laughed.

"Come on, let's cut the cake," Doc said. "We still have to go see your Mama, and then Daddy's gotta go play. I've got an early gig tonight."

"Nick, let me hold the kitten," Shay said. "He's little but he cheers me up a *lot*."

"Yeah, you can hold him. Maybe he'll make *you* purr, Shay! But be careful."

"I will! Who do you think's gonna be babysittin' him while you go see your Mama?"

"Okay. But don't forget he's *mine*. I'm a Daddy now, and Sylvester's my son."

Shay rolled her eyes as she took the kitten. "You are *so* weird."

Nick felt a tap on his shoulder and looked up at Calvin, who smiled and handed him a large envelope. When Nick tore open the envelope, he let out a screech.

Pearl was cutting the cake, and her hand jerked, splattering chocolate icing onto the wall. "Dammit, boy! You scared the hell out'a me! What in the world are you screamin' about?"

"It's a United Airlines ticket, Aunt Pearl! I'm really goin' this time, Uncle Calvin?"

"Yeah, buddy. I talked it over with Doc and Pearl, and they said it was okay. I got some good contacts in Los Angeles and I think we can get you in a studio for some recording."

"In that studio you told me about? That house that Nat built?"

Doc's eyebrows shot up. "That's Capitol Records! How'd you know they called it that?"

"Uncle Calvin told me it's named after Nat King Cole and Mama played on his records."

"She sure did, sugah," Pearl said, smiling up at Calvin. "How'd you know that, Calvin?"

Calvin shrugged. "I heard you mention it, and I saw her name on some liner notes is all."

"I'ma practice real hard," Nick said. "I been singin' in church and I'm in the choir now!"

"He sure is," Pearl said. "Here. I'll put the ticket someplace safe."

Calvin rubbed Nick's head. "Okay, how 'bout I take you to the arcade, whadaya say?"

Nick handed the ticket to Pearl, then patted his hair back into place. "Can't, Uncle Calvin. I gotta take Mama some birthday cake. Daddy's takin' me to see her."

Pearl gave Calvin a pointed look as she tore off a piece of wax paper and wrapped up a slice of cake. "It's chocolate," she said. "His Mama's favorite."

Chapter 27

The Calhouns could only afford a small Christmas tree that year, but it appeared taller once Pearl placed it on a card table in the corner. She surrounded it with a mountain of homemade gifts and dime-store trinkets, and trimmed it with ornaments and the last working string of multi-colored lights. Every light on the string was chipped and one of the points was missing from the star, but a hefty dose of silver tinsel camouflaged all the flaws. When the decorating was done, Nick and Shay agreed that their tree was almost as grand as the one in Rockefeller Center. Pearl prepared a Christmas Eve dinner of roast chicken, mashed potatoes, greens, and apple pie. Doc passed on the pie, opting for jazz and a beer instead. The house was noisier than usual, and happily hectic.

After Shay and Nick went to bed, Edward turned the radio dial to WWRL and flopped onto the sofa next to his father. As he tucked a blanket under his feet and mushed his pillow into a comfortable shape, he saw Doc glaring at him wordlessly. Edward held out his hands. "What? Your program was over, wasn't it? Come on, Daddy. Equal time for Motown! You *do* want me to be a musically well-rounded young man, don't you? Time for my music!"

"Music? Man, those singers haven't hit a right note yet," Doc growled. "Go to bed."

Edward laughed and pulled the blanket up around his chin. "I *am* in bed, Daddy!"

"Not on Christmas Eve, boy. Get'cha tail in there and squeeze in with Nick."

"In that little midget bed with Nick *and* the cat? Man, Daddy! I'm sixteen, remember? What? You afraid I might see *Santa Claus* or sump'm?"

"Well, Edward, I'll put it this way. Your present's gettin' mighty damn cold standin' out in the hallway in her bikini, man. So if you don't get to bed so I can wrap the poor thing up—"

"A hooker!" Edward said, grinning. "*Finally* I get what I always wanted for Christmas!"

Pearl walked in and smacked his arm. "Where'd you hear about hookers, boy?"

Doc laughed. "Just 'cause he's *heard* of 'em doesn't mean he *knows* about 'em."

Edward's eyebrows bobbed up and down and he rubbed his chin. "I'm shavin' now, Daddy. You might be surprised at the things I know."

"Bed! And turn off those howlin' squirrels before you go. Put my jazz back on."

Edward sighed, then got up and turned the radio dial until Ella Fitzgerald's "Have Yourself a Merry Little Christmas" filled the room. "G'night, Mama," he said, kissing Pearl. Then he doubled up his fists. "You too, Santa Claus. Can't wait to unwrap my hooker."

Doc grinned and took a swing. "You better duck before you get a shiner for Christmas! Uh-huh. You flinched! You're slowin' down, boy."

"You the one slowin' down, ol' man! And don't blame me if Nick and Sylvester look like two pancakes tomorrow. 'Cause I am *not* gonna be the one all squashed up against the wall."

"Last time, Edward," Doc said, pulling off his house slipper and aiming it at him.

Pearl snatched the slipper from Doc's hand just as he was about to let it fly, and Edward darted into Nick's room, laughing.

"He's gettin' big, huh?" she said wistfully.

"Shit! Big in the mouth. And gimme my slipper."

She dropped the slipper into his lap. "Liar. You so proud of him you about to bust."

Doc snorted. "Don't tell *him* that. His head's too big as it is. Big head, big mouth… Hey. Is Calvin comin' over?"

"Mm-hmm. He called about an hour ago."

"We got any more beer?"

"Calvin said he'd bring some."

"Hey, come here a minute," Doc said, pulling Pearl onto his lap. "Why don't you come out to the club next week for New Year's Eve? I'll lay out for a few songs and we can dance."

Pearl wrapped her arms around his neck and smiled. "You romancin' me, old man?"

"That's my plan," he said, taking a gentle nibble at her earlobe. "You still got those silk stockings and black high heels you use'ta wear?"

"*Silk* stockings?" she chuckled. "Hell, man, I'll be lucky if I can dig up one or two *nylons* that ain't got runs. But I do have a pair of high heels I keep for emergencies."

He nuzzled her neck. Her pulse thumped softly against his cheek and he breathed in the smell of her hair—a sweet familiar blend of shampoo and Dixie Peach, with just a trace of cigarette smoke. "So does this qualify as an emergency?" he whispered.

Her deep laugh vibrated like a sustained note on a bass string. "Well, let's see," she said. "All these kids runnin' around—one of 'em big enough to shave—and you still talkin' about dancin' and romancin'? Oh, yeah. That sounds like a high-heel emergency to me, sugah."

Doc grinned. "Good. 'Cause I sure do love the way those long brown legs of yours look in high heels and stockings. And I don't give a good goddamn if they're silk *or* nylon."

"Well, then. Looks like you got yourself a date, busta." She heaved a tired, shaky sigh and slowly stood up. "But right now I got things to do and I need to find them damn scissors."

"Aww, hell!" Doc protested. "The brush-off! The gate! But it *is* Christmas, so I guess it's arts and crafts time. What's left anyway? More stuff to wrap?"

Before she could answer, there was a knock on the door, followed by a soft "Ho, ho, ho."

Doc got up to open the door. "Must be Santa Claus, Mama," he called.

Nick and Shay giggled from the back bedroom, and Edward groaned loudly.

Calvin stepped inside, carrying two bags of groceries. "Merry Christmas, folks!"

"Merry Christmas yourself," Doc said, peeking into one of the bags. "Where's the beer?"

"Wrong bag. Here. It's the cold one."

"Hot damn!" Doc cheered. "Budweiser! Gimme about fifteen minutes of guzzlin' and maybe I'll catch some'a that Christmas spirit too."

Pearl was quietly sorting through some old rolls of Christmas wrapping paper. "Merry Christmas, Calvin. Don't tell me that's *all* beer. How drunk you two fixin' to get?"

"Uh, naw. I got a few presents here for the kids."

"Aw, man, that's real nice," Doc said, taking one of the grocery bags. "But those hyenas don't deserve it. Here, let me open you up a bottle of that beer you bought yourself, man."

Calvin handed the other bag to Pearl. "I ain't had a chance to wrap 'em up or nothin'."

Pearl reached into the bag and smiled. "A transistor radio," she whispered. "This must be for Nick. That's all he's been talkin' about, Calvin."

"Well, actually, that's what I got 'em all. And I got this little collar for the cat."

Doc eyed the collar as he handed Calvin a beer. "Oh, great," he groaned. "Silly Sylvester with a goddamn *bell* around his neck? Calvin! That crazy cat already acts like he's on Bennies, man! So now I'll have three blaring radios and that cat makin' like one of those Swiss bell ringers from the Ed Sullivan Show! Thanks, man. That ought'a send me right over the edge."

Calvin laughed. "Why the hell you think I brought all this beer? Besides—look at this." He held up an earplug attachment on a wire for one of the transistor radios.

"Hey, look at this, Pearl!" Doc said, smiling. "Just for my sanity! It's got one'a those—"

"Shh! Keep your voice down," Pearl cautioned. "I see it."

"And you won't be able to hear that little bell even across the room," Calvin whispered.

Doc rolled his eyes. "Well. Jury's still out on that one, but thanks, man."

"Ignore that grouch," Pearl said. "It was real sweet of you, Calvin. Now, you gonna help us? Doc's still got lots'a wrappin' to do while I finish up here."

"Sure, I'll help. What's that you workin' on?"

Pearl carefully tore apart an empty Chesterfield cigarette carton. "Jus' makin' some presents," she said as she began drawing on the blank inside section of the carton.

"With cigarette cartons?"

"Mm-hmm." She sighed and erased a crooked line. "Damn, I knew I should'a done this yesterday," she murmured. "I'm usually a better artist than this. Oh, Calvin, I nearly forgot. You never did say whether you'll be goin' with us tomorrow to church. Nick wants to surprise you. He's doin' his first solo with the choir."

"Oh, I ain't gonna miss that." He directed his gaze at her artwork and his eyebrows pulled together in a perplexed expression. "Hey, what's that you drawin' anyway?"

Pearl dabbed at her forehead with her sleeve as she explained. "This, Mr. Bailey, is the glamorous new Chesterfield model named Babette Latour." She smiled. "I thought that up last night. And for your information, Miss Babette's fixin' to take the fashion world by storm."

"Oh, really?" Calvin said.

"Yeah," Doc said, grinning. "That's a fancy way of sayin' it's a paper doll for Shay."

"Shh! Would the big loud ox in the room keep his voice down, please?"

"Hey, you draw real good," Calvin whispered. "But ain't Shay too big for paper dolls?"

"She's been takin' that art class in school, sugah," Pearl murmured. "She designs clothes for my little cigarette-carton models. My baby's gonna grow up to *be* somebody in this world. Might be a big fashion designer—like Oleg Cassini or somebody." After one last touch, she stared at her art work. "Guess you pretty enough, Babette. Doc, you got the scissors, baby?"

"No. —Oh, wait. Here they are. So that's what I been sittin' on. Here ya go."

"Thanks."

"And what was that you said about Oleg Cassini?" Doc snorted. "Shows how much you know. Shay's gonna play trumpet in her own trio."

Pearl lit a cigarette and blew out the smoke through bared teeth. "Cool. And the trio's gonna be wearin' original designs from the House of La Belle Shay Calhoun. How 'bout that?"

Doc peeked over at Pearl's drawing. "Cool. But they're gonna have to be a hell of a hot band so the audience won't notice they're in drag. All but Shay, of course."

"They won't be in drag, fool. They'll be women."

"Name one woman jazz drummer," he said, taking a playful jab at her. "Just one."

"Don't mess with me, old man. I'm busy here, and I don't feel like it right now."

"Okay, that was just one 'old man' too many," he said, rising slowly from the sofa. He reached into the grocery bag and rattled the cat collar. "Time for the main event, ladies and gentlemen! And here goes the bell for round one! Come on, woman. Put 'em up."

"Oh, Lord," Pearl murmured as he pulled her to the floor. "You gonna knock my cigarette out'a my mouth and burn the house down!… Come on, sugah, not so rough!"

"Oh, you ain't seen rough yet, baby!" Doc said, grinning.

"Man, you two are crazy!" Calvin laughed. "Rompin' on the floor like kids! Hey! I almost forgot. Y'all mind if I bring somebody over tomorrow morning before church?"

"Male or female?" Doc said with a stern expression.

"Female."

Doc rolled to a sitting position and pretended to fuss with his shirt collar. "Damn, Pearl! Control yourself, baby!" He grinned and snatched her cigarette out of her mouth for a quick drag.

"Gimme back my cigarette and let me up," Pearl said, slowly getting to her feet. "You still got presents to wrap. And be careful with Babette, too, ya clumsy ox. Mind you don't tear off one of her legs or sump'm." She clapped her hand over her mouth and glared at Doc. "Aw, hell, now you got *me* talkin' all loud! Okay, that's right," she shouted in the direction of the children's room. "Her name's Babette! That's one surprise gone, Miss Big Ears Shay Calhoun!"

Shay and Nick giggled, and Doc covered a laugh with a gruff reprimand. "You kids go to sleep in there! Okay, Calvin. So who's this female you're bringing by?"

"Her name's Donna. She's one'a them receptionists at a little record label out here. I been meanin' to ask her out for a long time, but—"

"And you finally did. Good. Bring her to church too, if she wants to come." He glanced back and saw Pearl leaning unsteadily against the back of the sofa. "Hey, baby, you okay?"

Pearl shook her head and hurried toward the bedroom door.

"Oh, so now that the artwork's done, you're knockin' off for the night?"

"No," she said, turning back to look at him. "I—I got one little errand to run is all."

Doc's smile faded. "Now? But it's late. The stores'll be closed by the time you—"

"I'll be right back," Pearl said quickly.

"Look, Pearl—"

Calvin stood up. "Uh, I'll be in the kitchen for a minute."

When the kitchen door closed, Doc grabbed Pearl's arm. "Not tonight."

She eased out of his grip. "Look, I don't wanna be sick while the kids open their presents tomorrow. It's gonna be a long day—church and visiting, and then I gotta cook."

"But you're not sick, Pearl," he said. "You've been fine all night."

Pearl grabbed his hand. "Feel my forehead. Go on, feel it! I'm clammy, and I been hidin' the shakes all night. And then you go to rollin' me on the floor till I'm 'bout to throw up."

"I'm sorry. I didn't know. But come on now, I've seen you sicker. This isn't *that* bad."

"Look. I'm tellin' you I *need* to go. And—I'll be back in a while."

Doc expelled a frustrated sigh. "Then I'll go with you."

"No, man!" Pearl snapped. "Look—you know I don't want you there."

Doc glared at her, then sat down and lit a cigarette.

After a few moments of tense silence, Calvin walked back in. "Everything awright?"

No one answered. Pearl was putting on her coat, and Doc was staring at the wall.

Pearl walked over and stood directly in front of him, but Doc refused to look up. "I won't be long, baby," she said softly.

He didn't say a word until she opened the front door to leave. "Pearl—"

"Yeah, sugah?"

"Be careful."

≈∞≈

125th Street was still hectic when Pearl joined the crush of last minute shoppers on their way to the subway. On the short ride to her stop she tried to shake off the feeling of guilt. It was always at this point—riding to the quarter house—that she dreamed up elaborate fantasies about kicking heroin and reclaiming her life. But when the subway doors opened, she made the same choice she always made. Hurrying up the stairs, she pulled up her collar against the chill. As she stood staring at the pavement of St. Nicholas Avenue, still fighting for control, a woman startled her with a cheery "Merry Christmas." Pearl managed a smile, then ducked into a nearby coffee shop.

Taking a table near a window framed with red and green lights, she ordered coffee and gazed out at the corner of a dead-end street with no sign to identify it. Margaret Jackson did business on that street, and Pearl was sure that she had chosen her location carefully. She had always doubted that Margaret Jackson was even her real name, but she was dependable, as dealers went, and discreet. She met her customers in an old yellow fourplex at number 441¼, which explained its street code among addicts as "the quarter house." But she did not live there.

Pearl had only meant to sip the coffee to warm up, but her hands began to shake and she realized that she had drained the cup. Lately her fingers had been swelling so badly that her wedding band was cutting off her circulation. Forcing the ring over her knuckle, she rubbed the sore spot and licked her lips, thinking about the ecstasy of the heroin dancing through her bloodstream. *Hydra.* That was the name of Margaret's product. It was a word that Pearl either hated or loved, depending on her state of need. At the moment, she hated it.

So what if I'm sick on Christmas? It'll be worth it... I can kick, dammit. I know I can.

A faint voice began mocking her, telling her that was what she always said, but she stood up resolutely, ignoring it. She left some change on the table and stepped outside. Across the street in a bright shop window was a large silver Christmas tree surrounded by gifts and child-sized mannequins. With a quick glance at Margaret's dead-end corner, Pearl lit a cigarette to ease her craving, and then crossed the street. The smallest mannequin was dressed in red, with dark hair and blue painted eyes, and Pearl thought of Magda. *I could'a gone to see her with Nick on his birthday. But where was I? Right down the damn street handin' over my grocery money to Margaret for a fix.* She jerked up her chin and wiped her eyes. "God, help me—it's time to stop this shit. I'ma go visit my friend and then I *am* goin' home."

After all these years, she could still hear the sound of Magda's voice speaking the words she always said when she was afraid: *I make my courage.*

Pearl turned her back on the street with no sign, then walked quickly back to the subway entrance and hurried down the steps. "I make my courage too, sugah," she whispered breathlessly. "Tonight—dammit—I make my courage."

$$\approx\infty\approx$$

All was quiet at Genesco Medical Center when Pearl arrived. She tiptoed softly to the nurses' station and saw Hattie scribbling on a chart. "Hey, girl," she whispered. "Merry Christmas."

Hattie looked up and smiled. "Merry Christmas to you too, Pearl! How you doin'?"

"Oh, I'm okay, I guess. How's the family?"

"Just fine. Everybody's comin' to our house for dinner tomorrow and I *should* be home cookin' and cleanin', but I sure needed this overtime, girl."

"Oh, I know how it is. I need to get back quick too, but I just wanted to come look in on Magda. Okay if I go in just for a minute or two?"

"Stay as long as you want to, Pearl. We're down to a skeleton staff and nobody cares."

When Pearl reached Magda's door, she nearly collided with a young blonde nurse she had never seen before. "Oh, I'm sorry!" the nurse said. "I'm Sharon Atkins, the new trainee. You must be Mrs. Calhoun."

"Yes, I am. It's—it's real nice to meet you. "

"Nick told me about you a few weeks ago when he came on his birthday. He asked me to roll in one of the portable television sets to see if his mother might watch it." She smiled. "I'm leaving, but I'll leave it on for you. It was nice meeting you, Mrs. Calhoun. Merry Christmas!"

"Merry Christmas to you too."

The room was stifling, and Pearl pulled a handkerchief from her pocketbook and pressed it to her perspiring forehead. Slipping off her shoes, she climbed into the bed next to Magda. "Hi, sista. Guess you didn't expect to see me tonight, huh? But don't worry. We're still bringin' Nicky to see you tomorrow. I just thought we could have a little visit by ourselves tonight. So what's on TV? Oh... *It's a Wonderful Life.* Yeah, I like that one. It's almost over though, huh?"

Magda's head jerked and she made her usual grunting sounds. Then her fingers clutched at the air until Pearl clasped her hand and patted it. "Okay, sugah. Guess this must be your favorite part, huh? I know, girl. I love it when old George Bailey goes runnin' back home all happy."

She tried to ignore her pounding head and stomach cramps as she stared at the grainy images on the set. George Bailey running through the snowy streets of Bedford Falls; greeting the bank examiner; kissing the broken knob from the banister post; and then the big reunion with his family and friends. Pearl frowned, suddenly resentful of George Bailey's happy ending. *You ever met the Hydra, George Bailey?*

Suddenly, she felt Magda's body sag awkwardly against her. It was a struggle, but Pearl managed to steady her just as Magda's head dropped onto her shoulder. Then she was still.

Pearl patted her hand and then positioned the pillows to keep her from falling again. "You got your own way of huggin', don'tcha, sugah?" she whispered.

Leaning back, Pearl took several deep breaths. "You 'member the old days, sista?" she whispered. "You'd—come to our house like it was home, bringin' me flowers, and playin' with the kids. And me and you and Doc—we'd dance and laugh—" She chuckled weakly. "And Macy's—Remember Macy's? When you chased those old prejudiced heifahs off that elevator—and then knocked down that model? Lord, we sure got us some memories..."

She felt Magda's body jerk. "Don't fret now, sista. I'ma—watch this movie with you."

God, help me make it to the end of this movie. Then if I can just make it home, I can—

But a sudden, internal tremor reminded her of the reason Margaret called her product Hydra. In mythology, each time a hero dared to battle the Hydra by lopping off one of its multiple heads, two heads grew to replace it, each more gruesome than the one before. She thought back to the night when Margaret had whispered that word into her ear for the first time. *Hydra.*

She remembered shivering on the porch of the quarter house, thinking that she would die if Margaret didn't hurry and open that door. Pearl didn't realize what she had done until it was too late, and she was lying back on that faded green sofa gazing at her own reflection in Margaret's eyes. Margaret leaned so close to her face that their lips brushed and her hot breath tingled down Pearl's neck. "The Hydra done come inside you now, baby," Margaret had whispered into her mouth. "He done turned you out and he ain't never lettin' go. Oh, he'll be sweet to you—give you that gooood feelin' down low—like you feelin' right now. Oooh, ain't it gooood?… But baby, don'tchu try to leave him, 'cause he can get real mean and jealous if you try to leave him. Get to howlin' and growin' them heads. But when you come back to him, then he grow them feel-good heads." Margaret laughed lewdly and Pearl closed her eyes. The Hydra was making love to her, moving with the skill of an experienced lover, and exploding like a separate climax in each nerve of her body. When she felt him hit that spot "down low" again and again and again, she remembered screaming and then seeing herself smiling like a trick in Margaret's eyes.

The memory popped like a bubble, and the hurt was more intense than ever. Pearl stared at the television and laughed at herself for thinking that she could quit. She had kicked heroin once, but it had not been Hydra. Hydra was a high-grade beast. And she had angered him. She had brought him into this room with Magda, where he didn't belong. And now he was screaming inside her head like a siren, and growing heads by the dozens. She squeezed her eyes shut. She felt her nerves twisting and cutting their way through her skin, and her eyes flew open. *Razor blades! Oh, my God… Ronnie!*

Desperate for a distraction, her eyes darted around wildly at the four drab gray walls. Three mismatched chairs making skeletal shadows in the glow of the television set. Nick's school drawings on drooping paper, taped to the wall near the dark window. Nighttime always fell so heavy and cruel in this sad little room. Magda's sad little world.

She took a breath and tried to lick her lips, but her tongue was too dry. A child's shrill voice was bouncing around inside her head, talking about an angel getting his wings.

Then the Hydra rolled over inside her with a piercing howl, and Pearl barely made it to the bathroom sink in time to throw up. "Oh, God," she groaned, sinking to the floor. Her whole body was rattling convulsively as she struggled to her feet. She tried to clean up the mess and dropped the soiled towel into the trashcan, then grabbed a fresh towel to scrub her face and hands. After rinsing out her mouth with water, she gazed at her gaunt reflection in the mirror and muffled a sob. Returning to the bed, she slipped on her shoes, and kissed Magda's head.

"G'night, sugah," she whispered quickly. "I'm sorry, but I gotta go—right now."

≈∞≈

Doc had no recollection of falling asleep until he heard a meow and felt someone tugging on his arm. He opened his eyes and saw Nick and Sylvester staring at him in the predawn darkness.

"Wake up, Daddy! It's Christmas! What'cha doin' sleepin' on the sofa?"

Before Doc could gain control of his vocal cords, he heard Edward laughing. "Here ya go, Daddy. Some Doc Calhoun wake-up music…"

Dave Brubeck's "Blue Rondo a la Turk" blasted from the radio.

Doc groaned as he sat up. "Turn that down a little. Where's your mother?"

"Right here, baby," Pearl said, appearing suddenly with a cup of hot black coffee.

Doc looked up at her. Her hair was combed back, still wet from her shower, and her face was scrubbed clean. She was wearing the white sweater that looked so nice on her. Aside from the unnatural shine in her eyes, she looked angelic. Instead of taking the coffee, he reached up and placed his palm gently on the side of her face. "You all right?"

"Mm-hmm. I got in about two," she whispered. "Here, sugah. Drink it 'fore it gets cold."

Doc pressed a small white box into her free hand. "Sorry I didn't wrap it."

She stared at the label and gasped. "Eau de *Joy*? My God, baby, this stuff costs a fortune!"

"It's just a quarter ounce. I wanted you to have sump'm nice this year—for a change."

A look of abject shame fell across Pearl's face. "Oh… baby—I don't deserve this."

"Shut up and kiss me," he whispered.

Sinking down next to him, she leaned into his arms and held on for a long moment.

"Come on, Daddy!" Nick whined. "Can't we open the presents now?"

"All right, all right! You can open a *few*. But turn on the Christmas tree lights first."

Nick and Shay bolted for the tree. Pearl smiled and dabbed a bit of perfume behind each ear.

Doc swallowed a sip of coffee, then leaned back and closed his eyes until the noise was too loud to ignore. The children were tearing open their presents while the cat leaped into piles of wrapping paper and batted an ornament around under the tree. Doc opened one eye, then sat up straight. "Hey! I said you could open a *few*! And what the hell's wrong with that crazy cat?" He leaned back on the sofa and began muttering. "I ought'a slip that damn cat a Mickey… Calm his hairy ass right down…

Hey, Edward, turn the damn station, boy. It's too early for that. Turn it to that crooner station your Mama likes."

Edward turned the dial until Nat King Cole was singing "The Christmas Song."

"That's better," Doc said. "And you kids stop opening presents till Calvin gets here."

Shay pointed toward the open kitchen door. "But Daddy... Calvin's right over there."

Doc looked over and saw Calvin and a young woman peering at him from the kitchen.

"Thought you was dead for a while there, buddy," Calvin laughed.

Doc cleared his throat and checked his fly. "Anything else happen while I was asleep?"

"It was all that beer you had last night," Pearl said with a lazy laugh.

Nick sighed impatiently. "So *now* is it okay to open all the presents, Daddy?"

Doc's groan faded into a sigh. "Nick, go crazy, man."

Calvin stepped into the room with his arm around the woman he had brought. She had a medium brown complexion, and wore her black hair in a straightened, shoulder-length flip, with a small white bow just above her left ear. She smiled and her face was suddenly twice as pretty.

"This is the lady I told y'all about," Calvin said. "Donna Carlisle. Donna, this is Doc."

"Nice to meet you, Doc," she said. "Sorry we woke you up so—uh, suddenly."

Doc drained his cup and smiled. "Donna, around here, everything is *always* suddenly."

Nick ran over to Calvin. "A transistor radio! Awright! Thanks, Uncle Calvin!"

"Good! You finally opened it. Now you can practice your singin' like we talked about."

"It's a deal!" Nick switched on the small radio and grinned. "Hey, it even got batteries!"

Doc winced. "It's got an ear-piece, too. Use it, please. At least till Daddy sobers up."

Calvin pointed at a flat, rectangular-shaped gift with a large red bow that was leaning against the wall near the Christmas tree. "Nick, bring that present over here."

Nick retrieved the gift and grinned as he handed it to Calvin. "Is it for me?"

"Well, actually it's for your Mama."

Nick let out a yelp and hugged him. "Can I open it for her, Uncle Calvin?"

"Sure, boy. Then we can take it to her when we visit after church."

Nick tore through the wrapping paper. "It's a picture!" he squealed. "For Mama's room!"

Pearl gazed at the painting and smiled. "You know what that looks like? It looks like that marketplace she use'ta tell me about from her home town. This is just how I pictured it, Calvin!"

Calvin shrugged. "It ain't no big thing. You told me she was from Greece, and I know this Greek painter in the Village is all. He painted it for me. It ain't no big thing."

"It *is* a big thing, Calvin. It was so thoughtful. What kind of trees are these?"

Calvin shrugged. "Hell, I don't know, Pearl. Greek trees, I guess."

"That was such a sweet idea," Pearl whispered. "You sure made Nicky happy."

Calvin rolled his eyes, and Donna laughed. "Don't be bashful," she said. "It *was* sweet!"

"Okay, everybody!" Pearl called. "It's time to get dressed for church, and no groanin'! We gotta be there early—and nobody better ask me why. It's a surprise. So let's get movin'!"

≈∞≈

The Calhouns made a noisy entrance as they filed up the center aisle of St. Philip's Church, despite Pearl's repeated shushes. With the addition of Calvin and Donna, they nearly filled an entire pew. The children's choir was already assembled, with Nick standing in front.

Doc leaned over and whispered to Calvin, "You look as nervous as the boy, man!"

Calvin shook his head. "Last time I set foot in a church, it was my brother singin' with the choir. That was a long time ago, I ain't gon' lie. And it sho' wasn't no grand joint like this."

After the Pastor's opening prayers, the organ sounded the intro, and Nick's clear, high voice echoed through the church as he began to sing "Ave Maria."

Doc nudged Calvin's arm. "Sounds a lot better than that rock and roll Motown mess he's always squawlin' around the house," he whispered. "I bet'cha—" He stopped when he saw the odd expression on Calvin's face. He was staring at Nick as if he'd never seen him before.

Suddenly, and without a word, Calvin stood up and walked out of the church.

Chapter 28

All through February, Harlem was buzzing about the upcoming heavyweight championship fight between Sonny Liston and Cassius Clay.

On the night of the fight Doc hurried into the apartment with two bulging grocery bags. "Where's everybody?" he called.

Edward walked in from the kitchen. "Everybody's here but Calvin. He's comin', right?"

"He'll be here shortly. Man! I got the last six-pack in the store! Everybody was stockin' up on beer and party food. This is *some* big fight. Hey, where's your Mama?"

"In the bedroom asleep. She wasn't feelin' too good."

Doc's smile disappeared. "Headache or sump'm?"

Edward gave him a pointed look. "Throwin' up again."

There was a sudden knock at the door, and Doc patted Edward's shoulder. "I'll go check on her. You go let Calvin in, man. And then go put those chips in some bowls."

When Calvin walked in, Nick greeted him loudly. "You was almost late, Uncle Calvin!"

When Doc walked back into the room, he reprimanded Nick in a soft voice. "Hey, lounge, man! Your Aunt Pearl's tryin' to rest, so lay off all that jumpin' and loud talkin', you hear me?"

"Sorry, Daddy," Nick murmured. Looking up at Calvin, he made a big show of silently mouthing the words, "Sit down, Uncle Calvin."

Calvin sat down next to Shay. "Hey, big girl. What'cha doin' wit'cha Daddy's horn?"

Shay's bottom lip poked out in a pout. "He's gonna give me a lesson tonight and teach me how to clean the valves—if the stupid fight ever gets over."

Doc placed the chips on the coffee table, then carefully took his horn from Shay. "Let's put baby back in her case. 'Cause if you put a dent on Daddy's baby, Daddy'll put a dent in you."

Shay rolled her eyes and laughed. "I'll be careful. But I'm still gettin' my lesson, right?"

"Yes. But we're just studying a chart tonight. We're keeping things quiet for your Mama."

"What about tomorrow? I'll play real soft—"

"Tomorrow's a work night. You know that. Daddy's gotta go play. So tonight you learn your valves and study this chart. Then by Thursday, you'll be ready to *begin* playing."

Shay sighed. "Yes, sir."

When the announcer began the introductions for the preliminary fight, everyone fell silent. "Turn it down a little, Edward," Doc said softly. "You want a beer, Calvin?"

"Thought you'd never ask."

"Hey, Daddy, when are we gonna get a TV set like Miss Rose?" Edward called.

Doc looked in from the kitchen and pressed his index finger to his lips. "Shh! How many times do I have to tell you knuckleheads your Mama's restin'? This fight isn't on TV anyway."

Nick hugged his knees to his chest and grinned. "This is a *big* fight, huh, Uncle Calvin?"

"Yeah, buddy. This is a title fight for the heavyweight championship of the world, man."

"The whole world?" Nick asked.

Edward sighed. "Why you think they call Liston champion of the world, dummy? Ain't nobody callin' him heavyweight champ of Brooklyn or 125th Street or sump'm, are they?"

"So then he be kind'a like the king of the whole world?"

"Well—the boxing world, at least." Calvin rubbed Nick's head. "You know, when I was a kid I use'ta listen to the fights with my Daddy. Mostly, we use'ta listen to Joe Louis. He was the heavyweight champ back then. For twelve whole years, too. You ever heard'a him?"

"The Brown Bomber! Daddy told us he whupped that Nazi man! And everybody in Harlem got drunk and they was dancin' in the streets! Hey! You think they gonna do that tonight?"

"No, man. That fight was different. See, America was fightin' Germany in World War II, and Schmeling was a German. So it was like Joe Louis was representin' America in that fight. And folks wasn't just dancin' in Harlem. Folks was dancin' all over the USA that night—white *and* black. I'll never forget *that* fight. Me and Daddy sho' was happy that night."

A dreamy expression crossed Nick's face. "And my Daddy too? My blood-Daddy?"

Calvin frowned. "Nah. Joe listened to them big bands. Me and Daddy—we liked the fights."

"Wish I could'a been there," Nick said wistfully.

Calvin stared at him for a few seconds, and then smiled. "So, who you kids bettin' on?"

"Cassius Clay!" Nick and Edward said in unison.

"Aww, man! Cassius Clay? He's all mouth, man! That skinny little wise guy ain't gon' put no whuppin' on my man Liston! What about you, Shay?"

Shay curled up one side of her top lip. "Shoot! I'm just waitin' for my lesson. I don't care 'bout this daggone fight or ol' daggone Cassius Liston *either*."

"Not Cassius Liston! Cassius *Clay!*" Nick said, rolling his eyes. "Ya dumb *girl!*"

Doc swatted Nick lightly on the back of his head. "Apologize to your sister, man—quietly."

"Sorry, Shay," Nick mumbled.

"That's better. Anyway, Liston's gonna send that youngster home cryin' to his Mama."

"Nuh-uh!" Edward said, grinning. "Float like a butterfly! Sting like a bee!"

"Rumble, young man, rumble!" Nick shouted.

Doc sighed loudly, and Nick clapped a hand over his mouth. "Sorry... Hey, Uncle Calvin," he whispered. "Do Cassius Clay represent America like the Brown Bomber?"

Calvin snorted. "Cassius Clay don't represent nothin' but his mouth."

"Well, then... do *Liston* represent America?"

Doc nudged Calvin and they both laughed. "Naw, Nick. Liston represents the mob!"

"Never mind," Doc said. "They're both from America and there's no big war goin' on, so don't be expecting any dancin' in the streets tonight."

"Okay," Nick sighed. "But Clay gon' *win*, Uncle Calvin. You just wait and see."

Calvin nudged Nick's knee with his shoe. "Wanna bet? How much money you got?"

"A lot! From my job, and then every day I go down the alleys lookin' for soda pop bottles and turn 'em in for deposit money. *And* today I had me the best day of my whole career!"

"Your whole career, huh? And just what *is* your career, Nick?"

Nick stared upward for a moment in deep thought. "I'm a—box-man!"

"A box-man? Okay, so why was today the best day of your career, Mr. Box-Man?"

"Well, I was helpin' Edward stack up our boxes, and this lady asked me to help her. So I helped her take about ten bags of groceries to her car and she gave me a dollar!"

"It was *three* bags," Edward said, "and nothin' heavy, so you were overpaid, chump."

"Nuh-uh! Anyway, now I got me three dollars, three quarters, and a nickel saved up."

"Okay, Mr. Box-Man," Calvin said. "I ain't wanna take *all* your money, but I bet'cha a dollar Liston mops the flo' wit' Mr. Big Mouth. What about you, Edward? You wanna bet?"

Doc shook his head disapprovingly at Edward, who was staring at the floor. "Nick saves his money, but Edward blows his faster than a drunk at a brewery."

"How?" Calvin asked.

"Shootin' craps with those juvenile delinquents in the damn alley back behind the store."

Edward grimaced. "Come on," he whispered to Nick. "Loan me a buck so I can bet too."

"No," Nick said dryly. "You blew yo' money like a drunk at a booery. Too bad, chump."

"It's a *brewery*, stupid, and you don't even know what it means!"

"Yes, I do!"

Doc sighed and reached into his pocket. "I'll give you a dollar to bet. But you better not start cryin' the blues when dancin' boy gets knocked unconscious and you gotta pay up."

Edward grabbed the dollar and grinned. "Thanks, Daddy!"

"Okay, wait!" Nick dashed to his room and returned with a dollar. "Me too! It's a bet!"

By the end of the seventh round, the world had a new heavyweight champion, and Nick's savings had increased to four dollars, three quarters, and a nickel.

Doc grinned as he reached over to change the station on the radio. "Lucky li'l knucklehead."

Nick was strutting around the room, loudly imitating the new champ. "I'm a *baaad* man!"

"Hey!" Doc said sharply. "I ain't gonna tell you again, boy! Your Aunt Pearl's asleep."

At that moment the bedroom door opened and Pearl walked in. "It's okay, sugah. I'm up."

Doc's jaw tightened when he saw her putting on her coat and gloves. The radio announcer's voice grated against the silence in the room:

> *And now, a mellow performance by the great John Coltrane, with Johnny Hartman on vocals. This is Billy Strayhorn's "Lush Life."*

Pearl gazed vacantly at Doc. "You gonna be here with the kids, sugah?"

"Don't go out, Pearl." There was an angry finality in Doc's eyes and in his voice.

Calvin stood up. "Why don't you boys show me your baseball cards. You too, Shay."

"But I don't have any baseball cards," Shay whined, "and I been waitin' for my lesson."

"All you kids go in your room with Calvin," Doc said. "I need to talk to your Mama."

Nick picked up the cat and gazed sadly over his shoulder as he followed Shay out.

As soon as Doc and Pearl were alone in the room, he blocked her path to the front door.

"Not tonight, Pearl. It's time for this shit to *stop*. You're not going out."

Pearl stared at him for a moment, then reached around him for the doorknob.

As Doc nudged her away from the door, he was desperately searching for words strong enough to fight that needle that was calling her out into the night. But he couldn't think. The song on the radio was wearing on his nerves, but he didn't dare step away to turn it off.

He moved to his left to block the door again, and again Pearl shifted her body subtly to get around him. A thought flashed in his mind—they were like two boxers in a ring, sizing each other up before the first blow. "Pearl. Did you hear me? We gotta deal with this now."

"No, you gotta let me *go* now… *Now*, baby."

The edge in her voice sent a chill down Doc's neck, but he held his ground. "No. It's time to face this shit. Come on, now. You gotta dig down deep and really try this time."

Pearl squeezed her eyes shut and shouted through clenched teeth: "What in God's name do you think I been tryin' to do in that damn room for the past two hours, man?"

"Keep your voice down! And where the hell did you get the goddamn money anyway?"

Pearl jerked her head up. "I ain't gonna lie! I cashed one'a Nick's checks."

"You *what!*" he yelled. "Pearl, goddammit!" He paused and lowered his voice. "That's the boy's college money! That man didn't send those checks to pay for your goddamn smack!"

He could tell that Pearl had hit that turning point that always transformed her into a dangerous stranger. But he couldn't lose this time. He had to keep fighting.

A blistering hate radiated from her eyes and her voice dropped to a feral growl: "We had a deal, remember? I don't bring up all your mess from the past, and you don't bring up my mess. We had a deal! So *don't* pick a fight with me, man. Don't you *dare*."

"To hell with a goddamn deal! 'Cause if I gotta fight *with* you to fight *for* you… then hell, that's just what it's gonna have to be."

"Get *out* of my way!" she screamed.

He grabbed her hands and held them firmly. "That ain't gonna work this time, Pearl."

Now she was shivering, and her voice dropped to a whimper: "You gunna kill me, man."

Her hands began to shake so violently Doc could no longer hold them still. And he realized that this was how the needle always defeated him— by showing him the raw inevitability of her suffering. He changed his mind twice before releasing his grip and stepping out of her way.

Before he could say another word or think another thought, she was gone.

For a moment he stood there staring at the open door, but finally closed it and walked into the kitchen. Dropping heavily into a chair, he cursed himself for not turning off the radio in the living room. He could still hear Johnny Hartman singing that lonely, painful song.

Doc was still sitting at the table when the light of dawn began to cast pale shadows in the kitchen. From the small eastward-facing window he could see the sun's corona blinking like a 4th-of-July sparkler in the narrow space between two brownstones across the street. He closed his eyes, but the image was still sharp and bright under his eyelids. After a while, the children began drifting in for breakfast and asking questions he couldn't answer.

It was nearly noon when he called the first hospital, and after two when he called Calvin.

"I need a favor, man. I was gonna grab a cab but— Look, I need—I need a ride to—"

"Don't waste time explainin'. Just hang up. I'm on my way."

Doc nearly bumped into Calvin as he ran down the stairs to meet him. Without stopping, he grabbed at his coat sleeve and mumbled, "I saw your car pull up. Come on, man."

They hurried across the street and got into the car. "Harlem Hospital" was all Doc said.

Calvin drove quickly to the hospital and parked at the emergency entrance. When they reached the admittance desk, Doc said, "Uh, I called earlier and somebody called me back—about an hour ago—somebody named Fenton—about… about the Jane Doe they brought in."

Calvin's low moan had a slurred prayer to Jesus in it.

"Oh, yes, sir," the nurse said. "Let me get Jamie for you. He's the attendant down there."

"Down—where?"

She blinked hesitantly. "Well—the morgue, sir."

Doc swayed, and Calvin steadied him. "It ain't her, man. She had I.D., didn't she?"

Doc nodded with a glimmer of hope in his eyes. "She had her pocketbook when she left."

Several minutes passed before a dark-skinned man wearing a white smock and horn-rimmed eyeglasses approached them. "Mr. Calhoun?" he said with a faint West Indian accent.

"Yes."

"I'm Jamie Fenton. Follow me and I'll take you to the identification room." He smiled reassuringly. "You know, a lot of times these John and Jane Doe bodies are never claimed. So chances are that it's probably not your wife, sir. And we'll get this cleared up for you without another moment of worry."

They stepped into an elevator that reeked of disinfectant, and Doc felt a wave of nausea. He glanced over at Calvin, who was staring at the floor; then he turned back to Jamie Fenton. "Where'd they find—this woman? I mean, who brought her in?"

"Well, this poor lady was found in an alley not too far from here. A couple of garbage men found her on their morning route. They should've called the police, but they'd never come across such a situation before. So they wrapped her up in one of their coats and brought her in."

"And she didn't have any I.D.? No—pocketbook or anything?"

"No, sir."

"Well, didn't anybody—call the police?"

"We did. And they reprimanded those garbage men—for disturbing a possible crime scene—but once they checked everything and decided there was no murder, they let them go."

The word "murder" echoed in Doc's mind and he felt a rattling down the back of his neck. The whole day had seemed like a bad dream, but now he was wide-awake, and death was standing right next to him—a long-feared enemy with sharp, discernible features.

When the elevator doors opened, Doc hung back. "Mr. Fenton, was this woman—tall?"

"Well—yes. Fairly tall."

Doc nodded, and slowly followed him down a long corridor. When they reached the door marked "MORGUE" in bold black letters, Jamie Fenton looked over his shoulder at him.

"Mr. Calhoun—it might be a good idea for you to prepare yourself—just in case."

Doc gave him a blank stare. "Do you know yet—how this woman died?"

"Well—all indications point to a heroin overdose."

Doc closed his eyes. "You just prepared me."

They walked into the cold room and Fenton turned on a light. It was a bare light bulb hanging over the door that sent crawling shadows along the floor beside Doc as he walked. Along one wall were rows of stainless steel drawers gleaming blue in the dim light, and at the far end of the room were three tables. Two were vacant, but stretched out on the third was a body, covered by a white sheet. The only exposed part of the body was the right foot. Fenton uncovered the face and stepped aside. "Let me turn on the overhead light so you can see—"

"No! —I mean, this light's okay." Doc's eyes remained fixed on the toe-tag. *Jane Doe #3.*

After waiting for nearly a minute, Fenton said, "Please, Mr. Calhoun..."

Doc nodded. Forcing his gaze away from the toe-tag he finally looked at Jane Doe #3's face. His entire body felt as if it were crumbling inside his clothes. He stared down at the gray color of Pearl's face and the ink-colored flecks on her eyelids and lips. Aside from the discoloration, her features were relaxed and serene, as if she were enjoying a pleasant dream. She was still beautiful, even in death.

He stared at her right hand, which was resting just under her throat. Then he moved the sheet and his eyes traveled down her left arm, which was stretched out beside her body. Her ring finger was bare. The horrible speculation of what had happened to her wedding band was replaced by a merciful rush of memories: her hands moving efficiently through their day—braiding Shay's hair so carefully because she was tender-headed; placing hot food on the table for supper; making those soft, gentle circles on his back to relax him when he couldn't sleep. But then his mind flashed back to the tremors in her hands the last time he had touched her, and he remembered the only words she had spoken at Ronnie's burial: *This is a damn mean world.* He gazed down at the needle scars on her arm. How many times had she tried to quit and been wounded by failure? One by one, each wound deeper than the one before, and now, just like Ronnie, Pearl was a casualty of this damn mean world. Leaning down, he kissed her scars, then her hands, then her face. She was cold.

Though he knew the futility of it, he tucked the sheet about her shoulders, trying to make her warm. Reason told him that he should leave, but the idea of taking the long walk back to the door struck him as impossible. As long as he could see her face, she wasn't really gone. He stared at her until he heard Jamie Fenton clear his throat, and he knew his time was up. He tried to step back, but his head suddenly felt too heavy to hold up. To keep from falling, he lowered himself in a series of jerks to a sitting position on the floor. He saw a blur of movement as Calvin rushed over to him, and Doc held up one shaky hand in a "stop" gesture. Calvin didn't touch him. Instead, he quietly sat down on the floor next to him. Doc gave him a grateful look and saw a trail of tears running down his face. They sat together on the floor in absolute silence for several minutes as Jamie Fenton maintained a respectful vigil near the door.

An overwhelmingly real feeling came over Doc just then—that he was sitting in the middle of a still photograph, where there was no such thing as time. He was keenly aware that some new, unbearable level of pain was hovering in this room on the brink of attack—but if he didn't move, perhaps it wouldn't find him. He tried not to breathe.

It was working fine until he saw something move under his chin— two small splashes on the gray linoleum floor. He hadn't even felt himself crying, and now the spell was broken. And just as he had feared, the pain of absolute loneliness clawed at him like a hundred cold fingers, and a scream rose in his throat. The sound of his own voice was like a jarring explosion, but to his surprise, it did not scream. It simply said, "Jamie Fenton?"

"Yes, Mr. Calhoun?"

Doc got to his feet slowly, pulled a handkerchief from his coat pocket, and pressed it hard against his eyes for a few seconds. Then he jerked up his chin and looked directly at Jamie Fenton. "Listen… I know what folks think about junkies."

"Oh, Mr. Calhoun. There's no need to explain anything to—"

"*Listen* to me, man… I know it's an unacceptable—habit, but—" He stopped cold; the realizations were flooding his mind too fast. He had said *habit*, not *addiction*, and the second he had said it, he knew why. He couldn't allow that word to claim ownership of her. This was his last stand, his last chance to protect her. And for some reason, that meant making this stranger understand. "It's an unacceptable habit," he repeated. "Some folks might even call it—dirty, but she's a *clean* woman. Clean *inside*, in her soul, man. Where it counts. You understand?"

Jamie Fenton nodded quietly.

"So take that Jane Doe tag off her. Her name is Pearl Marie Calhoun. And she's the finest person—I ever knew. So you—you make *damn* sure you treat her with dignity—and respect."

Jamie Fenton hurried to the table and removed the tag. When he returned to the door, his eyes were moist. "Pearl Marie Calhoun," he said. "She will receive my most respectful care, sir."

≈∞≈

When Calvin pulled up to the apartment building, he looked over at Doc, but neither man moved for a moment. Finally, Doc leaned out the passenger-side window, looked up, and then groaned.

"Well, come on. Let's get this over with. Edward's sittin' up in that damn window lookin' at the car. He knows sump'm's up. He hasn't said a word since I started callin' hospitals."

Calvin opened the door. "I'm right with you, man."

Edward met them at the halfway point in the stairwell. After exchanging a fearful look with his father, he managed to whisper a one-word question: "Mama?"

Doc stared at him. His chest rose and fell twice before the words finally came: "She's gone, Edward. She… Your Mama… died."

Calvin's eyes welled up as he watched Edward battle to keep his manly pride. The boy's shoulders shook, then he let out a jarring scream from some deep primal place. "Mama!"

Doc reached for Edward and jerked him against his chest. "Goddamn," he whispered.

Edward let out a racking sob and moaned something unintelligible into Doc's shoulder. Calvin leaned on the wall and closed his eyes to shut out the agonizing scene, but it had already burned itself indelibly into his brain. He began to wonder how much worse it could get. Nick and Shay still had to be told the news.

He didn't have long to prepare. Although several curious neighbors were standing in their doorways murmuring, the sound of Shay's gasp cut through all the noise. She stood frozen at the top of the landing, staring at Edward sobbing in her father's arms. "No!…Where's Mama?"

As she ran down to her father, her crying grew into a shrill scream. Doc caught her in his free arm, and, with both of his children clinging to him, he slowly made his way up the stairs and walked into the apartment. He looked at Calvin and nodded in the direction of his bedroom.

Calvin understood. That's where Nick would be. As he walked into Doc's bedroom, he heard the faint sound of music. It was a Jackie Wilson song—"To Be Loved." He opened the closet door slowly and found Nick sitting in the corner hugging his knees to his chest. His head was resting on one arm, and he was clutching his transistor radio tightly in his hand. Sylvester was sitting next to him like a bodyguard.

Nick had grown too big to be picked up and carried around, but as Calvin stared down at the boy's shaking shoulders, he heard a rattling sob, and pushed aside the clothing to reach for him. He pulled him up into his arms in a quick motion and held him close and secure against his chest. As Nick grabbed Calvin's neck, the radio slipped from his fingers to the floor, and Jackie Wilson's voice disappeared in a sea of static.

"You okay, son?"

"Naw, sir," Nick croaked. "I ain't okay… Uncle Calvin?"

"Mm-hmm?"

"I awready heard Shay screamin'. Aunt Pearl's—dead, huh?" He wiped his nose on his sleeve and shot Calvin a fierce look. "Don't lie!"

"I ain't gon' lie to you, Nick. Your Aunt Pearl's gone to God."

Nick's head sagged back down onto his shoulder. "Ya know what, Uncle Calvin?"

"What, son?"

Nick's entire body stiffened as he shouted through a choked sob, "The blue hawk finally came just like you said! He killed Aunt Pearl—and now he's laughin' at us!"

Chapter 29

Doc Calhoun was a devout believer in Johnnie Walker Red, and for good reason.

When there was nothing else left to believe in, Johnnie Walker was the best kind of old-time religion. Johnnie was a tent revival, complete with a shout-choir, tambourines, and the power to heal you to into blissful unconsciousness—if you drank enough.

But if sleep was bliss, then waking was the seventh circle of hell. Each time Doc fell into a merciful sleep, he woke with the alcohol-induced belief that time actually stopped in the hours between midnight and dawn, maliciously dragging minutes into some dark eternity. He had no idea whether it was Sunday or Thursday, and didn't care.

He lifted his head from the damp flattened pillow and reached for his cigarettes. The house was too quiet, the air was stale, and the bottle was empty again. The matches looked blurry in the pale glow of the night-light near the bedroom door. Pearl had left it on that night, and nobody had turned it off. When he touched the matchbook cover, it was limp and soggy, and he vaguely remembered spilling his scotch on the nightstand.

"Shit."

He attempted to stand up, but lost his balance and fell back onto the bed. This time he grabbed the headboard to steady himself and finally got to his feet. As he made his way to the kitchen, his steps were slow and heavy. Then he heard an eerie, repetitive sound that seemed to match the dragging rhythm of his feet: *Sh-shwup—sh-shwup—sh-shwup…* After a moment of confusion, he remembered the record he had left playing on the hi-fi.

When he got to the kitchen, he found matches in the drawer near the sink and lit his cigarette. The sound was still calling: *Sh-shwup—sh-*

shwup—sh-shwup... Heading over to the hi-fi, he lifted the tone arm, ending that maddening eternal groove. As he squinted at the needle, trying to place it at the beginning of the record, he had a brief flash of philosophical clarity. Something about addiction—junkies and heroin, musicians and jazz, hypodermic needles and phonograph needles. But Johnnie Walker quickly garbled it into a loud jumble in his head that sounded like Ornette Coleman on his most self-indulgent high-horse. Doc shook it off—probably not important enough to remember anyway— then slowly walked back to his bedroom and listened to what was left of the intro to "Lush Life."

"Bet you don't even know what day that goddamn funeral was," he whispered to the walls. He fumbled in the nightstand drawer until he found the last bottle of scotch and broke the seal. He took a gulp that burned his throat, and then smiled. How many times had he played that record, sadistically trying to burn himself with its lyrics? He thought of Ronnie, and yelled at him. "It's your fault too, goddammit!"

As he took another gulp, a drop of rational thought fought its way through to his brain:

"Wait. Did the kids eat today?" he whispered, staring into his glass. "Shit... I don't even know."

Johnny Hartman kept crying from the hi-fi about loneliness, but that was his job, after all, and the main reason he had been invited to this party. But Doc finally hit his tipping point, and felt the glass shaking in his hand. "I can't—do this," he moaned. "Jesus Christ... Okay, Ronnie! I get it now, man. I get it!" He threw the glass at the wall, sending the scotch flying in a sweeping arc. "Razor blades, Ronnie? I always wondered about those goddamn razor blades... Aww, man, I bet you ate that shit up like candy! I bet—"

He stopped, and his voice fell to a whisper. "Oh, God—that can't be me yellin' like that..."

A fleeting thought crossed his mind about souls. If he had one, it was surely dying now.

But then Trane's solo poured over him like cool water on a third-degree burn. Doc closed his eyes and leaned toward the sound with a desperate concentration until he could see each note written out on a chart that he could see clearly in his mind. His fingers moved, the way they sometimes did when he slept, playing the melody as if working the valves on his trumpet. And the pain left him for a moment—actually got up off him and drifted over to the corner, where it waited, respectfully, for the great John Coltrane to finish his solo. Doc smiled.

But the solo resolved too soon and Johnny Hartman began to sing those razor-blade lyrics again. And just like that, the pain was back. And the chart was gone. And Pearl was dead.

Doc's ears followed the last note until it was gone. Until the only thing left to do was light another cigarette and wait for that sound:

Sh-shwup—sh-shwup—sh-shwup—sh-shwup...

Chapter 30

Over the next few months, the Calhoun family slowly returned to a robotic semblance of its old routine. Edward had to buckle down hard with his Algebra homework to catch up on the assignments he had missed, and Shay tentatively approached her father to remind him about her trumpet lessons. Nick was withdrawn and quiet, but went to school without argument. After a long drinking spell, Doc finally returned to work with King's quartet, but bookings were scarce. Overall, there were two noticeable changes: Pearl's absence left a painful silence in the apartment. And Calvin Bailey began spending nearly all of his time there.

After thinking things over for weeks, Doc finally called everyone together in the living room. He avoided Calvin's eyes and came right to the point.

"Edward. You got any ties here, son? I mean *real* ties?"

"What'chu mean, Daddy?" Edward asked.

"I wanna know how you'd feel about moving—for about six or eight months."

"Well... movin' where?"

"Don't answer a question with a question. Do you have any ties that'd make you miserable to leave? Like a girlfriend? And what about graduation? This would mean you missing graduation with all your friends."

Edward shrugged and gazed at the floor. "In case you didn't notice, I ain't been much in the mood for dates lately," he said softly. "And school's school. Wherever we go."

Doc nodded and looked over at Shay. "What about you, baby?"

Shay fidgeted with a patch on the knee of her pedal-pushers and dropped a few tears. "I just miss Mama. I don't care what happens to me."

Doc stretched out his arms. "Come here, baby."

Shay collapsed on his lap, an adolescent tangle of bony arms and long legs, and sniffled softly. "I don't care where we go, Daddy. Just don't die, okay?"

Nick was sitting on the sofa with Sylvester sprawled across his lap, belly up and sound asleep. "Well, I ain't movin'," he said, scowling.

"And you and Uncle Calvin need to quit smokin' them cigarettes, Daddy, or else you *both* gon' die. That's what the *general* said."

"You move where *we* move, boy. And you're talkin' about the *surgeon* general, aren't you? Hell, he doesn't even know me! And Shay?" He handed her his handkerchief. "I am *not* dyin', baby. I'm too grouchy to die. God'd take one look at me and throw me back."

Shay managed a slight smile and then wiped her nose.

"But why we gotta move, Daddy?" Nick asked. "And where are we movin' to?"

Doc shook his head. "Cassius Clay in miniature. Mouth always movin'."

Nick corrected him quietly. "Muhammad Ali, Daddy. He ain't Cassius Clay no more."

"*Isn't*, not ain't. And it's *any*more, not no more. And we're moving to—Paris."

Calvin spoke up for the first time. "Paris? As in—*France?*"

"It's not as crazy as it sounds," Doc said. "Jazz is red hot in Europe right now, and Paris is the jazz capital over there. King booked the band for a full six-month gig, alternating between these three clubs in Paris. He made all the arrangements, even a cottage for us to live in. Now, for one thing, the bread's too good to pass up. But really, the best thing about it is the change." He sighed. "Look at me, Edward. None of us is ever gonna forget Mama, but you know what? She wouldn't want us cryin' forever. She'd want us to try to be happy."

"I know. But we don't speak French, Daddy. We won't know what anybody's sayin'."

"We could learn French," Shay said.

"And a lot of folks speak English over there," Doc said. "But we *will* have to learn French—all of us. And maybe you won't butcher it up the way you do English."

"Wait a minute," Calvin interjected. "Only six months? You said a six-month gig, right?"

Doc stared at him. "Uh, why don't you kids go outside so Calvin and I can talk."

Nick slid out from under the sleeping cat and stood up. "What about my Mama?"

"We're gonna work that out," Doc said. "But right now I need to talk to Calvin."

"Come on," Edward said. "Let's go to the store. You too, Shay. I'll get us all a Coke."

Nick shot Calvin a pleading look, and then followed Edward out.

With the children gone, all that was left was an uncomfortable silence. Finally, Calvin murmured, "Please... please don't take that boy so far away from me."

"Calvin, I've gotta go where the work is, man. You know that."

"Then let him stay with me. I'll take care of him."

"Calvin! I *raised* that boy since the day he was born. I'm the only Daddy he ever knew."

"I know that. And I ain't got no right tryin' to take him now. It's just—"

"Just what?"

"He's the only blood relative I got. Look, I know you and Pearl always wondered why I ain't showed up sooner. And there's sump'm I should'a told you a long time ago, but—"

"Calvin, if you got sump'm to say, just say it, man."

"Okay, okay. Look, I got no excuse for not showin' up sooner in the boy's life. I'm carryin' a lot'a guilt for that, and, well, for Joe, too."

"For Joe? I'm not followin' you, man."

"Look, I did some things to him—to Joe. I was pretty violent back then, so I can't blame him for runnin' away. He probably thought I'd kill him next time."

Doc sighed. "I'm sorry you feel guilty, Calvin, but whatever happened between you and your brother when you were kids has got nothing to do with me. And as for Nick—"

"Yeah, it does, Doc. It's all tied together. It should'a been *me* takin' care of that boy, but—well—I was in prison. I was innocent, I swear, but I was still locked up."

"I'm really sorry to hear that, man. What for?"

"Well... murder," he said, "but let me explain. See, Joe ran off and everybody thought he was dead, so they convicted me for killin' him 'cause I was always beatin' on him. That's how come I ain't never been back to Mississippi. Nothin' but bad memories and a bad reputation."

A look of surprise crossed Doc's face. "Mississippi? Joe always said he was from New Orleans. But wait— He must'a lived in New Orleans—at least for a while."

"Why you say that?"

"Somebody from New Orleans contacted us after Joe passed. Said he was a friend and he was concerned about Nick. But never mind that... So Joe was from Mississippi. What part?"

"Just outside Natchez on one of them work farms. Daddy was a sharecropper, so all we had was a little raggedy house. Out there off Highway 61."

Doc was about to light a fresh cigarette, but his thumb froze on the lighter wheel as his gaze shifted to Calvin. "Highway 61?"

"Yeah, why?"

Doc finally lit the cigarette. Inside the silence that stretched between himself and Calvin he could hear the distant echo of Robert Johnson's guitar.

Calvin narrowed his eyes at him. "So—which one?"

"Which one what?"

"Which one of us you figure sold his soul? That's what you thinkin'. Was it Joe—or me?"

"A man can't sell his soul, man. That's nothin' but an old superstitious drinkin' song."

Calvin stared at him blankly. "You think so, huh?"

"Let's get back to the subject of Nick."

Calvin nodded. "Look, I just don't wanna lose him, that's all."

"Calvin, I'm sorry your life was so tough, but look—man to man, if you're askin' me for my child, the answer's no. It's gotta be no."

Calvin stared down at his hands. "But you got two other kids—"

"And you got none, so I'm supposed to give you one'a mine? Let's make that *hell* no!"

Calvin was about to answer, but Doc nodded in the direction of the doorway. Nick was standing there staring at him.

"Daddy?" Nick said softly, "I wanna say sump'm."

Calvin and Doc exchanged a worried look. "Boy, how long have you been standin' there?"

"Only a minute."

Doc sighed. "Okay. Sit down and tell me what's on your mind."

"Could you leave, Uncle Calvin?" Nick said. "I gotta talk to Daddy alone for a minute."

Calvin blinked at Doc and shrugged. "Okay, Nick. Guess I'll—go for a walk or sump'm."

Nick sat down and watched Doc crush his half-smoked cigarette in the ashtray. "I can't leave, Daddy," he said simply. "I can't leave Mama and I can't leave Uncle Calvin. They'll be all alone without me. And what about Sylvester? Sylvester can't go to no Paris!"

Doc smiled. "Okay, look, Nick. Calvin is a full-grown man. He'll be okay. And Sylvester *can* go to Paris. There *are* cats in France, you know. Now, as for your Mama—" He paused and chose his words carefully. "She's got all those doctors and nurse-friends takin' care of her."

Nick shook his head. "But I'm her blood. You know how important *blood* is? I'm blood to Uncle Calvin too. He needs me."

"Well, Nick—here's my problem. If I don't go with the band, then I'm out'a work. I'll have to go on auditions, and that can take weeks. What are we all supposed to eat in the meantime?"

"No, Daddy, you don't get it. *You* can go. I just can't go. Not to no *Paris*."

"So what are you sayin'? You don't wanna be a member of our family anymore?"

"I ain't sayin' that! I just think— See, sometimes when bad things happen, it makes you have to grow up real fast, that's all. I gotta start growin' up, Daddy. I got responsibilities, man."

Doc hid his smile and nodded. "Well, okay, Nick, but you're not old enough to work."

"I got me a job with Mr. Goldstein."

"Come on, boy! I'm talkin' about a full-time job. Mr. Goldstein keeps you in pocket money, and that's not enough to live on. You know that! Besides, you can't live by yourself."

Nick's far-fetched plan spilled out in a frantic rush of words: "Me and Sylvester can live with Uncle Calvin. I heard him say so. And I'ma have a job, awright, 'cause I'll be makin' a record in the studio! Then all I gotta do is get the deejays to play it, and I'll get me some money. I aready met Mr. Leadbelly and Ravishin' Ray, Daddy. I *know* they'll play my record. Then I can help Uncle Calvin pay the rent and buy Mama some dresses and stuff." He stopped and gazed sadly at Doc. "She ain't got no dresses, Daddy. Did you know that? Only nightgowns."

"Okay, look," Doc said, rubbing his temples. "I know you think you got this all figured out, but you need to be realistic about this record business. Just 'cause you met a couple'a deejays does *not* mean you'll have an instant hit record. This is a damn hard business, boy. I know."

Nick tightened his lips in a stubborn line. "I could *try*. And Uncle Calvin's gonna help me."

"Nick, you know Calvin's out of town a lot and he can't always take you with him. And what about Sylvester? If you go off with Calvin, then who's gonna take care of Sylvester?"

"Miss Rose *loves* me and Sylvester, Daddy. She'll take care of us when Calvin's gone."

"Uh, huh. And her kids, and your Mama, and everybody else in Harlem, I suppose."

"No, *I'll* take care'a Mama. See, Daddy, them doctors and nurses ain't like—*real* friends to Mama. I told 'em a hundred times she don't like that ol' boiled rice stuff for supper, but they still give it to her anyway. She likes mashed potatoes, like me. If they was *really* her friends, they'd remember and give her mashed potatoes and extra gravy. Wouldn't they?"

Doc sighed again. "I guess so, Nick. So you wanna stay here to remind 'em, huh? But wouldn't you miss Edward and Shay? And me? Have you given that any thought?"

Nick's lower lip quivered. "Well—" After a pause, he brightened. "I know! Me and Uncle Calvin can stay here in the apartment till you come back. And you can go for six months and save up all your money, Daddy. You *said* six months, right?"

Doc rubbed his chin thoughtfully. "You know what, Nick? That really isn't a bad idea. I can't believe I didn't think of it. Instead of lettin' the apartment go, Calvin could just sublet it. I mean, he *is* family, so it wouldn't be like leaving you with some stranger— Okay, look. I'm not promising anything, but let me talk to Miss Rose and Calvin about it."

≈∞≈

Three weeks of hurried arrangements went by too fast. Nick sat staring sadly at Shay and Edward, who were at the front window waiting to catch sight of King's station wagon.

Doc stepped out of his bedroom and adjusted his necktie. "Edward, Shay—you two take your bags downstairs and wait for King on the stoop. I need to talk to Nick and Calvin a minute."

Shay hesitated. "Well, uh, Nick's comin' down to say goodbye to us too, isn't he?"

"Yes, of course. We'll all be down in a minute."

"Yes, sir."

Nick and Calvin followed Doc into the kitchen. After putting on his jacket, Doc reached into the inside pocket and pulled out a white unsealed envelope. Handing it to Calvin, he said, "This is a check for Nick and a deposit slip. He gets one on his birthday and one at Christmas, but with all that happened this year, I just never got around to putting this one into the account."

"Who's it from, Daddy?" Nick asked.

"It's from a man named Adam Delavigné. He lives in New Orleans, and he must've been a good friend of Joe's. He's the one I told you about, Calvin. We got the first letter from him when Nick was just a baby. He'd followed the story about Joe in the newspapers and magazines, and he wanted to help. I don't know how he located us, but he started sendin' these checks for a college fund." Doc fell silent for a moment. "We had to borrow a little money from it a while back, but we replaced it as soon as we could, so it's all there—every dime. It ain't millions, but it'll help when Nick's ready for college."

Nick frowned. "You mean I can't use it for nothin' else, Daddy?"

"No." He pressed his index finger against the center of Nick's forehead. "It's a deposits-only account. I'm the only one who can withdraw that money and it stays in the bank until you're ready for college. And you're old enough to write Mr. Delavigné a thank-you letter too."

"I will. But Daddy, you know Mama needs some dresses—"

The sound of a horn blast from downstairs interrupted him. Doc rubbed Nick's head and walked to the door. "No more time for backtalk, boy. It's time to go."

Nick froze. "Wait—Daddy—wait a minute," he stammered.

Doc turned around and saw Nick's eyes reddening. "Hey, Calvin," he called, "Go on down and tell King we'll be right there, would you?"

He waited until Calvin's footsteps died away, and then reached for Nick's hand. "Come here a minute, boy. I want to show you sump'm." He led Nick down the hallway, then handed him his handkerchief and knelt down on one knee near his bedroom door. "See that?" he said softly, pointing at the night-light.

Nick wiped his nose and nodded. "Yes, sir."

"Well, for centuries, when a loved one went away, the family kept a candle or some kind'a light in the window to guide 'em back home. Folks did it for soldiers in all the wars too, like a symbol of hope. And that's what this little light meant to your Aunt Pearl. It's not in the window, but she kept it lit so she could always see me come home safe at night." He stopped to clear his throat, and began to stammer. "And it—helped her through some things she was—"

Nick touched his face. "It's okay, Daddy," he whispered. "You could cry. I won't tell nobody. I *promise*."

Doc enfolded him tightly in his arms for a long time as he fought for emotional control. "Six months, Nick," he whispered. "You keep this little light on so me and Shay and Edward can find our way back home to you, okay?"

"Yes, sir," Nick croaked, wiping his nose again.

Doc stood up and grinned as he rubbed his eyes. "Aw, hell, now I gotta wash my face! You got a clean handkerchief I can take? You got mine all snotty and my other ones are packed."

Nick ran to his room for the handkerchief and brought it to Doc in the bathroom. "We're all through cryin' now, right, Daddy?"

"Right." Doc dried his face with a towel, then folded the handkerchief and smiled as he put it in his pocket. "And we better get goin'. Us two crybabies are holdin' everybody up."

By the time they stepped outside, Shay and Edward were waiting in the station wagon and King was pacing the sidewalk and smoking a cigarette. Dressed in a purple shark-skin suit, he was sporting a new goatee, a black beret, sunglasses, and his usual Errol Flynn grin. "Hey, baby!" he called, extending his arms. "Dig my new threads?"

"Oh, Lord," Doc groaned. "A goatee? So what're you? The Caucasian Dizzy Gillespie?"

"You dig me, Doctor Calhoun! You know they *adore* Birks in Paree, baby!" King grinned down at Nick. "Hey, shortie! Skin me! You been growin', huh? Thought you were gonna be a runt all your life, but you're gettin' to be a long, tall alley cat, just like Sylvester!"

"You sure are sharp, Mr. King!" Nick said. "Hey, could I get a suit like that, Daddy?"

"Like *that*?" Doc grinned. "Better ask Calvin about that. He's in charge of suits now."

Calvin rolled his eyes. "Thanks, man. We'll talk about that later, Nick."

Doc peered into the rear section of the wagon. "Damn, King! You think this ride'll roll?"

"Hell, I don't even have my drums back there, man. Sure it'll roll."

"Well, where *are* your drums, now that you mention it?"

"Shipped ahead with the equipment. What the hell you think this is? The chitlin circuit?"

"And what about the wagon?"

"My brother's pickin' it up at the airport tomorrow, and he can have it! I know your trip is temporary, but man, Paris is where I belong. I'm ready to parlez and sight-see, dig? Nothin' but jazz and cosmopolitan French frails with wavy frames! Ooh-la-la!"

"I need to say goodbye to my boy," Doc laughed. "So evaporate, *s'il vous plait.*"

Nick leaped into his arms. "I'll keep the night-light on all the time."

"You do that, Nick. I'm countin' on you," Doc said. "Hey! I bet by the time we get back, you'll be a big singin' star. And you *better* be a straight-A student too. That means do your homework and do what Calvin and Miss Rose tell you to do. Take care of Sylvester and be sure to clean up after him. And keep after those nurses about your Mama's mashed potatoes."

Nick grinned. "And gravy! You forgot!"

Doc messed up Nick's hair and laughed. "Okay, gravy too."

Edward leaned out the car window. "Hey, Nick, be sure to send us your record when it's done. I might be needin' a laugh by that time."

"Bye, Edward. Bye, Shay. You guys write me, okay?"

"You know Edward won't," Shay said. "He's gonna be too busy chasing those French girls around. But I'll write. I'ma miss you, little squirt—believe it or not."

Doc slid into the passenger seat and shut the door. "Six months, Nick. I love you, okay?"

"Me too," Nick squeaked. He stepped back and waved until the station wagon made the turn onto Lenox Avenue and disappeared.

Calvin stepped over and patted Nick's shoulder. "I know it's tough sayin' goodbye. But six months goes by faster than you think. And you know what? You gotta start practicin' that song I showed you, 'cause we gotta get into that studio so we'll be ready for our big trip to L.A., okay?"

Nick gulped and rubbed his eyes. "Okay. So I'm *really* gonna sing on a record?"

Calvin grinned and raised his right hand. "I swear 'fo God and three other white folks."

"Uncle Calvin. You think maybe I could use Daddy's name—Bluestone—on my record?"

Calvin stared at him for a long moment, then sighed. "It's your record, boy."

≈∞≈

After moving his belongings into the Calhoun apartment, Calvin took Nick to the Quarter Note Studio on 125th Street to go over the song with a piano player named Ron Dayton.

They walked in just as Dayton was stepping out of one of the soundproof rooms. "What's happenin', Calvin? Guess this short brutha must be Nick, huh? How ya doin', man? I'm Ron."

"Hullo," Nick said bashfully as he shook Ron's hand.

"Look, Ron," Calvin said, "Is this a good time to go over that song?"

Ron poured a cup of coffee and nodded. "Perfect timing. My next session doesn't start for an hour, so we can run through the song a few times. Grab some coffee and follow me."

He led Nick and Calvin into a room containing a piano and several stools. "This is the vocal rehearsal room. So, Calvin, you got some kind'a rough sheet music?"

Calvin pulled the chart from his satchel. "It's called 'When I Make My Baby Smile.'"

"Nice title. Let me run it down a couple of times and see what I can do with it."

Nick was checking the edges of his slicked-down hair, and Calvin laughed. "Boy, you could be a criminal facin' a firing squad, and all you'd be worryin' about would be that hair."

"But do my hair look *good*, Uncle Calvin?" Nick whispered. "My edges?"

"It's *does*. *Does* my hair look good, not *do* my hair look good. And yeah," he said, grinning, "you look clean as a jitterbug on his way out'a Sugar Ray's barber shop."

Nick stared at him with a bewildered expression. "Huh?"

Calvin laughed. "Before your time, boy. Your hair looks fine."

"Good lyrics for his age," Ron said. "Okay, Nick. Let's try it. The intro goes like this… and you come in right here. Got it?"

Nick nodded and began to sing. Then suddenly, Ron stopped to experiment with the chords.

"Nick, see if you can hit this note."

Nick hit the note with ease and Ron smiled. "Oh, yeah. This is the key."

This time, Nick closed his eyes and snapped his fingers as he sang.

Tellin' jokes and secrets / walkin' in the rain
Since I met my pretty baby / I'll never be the same…

After running through the song a few times, Nick saw several faces peeking in at him through the partially open door. He grinned and then jumped down off his stool to take a bow.

Calvin laughed. "What a ham! Okay, Ron, you available next Tuesday?"

"I *will* be. And I'll kill you if you hire anybody else! See you next Tuesday, Nick!"

"Thanks, Mr. Ron!"

As they headed to the exit, Nick said, "Uncle Calvin? When we go to California, you think you could introduce me to somebody? 'Cause I'm pretty sure she lives out there."

Calvin looked at him curiously. "Who?"

Nick grinned bashfully and squeezed his eyes shut. "Mary Wilson."

"Mary Wilson? You ain't talkin' about the Mary Wilson that sings with the Supremes?"

"I thought you might know her, Uncle Calvin. I sure would like to meet *her*."

"Nick, you're eleven years old. And Mary Wilson's a grown woman."

"I know. And *fine*, too."

Calvin chuckled. "Tell you what, Romeo. How 'bout we get the record cut first. And then you can worry about gettin' Mary Wilson to fall in love with you later."

Chapter 31

The next few months were a series of firsts for Nick—his first recording date, his first flight in a jet, and his first trip to Los Angeles. But the most important first was the signing of his first contract with the Atlantic label. He almost didn't notice that six months had turned into a year.

He was returning with Calvin from a promotional trip through the tri-state area, and all he could think about was his reunion with Sylvester. As Calvin unlocked the front door and began dragging the bags inside, Nick ran across the hall and knocked on Rose's door.

"It's me, Miss Rose! Nick! We're back."

"Hey!" Calvin called softly. "Don't be wakin' folks up at this hour! The cat can wait—"

But Rose was already stepping into the hallway, tying her bathrobe. She looked sleepy, with pink hair curlers dangling from her head, but she smiled broadly at Nick and then hugged him. "Oh, baby, it's so good to see you back safe! Did you knock 'em dead, Killer?"

"I ain't killed nobody, Miss Rose!" Nick laughed. "Hey, where's Sylvester?"

"Well, here he is under my feet, as usual. Take him on home. I know you missed him."

"Hi, Sylvester!" Nick said, picking up the cat. "Hey, you got fat! Were you a good boy?"

"Thanks for keepin' the cat, Rose," Calvin said. "We're takin' you to breakfast tomorrow. Hey, Nick, come on. Get on in here and you and the cat can talk your heads off."

As Calvin shut the door, the phone rang. He hurried to the bedroom to answer it. "Hello?"

"Calvin? That you, man?"

"Doc? Hey, man! How you doin'?" He reached into his pocket for his cigarettes.

"We're all fine. Look, I hope you weren't asleep. I know the time difference is a bitch, but I just can't find the time to call when it's probably good for you. Is Nick asleep?"

"No, we just got in from a quick tri-state hop. Hang on... Hey, Nick! Get in here! Doc's on the phone, callin' from France. And hurry up! Long distance costs a fortune!"

Nick ran in and grabbed the telephone. "What's jumpin', Daddy?"

"The jumpin' jive, Jackson!" Doc laughed. "What's the happle in the Apple, Scrapple?"

"We're just diggin' the scene, Maybellene!" Nick shouted. "Hey, Daddy, guess what?"

"I bet'cha I can guess. I bet your record's gettin' played a lot on the radio, right?"

"How'd you know?"

"Because I'm holdin' this record called 'When I Make My Baby Smile' by Nick Bluestone right in my hands. I got your letter about it too. But Nick, now it's your turn to guess what."

"What?"

"Shay and Edward told me they've been playin' it out here."

"My record? In Paris?"

"Yes, in Paris. So I know if they're playin' it here, it must be red-hot in the States."

"Daddy wanna know is my record red-hot, Uncle Calvin."

"Hotter than red-hot!" Calvin said. "And the rest of the album's nearly finished!"

Doc laughed. "Did he say a whole album?"

"Yes, sir! I did six songs awready! And I'm fixin' to be on the Ed Sullivan Show too!"

"Ed Sullivan? Well, that's big-time, boy! That record must be sellin' like crazy!"

"It is! And I got girls writin' me letters and everything. I'm a star now, Daddy!"

Calvin rolled his eyes and laughed. "Gimme the phone a minute, Mr. Star. Hey, Doc?"

"Goddamn, Calvin!" Doc said. "That record's really selling, huh?"

"Only problem now is his big head. It wasn't so big when he was just Mr. Box Man."

Doc laughed. "I still can't believe you got him signed to Atlantic Records!"

"Well, I been knowin' their A&R man a long time, and he owed me one. But when he heard the demo, I saw them dollar signs in his eyes. Nick's voice and personality got him the deal. Best part is I'm the main promotion man on the project, so I can keep my eye on Nick."

"Yeah, but how's he doin' in school? Did he bring up that D from last semester?"

"Sure did. He brought it up to a B. I got his teacher to give him assignments for when we're on the road, and it's workin' out okay. Then she lets him make up his tests when he gets back."

"Aww, man, that's great. And this Ed Sullivan business—on the level?"

"It looks pretty definite. We'll let you know as soon as we find out."

"Well, I'm glad things are goin' so well for him. Takes his mind off all the bad times." Doc's tone deepened. "And maybe it'll take the sting out'a what I called about."

Calvin looked down at Nick and rubbed his head affectionately. "What's that?"

Doc sighed. "You know that last batch of mail you forwarded to us? Well, there was a letter in there—from the draft board. They want Edward back in the States for his physical."

"Oh… " Calvin's voice faded as he realized the full impact of what Doc had said. "That's right. He's eighteen now. So does that mean—what I think it means?"

"It means we're not coming back. I'm not sendin' my son to Vietnam, Calvin."

"Whoa, wait a minute, Doc. That's a pretty serious decision—"

"That's why Edward and I sat up all night talkin', so we could make the *right* decision. Look, I keep up with the American papers, Calvin, and I know war propaganda when I read it. But France already fought the Vietnamese, so I'm gettin' a whole different take on things over here. My friend Jacques fought over there in '52, and he says the U.S. is a damn fool to mess with Vietnam. He told me the French newspapers were full of the same kind'a overconfident bullshit when they first sent troops over there in '45. And that war dragged on for nine years. Then the government refused to admit they got their asses handed to 'em! Called it a 'ceasefire' to save face. So now, every time I read those interviews in the *Times* with McNamara doin' all his shit-talkin', that old saying pops into my head. You know—the one about how history repeats itself. So maaan, I'll be *goddamned* if I send my boy over there. Folks back home can call me unpatriotic if they want to, but this is a whole other kind'a war than the one I was in."

"I didn't know you were in the service," Calvin said quietly. "Korea?"

"World War Two, when the army was still segregated. And you didn't know about it because I don't talk about it… Look, Calvin, right or wrong, I'm not sendin' my son to die for some shit that doesn't even make sense. Let McNamara and those cats send *their* sons."

Calvin smiled weakly at Nick. "I understand, man. But what do we do about—ya know."

"Look, man. I know how you feel about Nick, but we're pretty settled here. Shay loves her school, and the band's gettin' so much work, we have to turn some gigs down. And everything Miles and all those cats told me about France is true. I made more white friends since I've been here than I made in my whole life in the States. Then this thing with Edward being drafted— I've got no choice but to send for Nick. He belongs with his family, Calvin."

Out of a long silence, Calvin said, "Well—when's that supposed to happen?"

"Well, the record takin' off and the Ed Sullivan Show are pretty big commitments, so I guess we'll have to wait. But don't mention this business about Edward and Vietnam. I don't want to worry him. I'll just tell him we're—delayed. How do you think he'll take that?"

"Guess you'll have to ask him."

Doc sighed. "Okay. Put him on."

Calvin handed the receiver to Nick, who gave him a curious look.

"Hi, Daddy... Mm-hmm." His smile faded. "Oh. Yes, sir..."

Calvin sat on the edge of the bed staring at the floor until Nick said his goodbyes to Doc. "I love you too, Daddy... I will. I'll keep the light on. Okay... Okay, bye."

When Nick hung up he was on the verge of tears. "Daddy said—six more months."

"I know, son, and I'm sorry. But don't worry. The time'll go real fast. Remember we got that Ed Sullivan Show to do, and then we'll be hittin' the road for another little tour."

Nick looked up. "Another tour? For how long?"

"Well, if you can follow up this record with another hit, who knows? And the time's gonna fly so fast—you'll be seein' your Daddy and Shay and Edward before you know it."

≈∞≈

Nick and Calvin walked quietly along 53rd Street until they reached the corner of Broadway. They stopped, and Nick stared up at the marquee—*CBS TV, Studio 50*. His heart began to thump.

"Well, boy," Calvin said, "this is it."

"Yes, sir," Nick murmured softly.

"Aww, come on, now. Ain't nothin' to be nervous about."

"Yes, it is, Uncle Calvin! What if I—fall down or sump'm?"

Calvin laughed. "Fall down?"

"My legs feel like two spaghetti noodles!"

"Boy, you ain't gonna fall down. Remember how scared you were when you sang in Philadelphia? Soon as you sang that first line, you weren't nervous anymore. Remember that?"

"I guess so."

"Well, this ain't gonna be *that* different. And you been rehearsin' every day for weeks. Shoot. You could do this with your eyes shut, boy. Now come on. Let's go in."

They stepped inside and a tall white man greeted them. "Name?"

"Nick Bluestone," Calvin said. "He's here for the Ed Sullivan Show—dress rehearsal."

The man checked the list on his clipboard, and then motioned to a younger man in a loud plaid sports jacket who was rushing past. "Chuck! I got that kid singer here. Nick Bluestone."

The man hurried over and shook Nick's hand. "Hey! So I finally get to meet the kid that Jerry Wexler's so wild about! How ya doin', Nick Bluestone? I'm Chuck Ellis from Atlantic. Hi, Calvin. We met in Pete's office last summer, remember?"

"Oh, yeah," Calvin said. "I remember. So you're like our—liaison with CBS?"

"That's me, at your service, gentlemen." Ellis checked his wristwatch. "Okay, now, if you'll follow me, I'll do my first job, which is to show you around. The band's already here and set up. They're getting a bite to eat, so we have a few minutes before rehearsal starts."

Nick and Calvin followed Ellis around the perimeter of the theater seating area, and then through a door that led backstage. As Nick took it all in, he touched his thumping chest and wondered how old a person had to be to have a heart attack. The backstage area was alive with colors and rushing people until suddenly, a blinding light caused him to blink and cover his eyes. He felt Calvin and Ellis nudging him out toward the light. After a moment, his vision adjusted.

He was standing at center stage. His mouth dropped open as he stared at dozens of camera operators and crewmen, all shouting directions at each other and rolling huge television cameras around the perimeter. Unsure of which way he was facing, Nick turned around and saw the drums set up on risers behind him, and then blinked at Calvin. "This ain't gonna be *nothin'* like Philadelphia, Uncle Calvin! I can't sing to them giant cameras! I need some girls to sing to!"

"Well, there'll be girls," Calvin said, glancing at Ellis. "It'll be a live audience, right?"

"Sure!" Ellis said. "And don't worry. You'll be able to see past the cameramen. And believe me, there'll be plenty of girls with the way your record's climbing the charts. Oh, wait… here comes Tim. Nick, Calvin— I want you to meet the show's director, Tim Kiley."

As the director shook hands with Calvin, Nick began to feel dizzy, then nauseous. "Uncle Calvin?" he croaked. But Calvin was talking, and Nick could tell that he hadn't heard him. He pulled at his uncle's sleeve. "Please—"

"Uh, wait a minute, Mr. Kiley," Calvin said, leaning over Nick. "Boy? You okay?"

"I think… I think I'ma—"

Ellis steered Nick offstage and into a washroom. "It's okay, kid. Happens all the time."

Before Nick knew what was happening, he was throwing up into an empty mop pail near the door and Ellis was handing him a cool cloth for his face. When Nick saw Calvin's worried expression, he broke into a grin. "Don't worry, Uncle Calvin. I feel better now!"

Ellis laughed. "That'a boy! Look, I'll go get you a soft drink. The bubbles might settle that stomach. Then you think you'll feel okay to rehearse?"

"Yes, sir. I think so."

After Ellis returned, Nick took a few sips of soda and they headed back to the stage. The director smiled, patted Nick on the back and then began rattling off a litany of instructions.

"And the most important thing, Nick—try to sing directly to this center camera when the red light goes on. That's your close-up, so smile like it's your best girlfriend and you'll do fine."

Nick nodded, terrified that he would forget something—or everything. But when the drummer counted off the intro to his song, he hit his mark and sang on cue. After a few run-throughs, the director took him to the makeup department, where he met Ed Sullivan.

The next hour passed in a blur, and then Ellis came into the dressing room to round up the band members. "I'll be back for you in five minutes, Nick. Just take the time to relax, okay?"

"Yes, sir, Mr. Ellis."

Nick rummaged in his bag for his transistor radio, and then adjusted the dial until he heard Smokey Robinson singing *Shop Around.* "Uncle Calvin?"

Calvin looked up from his copy of *Billboard.* "Yeah, boy?"

"Does my hair look okay?"

Calvin nodded. "Yup."

"But does it look real, real good, Uncle Calvin? Like I went to Sugar Ray's barber shop?"

Calvin grinned. "Like a jitterbug on his way to the Savoy on kitchen-mechanics night."

Nick stared at him with a bewildered expression. "That's good, right?"

"That's *real* good. Hey, you sure you awright, boy? Them spaghetti legs okay now?"

Nick rolled his eyes. "Yes, sir. And I ain't gonna throw up again."

"Well, that's some good news."

Nick inspected his new baby-blue suit in the mirror; the jacket felt hot, but the sleeves were the perfect length to show off his father's aquamarine cuff links.

"Those sure are nice links," Calvin said quietly. "Look custom-made to me."

"Yes, sir. Real gold too. That's what Daddy told me." Nick straightened his white bow-tie and sighed. "Well, I guess I'm ready now... Hey, Uncle Calvin?"

"Yeah, boy?"

"How come everybody keeps on tellin' me to break my leg? Even Mr. Sullivan said it."

"Oh, that's just show business talk, Nick. It just means good luck."

"That's what I figured," he said as he stared at his own reflection in the mirror. "Uncle Calvin, it's dumb, but I feel kind'a—sad. I mean, I feel happy, but sad too. That's dumb, huh?"

"No. It ain't dumb. But why you think you feel sad?"

"Well... I just miss Daddy and Shay and Edward... and Mama and Aunt Pearl too."

"I know. But you still got me. And your Aunt Pearl's watchin' from heaven. *And* I'ma be doin' that long distance call to Paris when you go on so they can hear you over the phone."

Nick smiled. "Make sure they hear all my applause, Uncle Calvin. Don't hang up too soon."

"What a ham! Okay, I'll make sure they hear all the applause."

"Thanks, Uncle Calvin."

"So you feel better? That sad feelin' gone now?"

"I guess so. But I just wish—"

Before Nick could finish, there was a knock, and Chuck Ellis hurried in with the makeup lady. "Okay, Mrs. Steinberg's gonna touch up that face one more time, and then you're on!"

"Yes, sir." Nick shut his eyes as Mrs. Steinberg patted his face with the powder puff.

"Okay, handsome!" she said. "You go break a leg and knock 'em dead!"

Nick grinned. "Okay, Miz Steinberg. I'ma break my leg—and kill everybody!"

"Such a comedian, this one!" Mrs. Steinberg cackled. "Shecky Greene should be so funny!"

"Bye, Miz Steinberg," Nick called over his shoulder. "Thanks for the powder!"

Calvin shook his head as he guided him out the door. "Come on, Shecky."

When Nick returned to the stage, the curtains were closed but he could hear the audience murmuring. "There's your mark," Kiley whispered. "Lights, curtain, and watch for my signal."

A drop of perspiration rolled down Nick's face as the lead-in music played. Ed Sullivan's familiar voice boomed through the theater, and Nick knew that his life was about to change.

And now we have for you Atlantic Records' newest young recording
star—Nick Bluestone!

The curtain opened, the lights blazed on, and the drummer kicked off
the intro to "When I Make My Baby Smile." Nick could barely hear the
band over the girls' squeals from the audience. The center camera was
moving toward him and the red light came on. *Close-up.* He flashed the
smile he had been saving for Mary Wilson in case he ever met her; then
he spun into his best dance step, and the squeals rolled into an earsplitting
echo of screams.

Chapter 32

August 1965

Nick woke up abruptly, and sat up. "What happened? What was that—
noise?"

"Which noise?" Calvin asked. "The bump we just hit or you singin'
in your sleep?"

Nick grinned. "I was singin' in my sleep?"

"Yup. And it was *pitiful*. Guess you didn't wanna upstage your
girlfriend on the radio."

"Yeah, that's Mary, Uncle Calvin. You hear Mary singin' that
background?"

"I hear her. And Florence too. And even that Diana somebody-or-
other. But mostly I heard your voice crack. You ain't turnin' baritone on
me, are you, boy?"

"Man! Did my voice really crack?"

"Yeah. We'll just adjust the keys of your songs, that's all... Damn!
Another bump!"

"Why so many bumps?"

"Construction work on the highway. You slept through the worst of it
though."

"How many cities we been to on this trip, Uncle Calvin?"

"At least ten. We 'bout to roll into L.A. now. You slept right through
Las Vegas."

Nick scowled. "Aww, man! I wanted to see that giant cowboy all lit up."

"I tried to wake you up! We'll see it on the way back."

"It sure was faster when we flew on the airplane," Nick said, yawning. "But it's—"

Calvin cut him off. "Hush! What did that deejay just say? Turn up the
radio, Nick."

Nick turned up the volume. The deejay was obviously off-script, and
talking rapidly:

... The one thing we know is that it all started with that arrest in Watts yesterday. Callers from the area report that it was another case of police brutality that went too far. So we're asking our listeners to please steer clear of the Watts area... They're calling it a riot now. Confirmation of several blocks burning and... we're getting calls saying that the police are in their riot gear. So if you don't live in Watts, the best thing to do is stay away from the area... Okay, we're getting more information and we'll have an update for you shortly. Stay tuned...

Then—a moment of dead air, followed by a Doublemint Gum commercial.

"Ain't that where Jimmy lives?" Nick asked softly. "In Watts?"

"Yeah, so we'll have to stay someplace else. I ain't takin' you into that mess."

"Is Dr. King there, Uncle Calvin?"

"Naw. He's handlin' all that business down south, remember?"

"Mm-hmm." Nick slid down in his seat and crossed his arms. "That's where they got all them big dogs—and fire hoses. And the people got all beat up on that bridge. I sure hope they don't try to cross that stupid bridge again, Uncle Calvin."

"It's the Edmund Pettus Bridge. Get the name right, boy. And they crossed it for a reason."

Nick frowned. "What reason? They just let them dogs chew on 'em and can't nobody fight back or they throw 'em in jail! Wait! You think they got some'a them dogs in Watts too?"

"We ain't goin' anywhere near any police dogs, Nick. Now hush, here comes another report so let's find out what—" Calvin stopped in mid-sentence and turned off the radio.

Nick looked over at him. "Why'd you turn it off?"

"See that roadblock up ahead? Now listen to me. We gotta stop and you need to stay quiet about where we goin', hear me? Keep that long-playin' mouth a'yours shut for once and let me do the talkin'."

Nick stared fearfully at the flashing red lights on the patrol cars. "Yes, sir."

The car rolled to a stop, and two highway patrolmen approached the car. One came to the passenger door, and the other to the driver's side. Placing one hand on his pistol, the patrolman leaned down and stared at Calvin through a pair of dark glasses. "Out of the vehicle."

Calvin opened the door, but Nick grabbed his arm. "No, Uncle Calvin! Don't get out!"

"Stay in the car, Nick," Calvin said. "Everything's gonna be okay."

"No! They might have one'a them big dogs in that car!"

Calvin gave him a hard look. "Ain't no dogs, so stop that back-sass and do what I tell you!"

The second Calvin stepped out, the patrolmen pushed him over the hood of the car.

"No!" Nick yelled. "What're you doin' to him?"

Calvin glared at Nick through the windshield. "Stay in the car!" he shouted. "I'm okay."

One of the patrolmen pushed Calvin's face back down on the hood as his partner fished out the wallet from his trousers pocket. After yanking out the wallet's contents and tossing it to the ground, he studied the driver's license, then leaned down. "So you're Calvin Bailey from New York. You're a real long way from home, Calvin Bailey. Where are you headed?"

"Los Angeles. I got business there."

"You got *business* there?" His voice was laced with sarcasm. "What kind'a business? You one'a those Black Muslim troublemakers? Comin' out to Watts to stir up more trouble?"

Calvin raised his head to look at the officer. "No, I'm not tryin' to stir up any trouble."

"Keep your head down! You eyeball me again and I'll cuff you, you understand?"

"Yeah."

The officer thumped Calvin's temple with his knuckle. "Try yes, *sir*," he barked.

Calvin's control was stretched to the breaking point, but he caught himself just in time and forced a response through his teeth. "Yes, sir."

"Okay. So what business you got in L.A. anyway? You a thief or something, Calvin?"

"No, sir. I'm in the music business."

"The music business? Come on, Calvin, try the truth. You a dope dealer or what?"

Suddenly, Nick jumped out of the car, waving one of his records in the air. "You shut-up! My uncle ain't no dope dealer! He *is* in the music business! He's promotin' my record and—"

"Nick!" Calvin yelled. "Get back in the car—right now!"

The officer waved his hand. "No, it's okay, let me see what the boy's got here." He reached for the record and stared at the label. "Nick Bluestone. So this is *your* record?"

"Yes, sir. I got pictures in the trunk too. And my bio."

"Your *bio*, huh?" the officer snickered. "Well, Nick. I just don't know if I believe you."

"It's my record!" Nick fumed. "I was on the Ed Sullivan Show and everything!"

The officer restraining Calvin stepped back. "Hold on, Ben," he said, nodding. "I saw the kid! Yeah. Damned if it wasn't this kid! He really was on Ed Sullivan a few weeks ago."

"For the second time," Nick snapped. "Look, maybe you better let my uncle go."

"Hush, boy!" Calvin shouted.

The officer's mocking grin hardened into a frown. "Maybe I *better* let your uncle go? You're a real wise guy to be so little. You better *fix* that before you grow up."

Nick swallowed hard. "Yes, sir... How 'bout if I say *please* let my uncle go?"

The officer removed his sunglasses and stared at Nick for a long time with a pair of cold blue eyes, then handed Calvin's driver's license back to him. "You better educate this brat about the way things are, Calvin. And stay away from Watts, you understand?"

Calvin jerked his head in a nod and nudged Nick back into the car.

The officer kicked Calvin's wallet toward the driver's side door, then put his sunglasses back on and smiled sardonically. "Don't forget your wallet, Calvin."

Calvin picked it up and shoved the contents back inside, then eased into the car and started the engine. As they pulled away, Nick stared at Calvin's profile, then turned in his seat.

"Don't look back," Calvin snapped. "You keep your eyes front, hear me?"

"I wanted to *kill* them cops, Uncle Calvin!"

"You ain't killin' anybody, boy," Calvin said, without looking at him.

"But he made you say yes, sir, Uncle Calvin! Like you was a little kid!"

Calvin didn't answer.

"Did they—hurt you?" Nick asked quietly.

"Naw. I'm fine as wine. It's all over."

"Fine as wine? But—ain't you mad?"

Calvin took his time about answering. "I'm a black man, Nick. I *stay* mad."

Nick wiped his eyes and then crossed his arms. "Me too."

"And that's okay. But inside yourself, you gotta stay calm—fine as wine. That's the trick." He glanced at Nick and sighed. "Look, boy. I had a choice back there. I knew who was right and who was wrong, and if I'da lost my temper and bashed that cop's head in, it would'a felt real good—for about ten seconds. 'Cause they were lookin' for any excuse to

throw my ass in the jailhouse—maybe worse. They might'a shot me...
So you think I made the right choice?"

"I guess so." Nick shrugged and stared at the broken lines in the road
ahead. "You think that's why Malcolm X got killed? 'Cause he got mad?"

"Actually, Malcolm was real good at keepin' his cool. You never saw
him get arrested for any kind'a violence, did you? What happened to him
was a lot more complicated than what just happened to me. What
happened to me happens every day. Someday it might even—"

Nick looked up. "It might even *what*?"

"It might—happen to you someday, Nick. I hope not, but it's
possible. And if it does, I want you to make the right choice, that's all."

"But they treated you like a—a criminal, Uncle Calvin! That ain't fair!"

"Life ain't fair. That's why you gotta learn to control yourself. But
look. Things ain't as bad as they use'ta be. Like what I saw my Daddy go
through. Things are startin' to change."

"Things need to hurry up and change faster," Nick said bitterly.

"Things change in they own time. Says so in the bible. There's a time
to live and a time to die. A time for war, a time for peace." Calvin gazed
at him. "How old are you now? Twelve?"

Nick sat up straight. "Yes, sir. But I'll be thirteen in three months."

"There's a time for everything, boy. And for you, it's time to grow up."

Chapter 33

From 1965 to 1968 America was in chaos. Change was long overdue,
and now it was coming in seismic convulsions. Each night Walter
Cronkite reported on the divisive issues of the day—Vietnam, Civil
Rights, and the Women's Movement. When President Johnson
announced that he would not accept his party's nomination for President,
Robert Kennedy embarked on a late but electrifying campaign with a
focus on racial issues, poverty, and ending the Vietnam War.

An entire generation was breaking the constraints of a repressive
society, creating a new counter-culture dedicated to peace and equality
but drawn into a dangerous obsession with hallucinogenic drugs.
Conscientious objectors were burning their draft cards in Times Square,
and Nick was glad that his brother Edward was safe in France.

He wished bitterly that his friend Ernie could have figured out a way
to avoid the draft, but he was gone now—drafted, deployed, and fighting
alongside all the other young soldiers in Vietnam. It frustrated Nick that
no one could ever explain to him what it was they were really fighting
for. Finally, it was Ernie who answered the question for him in a letter
with a Saigon postmark:

... What are we fighting for? Shit, I don't know, man. Every time I fire my weapon, I wonder who I'm shooting—the enemy? Or the folks we're supposed to be helping? I mean who the hell's who? I don't know about these other guys, but I sure didn't expect all this. Seems like <u>every</u> <u>day</u> all I'm doing is fighting for my life. So I guess that's my answer, Nick. I'm fighting for my life.

≈∞≈

Nick began rehearsing a new show that March, which was a welcome distraction from his worries. The show featured a star-studded lineup, and it would be Nick's biggest appearance to date. Advertised as "Soul Under the Stars," the first show was scheduled in Indianapolis, Indiana on the first Wednesday in April. By the time Nick's flight landed that Tuesday, the tickets had completely sold out. He and Calvin arrived at their motel just as the sun went down.

"Hurry, Calvin," Nick said as he dragged his suitcase up the steps.

Calvin dropped his bag and unlocked the door. "Calm down. It ain't that late."

"If she's already asleep, they won't wake her up. Come on, man!"

"Okay, okay, we're in."

Nick dropped his suitcase, dove onto one of the beds and grabbed the telephone. Calvin began unpacking, and saw Nick's reflection in the mirror grinning and giving him a thumbs-up.

"Hilda? Hey, what's happenin', baby? How's that knee treatin' you?... Aw, that's good. Listen, is Mama still awake? Could you hold the phone for her so I can talk to her a minute?... Oh, you were?" He covered the receiver and whispered, "Calvin, she already punched out for the night, but she was waiting for me to call before she left!... Aw, Hilda, you're a livin' doll. You are gonna get *such* a bouquet of roses when I get back to the city!"

Calvin shook his head and laughed. "Hilda's what? About sixty?"

Nick covered the mouthpiece again. "Sixty-two last December. And for your information, she digs it when I flirt with her! She's my girl!"

"Yeah, Hilda and anything else in a skirt. Well, tell her I say hi."

"Okay... Oh, hey, Calvin says hi... What? Really? Hey! Go on wit'cho bad self, Hilda! Hey, Calvin, Hilda got a raise today!"

"Congratulations, Hilda!" Calvin called.

"You hear that? Yeah... Okay, I'll see you next week... Okay, thanks... Hey, Mama! It's me, your healthy brown boy! And I got some big news for you tonight. I mean some *really* cool news, so hang onto Hilda. Okay, I'm here in Indianapolis for this big concert, Mama, and guess who's gonna be on the show with me? Only Wilson Pickett, Booker T and the MGs, the Bar-Kays, and—who else? Oh, yeah, the Staple Singers. But I saved the best for last—the Supremes, Mama! I'm *finally* gonna meet Mary Wilson! And guess what else—"

Calvin grabbed a motel ashtray, then slipped outside and shut the door. Leaning against the rail, he lit a cigarette and stared out at the traffic, hoping its noise would drown out the sound of Nick's one-sided conversation with a mother who couldn't answer him.

≈∞≈

When Calvin stuck his head into the dressing room the next evening, Nick was putting the finishing touches on his afro as he worked out background harmonies with Benny.

Benny played rhythm guitar, and was the most disciplined musician in the band. He was a short, dark-skinned man with a wiry build, a serious disposition, and a conservative wardrobe. No ruffled shirts or psychedelic bell-bottoms for Benny. He was older than the others—about thirty—and he had a settling influence on Nick. It was no surprise that Calvin adored him.

Nick grinned and put down his afro pick. "How's my hair, Uncle Calvin?"

Benny laughed and Calvin groaned. "You and that damn hair. It's perfect. Now get your face out the mirror, boy. I got somebody I want you to meet."

A light-skinned gentleman in a neatly pressed brown suit stepped in beside Calvin and pulled his dark glasses down to the end of his nose to peer at Nick. "I hear you're makin' a lot'a noise on those charts, son! It's good to meet you."

Nick smiled broadly as he grabbed the man's hand. "Jack the Rapper! I finally get to meet the legend! Calvin told me a million stories about you, sir!"

Jack laughed, and his voice dropped to an imperious baritone. "Good work, Calvin. Gotta school these youngsters about payin' respects to us legends. Did you tell him how we met?"

"I don't think I told him that story. My first music business job was workin' as Jockey Jack's assistant. 'Least that's what I told folks. I was really more like his personal slave."

"Damn right," Jack said, laughing. "It was his first job and he needed schoolin'. Son, you're lookin' at the man that put your uncle through the school of hard knocks. The music business was rough back then, man, especially for black radio. But that shouldn't surprise you."

"Not a bit. Oh, I'm sorry," Nick said, offering him a chair. "Have a seat, sir. But wait a minute… What did you call him, Uncle Calvin? Jockey Jack?"

"Jockey Jack, the Morning Mayor of Louisville!" Calvin said, laughing.

"Man, I'll never forget that first mornin' if I live to be a hundred," Jack said.

Calvin grinned. "Me neither. But now you're at Motown. And *that's* your payback."

Jack laughed, then glanced back at some commotion in the hallway. "Oh, looks like the *Jet* photographer got here. He's doin' a spread on the girls and I better get over there to run interference, or else they might never get to the stage on time. I'll see you guys after the show."

Nick stared into the hallway, and his mouth dropped open. Calvin turned around to look, but only saw the backs of two women. "What's wrong with you, boy?"

Benny laughed and pointed. "His love jones, Calvin."

"What love jones?"

"It's—it's her, Calvin!" Nick whispered. "*Mary Wilson!*"

Calvin laughed. "Oh, Lord! Hang on a minute, Jack. I hate to ask, but could you—"

"I'm way ahead'a you," Jack said, grinning. "And I can dig it, young brother! Follow me."

When they approached Mary Wilson she looked up and smiled warmly. "Oh, there you are, Jack," she said. "We were lookin' for you. Who are your friends?"

"Mary, I'd like you to meet Calvin Bailey and your number one fan, Nick Bluestone."

"Hi, Calvin. Hi, Nick. Hey, and that fan thing goes double. I've been a fan ever since I heard 'When I Make My Baby Smile.' But you sure have grown up since then, huh?"

Nick stood there gawking at her, unable to speak. No photos he had ever seen could live up to the flesh-and-blood Mary Wilson. She was wearing a long, strapless gown made of gold bugle beads that glittered every time she moved. Her honey-colored complexion was almost a perfect match for her hair, which was swept up in a curly bouffant. Then she smiled widely, just like a regular girl, and Nick grinned back. *Even her teeth are sexy!*

"Tell you what," she was saying. "Let's exchange autographs, okay, Nick?"

Nick's protruding Adam's apple bobbed up and down with a dry gulp. "Huh?" he croaked. "Uh, I'm sorry, Miss Wilson. What did you say?"

"I said that if you give me your autograph, I'll give you mine. Here," she said, turning around suddenly. "Use the program and you can rest it on my back to write."

Nick gazed at her bare shoulders and his knees went weak, but he managed to scrawl his shaky autograph. When he finished, Mary signed another program and kissed him on the cheek.

Nick blinked. "Uh, Miss Wilson?"

"Call me Mary."

"Okay. Uh… I, uh, just wanted to tell you that—I think you're the star, not Diana Ross. She's too skinny." He rolled his eyes. "Oh, God. I can't believe I said that."

Mary laughed. "It's okay, Nick! That means a lot to me. But you better not ever let her or Berry hear you say that. Hey, you knock 'em dead tonight, baby, you hear?"

"Yeah, you too! Break a leg, Mary."

Calvin laughed as he guided Nick back to the dressing room. "Come on, Casanova."

"She kissed me, Calvin! And she called me *baby*! You hear that?"

"Yeah, I heard. Must'a been all that smooth rap you laid on her."

≈∞≈

Nick's performance that night was his best to date, but he had little time to savor it. Calvin had arranged on-air interviews at two Indianapolis radio stations, and appearances at three record stores over the next day and a half. They survived on coffee, donuts, and very little sleep. When they finally got back to their motel room, it was nearly three in the afternoon.

Calvin undressed and fell into bed. "Put the do-not-disturb tag on the door, Nick. And listen to me now—do *not*—I repeat—*do not* wake me up until eight-thirty tonight. I'm all packed, so all I need's a shower and we can still make our flight. And don't forget to set the alarm."

≈∞≈

The room was pitch dark when the alarm clock jangled that night. Calvin was still muttering and cursing when Nick turned it off and flipped on the light switch.

"Get up, ya evil old bear," he said loudly. "It's almost nine."

"Boy, do *not* piss me off when I'm this damn tired," Calvin grumbled.

Outside someone was running past their door and there were voices shouting in the distance. Calvin stood up slowly and pulled on his robe. "What the hell's all that damn noise?"

"Somebody must be throwin' a party or sump'm. Come on. We gotta get to the airport."

"Okay, okay." Calvin cut his eyes at Nick and then chuckled. "You still grinnin', huh?"

"Three encores, Calvin! Nobody else got three. Not even Beauty and the Beasts."

"Beauty and the *what*?"

"The Supremes!"

"Nick. What the hell have you got against Diana Ross anyway? I think she's great."

Nick fastened his suitcase. "Too skinny. And anybody's a beast next to Mary."

"Well, I hate to break it to you, but I heard your Mary's engaged."

"I know and I don't care," Nick said, grinning. "I got a *real* vivid imagination."

"Oh, Lord. Just get all the bags together while I take my shower, awright?" But before Calvin made it to the bathroom, someone began pounding on the door. He motioned at Nick to stay back, then hurried over to the door and stood at the hinge side. "Who is it?"

"It's Benny. Let me in, man!"

Calvin blinked at Nick. "I thought—didn't he fly out after the show?" He opened the door, and Benny stumbled inside, sinking to his knees on the floor. He was sobbing.

Calvin slammed the door shut behind him and locked it. "Shit, man! You hurt or sump'm?"

Benny shook his head, but said nothing as he struggled to his feet. Calvin and Nick helped him into a chair and Calvin pushed Nick toward the bathroom. "Get him a towel, man."

Nick hurried back with the towel and Benny pressed it against his face for a moment. Then he blinked at them with new tears forming in his eyes. "Ain't you heard?" he croaked.

Nick sat on the edge of his bed. "We been asleep all afternoon. What happened?"

"He's dead, man!" Benny cried. "Okay, look—we went to see— Nick, you were there when my brother came backstage after the show. See, Calvin, I postponed my flight 'cause my brother found out Bobby Kennedy was comin' to Indianapolis for a campaign stop and—"

Nick jumped to his feet. "Bobby Kennedy's *dead*?"

"No, man!" Benny shouted, shaking his head. "Not him! Wait. I—I ain't tellin' it right. See, we was waitin' a long time for him to get there and then—"

Calvin cut him off. "*Who* is dead, man?"

Benny took a breath and stared at the floor. "Dr. King… They killed him."

Calvin flinched as if someone had hit him, and Nick slowly sank back down onto the bed. In the sudden silence of the room, the noise from outside began to make sense. The shouting was louder now. Women were crying, and blaring motel televisions competed with car radios emitting muffled news updates. Finally, Benny began his halting story.

"See, Bobby Kennedy was supposed to make a campaign speech at that park over on 17th and Broadway, so everybody was crowded around the platform waitin' for him. When he got there, the secret-service guys kept pullin' on his arm to keep him from talkin', but he ignored 'em. My brother was *just* sayin' sump'm must be wrong, and then—that's when he told us. He said he had some real sad news—Martin Luther King was shot and killed in Memphis. So folks started shoutin' and I thought things were about to blow up. But then he said sump'm—" Benny stopped, apparently too choked up to continue.

Calvin urged him on. "What? What did he say?"

"First, he said some kind'a poem—maybe it was after, I ain't sure. But it was sump'm 'bout the grace of God—sump'm like that. And then he—he said he understood we were angry 'cause he was angry too—when *his* brother got killed. But he said we ought'a stop and think before we ran out to kill all the white folks—'cause we all knew it had to be a white man that killed Dr. King. But he told us it wouldn't make no sense. 'Cause it was a white man that killed his brother too." Benny looked up at Calvin with a look of awe in his eyes. "And for some reason, that calmed everybody down—soon as he said it."

≈∞≈

Calvin waited for the French operator to ring *Le Petit Journal*, then heard a male voice answer over the noise of clinking glasses and conversational French: "Bonjour. Comment ca va?"

"Uh, oui, bonjour," Calvin said haltingly. "Uh—connaissez-vous Doc Calhoun? Merci…"

Nearly a minute passed, and then Doc answered in a somber tone. "Hi, Calvin. Jacques said it was a call from the States, so I knew it was you. I was gonna call later, but you beat me to it."

"So I guess you heard all about Dr. King then."

"It's all over the news in Paris. Damn, Calvin. So… how'd Nick take it?"

"Pretty bad. You know how he gets when he's upset. So I'm movin' up the vacation, and we'll be flyin' out there. If I can get him through these last few commitments, the schedule's clear. Last show's in Syracuse, first week of June."

≈∞≈

The Syracuse show was held in the afternoon, so Calvin decided to drive back to Manhattan that night. The flight to Paris was scheduled for the next evening. After the show, they hurried to the motel to pack, and Nick turned on the television set. He had been closely following Bobby Kennedy's presidential campaign ever since Dr. King's assassination two months earlier, and the California primary had been held that day. Walter Cronkite was reporting that the polls had closed and the returns were beginning to come in. The telephone rang, but he ignored it.

"Guess I'll get the phone, even though you right next to it," Calvin grumbled as he reached over Nick for the receiver. "Hello?... Oh, hi, Rose." He turned his back and walked away from the television. "Yeah... Oh... Oh, no... Do they know... ? Oh... Well, I'm not sure, but we're on our way home tonight. Meantime, give 'em our—our best."

Nick gave him a suspicious look when he hung up. "What's wrong?"

Calvin stared at Nick. "Uh—when did you last hear from your friend Ernie?"

"Ernie? Couple'a weeks ago. Why?... Wait—nothin' happened to Ernie—"

Calvin hesitated just long enough for Nick to figure it out. Walter Cronkite's voice seemed louder as he began reporting the election results. Nick stood up slowly, shaking his head. "No, Calvin! *Not* Ernie! Don't tell me that!"

Calvin reached over and turned off the television set. "I'm sorry, boy, but... look. Rose saw the military car out her window this afternoon and—"

Nick backed away from him. "No! That doesn't mean anything! There's three other guys in Ernie's building that went to 'Nam—"

"Listen—" Calvin reached for his arm, but Nick jerked away. "Boy, *listen* to me. Rose went over and talked to Miz Watson," he said gently. "I'm sorry, son, but Ernie's—gone."

Nick glared at him for a long, tense moment, then went back to packing.

Calvin sighed. "Nick—let's just sit down and talk a minute."

"I don't want to talk about it, Calvin."

Calvin handed him a tissue. "There's times it's okay to cry, boy. This is one'a them times."

Nick wiped his eyes and stepped away from Calvin without looking at him. "I'm all right, okay? But let's get out'a here. Let's just pack and get out'a here."

They finished packing their bags in silence. But as Calvin was checking the bathroom for any overlooked items, the telephone rang again. Nick froze, and Calvin hurried over to answer it.

"Hello?... Oh, that's right. He did, huh?... Well, *that's* some good news anyway. Thanks for callin', Rose... Yeah, we were just leavin' out."

Calvin smiled at Nick as he hung up. "She wanted to tell us Bobby Kennedy just won in California and he's makin' a speech. You feel like watchin' a minute 'fore we hit the road?"

Nick shrugged and took a seat on one of the beds. "I guess so."

Calvin turned on the set and a close-up of Bobby Kennedy's smiling face filled the screen. He was in the middle of his victory speech in a room crowded with balloons and cheering supporters. Standing beside him, wearing a matching smile, was his wife Ethel.

"How 'bout that?" Calvin said as he patted Nick's shoulder.

"Calvin," Nick said softly, "do you think—you think he can really stop the war?"

"Boy, the way he's been talkin', I think that's gonna be the first thing on his list."

"But too late to save Ernie," Nick said bitterly.

"I know. But he'll save a whole hell of a lotta other Ernies over there. And he'll save you from havin' to go. So for now, let's just hang onto that."

Nick stood up and Calvin wrapped his arm around his shoulder. "Let's go home, boy."

As he reached over to turn off the television set, Bobby Kennedy was just wrapping up his speech: "... *And now it's on to Chicago and let's win there!*"

PART IV

A LOVE SUPREME

Chapter 34

1976

Emily Johnson was a one-woman crusade against nonsense. There was little, if any, deception in her. With no patience for cruelty or careless stupidity, she believed that intelligence and education were tools to be utilized, not prizes to brag about. She was plump, in a healthy sort of way, with a smooth, brown face that was quick to smile unless something ignited her temper. She was a force of efficiency balanced by a kind spirit—the embodiment of an ideal nurse.

Since the death of her husband Jake two years earlier, Emily had been living with her daughter Shelly in the big family house. Her sons Tim and Jake Jr. were both married with families of their own, so when Shelly took a night job at the train station to help pay college expenses, Emily applied at Genesco for a night position. She started on the first of November and worked the 3:00 p.m. to midnight shift. She liked her new job, but quietly made up her mind to change a few things—especially when it came to the curious case of Magdalena Bluestone.

She discovered that all new trainees were assigned to Mrs. Bluestone, and the reason soon became clear. If mistakes were made, the helpless mute woman couldn't complain. So new nurses breezed through their first few weeks, and supervisors had fewer complaint reports to file.

After punching her timecard, Emily went to check on her patient. She stepped into the room quietly and looked at the frail white woman with the pale, staring eyes.

"Hi, Mrs. Bluestone." She placed a large canvas travel bag on the table and cranked up the bed to a sitting position. "You know, one of these days I wouldn't mind you shockin' the hell out'a me by saying 'Hello there, Emily!' Sure would shake things up around this place, wouldn't it? But it's okay. For now, I'm perfectly capable of doing the talking for both of us."

She reached into her bag and pulled out a small Tupperware bowl and a spoon. "Okay, now. I've decided that my mission as your nurse is to put some meat on those skinny little bones of yours, so I brought you some of my world-famous chicken and dumplings. Oh, good! It's still warm." She dipped out a spoonful and held it to Magda's lips. As Magda slurped it down, Emily laughed. "I know, honey. This is a treat after all this hospital food you've been used to. I had a feelin' that was why you were so skinny. Well, things are about to change 'cause Emily's here now, and I'm no novice. I've got fifteen years of experience! I had to leave that last corrupt hell-hole I was at, but I know what I'm doing, so don't you worry." She smiled and dabbed Magda's chin with a napkin. "They're gonna wonder what happened to you—take a bite of this bread now—I'm gonna put some color in those cheeks and you're gonna—"

The sound of a man clearing his throat startled her, and she nearly dropped the bowl. Scrambling up, she blinked at a tall man standing in the doorway. His complexion was cocoa-brown and his hair was cut in a short, neat afro. He was well-dressed in a crisp navy blue blazer, turtleneck, and slacks, and he was holding a duffel bag. He was not smiling.

Uh-oh, who the hell's this? Probably some management trainee five minutes out'a college.

Emily smoothed her skirt and stepped over to greet him. "May I help you, sir?"

The man shut the door without taking his eyes off her. "Smuggling in contraband, Nurse?"

Emily's eyes widened. "Contraband? Oh, you mean this little bowl of chicken and dumplings? No, sir! This is *my* dinner. And I was just—"

Suddenly, the man laughed and startled her with a bear hug. "Relax! I'm Nick! The Nick that's been calling every night and asking you to hold the phone for Mama. You must be Emily."

Emily blinked at him. "*You're* Nick? You're the son?"

Nick grinned. "I'm the son. You *are* Emily, right?"

"Yes! Emily Johnson," she said, extending her hand. "I'm sorry, Mr. Bluestone, but it's just that you don't look anything like— Okay, I get it. Black daddy, right? White mother, brown child. I get it." She rolled her eyes. "Slow as molasses in January, but I get it now."

Nick laughed as he walked over to his mother's bed. "It's okay. Every new nurse has to get used to our color difference." He sat down and gently pulled Magda into his arms. "Hi, Mama."

Emily turned to leave them alone, but then stopped and gasped. "Oh! Bluestone! Oh, Lord, I *am* slow! I just realized who you are. You're that singer, aren't you?"

"Yes, ma'am. That's me, all right. In fact, I just got back from a long road trip. Gotta croon to pay the Genesco bills, ya know."

"Well, it's wonderful meeting you! Oh, but I'll leave now so you two can visit."

"No! Stick around! We're fixin' to have a little party." He reached for his duffel bag and pulled out a small chocolate cake. "Today just happens to be my birthday."

Emily laughed. "You're full of surprises, aren't you? Well, happy birthday to you!"

"Thanks. The chocolate cake is our little tradition." He cut a piece of the cake, and held a forkful to his mother's lips. "Birthday cake, Mama! Open up."

Magda's pale blue eyes stared past her son, but her mouth dropped open for the cake.

"I'm twenty-four today, Mama. Can you believe that?" He kissed her forehead and then smiled back at Emily. "So you're Mama's night nurse. And you talk to her. I *heard* you talking to her. That's great, Emily. Ever since Hilda retired, none of these new nurses ever talk to her. So, how do you like it here at Genesco so far?"

"When you love your work, it doesn't matter where you do it. Listen, Mr. Bluestone—"

"Call me Nick."

"Okay. Nick. I was going to say—I know you worry about your Mama, but please don't. I've worked in special-needs facilities and I know how important it is to be somebody's voice."

Nick's smile faded. "What do you mean—somebody's voice?"

Emily smiled. "Your Mama can't speak for herself, so I'm her voice. I know what signs of neglect look like, so I check after that day nurse to make sure she's treatin' your Mama right."

Nick stared at her with a stunned expression. "Like—what signs?"

"I give her baths. And if I *ever* found a bruise, I would report it to you *immediately*. And her breath better smell nice and minty too, 'cause we're supposed to brush her teeth twice a day. And as I'm gettin' to know her better, I can tell when she's happy. At first, she didn't eat much of the food I brought her, which I knew was a sign of sadness. 'Cause, baby, I *know* my cookin' is good." She smiled sadly at Magda. "I think she was lonely. She just couldn't say it in words."

Nick stood up slowly and hugged Emily in a way that brought tears to her eyes. "Oh, baby," she said, patting his back, "you sure do love your Mama, huh?"

Nick leaned away from her and grinned. "New record. You went from 'Mr. Bluestone' to 'Baby' in under two minutes. I have that effect on women—but not usually that fast."

"Oh, Lord!" Emily cackled.

"No, but seriously, Emily. I had a good feeling about you—when I saw you talking to Mama and feeding her that soup."

"Dumplings," Emily said. "Chicken and dumplings—my specialty." She patted her own hips and laughed. "My husband loved my chicken and dumplings. And God bless him, he was partial to women with curves! Good thing too, 'cause I never could resist my own cookin'!" She leaned closer to Nick and glanced at the doorway. "That's why I've been bringin' your Mama evening meals. Between you and me, the food's not very good here."

"I know," Nick whispered back. "But don't you worry, Emily. Big changes are in the works here at Genesco. And with you makin' sure she eats, maybe we can get some curves on Mama too! But you know, what's really important is for you to keep talkin' to her. She really does better when everybody talks to her. She tries to talk sometimes. She makes sounds like she's trying to form words."

Emily peered over at Nick as she filled a cup from the water carafe next to the bed. "Really? I've never heard her do that. I was told—"

Nick cut her off. "Well, there are gonna be a few new specialists here soon, and there's some new research being done. So just keep talkin' to her, Emily. Promise me."

"Well, you can count on me. And that's great news about the new doctors. Oh, Lord! Where is my brain? If my daughter finds out I met you and didn't get her an autograph, she'll kill me! I know she likes your music."

"Well, then, the next show I do out here, you and your daughter have got free tickets."

"Oh, she'll be thrilled! Thank you, Nick!"

"That's 'Baby,' remember?" He pulled out a picture. "What's your daughter's name?"

"Shelly."

Nick scribbled a message on the picture, then handed it to her.

Emily smiled at the picture and headed for the door. "I'm gonna call her right now and tell her. So I'll be out here at the nurses' station if you need anything."

Nick gasped in mock indignation. "What? No goodbye kiss?"

Emily rolled her eyes. "I bet you run these young girls ragged, don'tcha?"

Nick grinned devilishly. "Actually, it's the other way around. It's the young girls who are running *me* ragged, Emily." He sighed deeply. "It's a curse, but I manage to live with it."

As she walked out, he could hear her cackling. "Hey, Emily," he called, "I'm partial to curves too, baby!"

≈∞≈

A week after his birthday, Nick had an early appointment with Ed Bridges, a new record producer he was interested in hiring for his next album project. Calvin had set his alarm for 7:30, but Nick woke him at 7:05. "Hey! Get up, you evil ol' bear. Coffee's on."

Calvin groaned as he blinked at the clock. "Boy, you must be dyin' to get back in that studio. When was the last time I ain't had to drag yo' ass out the bed kickin' and cussin'?"

Nick plopped down on the end of Calvin's bed. "I've been thinkin' about what this Bridges guy did for Rollo's last album. I want to see what he can do with some real talent like me!"

Calvin peered over his shoulder at Nick, who was wearing a baggy set of fire-engine-red silk pajamas. "Who you supposed to be? Charles Boyer? Where the hell'ja get them fancy pajamas?"

Nick grinned as he curled an imaginary handlebar mustache. "Nyah-ha-ha! Sweet Nell bribed me with 'em so I wouldn't foreclose on Granny's shack and tie her to the railroad tracks."

Calvin rolled to a sitting position, plunked both feet on the floor, and reached for a cigarette. After he lit it, he rested his elbow on his knee and gave Nick a long look. The boyish roundness of his face was gone, leaving him with the angular features shared by Calvin and his brother Joe—from the almond shaped eyes down to the dimple in his left cheek. He was a few shades lighter than Calvin, with a mocha velvet finish to his skin, and a toothy smile that sometimes made him look too much like Joe. When he was troubled, there was a vacant look in his eyes—like a lost creature searching for its soul. But when he was happy, as he was now, Nick was his own creation—unique, exasperating, and commanding laughter.

"Boy, you watch too many cartoons," Calvin muttered. "So which one's that?"

"Dishonest John from Dudley Do-Right! Man, Calvin, you'd never make it on Jeopardy."

"Whatever the hell that is. Look at'cha! Nappy hair, and swimmin' in them giant pajamas!"

"A fan sent 'em to me. She must'a thought I was seven feet tall, but this silk feels smooth!"

"Boy, I ought'a snap a Polaroid right now and make that your next album cover."

Nick flexed his biceps and showed his teeth. "Number one with a bullet?"

"Get your crazy ass off my damn bed and let me get in here and take my shower."

≈∞≈

The meeting with Bridges went well. Nick took an instant liking to his easy-going personality. With his longish dark hair, goatee, and blue eyes, Ed Bridges looked like a cross between James Taylor and every white Jesus portrait Nick had ever seen. The ballad he presented to Nick was a soulful, three-o'clock-in-the-morning torch song, and the other was a funky thumper with clever lyrics. The only drawback was his availability. Bridges would not be able to start work on the album for at least four months.

As Nick drove home, he and Calvin were discussing ways to convince the label to postpone the start date when he made a sudden sharp turn into a Chevrolet dealer's parking lot.

"Boy!" Calvin yelled. "What the hell's wrong with you?"

"Sorry, Calvin. But I just saw sump'm, and I need a closer look at it."

The car screeched to a stop, and Calvin's head jerked back. "That's what my dumb ass gets for lettin' you drive."

Nick jumped out. "Come on, Calvin!" he yelled as he sprinted toward the showroom.

By the time Calvin stepped inside, Nick was already behind the wheel of a cherry-red Corvette that was sparkling under a strategically-placed showroom spotlight.

Calvin crossed his arms and glared at him. "Aw, hell, no!"

"But it's *me*, Calvin!"

A smiling salesman suddenly appeared. "Thinking of buying your son a car, Dad?"

Calvin turned and nailed him with a look that bordered on serial-killer insanity.

The salesman backed away. "You gentlemen just take your time."

"Hey," Nick called, "Ricky's got one of these, Calvin. You know how fast this thing goes?"

"You know how many miles to the gallon it goes? About two. Guess you ain't heard about the big gas shortage, huh? And who the hell's Ricky anyway?"

"Percussionist, Calvin. The new guy, remember? And his car—man! It's a rocket!"

"Lord, boy, you are gonna put me in my grave. A gotdamn red rocket ticket-magnet."

Nick grinned. "A star has *got* to have a smooth car, man. And don't look at me like that! You're the one who promoted my records and *made* me a star."

"I liked you better when you were a box-man. Look. We live in New York and you're hardly ever in town, so you don't need a car... Boy, are you hearin' me? You don't really believe you *need* this car?"

"I need it *bad*, Calvin."

"Wrong. You don't."

"I'm an adult and I have my own money now. And *this* is what I want to spend it on. Besides," he said, grinning, "it matches my gigolo pajamas."

Calvin shut his eyes and sighed. "You know how much insurance is on this thing?"

Nick smiled sweetly and motioned for the salesman.

≈∞≈

Four speeding tickets later, Calvin went to his never-fail plan: a road trip. By court order, the Corvette was impounded until the tickets were paid and Nick had attended a safe driving course.

The car sat gathering dust in a midtown parking garage until Calvin finally convinced Nick to sell it. The new act was taking up most of his time anyway. Calvin had hired a road manager named Mike Adler and everything was set for the trip. But three days before their departure the bass player quit to take a higher paying gig on a European tour.

Mike was quick to reassure Calvin and Nick. "Okay, nobody panics. I know four guys I can call right now. Sight-readers. We'll bring 'em in to audition tomorrow. Do *not* worry."

The next afternoon was a jumble of late arrivals, missing background singers, and a mix-up with the itinerary. Calvin was standing in the hallway of the rehearsal studio, talking to the travel agent on a pay phone when Nick tapped him on the shoulder. Calvin waved him away.

"But Calvin, we found a bass man!"

"Okay. I gotta handle this and then I'll be right in. And *don't* hire anybody till I see 'em."

By the time Calvin finished his call and returned to the stage, the members of the band were packing up their instruments. "Wait a minute, Nick, what's goin' on?"

Nick jumped down from the stage, grinning. "Calvin! Meet TJ, my new bass man! He's ice-cold, man! You're gonna dig him, I promise. TJ, meet Calvin."

Calvin scowled at the weird character who reached for his hand. He was rail-thin and looked nothing like the other band members. They all dressed stylishly, but neatly, wearing afros of various sizes and shapes. Even the Caucasian drummer had permed his red hair into a huge curly afro to match the others. TJ's hair was straightened into a greasy, shoulder-length conk, and he was wearing a pair of worn-out, dirty jeans. His smile made Calvin cringe. TJ's teeth were discolored and crooked, and his eyelids never opened beyond half-mast. He spoke in a slow, Haight-Ashbury drawl, and his head bobbled when he spoke. "Faaar out, man."

Calvin said nothing to TJ, but blistered Mike with a look that threatened death.

Mike shrugged and whispered, "Nick's crazy about the guy, Calvin."

"'Cause he can really thump, man!" Nick gushed. "Wait'll you hear him."

"I was supposed to hear him thump *before* you hired him," Calvin growled.

Seemingly oblivious to the problem, TJ tapped out a Kool and lit it. "Smoke, dude?"

"No, thanks," Calvin muttered through his teeth. "I got my own."

"Faaar out," TJ droned. "Well, I gotta book now, man."

"Rehearsal tomorrow at ten, TJ," Nick said. "Don't be late."

"That's ten A.M., not P.M.," Mike called.

"No sweat, dude. Later."

Before TJ was completely out of earshot, Calvin grabbed Nick's arm. "What the hell *was* that? He looks like sump'm out of a goddamn Vincent Price movie! And what's he high on?"

Nick laughed. "I think that's just the way he acts. But wait'll you hear him play—"

Calvin cut him off with a groan. "Goddamn! I'm glad I ain't gotta travel with that—that conk-head *zombie*. I'm tellin' you now, boy, I'ma have Mike watchin' that guy. Close!"

"Grouch," Nick said, punching him lightly. "You just look in on Mama while I'm gone."

Calvin jabbed his forefinger into Nick's forehead. "Tell that zombie to take a bath!"

≈∞≈

Nick was on the road for two months, and Calvin filled the time with a new independent promotion project. First Shot Production Company had hired him to promote two new artists on the Capitol label. When he arrived for his first strategy meeting with the A&R group, he stared at the receptionist. She was partially turned away from him, with her head tilted against the receiver resting on her shoulder. After hanging up and scribbling a message, she looked up at him and broke into a smile. "Calvin Bailey! God, how many years has it been?"

"Donna Carlisle! I wondered what happened to you. Last I heard, you got married. Oh—guess that means your name's not Carlisle anymore, huh?"

"Well, it's Donna Stewart. I keep meaning to change my name back to Carlisle, but I just haven't gotten around to it. You see, the marriage only lasted a couple of years."

"Really? I'm sorry to hear that."

Donna laughed. "That didn't sound very sincere. Anyway, I'm free now and much happier."

"Well, that makes two of us, then!" Calvin reached into his pocket for his cigarettes. "Think anybody would mind if I smoke?" he asked, looking around the empty reception area.

"Well, I'd appreciate it if you didn't."

Calvin tucked the cigarettes back into his pocket and grinned. "Oh, that's right. I remember you worryin' me about my smokin' back when we dated before."

"I guess I worry about anybody who smokes. It's so dangerous for your health."

"Well, I know you're right about that. But it sho' ain't fair to folks my age. We all got hooked before anybody knew how bad they were."

"That's true. Have you ever tried to quit?"

"Once. It worked too, for about three hours."

"Well, you'll quit someday. They say the trick is to quit when you're real happy. Never try to quit when you're under a lot of pressure or upset about something." She shrugged and laughed nervously. "I just—heard that somewhere, I guess."

Calvin nodded as he studied her. "Your hair's different, but I like it."

Donna patted her short, curly hair. "Oh, Lord! I couldn't keep wearin' that flip, now could I? That's been out of style for years!"

"Well, you're still a knockout. And you really got it together, Donna."

"I can't complain. What about you, Calvin? Any kids?"

"Never got married. But I live with my nephew, and that's like raising ten kids."

"Oh, yes. Your nephew was the one that sang in the choir on Christmas. I remember him."

"Yeah, that was Nick." Calvin smiled. "You don't know who my nephew is, do you?"

Donna's face registered confusion. "Well, you just said his name's Nick."

"My brother went by the name of Bluestone."

Donna's mouth dropped open. "You mean that little boy I met is Nick Bluestone?"

"That's him, awright. Only he's not so little anymore. He grew up into a six-foot ham."

She laughed. "Well, I should've known he'd end up in show business with that voice he had. I can't believe he's all grown up. That goes to show us how much time is flyin' by, huh?"

"Mm-hmm. Listen, Donna, I gotta hurry and get to this meeting, but why don't you let me take you to dinner tonight so we can... catch up."

"I'd really like that. Stop by my desk after your meeting and I'll give you my number."

≈∞≈

Three weeks later, Calvin was enjoying a deep Sunday morning sleep when his ringing telephone woke him. He grabbed the receiver, croaked a sleepy hello, and heard Nick's laughter in his ear.

"Oops! Woke up the bear. Don't bother. I'll chop off my own head."

"Good idea," Calvin said, yawning. "Aw, man! Guess I'm not use'ta bein' out so late."

"What? No death threats for waking you up? Okay, bodysnatcher, what planet are you from and what have you done with my uncle?"

Calvin groaned. "Aw, shit, here he goes..."

"Nah, I'll spare you, but only if you tell me what's got you stayin' out so late."

"Well, I had me a date, that's all."

"What? With a real woman and everything?"

"Stop laughin', you little jackass. Why the hell are you wakin' me up anyway?"

"That's more like it. I'm comin' home tomorrow, Calvin! If you and your girlfriend ain't settin' up house or sump'm. I *have* been gone awhile and I don't want to *intrude*—"

"Aw, damn! I forgot about your flight tomorrow! What time was it again?"

"3:30 tomorrow afternoon. Continental 419."

"I'll be there. Now let me get back to sleep, boy."

"No way. I want details about your new woman! Where and when did you meet her?"

"I met her years ago. Her name's Donna Carlisle. Well, Donna Stewart now."

Nick gasped theatrically. "A *married* woman?"

"Shut up. She's a divorced woman."

"Is she a *fine* divorced woman?"

"Probably too fine for an old fool like me, but she lets me hang around. You met her."

"Me? When?"

"I brought her over for Christmas when you were little. You sang that solo at church."

"Oh, yeah," Nick said softly. "That was the last Christmas we were all together."

"Aw, it sure was. Sorry I brought that up."

"It's okay. Anyway, I do remember her—a little. She was real nice. So is it serious?"

"Aw, hell, I don't know. What the hell's serious?"

"Come on, Calvin. Tell me sump'm about her, man! She got any kids?"

"No kids. She works at Capitol, she's classy, got a pretty smile, and I'm real comfortable with her. And the romantic details ain't none'a your business. Oh, and she can cook her ass off!"

"Bingo! She can cook. That's all I need to hear. You got my blessing, Calvin!"

"Ain't nobody askin' you for no blessin'! And what the hell makes you think she'd ever be cookin' for your monkey ass anyway? I'll see you tomorrow and do *not* miss your flight!"

Chapter 35

For months everyone in the music industry had been buzzing about Stevie Wonder's upcoming album, so it came as no surprise when *Songs in the Key of Life* debuted at number one on the *Billboard* chart. But on the east coast, there was a secondary buzz about a reclusive new songwriter named E. L. Atherton, who had just moved from L.A. to open a New York office. As soon as Nick found out where his new office was located, he called and made an appointment.

As Nick waited in the outer office counting the number of Atherton's songs—three—on *Billboard's* top-forty list, an angry white man wearing a lime green leisure suit and a bad comb-over stormed in and demanded to see Atherton. After the receptionist asked him to leave for the third time, she finally picked up the telephone and murmured something into it.

Within seconds, the door to the inner office flew open and an attractive black woman in gray slacks and a matching turtleneck sweater walked into the room. With the tight set of her angular jaw and her long, purposeful strides, she was an imposing force, and Nick actually felt a breeze when she passed him. Her complexion was a smooth cocoa brown, and she was remarkably tall, without appearing gangly. *Like a pissed-off runway model,* he thought. She wore a short, neat afro, which matched her attitude, and her steely black eyes were like two guided missiles. She stepped up to the troublemaker like a school bully going for the first head-butt. Nick grinned.

The man rolled his eyes. "Great. First, I have to deal through nothing but lawyers, then a receptionist, and now a secretary. Look, I'm here to see E. L. Atherton. Would *somebody* tell him Sidney Summers is here to see him? That's Sidney Summers—the producer."

The woman gave her wristwatch a perfunctory glance, then looked at Summers. "*I'm* E. L. Atherton. I'm busy, you've got five minutes, and what can I do for you?"

She had a deep, resonant voice. Smooth, but commanding. When she said "what can I do for you," it was not a question, but a clear statement that she had no intention of doing anything for Summers, except possibly slapping him around and sending him home crying to his Mama.

Nick closed the issue of *Billboard* and placed it on the coffee table. E. L. Atherton was turning out to be a million times more interesting than the top-forty list.

"Uh, well," said Summers, blinking at her. "You're a woman!"

"Last time I checked," she said flatly.

"Well," Summers began tentatively, "I'm—here to talk to you about— Look, your lawyer called and told me you were pulling your songs from my project and… Listen, there's no reason for you to give me such a dirty look, or for you to be in my face like that."

"So sorry," she said. "I didn't mean to *intimidate* you."

Summers glared at her. "That's exactly what you're trying to do—intimidate me!"

Atherton looked at her wristwatch again. "*Now* you've got two minutes. Would you like to spend it talking about intimidation or would you rather get to the point?"

"I don't need this shit," he snapped. "I came here to discuss this—to find out why—"

She scowled and flicked up one hand dismissively. "Look. I pulled my songs because I found out your production company stiffed three musicians on the first recording date. One of those guys co-wrote one of the songs with me. Now, I expect my co-writers and musicians to receive the same respect afforded to me, which they were not. And just as you say, Mr. Summers, I don't need that kind of shit. I won't put up with it. I don't have to."

After a short, silent stare-off, Summers broke first. "I'll see you in court, bitch."

Atherton showed no outrage at the word "bitch." Instead, she curled her lips into a smile so sinister and saccharine, Nick was sure it would have made the great Snidely Whiplash tremble. He got himself comfortable on the sofa. All he needed now was a bowl of Captain Crunch.

Atherton handed him a business card. "Here's my lawyer's card. Feel free to call him about your lawsuit." One last glance at the wristwatch. "Time's up, Mr. Summers."

Nick almost applauded as Atherton blazed a trail back to her office on some kind of confident horsepower. He glanced at Summers, half-expecting to see Daffy Duck after a good cartoon brawl—featherless, skin hanging in singed strips, bill turned backwards, and smoke floating out the top of his head. But Summers only looked bewildered, standing in the center of the room in his ridiculous green suit. Nick suddenly couldn't wait to meet E. L. Atherton.

When the receptionist finally led him to the inner office, Atherton was seated with her back to him, involved in a telephone conversation. She turned her chair around slowly and made a circular gesture with her left hand to indicate that she was wrapping up the call. "Okay, Kenny. Yeah… I know… Will do… Listen, I've got someone in my office, so I've really got to… Yes, it's under control. Hey, KENNY! I'm hanging up now."

Kenny was still talking as Atherton hung up. She smiled at Nick. "*Please* forgive me."

He shrugged. "Nothing to forgive."

Atherton leaned forward and sighed. "Listen, I saw you sitting in the reception area, so I know you saw my tantrum. I hope I didn't make a bad impression on you, but Summers really had that coming. He's known for trying to cheat musicians and steal credit from songwriters who are just getting started. I have to admit I rather enjoyed that little scene, even if it did make me come off as a raving bitch. I guess it was my big chance to—to avenge them or something."

Nick grinned. "E. L. Atherton, the Avenger. Hey, no problem. I *love* superheroes. Especially fine ones. You got one'a them tight, black Emma Peel suits?"

Atherton blinked, and actually looked embarrassed for a moment before shifting gears suddenly. "So! Nick Bluestone—musical child prodigy, who somehow made the difficult transition into adult star. First hit—'When I Make My Baby Smile'—broke records for speeding up the charts. Consistently good follow-up product until your last album, which was better than most of the stuff out there today, but disappointing compared to your other efforts—at least to me. Well, all I can say, Nick, is that I hope you're here for the reason I think you are."

"And why do you think I'm here?"

"Well, I'm hoping you want me to write some songs for you."

"I do—if you have time. I'm hiring Ed Bridges as producer, and he has the rights to two good songs, but I'd love it if we could get you to write the rest. What I'm looking for is— Look. I've had hit records, but I'm really looking for that one *great* song, you know? My last album was a big jumble of formula songs that didn't have anything to do with each other. It sold strictly on the strength of my name. So I thought I'd try the concept idea—a little like Stevie, you know? Each cut a piece of the bigger story."

"I hear you. Once again, Stevie defies the status quo, and all us artistic oddballs benefit. What you want is a theme album with a statement, right?"

"Exactly. But subtle, you know?"

"Like an underscore—a *whispered* underscore, not a series of screaming pop vamps. And it's just the kind of thing I can sink my teeth into. But Nick, I've got one question."

He could feel her studying him closely. "Ask away."

"Why don't you take a crack at it yourself? I'm sure you could write a song if you tried."

"I tried, and believe me, I am no songwriter. I tried it once and when I looked at that mess I wrote down, I knew there was no way in hell I was gonna be the one to stand up and sing it."

Atherton laughed and stood up to extend her hand.

"Cool!" Nick said, taking her hand. "So I guess we'll do that 'my lawyer calls your lawyer' stuff and then get together to talk over ideas."

"I'm free Friday, so why don't you call your lawyer today? How's Friday for you?"

"Free as a bird, Ms. Atherton. I'll figure out a place and call you."

"Please call me Stella."

"Stella." As soon as he said her name he had a mental flash of Richard Behmer from *West Side Story* standing in a dark alley singing his heart out to Maria. The "Stella" version began playing in his head before he could stop it: *Stella! I just met a girl nay-hamed Stella!... Woo— Damn, I'm corny. Good thing this chick can't read my mind.* "Wait a minute!" he said out loud. "E. L. Atherton! But Stella starts with an 'S.' So why are your initials E. L.?"

She sighed. "Well, my name is—Estelle. E. L. is for Estelle Louise. Horrible, huh?"

"Not horrible. But I like Stella better."

Nick did his best to cover the silly grin he felt coming on. Now he was Marlon Brando in *Streetcar Named Desire*—wearing a torn t-shirt, dropping to his knees under a balcony, and screaming "Stella!" as he clutched his forehead in anguished passion. He snapped out of his daydream when he saw the perplexed expression on Stella's face.

"Hello?" she was saying. "Earth to Nick."

Nick slipped on his sunglasses and got the grin under control. "Okay, Stella," he said in his coolest double-oh-seven voice. "I'll see *you* Friday."

≈∞≈

The minute Nick saw Stella walk into Sylvia's Restaurant, all thoughts of business evaporated. She was wearing an African-print sheath dress that went just right with her hair, and a bone choker that accentuated her long neck. He stood up as the waiter pulled out her chair.

"Wow," he said. "What's the Swahili word for beautiful?"

"Actually, it's *nzuri*. And thank you, Nick. I'm really crazy about my African stuff. I've got a friend who's an importer. He goes back and forth from Africa at least six times a year, and I think I'm keeping him in business single-handedly. You should see my apartment."

"Is that an invitation?"

"Huh?"

"To see your apartment?" Nick grinned devilishly and raised his water glass to his lips.

Stella narrowed her eyes, but smiled. "Was that an innocent flirta-tion—or a doggish pass?"

Caught in mid-swallow, Nick began to cough. "Damn!" he sputtered. "It was *definitely* an innocent flirtation. And even if it wasn't, I sure as hell wouldn't tell you now."

Stella laughed. "I promise not to make you choke—again."

"Thanks. 'Cause I was seriously wondering whether or not to order food."

"Oh, come on. I'm not the black widow spider everybody makes me out to be."

"Who said that? Wait, I was just kidding around, Stella. I thought you were too."

"I was—sort of. But my antisocial reputation seemed to follow me here to the east coast. Actually, I was just a hermit in Los Angeles. Cocaine was everywhere, and if you said no, you were an instant outcast. So I just stopped socializing. But on the rare occasion I did go on a date—I don't know. I just didn't fit in. And all anybody wanted to talk about was how connected they were in the business."

Nick nodded. "Everybody trying to impress each other."

Stella leaned back and rolled her eyes. "And don't *even* try telling somebody that you didn't drive a Benz or a Jag. I never saw so many people in that status symbol bag in my life!"

"Uh-oh," Nick said, sinking into his chair.

"What?"

"Well… I have a confession, Stella."

"What, already?"

"Yup," he said, laughing. "I had a Corvette once. But don't worry. It was just a phase."

"But that's different. You're a guy. It was only the speed you were after."

"No, actually, it was the status symbol bag thing and *then* the speed. I'm busted."

Stella laughed. "Oh, very contrite. So let me brace myself. What phase are you in now?"

Nick sat up straight. "I'm proud to inform you, Ms. Atherton, that I am now in the grubby, air-polluting, New York taxicab phase. And when I'm feeling adventurous, I slide into the get-your-throat-cut-on-the-subway phase. Impressed?"

"Very! So Nick. What were we talking about before we took that detour?"

"You were leaving the coke-heads in L.A. with their Jags and coming to New York."

"Oh, okay. My parents moved here after my brother Donnie got accepted at Harvard. They couldn't stand being 3,000 miles away from him, so they bought a house in New Rochelle. Turned out to be that 'two birds with one stone' thing. Daddy could be closer to Donnie and still be near New York City so he could start making those all-important *connections*."

"Ah-hah!" Nick leaned forward and stared at her gravely. "*What* kind of connections and *what* kind of car does Daddy drive?"

Stella laughed. "A Lincoln! Okay, but don't you see? That's why I rebelled!"

"Yeah, sure. And the connections?"

"Okay, Mr. D.A., the picture starts to emerge. I clash with my parents. Daddy drives a Lincoln, so I drive a Volvo—not as flashy, but great gas mileage. And since I'm in show business, you can be sure that my Daddy has no show business connections. I think he was *born* a lawyer! And yes, the big eastward move was all about—at least I *think* it was all about—some kind of political ambitions. And let me punctuate that with a big *yuck*. Anyway, my work kept me in Los Angeles for a while, but then I started getting sick of the place, and I was missing Donnie too, so I dragged my little fledgling business out here." Stella sighed. "My family really gets on my nerves, but they're the only family I've got."

"Fledgling?" Nick laughed. "Come on, Stella! You're doin' a lot better than *fledgling!*"

"Well, most of my early hits I wrote for another company. I'm still new as an independent entity." She smiled. "But here I am on a date and about to start a big album project with one of the most popular R&B singers on radio today, so I'd say my business must be going pretty well."

"Hey! Things are lookin' up. Did you just say this is a *date* we're on?"

"Come on, brutha. You knew it was a date when you splashed on all that cologne."

Nick felt the heat rise in his face and grinned. "Uhhh... too much?"

"No. I rather like it."

"You *rather* like it? Man, Stella, you talk proper. I can tell you ain't from the projects."

She frowned. "What do you mean by that?"

"Oh, that wasn't an insult. I think it's great that you can speak actual English."

"Oh... Sorry for the knee-jerk. But I've had my share of labels—uppity, wanna be—that kind of thing. Just because I speak this way doesn't make me less—*down* than the next person."

"Hey, I knew you were cool when you suggested meetin' up here in Harlem. I know a lot of folks who won't come up here at all. And I'm talkin' about *black* folks. Ain't that a shame?"

"You're not talking about black folks, Nick. You're talking about 'Negroes.' So busy trying to integrate, they forget where they came from."

Nick smiled. Stella seemed to get better every minute. "Well, if you can stand my cussin', I can sure stand you not droppin' your—I mean, not dropp*ing* your G's and saying 'rather.'"

"Well, that's a deal then."

"You know what was funny? How so many people thought you were a man."

"Yeah, that *was* funny. All my mail said *Mr.* E. L. Atherton. But the word's out now."

"Yeah. We've all seen you now, baby, and you don't look *nothin'* like a Mister!"

Nick was encouraged by her smile. "Stella, do you feel as good with me as I do with you?"

She nodded and laughed. "So I guess this is where I say 'so tell me about yourself.'"

"And I say 'oh, nothin' much to tell. Just another singer lookin' for a hit.' Besides, you seem to know quite a bit about me already, judging from that speech you made in your office."

"Well, I might as well admit this now. I was excited when my assistant told me you wanted to meet with me. I adore the way you sing."

He grinned. "Really? Adore, huh? I'm flattered."

"So I asked around and got the lowdown on you."

"Ooh! Lowdown. You do know a slang word or two, don'tcha?"

She rolled her eyes. "*Anyway*—they told me all about how your uncle raised you after your father— Oh, God, I'm sorry—"

"It's okay," Nick said. "He killed himself. Blew his brains out all over a hotel room. Everybody knows that story. Hey, don't worry about me bursting into tears or anything, Stella. I never even met the guy and from what I know about him, I don't think I would'a wanted to."

"Oh... Well, what about your mother? Is she—still living?"

"Yes, she's alive—in a hospital. When I was a baby, she had an accident that sort of damaged her brain and she needs a lot of care. But the doctors are close to a breakthrough. So I'm hopin' to get her out'a there someday. I'll take you to meet her sometime."

"Oh, I've got a grandfather in one of those places myself. But he's too senile to ever get better. I'm glad there's hope for your mother."

"Well, she can't talk, but she can understand when I talk to her. I visit her all the time."

"Oh, that's really nice, Nick. So, then it was just you and your uncle? He raised you?"

"Yeah. Two road dogs, traveling the countryside. But don't get me wrong—he made sure I went to school and all that. In fact, that was the one thing he'd get really mad about, and then I'd get the speech— 'Boy, this education ain't no option! If you end up diggin' ditches or shinin' somebody's damn shoes, you best believe I'll be your *best* customer, just so I can put my shiny gotdamn shoe so far up your lazy ass you'll be tastin' shoe polish!'"

Stella laughed. "So it was education under duress!"

"No! Education under a foot! And I don't know where he got all that ditch-diggin', shoe-shine-boy stuff from! Like I wouldn't at least be smart enough to flip burgers or be the french-fry supervisor or sump'm! But anyway, he *did* get me graduated, even if I didn't get all A's."

"So then you never had a mother figure in your life?"

Nick's smile faded. "But—I *just* told you a minute ago—my mother's alive. I've *got* a mother figure. Just because she's sick don't mean she's not still my Mama."

"Oh—of course not, Nick," she stammered. "I didn't mean that at all. I just—"

"It's okay. Anyway, I had my aunt too." He smiled. "Hey! That's who you sound like! Aunt Pearl! She had a deep voice like yours."

"She did? You know, I used to hate it, but eventually I had to develop a sense of humor about it. It was actually funny when I'd answer the phone and somebody would call me 'sir.'"

Nick grinned. "You should'a heard Aunt Pearl read 'The Big, Bad Wolf.' Put chills in my bones! And she use'ta call everybody 'sugah'—you know, like Pearl Bailey, but baritone. I sure miss her. She was my second Mama—till I was eleven."

After a short silence, he said softly, "She died when I was eleven—tragic circumstances."

"I'm so sorry, Nick. You sure have been through a lot in your life, haven't you?"

"Well, most of it happened when I was a baby—all but Aunt Pearl dyin'."

"Was she your mother's sister or your father's?"

"No. See, Doc and Pearl were my mother's best friends, and after Mama's—accident, they adopted me. So legally, my name's Nick Calhoun."

"Doc Calhoun—the trumpet player—that's right. I heard you were related to him."

"He's my stepfather, and his kids, Shay and Edward, are my adoptive brother and sister. They all live in Paris. I'm the only one who lives here in the States."

"Why do they live in Paris?"

"Well, at first Doc went there for the work. Jazz is very popular in France. But they decided to stay when Uncle Sam came after for Edward. And now it's home for them. As a matter of fact, I'm goin' out there for a family vacation when we finish this album. You ever been to Paris?"

"No. I've traveled a bit, but never made it to France. Why? Is that an invitation?"

"Sure. The more the merrier. I want you to meet my family."

"Wait a minute," she said. "You're kidding—aren't you? Come on. I barely know you."

"By the time we finish this album, you're gonna know me a *whole* lot better."

Stella laughed. "Doggish pass?"

"Doggish pass. I ain't gonna lie... Hey, Stella? Did anybody ever tell you that you got a smile just like Mary Wilson?"

"Mary Wilson? Of the Supremes? I look about as much like Mary Wilson as you do."

"I didn't say you *look* like her. I said you *smile* like her. You know, real warm."

≈∞≈

Nick stepped into his apartment singing a loud musical goulash of *West Side Story* and *Streetcar Named Desire*. "I just met a girl nay-hamed Stel-lah! Hey, *Stellah!* I'll never stop saying—"

A familiar voice put an end to his performance. "Boy! Have you lost your damn mind?"

"Calvin!" Nick shouted happily, heading to the sofa. "When'd you get back?"

Calvin glared at him. "Eleven. What time is it?"

"Half past two."

"Damn. No wonder I'm so tired. I was sleepin' real good till you came dancin' your silly ass in here like goddamn Gene Kelly—singin' in the rain an' shit."

"Wrong movie, Calvin. What I was doin' was a scene from *West Side Story*."

"Are you plannin' on shuttin' up any time soon?"

Nick laughed. "What a grizzly ol' damn bear you are!"

Calvin got up slowly and lumbered in the direction of his bedroom. "Got*damn*, you watch too many of those late movies. And too many cartoons too! Read a book once in a while, boy!"

"G'night, Calvin," Nick called.

Calvin paused at the door and sighed. "Okay. So who the hell's this Stella, anyway?"

Nick grinned as he plopped down on the sofa. "The woman of my dreams."

"That shit again," Calvin groaned. "Boy, do me a favor and sleep it off this time."

Chapter 36

Stella set her alarm clock for 7:00 a.m. and sighed. She couldn't remember the last time she had stayed out so late, and she really needed sleep. Completing Nick's songs in time for his projected start date would entail many extra hours of work and a reshuffling of her current projects. After washing her face and brushing her teeth, she climbed into bed and closed her eyes. "Go to sleep, Stella," she muttered to herself. "Don't even start."

But after hours of tossing and turning, she gave up and went into the bathroom to run a shower. She looked in the mirror and gave herself a menacing look. "Stella Atherton, don't you dare do this again!" But a voice in her head began mocking her. *Too late...*

She took off her nightgown and stepped into the shower. "He's a dog, I just know it. He's too charming to be anything else. A charming—

singing *dog*—who walks onstage and ninety thousand women start screaming and throwing panties at him!... Then he probably howls. . . and then he goes to one of those—*orgies* or something... Oh, God, Stella! *What* have you gotten yourself into? A whole album project with an oversexed, salivating—charming dog!" Her scathing monologue was cut short by the distant ringing of the telephone. She grabbed a towel and ran to answer it. "Hello?"

"Estelle Louise Atherton. What took you so long to answer the telephone?"

"Oh, hi, Mama. I was in the shower."

"Why didn't you call me back? I left a message with the service. Didn't you get it?"

Here we go. Another interrogation. "I got in late, Mama," she said, hating her contrite tone.

"Well, didn't that silly operator tell you that it was important?"

"Yes, Mama."

"Then why didn't you call me first thing this morning?"

"It's not even seven yet, Mama! I was planning to call you right after my shower."

"Watch your tone, young lady! I called to remind you about the dinner party tonight."

"Mama—"

No, that's not her "Mama" voice. That's Mother. The one who named me Estelle Louise.

"Mother," she said, "It's circled in red on my calendar."

"I know you, Estelle. I don't want any of your last minute excuses because of some music business nonsense. This is a very important dinner for your father. Some of the partners in his firm will be here, and we're counting on you and your brother. Image is *everything*, dear."

Stella's jaw was so tight she thought her teeth would crack. The only words she had heard were "music business nonsense."

"Mama—" She paused, wishing she could speak the sharp retort forming in her mind:

For your information, Mama, I earned more money last year with my music business nonsense than Daddy did in the last two years put together.

She summoned all her courage, but the words failed to make it past her imagination.

"Estelle? Are you still there?"

"Yes, Mama. I'm here. And I'll be at the dinner party."

"On time and properly attired?"

A juicy image popped into Stella's head:

Shouldn't have said that, Mama! Properly attired? Let's see—torn jeans, granny glasses, a tight t-shirt—no bra. I'll be barefooted—and the t-shirt will say—what? I know! Down with the Establishment! Oh, and a joint! I'll be smoking a big, fat doobie. Image is everything, after all.

"I'll be there, Mama," she said, swallowing back a laugh. "On time and properly attired."

"I don't suppose I could talk you into doing something—different—with your hair?"

Stella did a quick mental revision of her imaginary fashion statement: *Grow hair into a huge Angela Davis afro with a black-power afro pick sticking out the top.*

"Mama," she said, "my hair is neat and in a perfectly acceptable style."

Audrey Atherton sighed. "Oh, all right, Stella. Cocktails are at seven."

"Seven. Got it, Mama."

≈∞≈

Stella enjoyed being the first one at her office in the morning. As she unlocked the door, she smiled at the gold script lettering: *E. L. Atherton Music.* Though the office was small, it represented the one part of her life that remained untouched by her parents.

After making coffee, she glanced up at the three gold albums and two platinum singles on the wall. The only honor missing was the elusive Grammy, but she knew that not even a Grammy would impress her parents. They saw her career as a disappointing flight of fancy, compared to their lifelong dream for her. Every class in every school Stella had attended was geared toward the legal profession. The one diversion Audrey Atherton had allowed was the study of music, which she considered the final touch to her perfectly designed "Estelle Louise."

Even as a child, Stella knew that her singing voice was a lost cause, but, to everyone's surprise, she was a natural at the piano. She possessed an uncanny ability to pick out melodies and mate them with chords until she was writing her own songs. Recognizing her desire to learn, her music teacher gave her several books and she began to dabble at writing her own musical charts. Neither of her parents ever suspected that her innocuous piano lessons were pulling hard at Stella's spirit and setting her feet on the path to her life's work.

To this day, she wondered how she had found the courage to drop out of pre-law at Stanford and move into an apartment in Hollywood. It certainly made it easier when a Motown producer picked up one of her songs, but she was still amazed at her audacity. She knew that her parents considered themselves lenient for allowing her to continue in the music business for a while. They were just waiting for her high ride on the charts to end with a crash into musical oblivion. Then their wayward daughter would come to her senses, finish law school, and take her rightful place as an associate at her father's firm.

Stella shivered at the thought. *But then why am I always craving their approval? I don't want to be like them.* She had to admit that even opening her small office had been somewhat a show of defiance against her parents, but mostly just a way to impress them. She thought of her younger brother, struggling through the same hell she had endured before her one mutinous act. Donnie had never wanted to go to Harvard and only Stella knew about his dream to study the humanities at Berkeley and then travel the world with the Peace Corps. But he was Donald Frederick Atherton Jr., so Harvard was inevitable.

"Poor Estelle and Junior," she muttered. "What horrible names they call us."

"Who are you talking to?" a voice asked.

Stella whirled around, unaware that she had been speaking out loud. Her assistant Dolores was smiling at her curiously from under the brim of a tweed apple cap. She was a tall, attractive Italian, who was an expert on R&B music, from picking hit singles to marketing.

"Oh, hi, Dolores," Stella said. "I didn't hear you come in."

Dolores laughed and flopped down into a chair. "So who the hell's Junior?"

"That's what my parents call my poor brother."

"Why *poor* brother?"

"Well, for one thing, they call him *Junior!*" Stella laughed. "Which ought to give you a clue about the rest... Hey, Dolores. Mind if I ask you something?"

"Not at all."

"Well, do you like working for me?"

Dolores gave her a perplexed look. "Sure. Why do you ask?"

"I mean, you could be working for the majors—more money, better benefits—"

"Please! We talked about this when you hired me. The majors? Shit! I'm too much of a free spirit to be stifled like that! Later for the majors and their cut-throat politics."

"Yeah, but I mean— Okay, look. Just tell me straight. Am I a bougie bitch?"

Dolores laughed. "What in the world brought *that* on?"

"I'm serious, Dolores. Really think about it and tell me the truth."

"Okay. No, you're definitely not bougie and you're not a bitch. You're—sophisticated, and you're a businesswoman. But it's nice to know you're concerned about what people think. Hey, and I *really* dug it when you stuck up for Ray and the guys with Mr. Leisure Suit the other day."

"Softened my sharp edges a little bit, huh?" Stella's laugh ended in a sigh. "God, Dolores. I just don't want to wake up one day and find out I've become my Mama."

Dolores grimaced and stood up slowly. "So that's what brought this on. Okay. Well, time for me to go. I know better than to try to give advice to somebody who's fightin' with her Mama."

Stella laughed, but it was joyless. "I don't blame you. But anyway, if you happen to see me still hanging around here at six tonight, please kick me out. I can't be late for this thing with—"

"Mama?"

"You got it. And hey, Dolores, thanks for the talk."

≈∞≈

Stella was met at her parents' door that evening by Carmen, the Puerto Rican maid that her mother really didn't need—except to dust the antique furniture in the too-many rooms of the too-large house—and, of course, on occasions like tonight, for sheer decoration. Audrey Atherton wouldn't be caught dead greeting her own dinner guests at the door.

"Good evening, Miss Estelle," Carmen said, reaching for Stella's beaded jacket.

"Hi, Carmen. Guess I'm early, huh?"

"That will please your mother, Miss Estelle."

"Carmen, would you mind calling me Stella from now on instead of Miss Estelle?"

Carmen's eyes widened. "I don't think Mrs. Atherton would like that, Miss Estelle."

Stella sighed. "You're probably right." She smoothed her basic-black cocktail dress—the only acceptable uniform for the evening. "Well, do you think I'll pass inspection?"

"Oh, yes, ma'am. You look very pretty."

"Thank you, Carmen. Is my brother here yet?"

"In the kitchen, Miss Estelle."

"Thanks. If Mother asks, please tell her that's where I am too."

Stella was always amazed at her ability to switch from "Mama" to "Mother" with such ease. "Mama" was all right in private conversation, but this was going to be a "Mother" night. She took a breath to calm her nerves and wondered what her employees would think if they could see her cowering in the shadow of her parents. *First I was the tyrant-bitch. Then I slew the dragon-producer and became—what was that Nick called me? Oh, yeah! The Avenger. Sorry, Nick, but I'm no Emma Peel.*

I'm just Estelle, the sniveling chicken—brought to her knees by her Mama... What a laugh.

With a resigned sigh, she cut through the living room to the kitchen. The white sofa and gray club chairs had been rearranged to make the room look larger, and the wet bar was stocked with wine from her father's collection. Hanging above the bar was a large red and black abstract painting that she hated and her mother loved. When she stepped into the kitchen, she saw her brother leaning into the refrigerator. He was wearing the trousers to the Pierre Cardin formal suit he looked so good in, and the jacket was hanging on the back of a chair.

"Donnie! When did you get here and why didn't you call me the minute your train got in?"

He turned around. There was a cold chicken leg clenched in his teeth and he was juggling a carton of milk and a tray of cheese. "Hey, Shtel," he mumbled. "Geshuumglashezh."

"What?"

Donnie placed the milk and cheese on the corner table and offered her a bite of the chicken leg. "I said—get some glasses. We mustn't get in the way of the cay-tuh-ruhs, dahling." He twisted his face into a pompous expression as he mugged the word "caterers." "Mumsy would be so annoyed." He pulled out a chair for her. "Shall we, my deah?"

She laughed and handed him the glasses. "Oh, let's, Donnie, dahling."

As they sat down for their traditional rebellious repast, Stella smiled at her brother. Now twenty, he had outgrown his awkward teen face and gangly physique to become quite a handsome young man. Since she had last seen him, his complexion had cleared up and what had once been a mouthful of oversized teeth was now a dazzling, confident grin. Donnie took after their father's side of the family, with a lighter complexion than Stella and their mother. His hair was sandy brown, and he was sporting the beginnings of a decent-sized afro.

"Hey, white sheep, your fro's bigger than mine," she teased. "Has Daddy seen it?"

"Yup. And he gave me the Hah-vud version of an ass-whippin'—you know—verbal, no belt, and perfect syntax, of course." Imitating his father, he leaned back in his chair and tucked his thumbs into his suspenders. "Well, Junior, I suppose a trip to the barber is out of the question at this late hour. You *do* have your tux in tow, I trust?"

Stella snorted. "Did he really say that? 'Tux in tow'? God, Donnie! How did we turn out so normal? Wait—we *are* normal, aren't we?"

"Shit, I doubt it—but hurry and eat some of this smelly cheese before the stuffed shirts get here." He let out a wicked cackle. "It's loaded with garlic so we can stink up the place with our horrible breath! And you are *not* gonna deprive me of the orgiastic joy of pissing Mama off when we pick at her zillion-dollar catered food like a couple of finicky birds. Come on, eat!"

Stella took a large bite of the cheese and continued their conversation. "Sho, Donnie, howzhhkool? Waivamumute—dijushay 'orzhiashtik'?"

"Yes, I did. I have acquired a veddy colorful vocabulary since attending deah old Hah-vud, with its ivy-covahed walls and all." He glanced at the door to watch for their mother. "Hey, Stel—think I ought'a throw 'orgiastic' into the conversation tonight?"

"I dare you. Wait! They'd *die* if their guests found out their daughter was in the music business! Gasp, Donnie! The scandal! So why don't you propose a toast to my hot new single climbing the charts— 'Orgiastic'—a song I wrote for—oh, who do they really hate?"

"James Brown!" Donnie chortled. "NO! Rufus Thomas! Remember when "The Funky Chicken" played on the car radio that time, and Daddy nearly went off the road? Let's tell 'em you wrote the X-rated part-two version—"The Orgiastic Chicken"—and watch their jaws drop."

"Right. Like we'd ever have the nerve." Stella threw a piece of chicken skin at him.

"Shit, Stel!" Donnie laughed, springing from his chair. "Now you got orgiastic chicken grease on my tow-tux! Mumsy will spank!"

The kitchen door swung open and Audrey Atherton glared at them as she approached the table. Stella hated herself for cowering like a child, and hated her mother for looking so imperious in her perfectly coifed hair and her perfectly beige gown.

"Why must the two of you behave like children whenever you see one another? Junior, put on your jacket and see Carmen about that stain. And as for you, Estelle—"

Stella nudged Donnie. "But I'm innocent, Mother! See? No stains on my tow-tux."

Donnie snorted at her unexpected bravado, and they collapsed against each other laughing.

Audrey Atherton lifted her chin and arched her left eyebrow menacingly. "Your father and I will expect you in the living room in ten minutes."

Stella cleared her throat and managed a meek "Yes, Mother."

When their mother was gone, Donnie tackled Stella in a gleeful bear hug. "The eyebrow, Stel! We got the eyebrow! Madame Atherton is *highly* pissed!"

"Oh, yeah, I'm sure we really got under her skin, Donnie," Stella droned sarcastically. "Life as she knows it is *over*."

Donnie nodded gravely. "Drug addiction, alcoholism. That's all that's left for her."

"Just shut up and do as Her Highness commands, *Junior*. I'll be there in a minute."

About an hour later, Stella was smiling for the guests and sneaking clandestine eyeball rolls at Donnie. It didn't take long for her to retreat into the world of her own sour thoughts:

Great. A rogue's gallery from some old Joan Crawford movie. Hello, Central Casting? Could you send up four pasty-faced lawyer-types and four blue-haired wife-types who look like they've been sucking lemons? Oh! Never mind, they're here.

Stella sat frowning at her father's stale jokes and stories, and watching her mother's reactions. Suspense, surprise, and delight all crossed Audrey Atherton's face with precision timing, despite the fact that she could have spoken the punch lines with him in perfect unison. It was the same old routine, all for the sake of connections.

Just then, the doorbell rang with a late arrival. "I'll get it, Mother," Stella said.

"No, dear," Audrey said sweetly. "That's what we have Carmen for."

The instant Stella opened the door she regretted it. "Alex," she said flatly.

As usual, Alex Monroe was unreasonably handsome. He stood an imposing six-feet-three inches in height and his complexion was the color and texture of liquid caramel. His hair was close-cropped with a blue-black sheen and his sharp features had always reminded Stella of the pretty boys who modeled tuxedoes in *Esquire*. But as she looked at him standing there in his tailored suit smiling his magazine smile, all she could think of was B.B. King. *The thrill is gone.*

She hadn't seen Alex in months. After catching him cheating for the third time, she had simply slipped off her engagement ring and shoved it into the newest other woman's hand.

The memory of the scene made her smile until her mother intervened.

"Alex, darling," Audrey gushed. "I'm so glad you're here. Estelle, baby, it's Alex!"

Stella stood rooted to the spot, like an action toy in need of new batteries.

Alex smiled, obviously amused at her dismayed expression. "You look beautiful, Stella."

Audrey linked arms with Alex. "Come in and let me introduce you to everyone, dear."

As they walked to the dining room, Stella crossed her arms and slunk behind them, muttering under her breath. After the introductions, everyone took their places at the long mahogany table, and Alex sat next to Stella. She felt his hand grasping hers under the tablecloth, and she firmly pushed it away.

"Come on, Stella," he whispered. "You can't still be angry with me about that girl. I can't even remember her name, for God's sake."

She gave him a hard, direct look. "I'm not *angry* with you. I'm just *through* with you."

"You'll never be through with me. I've still got the engagement ring, you know."

Stella had forgotten all about the garlic-laced cheese she had eaten until she noticed the change in his expression. Smiling sweetly, she leaned close and breathed hard into his face as she spoke. "*H-heavens*, Alex! *Haven't* you returned that ring yet? It's *high* time you did."

As Alex blinked and leaned away from Stella, Donnie's fork clattered to the floor and he disappeared under the table for an unusually long time to retrieve it. When he reappeared, his shoulders were shaking with silent laughter, and he stared only at his plate. Stella felt a laugh bubbling up, but managed to keep it under control.

"Anyway, why should I return it when I'm the man you're going to marry?" Alex was whispering. "I'll settle down, you'll see. Look, Stella, nobody will ever love you the way I do."

She gave him an icy look. "Scary thought. In any case, I'm just not interested. So I wish you well, but I'd really appreciate it if you'd leave now."

"Estelle!" Audrey hissed from across the table. "May I speak to you in the kitchen?"

Stella was about to stand up when her father's voice stopped her. "Now, Audrey," he said, "let's just enjoy our dinner. Stella and Alex can talk things over later."

"Of course, dear," Audrey said in a throaty, drawn-butter tone.

Stella stared at her with wide eyes.

Oh, my God! My mother just purred! Like a trained cat on a Friskies commercial...

When Alex touched her hand again, she dug her nails into his wrist, but he only chuckled. Then, for some unknown reason, Nick Bluestone crossed her mind again. *What is it about that guy?* she mused. *Well, he's—cute. And he's a lot more fun than Alex.* She smiled, remembering how many times Nick had made her laugh on their date. *And he's playful, like Donnie.* But there was more—a sensitivity in his eyes that added a dimension of mystery. Her daydreaming came to a halt when she realized that everyone was staring at her. She blinked at her mother. "What?"

"Your father just asked you to tell everyone how you and Alex met, dear."

Stealing a glance at Alex's smug grin, Stella felt the heat rising in her cheeks. "Uh, at Stanford—before I dropped out," she said, glaring defiantly at her mother. "He started dating me after he dumped his high school sweetheart. Actually, he was two-timing her until she found out about me and broke up with him, but I didn't find that out until later." She shot Alex a cynical look. "Wasn't that about right, Alex?"

He laughed easily. "Whatever you say, Stella."

But Stella's moment of insolent victory was short-lived. Her parents quickly smoothed over her inappropriate behavior and left her to her sulking.

Why don't I just leave? Why is an occasional childish outburst the best I can do?

Then she heard Donnie gushing: "Mother, the Hollandaise sauce was *so* delicious."

Stella's eyes zeroed in on her brother's empty plate, and she stared daggers at him. It was the first time he had betrayed her in their game of parental spite. *Oh, Donnie, you're such an ass.*

As the guests began to leave, Stella was looking for her opening to escape. But her father's grip on her arm told her she was staying. *I'm gonna get it now. But at least Alex is gone.*

Audrey waited until the last of the guests had left before she launched her attack. "Estelle Louise Atherton!" she snapped. "Have you completely lost your mind?"

Stella sank down onto the sofa and sighed. "I've got no correct answer for that, Mama, so I'm ready for my flogging. Bring on the cat-o-nine-tails."

Now her father was fuming. "Stella, where does this childish hostility come from? When do you plan to start acting like an educated woman, instead of a petulant twelve-year-old?"

Then came the expected barrage of "no-answer" questions. Stella glanced over at Donnie, who was fighting a laugh by staring intently at the floor.

"We were entertaining very influential people here tonight," her mother said. "And your father is counting on their support for—" She stopped and glanced uncertainly at her husband.

"Go ahead and tell her if you think she'll be interested. I'm going upstairs. I've got calls to make." He stood up and smoothed the lapel of his jacket. Not that it needed smoothing; it was just a bit of courtly Atherton body language. "Junior, I trust you're staying the entire weekend?"

"Yes, sir," Donnie answered. "I'll be taking the late train back on Sunday."

"Very good. Then you'll be going with us to the nursing home tomorrow afternoon."

"Oh, well, uh, yes," Donnie stammered. "What about you, Stel?"

Stella narrowed her eyes and fired a quick death-ray at him. "I've just got so much work—"

Her flimsy excuse earned her one last withering look from her father before he turned to leave. "I'll be upstairs, Audrey," he said. "Goodnight."

"Goodnight, dear."

The room was silent until Donald Atherton's office door closed with a slight slam.

"So what's this news Dad's talking about?" Donnie asked. "Politics, right?"

"Yes, your father has decided to take the plunge. Mr. Dawson and Mr. Weinstein seem to think that with his background he has a bright political future. They can be of invaluable assistance to him, and he needs their guidance and support. They believe that the time is right for some *responsible* black leadership. And your father has some wonderful ideas."

Stella's teeth began grinding the second her mother said the word "responsible." With that slight nuance, she had denounced every black leader from Dr. King to Shirley Chisholm. "What about Tom Bradley, Mama? He's black and responsible, and he's a Mayor."

"Oh, for God's sake, Estelle," Audrey snapped. "He's a Democrat. And don't change the subject. You owe your father an apology."

"Mama, I doubt that I hurt Daddy's chances at a political career, but if I did, I'm sorry."

"Well, I don't think any real damage was done, but Estelle, you've really got to learn to conduct yourself in a more dignified manner when…"

Audrey continued her lecture, but Stella managed to tune her out until the end.

". . . I *said*, do you understand, Estelle?"

"Yes, Mama, I really do understand."

It was a much sweeter answer than the militant translation in her head: *You're a couple of sellout Oreos buck-dancing for the Massah.*

"Oh, by the way, Mama—what was Alex doing here?"

"Alex has moved here to join your father's firm."

Stella groaned. "Great. But that's not why you invited him, Mama, and you know it."

Audrey lifted her chin and narrowed her eyes at Stella. "Just why *did* you break it off with Alex? You never told us. Could it be because your father and I approved of him?"

No, it was because he was screwing everything in a skirt and I wasn't in the mood to catch syphilis from the dog.

But, once again, Stella's prickly thoughts softened when they became spoken words. "He's a philanderer, Mama. And I got tired of it."

"Estelle, all men are philanderers at his age. A good marriage is—"

"Mama, we'll never see eye to eye on men or my career. So let's drop it, please."

Audrey sighed. "I've had a very long day, Estelle, and I'm too tired to do otherwise. Will you be going with us to visit Grandpa tomorrow or not?"

"I'll go. What time should I be here?"

"Two. With family comes duty, Estelle. Remember that… Goodnight."

Once she was gone, Donnie grinned at Stella. "Kitchen?"

She cut her eyes at him. "Yeah, Judas. Kitchen."

The caterers were just finishing the cleanup when Stella and Donnie sat down at the small corner table that had always been their meeting place for heart-to-hearts.

"I can't believe you ate," she whined.

He gasped comically. "I did? Oh, for God's sake! I gobbled my food like one of those Tom Bradley *Democrats*, didn't I? Aw, come on, Stel. They wouldn't care if we fasted like Gandhi!"

"I guess it was a childish game—but it was *our* game, Donnie. You switched sides tonight!"

"No way! Hey, the highlight of the evening for me was when you gassed Billy Dee with your garlic-cheese breath! *H-heavens, Halex! Haven't* you returned that ring yet?" he said, batting his eyelashes. "Holy shit, Stel! I about peed in my pants! I had to dive under the table!"

"He did turn sort of green, didn't he?" Stella laughed. "You are *such* a bad influence on me, Donnie. Good thing Mama didn't catch a whiff of my breath!"

Donnie shook his head. "Don't blame *my* influence, Stel. You came up with that all by your bitchy self. But I'm glad you told him off. I never liked that guy for you. He sure wasn't what you always talked about when you were a starry-eyed ninth-grader."

Stella grimaced. "Which was?"

Donnie placed his right hand over his heart and struck a pompous pose. "A nobleman."

"No, stupid! A noble *man*—a man who is noble. And there *is* a difference, you know."

"I know. They force me to read all that medieval shit at Hah-vud, you know," he sniffed. "But Alex doesn't qualify on either definition, and I'm glad you finally told Mama the reason."

"Can you believe she excused that dog? 'All men are philanderers at his age.' Please."

"Well," Donnie said, grinning, "She was right about that part. Arf, arf."

She smacked his arm. “White sheep! Don’t tell me you’re a hound in sheep’s clothing!”

“Hey, I’m just not ready to settle down yet. And stop calling me white sheep, you brown cow! Besides, I’m just a pup compared to Alex. He juggles girls like he’s Hugh Hefner!”

Stella let out an exasperated sigh. “And how did you know all those details?”

“Just because I’m up in Massachusetts doesn’t mean I don’t stay in touch with my friends in California. People felt more comfortable telling me things after you broke up with him.”

“Well, thanks for letting me in on it.”

“Hey, you’d already dumped him by that time. So I figured, let sleeping dogs lie.”

Stella groaned. “Oh, no. You just couldn’t resist one last lousy pun for the road. Well, I’m calling it a night. And if you bark right now, I’ll slap you silly.”

“Hey, don’t forget about our visit to Grandpa at the home tomorrow.”

“Oh, damn, I *did* forget that. Why do you suppose they bother? Neither of them cares about him. And he just stares at all of us like we’re strangers.”

“We are. He’s so senile, he has no idea who we are. Dad goes because it’d look bad if he didn’t. Maybe he’s like that because he was an only child. I’d be psychotic if I didn’t have you.”

“Yeah, me too. Makes it a more even fight. The kids’ team against the parents.”

“The Atherton rebels without the slightest trace of a damn cause. So are you going or not?”

“Okay, okay. But I don’t mind telling you it gives me the creeps.”

“So we’ll get it over with and then sneak off for dinner, just you and me. How ’bout it?”

“Okay, Donnie. I’ll go. But dinner’s on you.”

Chapter 37

When Nick listened to the first two ballads Stella had written for him, he was overwhelmed. Not only were the lyrics soul-stirring, but the melodic range was evidence that she had carefully studied his voice. He booked time at Big Apple, his favorite studio, which was on Greene Street in SoHo. Stella had managed to be at all the tracking sessions, but she was a no-show for the first vocal session. Nick’s preoccupation with her absence resulted in a lackluster lead track.

The engineer noticed it first, and whispered something to Ed. Ed nodded and called Nick into the control room. "Marco seems to think you need a break, and I agree."

Marco shrugged. "Your levels keep changin', man. And your pitch—hey, I know what you're supposed to sound like when you're hittin' on all cylinders."

Nick sighed. "Well, there's nobody's ears I trust more than yours and Ed's. You think we ought'a call the session and try again tomorrow?"

Before Ed could answer, the telephone rang and Marco answered it. "Big Apple... Oh, sure, he's right here. It's for you, lover boy," he said, grinning. "It's Stella."

Nick rolled his eyes and grabbed the receiver. "Hey, woman, where are you? We need you!"

"No, you don't, Nick. And have you looked outside lately? That's snow out there!"

"Yeah. One of the guys said it snowed a little. So?"

"Well—I can't drive in snow, Nick!"

"Why not?"

"Because—don't you have to have some kind of things on your tires or something?"

Nick laughed. "That's right, you're from California. First New York winter, right?"

"Well, my first *full* winter. All I saw last year was slush. And stop laughing at me."

"Stella. Those little puny flakes are not what hardcore New Yorkers would call *real* snow. That's a light dusting, not a blizzard. Just get in your car and drive over."

"Are you sure it's safe?"

"What're you? A hot-house plant? If you're scared to drive, then jump on the subway."

"No, thanks, Nick. I get lost on the subway. I have to see streets to know where I am."

"Well, then get in your car and you'll see plenty of streets! But please, Ms. Atherton, however you do it, get that fine chassis of yours over here. I got no inspiration, and the general consensus is that I'm singin' lousily."

"*Lousily?*" Stella laughed. "Okay, Mr. Linguist. Help is on the way."

≈∞≈

Stella's arrival improved Nick's vocal performance immediately. With her writing additions and Nick's interpretations, he finished two lead tracks before midnight. Things were going so well that Ed coaxed Marco to stay and work on background vocals. They ordered dinner and worked straight through the night before anyone even thought of the time.

"It must be late," Stella said, yawning. "I'm worn out. What time is it, Nick?"

"Little after seven."

"In the morning? Are you serious? My Lord, no wonder I'm so tired!"

"Yeah, but we got a lot done," Nick said. "Hey, Ed, wanna call it till tomorrow?"

"You mean tomorrow-today or tomorrow-tomorrow? It's already tomorrow technically."

"Tomorrow-tomorrow," Nick said.

Stella groaned. "Okay, that did it. I need sleep, 'cause that actually made sense to me."

Nick wrapped his arm around her shoulders. "Aw, poor thing. Here. I'll walk you out, so you can lean on me and catch a nap on the way to your car."

When they stepped into the foyer, an elderly dark-skinned man in a security uniform was walking in and shaking snow off his coat.

"Hey, Pop," Nick said through a yawn. "How was your vacation?"

Pop looked over his shoulder as he hung up his coat. "Oh, real good, son. Real good. I watched them Knicks on TV and just puttered around the house. Drove my wife crazy!"

"I bet! But what are you doin' working the day shift?"

"Gotta cover for Henry. He's goin' to see his family in Mississippi. Hey, what'chu fellers do? Pull one'a them all-nighters? Oh, 'scuse me, Miss. I mean you fellers and *lady*."

"Yes, we did, Pop," Nick said. "And us fellers and the lady are all beat. I'm sorry. I forgot my manners, if I ever had any. Stella, this is Pop Dawson, best security guard in the business. Pop, this is Stella Atherton, a soon-to-be-Grammy-award-winning songwriter."

Stella laughed. "Confident, aren't we?"

"Well, you must be good, young lady!" Pop said. "And it's real nice to meet'cha."

"Nice to meet you too, Mr. Dawson."

"Aww, honey, you just call me Pop. All the kids 'round here do."

"Okay, Pop. I will. And I'm sure I'll be seeing you again."

"Well, good luck, kids. Y'all gonna be shovelin' for a while."

"Shoveling?" Nick opened the door and squinted. The morning sun was a blinding reflection in a deep expanse of snow. "Oh, hell! It's three feet in some places! It's up to the car windows!"

Stella cut her eyes at him. "So this is what hardcore New Yorkers call a little dusting?"

"Hey, who listens to the weather? Okay, Miss California, you win and I pay. What you are lookin' at is the aftermath of a bona fide, hardcore, New York blizzard."

Ed appeared behind them and hooted. "Damn! When the hell did this happen?"

"While you were snoring in your chair pretending to listen to me sing. That's what we get for working in this off-the-beaten-path studio. The plows haven't gotten here yet."

"Nick!" Stella cried. "I can't even see my car! Do you see my car?"

He pointed across the street. "It's that blue bump in that Siberian wasteland over there."

"So who's gonna pull it out of the snow?"

Nick nudged Ed and they laughed. "Pull?" he said. "No, Stella. Nobody *pulls* your car out of the snow. You gotta go out there with a big heavy shovel and *dig* your car out." He grinned at her and began humming a loud rendition of "The Anvil Chorus."

Ed laughed, but then nodded solemnly. "It'll only take you about three hours, Stella."

"Oh, no," Stella said, crossing her arms. "If anybody's gonna be digging with big heavy shovels for three hours, it'll be Nick. He's the one who begged me to come here in a blizzard."

"Oh, cue the violins," Nick groaned. "Okay, here's what we'll do. The sun'll melt most of this soon. We'll all go home and get some rest, then I'll come back and dig out your car later."

"Well, okay," Stella said. "But how will we get home?"

"Not to worry," Ed sighed. "I'm the only one smart enough to have a four-wheel-drive truck. Only minimal digging. And then I'll drop everybody home."

"Thanks, Ed," Nick said, turning back toward the studio door.

Ed grabbed his arm. "Where are you going? You're gonna help dig my truck out, buddy."

"But—but, Ed! Manual labor? Have you forgotten I'm a star?"

"Not today you ain't. Stella, wait inside and we'll come get you when we're finished."

After digging for about twenty minutes, they cleared a path. Then Ed warmed up the engine and drove the truck as close to the building as he could. Nick went in to fetch Stella, but when she stepped outside, she glanced hesitantly down at her shoes.

"Uh, Nick, can't he get any closer with his truck?"

"Not without a lot more shoveling. Why?"

"Well—it's my shoes."

He glanced down at her feet. "What about your shoes? Or your *former* shoes, I should say, 'cause after you sink those babies into all this snow they'll probably be trashed."

"Oh, well," she sighed. "They cost three hundred dollars but—what's three hundred dollars? I sure can't stay here till it melts. Can I?"

"No, you spoiled-rotten California brat," Nick laughed. "Because around here in *reality*, where we have actual *weather*, you're supposed to wear ugly, functional snow-boots, not three-hundred-dollar-Barbie-doll shoes." He smiled sweetly. "So say goodbye to your shoes now, Stella. I'll give the three of you a moment alone."

"Wait! I know! I'll just walk in my stocking feet and *carry* my shoes. What do you think?"

Nick rolled his eyes. "Okay, then—say goodbye to your feet and hello to frostbite."

Stella was just about to protest when Nick suddenly hoisted her up into his arms. "Okay, okay, I'll carry you. But if I find out this was your plan all along, it's gonna cost you, lady."

Stella shifted her weight and surprised him by snuggling close to his chest. "I confess," she whispered. "So what's it gonna cost me?"

"Exactly three hundred dollars."

Stella cut her eyes at him. "Too bad. I was hoping you'd want to take it out in trade."

Nick cocked his head back and grinned at her. "No shit?"

"No shit." She rolled her eyes. "Great. Won't take Mama long to disown me after we finish this project. With your trash-mouth influence on me, I'll be cursing as much as you do."

"Impossible. And by the way, it's *cussing*, not *cursing*. Cursing is what the Republicans did when Jimmy Carter got elected. Hey, Stella—"

"What is it? Am I getting heavy?"

"Not at all. What do you weigh, anyhow?"

"Take a guess."

"Hmmm. Buck and a quarter? Naw, wait. Not that much. Buck and a dime. Right?"

Stella laughed. "That was some smooth backpedaling."

Nick winked. "I'm a smooth dude, baby."

"Mm-hmm. You're really thinking I weigh about a buck forty. Right?"

He laughed and helped her into the truck. "I'm stickin' to my original answer. It's safer."

Ed drove slowly through the snow-covered streets, sticking to main roads that had been cleared by snowplows, until he reached Stella's apartment building on Riverside Drive. "Looks like your landlord hasn't started shoveling yet," he observed. "But don't get any ideas, Stella. I'll do chauffeur duties, but I draw the line at shoveling other people's steps."

"Oh, no," Stella groaned. "I can't even see the sidewalk!"

Nick banged his head against the headrest. "No!" he cried. "I gotta carry you *again*?"

"Well, it *would* be a shame to get my shoes this far just to ruin 'em at the home stretch."

Nick sighed as he climbed out, then stuck out his arms. "Climb aboard, your highness."

After they made it to the top of the steps, Stella said, "How 'bout some breakfast?"

"Really? I finally get to see the royal African palace?"

"Well, if you're not too—tired."

"Too *tired?* Oh, no, baby," he said, grinning. "I'm never *that* tired."

Just as they stepped into the foyer, Ed's horn sounded. "Oh, shit!" Nick laughed. "We forgot about Ed." He put Stella down and stuck his head out the door. "Stella's makin' me breakfast," he shouted. "You— you wanna come in—too?"

Ed laughed and put the truck in reverse. "Call me later. I'll book the room for tomorrow."

Nick waved, then followed Stella to the top of the landing.

She opened the door to her apartment and they stepped inside. "Ooh, it's cold in here! Nick, why don't you start a fire while I see what's in the refrigerator."

Nick let out a long whistle as he surveyed the front room. Stella's taste ran to earthy greens and browns, and rugged textures, which enhanced her African theme. A sprawling L-shaped leather sofa faced a fireplace made of black, jagged-stones with two authentic Zulu masks hanging on each side. The room was the very essence of nature—the flora and fauna of some mythical African village. Rough wooden animal statuary decorated corners and shelves, with dramatic lighting accenting each piece. And the large exotic plants appeared to be growing not from pots, but from the steamy earthen floor of a jungle.

After a long silence, Nick finally said, "Stella! This is—beautiful."

"Thanks. I'm really glad you like it."

"No, I mean—it's *really*—I can't even find a word. Not like any room I've ever been in."

"Well, at first I didn't know what I was going for, so I let my instinct guide me. And the more tribal and raw it got, the more peaceful it felt, if that makes any sense."

"It makes perfect sense. Like your soul was guiding you."

"What a nice thing to say! Hey, have you read *Roots* yet?"

"Not yet. But I heard on the news that it's selling out every time they put it on the shelves. So that's what influenced your decorating?"

"Oh, no. I've been collecting my African stuff since college. I had to balance all that pre-law stuff with something I actually liked—like world history and music. So when *Roots* came out, I was ready for it." She shrugged self-consciously. "Well, let me get started on breakfast."

Nick built a fire that he hoped was worthy of the room, and then the smell of bacon lured him into the kitchen. Stella was standing at the stove beside an abnormally large cat with a glossy, blue-black coat and staring green eyes.

"How do you like your eggs?"

Without taking his eyes off the cat, Nick said, "Uh, scrambled. And what's with the panther? Your African importer bring you a kitten from Zimbabwe or sump'm?"

"Sorry to disappoint you, but he's just your garden variety house cat."

"No. I lived with a *normal* house cat named Sylvester—a *runt* compared to this bruiser."

The cat tilted his head and emitted a "waah" sound that was half-growl and half-rasp.

"Damn, cat! You must'a cut meowing class in school, huh? What's his name anyway?"

"His name is Miles. I adopted him from a shelter. Everybody was scared of him because he was so big and surly looking, but I took one look at him and I swear he smiled at me."

Nick pulled up a chair, turned it backwards, and rested his chin on the backrest. "*Surly* I believe, but smiling I'd have to *see* to believe. You name him after Miles or Wolfman Jack?"

Stella laughed. "You heard him meow. He talks like Miles."

"So you must be a jazz fan if you named him after Miles."

"I am. And I know you are too. I hear all that jazzy stuff you do in your ad libbing."

"Well, as much as I can get away with. But a real jazz singer? I wouldn't even try 'cause I ain't that good. But I listen to jazz when I wanna relax. It was my lullaby when I was a baby and the theme song to my whole childhood."

"That's a nice way of putting it. I didn't get into jazz until college. My roommate used to play all those great Coltrane ballads and I found myself humming the melodies. I had a pretty good musical foundation with my piano lessons and all that classical training. So I really got into the structure and asked my roommate to play me some of the more advanced stuff—you know, Monk and Brubeck and those guys. Before I knew it, I was hooked and started buying albums."

Nick tried to pet the cat. "Okay, Miles, you gonna be cool and let me hang around?"

Miles leaned his head back to avoid Nick's touch, but held his ground.

"Oh," Nick said, withdrawing his hand. "Stubborn, huh? Guess I gotta work on the wildcat. Maybe I'll bring him a juicy wildebeest carcass next time I come over. Whadaya think?"

Stella rolled her eyes. "Well, there went *my* appetite. Go on and eat before it gets cold."

"Thank you, Stella. It was really nice of you to cook 'cause I know you're beat."

"Actually, I'm still wired. You know, I've never done anything like that—staying up all night working on music, unplanned and just going with the inspiration. I usually keep to a strict schedule." She shrugged. "It was just a different experience for me, that's all."

Nick winked. "Stick with me, kid. I do a lot of that unplanned kind'a shit."

Stella turned on the radio and they settled down in front of the fireplace to eat their breakfast as Sarah Vaughan sang "Key Largo." Nick was watching Miles, curious about his interest in a large plant arrangement in the corner. "Don't look now, but I think Miles is eating your jungle."

"No, he's just getting a drink. Look what's on the side of that little tree."

Nick moved a large leaf that was obstructing his view. "Hey—it's a waterfall!"

"Just a little one. I'm surprised you didn't hear the trickling noise."

"Wow, Stella. I never knew anybody with a waterfall in their living room before."

"Well, you do now. Why don't you relax while I take a quick shower."

Nick grinned. "Need help? I could help you with those hard-to-reach spots."

She laughed. "Nice try. I'll be back in a few minutes."

Nick stretched and gazed up at a tilted skylight running the length of the room. A new snowstorm was swirling outside. He fought to keep his eyes open, but the fire was crackling in harmony with the trickling waterfall, and the blend of sounds hypnotized him into a deep sleep.

≈∞≈

When Nick woke up the fire was out. Stella was asleep next to him and Miles was lying on his chest staring at him like an imperious Sphinx-wrestler who had just pinned him to the mat. "Thinkin' of scratchin' my eyes out, Miles?" he whispered. "Think twice. Your Mama likes me."

The cat didn't move or even blink. Nick drummed his fingertips on one of the pillows. "I'm negotiating with a cat," he whispered. "Hey, Miles—whadaya weigh? About a buck fifty?"

Miles yawned widely, exposing an impressive set of large, razor sharp teeth. "Waaah."

Nick's eyes widened. "Shit! Okay, since you put it *that* way—" He began to stroke the cat's neck until he felt claws digging rhythmically into his chest. "Ouch!" he yelped.

Stella's eyes fluttered open, and she reached for Miles. "Oh, I'm sorry, Nick! They dig their claws like that when they're happy."

"I know that! But I'm used to happy little house-cat claws, not *meat hooks*, like this guy's got, for chrissakes!" He raised his shirt and peered down at his chest. "Am I shredded?"

"I'm really sorry," Stella said, inspecting his chest. "I hope he didn't break the skin."

"I'm tough. I'll survive," he said, grinning. "Okay, now it's my turn to take a shower."

"Bathroom's right down at the end of that hall."

"Band-Aids in the medicine chest?" he called over his shoulder.

Stella rolled her eyes. "Ha-ha."

By the time he returned, Stella was spreading a large down comforter over the bed of pillows on the floor. Nick liked the way things seemed to be going. "Let me get the fire goin' again," he offered.

"Mmm. You read my mind. Listen, are you hungry? I could fix something."

"No, relax. I guess I should be hungry, but I'm not."

"Me either," Stella said, leaning against the pillows. "Hey, I wonder what time it is?"

Nick squinted at his watch. "About a minute past eight. We slept all day. I never sleep that long! But this place is so comfortable."

"That's why we're in here. When my heater works, it only works in the front room. And when it doesn't, I've got this fireplace. I've really gotta call the super."

"Well, I got the fire goin' again so we're okay for now. And with all the plants and these paintings of Africa and that window on the ceiling, it's like sleeping outside. But it's warm."

"Oh, those aren't paintings. They're blown up photos—of the Serengeti Plain in Tanzania. I know the colors look too unusual to be photos, but they are."

"I sure would like to go to Africa—if it wasn't for that apartheid and everything."

"I know," Stella said softly. "The world is so beautiful, but there's so much hate."

"Sorry, Stella. I didn't mean to bring you down."

She smiled. "You didn't... Hey, my feet are cold. Are you a good foot warmer?"

Nick burrowed under the covers and rubbed his foot against Stella's ankle. "I can't believe I fell asleep with you layin' next to me without at least *tryin'* to make a move!"

"Well, the night is young."

"Ah, the lady is certainly agreeable tonight."

"Well—I'll just be honest, Nick. I didn't mean for it to happen, and I don't want to scare you off, but I'm starting to feel serious about you. I don't know how it happened so fast."

Nick propped his head up on one fist and gazed at her seriously. "I'm not scared. I've just been going slow with you, that's all. Look, I've never been very serious with just one girl, but when I met you, I knew you were different. And I really wanted to get to know you. In fact, I never wanted to know anybody the way I want to know you. And that's not a Mack line."

"What do you mean?"

"Well, it's way past physical attraction, 'cause that burns up pretty quick for me. It's *so* different with you." He stared into the fire. "I've been tryin' to figure it out these past few weeks, and it finally hit me what it was. We have one very important thing in common, and I think I've been looking for it. I just never knew it."

"Which is?"

"Well— See, when I was a little kid I really only wanted to sing because my father sang. It was the only thing he ever did that impressed me. He made a record that I could play on my little record player. He was dead, but I could still hear his voice. Then Calvin came along and told me I had talent. But I never thought about who I was or what I really wanted to *be*."

"Okay, and—?"

"And it bugged me. The other kids had things they wanted to be when they grew up. A doctor, a fireman, a teacher. You know, ambitions. I could sing, but it was just sump'm I could do, like Shay was the double-dutch champ of the block. No more, no less."

Stella shook her head and smiled. "I still don't see what you're driving at."

"Well, see, I went through a pretty tough time when I found out the truth about my father. I was out in L.A. doin' a concert when I was about sixteen, maybe seventeen, and this piano player came backstage and told me he worked with my father back in '51. He started talkin' about how sad it was, the way he died and all that, and then, all of a sudden I feel Calvin grabbing my arm. He says, 'Conversation's over.' I never saw him so rattled or so pissed in my life. I never even got the guy's name, and Calvin refused to talk about it. But he should'a known I'd be curious. I started thinking back and trying to remember things I'd overheard when I was little. I remembered Aunt Pearl sayin' sump'm about newspaper articles and pictures in magazines, so I went to the library and looked up the year my father died in the *Chicago Tribune* archives. Then I found it in some old gossip magazines, the *New York Times*, even *Down Beat*. And it was a whole different story than the one everybody told me all my life."

Stella touched his arm. "You don't have to talk about this, Nick."

"No, I want to. See, all those years I believed my father killed himself because of Mama's *accident*. When you're little, adults can get away with being vague, and I guess I sort of dreamed up my own romantic version of things. In my version, he killed himself because he couldn't live without Mama. But the real truth wasn't so romantic. He didn't kill himself *after* the accident; he killed himself *before* the accident. Him dying was what sent Mama into depression. And back then, they were still treating depression with some pretty barbaric methods."

"Nick—"

"No, I'm okay. I gotta tell you this because I really want you to understand. See, if my father had been man enough to face *life*, then Mama wouldn't be layin' up in that damn hospital today."

"I'm sorry, Nick. That must've been pretty hard to take, especially at sixteen."

"Yeah, but it made me stop idolizing him. And in an indirect way, it helped me find my own ambition. Me and Calvin went to France that summer to see my family, and I was still pretty messed up over what I'd read in those magazines. I told everybody I wanted to quit singing because I didn't want to be like my father. To be honest, I ain't the greatest at handling bad news. I have a history of overreacting, I guess. But anyway, one day we all went to the Louvre Museum, and I swear, sump'm happened to me at that place. All those ancient paintings and sculptures—I felt like I was in a church or some temple, and it hit me! I realized that my *voice* was a tool, like the tools that carved those sculptures or the paint and brushes that made those paintings. I wasn't like Joe Bluestone. All he wanted was to be a star. But I wanted to be an *artist*. And all of a sudden, I wanted it *bad*. Look, I know I kid around about being a star, but I don't really care about that at all. There are a lot better singers than me out there. But deep down inside, I'm proud of one thing—I *live* my songs. If it's sad, I can make 'em cry. If it's a dance cut,

I can make 'em so happy they forget their rotten day at work. And my songs are being recorded, just like your songs are. That's how people will remember us, Stella. Stars aren't eternal, but art *is*."

She smiled vaguely. "That's weird. That's sort of how I felt when I saw *The Starry Night* at the Museum of Modern Art when I first got to New York. Like he spoke to me."

"Wait—who spoke to you?"

"Vincent van Gogh."

"Oh, yeah—the guy who cut off his ear, right? The painter."

"That's what everybody remembers about him, but there was so much more. His big struggle was bringing the illusion of motion to the canvas. Some art critics even called it 'turbulence.'" Stella shrugged self-consciously. "Okay, so I was one of those girls with her nose always in a book. Anyway, so I read about his mental illness and how he killed himself thinking he was a failure, but when I saw that painting in the museum, there it was—the movement! The moon was glowing, the stars were spinning, the wind was blowing the trees... Don't laugh, but I actually started crying, and I kept babbling, 'You did it, Vincent!' It felt like he was right beside me—so pleased that I noticed. Everybody looked at me like I was crazy... So—do *you* think I'm crazy?"

Nick shook his head. "Not at all. You're an artist, and you were just having a talk with another artist, who happened to be dead. That's not crazy. We do it every time we listen to music. All those old jazz musicians like Coltrane and Billie Holiday—they all come back to life to talk to us the minute the needle hits the record. And we get to visit their world for a while."

Stella smiled. "I never figured you to be so philosophical, Nick."

"Yeah, I know. I'm always clowning. But I—have this other side too."

Stella gazed up at the skylight with a distant, dreamy expression. "You know what? You really make me feel good about the choices I've made in my life."

"You made great choices, Stella. You're an artist! You know how many people stuck in that nine-to-five hell depend on us for their escape from the rat race? Aunt Pearl used to say it's a damn mean world we live in, and she was right. And whenever I think about that, I realize that my job is to take the sharp edges off that meanness, and make people smile. And that's a privilege." Nick gazed into the fire. "How 'bout that?" he said softly. "Aunt Pearl's been gone for years, but she's still teaching me things."

Stella rested her head on his shoulder. "Nick, what time is it—right this minute?"

Nick gazed at his watch. "Eight twenty one. Why?"

"Well—I think I just fell in love with you, and I wanted to remember the time."

"Pretty smooth. Wish I'da said that." He touched her face. "Stella," he whispered, "I feel—so peaceful with you. Please make me stay peaceful."

Instead of answering, she kissed him. And the dance began.

Nick felt himself falling with Stella into some new place, deep in the unknown wilderness of that room. Where all the lines between fantasy and reality blurred, and dancing firelight urged them out of clothing to feel its warmth. A surreal elongation of time took physical pleasure to new heights, and disjointed thoughts tumbled freely in his mind. Tall green plants and Zulu masks framed Stella's face with ageless images of Africa, and Nick lost all track of time and space. Upon the sudden realization that he was completely inside her, a shiver ran down his spine; he couldn't clearly remember arriving at this essential point of lovemaking. He tried to focus. Had this been going on for seconds or minutes? Or had it been hours? He held her face with both hands and gazed into those black, penetrating eyes that never seemed to close. What was that look? He had never seen that look before, yet it was eerily familiar.

Stella was responsive, but quiet, with no over-zealous theatrics. Her breathing merged with the rhythm of his, and resonated like a whispered harmony in his ears. The only other sound in the room was the musical trickling of the waterfall. Another tremor ran through his body, and he held her tighter. At the point of climax her eyes widened, then finally closed. Again Nick surrendered to his fuzzy senses. A blink—the Zulu masks, a village. A sound—Stella's sigh, the waterfall, a River. An image of some long-ago place flashed in his memory—more feeling than visual. Some kind of primal compulsion came over him. His hands roamed over her hips with an unfamiliar urgency, and his fingertips tingled at the warm smoothness of her skin. He rolled her over forcefully and buried his face in her neck as he shuddered with the release.

When he looked at her face, her eyes had softened with a confused vulnerability. He wanted to reassure her—but she smiled unexpectedly, as if she had read his thought. And with that look, Nick knew that there was much more going on between them than just the first seductive dance of a love affair. And he knew that his normal urge to escape before daylight would not surface this time.

It didn't. Sometime during the night, he woke up and looked around the strange, exotic room. And he was perfectly content to lie there quietly thinking, surrounded by Stella's cherished bits of Africa, a waterfall, and a cat named Miles.

Chapter 38

Stella was nervous a few days later as she walked up the steps with Nick to his apartment. When he unlocked the door, she touched his arm. "Wait."

Nick looked back at her. "What's wrong? Aww, come on. Don't tell me you're nervous!"

"What if he doesn't like me?"

He grinned and opened the door. "It's *me* he doesn't like—most'a the time. *You* he'll love!"

Stella looked around the brightly lit living room. It was masculine but neat, with a long dark blue sofa. The coffee table was a large square made of rough slate, and the rest of the furnishings were utilitarian—two black club chairs, a stereo with large speakers, and a television set. Stella was about to take a seat on the sofa when she heard angry shouting from a back room.

"Where's my *got*damn blue shirt? If I miss my flight, I bet'cha I put my foot in that boy's ass!"

Nick smiled ruefully at Stella and sighed. "Ouch. Foot in the ass. Wait here a minute, Stella. Something tells me he didn't hear us come in."

"I don't know, Nick," Stella fretted. "He sounds—"

"I know. He sounds like a grizzly bear. But believe me. He's just a loud, foul-mouthed teddy-bear. Have a seat and I'll be right back."

Stella sat down, listening to the exchange of muffled male voices. A moment later, Nick walked back into the room with an amused expression. Behind him was a slightly taller brown-skinned man, who looked to be in his late forties. He wore a neatly-trimmed graying beard, and his head was shaved. His smile looked polite but uncomfortable.

"Calvin, I want you to meet Stella Atherton," Nick said.

Stella stood up and extended her hand. "Good to meet you, Mr. Bailey."

"You too," he muttered as he shook her hand.

"My uncle's embarrassed 'cause you heard him carryin' on back there like a fool."

Calvin took a chair across from Stella. "Which I would *not* have been doin' if some other fool didn't dirty up my good blue shirt and then not take it to the cleaners when he was supposed to. Hello, Stella. I promise I ain't this mean all the time."

"I'm sure you're not. Not after all the nice things Nick's told me about you."

"This knucklehead? He says nice things about me?"

"Yeah, when I'm not busy dirtying up all your good shirts," Nick cracked.

"I'll remember that next time we're in the middle of a knock-down-drag-out. And Stella, please call me Calvin. Mr. Bailey was my Daddy."

"Okay, Calvin. Listen, I understand you're a hot-shot promotion man."

"Well, I do a lot of independent promotion for different labels. I worked a few of your records, matter of fact. But I'm way too old to be called a hot-shot."

"Oh, please. You're not old."

"I am too! This youngster right here done aged me 'bout fifty years. You wait, young lady. You see this gray in my beard? Hope you ready to change your name to Miss Clairol."

"Hey!" Nick said. "You're supposed to tell her the good things!"

Calvin rubbed his chin and stood up. "Good things? Well, that's gonna take a lotta work and imagination, boy, and I'm about to miss my flight. Sorry, Stella, but this last minute trip just came up and I really gotta get goin'. But I got a feelin' I'ma be seein' you again." He leaned down and whispered, "The boy *sings* about you."

"He *sings* about me?"

Nick groaned loudly. "What time did you say your flight was, Calvin?"

"An hour from now, and if that driver doesn't get here soon, I'ma miss it. Oh! I nearly forgot. You got a call from somebody named Miller—Ted Miller. He said he got you a good price on that stock you were interested in. You playin' the stock market, boy?"

"Just some investments. Nothing risky, so don't worry. I'll tell you about it later."

Calvin looked at Stella, then back at Nick, and smiled. "Okay, man."

Just as he glanced at his wristwatch, a car horn blew outside. "Well, it's about damn time," he muttered. "Listen, Stella, it was real nice meetin' you."

"Same here, Calvin. Have a safe, successful trip."

"Thanks, young lady. And what about you, Nick? What'chu got to say for yourself?"

Nick laughed. "Sorry about the shirt, Calvin. I'll buy you a new one."

"Always throwin' your money away. Just take it to the cleaners, man!"

"Okay, okay. It'll be hanging in your closet when you get back. *Bye*, Calvin."

Once he was gone, Stella laughed. "You too are really close, aren't you?"

"*That* barkfest gave you the idea that we were close? We are, but how could you tell?"

"My brother and I are like that. Shoot cheap shots at each other all day long and miss each other like crazy when we're apart. Anyway, that stock you bought seemed to make him happy."

"Naaah. He just thinks it's a sign that I'm growing up."

"And are you?"

"Not until absolutely necessary."

"That sounds about right. Okay, so now what? Do I get a grand tour?"

"Okay, but it's just a two-bachelor flop-house compared to your place."

"My place isn't all that elegant or anything."

"Oh, yes it is. African elegant. I dig your place."

"Well, show me your room. I can tell a lot about a person by seeing his surroundings."

"Oh, I get it. You're lookin' for evidence—empty beer cans and *Playboy* magazines layin' around. Maybe the random red panties or a stray double-D bra under my pillow, right?"

"Hmm. That sounded pretty specific. So am I gonna bump into a bunny in there wearing red panties and a big, giant bra? With a beer?"

"No, Miss Wise-ass. She's been gone for hours. But I wouldn't mind if *you* dressed up like a bunny and brought me a beer."

"My highest aspiration in life, Nick—bunnyhood. How'd you guess?"

Nick laughed and led her through the kitchen to a second long hallway, at the end of which was his room. "Well, this is it. Come on in."

Stella's mouth fell open when she walked into the room. Every square inch of wall space was covered by photographs, newspaper articles, and posters. Moody black and white shots of jazz musicians— Thelonious Monk at the piano; Dexter Gordon in Zoot-suit slacks, undershirt, suspenders, and a porkpie hat, holding his sax; and the iconic overhead shot of Miles Davis onstage, his trumpet pointed downward. There were snapshots of Nick and Calvin with deejays they had visited across the country, and over Nick's bed was a row of school photos—a boy and a girl, in growth sequence—from missing-teeth years to graduation caps and gowns.

"Okay, you said you could tell a lot about a person by his surroundings. I ain't got a wildcat or a waterfall or anything—but what's the verdict?"

"Oh, Nick! I love people with a lot of layers."

"Who, me? I got layers?"

Stella turned in a circle, surveying the walls. "I've got a million questions to ask you!"

"Good. That'll give me plenty of time to make passes at you while I answer 'em."

"Okay, first question. I make the connection with the jazz—your parents and all that—and I suppose these old school pictures must be Edward and Shay, right?"

"Mm-hmm," Nick said as he nuzzled her neck. "Edward runs a travel agency in Paris and Shay's a school teacher in Marseilles. And don't ask to see *my* school pictures! They were too goofy to put up."

"I don't need to see your goofy school pictures. I saw your goofy first album cover."

Nick shoved her playfully. "Ha-ha."

"And this orange tabby cat—this can't be Sylvester?"

"Yup. My boy Sylvester."

"He's cute! Whatever happened to him?"

"Of course he's cute! But he needed stability. Miss Rose always took care of him when I was out of town, which was a lot, and he really loved her. Then when we moved out of the old building, I had to haul him back and forth in the car, and he hated that. So when Miss Rose retired to Miami with her son two years ago, Sylvester decided to retire too."

"You mean he's still alive?"

"Yup. He's thirteen and he loves Miami! He fits right in. He's got his little sunglasses and he wears these small little white socks with brown sandals—and Bermuda shorts—"

"Stop."

"—and he plays Mahjong with the little old Jewish ladies."

Stella groaned. "No wonder he moved away with Miss Rose. He's probably allergic to *corn*. But wait a minute. He's orange! Wasn't the Sylvester in the cartoons a black and white cat?"

"That's the same thing Shay said! You women got no imagination."

"I certainly *do* have imagination, Nick. It just doesn't stretch as far as a Bermuda-shorts-wearin' cat playing—what? Mahjong? In Miami?" She yawned theatrically. "Now *my* cat wouldn't be caught dead in that getup—and his game's poker."

Nick grimaced and nudged her to the next group of photos on the wall. "Who's corny?"

"Hey, wait. What's up with these protest photos? Is that you?"

"It was a Vietnam protest rally, that's all."

"Horrible war. I'm so glad it's over. But wait—"

"What? Ask me anything."

"Well, I was just thinking that if you protested the war, then you probably never went. Were you a conscientious objector like Ali?"

"Well, Daddy was trying to get me to France before my eighteenth birthday, but everything went wrong and I ended up having to register like everybody else. I had a few friends that— Well, most of my friends who were sweatin' the draft just turned to weed. You know, crank up the stereo and stay on a nice cannabis high—and hope your number doesn't come up."

Stella frowned slightly. "So is that what you did?"

"Nah, I turned to cartoons! Daffy, Bugs, Pepé le Pew, and Sylvester the cat, of course."

"That'd be the black and white Sylvester."

"Yes, Miss Smart-ass. Sylvester, the *actor*. Anyway, that was my escape—watching cartoons and trying not to think about the war. And somehow I never got into the whole pot-smoking thing. I tried it once and didn't care for it. That was enough for me."

"Well, that's good news."

"But I—I had a very good friend who died over there in '68."

"Oh, I'm sorry. 1968 was such a bad year. That was the year Dr. King was killed."

"Yes. And a couple of months later, Bobby Kennedy. And—my friend Ernie."

Rattled by his vacant expression, Stella said, "I'm so sorry about your friend, Nick."

"It's okay. It just bothers me whenever I think about it too much. All those guys died—and for what? Anyway, all you wanted to know was how I managed to avoid Vietnam... Okay, let's see. I turned eighteen in '71 so I had to wobble my scared-shitless ass in for my physical. My number ended up being 330, which was pretty high, and then they cut troop levels, so I got *very* lucky." He shrugged. "But you can feel real guilty bein' that lucky."

"Well, I'm glad you didn't go. And I think maybe we ought to change the subject, okay?"

"Good idea."

"Okay, now tell me about this picture," she said, pointing at a silver framed photo of a dark-skinned older man with his arm around Nick's neck.

Nick smiled broadly. "Oh, that's Daddy. The one and only Doc Calhoun."

"So that's him! He's got that look, all right. Like all those jazz musicians—that sort of distant, high-on-the-music kind of look. And the lip—he's got that horn player's lip, huh?"

"Yeah, it looks a little beat up, but that lip still works great. Okay, now, here's my favorite one of Mama and Pearl," he said, reaching for a photo on his nightstand. "See?"

Stella's eyes widened as she studied the two young women in the color-tinted photograph. They were sitting in a nightclub, wearing strapless, full-skirted dresses that were popular in the early 1950s—a style Stella's mother called "after-five." She stared at their shining eyes and red-lipstick smiles wide with laughter. The two women's joy at just being together seemed to leap from the photo in confetti-colors. Stella couldn't help laughing with them.

"What?" Nick asked. "What's funny?"

"Not funny—just— They're laughing, see? They must've really been close friends."

"They always found a way to laugh, even when things were rough. Guess that's why it's my favorite picture of 'em. And they were more than friends. More like sisters, from what Pearl always said."

"That's cool, considering how unusual it was back then. A black woman and a white woman as close as sisters? With all that prejudice everywhere? But how come you never mentioned that Pearl was—"

The doorbell rang suddenly, interrupting her question.

"I'm sorry, Stella. Let me go see who that is and I'll be right back."

"Take your time. I'll just browse the gallery."

When Nick returned, he was staring intently at a flat, square package in his hands. After ripping off the paper, he grinned and held up a phonograph album. "Listen to this! 'Dear Son: Now you aren't the only one who's a big recording star. Hope you like it. Love, Daddy.'"

The title on the cover was in French and written in bright blue script: *Cherchez la femme.* Nick turned it over and began to read the list of songs. "'What Are You Doing the Rest of Your Life,' 'When I Fall in Love,' 'Mood Indigo,' 'Autumn Leaves,' 'When Your Lover Has Gone.'"

"What label is it, Nick?"

"A French label—*Musique de Nuit.* It means night music… I wonder why he didn't tell me he recorded an album?"

"He probably wanted to surprise you, fool!" Stella laughed.

"Yeah. I guess," he murmured.

Stella took a seat on the edge of the bed. "I'd love to hear it, Nick."

"Stella," he said softly, "do you know what *cherchez la femme* means?"

"Let's see… I know *femme* means woman or girl, right?"

"It means 'look to the woman' or 'follow the woman.' And—the very last cut is 'Lush Life.' He played that song over and over after Pearl died… This whole album is about Pearl. All these songs—"

"Oh… that's beautiful! It's a love letter set to music. Don't be sad, Nick. Don't you see? This is his way of remembering their life together—the good times and the sad times too. It was probably like a catharsis for him after all this time."

"What's that mean—catharsis?"

"Well, it's a cleansing—a clearing of the mind and spirit. Like crying. That's a catharsis. But we don't have to listen to it now. We can listen to it another time."

"No, let's play it now," he said, carefully slipping the album out of its sleeve. "And don't worry—I won't be doin' any of that catharsis stuff."

Stella smiled. "Okay."

Nick placed the album on the turntable and positioned the needle at the beginning of "What Are You Doing the Rest of Your Life?" Then he stretched out on the bed. The instrumental arrangement was rich and atmospheric, and Stella rested her head on his chest, instantly entranced. Nick sang the lyrics in a soft whisper, leading her into a dream world where she saw Doc and Pearl, still young and in love, dancing to their song.

Chapter 39

Doc Calhoun took his regular seat at the bar and greeted the regulars of the nightclub he had called home for over ten years. Le Petit Journal was known for its twisting staircase that descended from the street entrance at 71 Boulevard St-Michel into one of the most popular cave clubs in Paris. He smiled at the bartender who quietly opened a new bottle of Johnnie Walker Red and filled a glass to the quarter point. Doc chuckled as he picked up the glass.

"Now, Jacques. What would you do if I decided to order a nice glass of Chablis one night?"

Jacques grinned. "I would go to za church and beg forgeevness of my seens, of course."

Doc chuckled as he lit a cigarette. "Mon frére! Pourquoi?"

"Because, mon frére, eet would mean zat za hell—she freeze over. Jacques has one reservation een zat hell, and no long-zhacks for such za freeze."

Doc laughed. "Not long-jacks, sil vous plaît. Long-*johns*."

Jacques tapped his forehead with his index finger and winked. "Long-zhohns. I weel master zees crazy Onglish language, my friend."

"And pour moi—le Français," Doc answered, and then drained the glass.

Several rowdy young people were making their way down the winding staircase, and Jacques sighed. "A busy night for Jacques, n'est pas?"

Doc tapped the bottle. "Just leave it, Jacques," he said. "Put it on my tab."

Jacques kept his hand on the bottle. "Mademoiselle Shay— You promised her."

"No nagging, Mother. I promise I won't gulp down the whole bottle."

Jacques turned to wait on another customer, and Doc caught a glimpse of himself in the wide mirror behind the bar. His hair was completely gray now, and thinner. He was stunned at how gaunt he looked in the dim light, so he smiled, hoping it would improve his appearance. After extinguishing his cigarette, he adjusted the stool, leaned against the bar, and watched the entrance. Sarah Vaughan's voice floated out of the jukebox: *The shadow of your smile...*

He was smiling at Sarah's warm voice and the buzz of the scotch when he saw Shay walking slowly down the winding stairs. He could still see her as a gangly fourteen-year-old taking those stairs two at a time, like an experienced mountain goat. She had always been more comfortable playing with the younger French children from the neighborhood and for years seemed unwilling to grow up. But she was a woman now, and she was smiling at the tall, olive-skinned Frenchman with her. That smile—it was Pearl's smile. Doc sipped his scotch and watched Shay greeting her friends.

A slender, gray-haired man in dark trousers and a white shirt with rolled up sleeves hurried over and kissed her cheeks. "Shay! Bonjour, dahling. We have meesed you!"

"Comment ca va, Henri?" she said, returning his kiss.

Henri shrugged and smiled. "Comme ci, comme ça, mon petit. We are all fine."

"Écoute, Henri—I want you to meet Phillipe Tourneau. Phillipe, this is Henri LeChampes. He's the Dutch uncle I told you about. Well, a French uncle, I guess."

"Bonjour," Phillipe said as he reached for the older man's hand. "Bonne foule ce soir?"

Henri smiled at Phillipe. "Oui, certainement! Pardon—" As he nudged Shay in the direction of the bar, he whispered, "Sh-sh-shoo, mon petit. Allez—ta Papa."

Shay nodded. "Oui. Come on, Phillipe. I want you to meet Daddy."

Doc stood up slowly and extended his arms as Shay ran over to him. "Hey, baby!" he said, hugging her and dancing her in a slow circle.

Shay took a nervous breath and smiled. "Well, here he is, Daddy—Phillipe Tourneau, the man I told you about. He's been dying to meet you."

"Bonjour, Phillipe. I hope you parlez some Anglais, and forgive my lousy French."

"But of course, sir. And your daughter has even taught me some of your jazz expressions, so I have been uh, digging the groove."

Doc laughed. "Diggin' the groove, huh? Well, all right, man—copacetic! Listen, I've been hearing a lot of wonderful things about you. Now, come on. They can't *all* be true."

Phillipe laughed. "Sir, you know this daughter of yours. She exaggerates, no?"

"She exaggerates, oui." Doc took a seat and groaned as Shay peered into the ashtray.

"I thought you were quitting, Daddy," she said softly.

"I am, baby. I'm down to four a day, believe it or not."

Shay narrowed her eyes. "Four, huh? Four cigarettes or four *packs*?"

"Oooh! You sounded just like your Mama just then. Suspicious *and* sarcastic," he laughed. "Well, for your information, it's four cigarettes, but there was a time it *was* four packs."

"Well, that makes me very happy. So where's King? I want Phillipe to meet him."

"Oh, hell, hit my nerve, why don't you! We have a temporary drummer sittin' in this week just because His Majesty had to go off to Germany to play one'a those jazz festivals. You know, Phillipe, those shows with about one or two *legit* jazz acts and about twenty pop singers or rock and roll bands—or R&B or whatever they're callin' it now. All I know is it is *not* jazz."

Shay grinned. "Daddy's sore spot."

"Damn right!" Doc said with a dismissive wave. "I mean, it's okay for King. You know he'll try anything when it comes to music. Remember what his favorite record was?"

Shay groaned. "Oh! That horrible Stan Kenton thing! What was it called?"

"'City of Glass.' He still plays that madness when he wants to light my fuse," Doc chuckled. "Hey, I like improvisation as much as the next cat, but that one escapes me. King's a little crazy, Phillipe, but he's my best friend so I tolerate him. Even his itch for the road. And he only goes out now and then. As for me, I like it right here. This place is my home now."

"Where the real jazz cats are!" Shay laughed.

"Well, what's left of us. All the great jazz artists are gone now. Bird and Trane and Lester Young. My friends in the States tell me you can't even find a decent jazz radio station anymore."

"But *you* are still here, sir," Phillipe said. "And you are a real jazz artist. And France has much jazz on the radio. Dizzy Gillespie is still alive, and Miles Davis and Horace Silver—"

Doc grinned. "Hey, this boy knows his jazz! So, Phillipe, has Shay played for you yet? Hey, that's what we'll do, baby! You come on and sit in tonight."

Before Shay could respond, Phillipe began asking questions. "But I did not know this! Why didn't you tell me you are a musician, cherie? What instrument do you play?"

"You mean you didn't tell Phillipe about your high school garage-band career?"

Shay groaned. "Great. Here come all the embarrassing lowlights of my childhood."

Phillipe grabbed her hands. "But I must hear you play! Please play, mon cher."

"No! And to quote my Daddy, make that *hell*, no! It's been years!"

Doc nudged Phillipe. "You should'a heard her play "Giant Steps," man. Hey, baby, didn't you win the high school talent contest playin' that?"

Shay glared at him. "Stop it! You know I came in third!"

"But I love "Giant Steps," cherie!" Phillipe said. "You *know* I love John Coltrane."

"Okay, that's it," Doc said, throwing his hands in the air. "The man loves Coltrane, so here's your blessing or stamp of approval, or whatever you two are lookin' for. So how long is it gonna take you to stop clownin' around and spring the news on me?"

Shay's mouth dropped open. "How did you guess, Daddy?"

"Baby. You sounded like you were bouncin' off the ceiling when you called from Marseilles last week. So break it down, Phillipe. You plannin' on stealin' my baby away, man?"

"Only with your blessing, sir. But it is true. We wish to be married."

Shay stuck out her left hand to show Doc her diamond engagement ring. "Don't worry, Daddy. I'm not gonna quit teaching or anything."

Doc stared at the ring for a moment, then hugged her tightly. "I never could afford to give your Mama a diamond like that," he whispered.

"Okay, Daddy. You only get sappy like this when you've been drinking too much."

"Aw, hell! Tonight, maybe. But I'm doin' better, baby. Really! Ask Jacques." He laughed and took a sip of his drink. "Well, maybe not Jacques. You know what a damn liar he is!"

"Daddy—"

"Come on, baby. I haven't had *that* much to drink. Am I embarrassing you?"

"You're kidding, right? High school garage-band, Daddy? You've been goin' out of your way to embarrass me since I walked in! And stop changing the subject. I'm worried about you."

"Well, stop worryin', baby. Matter of fact, why don't you go on back in Henri's office and call Edward. You know he's dyin' to see you. And that'll give me a chance for that man-to-man talk with Phillipe, so I can embarrass you some more. And when you come back I got a surprise for you—a special number just for you and Phillipe. Go on, now! I've only got ten minutes before the set starts."

"Yes, please go," Phillipe said. "Your father probably wants to show me your school pictures with pigtails and no teeth. Call your brother and I will find you when the show begins."

Shay sighed loudly as she walked away. "All my womanly mystery gone, just like that."

Doc grinned and signaled for Jacques. "Phillipe, let me buy you a drink. What'll it be?"

"Well, I see you have scotch. So scotch will be good for me too, I suppose."

"Not wine? I thought all you Frenchmen drank wine."

Phillipe adjusted his tie. "I am trying to impress you by acting American, you see."

Doc laughed as Jacques placed a glass on the bar for Phillipe. "Jacques, I want you to meet Phillipe Tourneau, Shay's fiancé. Phillipe, this is my good friend Jacques."

Phillipe reached over the bar to shake Jacques' hand. "Ah, yes. The damn liar."

Jacques laughed, and Doc nearly spit out the sip of scotch he had just taken. "Jacques, I swear—I don't know what sonofabitch called you a liar, but when I find out—"

"Mm-hmm," Jacques said. "Mon frère, you are—how you say? Busted."

Doc raised his hands and tried to look contrite as Jacques walked away laughing. "Okay, I'll pour," he called after him. "I know you're busy. Big tip for you though, mon frère!"

Doc grinned at Phillipe as he poured the drinks. "Shay's been a baaad influence on you."

"I joke with your friend, sir. He was on to us."

"Yeah, I guess he was." Doc took a sip of his drink as he gave Phillipe a long once-over, and then sighed. "Look, son. I don't have time to do anything but get right to the point. I hope you love my baby at least half as much as I do."

"I adore her, sir."

Doc smiled, pleased with that answer. "I adored her mother, you know," he said softly.

"Oh, yes. Your Pearl. Shay talks about her all the time. She showed me all of the pictures. Oh! And the, the, how do you say—les femmes du papier! She keeps them so carefully."

Doc looked up. "Les femmes—paper dolls? She's still got those? The ones Pearl drew for her when she was little?"

"But yes! She keeps them in a book, like a collection for the museum."

Doc stared quietly into his glass for a long time, wondering why the memory of those paper dolls hit him with such emotional impact. He finally looked up and managed a smile. "Phillipe, just make her happy— if you can. And don't ever take love for granted, 'cause when it's gone—" Again he fell silent, then finished his drink. "Maybe Shay's right. I *do* get sappy when I drink too much. So please forgive me. But it just makes me happy to see my kids doing so well."

Jacques grinned. "We hope to make you *very* happy. We plan to make you a grandfather."

Doc grimaced. "Okay, while I let that 'grandfather' crack sink in, why don't you tell me about yourself. I've been runnin' my mouth and all I know about you is that your Daddy operates a fleet of boats in Marseilles, and that you're the dreamiest damn dreamboat in the whole fleet."

Phillipe was still laughing when a short, light-skinned man wearing a black muscle shirt and a red porkpie hat approached them. He slapped Doc on the back and nodded a greeting at Phillipe. "Time to blow, baby," he said in a raspy voice.

Doc wrapped his arm around the short man's neck and smiled. "Phillipe, I guess I'll have to run my interrogation on you after this set. But first, I want you to meet the most frantic sax man on planet earth. This is Redbone Hamilton, from Detroit, U.S.A."

Phillipe shook Redbone's hand. "But I have heard of you! Many of my friends have seen the two of you play—oh, how do you say? The ultimate classic jazz."

Redbone scowled. "Classic? Did he just call us a couple'a old classics, Daddy?"

Doc stood up slowly and shook his head. "Like two ol' rusty Studebakers, Red."

"No!" Phillipe laughed.

Shay returned just as Doc was about to head to the stage. "What's so funny?" she asked.

Doc pointed at Phillipe, and Phillipe pointed back at him with an accusatory glare.

"Oh, you two are getting along great. Sarcasm loves company."

"Did you reach Edward?" Doc asked.

"Nobody was home. I was just back there catching up with Henri."

"Him and Anna are a couple'a late owls, but try later. He really wants to meet Phillipe."

"I will, Daddy."

"Well, guess it's about that time," he said, kissing her cheek. "Daddy's gotta go play."

Doc and Redbone ambled slowly to the stage, stopping to toss back a few wisecracks. "Hey, Red, you know "Giant Steps," don'tcha? My baby's just *dyin'* to sit in."

"My tour de force, baby," Redbone said dryly. "Before my *classic* days, that is."

Doc stepped up onto the bandstand and laughed at Shay's comical outrage. He had that sweet, energetic buzz he sometimes felt when he was about to play a great set—that feeling that he was young again and about to conquer some new, uncharted musical territory. He adjusted his necktie and felt the heat of the small spotlight on his back. Pulling a handkerchief from his pocket, he wiped down his horn, and then dabbed at the perspiration on his forehead and hands. "Hey, Pete," he said to the drummer. "Let's start with that new one we rehearsed. That cool?"

Pete nodded. Without an introduction, he kicked off a breezy, mid-tempo waltz and the bass player fell in with him. The piano player laid the harmonic foundation with a few chords, and Doc pressed his mouthpiece to his lips. The familiar Miles Davis arrangement of "Someday My Prince Will Come" rang brightly though the room and the audience broke into applause.

The song stretched freely as the musicians began trading eights. Doc began his solo and managed to interpolate a quick segment from "Giant Steps," then glanced up at Shay to see if she had caught it. Her laughter told him that she had. But just as he was about to resolve the solo, he felt a searing pain in his left arm, and then both arms dropped weakly to his sides. As he struggled to keep a grip on his horn, the pain seemed to leap from his arm to his chest, and he looked up in a sudden panic. He couldn't find Shay's face in the dark club, and he was falling.

Everything was a blur until he saw her leaning over him. The pain began to diminish, but there seemed to be no air in the room. Then he realized that there was also no sound. Shay's mouth was moving, but he couldn't hear what she was saying. In his confusion over the silence, all he could think of was holding on to his horn. He could feel it hanging loosely in his fingers, and he concentrated all his remaining strength on his grip.

Shay's mouth opened wide in a silent wail, and he tried to reassure her, but couldn't connect his thoughts to his vocal cords. *I'm okay, baby—if I could just catch my breath...* He could feel his heart thumping, but the rhythm was off, and his head was too heavy to hold up. *Shit! Come on now, man. Don't pass out in front of everybody...* He tried to turn his head, but couldn't. All he could see was one leg of the piano bench, and it was blurry.

The pain twisted again in his chest, but didn't last long this time. As he felt his horn slip from his fingers, his vision suddenly cleared up and that off-beat thumping in his chest finally stopped. The club's spotlight was brighter than usual, and it was shining on someone seated at the piano bench, facing him. From his prone position on the floor he could see a familiar pair of long, shapely legs in silk stockings and two black high heel shoes. Then, finally, the silence was broken—by a sweet whisper of the most beautiful music he had ever heard. He gazed up at the face he had missed for so long, and saw the understanding in her eyes. She smiled and began to sing a rich contralto rendition of "God Bless the Child."

Chapter 40

All week Stella had been working late hours on an uninspiring album project, and she hadn't seen Nick since Monday. By Friday, she was exhausted and missing him in the worst way. She grabbed the telephone and trudged into her bathroom, undressing as she went. After placing the telephone on the floor, she turned on the faucet and brushed her teeth as she waited for the tub to fill. Then she dialed Nick's home number and sank down into the warm water. It rang seven times before he finally picked up. She waited for a "hello" but heard only ragged breathing.

"Shaaay?"

Stella was alarmed at the slurred sound of his voice. "No, Nick, it's me—Stella. Wait, what's wrong? You sound—strange. Hey, are you—crying?"

Nick's voice was a breathless whisper. "Daddy—"

"Nick, I can hardly hear you. Did you say something about your—Daddy?"

"Where you, Shay?" Nick mumbled.

"What? Nick, what happened?"

Nick continued his fragmented babbling, paying no attention to Stella's confused interruptions. "Shay? Whuzzat—no uh can't, Shay… *Shay?*"

"What is wrong with you, Nick?" she said loudly. "Where's Calvin? Are you alone?"

"God, I shu been widdim," Nick moaned. "Daddy—"

Stella heard his voice crack and felt tears stinging her eyes. "Nick—listen to me. This is *Stella*—not Shay. Have you been drinking or something? Or Nick—did you *take* something? Some pills or something? What did you take? Tell me, please!"

"Shhh… S'okay," Nick whispered.

"No, Nick, it's *not* okay! Did you take something? Tell me, please!"

"Hell, yeah, I took sump'm!" he screamed hoarsely. "So what!"

Stella gasped and held the receiver away from her ear. "Nick, listen, please—"

He cut in with a raw whisper. "Don't hang up on me, okay? M'sorry I yelled…"

"I won't. But you've gotta stay awake, Nick. Do you have any coffee in the house?"

"Caawffee... Yeah... Lemme get muh keyzh." Now his voice was sliding like molasses.

"No! Don't try to drive! Just stay awake!" She grabbed a towel and tried to dry off with her free hand. "I'm on my way over there, okay?... Nick?"

There was an abrupt clattering sound, followed by a long silence.

"Nick!" she yelled. "Pick up the phone!... Oh, God!"

She hung up, dressed quickly, and grabbed her keys.

"Don't panic, don't panic, he's okay, he's okay," she muttered as she ran to her car.

She hoped for light traffic due to the late hour, but a tie-up on the FDR locked her in a bumper-to-bumper crawl. When the traffic came to a complete stop, she rolled down her window to see what the holdup was. An angry chorus of honking horns sounded for a minute, but slowly faded into a resigned silence. Just then something Nick had told her flashed in her memory:

> *. . . To be honest, I ain't the greatest at handling bad news.*
> *I sort'a overreact...*

Stella stared transfixed at the long line of red brake-lights for several minutes, then finally turned the radio to 1010 WINS to find out the reason for the backup. I was a two-car accident with fatalities about two miles up the FDR. The word "fatalities" kept echoing in her brain, so she changed the station in search of some distracting music. When she heard Don McLean singing "Starry, Starry Night," she slumped back in her seat and stopped fighting the tears.

Over twenty minutes passed before the traffic finally began to move. The instant Stella made the turn onto Nick's block she saw the flashing emergency lights. Parking at a haphazard angle, she jumped out of the car and ran up the steps. The front door was open and she nearly collided with Calvin, who was standing just inside. "Is he okay?" she sobbed.

Calvin handed her his handkerchief and steered her into the kitchen. "They're still in there with him, but they think he's gonna be okay. Shay called me at Donna's after she called Nick, and I rushed back here and found him passed out on the floor. So I called the ambulance and—"

"Why didn't *I* call an ambulance? Why didn't I think of that? What's wrong with me?"

"Calm down, Stella," Calvin said in a low, steady voice.

"Are you sure he's okay," she pressed. "It was Doc, wasn't it? Something happened to him. Nick kept saying 'Daddy' over and over."

Calvin nodded. "Yeah. Massive heart attack. That's why I rushed back here— I know how that boy is. I knew he'd take it hard—but it's a pretty long drive. Gave him time to—"

"Time to *what?*" Stella sobbed. "What was he trying to do, Calvin? *Kill* himself?"

Calvin stared at her for a long, silent moment, and then continued as if he hadn't heard the question. "Doc just fell out—right in the middle of a set. He was gone before the ambulance got there. Shay couldn't reach Edward so she called Nick, and then he got hold'a some damn drugs. I know he won't tell me who he got 'em from, but I'ma find out. You can believe that."

"What—what kind of drugs? He sounded really bad, Calvin."

"Ambulance man said it looked like LSD and maybe sump'm else. I ain't sure what."

"Oh, God," Stella moaned. "I knew he didn't sound right. Has he ever—"

"No, he never had problems with drinkin' or drugs. But he sure made up for it tonight."

"Will he be okay, do you think?"

"They're gonna take him to St. Luke's. He probably won't wake up till tomorrow night."

"I wanna go with him, Calvin."

"He won't even know you're there. Why don't you go on home and get some sleep so you can sit up with him when he wakes up. That's when he's gon' need you."

"But—"

Calvin smiled patiently. "Hey. You *know* that knucklehead ain't thinkin' straight, so don't you think we ought'a try to act like *we* got some sense?"

≈∞≈

Stella was shocked when she woke up the next afternoon and discovered that it was half past two. After calling the hospital and learning that Nick had already been released, she dressed quickly and fed Miles, then hurried out the door.

By 3:30, she was back at Nick's apartment. Calvin let her in quietly.

"Shh. We got here about one and he went right back to sleep. Come on in the kitchen."

"How is he?"

"Fine. Long as he's asleep."

"No, I'm not." Nick stepped into the kitchen, wearing only a pair of jeans. His eyes were rimmed with red and his face was puffy. "I'm not fine and I'm not asleep."

Stella walked toward him, but froze when he backed away from her.

"Just leave me alone," he said flatly.

Calvin intervened. "Stella's here to be with you in your sorrow, boy. You gotta face that funeral and you ought'a be glad to have somebody."

Nick fell heavily into a chair. "Get off my back, man."

"Nick, I'm so sorry," Stella said hesitantly. "I want to be there with you for the funeral."

Nick shook his head without looking at her. He didn't appear upset, just strangely detached. "No. I'll be back in a few days. I'll call you when I get back."

"But Nick—"

"I said *no*, and I'll call you when I get back."

Stella stared at him for nearly a minute, and then turned to leave. "Goodbye, Calvin."

Calvin followed her to the front door. "Stella, he don't mean it. It's that goddamn—stuff he took. Look, the flight's tomorrow and—"

"No, I know he's hurt, but he just doesn't want me around. Maybe—we hadn't gotten close enough to withstand something like this. And as for the acid—hey, nobody forced him."

"Give him a chance, Stella. I'll talk to him. He'll call you, okay?"

Before Stella could respond, she heard Nick calling for Calvin from the kitchen.

"I'll be right back, Stella. Don't leave yet. Please."

As Stella waited for him to return, she grew curious. Walking quietly across the living room carpet, she stopped just to the left of the kitchen door and watched their reflections in the glass of a large picture hanging in the dark hallway. She could see Nick slumped in his chair, staring into space, with Calvin standing beside him, looking awkward and helpless.

"You need me to get you sump'm, boy?"

Nick looked up at him, but said nothing.

"What is it, son?"

When Nick finally answered, there was a hard break in his voice. "He—smiled, Calvin."

"Who?"

"Daddy. Shay said he was layin' there—dead on the bandstand—but he was smiling."

"Well—that's good, ain't it?"

"I don't know, but I *need* to know! Do you think he was—happy when he died?"

"Well, he was always happy when he was playin' music. Just be glad he was smilin' and not—lookin' sad or sump'm."

Nick continued as if he hadn't heard him. "It was only supposed to be six months. Goddamn draft board—tryin' to get their hands on Edward. If it wasn't for that—"

"That's sump'm we'll never know, boy."

Nick looked up at him again. "Calvin?… Do you believe in God?"

Calvin leaned down and stared at him hard. "Yes."

Nick abruptly jerked back in his chair, knocking it over as he stood up. He was breathing hard and his arms were outstretched. "Why?" he screamed. "Why, Calvin?"

Calvin turned in a slow circle and covered his face with his hands. "Shit," he said softly.

Stella watched the two men as they stood there crying, despite their obvious efforts not to, until the tension was too much for her. She muffled a sob and hurried out the front door.

≈∞≈

With a project deadline looming, Stella spent the next day stuck on a simple verse that would complete the final song. As she watched the sun go down, she called CBS for an extension, then locked her door and dialed her brother's number. After four rings, he finally answered.

"Hey, hey, hello, hang on—"

Stella heard the receiver clunking against something, and then Donnie's laughter. "Hey, I'm sorry, whoever you are! I dropped all my books and started an avalanche!"

"It's me," Stella said, sniffling.

"Stel! Hey, you don't sound so good. What's up?"

"It's Nick. We—we broke up. At least I think we did."

"Aww, I'm sorry, Stel. From what you told me about him, he sounded like a pretty cool brother."

"Well, I'm just now finding out his bad points, I guess."

"Aw, shit. Sounds like you need to unload. Come on. Tell Donnie everything, po' widda baby," he said in an annoying baby-talk voice. "Big stwong Donnie make everything awwight."

Stella groaned. "I should hang up on you, but I really do need to unload. I'm so confused."

"Okay, so start with the reason for the breakup."

"Well, his father died," Stella began. "Actually, his stepfather, but they were really close."

"So you broke up with him 'cause he couldn't keep his Daddy from dying?"

"Sarcasm. Just what I needed, Donnie. And you didn't let me finish. There's more."

"I sure hope so, 'cause it sounds to me like you couldn't pick a worse time to split up."

"He took LSD, Donnie."

"When?"

"When he found out about his father."

"Stel! He was upset!"

"But *LSD*, for God's sake! Acid! That's pretty extreme, don't you think? What about his—stability?"

"Has he done it before?"

"Well, not that I know of."

"Trust me. You'd know if he was dropping acid."

"But he's got women chasing him all the time. I can't help worrying about that, Donnie."

"Well, shit! Does he chase 'em back?"

"Oh, I don't know. Not that I know of. But he's—he's just all wrong for me."

"Come on, Stel. I mean, he might not be that walking monument to nobility you always dreamed about, but the guy must have *some* good points."

"Of course, he does, Donnie. He's kind and he makes me laugh. Well, not lately, but usually. And he likes Miles. Most guys hated my cat, if you can believe that."

"Huh! Miles the man-eater? I tread lightly around that monster my damn self."

"Shut-up. You do not."

"Okay, here comes the sappy music—Cat Chow meets Hallmark."

"Stop it, Donnie. I *know* what you're doing. You're trying to cheer me up."

"No way. I'm *trying* to psychoanalyze you, Stel. Come on. Back to Superman's résumé."

"Well, he doesn't try to tell me how to walk and talk and dress and conduct my business, the way Alex used to. And he's a great—well, he's very romantic, if you know what I mean."

"Uh-huh. I know *just* what you mean, you trampy brown cow! Now I got dirt to tell Mama."

"Shut-up. Anyway, I just don't know if I can handle the way he flipped when his father died. He didn't even want me to go with him to the funeral. Can you believe that? And he—"

"Okay, stop right there and listen to me. You have *got* to stop being so afraid of love."

"I am *not* afraid of love! I *want* love, Donnie. What a weird thing to say!"

"No, Stel. What you want is *perfect* love. No such thing. Love's a messy business, baby."

"Oh, damn, Donnie," she groaned. "*What* are you even talking about?"

"Okay, I know you're touchy about this word, but Stel, you've always been pretty rigid."

"I am *not* rigid!"

"You're a goddamn ironing board, Stel. Just like Mama. Everything perfectly planned, no surprises. I hear you sniffling, but I'm on a roll here, so just blow your nose and listen. Nick sounds like a 'surprise' type'a dude, Stel. So loosen up and take a chance, for once in your life!"

"That's not fair, Donnie. What about when I quit Stanford? What about my music?"

"You're right about that. But the rest of the time you're playing some sick game of chess with Mama! But Nick comes along and it's good. So what's the worst that could happen? You get your heart broken. People have survived broken hearts since the Stone Age, Stel."

"But—some of the things he said, Donnie. I didn't tell you everything."

"You know what? You women think you're the only ones with the right to get upset and say things you don't mean. Contrary to popular female opinion, we men *are* humans, you know."

"Maybe I *was* hung up on that "noble" thing. Maybe—*nobody's* really noble anymore."

"For God's sake! Would you quit crying? I bet he calls you the minute he gets back. So instead of sitting around comparing him to Sir Galahad— Look, do you *really* want my advice?"

"Of course I do. Why the hell do you think I called you? So what do I do?"

"First, you need to stop playing games with Mama. And stop playing games with your life."

"Please! When did you switch your major to psychology? I do *not* play games with Mama!"

"Sure you do. We both do. Only my games are with Daddy."

"Then how come you get to play judge and jury here?"

"Because *you're* the one who called me for advice. And besides, we're talking about *your* psychosis, not mine. I'll let you delve into the far inner reaches of my weird brain another day. And stop changing the subject. You bitch and moan about how Mama looks down her nose at certain people, but then you turn around and do the same thing! You're doing it to Nick!"

"I am not!" Stella shouted.

"Look," Donnie said quietly. "I'm only going by what you tell me. It's obvious you love him. So if he's a good brother, just try taking that next step. Accept him, flaws and all. Simple as that. When he calls, just *be* there for him, Stel. Unconditionally. And see what happens next."

≈∞≈

Two weeks passed with no call from Nick, so Stella threw herself into her work, resigned to the fact that the relationship was over. She had just fallen asleep after a late night at the office when her doorbell rang, waking her. Slipping on her robe, she went to the front door and peered through the peep-hole. She saw Nick's brown jacket and slowly opened the door. Something in the way he looked at her told her everything she needed to know. Reaching for his hand, she led him back to her room, and they settled into a contented hug on top of the bedcovers. Then, with their heads close together on a pillow, they talked until the sun came up the next morning.

Chapter 41

Over the next few weeks, Stella began to feel a definite change in her relationship with Nick. As he began to open up to her emotionally, she found it easier to stop worrying and enjoy their time together. She was still nervous about meeting his mother, but finally agreed to go with him to Genesco Medical Center.

As they drove along the FDR, Nick regaled her with stories about his childhood. After a few minutes, she realized that she was only half-listening. When they finally pulled up to the sprawling group of red brick buildings, she felt as if they had been driving for hours.

"You actually rent a car twice a week to come all this way? Don't they charge you for mileage?"

Nick gave her a puzzled look as he opened his door. "It was only about twenty minutes. And believe me, when you start adding up a car note, insurance, and parking, this is a bargain."

"Oh. I guess so." As they walked through the courtyard, Stella began to fret over Mrs. Bluestone's mysterious condition. *What do you say to a lady who can't talk?* She thought about her last visit to her grandfather's nursing home and her parents' excruciating stiffness. They had hardly talked to the old man, speaking only to each other in hushed tones, as if he were asleep or dead. And Stella suddenly realized that their indifference had been passed on to their children—a learned response to an old man who meant nothing but inconvenience to his family. *We're all just waiting for him to die*, she thought, horrified at herself. *What if Nick's mother's like Grandpa? Just staring and drooling.*

"Hey," Nick said suddenly. "You sure are quiet."

"Oh, I was just thinking about something I've gotta do later, that's all. The grounds are lovely, Nick," she said, wondering why her voice sounded so chirpy.

"Well, they are now. But you should'a seen the place a few years ago."

"They fixed it up?"

Nick's enigmatic smile could have given the Mona Lisa a run for her money. "Investors," he said as they stepped inside. "It's a better place for Mama now."

Stella stared at him, half-expecting to see Anthony Perkins from the movie *Psycho*. She managed a smile, glad that Nick couldn't read her thoughts. *Oh, Lord. It's the Bates Motel.*

Every single face at the nurses' station smiled when Nick and Stella approached.

"Look who's here!" one of the nurses called. "Hi, Nick! How are you, baby?"

"Hi, Jackie," Nick said, as he kissed the nurse's forehead. "How're the grandkids?"

"Oh, those little devils are bad as ever. And who's your lovely lady-friend, Nick?"

"This is Stella Atherton. She's a very special lady-friend, Jackie, and a great songwriter."

"Really? Well, then you two ought'a make a good couple! All that talent! And honey, you *must* be special, because you're the first girl Nick's brought to meet his Mama."

Stella smiled crookedly. "Oh, really? That's—nice." Her heart was thumping so hard she wondered if Nick could hear it.

"And this is Dora and Ellen," Nick said, pointing at two younger women, who smiled and waved. "And that's Hazel over there, doing her favorite thing—filing medical reports."

"Hi, Stella," Hazel said, laughing. "Nice to meet'cha, girl."

"Uh, hi," Stella said softly.

Hazel leaned against the file cabinet and grinned at Nick. "Okay, so you *know* we saw you on the *Midnight Special* last Saturday, baby!"

Nick grinned. "You mean it finally aired? Okay, how'd I do? Give it to me straight."

"You know you tore it up, boy!" she laughed.

Nick bowed. "I know, but I'm a glutton for compliments. Hey, where's Emily today?"

"Day off," Jackie said. "She'll be sorry she missed you, but she's working tomorrow."

"Well, then tell her I'll be by to take her to lunch, will you? It's her turn."

"Sure will, Nick."

Nick waved at the nurses, then grabbed Stella's hand and grinned at her, unable to hide his excitement. "Come on. It's right at the end of this hall."

Stella's nerves had sent her imagination into overdrive.

Alfred Hitchcock's gonna jump out any minute for his cameo... Oh, God, Stella, you're being stupid. It won't be that hard. Just smile at her or something. Be spontaneous, like Nick.

But when the door opened and Stella stepped into the room, her nervousness gave way to shock. "*That's* your mother?" she blurted out.

Nick glanced back at her, obviously confused. "Yeah. Why?"

"Sh-she's—white!"

"So?"

"Uh, I mean, I'm sorry. I guess— I mean, I didn't know you were bi-racial, Nick."

"Bi-*what?* What're you—trippin'? I'm black just like you are, Stella."

"Oh, of course. I mean—okay."

Nick's annoyance was beginning to show. "You *saw* her picture."

"But—I thought that the white woman in the picture was Pearl, not—not your *mother*, for God's sake! I thought the *black* woman was your mother."

Nick grabbed her arm, a little roughly she thought, as he hissed a reprimand into her ear. "Look, stop talkin' like she ain't even in the room. She can hear you, you know."

"Oh, she can?" Stella whispered. "I'm sorry."

Nick walked over and hugged his mother. "Hi, Mama. Look who I brought to see you. This is Stella—the girl I told you about." He turned and shot Stella an expectant look.

"Oh! Uh—" As Stella gazed at the eerie, unfocused expression in the woman's pale blue eyes she became completely tongue-tied. "Uh—"

"Come closer, Stella," Nick commanded.

Stella finally managed a smile. "Hi, Mrs. Bluestone. I'm sorry. I'm just nervous, I guess."

Stepping closer to the bed, Stella allowed Nick to take her hand in his. Then he reached for his mother's hand to join it with Stella's, and a big smile spread across his face.

"I finished the album, Mama, and it's great. You know why?"

As Nick chatted amiably, his mother sat propped against several pillows, with all the animation of a fencepost. Stella was vaguely aware of Nick asking her something.

"Right, Stella?"

"Uh, right, Nick."

"And she sure can write songs, Mama. Stella wrote me the best songs I ever sang. I can't wait to play 'em for you. And believe it or not, she actually puts up with me."

Suddenly, Nick's mother made a grunting sound and squeezed Stella's hand spasmodically. Stella jumped, and then wished she hadn't when she saw Nick's withering look.

"I'm sorry. I—I—" Stella's voice faded as she stood up, and an awkward silence followed.

"Well, Mama, I guess we better go now. Don't worry. I'll make her understand. And I'll be back tomorrow for a nice long visit, okay?"

Stella watched Nick gently rocking his mother in his arms. It would have been touching, except for the dead flatness of the older woman's features. He appeared to be rocking a white lady with a bad case of rigor mortis. Again, Stella had to shake Norman Bates out of her mind.

When Nick stood up to leave, Stella smiled weakly at his mother. "Bye."

Nick said his goodbyes to the nurses as they left, but had nothing to say to Stella until they were well on their way back to Manhattan.

"I'm sorry you don't understand, Stella."

"No, Nick. I'm the one who's sorry. It's just that—well, I thought I was prepared for her condition, but then I guess her being—white—threw me off balance again."

"Okay, look. *What* is your goddamn problem with that?"

"I guess it's just a sore spot with me, that's all. So many brothers go after white women and leave us like yesterday's trash. It seems like all of a sudden everybody wants to be into this new "interracial relationship" bag. And to be honest, it just makes me sick, okay?"

Nick let out a sarcastic laugh. "All of a *sudden?* Man, you're naïve. Interracial relationships ain't nothin' new, Stella. I'm proof of that. Besides, what's my Mama got to do with your goddamn sore spot anyway? She's my mother, not my girlfriend."

"I *know* that," she snapped. "It was just a shock, Nick. I'm over it now."

"No, you ain't. You got your *sore spot* about interracial relationships and you're takin' it out on my Mama. Shit. It ain't like you're straight African yourself, you know."

"Well, unlike yours, my family is a hundred percent black. So just stop."

Nick grimaced. "Oh. So what're you now? The Mau Mau queen?"

"Let's drop the subject, Nick," Stella said in an icy tone. "You can't be objective."

"I can *too* be objective. What I want to know is what the hell happened to you to make you this damn—shit, what's the word?... Intolerant! That's it. Intolerant."

Stella sighed. "I am *not* intolerant."

"Maybe that's why you never introduced me to *your* family. Maybe I ain't good enough."

"That is *not* true, Nick! I hardly see them myself—only Donnie. And stop changing the subject! You called me intolerant, and I'm not! I'm just saying that with a white mother, you can't possibly be objective about the subject of interracial relationships, that's all."

"And you think *you're* objective? Besides, in my parents' case, it was *his* fault, not hers."

"What?"

"Stella. Did you ever see a picture of my father?"

"Well, no. Why?"

"So you don't know what he looked like?"

"No, I don't. So what did he look like?"

"He looked a lot like Calvin—except for the skin color. Stella, he was *passing*. Don't you get it? Remember when I told you how upset I was when I found those magazine articles about his suicide? I was upset because I found out *I* was the reason he blew his brains out! Mama has a little Buckwheat baby, and Joe Bluestone's cover gets blown. So goodbye, cruel world. Pow!"

Stella's eyes widened and her mouth dropped open.

"Mama thought he was white when she married him. So throw your intolerance at that muthafucka! He was *sick* with wantin' to be white. And I *know* you ain't comparin' me to *him*."

"No, I'm not. But I still say that it's harder for you to be impartial with a *white* mother."

Nick abruptly pulled over to the shoulder of the road, and the car stopped with a screech. After a tense silence, he spoke in a low, angry tone that Stella had never heard before. "So is that all you saw? A white woman? Let me get you straight on a couple'a points, Stella. My mother is a good, kind person with a pure soul—and she was a talented musician! And now all that's left of her life is that lonely little room. So I guess you're right. I guess I *can't* be objective. Because when I look at her, I don't see black *or* white. I see my mother. *Period*."

"I—I'm sorry, Nick," Stella said softly. "I won't bring up your mother again. I guess I just— I mean, I guess I was just surprised and it—it just triggered something in me."

"Yeah. That goddamn sore spot. Man, Stella, I never figured you to be so hung up."

"Hung *up*? Now, wait a minute, Nick. I apologized for my remarks about your Mama, but I will *not* apologize for my views."

"Goddamn, Stella! Get off my fuckin' back! You act like *I'm* chasin' some white woman around! I'm gonna remind you one more time. That was my *mother* you met, not some girlfriend!"

"Would you stop being so defensive? I'm not talking about you. I'm speaking generally… But now that you brought it up—have you?"

Nick slammed his palm against the steering wheel. "Have I *what*?"

"Have you ever dated a white girl?"

Nick groaned. "Shit. How the hell did I get *my* ass hung up on the goddamn white-girl hook? Look, all I wanted to do was introduce you to my mother. I apologize for her whiteness."

"I guess I'll take that as a yes."

"Let's go. I'll take you home since you ain't listenin' to a damn thing I'm sayin'."

"That's 'cause you haven't said anything, Nick. You never answered my question."

Gunning the engine, Nick swung the car back onto the road haphazardly. "I guess this was all a bad idea," he muttered. "Guess I forgot who you were for a minute."

"Forgot who I *am*?" she shouted. "And just who do you think I am, Nick?"

"*Everybody* knows who you are. Your superior attitude screams it all over the fuckin' place! Miss Stella Ass-on-her-Shoulders Atherton, that's who the hell you are!"

The rest of the ride back to Manhattan was a silent contest of wills. Before the car had completely stopped, Stella was halfway out the door. It was a clear statement that she punctuated with a contemptuous doorslam. Nick's response was a screeching of tires as he sped away.

≈∞≈

It was nearly 3:00 a.m. when Stella's telephone finally rang. She tried not to answer it, but grabbed it on the sixth ring. "Hello."

Nick picked up the conversation as if the past twelve hours had never happened. "So you asked me if I was ever involved with a white girl, and the answer is yes. But also a Puerto Rican stewardess, a Hawaiian chick—and she was a hooker—and a whole lotta black women, too, believe it or not. That direct enough for you? But if I'da known at the time that I'd ever have to make that confession to a black woman as *intolerant* as you, believe me, I'da thought twice."

After a short silence, Stella responded. "Goodbye."

"Wait! Okay, look, don't judge me, 'cause I ain't alone. I mean, I know it's the seventies and the Civil Rights movement is supposed to have changed everything, but all this 'black is beautiful' shit is still pretty new. So you never dated a white man—cool. You get the racial pride award. But just 'cause I dated a few white girls doesn't mean I *don't* have racial pride."

"It's more than a racial pride thing, Nick. It's a black-woman-pride thing. I'm just trying to get you to understand how painful it is when a sister sees a black man pass up a roomful of beautiful black women just to get to that one snaggle-toothed, bald-headed white skank in the corner. Drooling all over himself to get to her just because she's white."

"Stella, get serious. Do you want to hear the real story or not?"

A long pause, a sigh, and finally: "Well... I guess I can take the real story."

"Okay. There was a girl I met at one'a those protest rallies. Caucasian, liberal, and her name was Claudia. *And* by some miracle, she wasn't bald-headed *or* snaggle-toothed. She didn't even have a hump! She had hair too—a lot of it! And a whole mouthful of teeth. Okay. So I didn't exactly drag my feet when it came to gettin' her into bed—" He stopped and sighed. "Shit. I can't believe I'm tellin' you this."

"Go on. I'm listening."

"I *bet* you are! You're probably takin' notes too. But what the hell," he mumbled. "My ass is out on the end of the gotdamn plank now anyway... Okay, where was I? Oh, yeah. Claudia. Things were cool for a while, but it was like—like there was always this part missing—where we just couldn't connect."

"Don't tell me—she couldn't figure out how to break the news to Mommy and Daddy."

"Sorry to disillusion you, baby, but she did the whole guess-who's-coming-to-dinner thing and all that. I felt like a tiger in the zoo, but I went. And they were cool—you know, grinnin' and talkin' about Dr. King and playing Harry Belafonte records and—"

"No! They played Harry Belafonte records? The old Calypso tally-me-banana records?"

Nick couldn't help laughing. "Actually, that was their real hip stuff! And man, did I have a hard time keepin' a straight face when her Mom put on Leslie Uggams! What the world needs now is love sweet love? But they were just trying to be nice. They never gave us any trouble. It was other things with Claudia. We just never got into that comfort bag, I guess."

"Oh, well. Okay. But wait—did you say something earlier about a Hawaiian *hooker*?"

Nick sighed. "Yeah, I know your radar went off when you heard that. Okay, yes. I dated a Hawaiian hooker. But I wasn't a client! She was just a friend and we got pretty cozy for awhile, that's all. Look. She was just trying to survive, Stella, like everybody else. And besides, she had a pure soul. People who make mistakes *can* have pure souls, ya know. It's those perfect people—the ones who never *appear* to screw up—they're the ones you gotta look out for."

"Oh, no," Stella groaned. "Not the hooker with a heart of gold?"

"Yeah, as a matter of fact! She was real cool. Anyway, can we get back on the subject here?"

"I suppose so, but what about—with the hooker—didn't you ever worry about—"

"No. Look. Calvin made sure I knew a man's best friend is his raincoat."

"His *raincoat*? What in the world does that have to do with anything?"

Nick laughed. "A *condom*, Stella! You've seen 'em. You saw one just the other night."

"Oh, Lord! Good thing Donnie's not here. He would've had a seizure laughing at me!"

"I got a feeling I'm gonna get along great with Donnie."

"Who said you're gonna meet Donnie?"

"Oh, that's right. I forgot I was still beggin'—and bustin' my ass tryin' to convince this hard-headed, stubborn black Nubian princess I know to get back to bein' my woman."

"Hard-headed? And stubborn?"

"Women. All you hear is the negative things. Guess you didn't catch any of that 'Nubian princess' part, huh? And it took me a long time to dream that shit up, too."

"A Nubian princess sounds like one of those perfect people you're on the lookout for."

"Oh, no, baby. You ain't gotta worry. You got a *semi*-dirty soul, so you're cool."

"Mm-hmm. So can we cut to the chase scene now? We know where this is leading, so quit stalling. Believe me, baby, I'm ten steps ahead'a yo' ass every minute."

"Did you just say *yo'* ass? And what was that part about you bein' ten steps ahead'a *my* ass?"

"Ten steps, my racially proud brutha."

"Huh! Sez you."

"Sez me. Miss Ass-on-her-Shoulders Atherton."

"Okay. Then I guess that'll be me knockin' on your door in about thirty minutes."

"Then maybe you better get off this phone, grab your raincoat, and get *yo' ass* over here."

"Good thing I like the proposition, 'cause I *don't* like your bossy tone, Miss Ass."

Stella swallowed back a laugh. "Did you just call me Miss *Ass*?"

"Yup. Short for Miss Ass-on-her-Shoulders. But with a *much* more complimentary twist. It's my new lovey-dovey pet name for you, baby. Don't you like it?"

"Great. Can't wait to see Mama's face if she ever hears you call me that."

"Don't worry. I'll come up with a pet name for your mother too, Stella. Let me work on that awhile."

Stella laughed. "Okay, but listen, Nick. Speaking of mothers— All playing aside, I'm really sorry for the way I acted with your mother today."

≈∞≈

Nick tried to dismiss the incident at Genesco, but every time he thought about it, it disturbed him. He decided to talk to Calvin about it, but never found the right moment until their train trip to D.C. for a concert appearance. Calvin was reading the evening newspaper, and Nick knew that it was only a matter of time until the rhythmic clicking of the wheels on the track lulled him to sleep. So he seized the moment. "Hey, Calvin. You still awake?"

"I ain't sleepy, man."

"Right. I give you five minutes."

"What's on your mind?"

"Well—women, Calvin, women."

"Shit. I'm sleepy *now*."

"Come on, man. I need some advice."

Calvin folded the newspaper and sighed. "What the hell'd you do this time?"

"Damn! Nothin', man. I just—it's just sump'm I don't understand."

"And you think *I'm* some kind'a expert? Wrong! Women still confuse the hell out'a me."

"Well, see—it's about Mama. I—I took Stella to meet her."

"And?"

"And—" Nick stared at his hands. "I guess she's just like everybody else."

"What do you mean?"

"She just acted like it was useless to be there. She barely looked at Mama. And when she did, it was like she was looking at a piece'a furniture."

"Don't be so hard on her, man. You were raised around your Mama. You're used to her. Somebody meetin' her for the first time can't see her like she was before the—the—"

"The accident," Nick said bitterly. "That's what Aunt Pearl always called it—the accident. But Calvin, you're not like that. You look at her like she's there. And you talk to her."

"I been seein' you with your Mama for years. I got comfortable with it a long time ago."

"But Stella knows me. Why can't she be more understanding?"

"Give her a chance, boy. You only took her that one time, right?"

"Yeah, but there was sump'm else too. She was kind'a shocked that Mama was white."

"Oh. Did you explain about—"

"Yeah. I guess we kind'a smoothed that over okay, but I don't know. She just acted like she couldn't wait to get out'a there. I don't even want to bring up the subject of tryin' it again."

"Well, much as you like to visit your Mama, it's gonna come up again. If she loves you, she'll at least try. That's the test, boy. You don't need no selfish woman."

"Yeah. I guess you're right. Damn! How come it can't just be easy?"

"Nothin' in life's easy, Nick. Nothin' worth having."

"Yeah, but what about you and Donna? How come you two get along so great?"

"We just do. But sometimes she works my nerves over these cigarettes, and gets to lecturin'. She got this crazy idea that folks with addictions are really just lookin' for happiness and love. I *tried* to tell her that all I was lookin for was some nicotine, but she didn't wanna hear that mess. So she tells me I'll quit when I find *perfect happiness*."

"Huh?"

"Oh, yeah!" Calvin laughed. "Here's how it's supposed to go... When I'm happy as I'm ever gon' get, I'm supposed to get this overwhelming urge to quit smokin'. So I let her believe that shit... Aw, hell, I'll quit one a'these days and surprise her, I guess."

"Yeah, but other than that, you're happy with her. So what the hell's wrong with me and Stella? We get along great for a while, and then we're fightin' like Ali and Frazier!"

"You're both young, Nick. Life has a way of kickin' you around till you figure out what's important and what's not. And from all you told me about Stella, my advice is to hang on. I fell in love twice in my life, but I lost the first one. Donna was just an unexpected second chance, and I am *not* messin' it up this time. So hang on, boy, 'cause this might be your *only* chance."

"You never mentioned anybody before Donna. Not anybody serious. Who was she?"

Calvin settled back in his seat and closed his eyes. "None'a your damn business, boy. I was just a kid—and that makes it ancient history. You just worry about you and Stella."

≈∞≈

Three weeks later, after a short trip to Los Angeles for a *Soul Train* appearance, Nick sprinted through the airport to a pay phone and dialed Stella's office number.

After two rings, she answered in her business voice: "E. L. Atherton."

"Hey, Miss Ass! Guess what?"

Stella sighed. "If Sidney Poitier was my man, I bet he'd call me *darling*, not Miss *Ass*."

"Sidney Poitier's old enough to call you *daughter* so let's try this again. Guess what?"

"Don't I even get a 'hello, Miss Ass, I sure missed you?' This better be big news, Nick."

"I did miss you—insanely, as a matter of fact—but this *is* big news. Guess who eloped?"

"Okay, who eloped?"

"Calvin and Donna."

"No! Oh, how romantic, Nick! When?"

"Yesterday. He called me at the hotel this morning just as I was leaving and told me I'd have to take a cab from the airport because he was in Vegas on his honeymoon!"

"Well, I'm happy for them. We've got to get them a great wedding gift."

"We will. But now—" His voice suddenly deepened into a horrible French accent. "All Pepé wants is to get you into za prone pozeecion and make passionate love to you, Mon Cher. Pepé was plotting za evening of l'amour, you see. Za first sing Pepé weel do is to unplug za telephone. And zen to *peel* my leetle bon-bon away from za desk to *luuure* her over to za sofa." He shifted voices suddenly. "You know, you really need to get a sofa-bed in your office, Stella. I've been meaning to talk to you about that."

"A sofa-bed. You romantic skunk, you."

"Actually, I plan to wine you and dine you before luring you to the sofa. But first I've gotta stop by Genesco to see Mama before they shut down for the night. Wanna go?"

"Sure, Nick," Stella said, after a short pause. "I'd love to."

≈∞≈

On her second visit to Genesco, Stella seemed more relaxed. Nick watched her as she smiled and talked to his mother with passable enthusiasm. *At least she's trying...*

As they were walking out, Stella stared at the arrangement of pictures hanging on the wall—a large lithograph of a violin leaning inside a scenic window frame, an oil painting of an old marketplace at sunset, and a blown-up copy of the photo she had seen in Nick's bedroom.

"Oh, it's that picture—of your mother and Pearl laughing! I *love* that picture, Nick."

"Me too. I put it here so she can see it from her bed. And the paintings are of Greece, where she was born. Me and Calvin bought those for her over the years. And the violin—" He sighed. "She sure could play. Did I play you those Nat King Cole cuts she soloed on?"

"Mm-hmm, and you're right. She really played from her soul." Stella smiled at him. "I don't know why I didn't notice these pictures the last time I was here. You really made it nice for your Mama—the pictures and the sofa and everything."

"Well, the sofa's for me mostly. Sometimes I fall asleep here."

Stella kissed him softly. "You really are sweet, Nick."

Chapter 42

Nick and Stella had been spending all of their time together until the release of his album. It hit the Billboard chart at number 15 with a bullet, which prompted an immediate clash of schedules. Stella had to fly to Los Angeles for a music convention while Nick headed east for a string of appearances. It was their longest separation, and their telephone bills escalated.

After wrapping up her business in Los Angeles a day early, Stella rushed to the airport to fly home and surprise Nick. It was nearly 1:00 a.m. when her taxi pulled up to his building.

"Listen," she said to the driver, "would you mind waiting in case he's not here?"

"Well, it looks like a light's on in there, but sure, I'll wait."

"Thanks! And I'll come right back for my suitcases and pay you."

Stella hurried up the steps to the front door, smiling in anticipation of Nick's sleepy but delighted reaction when he saw her. She knocked, waited, then knocked again. When the door finally opened, she was face to face with an alarmingly attractive, unsmiling girl.

As Stella tried to think of something to say, she heard Nick's voice:

"Hey, don't be answering my door—"

When Nick appeared next to the girl, his face registered horror. "Stella! Come in! Why didn't you let her in, Gloria? This is Stella. My lady I *told* you about," he said pointedly.

Gloria stared at her maliciously; then she walked over to the sofa and flopped down on it. A clear, silent message that she was holding her ground.

With all his awkwardness, Nick tried to clarify the situation. "Time to leave, Gloria."

"Yes," Stella said, matching Gloria's stare. "Your replacement has arrived."

"Stella—" Nick began.

"It's all right, Nick. I didn't give you fair warning. No foul."

Gloria's glare intensified as she slipped off her shoes and tucked her feet up on the sofa.

"No!" Nick snapped. "I said time to *leave*, Gloria, *not* time to take off your shoes!"

She blinked at him sadly. "Take me home, Nick."

"Take the train, Gloria."

"But it's so late," she pouted.

"I don't even have a car. Look. You got yourself over here, now get yourself home."

"Oh, go ahead and call her a taxi," Stella said. "You might as well treat one of us right."

"Stella, wait. You got this all wrong."

"Oh, I wish you hadn't said that. That's what Alex used to say when he was cornered."

"I'm *not* cornered," he said sharply. "And I'm *not* Alex."

"Goodnight, Nick."

Stella ran down the steps and climbed back into the taxi. "Thanks for waiting."

"I kind'a figured it out when the girl answered the door," the driver said. "So where to?"

"Just drive!" she sobbed.

≈∞≈

When Stella's telephone rang a little over an hour later, she blew her nose and cleared her throat before picking up on the fifth ring. Before she could say a word, Nick started talking.

"She was nobody, Stella. I put her in a cab and she's gone."

"Nobody, huh?"

"Just somebody I dated a couple'a years ago. I did *not* bring her here, Stella. She just showed up at my doorstep."

"Then how'd she know your address? Calvin only got married a couple of months ago. You just moved into that place."

"Hell, I don't know! A lot'a people know where I live. She could'a found out from anybody. Look, I know what you're thinkin' and I am *not* like Alex."

"I just figured that you got lonely with me gone so long and—" As hard as she fought, her voice broke anyway. "Oh, Nick. I don't want to be just another girl to you."

"Aww, baby," Nick moaned. "You're not just another girl. Goddamn that Gloria."

"And I don't want to be one of those girls that's always interrogating you. But Nick, I can't help but wonder what would've happened if I hadn't gotten there when I did."

"*Nothing* would've happened, Stella. Damn! I wish you knew how much you mean to me. Look, I admit I was tryin' to be cool, but I had no intention of taking her up on any kind'a offer. I was tryin' to get rid of her when you got there. Why do you think the lights were on at one in the morning? If I'd been lookin' for a quick roll in bed, I'da just answered the door and walked back to my bedroom. Believe me, she would'a raced me down the hall."

"I believe that much anyway. That's what I get for trying to be spontaneous."

"Come on, Stella. Look, I'm sorry I didn't throw her down the steps the minute she showed up. And next time—not that there's gonna be a next time—but if there was, she'd get the treatment. It'd be exit, stage left... So, do I get a second chance to welcome you home?"

"Well—the lights *were* on, now that you mention it—"

"Heavens to Murgatroid! Blazing, even!"

Stella groaned. "Oh, no. Cartoons again? So which one is that?"

"Snagglepuss."

"You're nuts! You're doing cartoon voices in the middle of a fight?"

Nick continued his Snagglepuss impression with guileless abandon. "With a roaring television, even—in case you didn't notice. Very unromantic atmosphere, stage left, stage right."

"All right—stop it. And get over here so we can try this reunion again. But no Snagglepuss."

"Aw, no Snagglepuss? Well... let me think about that... Okay, you promise to talk dirty to me in that deep, sexy of yours?"

Stella's voice dropped to a throaty, subterranean register Nick had never heard before. "You mean... like this?"

"Damn, baby!" he yelped. "I'm on my way!"

≈∞≈

Three weeks later…

Once again, Stella showed up without calling—this time at the studio. As she stepped inside, she told herself that she wasn't checking up on Nick, but a sudden pang of guilt told her that she was. He was in the middle of laying down a vocal lead when she walked into the control room. Not wanting to interrupt Ed as he listened and adjusted levels, Stella stood quietly near the door and watched through the glass.

"How was that one, Ed?" Nick asked after the fade-out.

"It's a keeper, I think. All but that first entrance into the chorus. You'll have to do that line again. I clipped a breath or something, man. Just hold tight, and I'll find the spot."

As Nick waited to do the cleanup, he killed time by humming and conversing with himself in his endless repertoire of cartoon voices. He was Popeye, at the moment, regaling Woody Woodpecker with an R-rated account of his last trip to Singapore with Bluto.

Stella chuckled silently until she saw him look up and grin in the direction of the side door.

"The babes are here!" he said in his Popeye voice. "Shore leave! Awk, yuk, yuk, yuk, yuk!"

Three girls wearing huge, identical afro wigs and extremely short skirts filed into the vocal booth and headed straight for Nick. Stella knew them on sight. The Hedison sisters—Shawna, Davida, and Flora—the most in-demand background singers on the session circuit.

"Hi, baby," Shawna murmured with an overblown affectation of sex in her voice.

To Stella's horror, Nick dropped his Popeye act and welcomed Shawna with open arms and a kiss. And the kiss lasted far too long for Stella's liking.

"Leave some for me, girl!" Flora gushed. "Hey, Nicky, you fine devil! I been lookin' forward to singin' with you again!" Another kiss that exceeded the boundaries of friendliness.

"So tell me, Ed," Stella said tartly, "is he gonna make out with all three of them?"

Ed whirled in his chair and blinked at her. "Oh, shit!"

"Yeah," she said, stepping over to the console. "Oh, shit, Stella's here."

"Come on, Stella. Those girls are like that with everybody. He's never dated *any* of 'em."

Ignoring Ed, Stella leaned over his shoulder and hit the talk-back button. She had to fight to keep her voice cool. "So what's next? I guess the third one gives Popeye a blow job before everybody finally buckles down to work, huh?"

≈∞≈

The "Popeye incident," as it came to be known, took two days, a dozen roses, and five and a half hours on the telephone to rectify. Nick threw in a bonus—the Hedison sisters had worked their last session for him.

But even with all the bumps along the way, Stella had to admit that she was hopelessly in love with Nick. Whenever she convinced herself that he was wrong for her, the idea dissipated with his uncanny ability to make her laugh, or the need in his eyes when he told her that he loved her. She was unable to visualize anything as long-term as marriage, but resigned herself to spending every possible moment with him for the time being.

"I guess I'm addicted to you," she groaned after an inspiring night of make-up sex.

"Me too," he said, grinning. "I got me a baaad Stella-jones."

She sighed. "We should seek professional help."

≈∞≈

Relationship bumps were a completely different matter to Nick. Before Stella, if the path of love was not smooth, he simply followed a different girl down a different path. He was amazed at how effortless it had been to be true to Stella. As he reflected on his spotless record, he began to think about making things permanent. It was more than an impulse that prompted him to call her office to make a very special date.

"What's happenin', you long, tall, fine fox?"

"Oh, just trying to turn this sad, pathetic song I'm writing into a hit, what else?"

"Notice how I didn't call you Miss Ass? See, I'm kissin' up so you'll go on a date with me tonight."

"Mmm—well, a late supper, maybe. What have you got in mind?"

"Supper at DiMarco's and then a nice long safari in Tanzania."

Stella laughed. "Huh?"

"Inside joke, Stella."

"Well, don't I get to be on the inside?"

"No, my sexy bon-bon," Nick said in his Pepé le Pew voice. "Only Pepé gets to be on za eenside."

"Oh, sexual innuendo, huh? Well, for your information, Monsieur Pepé, Mademoiselle Bon-Bon is *always* on the inside. I *am* the inside. I just let you in for a visit now and then."

"Mm-hmm. Let's stick to dinner and talk about the mysteries of womanhood later. I got sump'm I wanna talk to you about. Serious too."

"Well, good. I've been trying to find the right time to discuss something serious with you too."

"Okay, cool. So I'll pick you up at our regular time. Eight twenty-one, on the dot."

"It's a date… And Nick? I love you. I really want you to know that."

"Pepé's heart eez panting for you, Mademoiselle Derrière. That's French for Miss Ass, ya know."

Stella laughed. "A heart *cannot* pant, you overheated skunk. And don't be late."

≈∞≈

The maître 'd seated them at their regular table. When the wine arrived, Nick toasted the mysteries of womanhood. "Okay, you first," he said, "What did you want to tell me?"

"Well—" she began, "—when I was in L.A.—"

Before she could finish, two teenagers approached the table—a tall, dark-skinned boy and a slightly shorter, slender girl with braces. "It *is* him!" the girl whispered. "We're sorry to interrupt you, Mr. Bluestone, but could we get your autograph on our menu?"

Nick nodded and smiled as he reached for the menu. "Got a pen?"

"Here, I've got one," Stella said, pulling a pen from her purse.

"What's your name?" Nick asked.

"Make it to Roland and Michele. I'm Michele, and this is my brother Roland. He was supposed to bring the pen. And that's our parents over there."

Nick smiled as he waved at the parents. "No problem, Michele. Here ya go."

"Thanks, Mr. Bluestone. We *love* your new album. Those songs are bad to the *bone!*"

"Thank you," he said, pointing at Stella. "This lady wrote the bad to the bonest ones."

"Really?" Michele gushed. "Could you sign our menu too?"

"Sure," Stella said, and then quickly signed her name under Nick's.

"Thanks!" Michele giggled bashfully as she backed away. "Okay, y'all can eat now!"

Stella grimaced at Nick. "Bad to the *bonest?*"

"Yup. But forget that. I'm dyin' of curiosity, here! *What* is your surprise?"

"Okay." She took a breath. "How would you feel about moving to L.A.? And before you object, you should know I got a great offer from A&M Records when I was there last month."

"Wait. You been thinkin' about movin' to L.A. and you knew about it since last month?"

"Well, we *were* having some problems. And I just needed to think things over."

"But I thought you hated L.A. Remember? The Jags and all that wicked cocaine?"

"There are Jags and cocaine in New York too. And besides, this is a whole different situation. I'd be heading up their writing department and I'd get to work with Quincy Jones."

"But you don't need to head up some writing department and you don't need Quincy Jones! You're a top songwriter *now*. What the hell do you need with goddamn A&M?"

"I never said I *needed* A&M, but what if it's just something I *want* to do?"

Nick extended his arms widely. "Fine. You wanna do it—go. I must've had the wrong idea about us, Stella. I thought we were gettin' serious. Guess I was wrong."

"Wait, Nick. Can we back it up to the beginning when I asked you to come with me?"

Nick gave her a crazed look. "Stella! What about my Mama? I can't just leave her here!"

"But L.A. has places like Genesco—probably better places. Why can't you move her?"

Nick stared at her with a wounded expression. "Because Genesco is my baby, Stella."

"What? What do you mean—Genesco is your baby?"

"I'm on the Board of Directors," he said quietly. "You should'a seen the place when I was a kid. It was run down and on the verge of going under, so when I finally started making real money, that's what I did with it. I've got lawyers handling things, but I'm the major investor."

"Well, that's a great thing you did, but—"

"But what?"

"Well… Nick, I know you want to believe that your mother's gonna get better, but—"

"Stop right there, Stella."

"But Nick, you told me she's been like that since you were a baby!"

"I *said* stop."

"I *can't* stop! Not when it affects us being together. Look, you can't realistically ask me to pass up opportunities like this, and I want us to be together, that's all… Nick, are you listening to me? I love you and I'm the one who's with you."

"And so is Mama."

Out of a tense silence, she muttered, "Great. I'm losing him to his null and void mother."

"*What* did you just say?" Nick yelled.

"For God's sake, face it, Nick! She's just like my Grandpa! She's just not *there* anymore!"

Nick pounded the table so hard with his fist, he broke a saucer and sent a fork clattering to the floor. "You don't know what the *fuck* you're talkin' about, Stella, and you are *way* out'a line!"

"Settle down, Nick," she said, trying to keep her voice calm. "Everybody's looking at us." She stared at the table for a moment and shook her head. "You know, it's really sad because sooner or later you're going to have to face the truth. Your mother wouldn't know whether you were in L.A. or—or China."

Nick stood up, his chest heaving with anger. "You know what? Fuck this and fuck *you*, Stella! Go ahead and take your uppity ass on to Hollywood where you belong. Maybe now you're ready to hang out with all the *beautiful* people and finally learn how to snort cocaine. Buy yourself a Jag and do all that other glamorous L.A. shit."

Yanking out his wallet, he pulled out a twenty, crumpled it into a tight ball, and threw it on the table. Then he leaned down and gave Stella one last icy glare. "You know who's null and void?" he said softly. "Us." Then he turned and walked out the door.

Chapter 43

After all his years of performing at large venues, Nick was still amazed at the speedy transformation that occurred at the end of each concert. One minute, he was standing in the blazing glory of adoration and stage lights, like some Greek god on the pinnacle of Mount Olympus. But the second he left the stage and began the slow push through the crowded hallway to his dressing room, all he could think of was a cold beer. Usually, the emotional drop was a relief to him. After gulping down his beer and taking a shower, he would slip into his comfortable jeans and relax in the knowledge that he was still just Nick—a brother who used to play stickball on 126th Street in Harlem.

But lately, the emotional drop was beginning to feel more like a car crash from a high cliff.

He had played the Los Angeles Forum three times as the opening act, but now he was the headliner, and it had been close to a sellout. After the show, he was sitting in the dressing room, hair still wet from his shower, wearing his comfortable jeans, and drinking his beer, but that guy in the mirror was frowning. Four months had passed since his split with Stella, and he was still alternating between anger and depression. Everyone was gone except TJ, who was droning in his slow-motion voice.

"What a joke," Nick muttered, interrupting him suddenly.

"Huh?"

"I ended up in L.A. after all, huh?"

"Oh, I can dig it, man. That's where your chick moved, right?" TJ said, nodding his head slowly. "Ironic, dude, ironic. Did she come to the show?"

"Shit! She wouldn't be caught dead at one'a my shows. Ain't you heard? We're null and void, man."

"Bummer," TJ muttered. "So, like—what time's our flight back to the Apple?"

Nick rubbed his forehead and looked up. "What did you say?"

"Man! You're on a wicked trip. No! A journey, dude!" TJ chortled at his own joke.

"Yeah, that's it, TJ," Nick said dryly. "I'm on a journey. So what were you askin' me?"

"What time's our flight tomorrow, man?"

A group of giggling females began pounding on the door. "Is Nick Bluestone in there?"

Nick was in no mood for groupies. "Bluestone's limo just left for the Marriott!" he shouted. As the girl-noise faded, he sighed. "Ask me that question one more time, TJ."

"Our flight, man. What time's our flight tomorrow?"

"Not tomorrow. I got a radio interview tomorrow night, so we're here till Monday. And the tickets are prepaid, so if you want to go earlier, you'll have to pay for it yourself."

"Whoa, man! Bummer. Good thing I brought enough party material to last me."

"TJ, I told you before. You better not let Calvin catch you with that acid. He hates that shit."

"Hey, man, mellow out. I pulled my shift. Now it's party time for TJ! But uh—where *is* your uncle, now that you mention it?"

"I don't know, man. Probably on the phone somewhere talkin' to Donna."

"Cool! Talkin' to his chick always mellows him out."

"Yeah, but he won't be very mellow if he catches you with that shit, TJ."

Another knock at the dressing room door stopped Nick's lecture. This time, TJ took a crack at fending off the groupies. "Bluestone's limo just left. The dude's at the Hyatt Regency!"

Nick groaned. "Goddamn, TJ! Marriott, man! You're supposed to tell 'em I'm stayin' at the Marriott. Now when I get to the damn Hyatt—"

"Oh, sorry, man! Like that scene last night—sex-starved chicks all over the lobby! Guess I fucked up, huh? But hey, if you ain't in the mood, you could always send 'em up to my room."

Another knock. "Who is it?" Nick shouted.

A male voice answered, "I got a telegram here for Mr. Bluestone."

Nick gestured toward the door. "Let him in, TJ, would you? But just him—no girls!"

When the door opened, a teenage boy in a Forum staff t-shirt slipped in quickly and handed Nick a telegram. Nick stared at it as he reached into his pocket for a tip. "Here, man."

"Thanks, Mr. Bluestone. Cool show, brutha! I got all your albums."

"Thanks, man," Nick said softly, still staring at the telegram. "Hey, wait! Do me a favor and get the rumor started that I'm stayin' at the Marriott, would you?"

The boy grinned. "Sure, man. You got it."

As he opened the door to leave, an attractive white girl pushed her way in. She wore a floppy Sly Stone hat over her long dark hair and a black leather skirt that was outrageously short and tight. "Hi, Nick," she cooed, smiling seductively.

Nick glanced at her and sighed. "Hi, uh, Annette. Look—"

"It's Angela," the girl pouted.

"Shit! Shut the door, TJ," Nick snapped. "Look, Angela, I'm busy tonight, okay?"

"How—how can you say that, Nick? After last night? We had such a good time last night."

Nick tore open the telegram. As he read it, Angela's voice faded out of his consciousness.

TO NICK BLUESTONE C/O FORUM 3900 W MANCHESTER BLVD INGLEWOOD CA = URGENT = PLEASE RETURN TO NY ASAP = YOUR MOTHER DIAGNOSED WITH PNEUMONIA = CONDITION SERIOUS MOVED TO BELLEVUE = WILL DO ALL POSSIBLE. R. BEARDSLY

The telegram slipped through Nick's fingers and fluttered to the floor. It wasn't until he looked at Angela and saw her tragic soap-opera expression that he realized she was still talking.

"Aren't you listening to me, Nick? I thought we had something special."

Out of a long silence he said, "Special?... *Special?* Angela, Angela. You need a dictionary, baby. You knock on my door at one in the morning, barely introduce yourself, and twenty minutes later we're goin' at it like a couple'a dogs. There *is* a word for that, but it ain't *special.* Look under the F's."

Angela gasped. "You bastard!"

Nick continued as if he hadn't heard her. "Don't get me wrong. I was happy to oblige. But the party's over, Angela. Time to go." He turned away when he felt his eyes stinging.

"You can't treat me like this!"

"Relax, baby," he said, taking an angry swipe at his tears with the back of his hand. "I hear the Ohio Players will be here next week. Maybe you can hound around and be *special* with Sugarfoot or sump'm."

"What?!"

Nick clapped his hands over his ears. "I can't take screaming, TJ! Get her out'a here!"

TJ pushed her toward the door. "Like he said, baby, party's over," he drawled. "Heave ho."

Angela slapped at TJ's arms. "No! Oh, you bastard! I hate your guts, Nick Bluestone!"

Once TJ had pushed her out and locked the door, she began pounding on it loudly.

Nick slumped into a chair. "Shit, TJ! Call security, man!"

As TJ picked up the phone, there was a commotion outside and Angela's screaming began fading down the hallway. "Looks like they got here already," TJ chuckled. "Hey, what happened anyway?" he asked gently. "That telegram bum you out?"

Nick stared at him. "You ever heard of the Blue Hawk, TJ?"

"Man, I'm from Chicago! Blue Hawk was *born* in Chi-Town!" His sleepy eyes registered confusion. "Uh—but I don't get it, man. It ain't cold."

"Never mind. It's just time for somebody else to die, that's all."

"Oh, bummer, man. That *is* cold, I guess. So—uh, who died?"

Nick laughed bitterly. "Everybody... Look, just leave me alone, okay?"

"Cool," TJ whispered, patting Nick's shoulder. "I can dig it, brutha. Take it easy."

"Wait a minute, TJ— How much of that party material did you say you had?"

"Oh. Yeah, baby, yeah," TJ murmured, pulling a vial from his pocket. "Gettin' stoned helps me when I'm bummed out. But just do a little." He tapped out a dollop of the liquid on Nick's hand.

Nick licked it up quickly and stuck out his hand again. "More."

TJ hesitated. "Wait a minute, man. You ain't used to it—"

"More!" Nick shouted.

"Okay! Be cool!" TJ said, unscrewing the vial again. "Damn! I hope you can handle it."

Just then, a security guard opened the door for Calvin, who hurried in with a big smile. "You see the size'a that audience, Nick? I bet—" Suddenly, he fell silent and his smile disappeared.

Nick quickly licked the acid from his hand as TJ shoved the vial back into his pocket.

"Goddamn!" Calvin roared. "Spit that shit out, Nick! Now!"

Nick waved his hand dismissively and turned around in his chair. TJ was edging his way to the door, but Calvin caught him by the collar and jerked him up until they were eye to eye.

"You get the fuck out'a here 'fore I have your sorry ass picked up for dealin' that shit."

"Dealin'? Naaww, man! Possession maybe—"

"I *said* get the fuck out!" Calvin yelled.

"Wow, man," TJ mumbled. "You mean— Does that mean—like— I'm fired?"

"*Listen*, boy. If I see you again, I'll lay your skinny ass out on a slab. That means *fired*."

"Okay, okay," TJ muttered as he reached for the doorknob. "Bummer."

Nick heard the door slam. He could feel his body going limp and his eyelids were getting heavy. Calvin's yelling was bouncing off the walls of the room with a reverberating backbeat.

"What the hell's wrong with you, boy? I told you never to touch that shit again. Goddamn! I guess if I ordered you to act silly and foolish, then you'd probably act right just to piss me off!"

Nick grinned stupidly at Calvin from the mirror. "Reverse psychology? Weak, Calvin, weak. How's this for a better idea—I'll just blow my brains out, like my Daddy." He held up his right hand in a gun pose, index finger pointed at his temple. "Goodbye, cruel world!… Pow!"

"Stop it, boy!"

"Shit, it worked for Joe Bluestone. So why—not—me?"

Calvin bared his teeth at him, but lowered his voice. "You ain't gonna do that."

"What the *fuck* do you know about it?" Nick yelled. "Huh? Suicide is—hereditary, ain't it? Mental illness and all that shit? My father was suicidal, so why shouldn't I be?"

"Shut up, boy! You got *no* idea what you talkin' about."

Nick opened his eyes wide, feeling the sting, and glared at Calvin. "Oh, but I do."

"Look. What the hell brought this on anyway?"

Nick ignored him and stared vacantly. "I ought'a do it. I lost Stella and now this shit—"

"*What* shit? Tell me! What the hell brought all this on?"

"I fuck everything up," he wailed, "just like my Daddy! And now Mama's dyin' and I lost Stella. Naw, that ain't right... I never really *had* Stella 'cause—"

"Wait a minute. What did you just say about your Mama—dyin'?"

Nick pushed the telegram toward Calvin with his foot.

Calvin picked it up and slowly sat down as he read it. "My God."

"Death, Calvin. Blue Hawk and his same ol' shit. And I'm sick'a bein' last in line. So I'm takin' cuts and gettin' the fuck out'a this damn mean world—before somebody else I love dies."

"The Blue Hawk? Shit, boy. That was just a kids' story I told you when you was little."

"Nooo, Calvin. He's *real*. And he's a stone cold killer, man."

"Okay, now, just shut-up," Calvin snapped. "You ain't killin' yourself. You gonna straighten up and act like a man. I'll get us a flight home and we'll go check on your Mama."

Nick's face twisted in a cynical sneer. "Oh, that's right. This must be one of those 'fine as wine' moments. Be strong, young man, and go watch your Mama die! Well, I pass. This time I'll be like Daddy and take the coward's way out. Matter'a fact, I need to go catch TJ..."

He stood up unsteadily and Calvin stepped up to him, chest to chest. "Here's your problem, son. You gotta go through that door to catch TJ. And you gotta go through *me* to get to that door. But if suicide's *really* on your mind, that'd be one way to do it, awright."

Nick glared at him. "Fuck you, Calvin! I ought'a just do it like my Daddy did it... Oh, but shit! All he leaves me is some fucked-up cuff links when he should'a left me his goddamn gun!"

Calvin grabbed Nick's shoulders and shook him hard. "I'm *through* listenin' to this shit, boy! You *ain't* like him. You hear me? You're just feelin' sorry for yourself and usin' him for an excuse. You *ain't* like him."

Nick cackled dryly. "Maaan, I'm *exactly* like him."

Grabbing a handful of Nick's hair, Calvin jerked his head back and stared at him. Then he squeezed his eyes shut and whispered, "You ain't like him. You *can't* be like him."

"Shit. Why the hell not?"

"Because—" Calvin stopped.

"Because bullshit!" Nick yelled.

Calvin shook him again. "Because Joe ain't your father!"

Nick blinked at him, genuinely startled.

Calvin's voice dropped to a grave whisper. "Joe Bluestone is *not* your father... I am."

Nick jerked away. "Maaan, just 'cause you took care of me a few years don't make you my goddamn *daddy*! I'm talkin' about my *biological* father. The one I got all my rotten genes from!"

"I *said* I'm your father, Nick. Your biological father."

Nick stumbled backwards into a chair, but managed to stay on his feet. "You're a liar!" he screamed, pointing at Calvin. "A goddamn liar!"

"I'm a lotta things, boy, but I ain't no liar. Now you need to calm down and *listen*, 'cause there's a lot you don't know."

"Like *what*?"

Calvin jerked up his chin and stared him in the eye. "I *knew* your Mama—*before* you were born."

Out of a tense silence, Nick walked slowly in Calvin's direction, his eyes glittering with an almost childlike curiosity. But suddenly, without so much as a twitch of warning, he crashed a straight right into Calvin's face. He was yelling incoherently and taking wild swings as Calvin did his best to deflect the attack. But then Nick managed to land a lucky punch—a sharp blow to the solar plexus—and Calvin's defensive reflexes went haywire. His arms dropped to his sides, his knees buckled, and he hit the floor.

By the time he found the strength to raise his head and look around, Nick was gone.

Chapter 44

Stella Atherton yanked the paper out of her typewriter and scanned the lyrics she had just written. "God, I hate deadlines," she muttered. "Hey, Norma! You still here?"

Norma appeared at the door. "Yes, Ms. Atherton?"

"Make about ten copies of this and deliver them to all the honchos, would you, please?"

"Yes, Ms. Atherton."

"And be sure to run one over to Quincy Jones. He's still in Room 'B' today, isn't he?"

"No, Ms. Atherton. I heard he finished up late last night."

"Oh, okay. Then would you have one of the guys run a copy over to his house?"

"Yes, Ms. Atherton."

Stella resumed her muttering as Norma rushed out. "Yes, Ms. Atherton, no, Ms. Atherton. I never asked her to call me that. Guess Mama would be impressed though. Big corporate office of the hot-shot head of the publishing department—Miss Ass-on-her-Shoulders Atherton."

When Norma returned, she handed her two pages. "There's an extra copy here for you."

"Thank you. Wait—Norma? Could you... Would you mind—calling me Stella?"

Norma gave her a deer-in-the-headlights look. "Uh, okay—S-Stella."

Well, that sounded like a cheap synthesizer. Artificial... Poor Norma.

After Norma left, Stella read the lyrics on her copy, and felt like crying. "Formula. My whole creative wellspring must have dried up if I'm reduced to writing formula crap like this."

The phone rang, and she grabbed the receiver, glad for the interruption. "E. L. Atherton."

"Hiya, Stel."

"Donnie! Oh, it's great to hear your voice! I really needed cheering up today. So how the hell are you, white sheep? Please tell me you're coming out for a visit."

"Well— Actually, we're all coming out there."

"All *who?* Aw, come on, Donnie. Don't tell me Daddy's throwing some political coming-out party or something. You know, I'm not in the mood for one of his—"

"Stella. Listen to me. Grandpa passed away last night."

Stella was quiet for a moment as the guilt crept in. She knew she should feel something—sadness, grief—but all she could think of was the blank expression on her grandfather's face the last time she had seen him at the nursing home. *Null and void.* Those were the words she had used about Nick's mother. Stella winced and her mood plummeted.

"Stel? You still there?"

"Yes, I'm here. And I'm really sorry to hear about Grandpa. I hope he went peacefully."

"Well, that's what the doctors told Daddy anyway. They said he just died in his sleep."

"Oh. So how'd Daddy take it?"

"Hey, you know Daddy. He sounded like Walter Cronkite reporting the news when he called me. I don't know. I'm sure it wasn't any surprise to him."

"Yeah," Stella said softly, "it wasn't much of a life for the old man after that last stroke, so I guess it's a blessing in a way. But it's still sad. When's the funeral?"

"The eighth. They're flying him back to California and having the funeral out there."

"Oh, that's right. They've got that crypt near his old house in Pasadena."

"Yeah. They'll stick him in there with his wife, I guess."

Stella let out a short, startled gasp. "Oh, God, Donnie! Please don't talk about *sticking* people into crypts! And don't call our grandmother *his wife* like she's some stranger."

"Well, she is a stranger! I mean, she died so long before we were born, it's hard to think of her as a grandmother. What was she—about thirty?"

"That's the story I heard."

"Anyway, I've gotta run. I just wanted to tell you the news so you can prepare yourself for the invasion. I'll get back to you later tonight, dahling, with the Atherton clan's itinerary," Donnie said, putting on his comic Harvard air. "Tah-tah, Estelle."

"You're nuts, Donnie. It'll be good to see you again, even if it is for a funeral."

$$\approx\!\infty\!\approx$$

It was late afternoon on the following Tuesday when Stella arrived at her grandfather's old house on the outskirts of Pasadena. The second she stepped out of her car she wished she hadn't agreed to help her mother. She stared at the tall, double entry doors and the two huge oak trees in the yard. Something about the place made her shiver. Then she heard her mother's voice calling and looked up to see her waving from an upstairs window.

"Come on up, Estelle. The door's open."

Stella climbed the porch steps and let herself in. Briefly blinded by the sun's glare on the white marble entryway floor, it took her a moment to focus and take it all in—the winding staircase, the fireplace in the great room, the smell of the old wallpaper. If she had been asked a minute earlier to describe it, she would have been at a loss, but now it was all startlingly familiar. As she touched the hand-carved banister, scattered images of the past flooded her mind. Visits here had usually been brief, but the atmosphere was burned into her memory. The absolute quiet. The sorrow. She reached the top stair and stopped. "Mama?" she called softly. Her voice echoed eerily down the hall.

"In here, Estelle. In Grandpa's room."

Stella followed the faded green rug into the room, and stood staring at her mother.

"Estelle! You look as if you'd seen a ghost! I'll get you some iced tea from the cooler."

"No, I'm okay, Mama. I just—didn't realize how much of this house I remembered."

Her mother grimaced as she glanced around the empty room. "Cold, unfriendly house."

"No, Mama. Not really unfriendly. It just feels—sad."

"Well, anyway, I had Donnie climb up into the attic and carry these boxes down from that safety closet up there. It's a good thing I brought these folding chairs for us to sit on. We've got to go through these boxes until we find those stock certificates your father's looking for."

Stella labored to keep the sour tone out of her voice. "Well, if he's the one looking for them, Mama, then why are we the ones here going through the boxes?"

"Estelle! Your father is handling all the estate matters. And yes, he *did* have to combine some business with this trip. He doesn't get out here that often anymore. You know that."

Stella sighed and removed the top from one of the boxes. "Have you checked this one yet?"

"No. So that's a good start for you. I'll keep going through this one."

"Where'd Donnie go?"

"He went out to pick us up some sandwiches. I don't know what's taking him so long."

Stella chuckled to herself. *Very smart, Donnie.* "So where's all the furniture, Mama?"

"Grandpa knew he wouldn't be coming back here when we moved him to the home four years ago. So we parceled out the furniture to your great aunt's children, with his permission."

"What great aunt?"

"Catherine's sister. She came from a poor family, from what I understand. God knows how they fought over that old stuff. Most of them aren't even employed."

"Well, if they're in need, why didn't any of them move into this house?"

Stella's mother peered at her over the top of her reading glasses. "This isn't just a house, Estelle. It sits on ten acres of prime California land. This is an *estate*."

Stella crossed her arms and scowled. "So Daddy lets all the poor relations fight over some furniture while he holds out for the *estate*."

"Don't take that judgmental tone with me, Missy."

"Never mind, Mother. Forget I asked."

"That's all you've been doing since you got here. Asking nosy questions that don't concern you and jumping to conclusions before you get the facts. This business about the house is in your grandfather's will. Your father and I spent a fortune on his hospitalization and placed him in the best facility in Los Angeles. And then there was the expense of moving him to the home in New York to keep him close. We could have rented this house to offset some of the costs, but he flatly refused. You don't know all we went through with him, Estelle, but we honored his wishes, and now we're entitled to this house."

"It's not a house, Mama. It's an *estate*, remember?" Stella said tartly, averting her eyes before her mother could land her blistering look.

"Just look for the papers, please. Your father said they'd be in a big brown envelope."

"Okay, but I have just one last nosy question. How in the world did Grandpa manage to buy this house in the first place? Wasn't it back in the 1920s or something? I studied some real estate law when I was at Stanford and I saw that racist language in the deed restrictions back in those days."

"Well, all I know is what your father told me. First of all, it wasn't in the '20s; it was actually earlier—1915 or 1916—just before the First World War. Anyway, Grandpa didn't buy this house. He and his brothers built it. Their father was a carpenter and brick mason, and he made sure his sons learned the trade when they were in their teens."

"I remember hearing that. That's how he got into the building supply business, huh?"

"I guess so. Anyway, this area was all countryside back then. An old farm, I think. Grandpa and his brothers bought the land from a white man they all worked for, acre by acre, and then built the house themselves. Your father told me that this house went to Grandpa because he was the first to marry. Then one of the other brothers—Harold, I think his name was—he got married next, and they started to build a second house for him. But then the war broke out and they all enlisted. I don't know all the details after that, except that Harold was killed over there and they never finished that second house."

Stella stared at her mother with wide eyes. "How horrible! But what about the other brothers? What happened to them? What were their names?"

"Oh, Lord, Estelle, I don't know. They've all been dead for years now. This is really all the history I know about your father's side of the family. Well, that and the story about your grandmother Catherine dying so young. She was a very sickly young woman."

"No wonder this house feels so sad, Mama," Stella said, sighing. "If Catherine wouldn't have died, they could've been so happy."

"They had their happiness, even if it was only for a while. They certainly had more than most Negroes back then. It was unusual for the times they lived in, Estelle, but it wasn't unheard of. All you Black Power kids think you're the first ones to take a stand for your race, but that's not true. This house is proof of that. So you see, we all fought the fight—in our own ways."

Stella stared at her mother's profile for a moment, then walked over and hugged her. "I know, Mama, but I guess you have to remind me sometimes."

"Well, enough of this, now, Estelle," she said, kissing Stella's forehead quickly. "We've got to get to work or we'll never get through all these boxes. She gestured to a small radio on the floor. "I brought that radio for you, dear, in case you got bored. It's got fresh batteries, too. Go ahead and turn it on."

Stella turned on the radio and laughed. "You like Bobby Womack, don't you, Mama?"

"You *know* I have no idea who he is, Estelle. We've definitely got a musical generation gap. But go ahead and enjoy yourself. I'll just tune him out. I can't understand a word the man's saying anyway."

The two women got to work searching for the documents. Stella was nearly finished with her third box when she saw a bundle of small envelopes tied with a faded red ribbon. On the top envelope she saw a name written in careful, elegant-looking handwriting: *Drew.*

"Mama? Who's Drew?" she asked, standing up to stretch her back.

"Drew? Oh, that's your grandfather, dear. No one ever called him Frederick. He went by his middle name, which was Andrew, and Drew was short for Andrew." She smiled vaguely, and shook her head. "Now, how in the world I remembered that, I don't know. Your father only mentioned it to me once—when he brought me home to meet him for the first time."

Stella slipped a small card out of its envelope. "Mama, listen to this: 'To Drew, my dear husband, on the occasion of your birthday. May we be together always. All my love, Catherine.' Oh, and look at her beautiful handwriting!" As Stella ran her fingertips over the words, thoughts of Nick filled her mind and she felt tears threatening. *My dear husband...*

"Estelle? What's wrong, dear?"

Stella looked up. "Huh? Oh—it's just that she died so young . So Grandpa never remarried, did he?"

"No, he never did. That's why it was so odd that he refused to let us sell this house or any of the land until after his death. Oh, now you're getting all emotional, Estelle. Give me those cards. We shouldn't be reading them anyway. They belong to your father now."

Stella handed the bundle to her. "So you always called him Grandpa? Never Drew?"

"Heavens, no! I called him Mr. Atherton until you children were old enough to visit him. Then I *had* to call him Grandpa. We couldn't have toddlers calling their grandfather Mr. Atherton! He didn't seem to enjoy being called Grandpa, but he tolerated it, I suppose."

"No, Mama," Stella said slowly, lowering herself back down onto the chair. "You're wrong about that. I just remembered something I haven't thought of in years."

"And what might that be, dear?"

Stella grinned and scooted her chair closer to her mother. "Okay, when I was little one time, we came here for a visit and Donnie and I were playing out in the back yard— Oh, correction. I mean, we were playing in all that prime California land back behind the *estate*."

Audrey laughed lightly. "All right, Estelle. Enough."

"Anyway, remember how much space there was back there before he put that fence in? Well, Donnie and I wandered off and found this big platform thing and we were running around playing on it. It wasn't that high, but it was huge and overrun with weeds—probably too dangerous to be playing on, but we didn't care. So, of course, I lost my footing and—" Stella stopped and gasped softly. "Oh, Mama! I bet that was the foundation for that other house they were building. The one you said they never finished because of the war. What did you say Grandpa's brother's name was?"

"It was Harold. And I bet you're right. It probably was that foundation. That's probably all that's left of it. Anyway, what happened after you fell?"

"Well, I remember crying, and the next thing I knew, Grandpa was scooping me up. He was probably keeping an eye out for us and saw the whole thing. Anyway, he started rocking me and told me to stop crying and not to be scared. All in baby-talk, Mama! 'I'm your Gwampaw, honey. Nothing's gonna happen when Gwampaw's around.' I can still hear him saying it. He was laughing and everything!" Stella grinned when she saw her mother's shocked expression.

"*Gwampaw?* Baby-talk? Are you quite sure, Estelle? That doesn't sound like him at *all*."

"Yup. *Gwampaw.* Just like that. I must've been about six or seven, but I remember it clearly. I guess it got buried in my memory till now. Oh, he was so sweet to me that day, Mama. He carried me back to the house and put a bandage on my little boo-boo, and then gave Donnie and me some ice cream. And for some reason, it makes me *so* happy that I remembered it."

"Well, I'm glad, dear. It's nice to have pleasant memories of the deceased."

Stella's smile faded. Her mother had already dismissed the story and was rifling through another box. *The deceased? Oh, Mama. What a horrible, impersonal thing to call somebody.*

She sighed and opened another box. "This looks like a bunch of ledgers or something."

"Look through them anyway, dear. The envelope might be stuck between the pages."

Stella yanked out the ledgers and saw a cigar box at the bottom. With a glance at her mother to make sure she wasn't looking, Stella studied the label: a colorful Indian chief on a horse and the words *Captain Jack Cigars—Markle & Co.* She lifted the lid and found a bundle of yellowed envelopes with foreign postage stamps. The one on top was addressed to Mr. Drew Atherton. It was tied with a faded red ribbon just like the envelopes she had found earlier, but the handwriting was distinctly different from the handwriting on the birthday card. The severe reverse slant was similar to Donnie's left-handed writing. As she nudged the box under her chair, her mother let out a yelp, and Stella jumped. "Mama! You scared the hell out of me!"

"I found it, Estelle! The envelope with the stock certificates!" Suddenly, her smile disappeared. "And since when do you use such vulgar language, Missy?"

"Music business," Stella said dryly. "We're all degenerates. We say hell all the time." The sound of a car pulling up outside saved her from her mother's reprimand, and Stella grinned. "Donnie. Leave it to that fool to get here the minute the work's all done."

"Well, I'm going downstairs to get one of those sandwiches. Coming, dear?"

"I've gotta run, Mama, but I'll take one home. I've got a million calls to make. But before I go, I'll get this stuff back into the boxes so Donnie can put them away."

"Thank you, dear... Oh, wait—I nearly forgot." She pulled a large card from her purse and handed it to Stella. "It's for you. The tribute card for Grandpa's funeral. What do you think?"

Stella scanned the black border and script lettering on the card, then stared at the photo. "Oh, he's in his uniform, Mama! I haven't seen this picture in years. Look how young he was!"

"It was just before he went off to war, and such a handsome picture of him, wasn't it?"

"Mm-hmm."

"Estelle, you *will* be wearing a dress for the funeral, and not one of those awful pantsuits?"

"I'm wearing a dress, Mother. Black, knee-length, with a Peter-Pan collar. Very sedate."

"That's good, dear. And thanks for all your help today."

As soon as her mother was gone, Stella took the bundle of letters and returned the empty cigar box to its place under the ledgers. By the time she got in her car, she was laughing. Whether it was the thrill of committing theft right under her mother's nose, or the prospect of uncovering some clandestine family secret that had been guarded for nearly sixty years, she wasn't sure. But whatever it was, she couldn't wait to get home and see what was in those letters.

≈∞≈

Miles was already standing at the door when Stella opened it and stepped inside. When she turned on the light the cat gazed up at her. "Waah."

"Waah, yourself, Miles. I know I'm late." Hurrying to the kitchen, she opened a can of cat food and dumped it into his dish. As he ate, she turned on the stereo and poured a glass of wine.

Sinking onto the sofa, she pulled the envelopes from her bag and looked at the return address. "London, England, ladies' stationery, and definitely *not* Catherine's handwriting. And addressed to a P.O. Box, *not* the house. Pretty suspicious if you ask me, *Drew*."

Phoebe Snow's voice floated out from the radio, and Stella sang along to "Poetry Man."

As Stella unfolded the fragile letter paper, she felt a fleeting pang of guilt for invading her grandfather's privacy, but quickly shook it off as she began to read the first letter.

> *February 3, 1919*
>
> *My darling Drew—*
>
> *It is a hundred times more difficult than I had imagined. Since seeing you off at Victoria Station, my life has been a series of empty, endless ticks on the clock. The days drag and the nights are worse. We knew that only our memories would sustain us, and it is so true. They are my only happiness now.*

Stella grinned and reached for her wine. "Oooh! Juicy trash! Grandpa was having an affair, just like in some corny romance novel!" But as she read, the ironic lyrics to "Poetry Man" caught her attention and she stared up at the radio. She listened for a moment, then gazed down at the cat. "Weird, huh, Miles?"

After a brief acknowledgment of her voice, Miles went back to his diligent paw-washing, Phoebe Snow went on singing, and Stella went back to her letter.

> *... Please forgive me, Drew. It was not my intention to write of my sorrows, but simply to speak to you through my letters. And so now for a cheerier try!*
>
> *My sister announced last Sunday that she is expecting her second baby, and her husband is over the moon! My brother comes 'round every day, fussing about and hammering nails, and the old house wears all the patched bits like medals of honor. People are smiling as the soldiers come home, and spring will be here soon. I shall find my happiness in these*

moments. If you knew my truest feelings, you would not worry about me. We must both take comfort in the knowledge that we helped each other through a terrible war. And we must believe that this is a pardonable indiscretion in the all-seeing eyes of God, if not in the blind eyes of society. Your grief was too heavy a burden for you to carry alone, and it helped me to know that you needed me. Therefore, no guilt for either of us, please, my love.

In closing, I shall say one thing more. You must find solace in your decision to remain with Catherine. In time you will find with her an enduring love that was never meant for us. It's strange, but I feel no jealousy when I think of her. My love for you will not permit it. Our time together is all behind us and we must march on like good soldiers. But I find no harm in visiting you in our small world of shared memories from time to time. With all my love—Erica

Puzzled, Stella placed the letter back in the envelope. "Grief? What grief?" She stared at the return address. "Erica Danbury," she whispered. "Who were you?"

A Coca Cola commercial blasted from the radio, followed by the smooth FM voice of the night deejay: "We've got a request from Pam Miller in El Segundo, who's got a jones for Marvin Gaye. So take a deep breath, baby. Here's Marvin comin' at'cha with back-to-back hits."

Stella took a sip of wine and turned up the radio just as Marvin Gaye began to sing the live version of "Distant Lover."

Then Stella remembered something her mother had told her earlier that day. "Oh, no. It was his brother... His brother got killed in the war. *That* was the grief." She sighed and unfolded the next letter, with a real need to know the rest of the story.

My darling Drew—

England has been foggy and gray these past few weeks— even drearier than usual—but reading your letter warmed my heart like the summer sun. I loved the description of your country home with its rolling acres of green grass and flowering trees. It sounds grand, my love, and I'm sure I'll visit it in my happiest dreams of you.

You should know better than to apologize for writing of your continuing sorrow over your brother. Losing Harold is our shared burden—a burden that we have carried together since the moment he took his last breath in my arms.

Stella gasped. "Wait—what the hell was Harold doing in *your* arms?" She read on:

Throughout this terrible war, I agonized over many deaths, but losing Harold was the worst. When your unit arrived from France with so many wounded men, it was through you that I found strength. Despite your own injuries, you never left your brother's side. I was determined to save him for you, but I failed. And I would give anything to bring him back to you—still.

Stella glanced at the clock. It was half past nine and Marvin Gaye was singing his anti-war anthem, "What's Going On?"

A shiver ran down Stella's neck, and a rush of scattered thoughts pulsed through her brain. Erica and Drew, and the miles and circumstances that separated them; an old war that she had only read about in books suddenly springing to life with all its vivid colors and emotions; and Marvin's voice ringing in her ears, telling her the whole story, as if he had lived it himself.

She stared at the radio, then searched for where she had left off in the letter.

... I begin my new assignment at St. John's Hospital in four days, Drew, and I will dedicate my future work to your brother's sweet, brave soul. I know that he watches over both of us, I just know it. Somehow it seems that only Harold and God could ever understand and forgive our indiscretion. Only Harold and God.

Common sense tells me that I should speak of our love in past terms, but my love for you has only grown stronger since our separation. I am sitting at my writing desk looking at a full moon shining down on the old River. Sometimes I believe that the moon alone knows why we fell in love. It looks so serene and forgiving that I expect God must be there on nights like this. I think of you watching that same moon and I know that we are united for eternity.

I will love you always—Erica

Stella stared down at her grandfather's funeral tribute photo. *The moon alone knows why...*

"Oh, Drew, you were so lonely, and none of us ever bothered with you." Then a harsh realization brought tears to her eyes. Drew's grief over his brother's death was reduced to her mother's offhand remark that afternoon: *Harold was killed over there and they never finished that second house.*

Stella walked to the window and gazed at the headlights winding along Mulholland's dark curves. Thoughts of Nick drifted into her mind. What would he think about Drew and Erica?

"My own grandfather with a white girl—she must've been white—but I don't care! Oh, boy, Nick, you'd laugh yourself silly if you heard me say that!"

She poured another glass of wine, unable to shake off the sadness of her grandfather's story. "Poor Drew. So you do the right thing and go back to Catherine, and then a few years later, she dies. But wait—why didn't you go back for Erica then?... Oh, right. Who am I kidding? Black man, white woman in the twenties? Forget it. You would've been lynched." She stared at the letters. As heartbreaking as it was, the story was too compelling not to finish. Shuffling through the envelopes, she found the next letter in the bunch, dated March 12, 1919.

> *My darling Drew—*
>
> *I received your letter yesterday morning, and I have been struggling for hours to write a response. But now, after reading your words for the second time, I have found the courage to tell you what I must. There is no other way to say it, Drew. I am expecting a child in September.*

Stella's mouth dropped open and she felt her heart racing.

> *I have spent many long nights wondering if I should tell you, but when a man has a child in the world, he has the right to know. And since Catherine is barren—*

Stella gasped. "What?! Barren?... Okay, enough wine for you, Stella." She set her glass aside, and then her eyes raced across the page:

> *... And since Catherine is barren, I knew it was doubly important that I tell you. You know that our racial difference is of no concern to me, Drew, but now we must face the fact that my family will never accept a half-Negro child. We were foolish to think only of ourselves. I considered a discreet adoption, but I know of no institution that will help me and the thought of our child being raised by strangers is too much to bear. So I must appeal to you. I have a proposal that is strictly in the best interests of our sweet baby. If Catherine would agree to an adoption, you could raise our son, Drew. You might tell her that our baby is the child of a fallen soldier you befriended.*
>
> *The most important thing is that he is raised by one of us, and by parents who will love him—or her. You must think me a selfish shrew for abandoning my own baby, but I see no other way. If he remains with me, he will suffer vilification at every turn. I am an unmarried white woman, and my family is struggling, as is all England. What sort of life could I provide for our sweet brown child? But when I envision him living*

with you and Catherine in the beautiful house you built with
your own hands, I have hope for his happiness. Am I so
terrible for that?

Again, she stared at Erica's left-handed writing that looked so much
like Donnie's. "And the sweet brown child was Daddy... My God. My
grandmother was a white Englishwoman."

≈∞≈

The next morning Stella pulled into the parking lot of the Church of the
Angels with a few minutes to spare. As she checked her appearance in
the rear-view mirror, she spotted Donnie grinning at her from behind the
car. Grabbing her purse, she got out and walked toward him.

"Hi, white sheep," she said softly, and then winced at the irony.

"Jeez, Stel! How come your eyes are so red? If I didn't know you
better, I'd swear you've been up all night blowin' a carload of weed!"

She gazed at her brother's face and wondered what Erica Danbury
looked like.

He gave her a puzzled look. "Hey. Earth to Stella."

"Sorry, Donnie. I just couldn't sleep last night, that's all."

"Well," he sighed, "let's get this shit over with. It looks like everybody's already inside."

"Damn, Donnie!" she snapped. "Drew's dead! Can't you show some
respect?"

Donnie laughed. "Wait a minute. Who the hell's *Drew?* And 'damn'
ain't your usual high-falutin' vernacular, *Estelle.* You know, we *are*
about to enter a church—"

Stella turned away from him and headed toward the church steps in a
huff.

He hurried after her and caught her arm. "Stella, what is *wrong* with
you?"

Stella softened her tone. "Drew is our grandfather. I guess some of
the stuff Mama told me yesterday sort of made him real to me for the first
time, that's all. I'm fine. Let's go in."

As they walked up the aisle, Donnie nudged her and pointed at the
row their parents occupied. They slipped in quietly, with only a
whispered reprimand from their mother.

Stella stared at the gray metal casket at the front of the church. A
spray of red and white roses covered the bottom half, and the top section
was open. From her seat, all she could see was Drew's forehead. A
dreary wash of organ music was occasionally punctuated by a soft cough
or someone clearing a throat, and Stella's thoughts drifted back to the

letters. It was nearly 2:00 a.m. when she had read the final letter that contained the most tender, crushing revelation:

> *... I am heartbroken, but proud of the courage you've shown, Drew. After much thought, I realize you were right to tell Catherine that the child she is raising is our son. I am humbled by her forgiveness and undeserving of the blessing that my child will be raised by this angel.*

Stella gazed over at her father. He was sitting next to her mother, with a dispassionate expression on his face. *He must know who his mother was. But—maybe not. Or maybe he just doesn't care.*

A man stepped up to the podium and introduced himself as Reverend Bennett. Stella barely heard his words, only catching occasional snippets that sounded like the empty rhetoric of a politician's speech—vague, sweeping phrases that covered everything without really saying anything. But suddenly he said something that did capture her attention: "Frederick was many things to many people. To his son Donald, he was Dad. To his grandchildren, he was Grandpa. So as we say goodbye to Frederick today—"

Stella felt a tremor in the pit of her stomach and balled up her fists in her lap. She began shaking her head and muttering loudly. "Not Frederick. No. His name is Drew!" She ignored her mother's shushes and felt tears streaking down her face. "No, Mama! *Not* Frederick! The people who loved him called him Drew! This is *his* day! Can't we call him by his name, like we at least *knew* him or something?" She leaned into Donnie's arms and cried on his shoulder for several minutes as the congregation buzzed. Then she felt him pressing a handkerchief against her face.

"Stel?" he whispered. "What the hell's up with you? Are you okay?"

She blew her nose and looked up at him. "Sorry, Donnie. I guess—I'm okay now."

After the long, uncomfortable interruption, Reverend Bennett asked the family to come forward for their final goodbyes. As Stella approached the casket, she gazed at the old man lying so still and tried to envision him as the young, tragic Drew she had come to know through Erica's letters. He was still wearing his wedding band. As she stared at it, she realized that she had never seen his hand without it. She leaned down to kiss his forehead. "Drew," she whispered, "please forgive me for being such a horrible granddaughter. And... wherever you are now—I hope you can hear me—'cause I want you to know something. I want you to know that Harold and God aren't the only ones who understand."

Chapter 45

Three days had passed since Nick's disappearance from the Forum. Calvin had checked all the hospitals and police stations in the Los Angeles area, and then he had tried the airlines, but none of them would release the names on their manifests. Out of ideas, he made the necessary calls to cancel the rest of the tour. Untangling the financial problems would have to wait. With a sick feeling in the pit of his stomach, he caught the red-eye to LaGuardia, hoping that Nick had gone home to New York.

Once the flight was underway, he closed his eyes, but couldn't sleep.

What if he really did it? That boy gets so damn depressed... What if he's layin' in some hotel room and ain't nobody found him yet—or in some alley? Some goddamn dirty ol' alley...

His eyes opened and a shudder ripped through him, bringing with it a clear, cold memory:

This poor lady was found in an alley not too far from here. A couple of garbage men found her on their morning route...

Calvin had pushed that day to the back of his mind years ago, but now, inexplicably, it was back—like an array of sharp color photographs in his memory. Driving to Harlem Hospital. The smell of disinfectant in the elevator that took them to the morgue. He even remembered the attendant's name—Jamie Fenton. And he could still see the pain etched on Doc's face when he sat next to him on the floor because he didn't know what else to do to comfort him.

As Calvin listened to the drone of the jet engines, he tried to fight back the tears. But these were patient tears that had been waiting for a weak moment, and now they overtook him.

≈∞≈

Donna was waiting outside baggage claim when Calvin got back to New York. He climbed into the car and kissed her. "You ain't heard from him, have you?"

"Oh, baby, I would'a told you first thing if I had. But he's all right. I feel it."

Calvin shook his head. "Wish I could believe that."

"Look, his Mama's just sick—not dead. And from all you told me about his relationship with her, I can't believe he'd abandon her like that. He'd *never* do to her what Joe did."

"Well, maybe. But what about the drugs, Donna? That can mess up any sense the boy might have. And even if he is okay, he ain't never gonna want to see *me* again."

"Oh, yes he will. You've got sump'm he needs—information. He's *dyin'* to know what you can tell him about your time with his Mama. No, baby, he's not through with you yet. He's just—shocked. But he's alive, all right. You mark my words."

Calvin smiled. "You know what? You make up for all the madness in my miserable life."

≈∞≈

Every morning Calvin called Bellevue to check on Magda's condition, but on Thursday his phone rang early. He answered it before the second ring. "Hello?"

"Calvin? It's Emily."

He stood up and gripped the receiver. "Emily. Please don't tell me—"

"Stop right there, Calvin. I'm not calling with bad news. I came out here this morning before my shift to check on Mrs. Bluestone. I just called to tell you they finally got that combination of drugs right, and her lungs are finally clearing up. She's doing much better."

"Thank God."

"Wait—let me finish. Nick visited her last night."

Calvin's knees nearly buckled. "Emily, if we wasn't on the phone, I'd—kiss you."

As he hung up, Donna walked in with a cup of coffee. "*Who* are you planning on kissing?"

Calvin set the coffee on the nightstand and wrapped his arms around her. "You. And here's the short explanation: That was Emily, Magda's doin' better, and Nick went to see her last night. He's okay, just like you said. Now let's just hope you're right about the rest."

≈∞≈

Two nights later Calvin woke to the sound of the doorbell. "Can't be nobody but Nick. That boy ain't got the sense God gave a pig! Ringin' the doorbell at two in the gotdamn mornin'—"

Donna laughed softly. "Aw, quit'cha bitchin' and go make peace with the boy."

Calvin chuckled and kissed her. When he got to the door and opened it, he stared at Nick flatly. He had lived too long to be caught with his guard down by the same man twice, even if it was his own son. Cradling his right fist in his left palm, he said, "Your Mama's doin' better."

"I *know*! I been checkin' on her."

"I know," Calvin countered. "I been checkin' on *you*."

Calvin was debating whether to step outside or shut the door when Nick's confrontational pretense collapsed into emotional stammering. "So—so—you really *knew* Mama?"

Calvin stepped outside and shut the door. "I *loved* her, boy. I didn't just *know* her."

Nick sat down heavily on the porch step. "So that time on the train—when you told me you had two great loves in your life—that was Mama? She was that first one that you lost?"

"Yes."

"I guess I shouldn'ta—hit you. I—I'm sorry I hit you."

Calvin chuckled. "Shit! I'm sorry I didn't hit you first."

"You did."

"Ouch. Guess I did, huh?"

"So you didn't say that just to keep me from—all that stupid shit I was talkin' about?"

"I told you—I don't lie. Not as a rule. And not about sump'm that important."

"So if you're my—*father*—" He paused, apparently still struggling with the idea. "Then that means Joe killed himself for nothin'. For *nothin'*! For some reason that really messes with me."

Calvin remained silent.

"But forget Joe. I wanna know about Mama. But I'm warnin' you—if she was some kind'a tramp, you better learn how to lie fast, 'cause I don't wanna hear any sleazy motel-room stories."

"Hey! Don't you *ever* use the word *tramp* when you talkin' about your Mama, you hear me? Damn, boy, I thought you were grown, but you got a lot to learn."

"What the hell do you mean by that?"

"Keep your voice down! My neighbors are sleepin'… Awright, look. First off, whatever she did in her life ain't none'a *your* goddamn business. She had her own life long before she even thought about bein' a mother. But she was—*is* a lady—with a good soul."

"I know that. I mean—somehow I just knew that."

"She made some mistakes, but she was the best person I ever met. There I was—a colored ex-con fixin' to be a two-time loser, but she saw sump'm else in me. Some—better man."

Nick stared at Calvin as if he were a stranger.

"I know. It's weird for me too—talkin' about my past. But you need to know all this. I'll tell you one thing you might not know about her… That little woman could make me laugh like nobody else."

"Mama? Mama was *funny*?"

The eagerness in Nick's eyes broke Calvin's heart and made him smile at the same time. "Oh, yeah," he said. "She could be a real goofball sometimes. Actually, she was the one who taught me how to laugh. 'Cause I ain't gotta tell you there wasn't much to laugh about in prison.

So she helped me with that adjustment. And then she just—changed my whole life."

"Okay, tell me about all that—how she changed your life and everything."

Calvin reached into the pocket of his robe for his cigarettes. "Okay. I guess it all starts with the real reason I was in prison."

"The *real* reason? I thought you said you didn't lie."

"I didn't," he said. "Think, Nick. What did I ever really tell you?"

"Well, I—I can't remember the details, but—"

"That's 'cause I never gave you no details... I was convicted for killin' Joe. I got life."

Nick's mouth dropped open, but he said nothing.

"Look. I'ma have to tell you some things about myself that I never told a livin' soul. I got lucky and didn't have to serve out that life sentence, but I paid for what I did to Joe." He stared hard at Nick and lowered his voice. "Don't ever end up in prison, boy. 'Cause it ain't losin' your freedom that's the punishment... It's the things that happen to a man when the lights go out."

After a long silence, Nick mumbled, "No wonder—you hated him."

"Hated him? Shit, hate don't even begin to cover it. When I got out the joint, I was like a goddamn hopped-up racehorse waitin' for the starter pistol! I couldn't wait to get my hands around Joe's neck." He sighed. "But then—everything got complicated when I met Mag."

"Mag?"

"Yeah. You never heard that name before. 'Cause I was the only one who called her that."

Nick stared into the distance, smiling vaguely. "Mag?"

Calvin lit a cigarette, took a deep pull, and then stared into the smoke as he exhaled. "Come on, boy. Let's go for a walk. It's a lot to untangle and I gotta figure out where to begin."

And now, for our late-night radio listeners—

A reprise—
Drumroll, please…
slow hands on black keys
Hard luck rondo
repeats and repeats
How high the climb
How high the moon?
High time for high noon
A duel of fools and
shadows of an unseen crime
Lies in rhyme
Played—
passionato, in twelve/eight time…

Chapter 46

I remember the day everything changed. For some reason, I was givin' a lot'a thought to a convict named Scat Jones that mornin'. Scat was like some kind'a comic book character. To the guards, he was just a square little sawed-off Clark Kent. But to the inmates, he was Superman—only more deadly... Damn, Nick, lookin' back on it now, I guess we wasn't supposed to get rehabilitated in there. Shit. Maybe we wasn't even supposed to survive...

≈∞≈

1949 — Parchman State Penitentiary
Sun Flower County, Mississippi

The 5:00 a.m. bell jangled through the cellblock inciting a chorus of groans.

Only Calvin Bailey was dressed and waiting for the guard. Since his mother's death, there had been no fluctuations in his daily routine—field work, three squares, no more visits, no more mail. The only thing he enjoyed was reading—something he had rarely bothered with before his incarceration. A trustee named Henry Till had left him a few books when he was released—*Native Son*, by Richard Wright, *The Street*, by Ann Petry, and *The Souls of Black Folk*, by W.E.B. Dubois. As he got lost in the stories, he realized that his imagination could carry him over the walls of Parchman to big cities he had only seen in the movies—Chicago, New York, San Francisco. The books became his most prized possessions; they were closest thing to freedom he would ever know.

His annoyance was growing as he waited for the guard. The sooner he finished his work, the sooner he could get back to his reading. He paced impatiently in the small confines of his cell until he heard the piercing, off-key falsetto voice of Scat Jones serenading the cellblock with "Don't Get Around Much Anymore."

Within seconds, the convicts began to curse and pound on the bars, but Calvin smiled, finding a perverse pleasure in their misery. He was the only man in the cellblock who tolerated Scat's screechy voice, partly because Scat and Henry Till were the only friends he had made in nearly four years at Parchman. Scat was the most entertaining little guy he had ever seen. It took guts—or a tin ear—to display that voice with such confident abandon. Besides, Calvin knew something else about Scat. Despite his size, he was a dangerous man—a trait not apparent upon first glance.

On Scat's first day at Parchman, Calvin watched him taking the long walk to his cell, and saw the effects of the other convicts' filthy catcalls. The new man was terrified and trembling so severely that he stumbled three times along the way. He was barely five-feet-two, and probably weighed a hundred and ten pounds soaking wet.

That night, the sounds of Scat's introduction to prison life at the hands of his cellmates made sleep impossible for Calvin. It was a harsh reminder of his own first night in Parchman and an inmate named Judge. Then he heard an unusual sound and sat up, wondering if the skinny kid had lost his mind. He was trying to sing. It was a slow, shaky version of "St. James Infirmary," and every few words were interrupted by a hard catch in his voice.

When the jeers and laughter started, Calvin slammed his head back down onto his cot. "Goddamn! That po' kid sings bad as me," he muttered.

A skin-tearing slap brought an abrupt stop to the singing, and Calvin made up his mind to straighten out a few people, which was a rare departure from his carefully cultivated "dangerous loner" persona.

He got his chance the next afternoon.

Stepping into the exercise yard, his eyes scanned the familiar faces of the men standing in their regular clusters until he spotted the three he was looking for. Lester, Too-Black, and Jerome leaned menacingly close to their victim near a shaded corner of the building with their backs to Calvin. He approached them quietly, then reached in with one hand to grip Jerome's bicep. Digging his fingers into the nerve between muscle and bone, Calvin made his point without saying a word. He pulled Jerome close and stared at him blankly as he calmly inflicted enough pain to bring him to his knees. Then he jerked up his chin. "What's up, Too-Black?"

Too-Black was an inch taller than Calvin and outweighed him by twenty pounds. His complexion was high yellow, but he boasted that he had guts blacker than darkest Africa, with a black heart to match—his own twisted version of racial pride. He smirked at Calvin, but didn't answer.

Calvin finally released Jerome, who groaned and scrambled to his feet. "I *said* what's up, Too-Black?"

"My foot—up yo' ass, man, if you don't back up off'a my piece."

Ignoring him, Calvin addressed the new prisoner. "You got a name, little man?"

"Scat—Jones," he muttered, his gaze fixed on one of Calvin's shirt-buttons.

"So Scat—was that you singin' last night?"

"Hey, man. I'm sorry, okay?" Scat said the right words, but his tone was a bit tart for someone surrounded by men twice his size.

Calvin was amused and impressed at the same time, but he didn't show it. "I'm *sorry?* That's a sorry answer, Scat, 'cause I like your singin'. Matter of fact, I want you to sing every night like that."

Scat blinked up at him in surprise, but Calvin's stare was fixed on Too-Black. "'Cause you know, Scat, my *high yella* brother use'ta sing—" With that, he stopped, well aware of the effect the mere mention of his brother would have. He had never denied beating Joe to death with his bare hands; it was too valuable as a tool of survival.

When the State of Mississippi had thrown Calvin into this pit of barbarism, he was eighteen—naïve and defenseless against a sudden onslaught of gang rapes and beatings led by a ruthless convict named Judge. Calvin's body was strong, so he survived the physical attacks, but mentally, he was breaking. Unlike the Natchez County Jail, Parchman's crowded environment yielded nothing for him but a small corner to curl up in each night—a bit of space in which to wait in dread of the next attack. No refuge, no compassion, and certainly no rescue. This was the last stop for hopeless, violent men, who made sport of terrorizing anyone showing the slightest sign of fear or weakness. When Calvin finally managed a stretch of clear thought, it was that word that saved him: *Weakness*. Whatever else he might be, Calvin Bailey was not weak.

When he made the decision to reclaim his mind and body, the change in him was swift. He dug deep beneath his fear to find a still-seething fury in his gut. He still blamed his brother for sending him to prison, so he used that hate to construct a useful illusion: Judge was Joe. But what about the gang? There were four others. Then Calvin heard his father's voice in his head: *If you cut off a snake's head, the body gon' die too.*

Instead of waiting for the next attack, Calvin hunted Judge down, with the explicit intent of gouging out one of his eyes. The element of surprise made his mission a quick one. Within seconds, Judge's left eye was gone, lost in the blood and muck of the laundry room floor.

The story quickly circulated among the prison population, along with exaggerated details about Calvin's fratricide conviction, cementing his reputation as a cold, clinical assassin. Since then he had been left alone—until Too-Black's arrival.

Thoughts of his revenge on Judge brought a cynical grin to Calvin's face. "So you sing all you want to, Scat. I think it'll give me just the edge I need—to stay good and pissed off."

Too-Black glared at Calvin, then retreated with a smirk. His group followed behind him.

"Damn!" Scat breathed, his eyes wide. "You sho' put a stripe down that nigga's back!"

"Naw, he'll be back. But he through with you, little man. He gunnin' for me now."

The inevitable ambush occurred two weeks later when Calvin was on kitchen duty. The handle of the spoon was so finely sharpened that it was lodged deeply between two of his ribs before he even realized that he had been stabbed. Too-Black backed away grinning as Calvin stared down at the bowl of the spoon protruding from his midsection, the pool of blood at his feet, and the rag Too-Black had used to mask his fingerprints.

He woke the next evening in the Parchman medical unit, amazed that he was still alive. The assistant warden went through the routine of questioning him, and Calvin went through the routine of stonewalling, ending with the standard "I didn't get a look at the guy" line. The handmade weapon had miraculously missed his vital organs, and after a few stitches and two days of bed rest, he spent two weeks in solitary for not cooperating. He spent the time wondering about how Scat was doing, now that he had no one to look out for him.

When Calvin finally stepped outside for his first walk in the exercise yard, Scat rushed over to him. "Calvin, ain't you heard?" he said, glancing over his shoulder.

"Man, I ain't heard nothin'. I went straight from unconscious to the hole, remember?"

Scat was as happy as a white kid on Christmas morning. "Too-Black dead, man."

"Good," Calvin muttered automatically, then jerked up his chin. "Who got him?"

Scat smiled and gave him a brotherly slap on the back. "Shit, I couldn't let him get away with fuckin' you up like that! You the only one stuck up for me. You my ace boon coon, man."

Calvin noticed a gap in Scat's smile where a tooth had been the last time he'd seen him.

"How'd you lose that tooth, man?... Naw, never mind. What'd you do to Too-Black?"

"Slit his throat like a gotdamn chicken, man. He ain't even know what the fuck was up."

"But how?" Calvin wondered if Scat was taking credit for someone else's handiwork.

"Got the drop on him, man. Same way he got the drop on you. Time he bus' me in the mouth, nigga awready *been* cut." Scat grinned. "Fallin' on the flo' smilin' with his neck! Shit! These mu-fuckas gotta *learn*! Li'l fella like me can be deadly as a mu-fuckin' train wreck, man."

Calvin said nothing. A churning feeling in his gut told him that Scat was telling the truth.

Despite all the unspeakable violence he had suffered, seen, or inflicted inside the walls of Parchman, Calvin was deeply disturbed by Too-Black's murder. He lay awake pondering the change in Scat, whose original conviction had been for armed robbery and assault with a deadly weapon. But the legal version sounded much worse than the actual crime. It had started as a simple liquor store hold-up, but the proprietor made a move to slap the small Saturday Night Special out of Scat's shaking hand. Since the gun was unloaded, Scat saw no choice but to use the butt of it on the man's skull in order to make his escape. And with all the confusion, he hadn't even remembered to grab the money. So one unloaded gun plus a failed robbery attempt plus a lump on a white man's head equaled ten years in Parchman for Scat, with a possibility of parole in a couple of years, with good behavior.

Calvin couldn't get a handle on Scat. He had gone from a scared, would-be stick-up man, who hadn't even loaded his gun, to a cold-blooded murderer in less than a year. Not that Too-Black wasn't asking for it, but it was the calculated detachment that bothered Calvin. It would have made sense to him if Scat had killed Too-Black in a spontaneous opportunity for payback, but Scat had waited and plotted, making sure that the murder occurred when Calvin, who would have been the number-one suspect, was in solitary. Scat had played it so cool that he threw the Parchman authorities into complete confusion. Even the guards, who prided themselves in knowing every detail of the infighting among prisoners, were stumped.

It took a few weeks for the final masterstroke to come to light. Even with all the snitches in Parchman—some of them large, frightening men—Scat somehow finessed a way to wear the killer's badge of honor among the inmate population without the guards ever suspecting him. Not only did he avoid solitary confinement, but he was never even questioned.

Two years had passed since Too-Black's murder, and Scat sang loud, long performances whenever the mood struck him. On this particular morning, his singing had served as an amusing distraction for a time, but now Calvin was growing agitated at the delay.

When the guard finally arrived, he opened the door and said, "Bailey! You got a visitor."

Calvin shook his head. "Must be a mistake."

"No mistake, Convict. Come on."

The guard took him through a series of security doors, then Calvin sat down at the table for non-contact visits. As he stared through the thick wire mesh, he wondered who would sit in the chair across from him. After several minutes, a tall, slender Negro Calvin had never seen before sat down. He wore a dark blue suit and a matching Fedora, which he removed to run a hand over his salt-and-pepper hair. Calvin blinked at him wordlessly, then stood up to leave.

"Wait!" the stranger said. "Please—are you Mr. Calvin Bailey?"

"Naw. I'm Mr. 87439, but all my *society* friends jus' call me Convict."

"Please, Mr. Bailey— You *are* Mr. Bailey—?"

"Look, who the hell are *you*? You ain't on my visitor list 'cause I ain't *got* one."

"My name is Ezekiel Templeton. I'm a lawyer, and I got a special pass to see you."

Calvin laughed bitterly and moved away from the table.

"Please!" Templeton said. "I'm not like your trial lawyer, I can guarantee you that."

"Naw, you ain't like *that* sissy. You got the extra handicap of bein' a nigga."

Templeton held up a hand. "Please, Mr. Bailey. Five minutes."

Calvin studied him for a moment, then slumped back into the chair. "*What* do you want?"

"I'm here to help you, if you'll let me. I'm pretty sure I can get you out of here."

"What'chu got? A shotgun down your pants leg? 'Cause that's the only way my ass gets out'a here."

Templeton leaned forward and stared into his eyes. "I know you didn't kill your brother."

Calvin felt a slight catch in his breathing. "How you know that?"

"Because nobody killed him. He's alive."

Calvin froze. For four years, he had known somewhere deep inside that Joe was alive, but hearing the actual words from this stranger was a jolt. "You—seen him?"

"Look, let me start over. As you said, it's not easy for a colored lawyer to begin with, and Louisville, where I'm from, isn't exactly crawling with big cases. But then I got one—a murder case without a corpse. The prosecuting attorney was going after my client like he'd found the body himself and was ready to present it as Exhibit A, so I started checking case law and came across your trial. When I read that you'd been convicted, I started investigating, and I found the newspaper photos of you and your brother. And I *had* to find out what really happened to Joe."

"Why the hell you think I *ain't* killed him?"

"A feeling. Then I found this." Templeton unfolded a newspaper clipping and he held it up.

Calvin stared at the grainy photo of a six-piece band above the words "Beat the Heat." His eyes were drawn to the man in the center. The straight hair and fancy suit made him look older and sophisticated, but there was no doubt in Calvin's mind. The "white" man in the photo was his brother Joe.

Chapter 47

I remember the first time I laid eyes on her. She come walkin' into that club wearin' this real pretty pink dress... What was it she called it? Moonlight pink? No—moonlight magenta! Now, how in the hell did I remember that? Anyway, all I kept thinkin' was how Joe always got what he wanted, and he must'a really wanted her. I even remember what song was playin'. It was a Billie Holiday song...

≈∞≈

Charles Jackson carefully studied the Café Nocturne sign before taking off his hat and opening the door. He had heard that there were no "white only" entrances in New York like the ones in the South, but he checked the window and door just to be sure. Studying his reflection in the entryway mirror, he rubbed his freshly shaved head, nodded, and looked around. It was the last night of 1951, and the bar was decorated with noisemakers and paper streamers. He took a seat.

A stout gray-haired bartender with a friendly Irish face walked over. "What can I get'cha, pal?"

"Beer, I guess."

"Shaffer okay?"

"Yes, sir. That be fine."

The bartender pulled a frosty mug from the icebox and filled it with beer from the tap. "Where ya from, buddy?"

Charles peered at him, trying to size him up. "The South."

The bartender placed the beer on a coaster. "You ain't been in town long, have you?"

Charles felt the heat of his fingertips melting the chill right off the mug's thick glass. "How'd you know that?" he asked suspiciously.

"The way you said 'yes sir.' That ain't necessary here in New York. At least not here at the Nocturne." He extended his hand and smiled. "I'm Ed. What's your name?"

Charles tentatively shook the white man's hand. "Charles."

"Welcome to New York, Charles. Let me know when you're ready for a refill."

"Thanks. I'll do that... Hey, wait a minute, uh, Ed."

"What'cha need, Charles? Some peanuts?"

"Naw. The beer's fine. I was just wonderin' about this band that's playin'."

"Oh, yeah. That's *Beat the Heat*. They're the house band."

Charles sipped his beer and gazed at the band—all white, except for a Spanish-looking sax player and one Negro, who was soloing on a trumpet. "I heard they had a singer or sump'm."

"Yeah, Joe Bluestone—one'a those crooners makin' like Sinatra. Had all the chicks dizzy over him, but he's sellin' records now. Too much of a hotshot to play this club anymore, I guess."

Charles finished his beer quickly, and laid a dollar on the bar. "Thanks, Ed."

"Hey, it's still early. Stick around and ring in the New Year with us. The crowd'll start rolling in any minute. Next beer's on the house, whadaya say?"

"Well—" Charles turned back and saw the musicians putting down their instruments.

"Hang on a minute, Charles. The band's takin' a break, so I gotta plug in the jukebox."

As Ed plugged in the jukebox, Charles saw the musicians pointing and smiling at someone coming in the entrance door. When he turned to look, he saw a petite white woman making her way to the front table. Her hair was raven black and gathered up into an arrangement of curls that hung over one shoulder. She was wearing a long, drop-waist gown, and when she looked his way, he was startled by the color of her eyes—the strangest, palest blue eyes he had ever seen. The jukebox sprang to life in the middle of a Billie Holiday song: "I Got a Right to Sing the Blues."

"So what were you asking me, Charles?"

"Huh?" Charles asked, quickly looking away from the woman.

Ed laughed. "I know. I bet you want to know who she is."

"Somebody's wife, I bet."

"Yeah, but not any of those jokers. That's Joe Bluestone's wife. He's that singer I told you about. She comes in sometimes with the other band wives."

Charles gazed back at the woman with heightened interest. "Oh, *really?*"

"Damn singers always get the prettiest dolls. So, Charles, how 'bout that beer?"

"Well, okay. Thanks, Ed. Hey, where's the uh—toilet?"

"Over there past the bandstand. I'll keep your stool for you."

"Okay, thanks." Charles made his way over to the men's room door, but didn't go inside. He hung back in the shadows, watching and listening to the conversation at the band's table.

The Negro trumpet player kissed the white woman on the forehead. "How you doin', baby?"

"Oh, I am fine, I suppose, Doc."

Charles looked around the room in disbelief. A black man had kissed a white woman and called her baby, and no one seemed to care. As he continued to stare at them, that Billie Holiday song began to wear on his nerves.

Just then, the drummer said something that made everyone laugh. Charles tried to tune out Billie Holiday so he could hear the conversation, but only caught snippets.

The trumpet player lit a cigarette. "Where's that missing-person husband a'yours?"

The woman shrugged and said something about "the road." Then she smiled and waved at an attractive woman with dark, Latin features who was making her way through the crowd. The band greeted the second woman with wolf whistles.

She laughed and twirled around in her gold sheath dress. "Get a load'a little Mama!"

The sax player wrapped his arm around her and muttered at the musicians. Charles could only make out a few Spanish words, then: "... eyes in your sockets and hands in your pockets!"

The blue-eyed woman hugged "Little Mama" as the drummer gave her his chair. "Okay, okay," he said loudly. "Break's over. Grab some alcohol on your way back to the plantation. Maybe it'll improve your lousy playing. Hey, Magda, fix my tie, will you? I screwed it all up."

Magda. So that's her name.

When the band reassembled, they started off with a ballad Charles had never heard before. He changed his mind several times before finally working up the nerve to walk over to the table. "S'cuse me, ma'am," he said, staring at the woman's strange eyes. "Would you like to dance?"

She gave him an uncertain look, then smiled shyly. "Yes. I—I dance with you, sir."

As she stood up, Charles said, "Listen, I ain't—a very good dancer."

"Is okay. I ain't very good too, so I now don't worry to keep up."

He danced her slowly away from the bandstand. "That's a real pretty dress, ma'am."

"Thank you. Is new color called 'moonlight magenta.' Do you hear of it?"

"No, I ain't never heard a'that color. Uh, mind me askin' where you from?"

"Greece. My English and my dancing is not so good, I'm afraid. What is your name?"

"I'm Charles. Charles Jackson."

"And I am Magda Bluestone. It is nice to meet you."

"Nice to meet you too, ma'am. Hey, you know what? You don't dance bad at all."

She smiled nervously. "I would dance with my husband, but he is on da road now."

"Oh. So you celebratin' New Year's with some friends, huh?"

"Yes, and my friend Pearl will be here soon. Mr. Jackson, you are not from New York?"

"Oh, you can call me Charles. And I'm from—the South."

She frowned. "Is very terrible for Negroes in dat South, Charles. I hear of dis."

Charles smiled. "That's exactly why I left, ma'am."

She gazed at him curiously. "When you smile dat way—you look like someone I know."

Charles rubbed his head and grinned. "That King of Siam I seen on them Broadway posters?"

Magda laughed. "Oh, yes! I see dat play! Dat angry king dancing all da time and having no hair! But no, not dat king. You look—in small way—like my husband."

"You mean—your husband is a Negro?"

"No! Dat is why it is strange thing. My husband is a white man."

"Well, well. That *is* strange, huh?"

The song ended, and Charles led her back to her table, keeping his back to the bandstand.

"Thank you for da dance, Mr.—I mean, Charles. I—I was feeling sad, you know? But you make me to smile. I wish to you good luck in New York."

"Thanks, ma'am. That's mighty nice of you."

≈∞≈

A week later Charles was standing at a window inside Maybelle's Flower Shop watching a crowd of people emerge from the subway on 125th Street. Then he saw her. Magda Bluestone. He turned his back and pretended to shop until he heard the door's overhead bell ring.

"'Mornin', Miss Magda!" the proprietor called.

"Good morning! How you are doing, Mrs. Maybelle?"

Charles glanced back and watched as Magda picked up a small bouquet of roses. He waited until she went to the cash register, then intentionally backed into her.

She looked up, startled. "Oh, my Gott! I bump you. I am such da clumsy woman!"

"No, it was my fault," he said. Then he smiled. "Hey! Magda, right? But I forgot your last name…"

"Bluestone. And you are—wait, I remember. Charles, yes?"

"Yes. Charles Jackson—from Café Nocturne. So what brings you up to Harlem?"

"Oh, I visit my friend Pearl—around da corner. And I bring to her flowers for her table."

"Oh, that's real nice, Miz Bluestone. She gon' love these."

"Please to call me Magda. Dat is da name everyone calls me."

Charles eased his hands into his coat pockets and smiled broadly. "Then I gotta call you sump'm else. 'Cause I hate callin' folks what everybody else calls 'em. What's your whole name?"

"Magdalena Philomena Bluestone."

"Oh," he said. "That's mighty pretty, but it *is* a mouthful. What if I just call you Mag?"

She laughed. "Mag?"

"Yeah," Charles said. "Unless you don't like it."

"No, I like! It makes me to feel very American and—modern, no?"

"Mm-hmm. Real jazzy."

Magda shrugged and backed away hesitantly. "Well, I now must pay for da flowers—"

"Oh…Well, it was good seein' you again—Mag."

"Yes. Well, Charles, goodbye now, I'm afraid."

"Goodbye—you're afraid?"

"Oh, my Gott! My English! How to say? Wait— I am afraid I must now say goodbye," she recited stiffly. Then she smiled. "I learn dis on my English language record, Charles."

"Oh, okay. Now I get it. But you know what? There's a great diner across the street. Let me buy you some lunch 'fore you *really* must say goodbye."

"But I—I am married woman."

"Oh. Guess married women can't eat lunch, huh? Against the law?"

Magda laughed nervously and shook her head.

"It's okay, I understand. Maybe some other time—if we ever run into each other again."

She stared at him for a moment, then shrugged. "Well—okay, Charles. Nothing wrong to go and eat lunch with you, I suppose. I buy da flowers after, and den I go to see Pearl."

"Good!"

Magda left the flowers with Maybelle, and Charles opened the door for her. As they crossed the street, he noticed her uneven gait and glanced down at her feet. "You okay?"

The color rose in her cheeks. "Is only my brace, Charles. You think I stumble, but—no."

"Oh, okay. So—you get Polio when you was a kid or sump'm?"

"Yes. Polio."

"You're lucky, Mag. Lot'sa folks died from it. Were you sick long?"

"Yes, very long time I am sick, almost to die when I am twelve years of age. I think always of not to walk no more. How afraid dat makes me! But Dr. Moskos…"

Charles saw her eyes reddening. "What's wrong, Mag?"

"Is only—I think of Dr. Moskos. Every day he come to put da hot towels on my leg for treatment. It burn so terrible, but he talk to me and hold my hand. But den—da Nazis come and take him away and—"

"And what?"

"And Hitler—*kill* Dr. Moskos and his whole family—because dey are Jewish. And I cry and dream to stay forever on dat bed and dat Polio to kill me too. And I dream of screaming." She glanced self-consciously at Charles and shrugged. "But dreams only. I make my courage, and I don't really scream."

"Yeah, that sho' was terrible—what happened to them Jewish folks. But don't think about it, Mag. You ought'a think about how proud Dr. Moskos would be that you walkin' again."

"Yes," she said softly. "I now walk okay—with brace."

"See? And I bet Dr. Moskos is smilin' down at you thinkin' that's a happy ending."

"I hope so, Charles."

They stepped inside the diner and sat at a table near the window. Magda stared out at the people passing by. "So many colors are your people, Charles," she murmured, then quickly looked at him. "Oh, I'm sorry. Dat was rude thing to say?"

"Not rude. It's true. We prob'ly all ought'a be dark like Africans, but with all the mixin' durin' slavery times and marryin' with Indians, we come in about every color of the rainbow."

"Very pretty rainbow. My friend Pearl—she is beautiful, with skin to glow like gold, you know? American white people say how healthy to be tan. You are *very* healthy people, yes?"

Charles laughed. "Well, I suppose so, Mag. But you're a very pretty lady yourself, you know. Even if you ain't *healthy* lookin' like us."

"Well, I thank you, Charles. But I—I don't feel so much like a pretty lady no more."

A waitress approached the table and Charles quickly ordered two coffees. When she was gone, he turned back to Magda. "Now, what were you sayin' about not feelin' pretty no more?"

"Oh, nothing. I am— You are stranger, Charles. I don't know why I tell dat to you."

"Well, maybe you just needed somebody to talk to today," he said gently.

"You know, is strange thing, but you are looking very much like my husband to me. But—also to look like my dear friend Doc too, who is with da dark skin like you, Charles."

"Well, maybe that's why you feel like you can talk to me... Can I ask you sump'm, Mag?"

"Yes, of course."

"I don't mean to get so personal but—are you havin' troubles in your marriage?"

She looked down at the table. "Oh, my Gott! Why—why you tell dat to me?"

"I'm sorry, Mag. It was when you said you ain't been feelin' pretty. I thought a husband was supposed to make his wife feel pretty. Aww, but I ain't never been married myself."

After an awkward silence, Magda's eyes filled with tears. "Oh, my Gott," she mumbled.

"Aww, look, Mag, I'm sorry I said sump'm to make you feel bad."

"No. You do nothing wrong, Charles. Is only too many things to understand."

"Tell me," he coaxed.

Another long silence. Then: "Why will a husband bring other women to his bed?"

Her words were so unexpected that Charles was too stunned to hide his anger. "Because some sorry bastards never change," he muttered.

Magda's eyes widened. "What?"

"Oh, I'm sorry, Mag. I ain't meant to use bad language."

"Charles—I think I go to da powder room—to wash my face. You will wait?"

"I'll wait. And listen. I ain't wantin' to make you feel uncomfortable. You take your time. And the minute you ready to go, I'll walk you straight back over to the flower shop."

She stared at him for a moment before walking away. Her eyes still made him uneasy.

When she returned from the ladies' room, Charles stood up and pulled out her chair. Then he pushed a cup of steaming coffee toward her. "Here, drink it, Mag. You'll feel better."

She gazed out the window as she sipped the coffee. "When did da snow start, Charles?"

"Just a couple'a minutes ago. Hope it stays light."

"Oh, no. So pretty is da snow. I would want it to snow until it is up to my window."

"You'd get snowed in! Now why would you want that?"

"Because den Joe must stay away."

Charles took a sip of his coffee. "You don't want him to come home? Things that bad?"

She blushed. "Oh, Charles. I must stop telling to you my troubles. You dance one time with me and I now make you to be my psych— psych— Oh, what is da word?"

Charles grinned. "Psychiatrist?"

"Yes. I am sorry. Please to talk about something else now."

"Okay. Well, why don't you tell me about Greece? And how'd you get here, Mag?"

"Oh, I don't tell to you! I am musician! I come for to play da violin for studio recording."

"Oh, and that's how you met Joe?"

"Please. We now talk about Greece, not Joe, okay?"

"Sorry. So then tell me about Greece. I ain't never been there and I prob'ly never will."

Magda closed her eyes. "Well, best time is da spring. With almond blossoms to bloom and trees are heavy with many olives. And near da sea, da breeze is blowing and fishermen bring in da catches of nets." She opened her eyes and smiled. "And da marketplace, Charles. I wish you can see da marketplace. Many faces are smiling and I am now missing dem."

"Sounds pretty," Charles murmured as he glanced out the window. "Hey! Look at that snow! It's really comin' down now, huh?"

"Oh, my Gott, Charles! I make dat wish, and it now comes true?"

"It ain't that bad. But maybe we ought'a head over and get your friend's flowers 'fore it gets worse."

"Yes, and I thank you for helping me to feel better. Dat is da second time you make me to feel better from da blues. Da blues means to feel sad. My friend Pearl teach me dat."

After leaving some change on the table, Charles helped Magda into her coat. They crossed the street and purchased the flowers, and then walked up the block until Magda stopped in front of an apartment building. "Please to come in, Charles. You will like Pearl and her family."

He still found it difficult to look directly into her eyes, so he aimed his gaze up at the building's details. The green paint on the cornice was chipped and the lamp hanging in the portico was cracked. It was an old building, but it looked clean and warm. "Naw," he said, "I gotta get goin'. But wait a minute, Mag." Pulling a matchbook and a pencil from his pocket, he wrote down his number and grinned as he handed it to her. "This is so you can call me if you ever want to use me for a psychiatrist again. Just to talk or anything."

Magda's smile faded, and Charles lifted her chin with his fingertips. "Hey, look, I ain't makin' a pass or none'a that. Just call if you need a friend to talk to, that's all."

Magda held up the matchbook. "To have talk-lunch again?"

"Anytime, Mag." Charles smiled, and then walked away into a heavy swirl of snow.

Chapter 48

Calvin Bailey stepped into his cold room and shook the snow off his coat, then hung it on a hook to dry. Cursing under his breath, he banged the radiator with the handle of the butter knife he kept beside it, even though he knew it was a waste of time. It was almost dark, and he needed sleep before checking in for the graveyard shift at Harlem Hospital.

Stretching out on the narrow bed, he shifted his weight, trying to avoid the broken spring that always jabbed him in the back. The other springs squeaked loudly in protest until he found a comfortable position; then all was still in the room. He listened to the sounds of cars and buses bouncing in and out of ice-filled potholes on the street below, the occasional blast of a horn, and the voices of Harlemites talking and laughing as they passed on the sidewalks. City sounds. Calvin was accustomed to prison noises—the slamming of steel doors and angry male voices, in varying degrees of volume, cursing each other and the world at large for their circumstances.

He still felt the old rage, but prison had taught him how to channel it. Pulling the thin blanket up around his neck, Calvin closed his eyes and went over his agenda. *Point 1—Get to New York. Check. Point 2—Get a job. Check.* It was only a low-paying custodial job, mopping floors in a hospital, but it paid for his room and board, and breakfast was provided free of charge in the hospital cafeteria. The hours were from midnight until nine in the morning—perfect for a man attempting to keep a low profile. *Point 3—Locate Joe "Bluestone" without him knowing that he had been located. Check.*

Which brought him to Point 4—a last minute addition—Mag.

Calvin's eyes fluttered open and he stared up at the ceiling at a large maple-leaf-shaped stain from a long-ago rainstorm that had saturated the leaky roof. Meeting Joe's wife at Café Nocturne had been a rare stroke of good luck; he had only gone there to search for Joe. It hadn't surprised him that his brother had been passing and consorting with white women. *Damn, Convict. While you was rottin' in that prison all them years, Joe got hisself a white wife and a white life. Shit... All his dreams come true.*

After all his careful planning, everything had changed the minute Calvin saw that colored horn player kiss Mag's face. She wasn't just another angle to work; he would turn her into his best weapon.

It had been a simple matter to follow her home and observe her routine for a few days so that their meeting at the flower shop had appeared accidental. After that, everything fell into place. Calvin's bitter memory of Joe in bed with Michele all those years ago became his new blueprint: Big-shot crooner Joe—catching his white wife in bed with his hated black brother. *Surprise, you muthafucka. I'm back.*

But was it possible?

Yeah. She awready trusts me... Naw, wait. She don't trust me. She trusts Charles Jackson. Shit! She'd run for the hills if she knew who I really was.

Then the sound of Mag's broken English interrupted his sinister train of thought:

Why will a husband bring other women to his bed?

Calvin shifted uncomfortably, vacillating between thoughts of pulling off his plan and an annoying feeling of pity for Mag. She seemed nice— nothing like the hateful white girls he had seen growing up in Mississippi. The debate began to tire him, but each time he tried to drift off, he saw that lost expression in her strange blue eyes. Exhaustion began to jumble his thoughts into a nonsensical half-dream that finally faded along with the traffic noise outside.

Sleep.

≈∞≈

Charles had made one friend at Harlem Hospital—Mel—an evening cafeteria cook with a small radio that he lent to Charles each night when his own shift was over.

It had been snowing heavily since Charles had talked with Mag, and all he could think of was her remark about wishing for Joe to stay away. Now there was a good chance that his flight might be cancelled. "Maybe your luck's changin', Convict." He placed Mel's radio on the cart with his cleaning materials, turned the volume low, and began to mop as he waited for word on airport closures. When he heard the news jingle begin, he steered his mop back to the cart.

... And the blizzard over the tri-state area is heading out. Flights have been resumed at LaGuardia, and the airport will remain open. Now a word from our sponsor...

Charles sighed and turned off the radio. The rest of his shift loomed before him like a ten-year sentence. The night nurse hurried past him silently in her white rubber-soled shoes, with only a perfunctory glance in his direction. He nodded and murmured a greeting, which she didn't acknowledge. He wrung out the mop and smiled. Applying for custodial work had been a stroke of genius. Everyone looked right through him, as if he were the invisible man.

Two weeks went by with no call from Mag, and Charles realized that he had badly misjudged her vulnerability. As he mopped the hospital floors each night, he went over their conversations in his head, analyzing every word and every nuance. *What if I just call you Mag...* The steady rhythm of his mop halted abruptly and he cursed himself for attempting to charm her. "Damn, Convict," he muttered. "That sound like some shit Joe would say."

As the third week began, Charles's frustration was beginning to eat away at his self-control. He hadn't actually seen Joe, but he could feel him, like the heat from a fever. Taking his anger out on the floors, he finished early that Monday and then approached the nurse's station.

"Pardon me, Nurse Tessler, ma'am. Think I could go on and do the emergency floors a little early? Ain't nobody been here since that last man come in."

"Well, all right, but put up the warning signs. And if it gets busy, you'll have to stop."

A few minutes later, Charles was mopping in the far corner of the waiting room when the double doors opened and he heard a familiar female voice: "Please to bring da doctor!"

A tall Negro woman walked in crying and carrying a small child, with Mag hurrying in behind her. Mag happened to look toward Charles, and he saw the recognition in her eyes. Then her gaze shifted to his mop and pail. Before he could react, an orderly rushed the two women into the emergency room and the doors closed. Picking up the pail, Charles fought the urge to throw it through the glass entry door and run away. But then the emergency room door opened again and Mag walked out, alone this time.

"Charles!" she called.

He stood rooted to the spot as she approached him. He couldn't think of a word to say.

"Charles?" she said, smiling shyly. "You don't remember me no more?"

"Oh, yeah. Sure, Mag. I was just surprised to see you here. 'Specially so late at night."

"I spend da night with Pearl and da children tonight, and Shay—dat is Pearl's little girl. She jumps on da bed to play, den she falls and cut her head on da table. Now da doctor tells to us he will stitch her."

"Oh, yeah. Stitches. Yeah, that'll fix it, awright."

"Is a very big cut, and she goes to sleep too."

"Oh. You mean she got knocked out?"

"Yes. And now Pearl is crying, so I must go to her."

"Oh, sure, sure, Mag. You go on ahead."

She smiled again. "But I wanted to say hello to you, Charles."

"Well, thanks. But you better go on back. And don't worry. We got real good doctors here."

"Good-night," she whispered.

He pushed his cart away as her heavy, uneven steps echoed on the linoleum floor behind him.

≈∞≈

At the end of another Tuesday shift, Charles placed his card into the time clock and waited for the click. *09:01.* A week had passed since he had seen Mag at the hospital, and he wondered why he had been delirious enough to think that she would bother with a colored man who mopped floors for a living. He bought a newspaper with his breakfast, and took a seat at his regular corner table in the cafeteria. As usual, he checked the entertainment section for any mention of Joe. He had just taken a bite of toast when he spotted an item that made him stop chewing.

> *There are artists and there are singers. Only last year this reporter was guilty of mistaking new vocalist Joe Bluestone for an exciting new artist on the jazz scene, but as it turns out...*

> Charles's eyes raced through the article to the end:

> *... I've been asked by the management of the Stork Club to pass along a little message to Joe: Married men are off-limits to Stork Club cigarette girls.*

> *Apparently, our boy Bluestone is a leg man.*

Charles slammed his tray onto the stack and strode out, ignoring the cashier's reprimand. Hurrying to the coat closet, he bundled up against the February wind he had heard howling all through his shift. He rushed outside and down the subway steps. When he was less than three feet from the train, the doors shut and it sped away. He cursed and then wondered why. "What the hell's the hurry, Convict? He can treat her like shit and she *still* ain't never gonna call."

≈∞≈

Calvin was lost. He walked along aimlessly until he suddenly found himself at the railroad crossing on Highway 61. Although it was night, he was sweating from an intense heat. A full red harvest moon was rising, and he squinted at its fiery color until he saw movement in the distance. Then, somehow, he was behind Gerald Moore's house watching two workers methodically stuffing cotton into long, trailing burlap bags. They were only dark strangers until one of them turned his way and he saw a face bathed in the crimson light of that moon. Calvin was too stunned to stop the tears rolling down his cheeks. He was looking at the face of his mother in her youth, and his father was at her side. The two worked as one, with a quiet dignity and efficiency that was like a graceful dance in silhouette.

It took him a minute to find his voice. "Daddy!" he called. He couldn't remember ever feeling such an overwhelming surge of joy in his life, and he let out a yelping laugh as he ran toward them. "Mama!" he cried. "Hold on! I'ma come help y'all!" He saw his father straighten up and peer over at him, shading his eyes with his hand. Calvin waved frantically. "It's me, Daddy! Calvin Jr.! I'm back! I'm back now!"

His father held up a hand. "Don'tchu cross over them tracks, boy! And go on back to school. I ain't havin' my boys diggin' no ditches or shinin' no gotdamn shoes! Go on, now!"

Suddenly, Calvin doubled over, shivering with chills. When he looked up, that red moon had turned cold and blue, and his parents were gone. He tried to run and find them, but the feeling of plowed earth under his feet had hardened into cement floors. He heard the echoes of prison doors slamming. Parchman. Somehow, he was back inside Parchman. Then, emerging from the shadows was a gang of men led by Judge, who was staring at him with both hateful eyes intact.

Three shots rang out. Again, Calvin tried to run. But his legs were too heavy for speed. Three more shots—closer this time. The faster his heart pumped, the slower his legs moved, until he heard a gentle voice calling: *Caal-vin... This way. Come back now, Calvin... Thiiis way...*

When his eyes opened, they were fixed on the water stain above him, and he heard his own voice speaking to it: "Why'd you call me? I—I was fixin' to find Daddy and... No, wait. You—you saved me from... You brung me back... It was you..."

But as soon as he sat up, it was already beginning to fade from his consciousness. The dream, the voice, the water stain. From the light in the room, he figured it must be late afternoon. The sheets were soaked with perspiration, and he jumped when he heard three knocks on his door. A quick flash of the dream: Three shots. Three knocks.

"Hey, man! You in there, Mr. Jackson?" a voice called.

He hurried over to the door and opened it. His neighbor Henry was standing there feeding his baby a bottle. "Phone's for you. Thought you might not mind gettin' woke up by a female."

"Thanks, man." Stepping into the hallway, he grabbed the receiver. "This is—Charles."

"Charles? You—you tell to me I can call—if I need talking. I come to talk to Pearl, but da neighbor tells to me she is sick so—" Her voice caught. "I am—at da diner—by da flower shop."

"Don't cry, Mag. I'll be there in a few minutes. Don't leave, okay?"

≈∞≈

It was snowing hard when he arrived at Delphine's Diner, and Mag was nowhere in sight. He was about to leave when he saw the same waitress that had served them on that first day.

"You lookin' for that little crippled white girl you was with before, Mista?"

"Yeah. You seen her?"

"Mm-hmm. She's in the ladies' room cryin' her eyes out." The waitress looked him up and down unsympathetically. "You two get in a fight or sump'm?"

"I don't know why she's cryin' and she's just a friend. Listen, Miss—"

"Myrtle."

"Miss Myrtle. Would you please go tell her Cal—I mean Charles is here waitin'?"

An amused expression crossed Myrtle's face. "*Miss* Myrtle? Where you from, honey? Dogpatch? That 'Miss' jazz is too square for the Apple. It's just Myrtle."

"Okay. Myrtle. Now would you please—"

"Sure, honey, sure. What was your name again? Charles?"

He nodded and watched Myrtle saunter over to the ladies' room. Then he sat down to wait. When Mag appeared, he got up and pulled out her chair, but she shook her head.

"Oh, Charles. We can go from here, please? I am—I make everyone to look at me."

Charles nodded and guided her outside. Then he took off his muffler and wrapped it around her head. "What'cha doin' goin' out without a hat and scarf in this weather?"

They passed two women on the sidewalk, who were already staring and whispering.

"Where you wanna go, Mag?" Charles asked, uneasy at being seen with a white woman.

"Walk. Only to walk, Charles. Where no people are all da time staring."

"That ain't gonna be easy, with you bein' the color you are and me bein' the color I am."

"Well—do you live near to here, Charles? We maybe have coffee and we talk."

It was the last thing he had expected her to say, and he suddenly felt split, like a cartoon character he had seen as a boy at the Grand Marquee. The red cartoon devil was tempting him from the right and a white-gowned angel was preaching at him from the left. He stared silently at Mag as the angel Charles made him feel guilty and the devil Calvin goaded him to do his worst.

"Where do you live, Charles?" Mag asked.

Charles hesitated, and Calvin wondered why. "Not far. Just up yonder 'round the corner."

≈∞≈

When they got to his room, Charles opened the door and shrugged. "It ain't much."

Magda slipped off her coat and took off the scarf. "Is fine, Charles."

He looked for signs of fear, but saw only sadness. *You way too trustin', Mag. If only you knew...*

She sat on the edge of his narrow bed. "Is cold. You can maybe—turn up da heat?"

"Wish it was that easy." He banged the radiator with the butter knife and smiled. "Well, I put in the request. Now we gotta wait and see what kind'a mood the super's in."

"Well, den, coffee will make us warm."

"Sorry, Mag. All I got is a hot plate. Guess we should'a brung coffee from the diner."

"Is okay for no coffee, Charles. Please to sit down and we talk."

Charles hesitated.

Come on, Convict. She's sittin' right on your bed and she gotta tell you to sit'cho ass down next to her?... Damn!

He felt a crooked smile working its way onto his face and tried to stop it, but couldn't. Silently cursing this unexpected wave of bashfulness, he finally sat down. "Listen, Mag. Before you tell me what's troublin' you, could you promise me sump'm?"

She looked at him curiously. "I try, Charles."

"You safe with me, 'cause I'm your friend, but please don't ever, *ever* go with a man into his apartment alone again. You can trust me, but it ain't a wise thing to do, okay?"

Magda stared at the floor and her face crimsoned. "Oh... Yes, you are right, of course."

He nudged her with his shoulder and smiled. "Don't be lookin' all sad, now. I'm just tryin' to be your friend is all."

"Yes. I try to be more careful, Charles."

"Okay. So how's your friend's little girl? She awright now?"

"Oh, yes. Da doctor sews her head with da stitches and she is now fine."

"Good. I'm glad. So now maybe you can tell me why you so upset, Mag."

She stared at her hands and spoke slowly. "Too many things... I fight with Joe—"

He noticed her rubbing a dark spot on her wrist. "How'd you get that bruise?"

"Is my fault, Charles. I pull too hard away from him. I tell to him dat I leave and he—"

"He hurt you like this a lot?"

"Oh, no, Charles. Is *my* fault. I pull too hard away from him."

"Mag, does he ever *hit* you?"

"No! Please to don't look angry dat way, Charles. Joe will never *hit* me."

"Well, what got you so upset that you wanted to leave? Tell me everything, Mag."

"Okay, I try. Joe got angry when I ask him about Al." She paused and looked around the room. "Is so quiet here. You have a radio, Charles?"

"No. I ain't never had no radio. My Mama use'ta have one though." He had a sudden, vague recollection of his parents and the dream, but remembering the details was like trying to catch clouds in the wind. He blinked distractedly at Mag. "Did you say just sump'm?"

"I say to you dat Al helps Joe to make records for da radio, but he now sues Joe."

"He now—sues Joe? What for?"

"He don't tell dat to me. But he don't know Al tells to me already on da telephone. Joe breaks da contract and goes to dat—Clef Records, and Al sues him with papers. So Joe tells to me, 'you don't have enough money, Magda? Why you are so worried?' But Charles, I don't care about dat money. I care because Joe is throat-cut to his friend who believes in him."

"Did you tell him that?"

"Yes, I tell. And he tells for me to mind my own business." She jerked her chin and took a swipe at her tears. "So I go—to mind my own business at da studio. Joe is not da only one with career. So he follows me and I tell to da guard don't let Joe come to holler on me."

Charles grinned. "So they wouldn't let him in?"

"No. Joe always make da trouble, so they call two men to throw him away." She glanced at Charles self-consciously. "No, dat is wrong. Throw him—outside? Dat is right?"

"Well, throwin' him away sounds like a great idea to me. But go on. Tell me the rest."

"Well, when I finish dat recording date, Joe is waiting outside for me and makes me to get into da taxicab. Den he tells to me nothing all da way home."

"And what happened when you got home?"

"He slam all da doors and is stomping like big mad horse all around dat house, Charles! So I tell to him nothing… Den guess what is da first thing he tells to me?"

"What?"

"He want to know who was da recording date for."

"Huh? What did that have to do with anything?"

"I don't know, Charles. So I tell to him, for Nat King Cole again."

"Nat King Cole? Really?" Both Charles and Calvin were impressed.

"Yes. He like da violins for songs. But when I tell to Joe 'Nat King Cole,' he is throwing da chair to break on da wall. I tell to him, 'Why now you are mad with Nat King Cole, Joe?' And he don't answer me. He go to da closet and get da suitcase." Her eyes narrowed and her lips tightened into a straight line. "And *dat* is when Magda gets mad."

"Good! So what'd you do?"

"I make my courage and I show him dat newspaper."

"What newspaper?"

"With da story about da cigarette girl—Joe's girlfriend." She paused and looked at Charles. "Do you ever go to dat Stork Club? And see da cigarette girls with da small costumes?"

"No, I ain't never been there, but I seen them cigarette girls in the movies."

Magda gazed silently at her leg brace.

"So what happened when you showed him the newspaper?"

"I tell to him, 'So you are da leg man now, Joe?' And he point at my brace—and he laughs."

Charles closed his eyes and felt his left hand curling into a fist.

"And—I cry, Charles. But still I am mad, so I tell to him I will leave. Why we are married with fighting all da time? I tell to him 'marry dat girl with da pretty legs and let me go.'"

"And that's when he grabbed your wrist."

"I am thinking he breaks my hand, is hurting so bad. I screamed, Charles. So he let go and den he tells to me—soft—dat he don't mean it, and 'please don't leave me, Magda. I need you.' I tell to him, 'to break my hand you need me? Please to let me go, Joe. I go to see Pearl. Dat is all. I come back later.' And for a while, he is very quiet—so I stand up to go—but den—"

"But then what?"

Magda stared at the floor and lapsed into a long silence.

"*Where* is he now, Mag?"

"Oh, no… You are now angry. I was wrong to tell you about Joe."

"Mag—*where* is Joe right now?"

"San Francisco. He go for one week. Please, Charles, no trouble."

He sensed her fear, and forced a smile. "Aw, come on. I'd never make no trouble for you, Mag. But you know what I think? I think he's jealous, so he tries to make you jealous too."

"But I never cheat on Joe!… Oh! But I come to dis room with you—"

"No, Mag! You ain't doin' nothin' wrong. You just talkin' to a friend, and that ain't what I meant anyhow. No, Joe's jealous on account'a you workin' with big stars like Nat King Cole."

She sighed. "No more talk about Joe, please. I want to forget Joe. We talk about you now."

"Me? Aw, I ain't nobody important. You seen where I work… Look, Mag, I ain't no doctor or no hot-shot singer or nothin'. I'm just the fella who mops up and empties out the trash, that's all. But—I work hard and I'm proud a'that. And I got dreams—like everybody else."

Mag was staring into his eyes, as if searching for something.

"What?" he whispered. "Why you lookin' at me like that?"

"Now I know why I call you today for talking, Charles. You are—like me."

He shook his head and grinned. "Like *you*? Come on, Mag! You ain't even gotta count the color difference! We from two different worlds! You just got through tellin' me you play on records with Nat King Cole. And I just got through tellin' you I mop floors at a hospital. You and me, we about as much the same as a—a hummin'bird and a—damn bowlin' ball!"

Mag laughed—a long, free laugh. "And Magda is da bird? Or dat damn bowlin' ball?"

Charles ran his palm over his shaved head, which sent Mag into uncontrollable giggling.

"You definitely the hummin'bird around here," he said. "So you gonna have to explain what you meant about us bein' alike, 'cause I just don't see it."

Mag dabbed at her eyes and tried to compose herself. "But is true, Charles. In Greece I was very poor skinny girl with Polio. Den Professor teach me to make my violin to cry and bring me to America. I send money to Papa and Mama each month because I now am not so poor."

Charles grinned. "You ain't so skinny neither."

She smiled, but it disappeared quickly. "I can never be no cigarette girl, Charles. I don't care, but is true. And I see da people stare when I walk so clumsy. And I make da bad English. I know I make dem to laugh at me. And if dey don't laugh, dey are sorry for me. And to me it makes da difference." She jabbed her chest hard with her index finger. "To *me*. So when you are mopping floors in dat hospital, you know it is good work—honest work. You have your proud and your dreams, but you know da people say, 'Look at dat poor man who must empty trash for work.' And it hurts you. It *hurts* you, Charles. I know."

The line between Charles and Calvin was blurring. He stared at her, feeling a genuine need to take her in his arms. "Look. There's sump'm else about me you ought'a know. I—I was incarcerated, Mag. Locked up." He sighed. "I ain't nothin' but a convict from the jailhouse."

After a long silence, Mag's startled expression softened to a smile. "You are da lucky one. You are free. Many people never get out of dat—house-jail to be free. A happy ending, no?"

Charles stood up and began pacing. "Now, see? This is just what I was talkin' about before. I don't mean to scare you or nothin'—'cause you can trust me—but I tell you I'm fresh out the jailhouse, and you *ought'a* be runnin' out'a here. You way too trustin', Mag. You worry me."

Magda shrugged. "But I believe you are—a good man, Charles. But you now tell to me please why you go to dat jail—house-jail?"

He stopped pacing and stared at her. "Okay. First—I didn't do the crime they locked me up for. I want you to know that. That's why they had to let me go. But see, I got in a fight with somebody and— No, wait. That ain't quite right… I beat up a man."

"But—"

"But nothin', Mag. I was stronger than him, and I beat him pretty bad." He gazed at her dismayed expression. *You blowin' it, Convict.*

"But—why?" she asked softly. "Why you hurt dat man, Charles?"

"'Cause he hurt me. He fought with—other kinds'a weapons. And all I had was my fists. That's the only way I can explain it, Mag. It was wrong, I know. But I *didn't* kill him. See, they thought I killed him 'cause he—he left town and couldn't nobody find him."

"But dat is crazy, Charles! Why da police don't just look for him?"

"They ain't got time to worry 'bout one mo' nigga goin' to the jailhouse."

Mag touched his arm and frowned. "Please don't call yourself dat name, Charles."

He smiled patiently. "That's just how it is, Mag, when the jury's all white."

"Oh. And da man you beat—he was white too—like dem?"

"Yeah, Mag. You startin' to catch on."

"Oh, I know about dat segur—uh, segur-gation, Charles. I see dat horrible picture-postcard and—" She stopped and gazed at him for a long moment with a pained innocence in her eyes. "And Dr. Moskos, Charles. Is segurgation too for Hitler kills Dr. Moskos, yes?"

"Yes, but slow down, Mag. What's this picture-postcard you talkin' about?"

Instead of answering she whispered, "Charles... how you get out to be free?"

"Well, this colored lawyer helped me. He traced the man to New Orleans. Then he filed papers with the court and now I'm free." He smiled. "See? Happy ending. But look, Mag, maybe you shouldn't tell folks about all this. Maybe it'd be best not to tell nobody about me at all."

"You mean Joe, of course."

"Well, it might not be a good idea to tell your friend Pearl either. She might get the wrong idea about us. You know, she might not understand that we just—friends."

Mag looked as if she wanted to say something, but stayed silent.

Charles sighed. His plan had gone up in smoke, but he didn't care. He was perfectly content to sit quietly with Mag locked in a long, reciprocal gaze. All the things he wanted to say ran through his mind, and the ticking of his alarm clock began to sound like music. When he felt her fingertips brush his face, he experienced a weird sensation of pleasure mixed with a pain so deep he couldn't begin to understand it. All he knew was that no one had ever touched him in such a gentle way—not that he could remember.

It was a ripe moment, and there was no other possible ending to it. He leaned close to Mag's face and let his lips brush hers. He expected her to resist, but she didn't. Just as he settled his hand on the small of her back to pull her closer, the alarm clock jangled loudly, causing them both to jump. He grabbed the clock and turned off the ringer, knowing that the moment was lost.

"This is when I usually get up for work," he explained. "I—work the graveyard shift."

"Da *graveyard*, Charles? But I see you work at dat hospital—"

"No, I don't work *in* a graveyard. That's what they call the late shift. I sleep durin' the day."

"Oh. Den I am so sorry to keep you awake, Charles. You have no sleep today."

"Oh, it's okay. I'm glad you came over. I just hope *you* feel better."

"I tell to you before, Charles. You make da blues to go away."

"Well, good. But I guess it's time for me to get you to the train."

They walked to the subway in silence. He stopped to look at her once, but she avoided his eyes. So he looked straight ahead and didn't say a word until they reached the platform.

"You know the way from here?"

She smiled. "I know da way." Then she slowly moved away from him toward the door.

"Mag?" he called. "You know I can't get in touch with you."

She turned around and looked at him sadly. "I know."

He took a tentative step toward her. "So you'll have to call me."

"I—would not bother you, Charles?"

"Bother me? Naw, Mag, you ain't no kind'a bother."

She smiled. "Goodbye, Charles."

He smiled back at her and watched the train speed away. Then he shook his head and groaned. "Aww, Convict... You such a gotdamn clown."

≈∞≈

For the next three nights, Calvin mopped the hospital floors, wrestling with thoughts of vengeance against Joe and sexual fantasies about Mag. He had heard somewhere that a woman can make the strongest man weak, and for the first time in his life he knew it was true. Mag had been his most useful weapon against his brother, but now the thought of using her that way was unimaginable. All he could do was wonder why she hadn't called. Her story about Joe's cruelty and that bruise on her wrist stirred up Calvin's killer instinct until it eclipsed every other thought and emotion, like a red flag waved before an angry bull.

At the end of the week when his shift was over, he went home and tried to sleep, but his gaze kept drifting up to that oddly-shaped water stain on the ceiling. It stirred his imagination in the manner of any transcendent work of art—a poor man's Sistine Chapel—or a map of some mythical kingdom in a book. He lost himself in it until daylight faded into the shadows of another lonely night.

≈∞≈

When sleep finally came, Calvin dreamed of a place beyond his memory. Back—way back—in time and in distance. A rolling indigo River lined with hazy trees of turquoise and emerald green, where coral-colored birds soared overhead, singing familiar songs in human voices. It had to be some other world—a pristine wilderness that existed only within the borders of that water stain.

But as Calvin dreamed, the earth was awake and moving with its own natural certainty.

Hundreds of miles away, the Mississippi Delta was sluggish and thick with humidity. Two warm air masses had collided there, merged, and then refused to budge. For several days, the stalled unseen presence gathered up the River's rich wetness, full of scientific microbes, historical memories, and spiritual voices. Then it rose and roiled into a massive cloud formation, high and dark, and began moving purposefully eastward.

≈∞≈

Calvin was washing his face when the telephone rang out in the hall. He wiped off the soap, then opened the door and reached for the receiver. "Hello?"

"Hello, Charles."

"Mag? You okay?"

"Yes. I—I was afraid to call, so I wait until da time is safe. Do you understand?"

"No, Mag, I don't. What'chu mean 'safe'?"

"Joe—he comes home tonight. I—I call you now because I will not be wanting to come to you. You see? If Joe is coming home tonight—"

Charles groaned. "Aw, Mag. I don't want you bein' afraid a'me. Listen, I'm sorry if things got a little too—close that last time you were here. Damn! I'd *never* do what *he* did to you."

"But how you know—" Her voice broke. "How you know—what he did to me?"

"He forced you—to have sex when you didn't want to, didn't he? You didn't have to tell me. I knew… Aw, Mag, don't cry."

"No, you don't make me cry. I cry because—I know if I see you again—"

"Wait— Look, I ain't handled this right—"

"No, Charles. You are a gentleman. You are more gentleman den my own husband."

"No. Truth is—I really need to talk to you— Mag, look—"

"Charles? I hang up now. I try to be da good wife. Is right for me."

Then he heard a click and the electronic buzz that cut him off from her.

≈∞≈

Charles volunteered to work two double-shifts the next week, thinking it would keep his mind off Mag. But no matter how tired he was when he got home, he always ended up staring at the ceiling in his small room—awake when the rest of the world was sleeping, and asleep when he needed to be awake.

His body jerked and he squinted at the alarm clock. *7:45*. Stretched across the faded rug on the floor were three glowing ribbons of light from the street lamp outside. The rest of the room was dark, and Charles wondered how long he had been asleep. Something had startled him—a thump. Then he heard it again, got up, and opened the door. Mag was down on one knee in the hallway, with her braced leg extended sideways.

She was fussing with a ribbon on a package. When she looked up, she lost her balance and would have fallen if Charles hadn't caught her.

"Charles! Why—why you are not working at da hospital?"

"This was my one off-night," he said as he helped her up. "Hey, what's in the box, Mag?"

"Is—is only gift—small gift for you."

A rosy blush warmed her face and Charles wanted to kiss her. "Come on in."

She smiled and stepped into the room. "It rains outside. Hear da rain, Charles?"

The soft sound of the rain suddenly intensified to a pounding downpour. "You got here just in time, Mag. And is that a smile? 'Cause you didn't sound so good last time I talked to you."

"For many days I am not so good, but I make my courage and I now feel better, Charles."

"Well, good! But Mag, you know you ain't had to bring me no present."

"Please to open it!"

"Okay, okay! Pushy, ain'tcha?" He tore off the paper and looked in the box. "Hey! A radio! With a clock! But that's too expensive, Mag, and it must'a been heavy for you to carry around."

"No, not too heavy, Charles. Bakelite, not wood. What dat salesman tell to me? Is stylish black Admiral clock-radio. To wake up with music."

"Well, that's just what I needed, 'cause I'm 'bout tired'a that noisy alarm clock."

"Charles—" She hesitated and her voice dropped to a whisper. "I—come dis time to bring da radio to leave by your door for a surprise, but I know I come again. If it is wrong, I don't know, but I think I am—*needing* you—like air to breathe."

He stared at her. *Like air to breathe.* The words were so sweet he wished he could swallow them. *Damn. You in trouble now, Convict.* Dozens of thoughts filled his head as he kissed her slowly. He hardly realized that he was speaking out loud. "But I don't care. I need you, too."

≈∞≈

He woke slowly the next morning, one lazy level at a time, to a rhythmic, chiming sound. He sensed something warm against his chest and tried to touch it, but his hand wouldn't budge. Then he felt movement against his thigh—something that felt like warm velvet. A sound near his ear reminded him of childhood summers in Mississippi—the low hum of a breeze blowing through the bulrushes in the River. This time his hand moved. The warm velvet became skin—the unmistakable touch of a woman's bare body—and the sound was her sigh. He opened his eyes and stared down at the tangle of limbs in his bed—his own brown legs entwined with the pale thighs of a white woman. Now he was awake.

"Good morning, Charles. Always you are waking up with smiling on your face?"

He laughed softly. "No, I ain't woke up with no smilin' on my face in a long, long time. Hey, you okay? You got enough room? That spring ain't stickin' you, is it?"

"I am very, very, and *very* comfortable, Charles. And you?"

"Fine as wine. I'm just tryin' to figure out what in the world you doin' here with me."

Mag snuggled under his chin and sighed again. "I am loving you, I'm afraid."

Charles swallowed hard and closed his eyes. "Mag—"

She interrupted him. "Oh, look. Da radio is still in da box. You don't like da present?"

"Sho' do. I just like this one a little better. Gimme a kiss."

"Okay," she said, "one more kiss for you."

Charles moaned softly through the lingering kiss, and then grinned as he stretched. "Hey, you know what? I just decided—I ain't never gettin' up out this bed."

"Is okay for me… Charles? Why da bed is crooked? How da bed turn dis way?"

"Leaky roof," he said, pointing at the ceiling stain. "Rain started drippin' on your arm while you was asleep, so I got up and moved the bed over a little."

Mag turned over and smiled down at the dented cooking pot that was catching the raindrops still falling from the ceiling. "Ding… ding… ding," she sang softly. "No wonder I dream of small bells to ring, Charles. A happy dream."

He rested his chin on her shoulder and gazed at the slow, hypnotic drip of the rain.

"Charles? Do you think I am a wicked woman to feel happy now?"

"Shoot. Happy ain't wicked. And if Joe was actin' right, you wouldn't even be here."

He wished he could think of something better to say, but figured that sounded pretty good.

"Many people will think dis is wrong, Charles. For me to come to dis bed with you."

"What people? I ain't worryin' about nobody in the world but you, Mag."

"I know only dat I try and try to not come to you but—I am here. And I am feeling happy here, Charles. More happy here den at my home. When I am at home, I feel—"

"Like a prisoner. I know the feelin'."

"You see, Charles? I tell to you we are alike."

"Oh, that's right. The hummin'bird and the bowlin' ball, huh?" He laughed lightly.

She turned over and smiled up at him. "Why you laugh?"

"'Cause you make me happy." Closing his eyes, he nuzzled into the warm hollow between her chin and shoulder. And he lay there quietly listening to the peaceful sound of the raindrops.

Chapter 49

You're my son, awright. No doubt about that. Me and Mag spent all our time together that March 'cause Joe was away on that road trip. Now you know we couldn't go out in public, so we spent a lot'a time in that room. Sometimes we'd cook up a little meal on my hot plate, but most'a the time we'd bring supper in from the diner. We talked a lot—really got to know each other. We'd listen to the radio and sometimes we'd dance. And yeah, okay, we spent a lot'a time in bed just like folks in love always do. And for that month I really felt married to her, Nick. I knew I loved her and I thought I knew everything about her. But then I saw this whole other side to her when she started talkin' about her music. She was just like you—real dedicated to that artistic part of herself. Anyway, one night this Nat King Cole record comes on and she shows me all the spots where she was playin'. So I told her I sho' wished I could see her play sometime. Then next time she comes over, she brings her violin. And that was one crazy night! I told you she could be a goofball. Man, we had a lot'a fun that night...

≈∞≈

Charles woke suddenly to the sound of a key in the door. "Zat'chu, baby?" he called.

"Yes, Charles. Is me. Please to carry for me dis bag."

Shivering in his t-shirt and pajama bottoms, he grabbed the suitcase and kissed her. "You should'a called, baby. I don't want you walkin' from the subway by yourself after dark."

"Is not very dark yet, Charles. Please let me tell to you da good news."

"Okay, tell to me the good news."

Mag smiled. "Joe is gone for da whole month. To California again."

"A month? Hey! That sho' is good news, awright."

"And you don't work tonight, so I bring a few little things—"

"But what if he calls the house lookin' for you?"

"I am sneaky woman, Charles. I tell to him I go to Pearl's house so I don't be lonely."

He laughed. "Okay, but what if he calls you at Pearl's?"

"Pearl will tell to him I am shopping or sleeping," she said with a careless shrug. "You see, I am now good for plotting, Charles."

"Yeah, you gettin' tricky, awright. But listen, Pearl don't know about me, does she?"

"No. She don't ask no questions. Pearl tells to me 'go and be happy, sugar.' Dat is da name Pearl calls people she like—sugar."

"Sugar, huh? And no questions? Yeah, that's a *real* good friend you got there. But listen now. You gotta promise me you won't tell her about us, okay? Promise me."

"I promise, Charles. But please to don't worry. We are sneaking good."

"And you sure it don't bother you?"

She waved her hand. "No! Joe is sneaking too, but he don't sneak so good like me."

"You in a silly mood tonight! Okay, Sneaky. So what'cha got in that little suitcase a'yours?"

She opened it and pulled out a nearly transparent black negligee. "I bring dis nightie—brand new from da Lord & Taylor. Dat saleslady tells to me is real sexy for honeymoon."

"Honeymoon?"

"Yes, I tell to her I go for honeymoon. I am now sneaky woman, remember?" She brushed the negligee across his head and smiled. "Is black, Charles. You like?"

"Mmmm-hmmm. I like a *lot*. Matter of fact, when you puttin' it on?"

"After one surprise more. Please to be patient."

"Okay, I'll try."

He watched her open a small, curvy black case and lift out her violin. All the colors of the polished wood grain gleamed in the lamplight as Mag sat on the chair, positioned the violin, and began to play.

The sounds rising from the violin were so compelling they ran a shiver down his neck. With each fluid sweep of the bow, Mag drew pure human emotion from the instrument—from low, sorrowful tones to bold, full-bodied drama. Her fingers were tiny magicians of movement, coaxing every colorful nuance from each string. The song was familiar, but he couldn't place it. He recognized the sound of pain, but was unable to identify the other feeling it conjured up. But by the time she finished playing, it came to him. Glory. Something about the music sounded like a choir of angels that had somehow made its way from heaven into his small room in Harlem.

When the last note faded, Mag opened her eyes, as if coming out of a trance. "You wish to see me play," she said softly. "So I play for you, Charles."

"Mag... How in the world did you learn to play like that?"

She smiled. "Practice, practice, practice. Many years to practice. You like da song?"

"I did. I *really* did. What was it?"

"Is a hymn for da church called 'Ave Maria.' Hail Mary, it means. Like da prayer."

"'Ave Maria,'" he repeated. "But it sounded real sad or sump'm. Was it supposed to?"

She touched his hand and smiled. "Charles! You hear dat? I make da violin to cry, you see? Only da violin will cry like people." She laid the violin on her lap and stared at it for a long moment. "Charles—I hope is not rude thing to say, but—do you think we are wrong to be together? For our souls?"

He was caught off-guard by the question. "No, Mag. Why? Do you?"

"Two times I am feeling like heaven, Charles. When I play da music and when I am here with you. How dat can be wrong?"

"Maybe it ain't. So let's stop worryin' about it. God'll let us know someday. But for right now, let's get back to my concert. Come on and play some more."

Her smile was back. "No, *you* play. I show you how, and you make da violin to cry."

"Oh, no, no, *no*, Mag!" he said, standing up quickly and stepping away from her. "Make it *cry*? Shoot, I'm liable to make it scream! And run for the fire escape!"

She laughed as she followed him, and he finally allowed her to push him into the chair. When she tried to hand him the violin, he waved her away. "No, now! I ain't touchin' it!"

Mag rolled her eyes. "So silly you are, Charles. You have da gentlest hands."

He heaved a sigh of resignation. "Aw, hell... okay."

Once she had positioned the violin under his chin, she showed him the proper placement of his fingers and carefully guided his hand so that the bow moved gently over the strings.

"You see, Charles? You make da music. Now, please to keep fingers like da way I show you and try by yourself. From one side to da other, with very light touch... Begin, please."

The violin felt too delicate in his hands. "Okay, Mag," he sighed. "You asked for it." An earsplitting screech sounded, causing them both to laugh, but he kept the bow and violin poised, afraid to move.

"Is okay, Charles!"

"Liar. Is lousy!"

Mag placed her hands on her hips and tried to look stern. "Please to try again."

"You a pushy woman, you know that? But you asked for it, so hang on to ya draw's and I'll play— Let's see. Hey, how 'bout 'Turkey in the Straw'? Mississippi white folks *loved* that one. You some Mississippi white folks, Mag?"

She covered her smile with her hand, but the corners of her eyes were crinkling with laughter. "No!" she sputtered. "Only immigrant—Greek white folks, I'm afraid, Charles!"

"Okay, immigrant Greek white folks. Get ready to pat'cha foot! Here we go—"

He clowned through a cacophony of grating squeaks and squeals, none of which resembled any form of music, swaying and stomping his foot until a neighbor started pounding on the wall. Mag fell on the bed, laughing. "Bravo! Dat was da best playing—ever I have heard!"

"Thanks, lady. So you think I'm ready to try out for that studio band a'yours?"

Mag dabbed at her eyes with her fingertips. "Few more lessons, I think, Charles."

"Aww, see? Now you just afraid I'ma steal your thunder wit'cha bandleader."

"Oh, yes, Charles. I am very jealous woman now. *Never* will I play so great like you."

He handed her the violin and bow. "Okay, quit lyin'. You give up on me takin' lessons?"

"Yes, Charles. I play da violin *only* now. You do da kissing."

"Deal." He leaned down and kissed her. Then, without interrupting the kiss, he turned off the lamp and reached over to turn on the radio. "Dance with me, Mag," he whispered, "like that first night."

Rosemary Clooney's dreamy version of "Tenderly" rose from the radio as Calvin and Mag swayed together quietly in their own uncomplicated dance.

≈∞≈

It was really killin' me, Nick. It just felt wrong, havin' this great big lie between us. But I got to believin' we'd have some kind'a future together anyway. That's how naïve I was about life, and I had zero experience when it came to women. But when Joe got back from California, all them notions of mine started fallin' apart, one by one. And I knew it wasn't gonna be no happily-ever-after ending for me and Mag. It all started with that phone call—when she told me about Paris.

≈∞≈

"Charles, he wants for me to go to Paris, I'm afraid."

"Who?"

"Joe, of course!"

"Oh. I thought maybe it was for work—with a band or sump'm."

"No. Joe will *never* let me go away with a band."

"Yeah, I *know* that's right," he said, unable to keep the bitterness out of his voice.

"I must go, I'm afraid."

"But Mag—can't you just tell him—"

"What, Charles? What I can tell him?"

"Nothin'," he murmured. "I ain't got the right to ask you not to go."

"Please to believe me, Charles. I feel so terrible to go away from you and go to dat Paris with Joe. But I am his wife. Not a good wife, but I belong to him."

"No. You do *not* belong to Joe. I know that don't sound right, but... Look, never mind. I shouldn'ta said that. I ain't got no rights here."

"Oh, Charles. You are hurt?"

"Yeah, but I ain't mad... I just wish I could change things for us."

Out of a long silence she said, "No one can change things for us, Charles. We are like a sad song on da violin. Very pretty music we make together, but sad."

≈∞≈

For the first few days after Mag left, Calvin alternated between depression and jealous rages until he finally had an inspiration. He felt better the instant he dialed the number.

After two rings, a familiar voice answered: "Ezekiel Templeton here."

"Zeke? Hey, it's Calvin Bailey."

"Calvin! Hey! How are things in New York?"

"Well, if you don't count this week, things been pretty heavenly."

"Heavenly? Ahah! A woman, right?"

"Yeah, a real sweet woman too. Her name's Mag."

"Mag, huh? Well, I hope things work out with her. So are you still working at the hospital?"

"Yeah, but see, that's what I was callin' about."

"Hard job, huh? I understand."

"Naw, it ain't that bad. But, see, I was kickin' around the idea of movin' someplace else. I was wonderin' if you might have a line on some kind'a job in another city."

"Well, well. I hear wedding bells. So you're serious about this girl."

"Real serious. But I gotta get her away from here. Look, Zeke, I'll do any kind'a work."

"Hmm… Wait, Calvin— Remember the inmate you asked me to look out for—Cyrano Jones? I think you called him Scat."

"Little Man's name is *Cyrano*? Shit! No wonder he went by Scat. He's okay, ain't he?"

"He's okay. I stayed in contact with him like you asked me to, and he finally wrote to tell me he was getting out. That was about three months ago, and he needed help getting a job in the Jackson area. So I put him in touch with a friend of mine—Blue Henderson. He owns a radio station out there. Maybe I could do the same for you—if they have another opening, that is."

"Thanks, but I can't go back to Mississippi. Ain't nothin' there for me but a bad name."

"Well, that's not the only option. Blue has a part-interest in a station here in Louisville—and a record business too, I think. I'll give him a call. If he helped Scat, I'm sure he can do the same for you."

"But I don't know nothin' 'bout music, Zeke. And what does Scat do anyway? Don't tell me your friend got Little Man singin' on the radio! Not with that screech-owl voice he got."

"No, I think he's learning radio announcing. But meanwhile, he's playing Man-Friday and everything else. Let me give Blue a call and see what he can do for you in Louisville."

"But I might not be able to get out there right away. What if he can't hold the job for me?"

"Look, Calvin. I can't go into detail, but Blue owes me a favor."

"Well… Louisville, huh?"

"I really think you'll like it here."

"Well, okay, Zeke. I'll definitely be callin'."

"By the way, Calvin… did you ever run into your brother out there?"

"I ain't seen him and don't want to."

"Well, that's probably for the best. Anyway, when you get things wrapped up out there, give me a call and I'll set everything up with Blue."

Calvin sighed. "Man, I don't know what I did to deserve all this. First, you give me my life back, and now this. I just wish there was sump'm I could do for you."

"You already did it, Calvin."

"Shit! What did I ever do for you but owe you money?"

"You changed your mind about killing your brother."

When Calvin didn't respond, Zeke laughed. "What's wrong, Calvin? Don't tell me that a square, buttoned-down college Negro like me could shock a hardened ex-con like you?"

"Who—who said I was thinkin' about killin' him?"

"Hell, Calvin. You might as well have been wearing a sign."

≈∞≈

They got back from Paris the last week in April. And when Mag showed up at my door that night with that lost look on her face, I knew sump'm was real wrong... It took her a while, but she finally told me she was pregnant, and to me it seemed like a good time to finally come clean with her. So I told her everything—who I was, who Joe really was, how I beat him. It was the first argument—well, the only argument we ever had. But it didn't last long. Mostly, we just sat there tryin' to figure things out— what was the right thing to do for you. It was the most painful night of my life. Not just 'cause I lost Mag—that was bad enough—but then it hit me that I was gonna be one'a those fathers who never gets to know his child. The hardest part was walkin' to the train, 'cause we both knew it was over. I kissed her goodbye and she got on, but she kept lookin' at me. After all these years, I ain't forgot that look on her face. She was cryin' her eyes out, but she smiled for me. Turned out to be the last time I ever saw her smile.

≈∞≈

Nurse Tessler was making notations on a chart when Charles approached her with the news that he was quitting his job at the hospital.

"You won't wait until Friday to collect your pay?" she asked, without looking up.

"No, ma'am. I got me a new job in Louisville I gotta get to," he said, handing her a slip of paper. "Just mail it to me at this address, care of Mr. Templeton, and I'll get it from him."

Without another word, he walked quietly down the corridor and out the side door of Harlem Hospital. Charles Jackson no longer existed.

≈∞≈

When Calvin returned to his room, he packed his suitcase mechanically and tried not to think about Mag. He checked the closet and all the drawers. Everything was packed except for the clock-radio she had given him. It was still sitting on the windowsill near the bed. He reached over to unplug it so that he could pack it, but stopped himself. "Nuh-uh, Convict. Just leave it. That belongs to Charles Jackson—may his dumb ass rest in peace." He buckled the suitcase and realized that he still had over four hours to kill before his bus was scheduled to leave. Placing the suitcase near the door, he stretched out on the bed to read the newspaper. He turned the pages quickly, unable to concentrate, until a large ad in the entertainment section caught his eye.

Don't miss the fabulous Count Basie orchestra featuring
vocalist Joe Blueston—Paramount Theater—One night only

It took less than an hour for Calvin to get to the Paramount. By the time he stepped inside, he was filled with a deadly cocktail of jealousy, sorrow, and hate. He took a seat and stared at the curtain. It was the only thing separating him from Joe. He gripped the armrests and felt his pulse thumping rapidly in his fingertips. Then the theater went dark and the stage blazed with light. The audience broke into applause and whistles as the Count Basie Orchestra slowly rose from the pit, blasting "Ready, Set, Go."

Calvin scanned the faces of the musicians. Two women in gowns sat in chairs next to the grand piano, but Joe was not on the stage. One by one, the women stepped up to the microphone to sing. Each song seemed to last an eternity, with extended horn and piano solos. Then finally, Count Basie said the words Calvin had been waiting for.

"Let's give a big Paramount welcome to tonight's featured vocalist— Joe Bluestone!"

Before he realized what he was doing, Calvin was on his feet. As he made his way to the front, he didn't take his eyes off Joe. There he was— the brother he hadn't seen in nearly eight years—striding across the stage of the world-famous Paramount Theater, waving at his adoring fans. Female screams filled the theater, and Joe flashed his smile.

That same goddamn smile...

Joe began to sing "How High the Moon," but when he got halfway through the first verse, he stopped singing right in the middle of a syllable. Calvin saw him staring directly at him, and Joe's smile melted like wax over a hot flame. But with the fluidity of a snake, Calvin eased behind a heavyset black woman and into the shadows. He smiled maliciously as he watched Joe's eyes darting wildly in his direction, searching. *Yeah, you seen right, brutha. It's me.*

Calvin was back on familiar ground—that burning in his belly—the physical manifestation of the hatred that had always driven him to violence. But now, for the first time, there was a conflicting sensation—a vague, distant voice warning him of danger. Suddenly, he was aware of the audience murmuring. Joe was still not singing, just peering out into the audience, shading his eyes with his hand.

Calvin felt a mental jerk, like waking up to a cold slap, and he began to retreat quickly, drifting away from the stage until his brother was nothing more than a blurry stranger. As he turned toward the exit, he heard him begin to sing again. Calvin turned and took one last look at him from a safe distance. Then he stepped outside and the door shut quietly behind him.

His mind was blank as he wandered down 43rd Street. He saw shoes walking past, the blurred colors of suits and dresses, neon signs, taillights on automobiles. His thoughts and emotions had completely shut down, and he was surprised when he found himself stepping off the subway at his stop.

Unaware of how much time had passed, he was suddenly back at his boardinghouse, climbing the stairs to his room. He unlocked the door, opened it, and turned on the light. The first thing he saw was the clock-radio, still on the windowsill where he had left it. And just like that, the merciful numbness was gone. With all its memories of Mag, his room was an emotional torture chamber. Without knowing why, he turned on the radio one last time and stared at it. When the static noise smoothed into the music of a full string orchestra, he reached over quickly to turn it off, but his hand froze.

If pain could be a sound, it would surely be the sound of the violin in this song. Then a singer began to tell his story—a singer that sounded a lot like Joe. The song was nearly over before he realized that it was Frank Sinatra, and not Joe. Calvin sank down weakly on the edge of the bed until the song ended. Then he turned off the radio, gathered his things and walked to the door. He stood there uncertainly for a moment before hurrying back to unplug the radio. Wrapping the cord around it, he placed it securely in his suitcase. Then, with one last look at the water stain on the ceiling, he left.

Chapter 50

Calvin had fallen into a long, private silence as he and Nick walked along the old non-working railroad tracks near his house.

The horizon was a long, blazing red haze that seemed to be melting what was left of the cool, dark night. It was a new morning, and the story Nick had waited so long to hear was told, complete with the missing details of his mother's life. The hypnotic rise and fall of Calvin's voice had taken him back to witness every moment of joy and sadness that had transpired in that small room with the water stain. But now the sounds of his footsteps and the chirping of the birds were slowly bringing him back to the present. He stopped walking and stared at Calvin. The pain of reliving his past was still in his eyes.

"So you just—left?"

Calvin lit a cigarette and looked away. "First I died, boy. Then I left."

"So then—you were gone by the time I was born."

"Long gone."

"Well… Guess I should thank you anyway, for telling me about her."

Calvin squinted at the sky. "Can't thank a man—or judge a man—for just *livin'*. We all do our best—and our worst too, sometimes… Come on, let's head on back. My neighbors are gon' think I done lost my mind, wanderin' around creation in my bathrobe."

When they got back to the house, the smell of bacon was heavy in the air. "Good morning, fellas!" Donna called. "Come on in here and get some breakfast. I kept it warm."

Calvin yawned as he walked into the kitchen. "What time is it?"

"Almost seven. I figured you two must'a either got lost or you talked the boy to death."

Calvin smiled back at Nick. "Don't worry. Donna knows the whole story."

Donna placed two cups of coffee on the table as Calvin sat down. "You two keep talkin'. I'ma go take my shower. Damn shame I gotta work on a Saturday!"

Calvin leaned back to kiss her. "Ain'tcha gonna eat breakfast with us, baby?"

"I ate. I knew better than to wait for you two. Anyway, there's more coffee on the stove." She paused at the door and smiled. "Nick, I'm really glad you're back safe, baby."

"Thanks, Donna. And listen—I'm really sorry for worrying you. And hey, thanks for the breakfast."

Donna's exit left an awkward tension in the room. The only sound was the jangling of Calvin's spoon in his cup. Nick cleared his throat and Calvin looked up. "So what else you wanna know, Nick?" he said, taking a careful sip of the hot coffee.

"Well, how'd you find out what happened to my—I mean—who told you about Joe?"

Calvin set his cup down and stared into it without responding.

"Calvin?"

When Calvin finally answered, his voice was so low Nick could barely hear him. "There's sump'm I ain't told you, boy."

"What?"

"Nobody had to tell me about Joe. I already knew… 'cause I was there."

Nick leaned back slowly. "What do you mean you were there? You were—where?"

"I was *there*… In Chicago… In his room."

Nick's mouth fell open and froze as if it had forgotten how to form words. Calvin held up one hand. "Don't try to say anything, boy. All night

I been tryin' to get by with just tellin' you part of it, but I guess there ain't no such thing as half a truth. So I'll tell it to you now. All of it."

He sighed deeply. "First off, everything I told you outside was true. I *did* walk away from him that night at the Paramount, and I *did* get on that bus and leave town, and I *did* go to Louisville to work for Jack. I really tried to let it all go, but I learned one lesson real good. The two most powerful things in the world are love and hate. And I was fightin' both of 'em at the same time. Every day I'm thinkin' about how far along Mag was. Wonderin' how she was feelin' and how he was treatin' her. Shit. I must'a killed Joe in my mind about ten times a day. But I stayed my ass in Louisville and I *might'a* kept my nose clean—if I just ain't heard that gotdamn announcement on the radio. But I *did* hear it—all about Joe's big show comin' up in Chicago."

He stopped to light a fresh cigarette and tried to read Nick's reaction, without success.

"So I took a Greyhound up there. Wasn't too hard to find out what hotel he was at. I hung out in the alley and slipped one'a the kitchen workers a ten to find out Joe's room number, but he wanted another ten for one of his uniform shirts. Shit. I *would* run up on a dish-washin', potato-peelin' *hustler*... Anyway, I ended up tradin' him my jacket for that uniform shirt and I put it on over my regular shirt. So then I could lay low, lookin' like one'a the staff. I still wasn't exactly sure *what* I was gonna do to Joe—not till that feelin' started comin' on me."

"What—feeling?" Nick's voice was barely a whisper.

"That feelin' I had in prison right before I snatched Judge's eye out his head. Vicious, and scared shitless, and happy as goddamn Disneyland—all at the same time. That's when I knew it was gonna go *real* bad for Joe when I got in that room... I *knew* I was gonna finish him off."

Taking a deep pull on his cigarette, Calvin gazed blankly at Nick's stunned expression and slowly exhaled the smoke. There was no turning back now.

"Then that article came out in the *Tribune* about you bein' born, announcin' to the world that Joe Bluestone had hisself a black baby. I remember them comparin' you to a Hershey bar... Anyway, that brought all them reporters and photographers to the hotel and I just faded back into the wallpaper. I was right there in the lobby when Joe punched that reporter and they took him to jail. That almost screwed up my plans. But I knew somebody'd bail him out and bring him back for his clothes. So I waited. When he got back the hotel manager wouldn't let the reporters follow him to his room, but I slipped up there in the service elevator without anybody seein' me. His floor was real quiet and I just went right up to his door. I remember thinkin' it couldn't be that easy—that he'd just open the door and I'd kill him before he even knew what was goin' on."

On the wall above Calvin's head was a large round kitchen clock—white face with black numbers and a black frame. The inner gears emitted a soft electronic buzz. Nick cut his eyes at it, annoyed by the sound. Calvin smiled, but his eyes were flat. "You got sump'm to say, boy?"

"Just get to the point," Nick said coldly. "It wasn't suicide. It was you… *You* killed him."

Calvin blew out a mist of smoke and continued, unfazed. "I heard him walkin' around in there. Then he turned up the radio real loud and it sounded like he was arguin' with somebody. But nobody was talkin' back, and I was sure he was alone. Man, he sounded so crazy. I knocked again, but it seemed like he wasn't hearin' it. So I just stood there listenin' for a while. I heard him say sump'm about suicide and then he got real quiet. Then—I don't even remember makin' the decision, but I was tryin' to force my way in. I grabbed the knob and the door opened before I could even put my shoulder into it. It wasn't even locked. So I walked in and saw him sittin' there with his eyes shut and that gun pointed at his head. Then he opened his eyes and looked at me, and I just knew he was gon' scream for help or sump'm—but he didn't. He just looked pitiful, and you won't believe what he said. He's lookin' me right in my eyes and he says, 'You ain't really here.' Kept sayin' that. So I figured he must'a been sittin' up all night gettin' drunk, or just lost his mind or sump'm. . ."

Calvin shifted in his chair. "Look, you probably don't need to hear the gory details."

"Hell, why not?" Nick shouted. "Let's have *all* the gory details. Don't stop now. He was pitiful, so what'd you do? Make him get down on his knees and beg before you killed him? Come on. The *whole* truth, remember?"

"Stop interruptin' me, boy! The whole truth ain't just a lot'a damn details! It's the shit you don't see—the shit that happens *between* the details. And there's a whole lot'a truth that happened to me in those few seconds. So shut up and let me tell it my own way."

Nick leaned back in his chair, glaring confrontationally. "Just get to it. *Truth.*"

Calvin leaned forward. "Awright, here's the truth. He was too miserable to kill. Shit, he was too miserable to hate anymore. So then I didn't know *how* to feel. That hate was like—food to me, or—or *air*. I didn't even know how to exist without it. How in the hell could I feel sorry for Joe? So I'm standin' there. Just *standin'* there. Big bad convict who snatched a man's eye out his head, and now I couldn't even finish

Joe's sorry ass off? After all he did to Mag? And me? I *had* me a gun—stuck right in the back of my belt, but I just—"

Calvin stopped and rubbed his face vigorously, as if trying to erase the muddle in his head. Then he opened his eyes and gazed at the kitchen wall. "I wanted to say sump'm... but I didn't know what the hell to say. So I held up my hands, and he was still mumblin' about me not really bein' there—kept sayin' that shit over and over. Then I asked him to put the gun down. I said, 'I *am* here, Joe. And we can talk this all out. I'm still your brother and I ain't goin noplace.' That's almost my exact words, Nick. I just kept tellin' him I ain't goin' noplace—I ain't goin' noplace till we talk it out. I was steady watchin' the way he was holdin' that gun, but then he said... he said he was dead already anyway... And the way he said it—"

After a long silence, Calvin lowered his head. "When he said it, I looked at his face—at his *eyes*—when I should'a been lookin' at his trigger finger. So when I jumped at him to get the gun, I was about a split-second off. And... he was dead before we hit the floor."

"So wait—you're tellin' me you tried to *save* him?"

"Yeah. But he saved me first."

"What the *fuck* is that supposed to mean?"

Calvin calmly crushed his cigarette in the ashtray. "It means I never pulled my gun, Nick."

Nick sighed and shook his head. "Shit, I don't understand any of this. This is all crazy."

"Well, maybe you ain't supposed to understand it. You ain't lived the kind'a life I did."

"Look, I've been through some shit in my life too! Just 'cause I never hunted somebody down and tried to kill him—"

"Boy, I ain't talkin' about no goddamn blues! I'm talkin' about *hate*—the killin' kind! Puts a fire in your belly so fierce it ain't even a choice no goddamn more! And *maaan*, it had a hold'a me—all them years. It was so strong I didn't even worry about goin' right back to prison—same place that damn near broke me the first time! Don't you get it? I was fixin' to get locked up for killin' Joe *again*! Wrap your youngster brain around *that* for a minute and *then* tell me how much shit you been through in your life!"

He gave Nick a long, probing look. "That's how he saved me, boy, don't you get it? All them years I dreamed about killin' him, but for those few seconds, *finally*, for the first time in my sorry life, I saw my *brother* sittin' there! A broke-down, miserable old man in a young man's body. With his last piece'a dream snatched away from him... I know, I know. He did a lot'a rotten shit in his life, but all he really wanted was just to *be* somebody in this rotten world. And yeah, I saw *all* that in those few seconds. I saw *him*—my brother. Not my enemy! My *brother*!" Calvin didn't fight the tears that were streaking down his face. "I—tried to save him, boy. I swear to God I did. But he saved me first. And that's the *only* reason I'm sittin' here today arguin' with my *son* instead of bein' dead or in prison. 'Cause that's where I would'a ended up. Guarantee ya."

Out of a long silence, Nick said, "Well… if *any* of that's true, then you're givin' *somebody* way too much credit. You not pullin' your gun doesn't exactly make you a hero. And saying that Joe *saved* you? Shit. All he wanted to do was pass for white."

Calvin jerked up his chin. "You weren't there, man. You didn't see him."

"So what? After what he did to Mama? And what about *your* Mama? He leaves her to worry herself to death, and leaves you to rot in jail, and then ends up takin' the coward's way out. But now I'm supposed to feel sorry for him? Shit."

"Oh. So now you ready to judge somebody you never even knew. You know what, boy? You ain't qualified. So just shut up."

"No, *you* shut up! You're a goddamn hypocrite, you know that? You're the one who went to kill him, remember? And now you're defending him?"

"Guess watchin' my only brother blow his brains out made me see things different. And if that makes me a hypocrite, then fine. 'Cause I'll *never* trade places with the man I use'ta be."

Each silence between them had stretched longer than the one before, building a tension that only broke when Donna walked back into the kitchen. "Gotta go, baby," she said, kissing Calvin on his forehead. When he didn't respond, she kissed him again and then gazed knowingly into Nick's eyes. "I know it's hard, baby. But listen to him. Give him a chance."

She picked up her pocketbook and patted Nick's shoulder, and then walked out.

"What did she mean by that?"

"I told you—she knows the whole story."

"The *whole* story? Even—"

"All of it. Now come on and ask your next question while I'm still in a goddamn answerin' mood. 'Cause I'm tellin' you right now—I ain't *never* talkin' about this shit again."

"Well, how'd you keep from gettin' caught anyway? Somebody must've heard that shot."

"Survival instinct. Dumb luck. Who knows? All I know is that after I knocked Joe on the floor and saw that hole in his head, to this day, I can't remember goin' down that fire escape. Seem' like all of a sudden I was just standin' in that back alley wonderin' what to do. Then I saw the blood on that white kitchen shirt, so I took it off. I was gonna leave it in the alley, but then I said naw, bad idea. So I turned it inside out and folded it up and stuffed it inside my regular shirt. Then I caught the first city bus I saw, and laid low on the south side a couple'a weeks. I checked the newspapers and when they said the cops ruled it a suicide, I figured it was safe to jump a Greyhound and leave town."

"Well, why didn't you come back for Mama then?"

"Where you think I went when I left Chicago? Don't you see? By then, Mag was already—"

Nick shut his eyes tightly. "Oh."

"I tried callin' the house first, but nobody ever answered. Then I took a real chance. The only friend she ever talked about was Pearl. And I knew she lived across from that flower shop, so I went over there and asked around till somebody gave me the apartment number. Rose was there watchin' Shay and Edward that day, and she told me that Doc and Pearl were at Mount Sinai with their friend. I didn't want to ask too many questions, but I figured the friend had to be Mag and that sump'm must'a gone wrong for her to be in the hospital so long. When I got there and asked about her, they told me she was in the psychiatric ward. Damn, that scared me. I went straight up there, but I couldn't get past the front desk, so I just hung around, tryin' to find some way to get in without gettin' arrested. Then I saw Doc and Pearl—comin' down the hall talkin' to a doctor. He was sayin' there wasn't no hope, and thankin' them for adopting the baby, which was you. And then he told 'em he'd be able to get Mag into a good facility. After that, I don't know what else anybody said. I just—left."

Nick shot him an icy look. "You just—left... again."

"Look. At that point in my life, I figured anybody'd make a better parent than me."

Both men fell silent again. Nick looked as if he were about to cry, so Calvin stared down at the table. When Nick finally spoke, his voice broke. "Aw, man, Calvin. Why didn't she just go with you? Why'd she have to stay with Joe? If she would'a gone with you, then they wouldn't have taken her to that place, and maybe she could'a—had a chance."

"Life's full of choices, boy," Calvin said gently. "We don't always get 'em right. Look, I'm sorry I had to tell you all this, but you wanted the story, and a lot of it was painful, I guess. The truth usually is."

Nick wiped his eyes and glared at him. "But *you* feel better, huh? Calvin Bailey repents. Hallelujah and cue the choir! You know what? I wish you hadn't told me *any* of this shit!"

Calvin shrugged. "Folks always say they don't want to be lied to, but if you give somebody a choice—maaan, they'll take the soft lie over the hard truth every damn time."

"Nah, man. Mama never even *had* a choice."

"She had a choice. We all had a choice." Calvin rubbed his temples. "Look, I'm carryin' my guilt, and I ain't complainin'. But don't judge me, boy. Your name ain't God, ya know."

"But you didn't even try to fight for her, Calvin."

"Boy, you got a baaad habit of talkin' out the side'a yo' goddamn neck! I didn't *fight* for her? I almost *killed* for her! Ain't you been listenin'?"

"But you never fought for *me*! Why didn't you come claim me? I was your son!"

Calvin hit the table with his fist. "*You* tell me what the hell I had to give a child! Tell me that, Nick! I ain't had a *got*damn thing! I went from moppin' floors in a hospital to sweepin' and unpackin' boxes at a radio station, boy! You were better off where you were."

"Then why the hell'd you show up at all? Be honest!"

Calvin leaned back in his chair and stared at Nick. "I had me a son," he said softly. "All them years, every single day, that thought use'ta blast through my brain. I got me a son out there! So when I finally got that promotion job—thank God for Jack—I decided to go see you. But all it took was that first Thanksgiving with y'all to see that you were Doc and Pearl's son, not mine. If I'da tried to take you, you would'a hated my guts, and they would too. And I had too much respect for the Calhoun family to risk that. You might not know it, but you had some quality upbringin', boy. Even with all their problems, they raised you right. So all I could do was just hang around, and it was real good of 'em to let me do that."

Nick gazed absently into his cup. "No wonder Mama always looks at you that way."

"Look at me? Mag? No, that was such a long time ago. She don't remember me."

"Yeah, Calvin. Somewhere in that lonely little world she lives in, you're familiar to her."

Calvin lit a cigarette and sighed. "Well, who's to say? But maybe it'd be better if she didn't remember me. I caused her a lot'a pain... I caused a *lot'a* people pain. All them years I blamed Joe for sendin' me to prison, but *I* was the fool tryin' to beat him to death on the road that night. Shit! All he did was bleed! Look, Nick. I know you still hate Joe for tryin' to pass. But you'll never be able to understand how things were back then. You don't know what it was like for a light-skinned man like him to go through life knowin' that the best thing he could hope to be called was *colored*. It was better than *boy* or *nigga*... but it was still third-class. Best thing your generation did was break it on down to *black*. You're a *black* man. Not Negro, not colored, not boy. Black! They use'ta insult us with that word, but your generation took it back, and now we *own* it. It means pride to us."

Nick nodded.

"So maybe you can understand better now. It's hard to admit, and it's ugly, but you wanted the truth. Joe could pass—and I couldn't. And I hated his guts for it."

Calvin jerked up his chin and stared at Nick with the last embers of the old hostility still burning in his eyes. "So how's *that* for honest? This white-folks world put us at each other like a couple'a dogs fightin' over a scrap'a rotten meat. And now the only one left to hate is *me*."

Another chilly silence passed; then Calvin finally said, "Speak your mind, boy."

Nick stared at him wordlessly.

"Boy, whether you believe me or not, every word of what I just told you was the truth."

Nick let out a tired sigh and stood up. "I know."

"You—know? So you believe me?"

"I've known you too long *not* to believe you. I know you said you *thought* about killin' him, but if you'da been cold-blooded enough to really do it—you sure wouldn't confess to it *now*. Not after you got away clean all these years. You're not dumb like that. Plus—"

"Plus what?"

"Mama loved you. And I gotta trust her judgment, even if it's—in the past."

They stared at each other quietly, and then Calvin smiled.

"I really beat you down with that story, huh? You look tired as a 75-year-old mule. When was the last time you got any sleep?"

"Couple'a days, at least… And now that you mention it, I feel like I'm about to pass out. Mind if I crash in your guest room for a few hours?"

Calvin crushed his cigarette in the ashtray and stood up. "You know that room's yours whenever you need it. And I gotta go to midtown for a couple'a meetings today, so you'll have the house to yourself. It'll be real quiet and you can sleep all day. Lemme just go unplug that phone in there so it don't ring and wake you up."

Nick began unbuttoning his shirt as he followed Calvin into the guest room. As he watched him unplug the phone and turn down the bedspread, he glanced at the clock-radio on top of the chest of drawers. "Hey, Calvin, does this old thing have an alarm? Or does it even work?"

"You seen me play that radio a million times, boy. 'Course it works. Alarm too."

Nick squinted at the time on the clock before slipping off one sleeve of his shirt. Then he stopped and turned back to take a second look. The radio had a smooth black finish and the brand name was written on a slant in the center of the yellowed clock face. *Admiral*.

"Calvin…"

"Yeah?"

"… Calvin…"

"What is it, man?"

"Is this radio the same one that… Calvin—how old is this radio?"

Calvin smiled. "Yes, it is the same one. And that makes it just a little older than you, boy."

Chapter 51

Stella had never been the type to waste time, but every evening since her grandfather's funeral she found herself standing at the west-facing window of her office gazing at the sunset.

"How long have I been standing here and *why* am I not working? There's got to be some rationale for this. I'm brainstorming. I'm creating… Oh, who am I kidding? I'm—what did Mama call it? Wool-gathering. Whatever that means." She sighed and dropped into a chair. "But it sure as hell isn't writing." Her phone rang, startling her, and she grabbed it. "E. L. Atherton."

"Uh, Stella?"

"Oh! Mr. Bailey?"

"Mr. Bailey was my Daddy. Please call me Calvin."

"Okay, Calvin. So you did get my message then."

"I sure did. Sorry it took me so long to call you back. I been out of town a couple of days and just got your message this mornin'. I was pretty surprised too. Is everything awright?"

"Yes. Well, no— I mean, not really. Listen, Calvin. Have you got some time to talk?"

"Of course. What's on your mind?"

"Well, I—I need to ask a favor of you."

"Happy to help if I can. What'cha need?"

"Well, it might seem odd, but I need you to tell me everything you know about Nick's mother. And then I'd like to fly out there and—I'd appreciate it if you'd take me to see her."

Calvin was quiet for a long moment. "Mind if I ask why?"

"Well, because he loves her so much, and I never— Well, I never even gave any thought to who she really was. I just want to start over, Calvin… Oh, Lord, I know I sound crazy."

"No, you don't. And actually, you came to the right person. I can tell you a lot about Mag."

"Mag? Oh—I guess I never heard anyone call her that before. But then I never knew my grandfather's name was Drew before last week either," she muttered. "So, Calvin, can you tell me about her now? Or would you rather wait till I fly in?"

"Why don't you book your flight and then call me back. I'll tell you some of it on the phone and the rest when you get here. Oh, and don't call Nick. I think maybe we ought'a surprise him."

"Whatever you say, Calvin. I just hope you know what you're doing."

"I don't. But for some dumb reason, that ain't been stoppin' me lately."

≈∞≈

After a series of flight delays, Stella arrived at JFK the next morning in the middle of a driving thunderstorm. Calvin was waiting for her inside, wearing a drenched overcoat and a smile.

"'Mornin', Stella. Nice flyin' weather, huh?"

"It was a pretty bumpy landing, but it sure is good to be back in New York."

"You got any bags to claim?"

"No. Just my pocketbook and this carry-on."

"Good," he said, taking her bag. "Then we can head on over, and I'll tell you the rest of the story. You're gonna feel like you're meetin' Mag for the first time."

As they rode to Genesco Medical Center, a second line of electrical storms hit the area, turning the drive into a two-hour crawl through traffic. It gave Calvin time to tell Stella the whole detailed story about his relationship with Mag and Nick's childhood. She hung on every word, without interruption, nearly emptying the box of tissues she had brought with her.

By the time they stepped through the doors of Genesco, she was in deep thought. "You were right, Calvin. I *do* feel like I'm meeting her for the first time. And as weird as it seems, I have my grandfather to thank for preparing me. And you, of course."

"Well, it's gonna be a new experience for me too," Calvin said cryptically.

"What do you mean?"

"Just sump'm Nick said that got me curious, that's all. We'll see. Come on."

As they approached the door to Magda's room, Stella stopped. "Calvin, what was it you told me Mag used to say? You know, about being brave or something?"

Calvin closed his eyes. "She use'ta say… I make my courage."

"I make my courage," Stella repeated. "Okay. I think I'm ready now."

Stella stepped into the room, half-expecting to see the Mag of Calvin's story, smiling and young, welcoming her lover with a kiss. But she saw only a small, frail woman, who looked older than her years, immobilized by a tragic, long-ago "accident." As she gazed into the pale, empty eyes, she tried to picture Mag smiling, and the thought made her feel like crying again. *Oh, I bet you were beautiful when you were young. Look what they did to you…*

She wasn't even aware of another person in the room until a nurse walked over.

"Hi, Emily," Calvin said, hugging the nurse. "How you and Shelly been doin'?"

"We're both fine, Calvin. Planning for the big graduation party and all."

"That's right! Shelly's graduatin' in June! You must be mighty proud."

"I am. I certainly am. We both worked hard for it." Emily turned and smiled at Stella. "And you don't have to tell me who this is, Calvin. This has got to be Stella."

Stella smiled back at her. "Yes, I am. But how did you know?"

"Well, I wasn't here any of the times you visited before, but the way Nick always talked about you, I would've known you anywhere."

Calvin gazed at Magda and frowned. "Hey, Emily. What's all this she's hooked up to?"

Emily patted his arm. "Don't worry. Ever since the pneumonia, we've been keeping her on oxygen and an I.V. drip and monitoring her vitals. You know, heart rate and that kind of thing. And you know what, Calvin? Your nephew was right about something."

Calvin exchanged a smile with Stella. "You mean my son."

"Huh? Oh, no, Calvin. I was talking about Nick. I didn't even know you had a son."

"Look, Emily. It ain't widely known—but Nick's my son, not my nephew."

Emily's mouth dropped open, and then she laughed. "Okay, you know you ain't gettin' out'a here without the story on that!"

"I promise. But now, what were you sayin' about Nick bein' right about sump'm?"

"Well. You know how he's always saying his Mama hears people talking and feels things? And we're all so skeptical? Well, he might not be wrong after all."

"Why? What happened?"

"Well, the last time Nick was here, I was monitoring her heart rate like now—see? On that machine over there? Anyway, as soon as he walked into the room, her heart rate went up."

"You mean—is that good?"

"Well, it's a definite reaction. It's only normal for a person to get excited when they see somebody they love. And then when he sat down and started talking to her, it went all the way back down to her resting rate. Nick's presence soothed her spirit. It was like—Nirvana."

Calvin grimaced. "Huh?"

"Oh, don't look at me like that, Calvin. I laughed too when Shelly first told me about all that transcendental meditation mess. Don't tell her I said this, but some of that stuff makes sense."

"Well, how's her heart rate now?" Stella asked.

Emily peered at the machine. "A little rapid—you know, like she's excited. But watch what happens when I sit down and hold her hand."

"Wait a minute," Calvin said. "Come here, Stella. Why don't you sit with her instead? And call her Mag—I mean, Magda, not Mrs. Bluestone."

Stella nodded, then sat on the edge of the bed. As she held Magda's hand, her emotions began to swirl with memories of her grandfather's letters and the story Calvin had told her in the car. Obeying a sudden compulsion, she wrapped her arms around Nick's mother and began speaking to her in a deep, soothing tone. "Hi, Magda. I sure hope you remember me. I wanted to come see you again because—we have so much to talk about now. Calvin was telling me about all those good times you had together. He told me how you played your violin so beautifully. And I *love* violins. Nick played me your records, but I wish I could've seen you play."

Magda emitted a low gurgling sound.

Stella looked over at Emily. "Is she okay? How's her heart rate now?"

"It's going down," she whispered. "Calm, like that Nirvana jazz. I told you. She *does* hear—in her own way. It's like Nick always says, her brain's only damaged, not *dead*."

Without taking his eyes off Magda, Calvin walked slowly toward the window. "So, Emily, when's the graduation?"

Magda's head leaned a fraction of an inch to the left.

"June 5th," Emily said. "I'll be sure to send you an invitation, Calvin. You too, Stella."

"Thanks. Wouldn't miss it." Now Calvin changed course, and walked in the opposite direction—toward the bathroom. Then he stopped and watched.

He saw Magda's head incline ever so slightly to the right, almost like a blind person might respond to a sound. It was a movement measurable in millimeters, and he had never noticed it before. He finally sat down on the chair near the bed, staring at her with a stunned expression.

Stella blinked at Emily, who shrugged and shook her head.

"What is it, Calvin?" Stella said softly. "You look kind of—upset."

"That's what Nick meant when he said—she *looks* at me."

Stella reached over to adjust Magda's pillows. "What do you mean?"

Suddenly, Magda lurched forward and emitted a puffing sound.

Stella looked at Emily. "Is she—okay?"

"P-puh—" The sound was clearer this time.

"Oh, no," Stella said. "Emily, did we overexcite her or something?"

"No. She seems fine. But I can't say I ever heard her make such a distinct sound before."

Stella looked at Calvin. "What's going on?… Calvin?"

Calvin shook his head, but didn't answer. The room became absolutely silent.

Stella sat back down on the bed beside Magda and stared at her. Again her mind flooded with all the stories that Nick and Calvin had told her about this woman who couldn't speak to her. And the details slowly came together in a vivid portrait: She was the daughter of a poor Greek fisherman; she had struggled through a deadly illness, survived a World War, and somehow made her way to America. A fiercely independent woman with a rare talent—she could make a violin cry. Despite the cruel damage inflicted on her mind, her spirit had remained strong. And now it was calling out—reaching for someone.

Stella wanted to respond, but couldn't think of a single word to say. Then it hit her—something Nick had told her when they first met: *Aunt Pearl had a deep voice like yours…*

Turning around, Stella gazed at the blown-up photo hanging near the door. Pearl and Mag in their after-five dresses, smiling at her from that happy night so long ago. Two sisters, one black, one white, eternally youthful and defiant against the divisive dictates of a damn mean world.

Stella leaned close to Mag until their foreheads were touching. And the words came.

"I'm sorry—sugah," she whispered. "I'm *so* sorry I was gone so long, but you and me—we're gonna have a nice long visit now. Get *all* caught up." When she felt Mag's fingers jerking at her hand to grasp it, Stella squeezed her eyes shut and smiled until her face hurt. "That's right, sugah. Pearl's back now."

Chapter 52

After three weeks in the studio, Nick's excitement about his new album project had dissolved into boredom. He had acquired three songs that he thought were potential hits, but his colorless vocal on the first one made him wonder if any of them would really fit his voice. As Ed worked on a rough mix in the control room, Nick sat at the piano experimenting with chords.

"Hey, Ed," he called. "Do yourself a favor and give up on that mix! We both know my vocal died an ugly death, so let's just get sump'm ready for the background singers tomorrow. You see the sheet music in there somewhere? I forgot the chord structure for the bridge and—"

Just then, the door squeaked open and Stella Atherton walked in carrying a notebook in her arms. Nick stared at her and stood up slowly. She was the last person he had expected to see.

"I'm gonna run out for a bite," Ed said, "while you two—uh, talk."

"Okay, man," Nick said as he watched Stella make herself at home on the piano bench.

"So what brings *you* to town?" he asked with a slight note of sarcasm.

Without looking at him, she pulled a page from her notebook. "I wrote you a song, Nick, in the car on the way over. I never wrote one so fast in my life. It needs work, but it's—good."

"Wait—you're here because you wrote me a *song*?"

"Let me just play it for you, Nick, while it's still fresh in my mind." She stared at her hand-scribbled page, played a few chords, and then began to sing softly:

Love letters lost in time / Whisper secrets / star-crossed crimes /
Nevermore, nevermore / brothers torn apart /
Nevermore, another war / Death by broken heart /
leaving only yesterdays / and lonely whispers in the dark

I make my courage / last the night /
for wrongs at last made right / As time slips by I realize /
the Moon alone knows why / but violins do cry

Sons and fathers / lessons lost / Brothers rage and wage a war /
Another war / At what cost? / As sisters love /
though far apart / A mother's sleeping heart /
living only yesterdays / and lonely whispers in the dark

I make my courage / last the night /
for wrongs at last made right / As time slips by I realize /
the Moon alone knows why / but violins do cry / Oh, how they cry...

Stella resolved the chord, then folded her hands in her lap. "It's not finished, but it's called—'I Make My Courage.'" Glancing up at Nick's stunned expression, she began talking rapidly to fill the silence. "Do you remember when you first came to my office and you said that you were looking for a great song—that one *great* song. Well, we recorded some good ones, but I think *this* is that great song you were looking for. Or at least it will be when I finish it. And that's not ego. It's not great because I wrote it. It's great because it's *real*. It's about both our families—your father and your uncle, my grandfather—" She laughed nervously. "—and wait till you hear the story I have to tell you about *him*. But mostly, I think it was about Pearl and Mag."

Nick's eyes widened. "Wait a minute. Where did you hear that name—Mag?"

Stella reached for his hand. "Nick," she said softly, "I visited your mother today…"

≈∞≈

Calvin was pacing in the lounge area near the coffee station, watching the wall clock as he pretended to listen to one of Pop Dawson's stories. He had heard Stella run through the song she had written in the car, but after that, nothing. And she had been in there for over forty minutes. Then, suddenly, he heard the song start up again, but this time it was Nick who was singing it.

He listened for a minute and then grinned. "'Scuse me, Pop. I'll be right back."

Hurrying to the control room, he peered through the glass. Nick was standing behind Stella as she played the piano. Stella spotted him and smiled. Then Calvin tapped on the glass to get Nick's attention. When Nick looked up, he stopped singing, but Stella continued to play softly as the two men stared silently at each other through the glass.

When the last chord faded, Nick leaned close to the microphone: "Thanks, Daddy."

Daddy.

The word clattered around in Calvin's brain. A crazy, unexpected word that meant *him*. And he was not prepared for the emotional impact. After a long, awkward moment, he nodded his head with a quick jerk, and hurried out to the foyer. Pop was still at his desk grinning at him.

"Them two gettin' back together?"

Calvin cleared his throat. "Yes, sir. Looks like it."

"Well, now, that sho' is good news. Real good news. I never seen that boy light up around no females like he do when he got that Stella on his arm."

"That's the truth, Pop. Hey, listen, did it ever stop rainin' out there?"

"Yup. Stopped a while ago, but them streets is still slick. You be careful drivin'."

"I will, Pop. G'night."

"Wait a minute, Calvin," Pop said, waving his hand. "Hold up—"

Calvin looked back over his shoulder. "Yes, sir?"

Pop smiled slyly. "You look a little misty-eyed there, brutha. You okay?"

"Fine as wine, Pop," Calvin said, grinning. "Matter of fact, I never been better. G'night."

Stepping outside, Calvin lit a cigarette and looked around. Greene Street was empty, except for two young blonde women with tall, skeletal builds, who were jaywalking. He chuckled at their hot-pink micro-minis and matching platform heels. They reminded him of the flamingoes from the Bronx Zoo that Nick had loved so much when he was seven years old. He closed his eyes and saw a clear image of that little boy and his toothless grin. *Thanks, Daddy.*

A cool breeze reminded Calvin of his running days, but he laughed at the idea of a middle-aged smoker with bad knees making like a track star in the middle of the night. Besides, he wouldn't want to frighten the two flamingoes. Taking a pull from his cigarette, he savored the just-lit sweetness and gazed up at the moon peeking through the breaking clouds. "Nice night," he murmured, exhaling a soft curl of smoke. "Real nice night." Suddenly, he held the cigarette out, looked at it, and laughed. "Oh, okay, Donna. This is supposed to be the night, huh?" He dropped the cigarette and stepped on it. "Aw, hell, I guess it's worth a try."

He glanced over at the blonde flamingoes. On an impulse, he spread his arms wide and shouted at them, "Hey! I got me a son!" Then he yelped with laughter when one of the girls let out a startled screech and they both tottered away, trying to run in those ridiculous shoes.

He could feel the silly smile on his face as he got into his car, but he didn't fight it. He started the engine and turned on the radio, which was set to 107.5—WBLS. When he heard what was playing, his smile faded. It was his favorite song—Sam Cooke's gut-wrenching masterpiece, "A Change is Gonna Come."

He had heard it dozens of times, but now it rang with new relevance, unlocking a room in his mind that had been locked for too long. It was a place where there was no judgment, no anger, no pain. And with blinding speed, the years rushed over him like the current of the Mississippi River he had known as a boy. He was too choked up to drive, so, sitting quietly in his parked car, he went back—back down the rough roads of his life, back down Highway 61, back down the levee road, all the way back to the River. And Calvin Bailey was singing again.